Cynthia Harrod-Eagles is the author of the contemporary Bill Slider Mystery series as well as the Morland Dynasty novels. Her passions are music, wine, horses, architecture and the English countryside.

Visit the author's website at www.cynthiaharrodeagles.com

The Mirage

Cynthia Harrod-Eagles

sphere

SPHERE

First published in Great Britain in 1999
by Little, Brown and Company

This edition published by Warner in 2000
Reprinted in 2000
Reprinted by Time Warner Paperbacks in 2002
Reprinted by Time Warner Books in 2005
Reprinted by Sphere in 2008 (twice), 2009, 2011 (twice), 2012, 2013,
2014

A CIP catalogue record for this book
is available from the British Library.

ISBN 978-0-7515-2546-5

Typeset by Palimpsest Book Production Limited,
Polmont, Stirlingshire
Printed and bound in Great Britain by
Clays Ltd, St Ives plc

Papers used by Sphere are from well-managed forests
and other responsible sources.

MIX
Paper from
responsible sources
FSC
www.fsc.org   FSC® C104740

Sphere
An imprint of
Little, Brown Book Group
100 Victoria Embankment
London EC4Y 0DY

An Hachette UK Company
www.hachette.co.uk

www.littlebrown.co.uk

THE MORLAND FAMILY

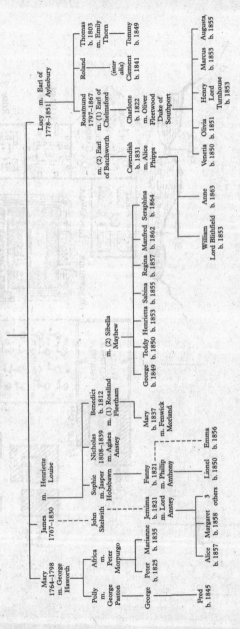

Mary 1764–1798 m. George Haworth — James 1767–1830 m. Henriette Louise — Lucy m. Earl of Aylesbury 1778–1851

Polly m. George Paston — Africa m. Peter Morpurgo

George — Peter b. 1825 — Marianne b. 1835

Fred b. 1845

John Skelwith – – – Jemima b. 1821 m. Lord Anstey

Alice b. 1857 — Margaret b. 1858 — 3 others

Sophie m. Jasper Hobsbawn — Nicholas 1808–1839 m. Aglaea Anstey — Benedict b. 1812 m. (1) Rosalind Fleetham

Fanny b. 1821 m. Phillip Anthony – – – – Emma b. 1856

Lionel b. 1850

Mary b. 1837 m. Fenwick Morland

George b. 1849 — Teddy b. 1850 — Henrietta b. 1853 — Sabina b. 1855 — Regina b. 1857 — Manfred b. 1862 — Seraphina b. 1864
m. (2) Sibella Mayhew

William Lord Blithfield b. 1853 — Anne b. 1863

Rosamund 1797–1867 m. (1) Earl of Chelmsford m. (2) Earl of Batchworth — Roland — Thomas b. 1803 m. Emily Thorn

Cavendish b. 1831 m. Alice Phipps

Charlotte b. 1822 m. Oliver Fleetwood Duke of Southport

(inter alia) Clement b. 1841

Tommy b. 1849

Venetia b. 1850 — Olivia b. 1851 — Henry, Lord Turnhouse b. 1853 — Marcus b. 1853 — Augusta b. 1855

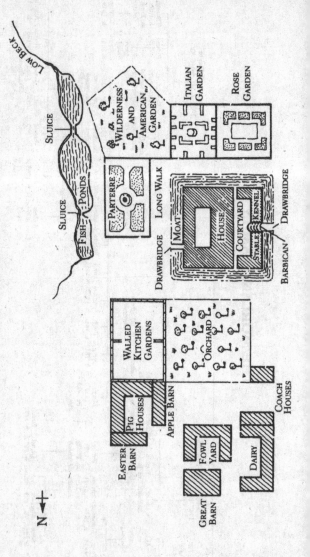

MORLAND PLACE AND GROUNDS

N

MORLAND PLACE IN 1830
GROUND FLOOR

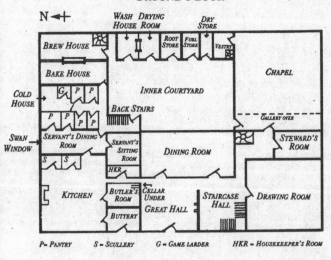

N

| BREW HOUSE | WASH HOUSE | DRYING ROOM | ROOT STORE | FUEL STORE | DRY STORE | VESTRY |

BAKE HOUSE

COLD HOUSE →

G P P

INNER COURTYARD

CHAPEL

P P P

BACK STAIRS

GALLERY OVER

SWAN WINDOW →

SERVANT'S DINING ROOM

S S

SERVANT'S SITTING ROOM

HKR

DINING ROOM

STEWARD'S ROOM

KITCHEN

BUTLER'S ROOM

BUTTERY

CELLAR UNDER GREAT HALL

STAIRCASE HALL

DRAWING ROOM

P = PANTRY   S = SCULLERY   G = GAME LARDER   HKR = HOUSEKEEPER'S ROOM

FIRST FLOOR

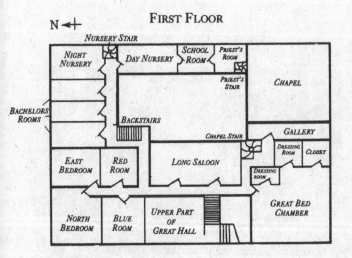

N

NURSERY STAIR

| NIGHT NURSERY | DAY NURSERY | SCHOOL ROOM | PRIEST'S ROOM |

PRIEST'S STAIR

CHAPEL

BACHELORS ROOMS

BACKSTAIRS

CHAPEL STAIR

GALLERY

DRESSING ROOM

CLOSET

EAST BEDROOM

RED ROOM

LONG SALOON

DRESSING ROOM

NORTH BEDROOM

BLUE ROOM

UPPER PART OF GREAT HALL

GREAT BED CHAMBER

BOOK ONE

Escape

At last, tenderly,
From the walls of the powerful, fortress'd house,
From the clasp of the knitted locks – from the keep of the
   well-closed doors,
Let me be wafted.
Let me glide noiselessly forth;
With the key of softness unlock the locks – with a whisper
Set ope the doors, O soul!

Walt Whitman: The Imprisoned Soul

CHAPTER ONE

May 1870

A shepherd has his dogs for company, and his sheep, and his thoughts; and on the whole he does not want for more. Old Caleb had been looking after Morland sheep for more than forty years, but he was not Yorkshire bred. He came from Wiltshire – from the Old Hills, as they called them – where his father had been shepherd to Mr Johnson, whose place was called Gilpin's Low. But times were hard in the South, and Mr Johnson's sons had both been killed in the wars, and when he died his daughter couldn't hold things together. The great flocks had been sold to pay off the debts, and what was left did not warrant more than one shepherd. So Caleb had said goodbye to his father and mother, to Gilpin's Low and White Sheet Down and the green, rounded hills he had been born to, and walked north.

Yorkshire was his goal, where there was always work – far away as a foreign land, but it was sheep country, and sheep men everywhere speak the same language. At first he'd done odd jobs, waiting for the hiring-time to come round. Then at the Michaelmas fair he had stood in his smock with his crook amongst the other shepherds, and there had caught the eye of Mr James Morland. Mr James had taken a fancy to him and hired him, and he'd been here ever since. He had never seen the Old Hills again, but a place in his chest still ached when the wind was in the south-west, smelling of green softness, and little turf streams, and home.

He had a good place here. He worked first for Mr James

3

and his wife, and then for their sons, Mr Nicholas, and after his death Mr Benedict. Thirty years Benedict Morland had been the owner: Caleb thought of him simply as *Maister*, without qualification.

Sitting on a rocky outcrop that served him for a chair, Caleb looked away over his flock, grazing quietly downwind of him. His dog, Watch, was at his side, his nose working, the breeze stirring the little hairs on the tops of his ears. He was a comical-looking dog with a face half white and half black, and a black patch over the eye in the white half. Looked like a clown, he did – and knew it! Liked to play the fool when he was off duty. The other dog, Monk, was away on the other side of the flock, out of sight. Caleb knew where he was. He could feel him with that sixth sense long partnership develops.

It was what Caleb called a shiny day, fresh and clear, with a breeze bowling light clouds across the washed sky. After the rains of last week, this good, drying wind was just what was wanted to stand the hayfields up for the sickle. A shiny day, and a quiet time of year, between lambing and shearing: a good day for wandering over his thoughts.

Maister, now: he was a queer one. Always restless. When he was only a young lad he had left home and gone off to be a railway engineer. It must have been an exciting life on the workings, Caleb allowed. After he inherited Morland Place, it seemed he missed the excitement, for he always had something on the go, some scheme or other. Always wanting to be somewhere else.

Went off all the way to America once, to visit his daughter, Miss Mary, who'd married an American, a cousin of sorts. Nearly got caught up in the war over there. Ah, that was a bad business! Civil wars were the worst kind – brother fighting brother. And Miss Mary, poor thing, had disappeared, and try as he might, Maister could never find word of her. It broke his heart – she'd been the apple of his eye. To Caleb's mind, he'd never been the same after that. What with that and then poor Mrs Morland dying, they'd had hard times of it, one way and another, up at the house.

A horse was cantering up from the direction of Rufforth. It was still a way off, but Caleb recognised the nice bay pony,

4

Dunnock, that belonged to Miss Henrietta, the Maister's eldest girl. You couldn't want better than a nice bay, he always said: blacks and chestnuts might be fancier, but a good bay was as smart as a Sunday suit, and lasted as long. Watch made a small sound in his throat and shifted his feet in excitement.

'Aye, lad, tha knaws who that is,' Caleb said. If a man couldn't talk to his dogs, who could he talk to? 'Coming up to see us. Well, we don't mind that, do we? She's a bonny lass, and a mind full o' queer starts.'

As he watched she slowed from a canter to a trot, because she was approaching the sheep – not like her brother Master George, the heir, who thought nothing of scattering a flock before him. She was riding bareback, her long legs dangling round Dunnock's grass-fat sides. Born on a pony, like all the Morland children – but getting too big for Dunnock now. Ought not to be riding about the countryside like that, for she was – he furrowed his brow in calculation – well, fifteen or sixteen, anyway. But who was there to tell her such things? Four years, it was, since Mrs Morland died; and Maister, to Caleb's mind, had turned a bit queer in the head. He took no more interest in the house or the estate, still less in his children; and these two years past he had been far away in a foreign land on some wild scheme or other, leaving Morland Place to take care of itself.

Watch looked at him and whistled softly, and Caleb said, 'Doos tha want to meet her, awd lad? Goo on then.' The dog raced away down the slope. The girl reined up at a little distance and slid off. She was not thin, but brown and wiry; and you wouldn't call her pretty, but she had a nice face. A lot like her poor mother, with the same narrow chin and red-brown hair, but her father's brown eyes. Like a little fox.

'Hello, Caleb!' she called.

'Now then, miss.'

'May I come and sit with you?'

'Set down and welcome,' he said, appreciating the politeness. Many folk would just assume.

The pony had lost no instant in getting his head down

5

to graze: short moorland turf, tougher than paddock grass, but sweet with wild thyme and 'eggs-and-bacon', and all the tastier for being different. Henrietta knotted the reins on its neck and let it go, and it walked away a few steps to establish independence before getting back to the serious business of eating. All creatures like their little bit of freedom, he thought.

'Run away from thy lessons, hast'ow?' Caleb asked slyly.

'You know I haven't done lessons for years,' Henrietta said. 'Anyhow, who is there to teach me?' She sat down on the grass, and Watch came up to paw at her, thrust his head between her updrawn knees, and generally play the fool as if he were a puppy. Soon she was tussling with him, and Watch was rolling on his back with one ear turned inside out.

'No fool like an old fool,' Caleb observed. 'Don't tha try that sort o' nonsense wi' Monk, or tha'll be sorry.'

'I know. I won't.' Henrietta said, sitting up and dusting herself off. Watch righted himself, shook vigorously until his ears rattled, and took up his duties again, refreshed by the interlude.

'No-one can't take liberties wi' Monk,' said Caleb. 'He's as good a dog with the sheep as you'll find, but he's no time for people.'

'Funny how different he is from Watch,' Henrietta said, clasping her arms comfortably round her knees.

Caleb nodded. 'Watch, now, he sleeps on the mat at the foot o' my bed, but Monk stops in the yard, even in the worst weather. I've coom out some winter mornings and found him covered so deep in snow he's nobbut a mound. But go into a house he never will; no, nor barn nor byre, nor anything men have built.'

'Is it because he was ill-treated once?'

'Nay, I bred him myself from my old bitch Meg. He were never any different. God makes a few that way, for His own reasons. They can't like the soft life, try as they might. Folks too,' he observed. 'I reckon your faither's one. Restless. Never one for stopping home.'

Henrietta nodded, watching the wind as it passed over the

6

uncut fields like a shadow. 'Yes, and the funny thing is that Mama warned me about it – at the end when she was ill and I was sitting with her so much. She said Papa would be off again one day. I thought she meant he would go back to America. I don't suppose even she could have guessed where he'd end up.'

'What's it called, again, that place he's gone?'

'Suez. It's in Egypt.'

'Oh, ayé? And what sort o' place would that be?'

Henrietta was flattered to be asked for information by someone so much older and wiser than her. 'It's a desert place,' she said. 'All sand. And camels.'

Caleb pondered. 'Like what our Blessed Lord wandered forty days in?'

'Yes, I suppose so,' Henrietta said. 'It's very hot there, so you're always thirsty, and there's something called a mirage, which makes it look as though there's a lovely pool of water ahead, but it's not really there, and when you get to it, it's just more sand.'

'The world is full of falsehood and deceit,' Caleb said wisely, 'put there a-purpose to lead men astray.' After some further consideration, he asked, 'What are camels, then?'

'Animals – like horses a bit, you know – but with bumps on their backs.' She drew them in the air.

'Whatever for?'

'They just grow that way.' A picture she had seen in one of the books in the library was the sum total of her knowledge, and she hoped he would not probe it too far. 'The people who live there ride them like horses. The bumps stop them falling off, I suppose,' she added inventively.

'Maister won't like digging a canal through sand,' Caleb said. 'No good, is that. Won't hold up.'

'That's why they sent for him,' Henrietta said, 'because he knows so much about it, after the Kilsby Tunnel. He was terribly proud to be asked, because the company that's digging the canal is French, and the French consider themselves better engineers than anybody else. Not that Papa agrees about *that*, of course; but in any case, he's what they call a specialist, so he knows things other people don't.'

7

'I knawt what folk want wi' digging canals in countries not their own,' Caleb said disparagingly.

'But the canal's a benefit, so Papa says,' Henrietta told him. 'Ships won't have to sail right round the bottom of Africa any more – the Cape of whatever-it-is – which will cut the journey time to India by half. And since most of the trade with the East goes in British ships, it will be especially good for us.'

If Henrietta's knowledge of geography was sketchy, Caleb's was non-existent. He didn't know where India, Africa or Egypt were, but they were Abroad, and that was enough for him. 'Well, but what's it to do with thy faither?' he said. 'If it was here in Yorkshire, mebbe it'd be different.'

'You think it wrong of him to have gone?'

'A man should not neglect his duty. He's Maister, and his duty is here.'

'I suppose he'll come back soon,' Henrietta said, but doubtfully. His letters, which had been frequent at first and more full of detail than anyone at home had the education or even the desire to assimilate, had grown shorter and rarer as the canal neared completion. Last year when it was finished he wrote that he must stay for the opening, to solve any teething problems that might arise; then that he was going up country to look at damming and irrigation systems. It was as though he were making excuses not to come home.

'We've had no letter from him for weeks,' she went on at last. 'We thought for sure he would be back for Georgie's twenty-first birthday, but that's not possible now, unless he's already on his way.'

'Will there be a celebration for Master George?'

'I don't know. Probably not, for who'd organise it? Besides,' Henrietta went on, 'Georgie's being twenty-one won't change anything. We shall just go on as we are.'

'Aye, as you are,' Caleb said, and it was plain from his voice he didn't think much of that.

They lapsed into silence, and Henrietta, squinting against the sun, thought of the way they were. Home, being what you know, has to be normality, but she wondered if other children lived as they did. The nursery, ruled over by Mrs Gurney, who'd first come to Morland Place when Georgie

8

was born, had always been like a separate kingdom, apart from the mainstream of the house. Her parents, busy about their own affairs, had been remote figures to the children, loved and admired, but distant, like the Queen at Windsor, and only nominally 'theirs'.

There'd been a chaplain-tutor in those days, the awe-inspiring Mr Wheldrake, but he'd only concerned himself with the boys, Georgie and Teddy. Henrietta and her sisters, Sabina and Regina, had been left to scramble themselves into whatever education they fancied. Girls were destined for marriage, so they didn't need to be clever. There was a library full of books, but with all the estate to roam over, and horses and dogs to roam with, it had only been on really rainy days that Henrietta had thought of opening a book.

She had always been a girl who needed someone to love, and from the time Sabina was born, when Henrietta was two, she had lavished all her affections on her. Together they had played, roved the country, and at night shared a bed in the nursery, where in the dark they continued in murmurs and whispers the unbroken stream of conversation that meandered through their days.

Golden days, she recalled: a golden age of happiness and security. Her father's departure for America had been barely noticed; his return, Odysseus-like, was a nine-days' wonder. The American war had seemed as remote as a Bible story, and her father's grief over the loss of Mary had not touched the children. Their lives were bound by the nursery walls and nursery rules; their aims beyond pleasure merely to get enough to eat – nursery food was always sparse – and to remember Gurney's prohibitions and avoid whippings.

Papa coming home had meant new arrivals to the nursery: first Manfred, then Seraphina. But 'Phina had only lived a year, and it seemed in retrospect that her death had begun the time of sadness which had ended the golden age. Henrietta remembered vividly the day they had lowered the tiny coffin into the crypt. Bewildered, not knowing what to feel or how to behave, she had looked at her parents. Papa was grim and grave; Mama – already then pregnant again – white and weeping. It had shocked her that they could show so clearly the effects of the event, when they ought to have been invulnerable and unchanging. An autumn day it had been: the chapel filled with chrysanthemums cut by the gardener for poor little 'Phina. Ever since, the memory of that time was mixed up with the smell of chrysanthemums and hot candle-wax.

In the cold and dark of February 1866, Mama had lost the baby, and after that she had never been well. From the security of the nursery Henrietta had emerged as suddenly and completely as a chestnut being shelled. For seven months she had attended her mother, run messages, fetched and carried, and, as Sibella grew ever more bedridden, nursed, entertained and listened. In her last weeks Mrs Morland had come to confide in her eldest daughter. A warmth and tenderness had grown up between them; and just as Henrietta began to depend upon this new intimacy, she became aware that her mother was dying, and that it must soon end. Sibella died the day before Henrietta's thirteenth birthday, and of all those who mourned, none felt the loss more keenly than the bewildered girl who had found her mother only when the shadow of death was already on her.

There had been no way back to the safety of the nursery for Henrietta. Before she had so much as begun to come to terms with her mother's death, during that dreadful winter when the house was paralysed with mourning, Sabina had fallen ill, and before the first hint of spring could lighten the gloom, had followed her mother to the grave. The world had become intractable and real. There were things that were so bad that a black draught and early-to-bed couldn't mend them; deeds had consequences that a beating from Gurney couldn't deflect. People could die, really die, and you couldn't turn the page back and have them alive again.

After that, life had seemed to unravel. Papa grew very strange, shut himself away and withdrew his controlling hand from the reins. Wheldrake departed, and the chapel stood empty. Servants left and were not replaced, and the house grew a little shabby. There was no more entertaining, no visitors, no visiting. Teddy went away to school and then to university, Georgie went his own way. The rhythm of the

10

masterless house slowed and, like a spinning top, seemed to grow unstable.

In the nursery Regina and Manfred were still cocooned to some extent by their youth and Gurney's authority, but Henrietta had nothing to do but wander, purposeless, lonely. There was no-one to tell her what to do. Since her father had gone to Egypt, Mrs Holicar, the housekeeper, ran the house, and Atterwith, the steward, took care of the estate. Officially he did so in consultation with Georgie, but Henrietta suspected the consultation mostly took the form of Mr Atterwith saying what he meant to do and Georgie saying that was all right by him – for Georgie never cared to be bothered with anything that took him from his own pleasures.

Henry Anstey, whom the children called Uncle Henry, was Papa's man of business and his agent while he was abroad; but he never interfered in their day-to-day lives. His wife had died not long after Papa left, and they never saw him at Morland Place any more. So Henrietta roamed the estate, looking for something to love, and something to be. She helped the estate people with their work, visited their cottages, ate with them and played with their babies; but she was not satisfied. The sweet intimacy she had shared with her sister and her mother, first as the senior and then as the junior partner, had left a hunger in her. Besides, she was sixteen years old, and childhood was behind her. What shape would the life ahead of her take? She wanted to know what she was *for*.

Caleb, abandoned by her conversationally, had taken up a bit of whittling. His old, weather-punished hands were all knuckles and swollen fingers, looking as stiff and unwieldy as rocks, but they turned and worked the wood with astonishing nimbleness. He had his place, his purpose and his work: he *belonged*. She envied him.

'What are you making?' she asked. He showed her silently. It was a bell. 'Will it ring?'

'Course it'll ring. What'd be use of a bell that didn't ring?' Caleb said, amused.

'Church bells are made of brass, aren't they?'

'Bronze,' he corrected. 'But I've all sorts. Bronze, copper, silver, bone, wood. I've thirty altogether.'

11

'Thirty?'

'Aye, and I wish it were sixty.'

'Do you need so many for telling where the flock is?'

He snorted softly in derision. 'Nay, miss, doosta think I need bells for that? A poor shepherd I'd be if I knawt where my flock was at! I've two good eyes in my head – aye, an' two good dogs.'

She was never sure with Caleb when he was roasting her: in his brown and wrinkled face his eyes seemed to glint with knowing laughter. 'Then what are they for?'

'They are music,' he said. 'Listen, and tha'll hear.'

She listened. The different sizes of bell produced different tones, from the sharp tinkling of the smallest to the deep clonk-clonk of the largest; and the sound varied, too, as they were differently agitated, quietly as the sheep grazed head-down, more rapidly as they walked, with a carillon as a sheep shook its head, or broke into a run from one grazing-spot to another.

'I hear it,' she said delightedly. It was a strange, remote, aching kind of music; beautiful like the cry of the curlew, or the way a silver band of light would fall far away from behind rain clouds.

Caleb nodded. 'It's company, too, for me and the sheep. It's lonely out on the moor, most of all when it's wet or cold and we're like not to see a sawl all day. The bells keep us from feelin' it too much. Aye, we knaw what we have 'em for, the yows an' me.'

'Are *you* lonely, Caleb?' she asked him shyly.

'Aye,' he said. He looked at her. 'Did tha think it were only thee? Nay, miss, all creatures are lonely – us human-folk most of all, because we've the minds to know it. It's being separate from God, that's all. We want to get back to Him, and we know we can't, not for a space; not till we've worked out His purpose.'

A cloud shadow chased across the moor; in the distance a windhover hung quivering on the air, its tail-feathers fanned to balance it. One part of her mind marvelled: it seemed living proof that the impossible was possible. The other part thought, perhaps the old man beside her had answers for her.

12

His face was as brown and old as a prophet's, the creases so deep in it, they were like the cracks in the riverbed when it dried out one year. An impossible face; just as his hands were impossible, seen beside hers, slim and flexible. But they were the same clay, and she felt a kinship with him. He knew solitude, understood it.

'And what is His purpose?' she asked him.

'To do His will, that's all.'

'But what *is* it?' she cried in frustration. 'What am I to do? I want to do God's will but I don't know how, and no-one will tell me. What's to become of me?'

'Nay, be still, miss,' Caleb said gently. 'Tha can't hear God's voice if tha makes all that commotion.'

She was silent. The breeze pressed lightly against her ear and stirred her hair; the sheep grazed to their bell-music, the bees droned in the gorse flower, and the sun lay hot on her head like a blessing hand. If that were God, she thought, it would be easy, for she saw it and knew it and loved it, and it was all around her. But there must be more to it than the sweet day and the warm smell of earth: *that* still left the question and the hunger – the feeling that was like the trembling cry of the curlew, for ever out of sight, out of reach.

'Nay, it will come to thee,' said Caleb, as if he had heard everything she thought. 'Don't fret, miss. Tha'rt still young. Only do thy duty and listen for God, and tha'll find out soon enough what He wants thee for.'

'Do you know what He wants you for?' she asked.

'Why, to mind the sheep,' said Caleb, 'and to love the beautiful world He made.'

'Is that all?'

'We must each do what we're fit for,' he said. 'See awd Watch, here—' He reached out a hand and the dog leaned into the touch. 'He doesn't fret because he's not a man and can't read and write. He serves by being what he is. Tha'rt a woman, and must serve in a woman's ways. I can't tell thee more than that.'

It didn't seem much; but Henrietta found that she felt comforted. Perhaps that was why she liked visiting Caleb. He seemed so contented with his isolated life that it rubbed

13

off on her. With a sudden sense of well-being she stretched her arms and then hugged her knees to her chest and said, 'It's a glorious day, isn't it?'

'Aye, thank God,' Caleb said. 'They'll be haying tomorrow. Grass is ready – they on'y wanted a bit o' dryin' wind. They'll be cutting Watermill Ings first.'

'How do you *know*?' she marvelled. 'You always seem to know everything. I think you must be a seer.'

His fathomless dark eyes twinkled at her. 'Mester Atterwith were by yesterday. Doos tha think I niver speak to anybody but thee?'

She spent the afternoon with the gamekeeper of Acomb Woods, and got home late, dishevelled, and with a brace of wood pigeons across her pony's withers. She was very hungry. In any other household, a girl of sixteen would have dined down, but nothing at Morland Place was like anywhere else now. Georgie was the nearest thing they had to a master, and when he dined at home, which wasn't often, it was with his bachelor friends. Henrietta took her meals in the nursery still. Nursery tea was at five; hers, in deference to her greater age, usually fortified with a bit of something left over from midday dinner.

When she rode into the yard, Askins, the home stables head man, took Dunnock's rein from her and said she had better go straight in, she'd been looked for, he would put the pony up for her.

'I s'pose you've been rattling him round all day in this heat, and never a thought o' resting him,' Askins grumbled, looking at the bright-eyed bay as if he were lathered and sagging at the knees.

'As if I would,' Henrietta protested, hurt. 'He's been dozing in the shade all afternoon, while I was going round the woods with Mr Ellerby.'

Askins's scowl intensified. 'You'll catch cold at that some day, Miss Henrietta, frolicking about with the likes o' that one! He's a bad lot, is Ellerby.'

'Everyone says he's a very fine gamekeeper.'

''At's as may be, but company for a young lady he is not!

14

I wonder Master George lets you run wild the way you do. I've a mind to have a word wi' 'im.'

'Why should Georgie mind what I do?'

'He'll mind all right when your name's ruined,' Askins said with gloomy relish. 'Dragged through the mire, it'll be. And it's time you had a proper lady's horse. Dunnock's too small for you. You'll have his wind going next. *And*,' he piled another complaint on to stop her answering, 'you s'd have a side-saddle. Ridin' across is not dacent for a young lady and daughter o' the house.'

'I'm not a young lady yet,' she objected.

'Aye, well you soon will be,' Askins retorted, and clucking to the pony, led it away to a diminuendo grumble of disapprobation. 'Riding across! No-one'll marry you, you'll see. Time the Maister coom back an' set a bit of order t' th' house! I never knew the like of it, harum-scarum ways, all to rack an' ruin, females running shameless, no-one where he should be day or night . . .'

Swinging the pigeons, Henrietta ran up the steps and into the great hall. Her brother George was there, still in his breeches and dusty boots, surrounded by a moving carpet of dogs. He had one of the hounds gripped between his knees and was holding it up by the forepaws, trying to examine its belly. The captive struggled wildly to get free, while the rest of the pack, with the general perversity of dogs, were thrusting their noses in, wanting to be the one to get the attention.

He straightened up as she appeared: a big, heavyset young man with a healthy, high-coloured face, rather small, round blue eyes, and thick, wavy brown hair that he wore a little too long, so that his outdoor life left it looking somewhat shaggy and unkempt.

'Where have you been?' George demanded. 'Gurney's been looking for you this hour.' And without waiting for an answer, 'Have a look at Philo's belly, will you? I think she may have picked up a tick.' Henrietta came over, and the dogs all caught the scent of the pigeons at once and closed on her. 'What've you got there?' George asked.

'They're for you. I went out shooting with Ellerby.'

'Give 'em here.' He freed one hand to take the pigeons and

15

sling them over his shoulder where they dangled like a strange grey tippet. The dogs lapped him like sea waves leaping up at a rock. 'You shot two pigeons?' he said, impressed.

Henrietta crouched. 'Well, no, I missed,' she admitted. 'Ellerby says "rabs" and "woodies" are the hardest things of all to shoot. Poor old Philo, then! What's the matter, old lady? Oh, I see it. It's not a tick, it's a great big thorn! Where've you been, then, you bad girl? Hold still, I think I can get it out. There!'

Philo, released, rushed across the hall, sat down abruptly and went into contortions trying to lick the sore place. George, without a word, was already leaving her, and Henrietta, hungry for company and conversation, said, 'Old Caleb says there'll be haying on Monday.'

'I thought you said you were with Ellerby.'

'That was this afternoon. I went to see Caleb this morning. Will there be?'

'Haying? Yes, Atterwith says it's dry enough now. He wants to cut Watermill first.'

'That's just what Caleb said. He always knows everything,' Henrietta said with satisfaction. 'Has there been any word from Papa?'

'No. Why should there be?' George seemed to find the question odd.

'Only that we haven't heard for such a time. I just wondered if there'd been a letter today.'

'He'll write when he's got something to say.' George turned away.

She searched for something to keep him back. 'Will you have the pigeons tonight?'

He answered over his shoulder. 'It's the Greys' ball tonight. Mrs Pretty can make them into a pie for tomorrow.' And he went off down the kitchen passage to deliver the pigeons to the cook.

Cheated of her conversation, Henrietta started upstairs. She met Mrs Holicar coming down. 'Oh, there you are! Mrs Gurney's been looking for you this half hour.'

'I know: bath night,' Henrietta said. 'I'm awfully hungry.'

'Your tea's upstairs,' Mrs Holicar said, surveying Henrietta with a professional eye. 'You've torn that skirt again – what've you been doing?'

Henrietta looked down. 'It was a bramble. I was in the woods stalking pigeons. But it's only the old tear opened again,' she added in anxious mitigation.

'Old or new, it's just as much work to sew it up,' Mrs Holicar grumbled. 'Make sure you give it to Bessie to mend before you wear it again, or it'll go all the way. You ought to be dressed in sacking, Miss Henrietta, the way you go through your clothes! I don't know, miss, look at you! Hair like a rook's nest and a scratch on your nose—'

'That was—'

'Yes, I know, the brambles! What business have you rampaging about in bramble bushes at your age, I'd like to know? Daughter of the house, and look at you! That's what comes of a house with no mistress. It's never anything but grief.'

'I'm sorry,' Henrietta said, subdued.

Mrs Holicar softened a little. 'You should take more care,' she said. 'Think of others instead of yourself. And it's time you started behaving like a lady instead of like a child. Seventeen in September, only three months away; some girls are married at seventeen.'

Henrietta looked at her with wide unhappy eyes for a moment, and then fled upstairs to the nursery. Doing God's will in a woman's ways – that's what Caleb said, wasn't it? And a woman's way was to get married, she knew that. The servants were always talking about it, if you were a girl. She wanted to do God's will, but getting married would mean leaving Morland Place, and she dreaded it. It was the one thing she had left to love, the one thing that was safe and sure and good and beautiful. Outside Morland Place was a world full of incomprehensible dangers and duties. They circled like wolves beyond the fire, seen only as a glint of eyes. Out there she wouldn't know how to behave, and would always be offending.

She ran the whole length of the upstairs corridor as though pursued by demons, and burst into the day nursery. In front of the nursery fire, on spread sheets, the big bath was set up, and

Regina was sitting in it, her thirteen-year-old 'chicken-wing' shoulder blades sticking out as she bent her neck for scrubbing by Katie. Her head was nobbly like a strange, exotic fruit with the curling-rags. She was the pretty one of the family, and knew it: always left behind by Henrietta and Sabina, she had been thrown much more onto the company of servants, and learned how to manipulate them with her prettiness and taking ways. She was vain and vapid and harmless, as long as someone was petting her. Henrietta loved her as she might love a puppy or kitten: she hardly thought of her as human.

Eight-year-old Manfred was enthroned in the big armchair like a small Chinese emperor, still damp from his turn in the bath, one skinny leg stuck out from his nightshirt while Mrs Gurney crouched before him to cut his toenails. Manny lived a rich inner life of imagination, and hardly knew anyone but him and Gurney existed.

Mrs Gurney looked up. 'There you are at last! Don't you know better than to be late this night of all nights? Your hair wants washing, and thick as it is, it'll take all evening to dry.'

'Sorry, Gurney,' Henrietta said.

'And look at the sight of you! Wild as a gypsy! If you think you're too old for a whipping, you'd better think again.'

Henrietta felt happier, her panic dispelled. This grumbling was as natural as birdsong to her; the unseasonable heat of the fire, the steam, the smell of soap and scorching sheet, the sloshing sound of water being scooped over a bent back – everything was as normal as could be. She feasted her senses. Ah, and there, the crowning glory, was the table with the cloth folded over half of it, and her tea waiting for her: a plate of thick bread-and-butter, a big piece of pork pie, a dish of cold rice pudding, some stewed apples, and a slab of cake.

'Wasn't it a glorious day?' she offered Gurney, by way of payment.

'Glorious days are not my business,' Gurney said repressively. 'Katie, get Miss Regina out and dried, and then go down and ask Thomas to bring up fresh water for Miss Henrietta. That lot'll be cold by the time she's eaten. Eat your tea, now, Henrietta, or we'll never get you done.'

Henrietta needed no second urging. Mrs Gurney watched her for a moment. 'No need to choke yourself. Chew properly! And sit up straight. Eating like a wolf! Not that nursery tea's what you should be having, at your age. It's high time you were stopping down to dinner, and if the mistress was alive or the master was home, things'd be different, I promise you. How you'll learn your manners in time to go out into company I don't know; and if you don't learn 'em you'll never catch a husband.'

'What if I don't want to catch a husband?' Henrietta said, reaching for more bread. Was there anything a female could do, she wondered, apart from get married? She could be a nun, but that would mean being shut indoors all the time, and she would hate that. 'Suppose that's not my destiny?'

'Never mind supposing. You'll do as you're told, and like it,' Gurney said unanswerably. 'And what have you done to that dress? Lord, will the trials of this house never end?'

'Haying Monday,' Henrietta offered, to distract her. 'If the weather holds.'

CHAPTER TWO

Askins was annoyed at having to get the carriage out. Two horses to groom afterwards, harness to clean, and though the roads were dry, there'd be a wilderness of dust, so the carriage would have to be washed. Fitton, the coachman, would be bound to blame him, as bearer of the bad news, for having to spend an evening away from his comfortable hearth and wife.

'I don't know why you can't ride to Rawcliffe Manor,' he grumbled. 'It's a fine night.'

George thought of himself as an easygoing, genial sort of man, and in that his wants were uncomplicated and generally fulfilled, that was true. But the heir to Morland Place expected to have his own way. 'Nonsense!' he frowned. 'Ride in evening dress? A fine mess I'd be by the time I got there.'

'There's the gig, then,' Askins said, encouraged by the argument. If he had to clean something, he'd sooner it was the gig than the carriage, and one horse than two.

George lost patience. 'Oh, get on with it, man! Gig indeed! And don't keep me waiting. I don't want to be late.'

'Yessir,' Askins said sulkily, turning his mouth down. 'Who d'you want to take with you?' he asked in martyred tones. Two horses meant a groom as well as a coachman – another person to blame Askins for what was not his fault.

George was half inclined to tell Askins he must go himself, just to serve him out, but then considered the weeks of recrimination he'd have to endure, and thought better of it. 'I'll take Oadby,' he said, and added on impulse, 'in livery.'

'Livery?' Askins's jaw dropped. No-one had gone out in

livery since the mistress died. Fitton and Oadby would slay him. 'I doubt it'll be fit to wear.'

'Whyever shouldn't it be?' George said in surprise.

'It's been hanging in the wardrobe these five years.'

'Then it should be clean and ready, shouldn't it?' George said with mad logic. 'Get on and stop arguing. A fine thing if a gentleman can't have livery when he wants it.'

He turned away to end the argument. It would still be daylight when he arrived at Rawcliffe Manor, and there was just a chance he might be seen by the person on whom he wanted to make an impression. He had a pleasing picture in his mind of a well-turned-out equipage bowling up with the two smart servants on the box. Oadby was a well-set-up young man with shoulders that would do justice to the coat.

A few weeks ago, anyone suggesting to George that he might care how he looked when arriving at a house for dinner would have provoked a stare. It was not that he had no vanity, but it was of a particular order: as eldest son, and heir to Morland Place, it had never occurred to him to wonder what anyone else thought of him. From birth the servants had petted and spoiled him; and his tutor, Mr Wheldrake, did nothing to lower George's self-regard. Wheldrake was a man of moderate abilities, large consequence and a magnificent manner, who, realising his own status depended on that of his pupil, encouraged George to see himself as a *grand seigneur* in the making.

On some characters this influence might have had a malign effect, and there'd been times in his childhood when he'd enforced his will on servants and other children with his fists and boots; but as he grew up, George's strongest trait was laziness. As he could never be bothered to exert himself to acquire accomplishments, so he would have regarded it as 'too much fag' to be a monster or a tyrant.

George was sixteen when his mother died and his father retreated into grief, taking his meals alone and seeing no-one. As the routine of the house began to fall gently apart, Wheldrake found his comfort compromised in small but annoying ways. He saw, too, that a Morland Place grown shabby and reclusive was not worthy of him, and would do nothing to advance his career. He found another position, gave his notice, and left. No replacement was hired: Teddy was sent to school, and George was to 'learn the management of the estate' – in effect to please himself in idleness.

When Benedict departed for Egypt, life for Georgie became more or less perfect. With his father absent, he became master of Morland Place in all but name. The 'all but' was crucial. He could enjoy the advantages of the position – eat and drink what and when he pleased, entertain his friends, run up bills, have first pick of the horses, and parade the consequence of the Morland name – without having any of the work and responsibility. Atterwith ran the estate; Mrs Holicar ran the house; and the children, as far as he ever wondered about it, seemed to run themselves. All he had to do was to give orders about his own comfort, something he did not find a chore.

It was fortunate for Morland Place that he took his pleasures so harmlessly, for with no check on him he could have plunged the family into scandal and ruin. But George was not made that way. Though lazy in mind and temper, he was vigorous in all the outdoor activities of the country squire, and long days in the open air left him too healthily tired even to contemplate vice. In the hunting season he went out four times a week; he shot, rode, fished, point-to-pointed, played a hearty game of cricket, bred and trained his own dogs, and took a keen interest in the racehorse stud at Twelvetrees. But though he regularly attended the races, it was the horses that interested him: he had no love of gambling in any form. Dice bored him, he could never remember the rules of games of chance, and with playing-cards he had difficulty telling the knave from the king. He liked to eat and drink well and often, but he disliked the sensation of being drunk, and tended to fall asleep too early to make carousing either possible or a pleasure.

As for women, they were a closed book to him. Wheldrake had been a celibate by both calling and inclination, and under his influence George had remained young for his age, and profoundly innocent. He tended to choose his friends from the age group a year or two below him, and in the unlikely event that any of them referred to the mysteries of sex, he merely shrugged indifferently and said that he was 'not in the petticoat line', without having any clear idea what that meant. Women for him were divided into two categories: servants, and other people's mothers and sisters. They were an inferior species, and nothing to do with him, except in so far as they ministered to his comfort.

It was as great a surprise to him, therefore, as it would have been to anybody, that as the carriage jolted over the track towards the city that evening, his thoughts were dwelling with excitement on a female. He would see her tonight. He had enquired whether she would be at the Greys' before accepting. He did not like balls: friends of his parents would invariably button-hold him, make coy enquiries about his unmarried state, and oblige him to dance with their dull daughters. But for the chance of seeing Miss Turlingham, he was willing to endure even that.

He had met her at an evening party at the Aycliffes'. They had made their money out of flour milling, and were now rich and genteel enough to have bought Holgate House, a neat place with a front sweep and a small pleasure-ground, and joined the carriage-folk. Mrs Aycliffe had been Dolly Peckitt, daughter of Peckitt's boots and shoes, and her younger brother Arthur was one of George's bachelor friends, so he had not been surprised to be asked. He had accepted in expectation of a good dinner and a comfortable chat with one or two friends, while the older people played whist. What he had not expected was to fall in love.

'Oh, Mr Morland, I must present you to our house-guest, Miss Turlingham,' Mrs Aycliffe had said with a little flutter in her voice. 'Or I should say, the *Honourable* Miss Turlingham.'

George had turned with a patient sigh, only to be smitten as with a lightning bolt, a feeling like a soundless explosion inside the head. Mrs Aycliffe went on with an eager smile: 'She and I were at school together for a year, in London. I hope she will be making a long stay with us.'

George knew he was gaping, but he couldn't help it. He had never seen anyone so beautiful in his life. Her white skin, the cold purity of her features, the magnificence of her figure dazzled him. Her glossy chestnut hair was dressed under an elaborate headpiece to fall in heavy ringlets behind, one of which had strayed artfully over her shoulder to lie against her white breast, exposed by the *décolletage* of her puce satin evening gown. George knew little of female attire, but he would have been willing to swear that the gown was the latest shriek of fashion. It seemed in the same style as other women's – with the straight front and large draped bustle behind – but she wore it with such an air that he was sure every other female in the room must be withering with envy.

Above all it was her manner which captivated George. Unmarried girls usually blushed and fluttered, giggled and languished when presented to him, for he was very much a 'catch'. But this goddess, so obviously superior to all her company, gave him a look of utter indifference, and as he made his bow, returned the slightest curtsy worth the name. Everything about her conveyed exquisite boredom mixed with the controlled outrage of a queen forced to make small talk with a chimney sweep. George was entranced.

It was for Miss Turlingham's sake that he was anxious his evening trousers should arrive unsullied by horsehair, his rosetted slippers undimmed by dust; her he hoped to impress by bowling up in a smart carriage with a well-looking footman and the best match-pair in Yorkshire. As the inequalities of the track flung him now ceilingwards, now against the window, he contemplated the evening to come with a surprising modesty. He wanted her to notice him; he hardly thought of more than that. He had been in company with her three times now, and not once had she smiled at him, or showed him more than bare civility. He was an eligible bachelor, heir to a fine estate, and generally thought of (he generally thought so himself) as handsome; but in the throes of first love, he did not think of that. He only knew that she was as far above him as the stars, and as unattainable.

In spite of Askins's efforts, he arrived early at Rawcliffe Manor. The orchestra was playing half-heartedly to an empty ballroom, and a single glance round was enough to prove that the Aycliffe party had not yet arrived. In front of the fireplace in the ante-room Lord Grey, the host, was standing with three gentlemen, discussing the affairs of the day, and in the thinness of company George could not avoid being drawn into the group, especially as one of the gentlemen was Henry Anstey.

'Hello, George, my boy,' he said kindly. 'I hear you'll be starting the haysel on Monday?'

George had to stop and answer the question. Of the other two in the group, Colonel Wilby was well known to him; Lord Grey presented him to the stranger. 'Fortescue, let me make George Morland known to you – scion of Morland Place, you know. Morland, this is my old friend Edgar Fortescue, rector of Bishop Winthorpe, who is paying me a long-overdue visit. We were up at Oxford together.'

The two exchanged the blankest of bows. Mr Fortescue was an ascetic-looking man in his forties with the pale and lined face of the scholar – as different as could be from young George with his ruddy outdoor cheeks. Eyeing the two, Lord Grey indulged his humour a little by adding, 'Fortescue is a noted biblical commentator, of course. I dare say you will have read some of his papers, eh, Morland?'

Henry Anstey, with diplomacy in his veins, jumped in to rescue George. 'We've been talking about the Education Bill, George, trying to determine whether universal education is desirable or not. You'll be governor of St Edmund's School one day, so I suppose the question will affect you.'

As some response seemed to be required of him, George said vaguely, 'Education is an excellent thing, of course.'

Colonel Wilby jumped in eagerly. 'Yes, yes, just so, quite so – excellent for a gentleman, you were going to say, eh, Morland?' George did not dissent, and Wilby went on, 'You see now, young Morland puts his finger on it! What use would Latin and Greek be to the lower orders?'

Henry Anstey concealed a smile. 'There are other things that can be taught, Colonel.'

The colonel looked blank. 'When I was at Harrow we studied Latin and Greek. Latin and Greek, sir. What did your brother do at Eton, Morland?'

'Latin and Greek, sir,' George answered obediently.

'There you are, then,' the colonel concluded triumphantly. 'That's education. And I say again, what do the lower orders

25

want with it? As well give Tacitus and Xenophon to my horse!'

George laughed at this, but stopped when no-one else did.

Fortescue said gravely, 'The National Education League's proposals must be unacceptable to any gentleman who regards himself a Christian. To divorce education from religion is an appalling betrayal of the whole of society. It is a step towards barbarism.'

'Quite right, sir,' Wilby agreed. 'And I say if they can read the Bible and write a letter home, what the devil – I beg your pardon, sir – what the *dickens* more do they need?'

'That's a question that naturally arises out of the Reform Act of '67,' Anstey answered him. 'Extending the franchise had certain consequences.'

'You believe that we ought to educate our new masters?' Mr Fortescue enquired with chill irony.

'Should never have given 'em the vote in the first place. It's a damn' disgrace!' Colonel Wilby barked. 'I wouldn't have expected it of Derby. Always thought he was a sound fellow, up until then.'

'There is a natural division between the governors and the governed,' said Lord Grey, 'which ought to be observed.'

'Quite right!' Wilby said. 'Go confusing the issue and there's no knowing where it will lead. Discontent, violence, revolution – and, mark me, that sort of thing always starts with the very people the Reform Act promoted: back-street town dwellers, upstart artisans, and grimy-handed malcontents!'

'Perhaps if they were educated they would not be malcontented,' Henry Anstey said equably. 'It's surprising how well people behave when you give them responsibility and the wherewithal to fulfil it.'

'The government of the land should be in the hands of those who own the land,' said the colonel with finality. 'I should have thought anyone could see that for plain common sense, and if you can't, Anstey, well, I'm sorry for you.'

'Thank you, Colonel,' Henry said with a smile. 'But what's done is done, and we can't take the franchise back now. So hadn't we better see that those we have given it to think as they ought?'

'But to what purpose, sir?' Mr Fortescue said.

'To exercise their vote wisely,' Anstey said patiently.

'Let 'em vote the way their masters tell 'em,' Lord Grey said. 'If any of my people voted against my interest, they'd know all about it!'

'Yes, by God!' said the colonel. 'The lower orders settin' up their opinions in the face of their betters? Intolerable! Can't have one's own servants disputin' with one, hey? What do you think, Morland?'

George, who had been looking around for the Aycliffes and had not been listening, was startled to attention. 'I agree with you, sir,' he said, since it had worked the last time.

Lord Grey said reasonably, 'Besides, Anstey, the lower orders can't afford to send their children to school: they need their wages. How many of the free places at St Edmund's are empty, Morland?' Lord Grey asked.

George opened and shut his mouth, having no idea. Henry Anstey answered for him, 'All of them.'

'The poor don't value education!' Colonel Wilby said.

'The reason for that is simple,' said Henry Anstey. 'You have to have it to value it.'

'A circular argument, sir,' said Fortescue disapprovingly.

At this point George spotted the Aycliffe party entering the room, and with profound gratitude for deliverance, made his muttered apology and left the gentlemen to their jaw-breaking.

Miss Turlingham was in the best of looks, and when George made his bow, seemed to regard him with a degree less indifference than before. This encouraged him to ask, with great diffidence, whether Miss Turlingham had a dance free that she would be willing to bestow on him. She not only said yes, he might have the last dance before supper, but that he might also take her down to supper afterwards.

In a dream of anticipation, he went entirely unaware of all the other young women in the room and the efforts of their chaperons to get him to stand up with them. He stood at the edge of the floor, his hands in his pockets, watching in admiration as Miss Turlingham circled languidly with select partners. When his moment came, George was almost too thrilled to enjoy it. He danced well – Mr Wheldrake had considered it an essential part of education, and he had the natural grace of the athlete – and given the state of his mind, Miss Turlingham would have had actually to fall flat on her face for him not to think she danced like an angel. But he was too nervous, tongue-tied and overcome to talk to her, and they circled the floor in silence.

When he escorted her down to supper it was better, for they were at a table with Jack Anstey (heir to the Anstey title and fortune, and Henry's great-nephew) and Jack's cousin Polly Micklethwaite, who kept a conversation going. Jack felt sorry for George, who was obviously smitten and had no idea how to cope with it. He, Jack, had always been precocious, and found women no mystery. He had sat beside Miss Turlingham at a dinner at the Coweys', and thought her a shocking cold fish, but he knew George well enough to know he had never noticed a girl before, and that this was a bad case of first love, which would probably wear off as quickly as it came on.

Afterwards Jack said privately to Polly what a good thing it was that George wasn't of age and had no independent means, otherwise he might have made a fool of himself.

'Miss Turlingham is very beautiful,' Polly said in fairness.

'Too old for him,' Jack said, 'and cold and disagreeable. *And*, if I'm not mistaken, she's hanging out for a husband.'

'Don't be cruel, Jackie,' Polly reproached him.

'I wouldn't say it to anyone but you,' he reassured her. 'But as the friendship between her and Mrs Aycliffe seems to have been of the remotest, and she's so obviously above her company, I can't think what else she's doing here.'

'But she hardly danced at all, and she refused any number of unmarried men: Rupert Coake, Billy Cox, Ned Wilby—'

'Not rich enough,' Jack said succinctly. 'She accepted *me* when Lady Grey obliged me to ask her.'

Polly slipped her arm through his. 'But you're spoken for.'

'Ah, but she didn't know that. I'm *very* glad I have you

to protect me against predatory females, Pol. I don't know what would happen to me otherwise.'

Polly laughed. 'Don't talk like a coxcomb, or I might change my mind.'

Rawcliffe Manor was on the north side of York, on the Northallerton road, and though it was not far from Morland Place as the crow flies, it was a long drive by carriage, necessitating going into York by one gate and out again by another. George passed the journey home in a state of bliss, going over his memories of the evening. The Greys had naturally chosen a moonlight night for their ball, but by the time the Morland carriage passed out of York by the Micklegate, leaving the gaslit streets behind, the sky had clouded over. Turning off the main road onto Morland land, the carriage slowed to a walk: it was now quite dark, and Benedict had been too distracted and George too indifferent to order road repairs. Oadby got down and walked ahead to look out for potholes, and they crept along at snail's pace while Fitton cursed and fretted about his horse's legs – quite audibly to George, who had the window down. When they reached the coach house George called impatiently for him to stop, annoyed at having his dream disrupted.

'Let me out here, for heaven's sake, and I'll walk the rest.' He scrambled out and slammed the door. 'I could have been home an hour ago on my own feet!'

'''T'en't my fault, Master George,' Fitton defended himself robustly. 'If I've mentioned that road once, I've mentioned it a hundred times. It's not fit to be driven in daylight, isn't that, let alone in t'dark.'

'It's not my fault the moon went in,' George retorted, annoyed at being chided. But Fitton had been with the family too long to be deferential, especially to one who had taken his first driving lessons under Fitton's tutelage.

'The moon's nowt to do wi' it. If you don't get them holes filled, the end of it'll be brokken legs! It'd be different if we had a mistress,' he mourned. 'A lady'd never stand being jolted over them tracks every day. It's allus the same when a house lacks a mistress – everything goes to pot.'

His words brought a glorious vision to George's mind: he saw Miss Turlingham stepping out of a carriage before Morland Place, himself leading her in through the great door to take her place as mistress. It was the wildest dream, but it was so delicious that his scowls disappeared, and Fitton was surprised to find the young master reaching up to pat his leg consolingly.

'You're quite right, of course. I'll talk to Mr Atterwith in the morning. You did quite right to mention it, good old fellow.'

And he strode off towards the house with a dreamy smile. Fitton stared after him, amazed, and said to Oadby, who was holding the horses' heads, ''At young man has tekken on plenty tonight. Regular grassed, he must be. "Good old fellow", indeed! I nivver heard the like!'

'That's the way of it, Mr Fitton,' said Oadby. 'I shouldn't like to 'ave 'is 'ead in the morning.'

'Tha'll be lucky to have a job in t'morning if tha doosn't mind thy sauce,' Fitton said. 'It's not for thee to criticise t' gentry.'

'But I only said—'

'I heard what tha said. Now are tha going to turn them horses or are we going to stand here all night?' Fitton snapped. He had been heartily regaled in the kitchen at Rawcliffe Manor on cold beef, pickled onions, apple pie, cheese and beer, and his stomach was a molten lake. He thought perhaps the apple pie had been a mistake.

Reaching the barbican, George found the gates closed, which did not surprise him, since the gatekeeper would have been looking out for the carriage, not a pedestrian; but when he went in through the postern the gatekeeper was not there. The great door of the house was standing open, laying a slice of light down the steps and over the cobbles. George stood listening for a moment. The dark air was warm and still, apart from a flickering of bats swooping back and forth above him – he could hear their tiny needle shrieks – but there was a sense of disturbance which alarmed him. He was not an imaginative person, but he had a feeling of foreboding which, despite the warmth of the night, made him shiver. Part of him wanted to run away; but he was hungry and sleepy and needed a second supper and his bed, so he crossed the yard and went up the steps into the hall.

A group of upper servants was gathered there in a state of suppressed agitation, while the dogs, which slept in the hall, milled around them excitedly. There was Atterwith, who lived in the barbican, with a dressing-gown over his nightshirt; Battey, the first footman, in shirt-sleeves; Mrs Holicar fully dressed; Mrs Pretty, the cook, with curling-rags sticking out from under her cap; the missing gatekeeper, shifting nervously from foot to foot; and Askins, with a face as long as Monday, attended by the shock-headed stable boy whose eyes were round as marbles and whose mouth, left unsupervised by his brain, had fallen open.

As George appeared the dogs rushed at him in a solid blanket, and the servants turned in a single movement. Mrs Holicar cried, 'Oh Master George, thank heaven you're home!'

'I were just on't brink o' riding off to fetch you,' Askins added, his face shortening with relief to merely its usual degree of gloom. He turned to the housekeeper. 'I told you there weren't no point to it. I'd've on'y passed him on't road.'

'Well, I didn't know,' Mrs Holicar defended herself. 'We couldn't just do nothing, could we? You see,' she explained to George, 'there's been a telegraph come, and there's no making head or tail of it.'

'Telegraph?' George said, handing his hat to Battey. 'At this time of night?'

Atterwith tried to take over the tale. 'Potter brought it up himself, thinking it must be urgent—'

'*And* we've only just got rid of him,' Holicar grumbled. 'He stuck like a limpet, wanting to know what it was all about.'

'And then Mrs H. would 'ave it that I'd to saddle up and ride off to fetch you,' Askins reverted to his own complaint. 'I *said* there weren't no point to it.'

'The telegraph,' Atterwith said with emphasis, raising his voice a little, 'is from Port Said.'

He held it out to George, and George took it in a sudden silence. He felt all at once rather strange, remote from himself,

31

as though he were viewing everything through the wrong end of a telescope. His hand holding the scrap of paper seemed an inordinately long way away, and his fingers seemed to belong to someone else. Only the dogs, leaning heavily against his legs in a hot and hairy mass, were real.

Battey stepped close with a candle to illuminate the tiny black words for him.

DEEPEST SYMPATHIES FOR YOUR BEREAVEMENT STOP EMBALMED BODY HAS NOW SAFELY ARRIVED STOP DO YOU REQUIRE BURIAL HERE OR SHIPPING TO ENGLAND STOP PLEASE ENSURE INSTRUCTIONS ARE CLEAR AND DETAILED STOP REPLY URGENTLY NEEDED END

He looked up. Everyone was watching him. Mrs Holicar's lip was trembling. The cook's eyes were moist.

'Oh sir,' Mrs Pretty said, 'is it the master?'

'What can it mean?' Mrs Holicar asked. 'What are we to do?'

'Is the maister dead, Master George?' asked Askins. 'Is that it?'

George opened and shut his mouth and no sound emerged. He suddenly felt very young, not more than ten years old, and wished they would not all look at him so appealingly, as if they expected him to know what to do.

Atterwith spoke, gently and firmly. 'It could be a mistake. We must get confirmation. A telegraph should be sent, perhaps?'

'A telegraph, yes,' George said blankly. But to whom? How could one word such a question? His father dead? He had been gone so long George had all but forgotten him, but a father elsewhere and a father dead were very different things. It was like stepping into your house and finding the back wall missing. His brain felt as unhinged as the stable boy's jaw.

'Perhaps Mr Henry Anstey might be consulted?' Atterwith suggested.

Relief flooded over George. 'Yes, of course. He'll know what to do.' Thank God for Uncle Henry! He would take care of everything. The responsibility slid off George's shoulders, and in his relief he felt almost lighthearted. He smiled at the woebegone women and said, 'It's a mistake, depend upon

32

it. This is meant for some other family. Probably a quite different telegraph intended for us has gone to them, and we have theirs.' They examined the proposition, and seemed to find it comforting.

Atterwith spoke again. 'In the morning, perhaps, will be soon enough? No need to be dragging Mr Anstey from his bed at this hour.'

'Oh, certainly, there's nothing to be done now,' George said gladly. 'We should all go to bed.'

'And, if I might suggest,' Atterwith went on, 'nothing should be said about this until the truth is known. It would be better if the contents of the telegraph were known only to those present.'

'Quite right. It should be kept secret,' George said, happy with his role as translator of the steward's ideas. He looked round at the servants sternly. 'None of you is to mention it to anyone, do you understand?'

Henrietta had been asleep when the telegraph came, but the subsequent bustle in the house had woken Mrs Gurney, who had gone out into the passage to see what was happening, and had encountered Mrs Pretty toiling up the backstairs on her way back to bed. Their whispered conversation and the light from the door, left ajar, had woken Henrietta, and while the two dames were still wagging their heads together she appeared, sleepy and enquiring, her feet bare on the drugget and her nightgown too short for her.

'What is it? What's happened?'

Gurney's automatic reaction was, 'Dear Lord, look at you in that nightgown! If you haven't outgrown everything in the wardrobe!'

Henrietta tugged at the sides as if that might lengthen it. 'Is something wrong? What time is it?'

'Time you were in bed and asleep. Go back now, before you wake the others.'

'Time she had a room of her own, if you ask me,' Mrs Pretty sniffed. 'Sixteen and still sleeping in the nursery! This'll change a few things, mark my words. There'll be some growing up done in a hurry – and not before time.'

'Tush!' Mrs Gurney said warningly.

'She's got to know some time.'

'Know what?' Henrietta asked. She was wide awake now. She looked from one to the other and caught the thought out of mid-air. 'Has something happened to Papa?'

Gurney was thrown off balance. 'Now whatever made you say that?' she asked in a shaken voice. There was something unchancy about the child sometimes. Henrietta stared at her pleadingly, her eyes wide in her pale face. Gurney took pity on her. 'It's not sure yet, Miss Henrietta, so don't go fretting about it, but a telegraph's come.'

'About the master, or it looks that way,' Mrs Pretty put in, wanting her share of the news.

'Dead?' Henrietta asked starkly. There was a pause, as the women looked at each other, and then both nodded, slowly, like some strange, two-headed mechanical toy. Henrietta's mouth trembled and her eyes filled with tears. In the shadowy passage, lit only by the cook's candle, the night seemed profound and death suddenly a close and awful thing. She had had nightmares when she was a little child about a formless monster that lived in the dark corner of the nursery. Now she felt it close again. It had taken up her father in one curved, glittering black claw, and was passing its dead, blank gaze with terrible dispassion over the rest of the household.

'Well, nothing's known for sure yet,' Mrs Gurney said hastily, 'so don't you start upsetting yourself.' It was she who had stumbled awake all those nights, scraped painfully out of her sleep by a child's abandoned shrieks, and she didn't want a recurrence of it, not tonight of all nights, when her own nerves were upset. 'Go back to bed and think nice thoughts, and in the morning we'll see. And no need to talk to the others about it, either. Mr Atterwith says we're all to keep our mouths shut until word comes back and it's certain.'

Henrietta nodded dumbly and began to turn away, but turned back again to ask, 'What will happen to us, if it's true?'

Gurney looked at her with a mixture of pity and exasperation. 'Why, what should happen?' she said briskly. 'We'll go on just as before. Go on back to bed, now.'

Henrietta went; but she lay a long time before she slept, hearing the soft voices of the cook and the nurse washing in from the passage, rising and falling like slow sea waves, discussing the future which, whatever it held, would not be 'just like before'. And when she slept, she dreamed of them, standing in the small cave of light as she had seen them, solemnly nodding; but in her dream they grew smaller and smaller as she fell helplessly backwards into the void, spinning slowly to nothingness like a dead star.

CHAPTER THREE

George's healthy young body marched him off to sleep the moment his head touched the pillow; but he woke at dawn with the clear sound of birdsong through the part-opened window, and lay for a while, his mind empty, watching the pale, translucent gold of morning slipping across his bedroom wall. When he began to think, it was not of his father, but of Miss Turlingham, and the delightful vision he had entertained briefly last night. He had thought it a mad dream; but after all, why not? He had always known that one day he must marry and get an heir; and he had always known that he was, in worldly terms, a desirable *parti*. The Morland estate was by no means negligible: manor house of great antiquity, mentioned in all the guidebooks; demesne, six farms, stud stables, flocks and herds; a quantity of property in York, a thriving commercial enterprise ditto, and a half-share in three cotton mills in Manchester; and besides all that, the distinction of an ancient name and a coat of arms that went back to the fifteenth century.

Of course, until now, that had all belonged to his father. It occurred to him that he had never had any personal income or fortune, and that had he wanted to marry, it must have depended on his father's settling something on him, or his bride living like him at Morland Place as Papa's pensioner. Had he seriously considered asking Miss Turlingham to marry him, he would have had nothing to offer her. He had no doubt that such a superior female would have regarded the proposal as an insult.

Ah, but now things were different! If Papa was dead – and

what else could that telegraph mean? – everything was his. Not only that, but in a week's time he would be twenty-one, and he would inherit absolutely, without trustees or guardians. Whatever Miss Turlingham's circumstances were, his suit would not be contemptible. If only he dared! He thought about proposing to her, and his cheeks went hot. Her beautiful, ice-goddess face appeared before his inner eye, her eyelids lowered in that haughty look that turned his knees to jelly. He saw himself kneeling, possessing himself of that white hand, kissing it fervently. She would say no, for sure; *but suppose she said yes?* In his private theatre she consented, graciously, to be his wife, and he rose, clasped her in his arms, laid his lips on hers . . . He shuddered with excitement at that part. Now he was leading her, draped in cloudy white, from the church to the carriage, bells ringing, crowds cheering . . .

He sighed and turned over on his side, and went over it one more time, a little smile fixed on his lips. And then something occurred to him, and the dream-cobwebs vanished. Naturally, it all depended on Papa being dead; but if Papa *was* dead, they would all be plunged into mourning. As soon as the confirmation came from Port Said, he would have to put on blacks. The door-knocker would be wreathed in crape, visitors except close family denied, social invitations refused for at least three months. He sat up, frowning. It was not possible for him to have any tender emotions for a parent so remote, but he knew he couldn't go courting in deep black. Every feeling must revolt, and hers most of all, for she was a semi-divine creature with more sensibility than common mortals. If he even attempted it she would recoil from him in horror and disgust.

In three months' time he might begin a quiet courtship – but in three months' time who knew where she would be? She was a house-guest of the Aycliffes, and however warm the friendship, she would hardly stay with them more than a month. She would leave, and he would never see her again. What possible excuse would he have to seek her out? Mere acquaintance was not enough. She would think it impertinent. And besides, his fevered emotions told him, in three months she would have met someone else, someone with a title probably, a lord with London manners and dashing whiskers who would sweep her off her feet.

He got out of bed and began walking up and down the room, his brow furrowed with the unaccustomed effort of thought. There must be something he could do. The one love of his life! He would never love again; he would die a broken-hearted bachelor and Teddy would inherit Morland Place. He saw himself slumped over his lonely dining table, reading about her in the society pages, a dazzling hostess with ten hopeful children. It was not to be borne. He would drink himself to death . . .

Then a thought occurred to him. It was not possible to initiate a courtship while in deep mourning; but if one was already affianced, there was nothing against visiting one's beloved – indeed, it would be considered quite proper for the fiancée to appear at one's side, supporting one through one's affliction. And there was nothing against getting married while in mourning. It would have to be a quiet wedding, of course, but a quiet wedding need not be dowdy. *And he was not yet in mourning!* Until the confirmation came, he was free to do as he pleased: if he proposed and she accepted him before that, everything would be all right!

His brow cleared, and his jaw firmed with decision. He would do it this very day, before his courage leaked away! She might refuse him – he wasn't worthy of her – but he would have given it his best effort; and if she didn't refuse him too hard, it would at least lay the foundations for him to approach her again in the future. A declared lover could seek her out, given the right circumstances. It might be bold, but it would not be impertinent.

He strode to his wardrobe and flung open the doors. What to wear? Lord, he had to go and see Uncle Henry, too! He couldn't get himself up too bright for the old fellow. Well, then, sober but not sombre; elegant, that was the thing. Oh, if only he had a valet! Why didn't Papa get him a valet when Wheldrake left? He wondered if a superior female could tell when a man had dressed himself. He must at least have someone hold up a looking-glass so that he could check his back view – disastrous if his parting were crooked, for

38

instance, or his boot-tab out! And on the subject of boots, he must persuade Battey to polish them for him – Battey had a way with boots – and bring them upstairs in a cloth, so there were no fingermarks on them. She would be bound to notice fingermarks . . .

He pulled the bell to summon the footman, and began rummaging through his shirt drawer.

Miss Turlingham sat before the glass in her bedroom at Holgate House, staring moodily at her reflection while her maid, Bittle, dressed her hair. She did not quite wish she had never come here – the alternative was Cousin Matilda, and she preferred only to fall back on Cousin Matilda in extreme necessity – but it was humiliating to be under obligation to a woman like Mrs Aycliffe. Not that Mrs Aycliffe saw it that way: it was plain that in her eyes the obligation was the other way round. She had responded with thrilled promptness to Miss Turlingham's suggestion that she might visit, and had done everything since she arrived at Holgate House to make her comfortable. This bedroom, for instance, was furnished with every convenience, and the newness of the carpet and curtains suggested they might have been bought specially for the occasion. But it was galling for the Honourable Alfreda Turlingham, daughter of Viscount Marwood, to have to accept favours from one who had been merely Dolly Peckitt, the tanner's daughter – a girl whom, when they had been at school together, Miss Turlingham had despised for her provincial manners and shocking accent.

How her head ached! 'For God's sake, can't you dress hair without pulling me to pieces!' she snapped.

'You'll have to keep your head still, Miss Alfreda,' Bittle said colourlessly. 'I can't help pulling if you fidget about.'

The ball last night – *quel ennui!* Lord Grey was far too open in his invitations. Some of the guests were barely genteel. Besides, what pleasure was there in a ball for someone in her position? She was twenty-seven, penniless and unwed. All other circumstances counted for nothing against that hideous phalanx of facts. Twenty-seven. She was beautiful, and in the kindness of candlelight she still looked like a lovely girl, eighteen or nineteen at the most; but now in the cruel light of day she could see the effects of time. Beautiful, but no longer a girl. How long before the dread print of the crow's foot sealed her doom? *Twenty-seven!* These days it was the only thing she could think of when she looked in the glass.

Oh, that ball last night! She remembered her first glittering Season, the London balls in the great houses: the lights, the music, the flowers, the powdered footmen, the throng of carriages. Huge frilled crinolines, bare shoulders and little ringlets – the styles were so pretty then! Witty young men in uniform bringing one champagne and ices! Always the first in beauty, she had never lacked for partners. She had been presented, of course. The Prince Consort was still alive then, and the Queen wore white. She had been fêted; looked forward to a brilliant marriage and a future as a great hostess. An earl, a duke – a prince, even? Prince Alfred was just her age. What could be too good for the lovely Miss Turlingham, voted almost without dissent the most beautiful débutante of 1860?

How could she have known it was all an illusion? And yet, even at the moment of her greatest triumph, had she not been aware of an undercurrent? Had she not seen, when she came into a ballroom, the small whisper that ran along the seated row of chaperons like a chilly breeze bending a line of oats?

If only her father had been a different man, had not drunk and gambled away his entire fortune, before finally putting a bullet through his head one appalling day in the gun-room at Turl Magna, the family seat; one autumn day of rich, mellow sunshine with the smell of woodsmoke and crisp, dying leaves on the air. Miss Turlingham had been the first to reach him: even now the smell of dying leaves made her think of cordite and blood.

That wicked act was the last nail in the coffin of Miss Turlingham's golden future. Financial ruin was hard enough, but the scandal and shame of Marwood's suicide prevented even her beauty from rescuing her. She hated her father for his selfishness. And she hated her mother, who, unable to face shame and poverty, had pined away in a matter of months, never caring what was to become of the children she left behind.

Alfreda and Christopher: in their childhood they had been acknowledged the prettiest children in Leicestershire, and the cleverest. Their portrait, by Torquato, with two large mastiffs, had caused a sensation at the Summer Exhibition of '52, and hung thereafter in pride of place over the chimneypiece in the green drawing-room at Turl. Oh, beautiful Turl! It had been a bitter thing when it had been sold – especially hard for Kit, who inherited a tainted title and nothing else . . .

Poor Kit! Her expression softened even thinking about him. The one creature in all her life that she had loved was her brother. Always close, even as little children, they had grown up to be each other's fondest admirer. Alfreda was the level-headed one, Kit the volatile; she inherited her mother's beauty, he his father's charm. Fortunately his commission had been purchased before the money ran out, but living was expensive in the Blues, and there was no knowing how much he had contributed to his father's indebtedness. And then Papa had done that wicked thing, and when Turl was gone and the debts had been settled, there was nothing left. Mama had a tiny income of her own which was not taken by the creditors, and which, when she died, provided the slimmest of annuities for her son. Kit survived by remaining unwed and living in bachelor rooms, but an officer had to keep up appearances, as well as horses, and it was not in his nature to bear economies. It had soured his sweet disposition, and made him hard. He fretted, complained, and ran up debts of his own.

Alfreda had nothing at all, and was reduced to this gypsy life, depending on the charity of relatives, who passed her from hand to hand like a tiresome burden. The humiliating monotony was broken only by the occasional vacation solicited from ever more remote acquaintances; Mrs Aycliffe was surely the bottom of the barrel. And she was aware that, bad as it was, it could only get worse. In a year or two her beauty would be gone and her relatives would know that any chance of her securing an establishment was over. They would expect her to wear caps and look after their children and fetch and carry for them in return for her keep. She thought death would be preferable.

If only she could marry! She was desperate to marry. It must be a gentleman; and if she was to help Kit, it must be a gentleman of means, for much as she loved him, she could not deny that he was expensive. But her lack of dowry and the taint of her father's suicide clung about her like a bad smell. She had thought in York, away from London and the world of fashion, she might find someone who did not know, or at least would not care. But the only person she had met who was at all suitable was Lord Anstey's heir, and he, it rapidly became plain, was all but engaged to the mousy cousin with the vulgar name. Oh, the waste!

For the rest, she hated York, with its narrow streets, strange accents and impertinent servants. She hated the Aycliffes and their middle-class gentility. She hated going to balls. And – as she moved her head restlessly and got her hair sharply tugged for it – she hated Bittle most of all. Bittle was not a proper lady's maid: she had been head nurse to Alfreda and Kit. In those days the nurseries had taken up a whole floor of the west wing of Turl Magna. Under Bittle there had been four nurses, a sewing-maid, a still-room maid, a laundress, a footman, two grooms and a coachman.

When everything else had gone, Bittle had remained, mutating into Miss Alfreda's personal maid, learning to dress hair and alter gowns with surprising skill, and becoming year by year more undismissible as she was owed more and more wages. Alfreda hated her because she knew everything, had been party to all the shameful contrivances and makings-do, the turned gowns, mended stockings and cleaned gloves, the small humiliations and insults Alfreda told herself she could perhaps have forgotten if Bittle had not witnessed them. Alfreda hated her because though she was a servant she was not under her control; Bittle was an unknown quantity, who might do or say anything at any time, who had the power to hurt Alfreda as no-one else could. Oh yes, she hated Bittle as fervently as anything in her shabby, make-shift life; and she couldn't do without her. Who else would work for her for nothing? Miss Turlingham half believed that Bittle had become skilful at dressing hair purely to annoy her.

'There,' Bittle said, pressing in the last pin. 'Though how I managed it with you heaving about like a rough sea I don't know.'

'Hold your tongue!' Alfreda snapped.

'My, we are prickly this morning.'

'Don't be impertinent, or I'll—'

'Dismiss me without a character. I know.' Bittle turned away to pick up the morning gown. 'Was it a nice ball last night? You never said a word while I was undressing you.'

In the glass Miss Turlingham watched Bittle shake out the pink barathea. Pink again! A hand-me-down from Cousin Emmeline, who loved pink, altered by Bittle's patient hand. Pink was not Miss Turlingham's colour. Made-over clothes were bad enough, but pink made-over clothes were the limit!

'No, it was not a nice ball,' she said fretfully. 'A parcel of dowdies and their red-faced, thick-witted husbands; insolent, half-trained servants; and conversation so tedious I could scarcely be civil. Oh, whatever possessed me to come to a place like this?'

'At least it makes a change of scene,' Bittle said, holding the gown for Alfreda to step into. 'And who knows what might come of it?' *What*, in this context, always meant an offer of marriage.

'What could come of it?' Alfreda said bitterly. 'I hate Yorkshire! I should never have come.'

'Well, you needn't be so niffy-naffy,' Bittle said. 'Beggars can't be choosers.' She saw she had irritated her mistress to the top of her bent, and, as was her wont, now became kinder. It pleased her to be able to feel sorry for Miss Alfreda, who after all could not escape her situation, as Bittle could any time by walking out and finding another position. 'If you don't like it here, there's the Reeces,' she suggested. 'You haven't been there in a while. Why don't you write and see if they'll have you?'

'Not without new clothes. I shall never forget how Clarissa Reece looked at me last time and asked where I had that rose-fawn merino from.'

'Maybe Mr Christopher could advance you the price of a gown?'

'Kit can barely pay his mess-bills,' she said impatiently. 'He has nothing to spare for me.'

'Well, then, Miss Alfreda, you'll just have to stay put and find someone to marry you,' Bittle said, hooking up the gown. 'I hear tell there was a gentleman very struck with you last night, and eager to pay court. If you was just to *try* and be pleasant for once—'

'What gentleman?' Alfreda asked with faint hope.

'A Mr Morland – a nice young gentleman, and heir to a very fine fortune, so the cook says.'

The hope collapsed again. 'A country booby with a red face,' she said; though she had been surprised at how well he danced.

'The Morlands are a very old family,' Bittle said, 'and there's a little bit of queerness about them that'll very likely make nothing of your background, so you shouldn't put up your nose too soon. Your Mr Morland's father is quite eccentric, Cook says.'

Alfreda gave her a look of savage dislike. 'He's not my Mr Morland,' she said. 'Besides, he's the merest boy, barely out of school by the look of him. I couldn't think of him.'

'You should think,' Bittle said. 'Though his father's abroad, they say he's bound to come back soon. And he'll be wanting the boy to marry and get an heir. You should be concentrating on keeping Mrs A. sweet, so that you can stay here long enough to make sure of Mr George Morland: that's what you should be doing, if you want my advice.'

'I don't want your advice,' Miss Turlingham snapped. 'What you can be supposed to know about – *ow!*'

'Oh, sorry, Miss Alfreda, did I pinch you?' Bittle said sweetly.

Miss Turlingham relapsed into silence. Why was nothing ever simple? She knew, of course, that George Morland was attracted to her, though she had not encouraged his preference. What use, a boy under age? Even if Bittle was right and he was an heir, an heir was no use to her. She must have a man in possession of his fortune. Kit had debts to pay, and she needed an establishment. Besides, even if he wanted to propose, he wouldn't be able to do so while his father was abroad, and with boys, these fancies came and went. By the time his father returned he'd be courting some well-dowered local girl of seventeen. She stared at her reflection with despair. She hated the pink barathea. She was sure it made her look near to her age, and her age was like a poisonous toad squatting in the corner of her mind, which she was at pains never to disturb.

Amid the concern, anxiety and pain that Henry Anstey felt on reading the telegraph which George brought him in the morning, he found a corner of his mind to register surprise and approval that George had dressed with so much care for the visit. Usually to be found in riding-clothes, his hair a shaggy mane, he had presented himself this morning in black cutaway, grey trousers and a restrained waistcoat of lavender silk; his hair was parted down the middle, all the way from brow to nape, the front hair wound into two little horns over his temples, and the whole heavily pomaded. Young people in general were so careless about form these days that it seemed to argue a very proper realisation of the solemnity of the moment, and a respect for Henry himself which he had not much noticed before. He was touched.

'We must not jump to conclusions,' he said, 'but I am bound to say that it looks very much as though your father has met with some accident. The possibility was always there. It was a dangerous place to be visiting, and particularly when he went up country. And then, you know, we have wondered why there has been no letter these last weeks. I'm afraid—' He broke off to draw out his handkerchief to wipe his eyes and blow his nose.

'Well, sir, will you send a telegram?' George prompted.

Henry winced at the word. 'Telegraph, George; no slang, please. Yes, I shall put the necessary enquiries in hand at once. You did quite right to come to me, my boy. Oh dear, oh dear, I do so much hope . . . But there may be some mistake. We must not despair.' He looked down at his hands, resting on the desk. They were shaking a little. First his wife, and now

Benedict, his oldest friend! He drew a steadying breath. 'We must be discreet,' he said. 'I advise you not to speak of this to anyone until we are sure. You would find yourself the target of some very impertinent attentions if it were known – and then, if it should be untrue, the most distressing gossip.'

'Oh, quite. I've told the servants to keep their mouths shut,' George said. 'Well, I'll leave it to you, then, Uncle. I have some business to conduct in York, so I'll come back later and see what the news is.'

Henry stared in surprise as George stood up, preparing to leave. Business to conduct? At such a time? 'You are very calm, George. How can you – but no, I understand. Best to keep busy, eh? I shall have my occupation this morning, and you must have yours. Off you go, then.' He got to his feet to see George out, and laid a hand on his shoulder. 'We will continue to hope until no hope is left.'

'Yes, Uncle,' said George. Out in the street he assumed his top hat and gloves and hurried away to collect his gig from the Bunch of Grapes. It was early for a morning call, but he could not risk finding anyone else there: he must have Miss Turlingham alone to make his declaration. His hands were sweating and he was trembling with nervousness, but his determination drove him on. He had only this one opportunity, and he was not going to waste it, whatever the outcome.

Mr Potter of the telegraph office had mentioned the matter only to his wife, in confidence, for he had to explain why he was going out to Morland Place at such a time; and Mrs Potter had mentioned it only to her cook-housekeeper when she came for her orders first thing next morning – well, the woman had been with her twenty years and was almost family! The cook-housekeeper, enjoined to the strictest secrecy, would have thought it quite wrong to divulge it to anyone at all, except of course the milkman, who was betrothed to her daughter Jane, who was housemaid at Mrs Rawnsley's. Jane, given the story by her beloved at the back door, felt it was too good not to pass on to her mistress (who was a very good mistress) when she took up her morning tea – though she did

46

warn her that it was a great secret and not to be told to anyone else in the world.

Mrs Rawnsley mentioned it to no-one but her bosom friend Mrs Richard, whom she met outside Pemberton's, the confectioners, that morning, knowing that Mrs Richard was as deep as the grave and would never repeat it. Unfortunately the conversation was overheard by Mrs Beale, just coming out of the shop, the two ladies being too fascinated by the story to notice her or lower their voices. And Mrs Beale, with no silence bound upon her, paid an early and excited morning call on her friend Dorothea Aycliffe for the sole purpose of passing it on. Since Miss Turlingham was sitting with Mrs Aycliffe, she knew all there was to know about the telegraph within twelve hours of its arrival at Morland Place.

When Mrs Beale had left – sooner than might have been looked for, the story being too good to confine to such a small audience – Dorothea looked at Alfreda and said, 'Do you think there can be anything in it? Surely poor Mr Morland can't really be dead? What a horrid thing!'

'In a foreign place like that, anything might happen,' Alfreda said calmly, though her mind was working rapidly. 'Disease and accident cannot surprise as they might at home.'

'But it is odd that they heard nothing before, surely?'

'Letters go astray. The truth will be known soon enough, I suppose. But since it was something that Mrs Beale overheard, it was not proper of her to repeat it, and if I might give a hint, my dear Dorothea, we should not discuss it further, with anyone else or with each other.'

But Mrs Aycliffe found herself compelled to go on talking about it, though she had nothing to add but a reiteration of her wonder and concern. Miss Turlingham stopped listening to her in favour of frantic thought. If it were true – if Morland senior were indeed dead – it would change everything. George Morland suddenly became an interesting man. Possessed of his fortune, he was a match worth considering. But how old was he? It was hard to tell, and if he were still a minor, there would be tiresome trustees to get over. But, oh, what use anyway? By the time he was out of mourning, she would have left York, and before she could arrange another visit

47

with Dorothea and get to work on him, he would have been snapped up by some designing local mama. Why was Fate always so cruel to her?

There was the sound of the doorbell ringing below, and Miss Turlingham awoke from her bitter thoughts as Mrs Aycliffe said, 'Another early visitor? Could it be someone else who's heard the rumour? Of course, if they haven't heard it, it would not be proper of us to mention it,' she added quickly as she caught Miss Turlingham's eye.

But it was a male voice below. The two women exchanged raised eyebrows. What man would call at this hour, unless it was on business, and looking for Mr Aycliffe? But after a brief pause there was the sound of footsteps in the passage, and the maid opened the door and announced, 'Mr Morland, madam.'

George stepped past her, impeccably dressed, with his hat and gloves in his hand, the last person Mrs Aycliffe would have expected to see. She was so surprised she did not manage to conceal it, and stared at him in a way that, had he had his wits about him, would have told him rumour had run ahead faster than his horse could trot.

'Mrs Aycliffe. Miss Turlingham,' he said, making his bow.

Dorothea found her voice. 'W-won't you sit down, Mr Morland? How nice to see you.' He sat, placing his hat on his knee, cleared his throat nervously, but said nothing. He looked from one to the other, and then restlessly around the room. She searched frantically for something to say that would not touch on his father. 'Had you a pleasant ball last night?'

'Thank you, yes. It was a good one, wasn't it?' he said, and relapsed again into silence.

Dorothea was beginning to wonder whether she had dreamed Mrs Beale's visit. He was obviously not at ease, but did not seem to be consumed with grief or racked with worry. And what was he doing here anyway? He never paid morning calls that she knew of – and why would he do so at such a time? Her mind was so full of unaskable questions that she couldn't find anything else to say, and since Miss Turlingham never exerted herself to speak for mere politeness, and George wanted only to speak to Miss Turlingham, they all sat in silence for the next five minutes.

The doorbell rang again, and an exclamatory female voice was heard downstairs.

'It's Mrs Coake,' Dorothea said, and added, 'Oh dear,' looking at Miss Turlingham. Mrs Coake must have come for the same purpose as Mrs Beale, and since she was loud, overbearing and completely without sensibility, she would very likely put the question direct to George, which would be embarrassing and bring Miss Turlingham's disapproval down on Mrs Aycliffe for having such vulgar acquaintances. But there was no hope that the maid would deny her.

While she was wondering helplessly what to do, George got to his feet and, his normally bright cheeks reddening further, said rather hoarsely, 'I wonder if I might beg the favour of a private interview with Miss Turlingham? Mrs Aycliffe, would you allow me to – um—?'

Mrs Aycliffe was so grateful to be rescued she didn't stop to think what the request meant. 'Oh! Yes, what a good idea! Perhaps Miss Turlingham could show you the garden: the roses are very fine. Won't you step through into the other drawing-room? Then you can go out by the other door.'

Miss Turlingham was a ferment of emotions: indignation that George should have asked for and Dorothea granted the interview in such an awkward way and without consulting her; general anger at finding herself amongst people who hadn't the slightest notion of conduct; and palpitating wonder about what George could want to say. But she was so glad that the meeting between Mrs Coake and George was to be avoided that she raised no objection, only passed through the sliding door to the second drawing-room and, when she heard Mrs Coake admitted to Dorothea, led the way out into the passage and downstairs.

The Aycliffes' garden was very pleasant: neat lawns and gravel paths within a surrounding wall overhung with rambling roses, and at the far end a gate leading into a wilderness. Miss Turlingham, conscious that servants might well be watching from the windows, conversed firmly about the weather until they had strolled the length of the garden and then turned as casually as she could through the gate into the privacy beyond.

George followed her blindly, tongue-tied with embarrassment. He had hastened here with what he thought was an excellent plan, but finding himself in her actual physical presence wondered if he could bring it off. The words he had prepared seemed inadequate and wildly unsuitable; the very notion verging on the improper. Dare he mention it? Would she turn from him in loathing?

Miss Turlingham was also in some doubt. She could not think what a private interview could be for if not to propose, and yet she could not think how he could propose if he had just heard that his father was dead. And if he had not heard his father was dead, how could he intend to propose, having neither parental permission nor fortune? If he was free to ask her, it was improper; if he was not free, it was unacceptable. It was a conundrum. All she could do was to smooth the path for him. She led the way to a bench and sat down.

'Well, Mr Morland, you wished to speak to me?'

He stood before her, almost writhing with shyness, turning his hat in his hands, unable to meet her eye, only looking at her in little, fervent sips. He cleared his throat awkwardly. 'Miss Turlingham, I have something to ask you,' he began. But no, that wouldn't do. 'That is, I have something to tell you. You see, something has happened. Or at least, it may have happened – we don't know yet for sure. Though it seems likely.' He could feel his hands sweating. Oh Lord, he was making such a mull of this!

'I cannot understand you, Mr Morland,' she said coolly. Oh for the poised and witty young men of her London Season! 'Please be more explicit.'

He took a desperate grip on his wits and tried the words he had practised in the gig on his way there. 'Miss Turlingham, it can't have escaped your notice that I admire you. In fact, since the moment I first set eyes on you—' He lost his grip. 'Oh, Miss Turlingham, I'm mad in love with you, and that's the truth!' he cried, fixing his eyes on her at last, his face hot with passion. 'I've thought of nothing but you ever since I met you, but I knew you could never think of me. And besides, with me not being of age and Papa being away I couldn't have asked you even if I thought for a minute you'd have me, which obviously—'

Disappointment replaced curiosity. There was nothing for her here. She began to rise. 'Mr Morland, I must say that in the circumstances it is most improper of you to—'

'Oh no, please, you don't understand! Please, let me explain.' She subsided, but with obvious unwillingness. He felt foolish. The plan which had been so plausible to him this morning now seemed most likely to earn him the sharpest of rebukes. But it would be silly to have got this far and then give up. He took his courage in both hands.

'I know this is not the right way to go about things, but I can't see any other way round it,' he said. 'I had a telegraph last night, from Egypt.' He told her about it, and about his visit to Henry Anstey that morning. 'Uncle Henry thinks – and I do too – that it probably means my father is dead, in which case I inherit the estate as soon as I'm twenty-one, which is next week. That would mean I'd be in a position to ask you to marry me – except of course that once Pa's death is confirmed and I go into blacks, I can't. So it seems to me this is the only chance I have, before anyone knows about it.'

'I don't understand you,' she said – though she did, of course. She was running ahead of him; but she wanted to be sure.

'Well, you see, if I was to ask you now, and you accepted, by the time Pa's death was announced we'd already be engaged, so it would be quite all right. And we could get married as soon as we liked, because people do get married while they're in mourning, when they were engaged beforehand. A cousin of Jack Anstey's did, and no-one thought there was anything wrong in it.' She did not answer, her eyes lowered; and his hope sank again. 'I don't suppose you care for me. I know I was mad to think it, but Morland Place is a good estate, and though I'm not near good enough for you, I thought perhaps – well, I thought at least it wouldn't be an *insulting* offer,' he finished rather pathetically.

Now she looked up at him. She saw a red-faced and rather ridiculous boy; but he was in love with her, and could be

51

moulded. If the fortune was all right . . . In normal circumstances she would have told him that she could not decide at once, and sent him away until she had made discreet enquiries; as it was, she must take it on trust, though it was not likely in this sort of closed society that there could be any doubt about it. Henry Anstey was the man of business, and he was extremely respectable.

She paused not because she had any doubts about accepting him but because her mind was full of memories. She saw the handsome Palladian façade of Turl Magna, the servants lining the steps when her parents came back from Town in the summer; herself as a child being lifted up onto the saddle in front of her father, still smiling and handsome before the troubles came, to be galloped with him across the deer park. She saw herself coming down to the drawing-room in a white dress to play the piano for her mother's visitors and be praised for her prettiness and cleverness; she remembered her come-out and the high hopes that were cherished for her. And here she was in a miller's wife's garden, being surreptitiously proposed to by a tongue-tied Yorkshire farmer's son six years her junior.

She sighed. 'I do not think you are insulting me, Mr Morland. I am honoured by your proposal, even though the manner of it is unconventional.' She raised a hand to stop his protest. 'I understand your reasoning, but I think there are difficulties which you have not taken into account. Even if I were to accept you now, when it was announced it would be known exactly how the engagement came about, and we would be censured for lack of conduct.'

'Well, I did consider that,' he said hopefully. 'And I thought, if you wouldn't mind it too much, we could just – or rather *I* could – let people think that we had been secretly engaged for some time while we were waiting for my father's consent. I don't mean tell any lies,' he added hastily, 'but only hint a little and let people think it for themselves.'

'Mrs Aycliffe knows perfectly well that we aren't engaged. And she knows about the telegraph. Mrs Beale told us about it not half an hour before you arrived.'

'How the dickens— ?'

'Gossip travels fast, Mr Morland. It is not important *how*.

Mrs Aycliffe would have to be told the whole, and asked to keep the secret.'

'Oh, well, she is a good sort, I dare say, and won't mind,' George said. He looked at her shyly. 'Does that mean that you might consider marrying me?'

'I cannot answer a question that has not been asked,' she said.

'Oh.' He understood. Without hesitation he went down on one knee on the earthen path, his heart beating so fast he barely had a thought for his best grey trousers. His voice trembled as he said, 'Miss Turlingham, you are the most beautiful woman I've ever seen in my whole life. Will you marry me?'

There was no doubting the sincerity in his voice. He thought her beautiful; and she was nearly twenty-eight, and terrified of wrinkles, and Kit was running up debts he had no means of ever paying.

'Yes, Mr Morland,' she said sadly, 'I will marry you.'

She let him take her hand then, and he pressed his lips to it fervently. 'Thank you,' he said between kisses. 'Oh thank you! You won't regret it!'

Mrs Aycliffe was faintly shocked that George should have anything on his mind other than his father; and then she was shocked that Alfreda wasn't shocked. But when George explained the dilemma to her, and she saw how much in love he was, she had to forgive him. She had guessed Alfreda's plight, and was very glad that such a happy outcome was being arrived at, even if it had to be by an unconventional route. It was such a romantic match it was almost like a fairy tale: the lovely princess, cast into poverty through no fault of her own, raised by the hand of the handsome prince to the comfort she deserved. Morland Place was as good a fortune as any woman could want, and it would make a worthy setting for Alfreda's beauty. And Mrs Aycliffe, a mother herself, spared a thought for those poor motherless children who had now lost a father as well. Alfreda could provide them with the love and guidance they needed. It took some effort of imagination to see the icy Miss Turlingham as a substitute mother, but in the romance of the moment Mrs Aycliffe managed it. And then, more prosaically, she thought that if Morland Place had a mistress again, there would be a resumption of the parties, dinners, entertainments and balls the neighbourhood so missed.

So she promised to keep the secret, wished them happy; hoped, confusingly, that Benedict Morland would prove to be alive and well after all; and rang the maid to say she was not at home to any more visitors. Her mind was in such a whirl she was sure she wouldn't be able to speak calmly to anyone, or stop herself from blurting out the wrong thing. George took his leave to return to Henry Anstey's office, promising to bring news as soon as he had it, and Miss Turlingham, cheating Mrs Aycliffe of the conversation she craved, retired to her room to compose herself and think over what had happened. It was some time before she had recovered the tenor of her mind, and she rather knew that her position in life had improved, than felt it.

CHAPTER FOUR

Gurney did not want Henrietta to go to the haysel. It didn't seem right to her to be going about at such a time; but seeing the child so heavy-eyed and apprehensive, she couldn't deny that getting out in the fresh air would do her good, and she had sense enough to realise that to stay around the house doing nothing all day would drive Henrietta to distraction. So she said only, 'It's too hot for the little ones, at their age. You'll have to go on your own.'

Henrietta was grateful to be spared the burden of looking after Regina and Manfred when she had so much on her mind. 'Thank you, Gurney,' she said, and gave the nurse a brief but feeling hug.

Gurney was not used to hugs. She said gruffly, 'And mind you keep a hat on. I don't want you all freckled like a thrush.'

It was still early when Henrietta left the house, but the hay-makers had gone long ahead of her. It was a perfect morning, clear and cool, with the dew shining gold over the meadows where the low sun glanced, the sky a tender pale blue. The bridal look of May – the froth of hawthorn and kex, starry moon-daisies, the heavy candles of chestnut flower – had gone from the hedgerows and fields: now there were hanging festoons of voluptuous pink dog roses, wild honeysuckle, and the creamy, upturned lips of bear-bind. Everywhere was in full leaf, the rich grazing of midsummer, the darkening green of rising crops; lambs and foals no longer stotted and raced, but grazed head-down alongside their dams; everything in the natural world was preoccupied with the serious business of making growth.

As she followed the path at her usual swinging walk, her spirits rose a little. To be out of doors on a perfect day, to move and feel the easy meshing of her young and healthy body – simply to be alive was a pleasure. She passed one of the labourers' cottages. The woman of the house, with bare brown forearms, was hanging out linen on the thorn bushes by the door.

'Going to the haysel, miss?'

'That's right.'

'They're not much ahead of you. Going to be a hot one.' A toddling child in a cotton dress bleached of colour by washing came to the door; a curly-headed thing with a peg-doll clutched in its fist, too young for Henrietta to tell whether it was girl or boy. She smiled and waved her fingers, but it lowered its head shyly out of range and sucked the doll's head for protection. Henrietta walked on. As she passed the wooden shed at the edge of the cottage's cabbage patch, a grey striped cat slipped out from behind it and followed her, gliding along under the hedge on lion-coloured paws, pretending it just happened to be going in the same direction.

By the time she reached the edge of the hay meadow, the sun was well up, and the dew had vanished like a dream at cock-crow. The scythemen had already stripped off their jackets and rolled up their sleeves, and were strung out in a line across the field. While Henrietta had been visiting with Caleb, the men had been having a 'hanging day', declared by Mr Atterwith as soon as he saw the grass was ready. That was when the cutters took their scythes to the blacksmith for the blades to be sharpened, set and hung. There would be a hanging day before the corn harvest too. The occasion was a minor festival, always attended by a great deal of beer-drinking, paid for by the estate. Now it was time for the cutters to earn this small extra privilege. They must set the pace of the work, and never falter until it was done.

It was like a ballet, Henrietta thought. She loved to watch it: a smooth swing of the shoulders, the glint of the descending blade, and the grass sighed and sank as though into enchanted sleep. Then back and shoulders braced to contain and reverse the swing, and all in one movement the scythe came up like a pendulum, and the man moved on, spreading his spell over the ripe and rustling field. A good scytheman always looked effortless, as though the sickle swung of its own accord, drawing the man with it. Only when you were close by did you hear the grunt, smell the sweat, imagine the harsh burn of the wooden handle on the palms and the dead aching weariness of the physical toil.

The day broadened, and the line of scythemen became staggered across the field as their skill and the conditions separated them. Behind them came the men with the heavy rakes, breaking up the swathes and pulling the hay into windrows; behind again came the women and children gathering anything the men had missed. Henrietta helped where she was wanted, sometimes in the rows, sometimes helping to carry round water. The cloudless sky deepened to a deep, rich blue, the sun rose up burningly to its zenith, and the heat in the field became almost intolerable. The sweat of the workers attracted hordes of black flies, and when Henrietta straightened up to ease her back and look around, she saw that each hot body carried a dancing cloud of midges above it. The smell of bruised grass, so delicious at first, gradually grew sickening, seeming to replace all breathable air with its warm, cloying dampness; and strands of hay, which looked so soft and pretty in the mass, scratched wrists and necks like sharp wire.

Pausing to wipe the dust from her mouth, Henrietta saw the striped cat hunting mice along the uncut edge of the tall grass. A lark was shrilling over the next field; a train clanked slowly along the embankment between the hayfield and the river, emitting black smoke in puffs that stayed intact in the windless air like a row of full stops left behind it.

There was no chatter across the field: the workers laboured under the beating summer sun in silence, and Henrietta felt guilty that she had thought of haymaking as a pleasure. The fact was that she could stop whenever she wanted, and if she was tired tomorrow she could go and do something else. But for them, haysel was a time of hard labour, two weeks of long hours under the pitiless sun of midsummer. Meadow after meadow must be cut, the grass drawn into windrows, the rows turned every two or three days. Then the hay must be cocked, and loaded, and carted, and the stacks built and thatched; and every bit of the work, bar the pulling of the haycarts, had to be done by the labour of human muscles. Every hand was needed, even to the children who gleaned up the stray wisps, and while the weather held they would work from sunrise to sunset. After the corn harvest there was always a holiday, merrymaking and a sense of festival, for it was the culmination of the year's work with the crops. And the men were paid a bounty for the corn harvest. But there were no extra wages for the extra work of haysel, and when it was done, no holiday; for after haysel came shearing . . .

But though not a man in the field would have chosen to be there if he could have the choice of being rich and idle, there was a satisfaction in it all the same. There was a clear task to be done, and it was an important one: a good hay harvest meant fat beasts, good prices, and plenty – more meat and milk for all. It was work you could see the point of, work you understood the beginning and end of: grow the crops, feed the beasts, eat the bread and the beef. They were part of the cycle, they belonged to it, they depended on the land and the land on them; and though the work was always hard and often unpleasant, when it was over they were content. At a deep and wordless level, where men question what they are for, there was peace in their souls. Henrietta understood that, and wished she felt so about her own life. She longed for certainty, and for the sense of accomplishment that comes with service. She had cried to Caleb, 'What am I for?' These men and women need never ask that question: they knew.

At midday the head man – the 'lord' as he was known – called a halt. Tools were downed, aching backs straightened, and everyone sought what shade they could. There were no trees in the field, but there were hedges, the shade of the waggon, and on one side, the low, tumbledown walls which were the footings of a house long ago deserted and demolished: the Watermill House which had given the field its name. Baskets, boxes and cloths yielded up their contents to quiet the pangs of hunger sharpened by six hours of hard labour, and seven hours' distance from the last meal.

Henrietta joined a group sitting in the strip of shade along the ruined walls, and they made room for her companionably, with nods, smiles and 'Now thens', and a panting grin from a dog too exhausted by the heat to get up and greet her. At first there was no conversation, for everyone was too busy eating – Henrietta included. The parcel Mrs Pretty had hastily put up for her contained oat bannocks – rather dry and rough to eat in this heat, and Pretty had omitted to butter them – with slices of cold lamb and some faggots left over from yesterday's servants' dinner. Jugs of water were still being carried round, but one of her companions had a bottle of cold tea and kindly offered her some.

'When your gran'f'er were alive, we used to 'ave cider an' buttermilk brought us from up the 'ouse come dinner time,' he said. 'The old ways are dyin' out, seemin'ly.'

'I suppose with Papa away . . .' Henrietta said apologetically. She thought probably Georgie ought to see to things like that in their father's absence; but she had to admit she couldn't imagine Georgie bothering about anything that didn't relate to his own pleasure.

'Ah,' another man said, as if divining her thought, 'he were allus one to tek his coat off come haysel and harvest, was the maister. Always coom to 'elp when he were a lad, same as you, miss. But Master George, he 'as another cut to 'is jib.'

'Well, he's young yet,' said someone else philosophically.

'How is't with thy faither?' one of the women asked politely. ''As been any news?'

Henrietta collected herself and managed to say fairly normally, 'No, nothing for a while now. I expect a letter went astray.'

'Ah, that will 'appen when folks goes to foreign parts,' someone said wisely. There was general agreement.

'Lucky if that's all as gets lost.'

'It's a dangerous place, is Abroad. I don't know what t' maister wants wi' goin' there.'

'Ah, well, Maister 'as got furrin blood in 'im,' an old man offered as explanation. 'Not meanin' no disrespect, Miss Henrietta, but thy granny was a furriner.'

'She were a fine lady, and a good mistress,' a woman

reproved him severely. 'You remember that, Ebenezer Pike!'

The old man was unabashed. 'Ah niver said she warn't, Doris Simon! She were't best mistress we ever 'ad, but she were a furriner, an' there's no gettin' away from it. Coom from France, she did, time o' the Revolution. When the bad Frenchies killed their king, and the good Frenchies all coom over 'ere, 'cause we still had ours.'

It seemed a succinct summary of the history. Henrietta peeled the fat from a slice of lamb and threw it to the dog. 'I was named after her, though she died before I was born. I heard she was a French lady, but I wasn't sure if it was true.'

'True enough,' said Mr Pike.

'And she were a Roaming Catholic,' said Mrs Simon disapprovingly.

'We was all Roaming Catholics once,' said Mr Pike. 'Ivvry one of us. You remember that. York Minster were built by Roaming Catholics.'

A theological argument seemed about to break out, so Henrietta intervened by asking, 'I've never understood why the estate belonged to her. I mean, if she really was French? Or perhaps that was a mistake and it really belonged to my grandfather after all?'

'Nay, miss, it were hers all reet,' said Mr Pike. 'The way I understand it, the old mistress – thy great-grandma, that'd be – left it to her on account o' thinking she were t'best person to 'ave it. But why she thowt that Ah couldn't tell thee. That's the way it goes wi' Morland Place. The maister – or mistress – can leave it where they like, no questions asked nor answered. And to man or woman, too, just as they think fit.'

'How very odd,' Henrietta said.

'Aye, but it's historic,' said one of the others. 'Goes back time out o' mind.'

''At means mebbe tha could inherit Morland Place one day,' Mr Pike concluded jocularly.

'What, wi' two older brothers?' Mrs Simon objected.

'Ah just tellt thee,' Mr Pike said, 'it's all according to 'ow t'maister wants it.'

'Stands to reason he'd want to leave it to a son,' Mrs Simons said robustly.

Henrietta intervened again. 'I'm sure Papa means to leave everything to George,' she said; and then remembered the telegraph. It was one thing to talk blithely about people leaving things to people, but to do that they had to be dead. Suddenly she wasn't hungry any more. She gave the faggots to the dog, and turned her head away, staring at the shimmering horizon. Noting her silence, her companions politely let her alone and chatted amongst themselves of births, deaths and marriages.

Perhaps because she was attuned to the subject, Henrietta actually saw the news arrive. A woman appearing at the far end of the field with a basket of something spoke eagerly to the first person she met, and soon gathered a knot of listeners around her. Then someone broke off to go to another group; and island by island the whisper came round the field, a bending and turning of heads, jumping the spaces between the patches of shade where people rested like brush fire. At last it flickered about the edge of her own group, a low murmur and eyes turning on her, wondering if she knew and if she should be told. Finally one of them made a decision. Young Tilda Cook, not long married and bold with requited love, came over and hunkered down in front of Henrietta.

'Miss,' she said, 'miss, I don't know if anyone's told you, but you did ought to know, in my view. Mr Potter from the telegraph office says a message has come about your father.'

It was unfortunate that Mrs Potter's cook's daughter's betrothed was a milkman, with such excellent opportunities for spreading the word. So many back doors called at so early in the day: never had a secret less chance of remaining secret.

Henrietta brought her focus back to the kind, sun-brown, gap-toothed face before her, framed with the flaps of its cotton bonnet. 'If it was the message of last night, I know about it.'

Tilda Cook nodded. 'I'm very sorry about it, miss. I hope with all my heart it proves to be false.'

61

'He's a fine man, the maister,' said the woman next to her, and there was a murmur of agreement round the group.

'He is that!'

'A fine man and a good master.'

'We won't see the like of him again.'

'There'll be some changes round these parts if he's gone, you mark my words.'

Henrietta couldn't bear it. She wanted to shout at them, 'We don't know that he's dead yet!' But she knew: it was in their grave faces and reverent voices. They were already calculating the consequences, something she very much didn't want to do. After a moment or two she got up and walked away down the field, feeling eyes following her, murmuring voices nipping at her like gnats as they planned her future as an orphan.

The confirmation came: Benedict Morland was dead. He had died of liver-fluke disease, a sickness quite common in Egypt. He had been up country with a small party investigating some tributary waterways when he had taken violently sick, and though they had brought him back to the camp, he had died a few hours later. The letter explaining all this had gone astray; meanwhile the body had been embalmed by local practitioners, packed up and sent down the river to the company's headquarters at Port Said, whence, eventually, came the impatient reminder that instructions were awaited for its disposal.

Henry Anstey brought the news to Morland Place himself. He had known Benedict all his life; had run tame about Morland Place as a boy and shared a tutor with Benedict and his brother Nicholas. Nicholas had later married Henry's younger sister Aglaea, making them all brothers in law. After Nicky's death Benedict had become Henry's closest friend, and at one time it had been Henry's dear hope that his only son, Arthur, might marry Benedict's daughter Mary. Though that had come to nothing, still they had remained as close as brothers. Henry's personal grief was intense, and he could not do less than come in person to break the dread news to Benedict's son and heir.

And there was business to mention. 'You know, don't you, my boy, that I was named your trustee for the remaining period of your minority, though that ends tomorrow?'

In the drawing-room Henry sat on an upright chair with his hands resting on his knees, feeling all of his sixty-one years, and more. George sat opposite him, leaning one elbow on the table beside him and dressed as usual in breeches and boots, surrounded by dogs. He had taken it very calmly, Henry thought. In looks he resembled his father most, and Henry recalled his friend in younger days in just this pose, with his big hound Fand always at his heel. Everything about the drawing-room was familiar to Henry: the mellow panelling, the carpet – threadbare now – the furniture, the family portraits on the walls, the huge white marble clock flanked with bronze rearing horses on the chimneypiece. It was all just as it had been from his childhood: Aglaea and later Sibella as mistresses had done nothing to change this room. There was a sense of continuity here.

But now an era was ending. A new generation was to take the reins: George was to be master. What would he do with the position, the honour, the power over men's lives? It occurred to Henry that he didn't really know George. The lad called him 'uncle', was always polite, laughed at his little jokes; but Henry had no idea what went on inside that head. He had known Benedict inside out – at least until the end, when he had got so strange. He remembered the day Bendy set off for Egypt. The send-off at the station was very grand: York was proud of its famous son, who had done so much to bring the railways and prosperity to the city. Somehow the idea had taken root that he was going to dig the Suez Canal and open the trade route to the East for the specific benefit of York traders, and there had been a band, and bunting, and speeches, and the Corporation in full fig to wave the train out; and Benedict had raised a huge cheer by insisting on shaking hands with the locomotive driver before mounting into the specially decorated carriage. Benedict had grinned like a boy, excited, and more like himself than he had been for years. That was the last time Henry had seen him.

He drew out his handkerchief and wiped his eyes carefully

63

– they had a habit these days of watering. It was an old man's gesture, he thought; but when Celia died he had become an old man. He was tired. When his control over the Morland fortune ended he would retire from business completely. He would fulfil this last trust laid on him by his friend Benedict, and then Arthur could take over. That's what sons were for.

He sighed and went on. 'You become guardian of the younger children tomorrow, but I am Teddy's trustee until *his* majority. Of course, the legal processes will take time to complete, but in effect you inherit your fortune and your responsibilities immediately.'

'I see,' said George. The fortune he had long eagerly anticipated; the responsibilities were another matter. He had never thought of being guardian to his younger siblings, and spared it no more than the briefest thought now.

'I am executor of your father's Will, of course. Thank God I was able to persuade him to make a new one before he went to Egypt! He didn't want to, you know; had no idea he could ever die. Of course, I did not expect it, either; it was just my lawyer's caution.' He had to wipe his eyes again. George waited. 'So the Will is quite up to date, and there will be no difficulties about it. I will read it in due course to all concerned, as is proper, but I see no harm in telling you now that, as you must have expected, Morland Place comes to you.'

'Good,' didn't seem quite the right response, nor 'Thank you.' George compromised with a bow. Philo thought it was for her and reared up to rest her upper body across his lap.

'You will be free to make your own arrangements, of course,' Henry went on, 'but though my trusteeship ends, my firm will be happy to continue to administer the finances of the estate, if that is what you wish. I expect to be retiring from active business in the near future, but I hope you will always look upon me as a friend and mentor.'

'Thank you, sir,' George said.

'I recommend you have every faith in Atterwith, and consult him about the management of the land. Though he has not been here long, he is an excellent man with a most superior understanding of his business.'

64

George nodded neutrally.

Henry felt as though he were running through sand. 'To be master of Morland Place is a very great responsibility. There will be many things that puzzle or vex you, much that you want to ask. Come to me at any time; I will always help you if I can.'

'Thank you, Uncle,' said George.

Henry wondered if George were dazed with grief. 'Is there anything you want to ask me now?' he prompted.

George stirred. 'Well, yes, sir, there is.'

Henry waited, but George seemed to be having difficulty choosing his words. 'Well, my boy, out with it. Is it about the funeral, perhaps?'

'Oh, no. I'm sure whatever you arrange will do very well.' He pulled Philo's ears, and she jabbed her muzzle under his hand. 'No, it's something quite different: I want to get married.'

Henry was staggered. It was the last thing he would have expected to have raised at a moment like this; and George had never been in the petticoat line. 'This is rather sudden, isn't it?' he managed to say.

George avoided that delicate issue. 'The question is, sir, how soon would it be proper to have the wedding? I should like to marry as soon as possible, but I know one must wait a certain time for decency's sake—'

'For decency's sake? Your own feelings ought to tell you—' Henry interrupted, but was halted by a coughing fit. At last he found a husk of voice. 'Who – who is the young woman in question?'

'She is the Honourable Miss Turlingham,' George said with evident pride.

'Turlingham? Turlingham? I know that name.'

'She's staying with the Aycliffes. I danced with her at the Greys' ball. Perhaps you saw me with her.'

'Oh, yes, I know who you mean. I didn't know she was an honourable. Who is she?'

'Her father was Viscount Marwood,' said George, 'but he's dead now.'

Henry's eyes opened. '*That* Turlingham? No wonder the

65

name was familiar. I should think he is dead! Went bankrupt and blew his brains out. It was in all the papers – but some years ago now. You probably wouldn't remember. Marwood's daughter? George, my boy, you can't marry the daughter of a suicide! Good God, the Morland name! Your grandmother would turn in her grave!'

George frowned. 'I don't see what my grandmother has to do with it. Besides, it's not Miss Turlingham's fault. She can hardly have been expected to stop her father, can she?'

'You don't understand,' Henry said, shaken. 'When something like that happens, the whole family is shamed. The stain clings to all of them. The tainted blood runs in—'

'Well, sir, if I don't care about it, I don't see that it's anyone else's business,' George said impatiently. 'I love Miss Turlingham, and I don't care to have her abused by anybody, not even you, sir, with all respect.'

Henry saw in that moment that he had lost him. There was nothing he could do to stop George marrying, and his advice would not be heeded. His influence was finished, and this long chapter of his life was closed. Not only was Benedict gone, but with George, Morland Place, too.

Still, he couldn't help trying. 'How did you meet her? How long have you known her?'

'I met her at the Aycliffes, of course. I've known her for weeks, though we haven't been engaged for long.'

'I didn't know you were engaged at all,' Henry said. 'It was not proper to enter into an engagement when you were under age, with your father away, and without consulting me.'

'I only asked her yesterday morning,' George said. 'I went to the Aycliffes' house when I left you.'

'You went—! But – good God, George, you were waiting to hear about your father! You didn't know if he was alive or dead! Have you no sense of propriety?'

George pushed Philo off his lap and stood up, exasperated. 'Now isn't that just the sort of comment I was trying to avoid? If I'd left it until I knew for sure about Papa, everyone would have said it was shocking to go courting at such a time!'

'And they would have been right!'

'Yes, and if I waited until I was out of mourning, she'd have gone away, and I'd have lost my chance. I don't see what I was supposed to do,' he concluded resentfully. 'It seems to me I was damned either way.'

Henry held up a quivering hand. 'Stop, stop. I cannot speak about it any more. You must forgive me, but I am too overset by the death of my friend – *your father!* – to go on now. Another time, George, if you please.'

George subsided, sulkily. 'All very well for you to say another time,' he muttered. 'You ain't in love.'

'Help me up, please,' Henry said. 'I am damnably shaken.' George gave him his arm and Henry tottered to his feet. 'You can bring the young woman to see me at my office tomorrow and we will discuss the matter then.'

'I don't see what there is to discuss,' George began defiantly, but Henry held up a hand.

'I don't propose to try to dissuade you from this course,' he said. 'I see it would be useless. But you will need someone to draw up the marriage settlement; and until probate is completed someone will have to handle those formalities for you. You could, of course, instruct another solicitor—'

'No, of course not,' George muttered, a little shamefaced. 'I don't want anyone but you, Uncle.'

'Very well. Bring her to me tomorrow. And now, call my carriage, if you please. I must go home.'

An evening's reflection and a night's sleep did not reconcile Henry Anstey to the matter. He had a vague memory of Miss Turlingham at the ball, a tallish female in pink; he thought she had been handsome, though not in the first flush of youth. He could not doubt that she had 'caught' George: for all his airs, he was not up to the rig. Marwood's daughter could not have any dowry, and with the shame of her father's suicide must be supposed to be desperate.

There were things in favour of an early marriage for George. Aside from the question of providing an heir, it might prove a steadying influence. George had never shown any tendency to wildness, but he seemed to have no aim in life but pleasure, and inheriting a large fortune had turned harder heads. Then there were the younger children to consider. If George did not marry, it would be necessary for some female relative to be found to live at Morland Place: it wasn't right for the younger ones – especially Henrietta, who was at a delicate age – to be in the sole care of a heedless bachelor. Indeed, that was something that should have been arranged long ago, but while Benedict was alive it had been his decision, and he had neglected it.

But Marwood's daughter! What sort of influence would that be to introduce to Morland Place? How would it affect the chances of the girls, to have their name connected with Marwood's? It was only to be hoped that Miss Turlingham had not inherited her father's weakness, or she would run through George's fortune like water. Henry was deeply distressed, for there was nothing he could do to stop George marrying now he had turned twenty-one, and he knew enough of him to guess that opposition would only make him obstinate. All Henry could do would be to press for a long engagement, and hope that the thing would die naturally. George was young and volatile: first love cools quickly, and in a few weeks he might easily see someone else he fancied more. But if it were called off, the girl might cut up rough: it would do George's reputation no good to be known to have jilted her, and a court case would be costly and deeply embarrassing. The whole business was as bad as could be.

His first view of Miss Turlingham as she was ushered into his office was a welcome surprise. He had worked himself into such a state of mind he half expected a painted, gin-raddled harpy with bold eyes, bright clothes and a coarse voice. But though Miss Turlingham's pink merino gown and black-fringed paletot were not new by any means, she was dressed with elegance and propriety. She moved well, conducted herself with assurance, and was decidedly handsome, and her voice was well-modulated and refined. There was nothing in the least vulgar about her appearance or manner: on that basis she would not embarrass anyone in company, or cause the shades of Morland Place to writhe with shame.

On the other hand, as soon as she sat and Henry had a good view of her face, he could see that she was considerably older than George; and his questions soon elicited that she was dowerless – indeed, virtually penniless, and dependent on the charity of relatives for a home. She also seemed cold and haughty, displaying no warmth of affection towards her betrothed. Henry hadn't a doubt in the world that she wanted George for his money, and in spite of George's protestations of love, he would have bet that the whole thing was her idea and that he had been tricked into it.

Henry instinctively disliked her, and the thought of introducing her tainted blood into Morland Place, his second home, repelled him. For once in his life, his lawyerly caution abandoned him, and he spoke his mind.

'I cannot like this engagement. I have to tell you, George – with all due respect to you, ma'am – that I think it hasty and imprudent. The match is unequal, and the way you have gone about things presents an underhand appearance. When the detail is known there will be a scandal. If you do not care about it for your own sake, you might think of your sisters.'

George's face was reddening. 'The detail, as you call it, Uncle, won't be known unless you tell it! As for the match being unequal, I think myself very lucky. Miss Turlingham has birth, rank and beauty. As to dowry, I don't give a fig for it.'

Henry controlled himself. 'You are the son of my best friend, and it is natural I should want you to marry a well-dowered girl, just as your father would have wished. All the same, I should have nothing to say about that if other circumstances were different. I am very sorry to give you pain,' he bowed stiffly towards Miss Turlingham, 'but the lack of a fortune is nothing beside the shame of your father's bankruptcy and death.'

George, red as fire, wanted to jump in at that point, but Alfreda laid a restraining hand briefly on his arm and said with an icy calm that did not quite conceal her fury and chagrin, 'No-one can regret my father's failures more than I do. It was a long time ago, however, and I have nothing to reproach myself with in my own conduct. If Mr Morland does not regard it as a bar, I cannot see that it need concern anyone else.'

George looked at her with admiration. 'I wish I'd put it like that!'

She ignored him, addressing herself still to Henry. 'There is only one question for Mr George Morland to ask you. Have you the authority to prevent his marrying where his heart chooses?'

It was a bitter moment for Henry. 'No, I have not,' he said after a short struggle.

George smiled triumphantly. 'Then we'd better get on with the settlements and such.'

Henry and Miss Turlingham were still locked in a stare. 'I think,' Henry said slowly, 'that in the circumstances it would be better if my son Arthur were to deal with the matter. I shall be busy pursuing probate. And in view of what has been said here, Miss Turlingham would perhaps find it more comfortable not to have to talk to me.'

George shrugged and said, 'Just as you please. As long as we can get on and get things settled.'

Miss Turlingham merely inclined her head graciously, like a queen accepting a not very important service. Underneath she was burning: that this country lawyer should have the temerity to snub her, *her*! She would have liked to kill him. But he was right: she didn't want to deal with him. Apart from hating him, he was a great deal too canny. She had met Arthur Anstey and thought him no shadow of his father.

'I shall, of course,' Henry continued, 'tell Arthur nothing about the circumstances of the engagement. If you wish to let it be thought that it is of long standing, then it is best that as few people as possible know the truth.'

Miss Turlingham could not quite bring herself to say thank you, but she inclined her head again.

CHAPTER FIVE

Miss Turlingham's brother, Captain Lord Marwood, presented himself at Holgate House at an early hour. Mr Aycliffe, the maid informed him, examining him with unconcealed curiosity, had gone off to his business, and the ladies were not yet down.

'Perhaps you would let my sister know I'm here,' he suggested, and added the smile that had got him out of many a scrape – and into more. The maid blushed, curtsyed, and left him in the breakfast parlour with the paper and a last, lingering look.

Alfreda appeared only ten minutes later, hurrying in still buttoning a cuff. At the sight of him her face lit in a way few people ever saw. 'Oh Kit, Kit! Dearest, I'm so glad to see you!'

'I came as soon as I could get leave from the colonel.' He returned her embrace warmly. 'My little sister! Let me look at you. Why, you're more beautiful than ever!'

'Foolish!' She looked up into his face. Kit Marwood was not handsome in the conventional way: his features were irregular, his smile crooked, his eyes more grey than blue, his hair unremarkably brown, rather than chestnut like Alfreda's. Yet he had so much charm few women ever forgot him. Had his sister had half as much, their father's disgrace might not have proved such a handicap to marriage. 'But what can you mean by coming so early? This may only be York, but even family doesn't call before twelve. We haven't had our breakfast yet.'

'Neither have I,' he said. 'I caught some deuced awful

71

train at the most ungodly hour of the night, and I'm dashed hungry.'

She eyed the small bag at his feet. 'Why didn't you go to your hotel first? You could have had breakfast there and presented yourself at the proper hour.'

He made a sound of exasperation. 'Really, little sister, I think your sudden good fortune must have addled your wits. Where d'you suppose *I'm* going to get the rhino for an hotel? It was all I could manage to do to scrape up the train fare: I had to borrow from my batman to pay the cabbie. So I shall have to go back tonight – unless your lawyer fellow will cough up the oof to keep me here. Just because you are in clover doesn't mean the rest of us ain't still on poor grazing.'

'I'm sorry, love, I didn't think.'

'It's plain you didn't,' he said, 'but I suppose I can't blame you. I say, Alfie, you really have fallen on your feet this time! I stopped to have a chat with the stationmaster, and he told me all about your Morlands. They're full of juice! It's a very good estate – not just the land but commercial property as well, and some satanic mill or other in Manchester.'

'So I understand,' she said complacently, smoothing the front of her new gown. It was of the finest grey merino, trimmed with narrow bands of purple velvet ribbon.

'Yes, you look like the cat that got into the dairy,' he said. 'I like your gown – so good to see you out of that everlasting pink! Purple ribbons are a bit sombre, though.'

'A mark of respect to my fiancé and his family,' she said.

'I conclude he paid for it, then. So there's no trouble about getting at the blunt?'

She frowned a little. 'Don't be vulgar, please, Kit. I'm sure something can be contrived so that you can stay here, if that's what you mean. Actual cash might be difficult at present, but I'm sure we can arrange to charge your hotel and expenses to the estate.' She met his eyes. 'I'm treading cautiously as yet. Things are in a delicate balance.'

'I should think they are, with the body on the high seas and probate still to go through, not to say the bridegroom only just having reached his majority! If I were you Alfie, I wouldn't hold out for a smart wedding. Settle the thing quickly, before he changes his mind: marry him straight after the funeral, even though it means having things plain. Secure the fort before you stand the men down, that's the rule.'

She was a little nettled at the implication. 'I didn't force Mr Morland to propose to me! He's madly in love.' Then she sighed. 'But the sooner I can leave this place the better.'

'Don't they treat you well?'

'They are very kind in their way, but they are not of our station in life. The servants don't know their business, their friends are vulgar, and they dine just *anyhow*. Besides, it's intolerable to be mewed up here, dependent on them for the least thing. I want my own establishment and the freedom to spend my own money.'

He nodded sympathetically. 'You had better get to work on your betrothed, then. What's he like?'

She thought for a moment. 'Very young – I mean, young even for his age. But I think I can influence him.'

'I should hope so, if you're going to bale me out.'

She looked anxious. 'Oh dear, Kit, how bad is it?'

'Pretty bad,' he said lightly, but she could see the lines in his face when he let his smile drop, and it did not fool her. 'The tradesmen I can hold off. But I owe some of the fellows, and that don't do. And the sons of Israel are after me.'

'Oh, Kit!'

'It's no use *Oh Kit*-ing me,' he said. 'The money has to come from somewhere.'

'Well, it shall come from me in future,' she said firmly.

'That's my girl!' he said with a grin.

'As soon as I'm married I shall see to it,' she said.

'Love, I may need it sooner than that,' he said seriously. 'A fellow who don't pay his debts of honour can find himself cashiered.'

She looked at him bleakly. 'It's that bad, is it?'

'What's this lawyer fellow like? Anstey, is it?'

'The father is as sharp as steel, and he doesn't like me,' Alfreda said harshly. 'But he's handed over the drawing up of the settlement to his son. Arthur Anstey is not his father's equal. Seems to be a pleasure-loving, lazy man.'

'Good, good, then you'd better see about arranging a meeting for me with him, today if possible.'

'*You* to have a meeting with him?'

'There's a lot you don't know about the world, Alfie, smart as you are,' he smiled. 'As your only male relative, I have to give my consent to the marriage. Yes, I know you are of age and can decide for yourself! But it ain't modest to say so, and they'll think the more of you if we play propriety. And I can use the opportunity, by not seeming too eager for the match, to convince him of what a fine family we are.'

'Oh, do be careful, Kit,' she said anxiously.

He put his arms round her waist. 'What a nervous thing you are, Kitten!' It was his oldest pet-name for her: it had been *Kit and Kitten* when they were both in the nursery. The word and its associations made her relax against him, resting her head on his shoulder and feeling just for that moment safe and loved. It was a sensation she had not often known in her anxious life.

'Don't you know I wouldn't spoil your play?' he went on. 'Much better for me to talk finances than you – looks immodest, you know! And while I'm getting a good settlement for you, I can slip in a word about an allowance for me.' That made her start, and pull back so that she could look up at him. 'Don't worry,' he forestalled her, 'it's quite the usual thing, and your beloved can be grateful that he only has me to keep, and not a gaggle of younger brothers to put through school and a parcel of schoolroom sisters to find dowries for.' He squeezed her a little to stop her protesting. 'You have to give me a chance to work my charm – it never fails. Now, do you trust me?'

Before she could answer, the door opened and Mrs Aycliffe came in, much flustered. 'Oh, Lord Marwood, I'm so sorry to have kept you waiting. You quite took us unawares!'

'It's for me to apologise. I was villainously early,' Marwood said, politely detaching himself from his sister and looking an enquiry at her.

Alfreda performed the introduction.

Mrs Aycliffe blushed, and said, 'We did meet once, when Alfreda and I were at Mrs Holland's Academy in Kensington

– at a musical evening – but I don't suppose you'd remember me.'

Kit had not the faintest recollection of her. 'How could I possibly forget?' he said with a ravishing smile. 'I thought then that you were the prettiest of Alfie's friends, and you haven't changed a bit.'

Mrs Aycliffe, fluttering, said the first thing that came into her head. 'I'm afraid we haven't had our breakfast yet.'

'That is precisely what I hoped to hear, ma'am,' Marwood said, 'for, do you know, neither have I.'

Dorothea went down under his charm like infantry under grapeshot. She beamed. 'Oh, then perhaps you will do us the honour of joining us?'

'If I shall not be in the way?'

'Not at all! Nothing could be nicer than to have your company.' She rang the bell. 'I really can't imagine why people don't call for breakfast as they do for lunch or dinner. Alfreda will be so glad to have the chance to talk to you, and I should love to hear about London.'

Kit caught his sister's eye and gave her a secret and solemn wink.

Breakfast was such a success that the three of them were still chatting over the remains when George arrived for his usual visit to his beloved. He was faintly surprised but not much interested to meet Alfreda's brother, for he wanted only to be alone with her. It was a sign of Marwood's great address that within minutes George had been persuaded to walk out of doors with him for a smoke. Kit needed to get him alone to work his charm on him, and the smoke was a good excuse, for Alfreda hated the smell of it indoors.

The two men strolled along the sunny street together, while Kit lit a thin cigar. George had refused one. He smoked very little, and never this early in the day, and he was beginning to wonder how he had been detached from Alfreda, whom he wanted to talk to, in favour of this man, whom he didn't. But as soon as the smoke was going, Kit, who had been covertly assessing his companion, remarked that the trouble with June was that it was so long until the hunting season, and asked how early George favoured getting his hunters up. Five minutes later George was conversing more freely than he had ever done in his life, and ten minutes later he was thinking that Marwood was a first-rate fellow and that it was a damned shame that his father's weakness had left him so badly off.

'To tell the truth, Morland, I am deucedly embarrassed at present,' Kit said when the right moment came. He spoke lightly, as though his position were not embarrassing at all, but a source of wry amusement to him. 'Always worse towards the end of the month, as I dare say you know if you've ever been on an allowance?'

'Just so. An allowance never goes far enough,' George said, though he had never outrun his pocket in his life, so many of the things he enjoyed coming free from the estate.

'But I couldn't hold off any longer, when it was a question of an attention to my sister, and what will be my sister's new family. One had always rather do too much than too little. I came as soon as I got leave – couldn't wait to meet the man who will be my brother. So I hope you'll ascribe it to the right cause that my visit lasts only this one day. I must leave again this evening.'

George looked disappointed. 'Oh, but I hoped you'd dine with me,' he said, though he had only just thought of it. 'Surely the army can spare you for a few days?'

'Certainly it could, but that's not the trouble. I'm afraid I haven't the ready to pay for an hotel.'

'Oh, if that's all your trouble,' George said, his brow clearing, 'you can stay at my club and charge it to me. They'll make you comfortable there.'

'That's very good of you.'

'Not at all. Good Lord, we are practically brothers,' said George, who had never given his own brothers a thought. 'I tell you what, Marwood, we ought to go along to Uncle Henry's office and make you known. Uncle Henry's handling the estate until probate is through, and Arthur – his son – is drawing up the marriage settlement. I'm sure we could arrange for something for you by way of expenses. Miss Turlingham wouldn't want you to be embarrassed, and neither would I.'

Kit smiled sweetly. 'I should very much like to make both

76

the Mr Ansteys' acquaintance, and give my official sanction to the match.'

George had not thought about anyone else's having to give sanction. He was struck with the thought, and said, 'What do you say we go there now, since we're half way?' He changed direction and guided Marwood round a corner. 'And then on the way back I can show you my club and tell them to expect you. We might take a glass of something there, too. It will be late enough by then.' He had, for the moment, quite forgotten his interrupted visit to his betrothed: it was more natural to him to be in the company of his own sex; and besides, it was very flattering to have a man as senior in rank, age and sophistication as Marwood so ready to be his friend.

Henrietta was walking round the Italian garden, absently throwing a stick for Jacko, a stout, grey-muzzled, terrier. He scampered and wheezed after it indefatigably – retired from the hunt, he seemed to miss the activity, so generally attached himself to anyone who was going out of doors and presented them with one of his secret store of suitable sticks.

Henrietta felt miserable and bored, and didn't know what to do with herself. She felt she ought to be mourning her father, but the more she tried, the less she could remember what he had really been like. He was just a shape, his face a blur. It was over two years since she had last seen him, almost four since he had played any regular part in the life of the house – and even then, her contact with him had been formal. However hard she tried, she could arouse no tender emotion for him, and her failure made her feel that she must be wicked, hard-hearted and unfilial.

Jacko barked and reared up on his hind legs, resting his forepaws on her leg, the stick in his mouth, to remind her of her duty. But as she bent mechanically to take it, he suddenly turned his head, ears cocked, and then rushed away, yapping fiercely. Someone had come into the garden at the far end.

'What? What? Bite me to death, would you, old Jacko, old pensioner? Fierce old feller! Grr! Kill it then! Cats! Rats!' The young man bent to grab the stick Jacko had dropped, and engaged in a tug o' war tussle with the terrier, who was growling ferociously at the front end and wagging ecstatically at the rear.

Henrietta's face and heart lightened. 'Teddy! Ted! You've come home!'

'Hullo, Hen. Good Lord, you've grown like a beanstalk! You'll have to leave off soon, or you'll be pushing the roof off. Here, here, mind my necktie! What a greeting – you're as bad as Jacko!' He returned her wild hug, but then detached her arms from round his neck and straightened his bow tie carefully.

'Oh, it's so good to see you! Everything's been so horrid, I'm glad for your sake you've missed it; but I've missed *you*! Have you just arrived?' she asked.

'About half an hour ago. There doesn't seem to be anyone about, but Holy said you were out here, so I came to see. I say, what are you wearing? You do look a sketch!'

'It's one of the housemaid's dresses. Gurney was going to dye one of my frocks, but I've outgrown everything. I need mourning-gowns made but there's no-one to arrange it. But never mind me – you look very smart and handsome!'

'Flatterer!' She was only a sister, but still he smirked a little, for she said it with such passion.

'No, really. As fine as fivepence! I like your jacket.'

'Do you? The braiding was my own thought.' He was wearing a dark brown tweed sack-coat with brown-and-white twill edging, to match his brown-and-white check trousers. Looking down at himself, he sighed. 'I suppose I shall have to go into mourning too, and that means a frock-coat. No-one wears frocks at Oxford – too stuffy by half! But it won't do just to put on bands, though, not for the pater.'

Henrietta put her hand through his arm and squeezed it as she turned to walk with him along the gravel path. 'Don't talk like that, as if Papa's death meant nothing but a change of clothes. I can't bear it that no-one seems to feel anything for him.'

'Well, I won't then,' Teddy said agreeably. At almost twenty he was a pleasant, good-humoured, lazy young man with more of his father's temperament than George, though he favoured his mother in looks. Having a generous allowance, no particular talents, and no desire to outshine his fellows, he was very popular at Christ Church, where he occupied himself, as Oxford men always had, with cricket, fox-hunting, racing and dining, and just occasionally turning in a little work – enough, he hoped, to secure him a pass degree without incurring the stigma of being thought a 'brainy cove'. He couldn't remember ever having worried about anything in his life, so his father's death left him with no personal anxieties; and having been away at school and then at university for the past four years, he felt even more detached than his sister.

'I keep thinking, you see, how dreadful it was for Papa to die all alone,' Henrietta said, sitting down with him on the nearest bench. Jacko planted himself in front of Teddy, stick at the ready, swishing the gravel with his stumpy tail.

'Not exactly alone,' Teddy said. 'He was at the camp, wasn't he? There'd have been other chaps there, to say nothing of the natives.'

'But you know what I mean – not with anyone of his own. Anyone who loved him.'

'He was pretty sick, Hen,' Teddy said doubtfully. 'I don't suppose he really knew anything about it at the end.'

'I don't know that that makes it any better,' she mourned.

'I should have thought it must, a *bit*,' he said judiciously. Jacko pawed at his leg, and he reached down and threw the stick for him.

'And it was such a horrid death,' she went on. 'You get it from fluke-worms that live in the water out there. A worm sort of digs in through your skin while you're bathing and wriggles into your insides and lays eggs until you're just full of them—' She turned a little green and shut her mouth hard.

'Don't think about it,' Teddy said quickly. 'Who told you all that, anyway? It's not the thing to be telling children.'

'Georgie got it from Dr Bayliss and I overheard him telling Mr Atterwith. He didn't know I was listening, though,' she added in fairness to her brother.

'Let that be a lesson to you not to eavesdrop,' Teddy said, tugging her hair affectionately.

'I'm not exactly a child any more, either,' she pointed out.

'You can't expect me to see you as anything but my little sister. Do you remember how we used to sit on the top step of the grand staircase and talk?'

'You used to tell me the most awful stories, and I believed every word,' she said. 'Do you remember when Mama and Papa had dinner guests, and we used to look down through the banisters to watch the dishes going in?'

'Lord, yes! We were always so hungry!'

'Nursery tea was never enough,' she agreed. 'Do you remember the time you stole a pie, and we hid in the linen-room and ate it?'

'Remember? I got beaten for that. But at least we managed to scoff it all before they found out it was missing; and once it was eat, they couldn't get it back!'

They smiled at each other. Growing up in George's shadow, they had found themselves thrown together simply because they were *not* George; united in being the unfavoured two. Teddy had thought her clever because she had an imagination; she had admired his handsome maleness and the things he could do better than her – ride, fish, shoot. For a few years before he had gone away to school, they had been quite close, though it seemed a long time ago now.

'So what's all this about Georgie getting married?' Teddy said. He reached into an inside pocket. 'D'you mind if I smoke?'

'No, of course not. Oh, Ted, cigarettes! How dashing!'

He smirked modestly. 'It's quite the thing with some of the fellows – though I like a pipe when I'm taking my time, on the river, say. So when's the wedding to be? Have they decided a date?'

'I don't think so. I think it's awkward, because of us being in mourning. Gurney says they'll have to wait six months.'

'Not so long, surely? He won't like that, if he's really in love. Tell about her. Have you met her?'

'Well, no, because Georgie can't bring her here, because there's no mistress of the house. She's *very* particular. I suppose that's with being so grand – her father was a lord! And Mrs Pretty says Arthur Peckitt says she's very beautiful – you know she's staying with the Aycliffes?'

'Yes, I heard that. As to her father being a lord – I heard all about that from Codrington. It seems he was a shocking loose screw.'

'What, Codrington?'

'No, fool! This Miss What's-her-name's father. Gambled away his fortune and at the finish—' He was about to mention the suicide, but then recollected it wasn't the sort of thing to say to one's sister. 'Went bankrupt,' he concluded. 'Had to sell the family home and everything.'

'Oh, *poor* Miss Turlingham!' Henrietta cried feelingly. 'It must be the worst thing in the world to lose your home and have it sold to strangers and never to be able to go back there again.'

Teddy looked at her affectionately. 'You always see the best side of people, don't you?'

She blushed under his praise. 'But it can't be her fault that her father went bankrupt, can it?'

'Well, I hope she'll be as kind to you,' Teddy said.

'Oh, I'm sure she will. Georgie says she's beautiful *and* good. It will be so lovely to have someone to talk to, and to tell me what to do and how to go on.'

When she smiled, she looked quite pretty, Teddy thought. In a surge of affection he said, 'I almost forgot, I've got a present for you.'

'For me?' Her eyes widened. Because of her mother's death and her father's absence, spiritual and physical, presents were not things that had come much in her way.

He felt in his jacket pocket, and brought out a small, tissue-wrapped package. Henrietta took it with a wordless look of excitement and laid it in her lap to unwrap it. It was a necklace of silver filigree daisies. 'Oh, how *pretty*!' she cried, holding it up, looped over her thin fingers. 'Teddy, it's beautiful! Is it really for me?'

'Certainly it's for you,' Teddy said. He had in fact bought it for a certain accommodating girl in York with whom he was hoping to renew acquaintance, but what she did not know she would not miss, and it was nice to see Hen's bony little face light up.

'It's the nicest thing I've ever had,' she said, twisting round to kiss his cheek fervently. 'You are a great deal too good to me.'

'Steady the Buffs!' He tolerated the embrace good-humouredly. 'If a chap can't buy his sister a little trifling present . . .' He sat back, stretching his legs, enjoying the pleasant warmth of his own generosity. Jacko despaired of having the stick thrown again, and abandoned it in favour of lying down in the shade of the hedge and panting.

Henrietta turned the necklace round and round admiringly in her hands. 'I suppose I won't be able to wear it until we're out of mourning,' she said.

'You can wear it at the wedding,' he pointed out.

But her thoughts had gone elsewhere. She looked up at him gravely. 'Teddy, what do you suppose will happen to us?'

'Happen? I don't know. What should happen?'

'Well, now that Papa's dead, things will change, won't they?'

'I suppose so. I hadn't thought about it, really.'

'Everything feels so—' She struggled to find the word for her sense of insecurity. 'Like ghost-ash. As if it might fall apart at a touch,' she finished helplessly.

He struggled to understand. Of course, being a female was different, he thought. And she was growing up. The reason she looked so odd in her queer frock, he realised, was that under the shapeless cotton she was no longer physically a child. She had a figure, and at – what, sixteen? No, nearly seventeen! – it was about time.

'Well, I'm sure Pa will have provided for us,' he said at last. 'Uncle Henry would've seen to it that he did. At least, I don't know about me, but he will certainly have provided for you.'

'What do you mean?'

'A dowry,' Teddy said. 'You'll be old enough to get married soon.'

She seemed to shrink together, like a snail withdrawing from a touch. 'Oh don't! I don't want to get married. It would mean I'd have to go away from Morland Place, and then I should *die*!'

He laughed. 'No you wouldn't! You can't help growing

up, Hen. And girls always want to get married. When you come to it, it'll be the one thing in the world you want, you'll see!' She looked unconvinced. 'Your trouble is you think too much. You never see me fretting about what may or may not happen. Fretting won't change anything, you know.'

'I know,' she said glumly. 'I don't fret because I want to. Oh, I wish the funeral was over! It's like being trapped between two lives. Once Georgie marries and Miss Turlingham comes to live here, I'm sure everything will be all right. It's all this waiting that's so horrid.'

'Hmm,' said Teddy, at a loss.

'How long do you think it would take for the – the coffin to get here from Port Said?'

'Lord, I don't know. Two or three weeks, perhaps. It can't be long now. Well,' he threw away his cigarette and stood up, 'I think I'll go and get out of my town togs. Do you care to come riding with me? I'd like to have a canter about the estate, if there's a horse fit to carry me.'

'I'm sure there is. But is it proper?' she asked doubtfully.

'Why not? Riding ain't disrespectful. I'll get into my riding dress – I suppose one needn't get up in full blacks when there's no-one to see.'

'I'll put my habit on, then, if you think it's all right,' she said joyfully. 'Oh, Ted, I'm glad you're home! You must tell me all about Oxford. Do you have larks?'

'All the time,' he said solemnly. 'Sometimes we have them spit-roasted, sometimes on toast. Then there's confit of larks' tongues – always a favourite at the High Table—'

'Don't tease!' She punched his arm. 'Tell me about all the jolliness. I'm sure you have wonderful fun,' she added wistfully.

Agreeably, he put her hand through his arm and they turned towards the house, and as they walked he told her about the House, and Bullingdon, Loders, the river, cricket, picnics and races, and all the good dinners he had with the best set of fellows in the world. Jacko heaved himself up out of the shadows and trotted along behind them, stick at the ready in case they should happen to turn round.

★　　★　　★

On the day after Teddy got home, Henry Anstey asked him and George to call together at his office. An hour later, George was pacing up and down the morning-room at Holgate House, his heart burning with injustice, waiting for Miss Turlingham to come to him.

When Uncle Henry had told him, that first day after the telegraph arrived, that Morland Place was left to him, he had assumed that meant his father's whole estate. If it had never occurred to him to wonder how Teddy would make his way in the world, it was fair to say that it had never occurred to Teddy either. Younger sons generally had to fend for themselves: that was the way estates were kept together.

Uncle Henry had begun with a preamble about how he and Benedict and Nicholas had grown up together, how Benedict had gone off to be a railway engineer, how there had been a coldness between the brothers in later life. The old fellow was maundering, George thought, and let his attention wander until the change in the tone of voice told him that something of more substance was coming.

'So, you see, the thing above all your father wanted to avoid was any risk of the same discord between you two as there existed between him and his brother,' Henry concluded. 'His Will was drawn up with that in mind.' He turned to George. 'George, my boy, you are to inherit what your father and uncle before you inherited, everything which traditionally comprises the Morland fortune. Morland Place, the house and its furnishings, the demesne, the farms, the stud, and the stock live and dead; the property in Goodramgate, Water Lane and Bishophill, the warehouse on King's Staith – all this comes to you. In addition there is the half-share in the Manchester property: the three mills and the cottages known as Morland's Rents.'

George had listened to the list with a frown of concentration. There was something in his uncle's tone that roused his suspicion, and he was trying to calculate if anything had been left out. Something was coming: he didn't trust the atmosphere.

Henry turned to Teddy, who had been lolling negligently in his chair wondering what he was here for.

84

'But your father did not wish you to be in want, Edward. You perhaps are not aware that before he came into the Morland estate, he inherited a fortune from a very different source. Mrs Makepeace was a widow with no family—'

'Makepeace's!' George exclaimed, interrupting him. Now he knew what had been left out. 'Uncle— ?'

Henry held up his hand for silence. 'Mrs Makepeace left her considerable fortune to your father, and he regarded this as his own personal property, quite separate from the Morland estate. As he enjoyed it when he was second son with no expectation of inheriting Morland Place, so he wished you, Edward, to enjoy the same independence. You will therefore receive, on reaching your majority, what I refer to as the Makepeace inheritance: the shop and business in York known as Makepeace's, the three small factories, Makepeace House, the property in Clementhorpe, Nunnery Lane and Thief Lane, and the parcel of agricultural land between Shipton Moor and Overton Ings, including Overton Wood Farm and the small manor house called Moon's Rush.'

George gasped. 'But that's half the estate!'

Teddy merely looked dazed. 'It's too much.'

'Damn right it's too much!' George growled.

'Uncle, are you sure you've got it right?'

'My dear boy, you can't imagine I could be mistaken about such a matter,' said Henry.

'No, of course not – but, good Lord! I can't take it in. It's a fortune. Land and a manor house, too – I shall have my own place! I can live like a gentleman and not have to work.'

'Moon's Rush is in very poor condition. You will have a lot to do before you can live there in comfort. But Makepeace House is liveable, of course.'

It was at this point that George exploded. He flung to his feet crying 'It's not fair!' and the meeting deteriorated from then onwards.

Now Miss Turlingham entered the morning-room, exquisite in a gown of dove-coloured taffeta lined with lilac; the lining revealed where the overskirt was draped back into the bustle. There was real lace at the neck and cuffs, which she touched for reassurance when she saw the darkness of her betrothed's expression. Something had happened! She controlled her outward anxiety, appearing only more coldly calm for her effort.

'You seem agitated, Mr Morland. What's the matter?'

'It's the Will! Papa's Will! He's split the estate! I've been robbed of half my inheritance!' George cried passionately.

It was some time before Miss Turlingham could extract the information from him by patient questioning. 'But who was Mrs Makepeace?' she asked.

'Some old widow-lady who took a fancy to Papa when he was a boy. I don't know why,' George said impatiently. 'The point is I've been robbed! Makepeace's, the factories, *and* the land at Overton! It's too much, by God! It's half the estate! Pa had no right to split it. The Morland fortune has never been divided. If they think I'm going to give up all that to Teddy, just because – just because—'

'Just because?'

'Dammit, it's not right,' George ended in a grumble. 'I don't care so much about Makepeace's and the factories – dashed if I ever wanted to be a haberdasher anyway! It's the land at Overton that galls me. It joins up with Thickpenny, you see, only divided by the river, and I had a plan for it. If I could have persuaded Lord Howick to sell me his Scagglethorpe acres, my estate would have stretched all the way to Shipton! But that's no use now,' he concluded discontentedly.

Miss Turlingham had no clear idea of the geography involved. She wanted to know the whole before she commented. 'What of the others – your sisters and younger brother?'

'Oh, they're left to my charge,' George said carelessly. 'Now I'm twenty-one, I am their guardian until they come of age.'

'So you will have to provide dowries for your sisters and an education for your brother?'

'I suppose so,' George said. 'But those would have come out of the estate anyway, if Pa had lived.'

'Is no sum mentioned? Is it left to your discretion?'

'Oh yes, it's up to me,' George said.

Miss Turlingham was glad to hear that. There were ways the expense of the younger ones could be contained. 'But your brother Edward is under age, is he not? Is he also under your guardianship?'

'He is, but his fortune isn't,' said George. 'Uncle Henry's his trustee.' He was growing calmer now that he had spilled it all out to Miss Turlingham. It had been a shock to him, but now he was coming to terms with it, it wasn't so very bad, perhaps. The Overton land wasn't in good heart and the house was practically derelict; and Howick probably wouldn't have sold in the end. He just wanted to grumble a little more. 'It's a disgrace, and so I told Uncle Henry, but he says it was Pa's right to do as he pleased with his own – which I don't agree with at all. If the eldest son isn't to inherit all, what's to become of the world? *Why* should Teddy have it, that's what I say? What's he done to deserve it?'

'You must contest the Will,' Miss Turlingham pronounced.

George blinked. 'Eh? Oh! But – well, Uncle Henry drew it up, you know, on Papa's instructions. There can't be anything wrong with it. Uncle Henry's a downy bird.'

'No slang, please, Mr Morland. It is always possible that a mistake was made. Mr Anstey is an old man and his powers may be waning. If you are sure that everything was meant to come to you, then there is every reason to contest it. It may be that your father was . . .' She paused, delicately. 'His behaviour in going off to Egypt in that way—'

'Good God, you mean the pater was mad? Why didn't I think of it? Rushing off across the world at his age looks mad – and without making any arrangements before he went, for the house or the children or anything. Obviously he wasn't right in his head, that's why he changed his Will.'

'*Did* he change his Will?'

'Oh yes. Uncle Henry said he'd better have a new one before going to a place like Egypt, just in case. By Jove, Miss Turlingham, you have a head on your shoulders!'

Alfreda held up a restraining hand. 'I beg you will not be too hasty, Mr Morland. The law is a tricky thing, and you must take proper advice before beginning anything of the sort. And I beg you will say nothing of this to anyone until

87

the funeral and the wedding are both out of the way. It would cause gossip of the most unpleasant kind.'

'You're right,' he said, always willing to believe she was. 'Don't worry, I shan't make a fuss and spoil things.'

The maid came in looking for Mr Morland. 'Beg pardon, miss, sir, but there's a messenger from Mr Anstey's below. He brought this note, and he's waiting for an answer.'

George took the note and opened it. His face grew grave. He looked up at Miss Turlingham. 'The ship's arrived at London Pool – the one bringing Papa's coffin. It'll be put on the train tonight. Uncle Henry wants me to go and talk about the funeral arrangements.'

'It will be tomorrow, I suppose?'

'I expect so. No reason to delay that I can think of. I'd better go – if you'll excuse me.'

'Of course,' she said. 'You must do your duty.' And as soon as the funeral was out of the way, she would concentrate his mind on the wedding. 'You'll come back later and tell me what has been decided?'

He bowed, wishing he had the nerve to take her hand and kiss it. 'Nothing could keep me from you,' he vowed fervently, to the not entirely concealed delight of the lingering maid.

88

CHAPTER SIX

Henrietta stood at the door of the great hall, looking out across the yard. The stable cat was picking his way fastidiously across, his paw tips dazzling snow and his coat glowing thick-peeled marmalade, betraying only by one coral lick of his lips that he'd just had breakfast. Outside the buttery door, where the evening sun lingered longest, was an ancient kitchen chair with a broken back-rail, where Mrs Pretty liked to sit and smoke a pipe for half an hour. Ginger's arch enemy, the black kitchen cat, was enthroned on it, paws tucked under, and watched the progress through narrowed eyes, but was too comfortable just now to teach him a lesson.

From the open stable doors came the comfortable sounds of horses, champing feed, scraping hooves on the brick floor, jingling tether-chains, blowing hay dust. Somebody – Baynes, probably – said, 'Git over, tha lummock!' and slapped a rump percussively; the boy up in the hayloft whistled half a phrase and interrupted himself with a mighty sneeze. A flight of martins screamed past high overhead; Hogg, the gatekeeper, looked out of his little room, saw Henrietta and drew his head back in, like a tortoise; above her someone pulled a casement sharply shut.

Henrietta noticed all this unconsciously, and was comforted by it: home was to her a container for all the lives, animal and human, that mattered to her, and the sense of them around her, moving in their separate and indifferent orbits, close but not touching, was what sustained her. But with all her conscious mind she was staring at the sky, which was overcast, and willing the clouds to break up. Miss Turlingham was to drive to the church this morning in an open carriage. She wanted sun for her; rain would be a disaster.

The wedding was to be at St Michael-le-Belfry. Henrietta was sad that George was not to be married in the chapel at Morland Place, but Miss Turlingham (so Henrietta learned from Mrs Pretty who got it from her friend who was Mrs Aycliffe's cook's sister) had not cared for the idea. Nor was the wedding breakfast to be held at Morland Place, for Miss Turlingham did not believe Morland Place was up to it. Mrs Aycliffe's cook's sister's comments on this, too faithfully relayed, had incensed both Mrs Pretty and Mrs Holicar, who were now ostentatiously ignoring the whole wedding. But though Henrietta loved her home, she had to admit, looking at it from a stranger's point of view, that it was both shabby and grubby.

Henrietta had met Miss Turlingham now: George had brought her on a visit to Morland Place one day, with Mrs Aycliffe as chaperon. She had made a tour of inspection of the main rooms of the house, and though she had not said anything, she had looked grave. Henrietta hoped very much that when Miss Turlingham lived here she would love it as she did. Of course things needed doing, but she hoped Miss Turlingham would not change it too much.

She desperately wanted the wedding day to be fine, and she'd been darting back and forth to the window ever since she got up. 'No use looking,' Gurney had told her snappishly. 'That won't change anything.'

But Baynes, the elderly groom who worked under Askins in the home yard, came out of the stable with an armful of harness, and, seeing Henrietta looking at the sky, tacked across the yard to say to her kindly, 'Nay, that'll burn off, tha'll see. T'woan't rain today – on'y be too 'ot later. Mind tha teks tha sunshade, missy!'

He and Henrietta were fond of each other. He was a little, nut-brown man, an ex-ostler, bent by a lifetime's service to horses, and missing two fingers on his left hand, bitten off by a mad wheeler when he was backing it into the shafts of a mail coach. 'T'warn't a Morland 'oss,' he always said when he told the story. 'Morland cattle is allus good-natured. Eh, but 'osses is as 'osses is done by.' It wasn't easy for him to say the last sentence with most of his teeth gone, leaving just a lonely outpost here and there in his gums. 'Got more fingers than teeth,' was his proud boast, 'even wi' two missin'.'

Henrietta smiled and thanked him. The sky was seamless and impenetrable, a warm grey blanket laid over the world; but it was still early. She had woken practically at dawn, and even getting dressed had not used up the time, despite having to have her hair done up to go with her new gown. She smoothed the gown with a loving finger. Mrs Holicar had been scathing about it because it was bought already made-up from one of the new shops that had sprung up in the last ten years or so. Ladies never bought their clothes that way but had them made for them by a mantuamaker, she said. But Henrietta thought it lovely: white muslin over white silk, plain, but with a hint of a bustle – definitely a grown-up gown, not a child's frock. Miss Turlingham had chosen it and sent it to Morland Place. Regina and Manfred had new clothes too, but Henrietta couldn't help feeling her gown was different, that it denoted a special sympathy between her and Miss Turlingham.

Mrs Holicar, coming into the hall behind her, saw her at the door and stopped to look for a moment with a softened expression, reading the eagerness in the angle of Henrietta's shoulders and her taut back.

'The carriage won't be here for another half an hour,' she said. Henrietta turned her head. 'Why don't you go into the drawing-room and sit and read a book? It'll pass the time. Besides,' she added, 'if you stand there some dog or other will come running in and put its dirty paws on you. You know what they're like.'

Which of course was true. In deference to her new finery, Henrietta removed it to a safer place.

Miss Turlingham felt exhausted. She'd had to do everything herself, for George had no more idea than a baby how to arrange an occasion. Mrs Aycliffe, equally anxious for the wedding to be a success, had offered herself unstintingly, but Alfreda did not trust her taste, and would not delegate

91

anything to her, though she found her useful as a chaperon and parcel-holder.

She'd had no difficulty in persuading George to an early wedding. He wanted only to marry his goddess, and now that his father was buried he felt no more constraint on him. Henry Anstey wrote one last note begging George to reconsider, but glancing at it and seeing it was 'just more pi-jaw', George threw it away unread.

He had not so much wanted to marry at Morland Place as assumed he would; but Alfreda had vetoed it firmly. Her visit there had revealed everything to be far worse than she had expected. Her first sight of the courtyard alone had shocked her. Some of the cobbles were missing – dug up over the years by impatient hooves – and where they were gone pools of menacing brown water gathered. Manure and straw were scattered where the yard had not been swept properly, and there was a strong smell of horses and kennels. Paint was flaking from doors; the stable windows were opaque with dirt, and a crop of grass was growing in the gutter. Inside the house was not much better – nothing had been cleaned or refurbished for years. The staff was obviously idle and incompetent: she had seen George go off to shout for or even fetch a servant, for no-one answered bells. Worst of all, there were huge dirty dogs everywhere, and Miss Turlingham hated dogs: the first thing, she vowed, she would banish them all from the house.

But she also had good reason for wanting the wedding to be held in a public place. Since the engagement had become known, there had been little rivulets of gossip running about York. The history of her father had been revived, one or two of York's leading matrons had given her cold looks, and someone had made an impertinent and uncharitable remark about kidnapping behind her back in Hargrove's library.

Miss Turlingham was more incensed than hurt. The insolence of it! Dowdy provincials, clowns puffed up with rustic self-consequence, to look down their noses at the daughter of a viscount who had led her London Season? Still, it had happened, and it made it imperative that the wedding should be celebrated publicly and with great style. At Morland Place no-one would witness it except the servants and tenants. The Minster was out of the question, but St Michael-le-Belfry, being just opposite, was in a nice open position and would give space for a crowd to gather. That was why she had opted for an open carriage: driven slowly it would allow her to be seen by as many people as possible. George had given her *carte blanche* to spend what she liked, and no-one would be able to say there was anything hole-and-corner about this wedding!

Miss Turlingham had found by now that York was not so contemptible as she had first thought: a great many people of wealth and fashion lived in and around the city, and the tradespeople were accustomed to providing for their comfort, consequence and amusement. Given her taste and George's unlimited budget, she had no difficulty in getting what she wanted. She had even found a good mantuamaker, Madame Etoile (who was born a plain Miss Hegginbottam of Leeds, but had once in her career actually been married to a Frenchman, whose name, even more surprisingly, really had been Etoile). Brides with large budgets were plentiful, but those with taste and beauty as well were not, and Madame Etoile had thrown herself into the preparations with fervour.

The gown stood now on a dummy in the corner of her room; Alfreda could see its reflection glimmering whitely, like a headless ghost, as she sat in her underwear before the glass while Bittle dressed her head. The gown was of ivory silk taffeta, with a pearl-embroidered basque bodice. The height of fashion that year was for trimmings to be in a different shade of the same colour: the bodice was trimmed with cream silk tassel fringing, and a stiff little ruff at the neck, and layered flounces at the wrist, both of cream lace. Deep lace under ruched net edged the apron and hem of the skirt, and the back of the gown was decorated with a vertical row of silk bows, small on the bodice and becoming increasingly large over the bustle and down the long train. No-one seeing it would be able to doubt that it had cost a small fortune.

Bittle had been dressing her hair in a silence surprising to Alfreda, who had expected subtle abuse on this day of all days. But Bittle was worried. She had been told she was not to accompany Alfreda on the honeymoon. 'But you've never dressed yourself in your life!' she had protested.

'We shall be living simply,' Alfreda had said. 'We want to be alone together.'

This, Bittle thought, was not only a vulgar sentiment, but plainly a lie. What worried her was the thinking behind it. Alfreda penniless and dependent on charity was one thing; Alfreda married and wealthy would be free to pay Bittle what she was owed and be rid of her. Was that what she planned? Bittle did not want to have to find a new place and start again amongst strangers at her age. Suddenly she was vulnerable. It was not safe to grumble and snipe as she had done all these years.

'There, madam,' she said at last, stepping back from her handiwork. It had taken over an hour, and was as elaborate as confectionery: strings of artificial pearls, flowers and rosettes of feathers wound in amongst the coils and braids of chestnut hair. 'I'll just get you into the frame, and then I'll ring for Sarah. I'll need help lifting the gown over, if I'm not to disturb your head.'

Alfreda stood up in silence and stepped into the crinoline frame, which was collapsed on the floor. It was a Thomson's 'Empress New Resilient', a clever creation of watch-springs covered in white webbing, designed to give the flat-fronted, large-bustled shape: at the back the hoops went all the way up, but only half way up at the side, and in front only for twelve inches at the bottom. Bittle raised the frame and tied the tape round Miss Turlingham's narrow waist, and then the maid helped lift the gown into place.

Alone, Bittle fastened on the wreath and the veil of spotted net bordered with fine appliqué bobbin-lace, and then turned Alfreda towards the long glass.

'There,' she said. 'You look really beautiful, Miss Alfreda.' Their eyes met in reflection. 'I suppose,' Bittle said, gruff with the unfamiliar effort of unbending, 'I shan't be able to call you that any longer. It'll be all "Mrs Morland" and "madam".'

It was the moment for Alfreda to smile and thank her faithful maid, who had nursed her from babyhood and stayed with her through hard times, however prickly and difficult she had often been. But Miss Alfreda looked at Bittle and did not see the smile that was trying to work its way out through the dough of that sour face; she saw only the last link with the life of shame and humiliation, a link she wanted to sever. Bittle reminded her of what had been, and she did not want to remember.

'Hand me my gloves, will you,' she said, 'and then you can go and check if the carriage is ready. I shan't come down until it's at the door.'

Bittle's smile died unborn, and she turned away to do as she was told.

In the church Henrietta sat and gazed, her senses ravished. To add to the excitement of the occasion and the glory of the architecture, there was the beauty and perfume of the roses and lilies with which the church had been decorated, along with festoons of smilax and ivy (the florist in Parliament Street had bowed himself almost into knots at the size of the order). Listening to the organ music, she thought of her father's funeral: no music, no flowers, no guests but the servants and the tenants (though that was enough to fill the chapel at Morland Place). The service had been taken by Mr Hughes, the vicar of St Edward's. It didn't last long. She had forgotten, since her mother's death, how short the funeral rite was when unexpanded by sermon or homily.

And yet she had felt comforted by it, in the familiarity of the chapel with its memorials all round the walls; as though all those generations of Morlands were watching over her. Then the crypt was opened and her father's coffin was lowered in to rest beside those of her mother and sister, and it was over. She had not cried. She had wanted to, but there seemed no point when it was appropriate, no accommodation in the ritual for a pause for tears. Perhaps if there had been music . . . the music now was making her want to cry—

The doors of the church were flung open in a splendidly melodramatic manner by two sidesmen, who felt that at last they had got a bride worthy of their efforts, and at that very moment the sun broke through at last, so that Miss Turlingham entered in a perfectly theatrical beam of light.

Henrietta, standing and turning with the rest of the congregation, drew a breath of wonder. Miss Turlingham looked like something from a dream, gliding effortlessly on the arm of Lord Marwood, handsome and dashing in his regimentals. As she passed, Henrietta caught a glimpse through the veil of the beautiful face, and sighed with satisfaction. If there were such a thing as a perfect bride, surely lucky George had found one!

The service began, and as those most familiar of words rolled around the church, Henrietta was ravished anew by the solemn beauty of Cranmer's prose, and of Mr Fortescue's voice. It was Miss Turlingham's idea to invite him to officiate. She had met him before her engagement to George at dinner at the Laxtons', and was impressed with his erudition, and the fact that he obviously loathed the company he found himself in. When she met him again at the Greys' ball, and later walking in the Dean's Park with Lord and Lady Grey, she noted with approved his high connections. If she could not have the Archbishop, she thought, she would at least have a cleric whose name was known in the first circles. It did not occur to her to wonder why he had accepted, but in fact it was because Lady Grey had pressed him: she felt sorry for Alfreda, having known hard times herself in her youth as the daughter of an impoverished clergyman, and with her husband was doing all she could to make her acceptable in York.

Henrietta, made vulnerable by the occasion and all the beauty around her, was thrilled with Mr Fortescue's sermon. Others around her fidgeted when he passed the half-hour; Lord Marwood positively writhed in anguish when he reached three-quarters, and cast piteous looks around him for deliverance; but Henrietta listened, enraptured, to the whole hour, understanding not one word in three, but feeling that her mind was expanding and her soul was being lifted onto a new plane.

Then the solemn part was over; the organ struck up with Mendelssohn, and the bride, Miss Turlingham no longer, with her veil turned back to show her lovely face, came back down the aisle on the arm of a beaming George. The children scurried after; Teddy offered Henrietta his arm; everyone crowded out into the street, where the gathered onlookers cheered loudly enough to make it worth the couple's while to stand a few moments and be admired. The sun was hot now, in a viscous pale blue sky, and the day was rather sticky. Henrietta thought George looked splendid in black serge cutaway and pale grey trousers, black boots and a black 'topper'. The hat had been well dressed the night before by Battey with stout to ensure that it was glossy and sleek, and in the heat of the day it was now attracting a cloud of tiny black flies. Henrietta felt for him, and for Miss Turlingham, but the annoyance was perhaps a trifling price to pay for real elegance. Teddy, beside her, was wearing a grey top hat, which went well with his black-and-grey striped trousers, but Henrietta thought loyally that George looked smarter.

The couple mounted into the beribboned carriage (lent by the Aycliffes) with its splendid team of greys (hired from Willan's), and as it pulled away, pursued by the usual tumult of urchins, George flung out two handfuls of coins for them to scramble after.

'Well,' said Teddy, 'now for the feast. I hope it's lavish – I'm starved of hunger.' He grinned down at his sister. 'Now, little Hen, you can dry your tears. Why do females cry at weddings?'

'I'm not crying,' she pointed out.

'You're not so little today, either. You look quite a lady.'

Henrietta squeezed his arm gratefully. 'I have your necklace on.'

He squeezed back. 'Your turn next, I expect.'

'Oh no,' she said deprecatingly.

'Why not? The new Mrs Morland will bring you out, I dare say. And about time, too. You're not as pretty as Reggie, but you've more sense in your face. I'd marry you like a shot if you weren't my sister.'

'And I'd marry you, too,' she responded.

He laughed. 'Anyone'd marry me, now I'm a man of substance! God bless my generous father! Ah, here's our carriage. Where are the children?'

The wedding breakfast was held in the banquet room of the

Station Hotel, and if the circumstance seemed odd to anyone, it could be explained by the bride's having no settled home, and Morland Place having no hostess. The Station Hotel was delighted, not only with the trade, but with the opportunity to show respect to the memory of Benedict Morland, who had been so influential in bring the railways to York, and in getting the hotel built in the first place. The Station Hotel had once entertained the Queen and the Prince Consort, and felt itself quite equal to the occasion. It only wished the wedding party had been four times as large.

Henrietta, who had never been in an hotel before, let alone eaten in one, could not have been more thrilled. The long tables were decorated with flowers and trails of ivy, and glittered with crystal and silver; waiters brought a succession of dishes which, to one reared on nursery food, was almost bewildering. Henrietta began to feel exhausted and confused, and Teddy, leaning across, whispered that she must be drunk. But she had only sipped at a single glass of champagne: it was the surfeit of sensations that was befuddling her.

After the meal, the toasts and the speeches, Miss Turlingham retired to a room upstairs where Bittle was waiting to change her clothes. She reappeared shortly in a delicious travelling costume of pearl grey trimmed with emerald velvet and a tiny bonnet of ruched silk with long trailing ribbons, and after a prolonged round of goodbyes, the couple were seen off on their honeymoon. George had been keen to take her to Paris, but the situation in France was too volatile. They were taking the train straight to London and, after a few days there for shopping, going on to Brighton.

When they had departed, the company went back into the ante-room, the ladies to discuss the wedding, the gentlemen politics. Teddy slipped a hand through Henrietta's arm and drew her aside. 'I'm off to the club to blow a cloud and sink some brandy with Marwood. We're both vexed to death with doing the polite. You won't mind, Hen? You'll be quite safe going home with Fitton – and you'll look after the children, won't you?'

Before Henrietta could answer, he was gone. Anticlimax

98

struck her. The fun was all over, she had been abandoned, and she had no idea where the children had got to. While she was looking about glumly for her young brother and sister, she came up against Mr Fortescue, also for the moment unattached.

'Ah, Miss Morland,' he said vaguely. She looked at him, blushed deeply and lowered her eyes. He found that rather charming; as a middle-aged and scholarly bachelor he was unused to making young females blush – indeed, few young females ever came in his way. He searched for something to say. 'A lull in the proceedings. All this bacchanalian excitement is rather exhausting, don't you find? But no,' he corrected himself, 'as a young lady on the threshold of life, I dare say you don't feel you can have enough of it?'

Henrietta, overawed at having him address her personally, only managed to reply, 'I'm not much used to company, sir.'

He regarded her with increased approval. Young people were generally so frivolous, but she had a serious and, perhaps, other-worldly air, and she did not look as if she were enjoying herself. 'You prefer the quiet of contemplation and study?' he said hopefully.

She tried to find an honest answer. 'I have enjoyed the wedding very much, sir, but I am rather tired. We live very quiet at Morland Place.'

'And what did you like best about the wedding?' he asked genially.

She dared to raise her eyes a moment, and saw he was almost smiling. Emboldened, she stammered, 'Y-your sermon, sir.'

He was not immune to flattery. 'You liked it, eh?'

'I thought it *beautiful*,' she said, with such obvious sincerity that he was forced to reassess his opinion of her. He had thought her a mere child; now he remembered how all through his sermon she had sat with her eyes fixed on him. He had remarked it at the time without attributing any cause to the phenomenon. But perhaps, though young and female, she was able to appreciate scholarship.

'You approved my subject matter? The transitory nature

of all human happiness is not a precept which usually recommends itself to the young mind, but I fancy it a not inappropriate consideration on such an occasion, when earthly pleasures seem to offer a permanence of bliss. The Greeks said it better, of course.' He said something that sounded to her like birdsong – fluid, but meaningless – and seeing her incomprehension he translated: '"Call no man happy until he dies; he is at best but fortunate." Herodotus. Naturally, you know no Greek.'

Henrietta blushed deeper and hung her head, afraid she had disappointed him. 'I wish I had learned,' she said, very low.

'Such an extreme of erudition is neither to be expected nor even desired in the female sex. My dear Miss Morland, you must not be ashamed! A woman's condition is very different from a man's, and was it not also in my sermon: "The love of virtue is virtue itself"? In showing a love for learning you have done all that is required. Innocence is the most desirable state, after all, but not all can aspire to it – if I might permit myself the paradox.'

He gave a little chuckle, and she smiled shyly in response. She had little idea what he was talking about, but longed for him to go on. She felt the honour of it, that he should stoop to bestow the fruits of his mind on her; and, always lonely, she was grateful for his notice. She wanted to show her gratitude, to offer him something in return, but she was so stupid and ignorant, what could she say that would not disgust him? And then she remembered something Caleb had said. Caleb was wise, and shepherds were the favoured of God, so perhaps it would be good enough for Mr Fortescue. She seized her courage and ventured humbly, 'Perhaps – perhaps, sir, we can each serve God in our own way by being what we are?'

As soon as she said it, she wished it unsaid. He would know she hadn't understood him, would think her stupid or merely impertinent.

But, wonderfully, now he really did smile, seeming struck by her words. 'You are quite right! Indeed, I see you understand me exactly. Ah, but Lord Grey beckons – I believe the carriage is waiting. I must not indulge myself to his inconvenience. Pray excuse me. I have so enjoyed our little interlude, Miss Morland – "a small pool of quiet in a restless sea". I bid you good day.'

He bowed and walked off, leaving Henrietta feeling weak with relief that she had got through it unscathed, thrilled that he had chosen to talk to her, and more admiring of him than ever. It was as if a winged messenger had stooped down from heaven, and she had managed, miraculously, to entertain it. The despondency of anticlimax had left her, and she felt quietly exultant; detached from her surroundings, as though she were being borne through the air on a cloud.

Mrs Aycliffe found Henrietta sitting in a corner with her hands in her lap, and mistook her reverie for melancholy.

'My dear Miss Morland,' she said kindly, 'here you are all forlorn! You must feel flat after all the excitement. I've been looking for your brother Edward to tell him the carriage is here to take you home, but I can't find him.'

'He went away with Lord Marwood,' Henrietta said, dragging herself back from her dream. Mrs Aycliffe raised surprised eyebrows. 'They went off to the club together to smoke. He said we'd be quite all right going home with our own coachman.'

Mrs Aycliffe thought it a shame the way the young Morlands were neglected, but it wasn't her place to say so, and she supposed one could hardly expect a young blade like Teddy Morland to act responsibly in the absence of parents or even an older brother. Alfreda's influence was plainly needed at Morland Place!

'Well, never mind,' she said, giving Henrietta a warm smile. 'Boys will be boys. I expect my brother would have done the same thing. Are you ready to go? Your brother and sister are waiting at the door. They're quite worn out, poor things. It's a long day for little ones, isn't it?'

Regina and Manfred were indeed drooping, as was their finery, and Regina was fretful because her hair was coming out of curl. 'I'm hungry,' Manfred complained at the carriage door.

'You can't be,' Henrietta said simply.

'I *am*,' he said, sticking his lip out at her. 'It's my stomach, so I ought to know.'

'I'll tell Gurney you said "stomach" in front of everybody,' Regina said, pinching him.

'Wasn't everybody,' he retorted, pinching her back. Regina let out a yell out of all proportion to the offence.

'Oh hush, Reggie! And do get in, Manny,' Henrietta said impatiently, catching Harris's rolling eye as he held the door for them. It had been a long day for him and Fitton, too. 'Don't keep people waiting.'

At that moment a chill voice from behind her said, 'Excuse me, miss,' and she turned to see a hatchet-faced woman in an old-fashioned bonnet and cloak, holding a large carpet bag. 'I am Mrs Morland's maid,' the woman intoned. Henrietta stared, unable to think for a moment who Mrs Morland was. 'Madam's instructions are that I'm to come back to Morland Place with you.'

Henrietta looked at her blankly, with wandering wits. 'Mrs Morland?'

'Mrs George Morland, your sister-in-law,' Bittle said with a chilling raise of the eyebrows. 'My mistress wants me to start getting Morland Place in order, against her coming back from honeymoon.'

'Oh, yes, I see,' Henrietta said. Everyone was waiting, looking at her for orders. She pulled herself together. 'There's plenty of room in the carriage for you, now Teddy – Mr Edward – has gone to the club. Would you like to give Harris your bag, Miss – Mrs— ?'

'Bittle,' said she, with a contemptuous look at the gogglingly interested Harris. 'And I'll keep the bag with me, thank you. Please to get in, miss,' she added impatiently, as Henrietta seemed to want her to get up first. No idea of what was what, that was plain. Daughter of the house, and she hadn't an idea how to go on! Miss Alfreda was going to have her work cut out, Bittle reflected as she climbed up after the children and took the backward seat. There was room for all three of them on the forward seat, and they sat in a meek row facing her, feeling too intimidated to chatter.

Bittle was relieved to know that she was to be going to Morland Place, at least, and not to be dismissed out of hand; but she was still bitter and suspicious about being excluded from the honeymoon, and in no mood to make anyone else feel better than she did. She glared fiercely at the children, daring them to move or speak; and when the carriage left the road for the ruts of the track, and they were all flung about like peas in a rattle, she felt only a grim satisfaction at this fresh cause for complaint.

CHAPTER SEVEN

Benedict Morland's father, James, had had a younger sister, Lucy. She had married an earl, and the marriage had lifted that end of the family willy-nilly into a different sphere of society. But Benedict had always remained close to his Aunt Lucy's youngest son, Thomas Weston, MP. Each of them in his own way was something of an outsider, and it had formed a bond between them. Outside of Morland Place, Weston was probably the person most deeply affected by Benedict's death.

Weston was sixty-seven, but had still kept his hair, his springy walk, and his sense of humour, though he looked unusually solemn now.

'It's a hard thing to be the last of one's generation,' he was saying to his niece Charlotte, Duchess of Southport. Her mother, his sister, had died three years ago. 'I remember Mama saying the same thing to me when Uncle James died, leaving her the last of her generation. But I suppose that's the penalty for being the youngest.'

'At least you had the pleasure of being brought up with brothers and sisters and cousins. You can't lose what you've never had,' said Charlotte, who had had a lonely child-hood. She was resting on the sofa, recuperating after a bout of the strange, intermittent sickness which affected many who had been in the Crimea. It took the form of a low fever, headache, and sometimes agonising pains in the joints and the spine: very unpleasant when it was going on, and debilitating afterwards. No-one seemed to know what caused it.

Weston had come to visit her, bringing his adopted son Tommy. He had also brought a bunch of grapes, which were perfectly redundant, since Southport had hothouses to provide as many of them as she could eat. She found the gift the more touching for that.

'It's odd that you weren't invited to the funeral,' she said. 'I didn't expect they would ask any of us, but you and Benedict were always such friends.'

'I dare say things are at sixes and sevens at Morland Place, with Benedict having been abroad so long,' Weston said with a shrug. 'It wasn't young George who wrote to me. Harry Anstey informed me, otherwise I'd have had to wait to read the notice of his death in the paper.'

'Poor Benedict,' Charlotte said. 'Always looking for adventure. But he could be proud of his achievements. In the Crimea alone, he made an enormous difference.'

Weston looked at her narrowly, with a gleam of his old humour. 'D'you know, I half think you miss that place, with all its horrors!'

Charlotte did not smile. 'If you'd been there, you wouldn't joke about it. But it was something we endured, and survived. It's natural that we should remember it. And feel an attachment to those who were with us.'

Weston's son, standing by the window looking out, turned. 'I'd have liked to go to the funeral, to pay my respects. Cousin Benedict was very kind to me. I'll never forget how he took us on a special trip on the underground railway, before it was opened. It was thrilling!'

'But perhaps your principal wouldn't have given you leave,' Charlotte remarked.

'If he hadn't, I'd have taken the time anyway.'

'No you wouldn't, my lad,' his father said. 'That's no way to talk. You've accepted the position and you must fulfil it responsibly.'

'I know, Dad.'

'Suppose I gambled everything away on 'Change?' Weston went on. 'You'd be glad to be able to earn your living.'

Tommy smiled at him affectionately. 'As if I wanted your fortune! You and Mum have given me everything already.'

'Not everything,' Weston said. 'It was the duchess who rescued you from the chimney in the first place!'

'Oh, don't remind the poor child of that!' Charlotte protested. Tommy had started life as a sweep's boy, an orphan bought for a few shillings from the parish, who would have died stuck in a chimney at Southport House if Charlotte had not insisted, against the wishes of her servants, on having the wall demolished to get him out. Weston, whose wife Emily could not have children, took a fancy to the pathetic child, and adopted him.

There was nothing pathetic about Tommy Weston now: he was a well-dressed, well-spoken young man of twenty-one with quiet, pleasant manners. But to Charlotte, who had worked a great deal in the slums, there was an indefinable look to his face that she had seen many times before in the very poor. It was as though they were not quite finished properly; as though they had only just managed to get born by the skin of their teeth, and had a less than tenacious grip on life. She knew Emily worried about his health; if Weston did, he hid it better. He had dearly wanted his son to follow him into Parliament, but Tommy seemed not to have the ambition. Charlotte suspected his taking the position as secretary to another MP was a sop to his father, for he didn't seem to care much about that, either. Certainly there was no need for him to earn his living. Weston had inherited both his mother's and his stepfather's fortunes, and Tommy would one day be an extremely wealthy man, in anticipation of which Weston had settled a handsome allowance on him.

Charlotte changed the subject to spare Tommy's blushes. Her children teased him a good deal about chimneys and he took it very well, but she did not suppose he could enjoy it. 'I'm sorry to think I've had so little to do with Benedict in recent years. And I know nothing about George. We all seem to have drifted apart so – I haven't even seen you in months.'

'Weeks,' Weston corrected her. 'You exaggerate. But it's the penalty of age: everything falls away – hair – teeth – one's social circle. And poor Benedict did get rather odd at the end. What with losing Mary, and then Sibella dying, I

106

suppose there was nothing for him but to take up another of his projects to occupy his mind. If it hadn't been the canal, it would have been something else. At least he died in the saddle, poor fellow, which is what he would have wanted.'

'Who would have wanted what?' said a tall young woman coming into the room at that moment. She went over to kiss Charlotte. 'Good morning, Mama-duchess. When are you going to get off this old sofa?'

'Who is this luminous creature?' Tom enquired.

'Hello, Uncle Tom.' Lady Venetia Fleetwood bestowed a kiss on her great-uncle and a smile and nod on Tommy. 'I haven't seen you in an age.'

Weston looked ostentatiously at the clock. 'You're up early! Only half-past twelve, and I suppose you were dancing until four or five this morning with some Blues officer?'

'Only until three, and he was in the Greys,' she corrected him with nice literalness. 'Heavy cavalry, but he was light on his feet. Am I luminous?'

She was a tall girl, slender, and her harebell-blue dress, though in the fashionable style, was very plain and almost without trimming. But her face, though not conventionally pretty, was full of life, and her skin and her grey eyes shone as though she was twice as healthy as everybody else. She carried herself well, and wore her hair coiled at the back of her head, which made her look queenly.

'Olympian,' said Weston. 'Fresh down from the mountain.'

'That's nice,' she approved. 'Who would have wanted what?'

'There's no diverting her,' Charlotte warned.

'Cousin Benedict,' Weston explained. 'Would have wanted to die the way he did.'

Venetia's brows went up. 'Why does everyone always make suppositions about the wishes of dead people?'

'Because they can't contradict, of course,' Weston said.

'Besides,' she said firmly, 'no-one could want to die of bilharziasis. It's extremely unpleasant.'

Weston rolled his eyes at his niece. 'My God, she's another one of you!'

107

Charlotte looked grave. 'She surpasses me. I only wanted to open a hospital: Venetia wants to be a doctor.'

'That's madness on a grand scale,' said Weston. 'What possesses the women of this family?'

'I think it's a perfectly reasonable ambition,' Tommy exclaimed loyally. 'And I think she'd make a splendid doctor.'

'That is more of an insult than a compliment, my son,' said Weston.

But Venetia thanked him. 'You are my only supporter. No-one else wants a woman to do anything. Even my sainted mother would sooner have me a conventional husband-hunter – wouldn't you, Mama-duchess?'

'I want you to be happy, as every mother does. And people who try to swim against the stream are usually unhappy.'

Venetia moved her slim shoulders impatiently. 'Oh, happiness! Happiness is what comes when you are doing what you ought to do.'

'Very Methodistical, of you,' Weston teased.

'I have a mind. I can't pretend otherwise, even for the sake of attracting the herds of suitors that mothers seem to need, to reassure them their daughters are normal.'

'From what I hear, you have no shortage of suitors,' Tommy said, and if it came out a little wistfully, fortunately no-one noticed. 'You must have dazzled them in Berlin.'

'Have you been in Berlin?' Weston asked with interest. 'I didn't know that. What were you doing there?'

'I was supposed to be being finished. Mama thought if I was taken away from London I might forget all this medical nonsense and learn to giggle.'

'I *never* wanted you to giggle!' Charlotte defended herself vigorously.

'I thought you went to a school in Paris?' said Weston. 'When did the plan change?'

'It didn't. I went on from Paris to Berlin to improve my German. And then, just when France declared war and things started to get interesting, I was forced to come home.' She gave her mother a resentful look, which Charlotte shrugged off.

'Where did you stay in Berlin?'

'At court. It wasn't the best arrangement. They have the most rigid rules and etiquette there: you aren't even allowed out of the palace except on official engagements, unless you get special permission.'

'You do move in exalted circles!' Weston said. 'Who do you know at the Prussian court?'

'The Crown Princess. The Queen arranged it,' Charlotte explained. 'She really is quite extraordinarily kind! She never minds how much trouble she goes to when she sets herself to help a friend.'

'The Princess is kind, too, and *extremely* intelligent,' Venetia said. 'We had long talks about the lot of women. She said sooner or later women will be accepted in all the spheres they are now denied, so my chances were better than hers simply because I'm younger, and time and history are on my side.'

Weston saw that this direction worried Charlotte, so he tried to divert Venetia. 'What did you think of German Society?'

She wrinkled her nose. 'Oh, it was hideously dull! Not a patch on London.'

'Really? One is accustomed to thinking of Germany as the natural home of culture: music, literature, politics, liberal thought – one only has to remember Prince Albert.'

Venetia frowned. 'Yes, I've heard other people say that. But either he was unusual, or things have changed in the past twenty years.'

'I suspect the latter,' Charlotte said. 'Bismarck—'

'*Someone* had to mention Bismarck!' Tommy said with a grin. 'Sorry, ma'am.'

'Well, I saw no signs of this marvellous culture in Berlin,' Venetia said. 'Prussians think about nothing but soldiering. You simply wouldn't believe how many conversations it's possible to have about manoeuvres and tactics and all the rest of it! Agonising! *Our* young men here would die rather than bore you with such stuff. Germans go to military reviews the way we go to the theatre; and their gossip is all about who's getting his promotion and who's got his regiment and so on.'

'Don't the ladies talk about love?' Weston asked.

'They talk about clothes. When they found I'd just come from Paris, all they wanted to know was what the latest fashions were. They weren't a bit interested in the new constitution, or who it was who really ruled France now, or what Prime Minister Ollivier meant to do: they just wanted to know how Empress Eugénie was dressing her hair.'

'Shocking!' said Weston.

'Oh, but they love the army, too: they manage to combine the two by endlessly discussing the niceties of uniform!'

Weston laughed. 'You must have seemed a positive bluestocking to them: a female interested in politics?'

'I can't take any credit,' Venetia said. 'It's having a former diplomat for a father – one absorbs things without knowing it. I must say,' she added thoughtfully, 'I liked the Empress and Napoleon much more than the Prussian royal family – except the Crown Princess, and she's English, of course. But I know it's not fashionable to say so.'

'The newspapers are full of the decadence and tyranny of France,' Tommy agreed, 'while Germany is held up as the model of enlightenment.'

'Well, the French are Catholics and the Germans Protestants,' Weston said, 'which makes the Germans our natural allies. And perceptions take a long time to change. But I must say I've been feeling nervous about the way things have been going over there. I believe uniting the north German states was just the beginning of Prussia's ambition – not the end, as some papers have been saying. I can't see Bismarck resting until the Hohenzollerns rule the whole of Germany.'

'Oh, yes, they all talked endlessly at Court about a united Germany,' Venetia agreed lightly. 'But does it matter?'

'It will matter a great deal to the French, as their next-door neighbours.'

'That's why France declared war,' Tommy said.

'Yes, but I think it's a bad move. All it does is play into Bismarck's hands. Look how the war with Austria was turned into an excuse to force the north German states into confederation. Now he can use the threat to the Rhinelands

110

to unite the southern German states – "unite" in the sense of "annex", of course.'

'France might win,' Venetia said. 'When I was in Paris, Leboeuf, the War Minister, was saying the army was ready down to the last gaiter-button.'

Weston shook his head. 'How can they win? France has no friends and Germany no enemies.'

'But need it concern us?' Charlotte said, anxiously.

'I don't think we'll be anything but firmly neutral,' Weston said. 'But consider: if Prussia unites Germany by force of arms, what will it find to do next with that well-tuned military machine? Will it be content to disband it, or leave it idle?'

There was a short silence. Venetia, seeing her mother was troubled, introduced a new topic. 'By the way,' she began brightly, 'I was accosted last night at the ball by a guardsman who claimed cousinhood with me, though I'd never seen him before in my life. He looked a shocking rake, and Baby Sutton said he's a loose fish I should have nothing to do with. But I have to say he was horribly charming, and flirted *most* satisfactorily!'

'Venetia!'

'Don't "Venetia" me, Mama-duchess! Flirting is what balls are for, surely you remember that?'

'And what was the name of this loose fish?' Weston asked, amused.

'Lord Marwood. He said his sister has married my cousin in Yorkshire. Who could that be, Mama?'

Charlotte shook her head. 'No-one's married that I know of.'

Weston answered. 'Didn't you hear? Stirring events at Morland Place: the new head of the family has taken a bride. There was an announcement in *The Times*.'

'I didn't see it,' Charlotte said.

'Well, you have been ill.'

'It seems a very unseemly haste, so soon after Benedict's death. Were you invited to the wedding?'

'No.' He shrugged. 'Young George seems to do things in something of a ramshackle way, but at least one can acquit him of mushroomery, if he didn't seize the opportunity to send an ingratiating letter to his great cousins in London!'

'I don't think you should joke about it,' Charlotte said. 'It shows a want of conduct.'

'You wouldn't have wanted to go to the wedding,' Weston assured her. 'A pretty stir there'd be in York to have a duchess turn up for the occasion! You'd have been toad-eaten to death.'

'He seems to have done well for himself, at all events,' Tommy remarked, 'if he's marrying the sister of a lord.'

'That rather depends on the lord,' Weston said. 'Marwood's father was all to pieces – a gamester – went bankrupt and shot himself.'

'Good God! Yes, I seem to remember hearing something about that,' Charlotte said.

'And Marwood *fils* has the same proclivities, I understand, but fortunately much shorter credit. He has no fortune to gamble away. Not at all the sort of person you should be consorting with, Venetia.'

She laughed. 'Yes, that was very apparent! He was obviously a detrimental!'

'A detrimental?' Weston enquired, eyebrows arched.

'Don't you know, Dad?' Tommy said colourlessly. 'A detrimental is a man girls like to flirt with, but who is not a marriage prospect.'

'Either because he's not serious – like Cleveley, for instance,' Venetia took it up, 'or he's a younger son.'

'Or he has pockets to let,' Tommy finished for her.

Venetia glanced quickly at him, but he would not meet her eyes. A thought occurred to her, and her cheeks coloured.

Charlotte said, 'Well, darling, he sounds most unpleasant to me, especially if he's claiming acquaintance with you in that improper way. You must have nothing more to do with him.'

'Can't cut a relative!' Venetia said lightly. 'But don't worry, I shan't let him hang around the house and bother you. I dare say he'd love to marry me for my portion, but I'm sure he knows he has no chance, for I must say he didn't seem at all *stupid* – which rather singles him out from the crowd.

If men only knew how much we appreciate intelligence, they wouldn't put all their effort into growing whiskers!' She said it with a glance towards Tommy, who was clean-shaven, and he understood that she meant it for an apology, and smiled. The fact that she cared enough to care was something.

'You don't seem to object to Captain Winchmore's whiskers,' Charlotte said.

'Captain Winchmore is an elegant accessory to one's *toilette*,' she said, 'but one doesn't take him seriously.'

'Poor Winchmore,' said Weston. 'How cruel you acknowledged beauties are!'

In the afternoon, Charlotte felt strong enough to leave the sofa and go and visit Fanny. Fanny Anthony was Charlotte's second cousin, the daughter of Benedict's sister Sophie. They had first met when making their come-out together, became intimate friends, and lived together in London until they married. Because of the peculiar circumstances of Charlotte's childhood, Fanny had been her first, and perhaps only close female friend.

Fanny's marriage to Dr Anthony had been a disaster, and she was driven at last to run away from him, abandoning her fortune, her son, and her reputation. She had disappeared, and everyone had assumed her dead. But years later, while doing charity work in the London slums, Charlotte had found her again, destitute, starving, and with an illegitimate daughter, Emma.

Charlotte had taken Fanny in and nursed her back to health, and Fanny lived in Southport House still. Thanks to the efforts of Charlotte's stepfather, Fanny had an ample income now, but her experiences had taken their toll of her, and she would never be strong again. All she wanted was to live in seclusion and see her daughter safe and well, and she spent her days in reading, sewing, and writing letters. Her life passed blamelessly and quietly, and out of the stream of the world; but it was surprising how often troubled members of the household found their way to 'Fanny's room' and the willing listener there.

Charlotte found Fanny sitting in her favourite rocking-chair, which she had drawn up near the window, alternately setting stitches in a doll's dress and looking out at the garden beyond. A tabby cat was dozing on the window-seat in a slant of sunshine. It had found its way to her mysteriously one day and adopted her. It came up after luncheon, slept all afternoon in her company, and at five when the maid came in with her tea, would get up, stretching and yawning, step delicately across to brush against her legs in farewell, and follow the maid downstairs to be let out into the garden and its other, enigmatical life.

Fanny looked up and smiled as Charlotte came in. 'This is nice,' she said. 'I'm glad to see you on your feet again. Poor Charley, you look very pulled! I should have come to see you, but I was afraid I might disturb you.'

'I know you don't leave your room; I didn't expect you. And I'm sorry I've neglected you so long. This tiresome fever makes me so weak. But I'm much better today. How peaceful you look! What are you making?'

Fanny offered it for inspection. 'A dress for Augusta's doll, to match the one I made for Emma's – only in a different colour, of course, or there'll be quarrels!'

'How small the stitches are!' Charlotte marvelled. 'You're getting very clever at these tiny things.'

'Yes, and when I think how when I lived with the Wellands I couldn't even hem a sheet straight, I amaze myself. What a useless creature I was then!'

'I don't suppose I could hem a sheet straight,' Charlotte said, amused. 'Boredom would prevent.'

'I suppose that's what it is. I've learned to take trouble because I'm interested,' Fanny said, taking back the little garment. 'It's nice that Augusta and Emma are such friends,' she added. 'I do think it very broad-minded of Southport to let them share a governess, when you think what Emma is.'

'Emma isn't a "what",' Charlotte said firmly. 'She's herself, and we love her very much.'

Fanny smiled calmly. 'Dear Charley! You know exactly what I mean. And I'm grateful for what you're doing for her – even though it means her living down at Ravendene.'

Charlotte drew a chair up and said, curiously, 'Why is it that you love Emma so much, when you hated poor Lionel and don't miss him at all?'

'I didn't hate him,' Fanny protested. 'But he was so much Philip's son. And I was a different person then, too – vain and silly and selfish. I feel guilty about Lionel sometimes,' she added, 'but I'm sure he does very well without me. And he wasn't a very nice baby, if you remember.'

'Oh Fanny! All babies are nice.'

'Hmm. Well, we won't dispute over that,' Fanny said. 'At any rate, all of yours are nice. Venetia came to see me yesterday, to tell me all her balls and flirts. She's so amusing, she does me good!'

'She seems to have one flirt too many at the moment,' Charlotte said, and told her about Lord Marwood.

'How time flies,' Fanny said sadly. 'Uncle Benedict's wedding to Sibella was just a few months before yours and mine; and now here's him and Sibella both dead, and little George getting married. It makes me feel very old.' She shook off the melancholy. 'But you needn't worry about Venetia. She has her wits about her. I'm sure she won't be taken in.'

Charlotte hesitated before going on. 'Fanny, has it ever occurred to you that Tommy Weston—'

'That he's in love with Venetia? Oh Charley, stale buns!' Fanny laughed. 'You needn't worry about him, either. He knows there's no chance.'

Charlotte frowned. 'Well, she doesn't love him, of course, but if she did there'd be no reason—'

'No reason? How republican of you! But what do you think Southport would have to say?'

'Oliver's not proud in that way.'

Fanny shook her head. 'Sometimes I think you don't know your husband at all! How you can be so wrong about him time and again defeats me.' Charlotte was silent, and Fanny went on, 'Venetia says she wants to study medicine – to be a doctor. I suppose she's talked to you about that?'

'Yes, of course. I hope it isn't a serious ambition.'

'Why don't you forbid her?'

'Given my own history, and Grandmama's, it would smack of hypocrisy, don't you think?'

Fanny laid down her needle. 'Nursing is bad enough, but do you really want your daughter to be examining men's bodies and cutting them about and so on? Especially lower-class men?'

'No,' said Charlotte, 'of course not.'

'Of course not. You want her to love a nice young man of rank and fortune and marry and have children. And why not? Only misery comes of flouting convention. You and I have proved that in our separate ways.'

'But if it turns out to be really what she wants?'

'You must make sure she stops wanting it. Charley, even if by some miracle she succeeded, what a waste for her to strive with so much pain to be a third-class man, when she could be a first-class woman!'

'I wish you would tell her those things,' Charlotte said ruefully. 'If I tell her, it will only make her more determined. She's very stubborn, and opposition only braces her.'

'Yes,' Fanny said thoughtfully. 'I do see that for you to be saying *don't do as I do, but as I tell you* might set her back up. Well, perhaps if you could put her in the way of seeing the most unpleasant side of it, she might decide it's not for her. When you're young and full of life, there's a romance to misery and death, when you've no experience of it.'

Charlotte considered. 'It might work. But if it didn't—'

'Then you'd just have to hope for love to sweep her off her feet.' They were silent a while, and then Fanny said, 'I can't get used to the idea of Morland Place without Uncle Benedict. I wonder if it's changed much. Don't you wish you could see it again?'

'Yes, and it seems sad that there's no contact with the family there any more. But there are lots of places I wish I could see again. Do you never wish you could go home?'

'To Hobsbawn House?' Fanny asked. 'I don't think of it as "home" any more. I thought I should, but now I just see Anthony there.' She set another tiny stitch in the green velvet dress. 'I shall never go there again,' she said.

*   *   *

At two o'clock, the hour of 'morning visits' found Lady Venetia Fleetwood with her sister Olivia in the Chinese drawing-room, doing the honours for her mother, receiving the stream of visitors who came to leave cards of form, or enquire after the duchess's health. Since everyone in Town knew that the duchess was not seeing anyone yet, these visits only took up the first hour or so, after which a more relaxed and youthful crowd began to appear, calling on the young ladies rather than their mother, and behaving much more as if they were making informal 'five o'clock tea' visits.

By half-past three a coterie had gathered around Venetia and Olivia: Lady Cordelia Stratford, a second cousin on their father's side; Miss Edith Wood, a frequent companion; and a gaggle of young gentlemen, mostly Guards and cavalry officers, who had come to idle and flirt.

Of the ladies only Olivia, in the strictest terms, was a 'beauty', with golden hair and her father's violet eyes; but Cordelia had countenance, Miss Wood vivacity, and Venetia was generally agreed to be magnificent if a little daunting. All had their admirers. Whenever the Fleetwood young ladies were 'at home' there was a constant stream up to the front door of Southport House. Not a little of the attraction for the young men was that of being sure of meeting all their friends there.

The company was discussing the sad affliction of a common acquaintance, whose grandmother had died, necessitating black ribbons. 'And in the middle of the Season, too,' Miss Wood said. 'It's too bad!'

'What a blessed thing it would be if one had no relations,' Lady Cordelia said. 'They do nothing but worry and contradict you during their lives, and then die just when it will be of the greatest inconvenience to you.'

'For shame,' laughed Viscount Freshwater. 'You can't suppose they consult your inconvenience at such a moment!'

'Little you know of it, my lord,' she replied sternly. 'Only let the thermometer stand at a hundred and something in the shade, with all of humanity disporting itself in butterfly radiance, and off will pop some ancient great-grandsomething

117

and plunge you into stifling black, at total variance with your feelings. My careful study of the subject has convinced me,' she finished largely, 'that they do it to annoy.'

'*Les femmes, les femmes*!' cried Augustus Sutton, a merry young man, rather small, and with a chubby face, whose inevitable nickname was 'Baby'. 'The prettier they are, the more unreasonable!'

'And the more heartless,' Lord Cleveley agreed. 'And Lady Cordelia is the most heartless of them all.'

'Upon my word, Sammy, you can't say that,' said Clement Chetwyn, a cousin of the Fleetwoods on their mother's side. 'It's simply not done, old fellow, to praise one young lady in the company of others.'

'I assure you we don't in the least regard it,' Venetia said. 'We are none of us hanging out for compliments.'

'Too cruel, Lady Venetia,' said Captain 'Beauty' Winchmore, her most devoted admirer, who had positioned himself leaning on the back of a chair where he could see her face, and hoped also to display his tight overalls to advantage. 'Would you grow roses and deny the bee? Would you forbid the blackbird to sing when he sees the sunrise?'

'Would you deny Beauty the mirror he practises his speeches in front of?' Sutton enquired ironically.

'I apologise, Baby,' Winchmore said with a bow. 'I know how address and polish can frighten the unsophisticated.'

Fred Paston, another Morland-side cousin, thought it was time someone looked at him. 'I count it very lucky that none of us is having to wear ribbons for Mr Benedict Morland. He was only cousin to our respective grandmothers, of course, but didn't your mother know him well, Lady Venetia?'

'Moderately well. He's been to our house on a few occasions, I believe, but I don't remember him. Mama would probably put on mourning for him, but she isn't going out at the moment; and she says we needn't.'

'So you will be at the Blues' ball next week?' Sutton asked.

'Oh, certainly we will,' Olivia answered for her sister. 'Since Captain Winchmore so kindly got us the tickets—'

'Yes, we're always amazed that Beauty can be kind,' said

Freshwater. 'If you'd seen him last week chasing poor Holford round and round the barrack yard uttering bloodcurdling threats, only because he borrowed his razor—'

'And nicked the blade, don't forget,' said Winchmore wrathfully. 'Imagine if my man hadn't noticed! I should have been horridly cut up.'

'Beauty would have been transformed into the Beast,' Freshwater agreed. 'What a loss to the world!'

'Holford's a great deal too fond of borrowing things,' said Clevely. 'Perhaps it's because his father is a banker. I know my banker would far sooner borrow my rents than lend them back to me. By the by, I saw Holford carrying a handsome bouquet along Grosvenor Street on Tuesday. Was it for you, by any chance, Miss Wood?'

'What an indiscreet question,' Edith Wood reproved him. 'Suppose it hadn't been?'

'No use supposing anything of the sort,' said Sutton. 'Everyone knows poor Holford is your poodle, Miss Wood, and that you treat him in the savage way all you great beauties torment your helpless admirers.'

'But I distinctly remember dancing with him at Lady Pakenham's on Monday,' Edith replied, affecting to search distant memory. 'What greater kindness is there than that, when one has so few dances in a Season to bestow amongst so many?'

'They would not be so few if Miss Wood had not such a great dislike of dancing,' Chetwyn remarked. 'But she is famous for it.'

'Are you?' Venetia asked her in surprise. 'I never knew. Whenever we are at a ball together I see you dance every dance.'

Everyone laughed, including Edith, who was good natured, and never minded being the subject of a joke. 'But really,' she said, 'it's not so far off the mark. One doesn't mind dancing with such as the present company—' She flirted a look round the assembled gallants – 'but to be obliged to have any and every man's arm around one, just for the asking, is intolerable.'

'Refuse them,' Venetia said firmly. 'I do.'

'Not everyone has your strength of character, darling,' said Lady Cordelia.

'But one must draw the line somewhere,' Edith said. 'There was one creature introduced to me last week at the Edgecumbes, who actually proposed to *shake hands with me*! Such a shocking breach of decorum you would never have expected to find in the middle of London in the enlightened nineteenth century!'

'Or the amiable Mr G – you know who I mean,' Cordelia nodded to Edith. 'The most delightful fellow, with the face of an angel, who flirts *à merveille*, but has only four thousand a year, besides a widowed mother to keep and eleven brothers and sisters to educate.'

'Now I know that you are quite, quite heartless,' Cleveley said happily. His own fortune was large and secure.

'Not at all,' Miss Wood protested. 'It's the greatest grief to us, for we have all too much heart. Every girl's duty is to marry as well as she can, but naturally we want to marry for love, too. The conflict of interest affects us *dreadfully*.'

She spoke the word with such emphasis and with an expression of such complete contentment that everyone laughed again.

'Talking of detrimentals,' said Beauty Winchmore, 'how come you allowed yourself to be accosted by that rogue Marwood at the ball yesterday, Lady Venetia?'

'I couldn't help it, Captain Winchmore. His sister has married my cousin in Yorkshire.'

'That *is* bad luck.'

'Marwood?' said Cleveley. 'I should think it is! He's not at all the thing, Lady Venetia. I beg you won't have anything to do with him.'

'Oh,' she said demurely, 'but what can one do? One can't be impolite to a connection.'

The gentlemen set themselves in a most gratifying way to assure her that she could, and that if the impertinent fellow became a nuisance they would be happy to rescue her in any number of bold and active ways. So the inconsequential chat and mild flirtations went on, until Lady Cordelia's carriage called for her. Since she offered to take Miss Wood up, and Lady Venetia seemed a little preoccupied, the gentlemen walked off, and the Fleetwood sisters were left alone.

Venetia had enjoyed it as much as anyone. She liked the company of young men, the flattery, the sense of power it gave her to have rivals vying for her attention. She liked chatting and flirting – artificial and trivial though it was; she liked dancing and clothes, dinners and tea visits, driving and walking in the Park, riding in Rotten Row – the whole pleasant, frivolous business of the Season.

But it was not enough to satisfy, she thought. It had not been enough for her mother, though nowadays age and illness confined her to the domestic scene. It would not have been enough for her father, and she dismissed out of hand what she guessed would be his objection, that it was different for a female. That it *was* different did not mean it should be! If one had an agile brain and energy and ideas, why should the fact of having a female body prevent one from being active and useful in one's chosen sphere, whatever it might be?

She came back from the depths of her thoughts to realise that Olivia had been talking to her and had apparently asked a question to which she was expecting an answer. Venetia had no idea what the question had been. She asked one of her own instead. 'Livy, do *you* think it's every girl's duty to marry well? Is that your goal?'

Olivia looked at her doubtfully, wondering what was under the question. Venetia's tongue could be barbed, and though she loved her, she was sometimes afraid of her. 'Well,' she said at last, 'it's what Mama and Papa want us to do.'

'You are a great beauty, of course,' Venetia said thoughtfully.

'But everyone admires you much more than me,' Olivia said loyally. 'You amuse them, but I'm so stupid, I can never think of witty things to say.'

'Most men prefer to have their wit admired, not matched. You do exactly right. I am often too sharp.'

'Captain Winchmore is desperately in love with you,' Olivia said, a little out of her depth, 'and he is the wittiest of them all, so everyone says.'

'Oh, I believe I must look higher than Beauty Winchmore,'

121

Venetia said sarcastically. 'He is only Lord Hazelmere's heir. To satisfy Papa I can hardly go below a marquess.'

'But I'm sure Papa wouldn't object to Winchmore, if it was what you wanted,' Olivia said.

Venetia almost laughed. 'That is a very novel view of our father! It's what Papa wants, not what we want, that matters. Imagine defying him!'

Olivia blenched at the thought. Both girls were in awe of him, as was natural, for he was not only their father and head of the household but hugely powerful in society and in the Government: a landowner who controlled vast acres and the welfare of hundreds of employees, a peer of the realm and legislator whose weighty deliberations in the House of Lords might alter the destiny of the nation. Neither of them had ever even considered going against Papa's wishes in anything. He had never had to forbid them: merely the information that something would displease him had been enough to govern them.

But now Venetia wanted something important. She hadn't yet broached the subject with him, largely because she was terribly afraid that she knew what his reaction would be. But this was not simply a matter of a sliding down the banisters or making a noise in the corridors, of a gown being too low-cut or of going shopping in Bond Street without a chaperon. This was a matter of real importance, and though Venetia had not yet gone so far as to think she might defy her father, she had got as far as considering whether his expected embargo might be wrong.

'Are we going to five o' clock tea at Lady Hope's?' Olivia interrupted her reverie wistfully. 'Lord Lansdowne's sure to be there. He'd be such a good match for you, 'Netia, if you think Papa wants you to have a marquess; and I know you find him amusing.'

Venetia smiled at this transparent device. 'Cocky Lansdowne hasn't an idea of marrying anyone yet. He's having too much fun as he is. But by all means let's go to Lady Hope's. Her refreshments are always good. Last time it was strawberries and cream and peaches, do you remember? And those delicious little cakes – and the best French coffee in London.'

CHAPTER EIGHT

The conflict between France and Germany filled the newspapers. Since the Crimea, war – even a war in which England was not involved – had ceased to be a private matter for soldiers and ministers. Now with photography and the telegraph, the public expected to be told everything that went on, and at once.

The Crimean episode had also made the plight of the common soldier a popular concern, and now heart-rending reports were being published every day about the suffering of troops on both sides. Public sentiment ran high, and in July a meeting was held in London, as a result of which the National Society for Aid to the Sick and Wounded was founded, with the object of providing medical aid impartially to the French and Prussian soldiers.

An executive committee was formed, of which Charlotte was asked to be a member, for her experience was unrivalled, except by that of Miss Nightingale. There had of course been letters and appeals in the newspapers for Miss Nightingale to take up her Scutari rôle again, and many of the contributions which poured in to the Society were addressed to her personally, reflecting how strongly she was associated in the public's mind with soldiers' welfare. But she refused to join the committee, preferring to continue with her other work of pursuing army sanitary reform.

Charlotte agreed to serve as long as her health held up, but she did so with some misgiving, knowing it must encourage Venetia in her dangerous ideas. But when Venetia requested a private interview one morning, her opening words were on a more conventional subject.

'Mama, I've had a proposal of marriage this morning. Well, two, to be exact.'

'*Two* in one morning?' Charlotte said. 'Good heavens, and it isn't twelve o'clock yet.'

'Oh, don't tease! Who comes calling so early? Why, cousins, of course!'

'Oh,' said Charlotte, disappointed.

Venetia explained. Fred Paston and Clement Chetwyn had come separately, and by coincidence on the same mission, using the privilege of relations to call at an unseasonable hour when they might hope to find Venetia alone.

'They missed each other by ten minutes,' she told her mother. 'I wonder what I said yesterday to set them off?'

She had received their proposals with different degrees of pleasure. Clement Chetwyn knew quite well he had no chance. Although his eldest brother, the Earl of Aylesbury, was a convinced bachelor, there was another brother, Titus, before Clement, and Titus was married and had two sons already. The likelihood that Clement would ever come into the title, therefore, was remote, and all he had to offer as a husband was his allowance and his captain's pay, which were just about enough to keep him in the style expected of an officer of the Blues. But Clement was moved by a very deep attachment to try his luck, and Venetia honoured his heart if not his head.

Fred Paston was a descendant of a collateral Morland line, great-grandson of Mary Morland, who was a sister of Venetia's great-grandmother Lucy. Having come early into his father's fortune, Paston was one of the wealthiest men in England – so wealthy that he felt his lack of a title did not disqualify him from offering for the daughter of the Duke of Southport, to whose dowry he could be supposed indifferent, but whose consequence would greatly add to his. Venetia was sure there wasn't an ounce of affection in the case.

'It was wrong of them to ask you before your father,' Charlotte said, when Venetia had finished.

'Oh Mama-duchess, this is 1870! If they were so Gothic as to ask Papa first I should refuse them even if I loved them! Which I don't, of course. I was sorry to hurt Clement, for I'm very fond of him. But I had no difficulty at all in snubbing that odious Fred Paston. His conceit knows no bounds! His papa was so charming, too, which makes it all the more strange that Fred didn't inherit a bit of it along with all that money. It's a great pity Paston senior pegged out so young.'

'Pegged out? Darling, your slang!'

'Never mind my slang. The thing is, Mama, that this marriage business is out for me. Girls are supposed to marry upwards, and how can I go upwards? I'm already a duke's daughter. Who is there for me: one of the royal princes?'

'The Queen wouldn't allow it,' Charlotte said. 'She doesn't believe in royalty marrying subjects.'

'So there you are,' Venetia said. 'You might as well face it bravely, and help me to become a doctor.'

'Oh Venetia, don't begin that again,' Charlotte pleaded. 'You know it's hopeless.'

'It's not hopeless! Miss Blackwell and Miss Garrett did it.'

'Two unusual cases. You can be sure there will be no more: doctors are the most determined of all the professions to keep women out.'

'But you could help me,' Venetia urged. 'You know so many people in the medical world.'

'It's because I know them that I know it's impossible. None of the medical schools will admit you. The examining boards wouldn't let you take the examinations. If you tried to storm the citadel, you would meet with hostility, mockery and abuse. They wouldn't regard your sex, you know—'

'I don't *want* them to regard my sex,' Venetia interrupted.

'I mean they wouldn't spare you. You would be treated with great impertinence, even called indecent names. Your rank wouldn't protect you.'

'Oh Mama! As if I care about that!'

'You can't know what you would care about, love, until you suffer it. You've been brought up gently. You haven't faced people whose delight it would be to see you blush, tremble, and cry – people who would deliberately set out to hurt and offend you, and crow over you when they succeeded.'

'You paint a black picture,' Venetia said, 'but *you* faced

those things to do what you thought right. Don't you think I have as much determination as you?'

'Times are very different now,' Charlotte said, 'and what I wanted to do was not in direct competition with men. You don't understand how hostile the medical profession is: half of them barely accept women as nurses – and nurses are sworn to follow doctors' orders at all times. They can regard nurses as servants. The idea of a female setting herself up as an equal, a competitor, is anathema to them.'

'I'll worry about that when I come to it,' Venetia said, waving difficulties away. 'If only you'll help me get into the Southport – you can't pretend you don't have influence there?'

'You overestimate it, if you think I could do that for you,' Charlotte said. 'I am only *one* of the sponsors now; and my direct involvement is long in the past. I might recommend you to the Medical Committee, but the most I can guarantee is that they'd be polite when they refused me. And I have to tell you, my love, that I don't *want* to recommend you.'

'You don't mean that!'

'I do. Darling, why do you want to be a doctor? Isn't it just because you want to be different, to do something that shocks?'

Venetia was hurt. 'How can you, of all people, ask that?'

Charlotte shook her head. 'I never even wanted to be a nurse. I wanted to help, yes; and when it came to it, I did the task that was to hand. But I never liked it.'

Venetia looked her disbelief.

'Oh, there was an intellectual fascination about it, I grant you,' Charlotte said, 'but the actual business of medicine is brutal and disgusting: pain, blood, stench, dirty bodies. Men dying in the most revolting circumstances. Death is not romantic, you know. Sick and wounded flesh is not lovely.'

'You talk as though I were a fool. I know those things.'

'I don't believe you do. You've read and studied, and you know in theory, but the reality is worse than anything you can imagine.'

'Well, then,' Venetia said, locking eyes with her, 'let me see the reality, and we'll find who's right. *Try* me.'

126

'I don't want you to be exposed to those things. It was hard enough for me, but your upbringing has been very different from mine. To survive it you would have to change in ways I don't want my daughter to change. Do you know what they said of Elizabeth Blackwell when she came to England? That she was a monster, a freak of nature. "How could a woman whose hands reek of gore be possessed of the same nature and feelings as other women?" That's what they said.'

Venetia's look burned. 'But I am not like other women! I can't bear the empty life of do-nothing any more than you could! You know that complete mental blankness is the ordinary condition of women, and if it weren't, they could never endure the boredom of their lives. I must have something to do! I must work!'

'But why *this*?' Charlotte protested.

'Because it's what I want! Mama, help me!'

Charlotte was silent a long moment, and then sighed, and said, 'I can't promise anything. It will depend on your father, and I don't suppose for a moment he'll agree.'

'But you'll speak to him?' Venetia was all eagerness now. 'Then it will be all right. He can't refuse you anything!'

Charlotte laughed, breaking the tension. 'Darling Venetia, how wrong you are about almost everything! It's very endearing.'

Having won her point, Venetia was prepared to be gracious. 'It's my age, Mama-duchess. I'll grow out of it.'

Later, that afternoon, Charlotte's husband came in to see her in her private sitting-room, which she sometimes called her 'office'. She was at her desk, going through the piles of letters that had flooded in to the National Society for Aid to the Sick and Wounded. Her secretary, Temple, began to rise – awkwardly, since he had a lap full of papers – and Southport waved him casually down again.

'It's very touching,' Charlotte said by way of greeting. 'The contributions sent to the Society come mostly from those who can least afford it. The rich and comfortable give when we ask, but every day I get small amounts scraped together by Ragged Schools, Sunday schools, Friendly Societies, a group of Concerned Factory Hands – there's one here from a Christian society of negroes in the West Indies. All people hardly better off than the soldiers they want to help. It's rather sad, somehow.'

Southport leaned over her shoulder to look. He was in his fifties now, and like many who had been at Balaclava all through that terrible war, his health had suffered and his vigour was impaired. But he was still handsome to Charlotte, in spite of his grey hair and careworn face. Theirs had been a troubled marriage at times, for they came from different backgrounds and were both strong-willed; but he was the only man she had ever loved, and she believed that he, too, had never truly loved another. One way and another, they always found each other again after their differences.

Since Gladstone had come into office in 1868, pulling together a heterogeny of Whigs, Peelites and radicals into the entity which the world now called 'liberals', Southport had been at the War Office under Cardwell, an able man three years his senior. Cardwell was determined to reform the army and used Southport's experiences in the Crimea to the full. But the army was notoriously reactionary and hard to persuade, and it was axiomatic amongst soldiers that civilians could never understand military matters. Cardwell used Southport as his go-between – or, as Charlotte put it, his whipping-boy. He came in for much of the hostility Cardwell's ideas provoked, and it was a strain on his nerves which affected on his temper.

Today, however, he was looking quite genial. 'I hope you won't knock yourself up with all this, my love,' he said, straightening up. 'I should have thought it was more in Miss Nightingale's line.'

'Her health is delicate too. I believe we suffer from the same thing,' Charlotte said.

'Her illness is all in her mind,' said Southport lightly. 'She's quite mad, you know.'

Temple stifled a smile. Charlotte looked cross. 'No, what an ungenerous thing to say! You had that from some soldier. They all hate her so.'

'From Cardwell,' Southport said. 'But the dislike is mutual.

I understand she hasn't a good word to say about him, either.'

'Well, I can't say I like her much,' Charlotte admitted. 'She's very cold – and sometimes fanciful, which is an odd combination. But I do her the justice to think her illness is as real as mine. It must add to her suffering to know people think it's imaginary.'

Southport shrugged. He cared not a whit for Miss Nightingale's ills, especially as he had been at the sharp end of some of her more robust criticisms, even while they were pursuing the same ends. 'She'd have more sympathy if she refrained from annoying people with her constant letter-writing. She's desperate to get back into government, but of course Gladstone can't stand her at any price. It would be better if she would go and be the Lady with the Lamp again out in Alsace, or somewhere. She might do that with everyone's blessing.'

'You shouldn't talk lightly. The suffering is very real.' Charlotte waved a hand at the newspapers on her desk. 'Hospital conditions on both sides are dreadful, and you and I know what that means.'

He nodded. 'The only comfort I can offer you is that it will be a short war. The French are in hopeless disarray, outnumbered two to one, and half of them without rifles, despite Leboeuf's boasts. They haven't a general to match von Moltke, and Napoleon is no better a leader now than he was during the Crimean war. I don't imagine he can hold out as long as a year. The German organisation and preparation have been faultless.'

'Not quite,' Charlotte said. 'Their hospitals weren't prepared at all. Which brings me to something I want to speak to you about. Mr Temple, would you be so kind?'

Temple gathered his things together, bowed and left them. Oliver sat on the edge of her desk and looked down at her. 'I can guess what this is about.'

'Can you?'

'My love, I am not blind and deaf, and nor are the servants. Don't you know by now that there can be no secrets in a house?'

She flushed a little. 'I hadn't intended keeping anything from you—'

'But you have been encouraging Venetia in this nonsense about being a doctor.'

'Not at all. I've told her it's impossible—'

'Quite impossible. Good God, I can't have her running around Town making a spectacle of herself! Even if it were possible, it would be grossly improper. Every feeling revolts. You should have told her so from the beginning, instead of encouraging her by engaging all those tutors.'

'You wanted her to be educated too,' Charlotte said, stung to protest.

'In a general way, yes. But when she started reading the medical books your grandmother left you, you should have intervened. In fact, it would have been better all round if you had thrown them away when they first came to you, and then they wouldn't have spread their corrupting influence over my daughter.'

'But Oliver, you always supported me in my work.'

'The cases are very different. For one thing, Society was a great deal more tolerant twenty years ago. You know that! Look at the difference alone between a Palmerston and a Gladstone.'

'I did tell her that,' Charlotte murmured.

'Not forcefully enough, it seems! And besides, your obscure background, your grandmother's position and history, your independent fortune, all gave you a freedom of action which is not appropriate to Lady Venetia Fleetwood. She was born to position. She is a duke's daughter. She is *my* daughter.'

Charlotte was nettled. 'Whereas I was just your wife?'

'Precisely so.' He looked at her steadily. 'You wish to take that as a barb to your heart. But I inherited you as a grown woman, with a character already fixed, with ideas and traits I had no control over. I could not make conditions if I wished to have you: you had the power of independent action – as you proved more than once. I hoped to influence you, but in the long run I couldn't prevent you from doing what you wished, however much I wanted to.'

'And did you want to?'

'Good God, can you doubt it?' he said impatiently. 'Do you think I *wanted* you to wash dirty bodies and pick maggots out of wounds? Would any man want that for the woman he loved?'

'Do you think I wanted to do it?' she flared back.

'Didn't you?'

'It was necessary! But when I think of the Crimea, of what I had to do in that field hospital, I shudder.'

'Yet you want it for your daughter – and worse.'

'*No*. But she has a burning ambition, and I know how it feels to be thwarted!'

'Well, as I was saying, I inherited you as a grown woman; but my daughter has been mine from birth, and fortunately I do have control over her. I will thwart this *ambition*, as you call it. She shall not unsex herself and disgrace her family.'

Charlotte lowered her voice and tried to speak reasonably. 'Oliver, she's not like the other girls. She's intelligent, and she wants to be useful, as I did at her age. Fortunately it was in my power to do something. But if Venetia is not allowed to act, she will be miserable.'

'There are plenty of ways she can be useful, suitable to her sex and rank. Committee work of all sorts.'

'But that's not what she wants—'

'She doesn't know what she wants. It's an idle fancy.'

'That's not fair. She's studied so hard.'

He rounded on her. 'Charlotte, I warn you, do not defy me in this!'

'Please hear me out,' she begged. 'You see what a wrangling we're in already. If you simply forbid Venetia point blank she won't accept it meekly. The house will be in uproar for weeks, and while you may escape to the House or Horseguards whenever you please, *I* shall be worn down with it! And in the end, who knows but what she might defy you and do something desperate?'

He looked at her, nostrils flaring. 'You paint a pretty picture. What do you propose?' he asked stiffly.

Charlotte took a deep breath. 'I believe that she has a romantic idea of what being a doctor entails.'

'How could it be otherwise?'

131

'If she is brought face to face with the reality, as you and I know it, it may be enough to drive it all out of her for good.'

'You can't mean— !'

'Please listen! The Crown Princess of Prussia has been studying sanitary reform, and she wants to do something about the war hospitals in Berlin – they're in a shocking state. She wrote to Miss Nightingale to ask for trained matrons to be sent from England to help her. Miss Nightingale's sending Miss Lees and Mrs Cox, and she's asked the Southport if we can spare our Mrs Draper to go with them. Now, how if we were to let Venetia go back to the Crown Princess and help her in the hospitals? She could travel with the nurses – they're all very respectable – and once there, the Princess would make sure no harm came to her. Venetia respects her and would accept her authority; and I believe the experience would be enough to convince her that it's not what she wants to do for a permanency.'

Oliver listened in silence, and then turned away and walked up and down the room, thinking. Charlotte knew that it would be hard for him to accept anything but simple obedience to his will, that his pride would demand no compromise. She waited quietly, hoping his sympathy and intelligence would work on him.

'I don't like it,' he said at last.

'I didn't expect you to,' she said. 'But for her to be returning to the Court in Prussia won't seem a remarkable thing, even at this time. And helping in the hospitals in that way can't be thought improper. She'll be quite safe – the fighting won't come there.'

He laughed mirthlessly. 'You can be sure of that! Well, I will think about it. It might be the solution, if it really does discourage her. But why the dickens,' he burst out wrathfully, 'couldn't she just fall in love like any other girl?'

'She may still. But at twenty she's had enough of frivolity, and if she hasn't yet seen the man she wants to marry, she will need something else to occupy her mind.'

'Hmm,' he said. 'And suppose this plan of yours sends her back to us more determined than ever to be a doctor?'

'Well, then,' she said gravely, 'don't you think in that case you might take the ambition seriously?'

'Never,' he said firmly.

'We'll cross that bridge when we come to it,' Charlotte said hastily.

When Venetia and Olivia rode in the Park they drew all eyes. Handsome young women superbly mounted were a rarity: most ladies preferred to ride in a carriage rather than expose their equestrian skills to criticism. And since Venetia had taken the trouble to mention to several people the day before that they would be riding that afternoon, she was not surprised when Winchmore, Sutton and Freshwater rode up and asked if they might join them.

It wasn't long before Captain Winchmore managed to manoeuvre himself and Venetia a little ahead of the others so that he could speak to her privately. Their horses had done this often enough by now to be accustomed to each other, and after a brief and explosive touch of muzzles, they walked quietly, keeping pace.

'I've heard the most alarming report,' Winchmore said. 'I hope and pray it isn't true.'

'And what could it be, I wonder?' Venetia said demurely.

'Oh, Lord, now I know it's true, or you wouldn't talk in that cozening way! You really are going back to Berlin?'

'Yes, why does it surprise you?'

'But you've only just come from there! London was a desert during your absence, and now you propose to punish us again? Society wilts like a thirsty flower when you leave us.'

'I didn't hear that you were pining in a corner last time, Captain Winchmore. Tell me that you didn't dance once while I was away!'

'My feet may have danced, but my heart crouched sobbing in a corner!'

'Very pretty! But don't talk to me of hearts. It's well known that you Blues officers haven't a working one between you.'

'I certainly haven't – I gave it to you long ago.' He lowered his voice. 'Seriously – why will you go back there? And at a time like this?'

'Seriously? Because I've been invited by the Princess Frederick to help her reorganise the war hospitals.'

'Well, that's what I heard, but I didn't believe it.'

'And why not?' she asked, annoyed.

'It's no business for a lady.'

'Is the Crown Princess not a lady?'

'It's different for her. She has a duty to her subjects. You haven't. Lady Venetia, let me beg you not to go!'

'You may beg all you please, but it won't change my mind. I'm so bored with London and balls and endless, pointless chatter. I must *do* something!'

'Then marry me,' he said abruptly.

She burst out laughing. 'Why, Beauty, what an elegant proposal! A thing of polished eloquence! How long did you rehearse it? I've never been so moved!'

'Don't mock,' he said, nettled. 'I hadn't meant to blurt it out like that, but you surprised me.'

'Not half as much as you surprised me!'

'*Did* it surprise you? I thought you knew how much I admire you.'

'No, I always thought you admired yourself most.' She saw she had hurt his feelings, and said more soberly, 'I'm sorry, I didn't mean that. I knew you liked me, of course, but I thought it was at least half gallantry. I know you officers must always be making love to someone.'

He smiled a little crookedly. 'The motley was meant as a defence against the cruel world. It was not meant to deceive *you*.' She looked at him consideringly and in silence, and he said, 'I do love you. Truly.'

'Yes,' she said after a moment. 'I believe you.'

'Ah, then I suppose that's my answer. I notice you don't say that you love me.'

'I don't think I love anyone just now,' she said lightly, not wanting to upset him further.

'Of course, I know my rank and my fortune are not what you are entitled to expect—'

'Oh Beauty, don't!' she said crossly. 'That wouldn't weigh with me.'

'It might with your father.'

'It might if you were penniless or vulgar, but you are a perfectly respectable match, so don't be hanging out for compliments! The plain truth is that I don't want to marry yet. I don't know if I ever shall. I want to do something that matters in the world. Don't you ever feel that?'

'Of course. But there's so little one can do that matters. Unless there's a war—'

'But there is one. You can't fight in it, and neither can I, but there may still be something I can do. At all events, I'm going to find out.'

'It may be dangerous. It will certainly be disagreeable.' She merely shrugged. 'You are a remarkable person,' he said. 'Not many people act on their good intentions or their better feelings. I honour you.'

'Thank you,' she said, with a smile that melted him. She laid her gloved hand briefly over his. 'You are the only person who understands and approves. Everyone else thinks I'm mad.'

He didn't approve, but he let that pass. 'When you come back – how long will that be, by the way?'

'Papa says I may go for three months, but I hope once I'm gone he may let me stay longer.'

'I pray not!'

'Well, the war will be over by Christmas, Papa says, so it can only be five months at the longest.'

He nodded. 'So, when you come back, will you allow me to address you again?'

'I shall always be glad to see you, Captain Winchmore. I enjoy your company.'

He saw she would not give him more than that; but he was hopeful. He felt she liked him. 'One more favour – will you allow me to send you my photograph?'

'I should be happy to receive it,' she said. 'Alas, I can't send you mine in return, since I've never had one taken.'

He grinned. 'I know. I can't tell you how glad I am that I've never come across it in anyone's collection! I can bear not to have one myself, as long as no-one else has!'

After the ride, when she and Olivia were going up to their room to change out of their habits, Olivia said, 'You were very thick with Captain Winchmore, 'Netia. The way you had your

135

heads together, Baby Sutton said he made sure Beauty was proposing to you!'

Venetia smiled to herself, but said only, 'He asked if he might send me his pho.'

Olivia said, 'Oh, how lucky you are! I wish I might have one too. My collection is very dull beside yours. I wish Papa would let us have ours taken. It's much easier to get other people's if you can exchange yours; otherwise it looks so mean.'

Venetia didn't answer, thinking of the photograph. The collecting of 'pho's' was all the rage, and having one sent you by a person of the opposite sex did not signify any romantic attachment. But Venetia could not help thinking that in this case, Winchmore was hoping that she would take it to Berlin with her, and hoping further that it might keep his face before her mind, and do for his cause what he could not do in her absence.

On the morning of her departure, another cousin invoked a relative's indulgence to call when the family was not at home to anyone. Tommy Weston was admitted to the yellow sitting room, the private room the girls used, where Olivia and Venetia were awaiting the hour of departure.

'You look very smart,' he said, making his bow to Venetia. She was wearing a raspberry-coloured travelling costume with caped shoulders, edged with black velvet bands and trimmed with sable tassels. 'Is that new?'

'Yes. Papa said I must have something good to travel in, to make up for having to dress plainly when I get there.' She made a face. 'I think he was hoping vanity would put me off this course – as if the prospect of not being able to wear finery would weigh with me.'

'I'm sure your father didn't think anything of the sort,' Tommy said.

She looked at him quizzically. 'I was only joking. So, Tommy, have you come to beg me not to go? I have to warn you you're behindhand. I've had twelve pleas already, in person and by letter.'

'No,' he said, 'I just came to say goodbye and to wish you good luck. I think what you're doing is splendid.'

Olivia looked at him quickly, and then got up and went across the room to the table under the window, where she picked up a journal and began leafing through it. Tommy hardly noticed her departure, but Venetia did, and it made her feel uncomfortable. But she said evenly, 'Thank you. I think you must be the only person on my side. Even my mother is against it.'

'That can't surprise you,' he said reasonably. 'The thought of *you*,' he made a little encompassing gesture of the hand, 'in the surroundings of a hospital – and a war hospital at that – is so incongruous it outrages the senses.'

'Even yours?'

'Even mine,' he agreed. 'But I understand why you want to do it, and I applaud you for sticking to your guns. And if there's ever anything I can do to help you, you know you can call on me.' He blushed suddenly. 'Not that I can think there ever would be. I mean, considering who *I* am and who *you* are—'

'Thank you, Tom,' Venetia said warmly, interrupting his descent into deprecation. 'It's good to know I can count on you.' She laid her hand on his arm, and he looked down at it, longing to lay his own over it, and not daring. She noticed him looking, and removed it.

'I have something for you,' he said, breaking into the awkward pause that followed. 'Just a little something – I hope you can accept it.' He reached into the pocket of his jacket and brought out a book. It was small, leather bound, very handsome. She took it. 'For the journey,' he added, as though some justification was needed. 'Small enough to fit in a pocket or reticule, you see.'

'*Gulliver's Travels*,' she read the title, and then looked up at him.

'I always think it's very important to have a good book about you on a journey,' he said gravely. 'In case of delays, you know.'

And suddenly they both smiled. Olivia, glancing covertly across at that moment, thought in surprise that cousin Tommy was not at all bad looking – at least, when he smiled like that. But of course, young men never smiled like that at her, only at Venetia. She thought it without resentment. She had come second to her sister all their lives, and no young man's admiration for Venetia could be greater than hers.

Venetia was gone, and the house seemed very quiet without her. Olivia, having just got used to having her back after her previous trip, now had to realise all over again how much she missed her. At first the young men called at the house in as great numbers, so that they could enquire of Olivia whether there were any news of the traveller, and to wonder at her going, and to marvel at their own desolation over it. But when that palled, Venetia's particular admirers dropped off, and other young men, who called because it was the fashion or because their friends did, also came less frequently. Olivia was a beauty, and as a duke's daughter and a sweet-natured girl would always have her following, but the 'young ladies at home' days lost a great deal of their sparkle when Venetia was gone.

Olivia was in danger of moping, and was glad that the Season was ending so that she would soon be able to go down to Ravendene for the summer, to join her younger sister Augusta, and cousin Emma. She liked the peace of the country, the ordered routines of the country house, the walking and riding in the delicious green spaces of the park. And her twin brothers, she hoped, would be there for at least part of the summer. She was very fond of Harry and Marcus; and when they were at home, they always attracted company to the house. Olivia's beauty brought her admirers, but she had not the personality to make them stay, and though she loved company she had always depended on others to assemble it for her. That was perhaps why, having just had her nineteenth birthday, she was still unwed – that, and the fact that, apart from her immediate family, she had never yet liked any one person better than another.

One morning about a week after Venetia's departure, her mother came into the yellow sitting-room, surprising Olivia, who was accustomed to being sent for rather than sought.

'I've had a letter this morning from Lady Augusta Stanley, one of the Queen's ladies-in-waiting,' Charlotte said. 'She's an old acquaintance: perhaps you've heard me mention her?'

'Yes, Mama.'

'The letter concerns you, my love.' Charlotte sat on the sofa and patted the seat beside her. 'Come and read it.'

My dear Duchess,

The Queen has commanded me to sound you as to the possibility of your daughter Lady Olivia's joining the Household in the position of Maid of Honour. A vacancy has arisen very suddenly with the unexpected resignation of Lady Alice Adair. Her Majesty remembers Lady Olivia from her childhood visits to Windsor, and considers, from all she has heard of her since, that she would suit. I should be grateful if you would give me your immediate reaction as soon as possible, as Her Majesty is anxious to have matters settled. If you and Lady Olivia look favourably on the proposal, we should discuss it further. I shall be in London on Tuesday and can call at Southport House in the p.m. if that is convenient.

Believe me, my dear Duchess,

Ever your Firm Friend,

Augusta Stanley

'Well, love, what do you think?' Charlotte asked when Olivia had finished reading.

'I don't understand, Mama,' Olivia said. 'Why would the Queen want me? The only time I've met her was when I was presented, and I can't believe she'd remember me.'

'Oh, I think she does. She has a phenomenal memory for people. Besides, I used to take you and Venetia to play with the royal children, when you were very young. Don't you remember going to Windsor?'

Olivia shook her head. 'I know that we did go, but I don't really remember it.'

'Well, never mind, it's enough that the Queen does. She likes to employ people from families she knows. Your papa, of course, has often advised her, and the Prince thought very highly of him. And your Uncle Cavendish did palace duty when he was in the Hussars. But in spite of the connections, it's a great honour, and one I hadn't expected.'

Olivia stared at the letter again. 'Would I have to go and live at Court, then?'

'Not all the time, only when you were in waiting. For the rest of the time you would be at home as usual. I don't know how long waiting is – I've never had much to do with the Household – but I'd guess it would be three or four months a year.'

'That doesn't sound too hard. I shouldn't mind that.'

'But there are strict rules of behaviour at Court. You would have to consider yourself as under discipline, like a soldier, twenty-four hours a day. That's a great deal to ask of a girl as young as you.'

Olivia was considering. 'I can't tell absolutely, but I think I should like it, Mama. It would be like visiting another country. I expect life is very different at Court. It would be interesting to know how things go on.'

'You'd be willing to give up your freedom and go away from home, and miss the balls and parties and so on?'

'You said it wouldn't be all the time.'

'Very well, I'll ask Lady Augusta to call and tell us more. But you must be sure that it's what you want. Don't feel you must accept to please me or Papa.'

'Her Majesty had a very good report of your other daughter from Princess Frederick,' Lady Augusta said, sitting in the green drawing-room with Charlotte. She put her teacup down in its saucer without the hint of a rattle, sign of her years at Court. 'I think that's why Lady Olivia came to mind.'

'I'm surprised the Queen remembers her,' Charlotte said frankly.

'There aren't so many duchesses in the kingdom that she's likely to mislay you,' Lady Augusta said with a smile.

'I'm sensible of the honour,' Charlotte said. 'My worry is that Olivia is too young.'

'She *is* very young, and I have my own misgivings on that score. You understand that a maid of honour cannot be married or even engaged to be married? Alice Adair announced that she was engaged only two months after accepting the position, and during her very first waiting – extremely tactless behaviour, for she certainly knew what was entailed when she accepted. The Queen was most put out.'

'I can see that she would be,' Charlotte said.

'She dislikes change, especially when it involves losing people. Naturally one cannot expect girls to renounce marriage for ever as though they were entering a convent, but it would be upsetting for the Queen if, having accepted, Lady Olivia did not remain for two or three years. That's a great deal to ask at nineteen, so I must be sure before I report back to Her Majesty that she is heart-whole and likely to remain so.'

'I don't know what assurance I can give you,' Charlotte said, 'except to say that she has never to my knowledge shown any interest in one young man more than another. She's a warm-hearted, affectionate girl, but I wouldn't say her emotions are easily stirred.'

Lady Augusta nodded. 'One can't do more than ask her. At nineteen there's no knowing how things may change. It's a volatile age. She would be the youngest of the present maids of honour by some years, and I was surprised when Her Majesty suggested it. But the Queen knows her own mind, and it's surprising how often she turns out to be right and everyone else wrong when it comes to judging people.'

'Shall I send for Olivia, and you can make your own assessment.'

Olivia was waiting in a room nearby, and came at once. Lady Augusta rose, took her hand and said kindly, 'Why, my dear, you have grown up a beauty! I remember you were always a pretty child, but now you have real elegance. You don't remember me, I dare say? Well, it's a long time since I saw you. Turn around and let me look at you.'

Olivia did as she was told. Her high-necked gown of lavender corded silk was fitted in the bodice and with a tiny waist, showing off her figure, and Lady Augusta noticed how neatly she managed the swing of the bustle and short train. She moved gracefully and when Lady Augusta sat down with her and engaged her in conversation, she noted that her voice was clear and pleasant.

'Well, my dear,' she said at last, 'your mother has told you what has been offered you?'

'Yes, ma'am.'

'There are eight maids of honour in the Household, divided into four pairs, and each pair is in waiting for one month at a time – which makes three months of duty in all during the year. The rota is set out in January, and the Court moves between Windsor, Osborne and Balmoral, so you may have to be on duty in any of those places.'

'What would my duties be, ma'am?'

'Attending the Queen: running errands and taking messages for her, chatting to her when she wishes, perhaps writing letters. You will soon learn what is required. An inexperienced maid is always paired with an experienced one. You might also be asked to attend one of the princesses, or accompany them riding. You do ride?'

'Yes, ma'am.'

'Olivia is an accomplished horsewoman,' Charlotte confirmed.

'That is good. And in the evening you might be asked to read aloud. How are your French and your German, my dear – are you fluent in them?'

'Yes, ma'am – and in Italian,' Olivia said.

'The Queen and the late Prince used to speak Italian together, but it's not much used now, except in singing. The Queen is very fond of music, and you may be asked to contribute to the entertainment. How is your pianoforte playing? Would you like to play and sing something for me now?'

Olivia had been well taught by one of her numerous tutors, and since she was accustomed to being called to the drawing-room to perform for her parents and their guests, she was not self-conscious. Her voice was small but pleasant, and she played well. Unlike Venetia, she had no academic bent, but she had a quick ear: she played better and was more proficient in all three foreign languages than her sister.

'That will do, thank you,' Lady Augusta said at last. Olivia returned to them. 'You can read music at sight? Good. Do you draw? Very good.' She turned to Charlotte. 'I see she has been well educated, Duchess. A credit to you, and to herself. Olivia, my dear, would you be so kind as to pour me another cup of tea?'

Olivia did so, managing it neatly and not seeming to know it was another test. When she was seated again, Lady Augusta said, 'There is one last question. A maid of honour cannot be married or engaged to be married, so I must ask you to be quite honest with me. Are you in love with anyone?'

Olivia's deep blue eyes met hers innocently. 'No, ma'am,' she said promptly, and with no great emphasis, as though it did not much matter. Then she added, 'I don't think I have ever been in love.'

'You don't *think*?'

'Well, ma'am, I'm not sure how you would know. But from what I've heard other girls saying, I don't think I have.'

'You are such a pretty girl, you must have lots of admirers. Is there one special one, who pursues you more than the others?'

Olivia considered. 'No, I don't think so. They all say a great many foolish things, but it's just funning.'

'Well, my dear,' Lady Augusta concluded, 'if you would like the position, I think I can tell the Queen that you seem very suitable to me.'

'I should like it very much, ma'am,' Olivia said.

'Very good. I go back to Windsor this evening, and I shall speak to Her Majesty. She will want to interview you, I don't doubt, before the matter is finalised.'

CHAPTER NINE

Matters moved more quickly than either Lady Augusta or Charlotte expected. On the following day a letter came from the Mistress of the Robes, who was officially in charge of the maids of honour, formally offering Olivia the position. Her Majesty was quite sure that Olivia would suit, she said. As Lady Alice's resignation had left an unfortunate gap in the rota, it would be convenient if Lady Olivia could go into her first waiting at once, when the Household moved to Osborne on the 28th of July. Lady Olivia should write her acceptance in a letter addressed to the Duchess but in terms suitable to be shown to Her Majesty, and should present herself at Windsor on the 27th.

'It's too soon,' Charlotte said, reading the letter. 'Everything is happening too quickly. You are being rushed into a decision.'

But Olivia's cheeks were flushed and her eyes bright with excitement. 'Oh no, Mama! I'm quite sure it's what I want. This is my great adventure, like Venetia's going to Berlin. And I'd much sooner go at once than have to wait for months to begin.'

'It gives us hardly any time to prepare. You ought to have a new gown. Oh dear, and with Venetia just gone! Now I shall lose you too.'

But there was not really so much to do, and Fanny helped, excited on Olivia's behalf. On the 27th of July Charlotte and Olivia took the afternoon train to Windsor, and spent the next few hours being introduced to various members of the Household and losing their way in the labyrinth of corridors, anterooms and staircases that everyone else seemed to navigate unthinkingly.

By half-past eight that evening, when they were waiting with the other dinner guests in the corridor outside the dining saloon, Olivia was in a state of near panic. She would never remember all the names and faces, never find her way around; and as for meeting the Queen face to face – the most important and powerful woman in the world, the anointed of God – the very idea paralysed her.

The clock struck the three-quarters, the normal hour of dining for the Household, and as if conjured by the sound, the Queen walked out from her private apartments and approached down the corridor. Olivia, trembling with nervousness, fixed her eyes on the floor and prayed her knees would not fail her, hoping she might escape notice for one more evening. But the Queen paused before Charlotte and said, 'Ah, Duchess. You may present your daughter.'

Charlotte did so, and Olivia, almost overcome with awe, sank to the ground in a curtsy. The Queen's small, ring-decked hand appeared before her eyes and Olivia kissed it as Charlotte had taught her, dumbly thankful that she had practised in her bedroom every moment of the last few days.

She rose from her curtsy, hoping only that she had done it right and not annoyed the Queen or disgraced her mother. She did not dare raise her eyes; but the black silk rustled and the Queen leaned forward and kissed her cheek like a kind aunt and said, 'I am very glad to have you in my service, my dear.'

Only then did Olivia look up, and saw the face, familiar from so many lithographs and portraits, but now close and alive and real, the eyes a brighter blue than she had expected, and a smile so warm and charming that for a moment she wanted, absurdly, to fling herself into the Queen's arms and beg pardon for having been afraid.

The Queen turned to Lady Augusta, who was standing at her elbow, and received something from her. Turning back to Olivia, she said, 'Now I must pin on your badge. Stand still, my dear.' The Maid of Honour badge – a miniature of the Queen set round with diamonds and mounted on a silk ribbon – was pinned to the left shoulder of Olivia's gown. 'My newest – and youngest – maid of honour,' said the Queen.

She moved on; and Olivia stood straight, her cheek pink as though the kiss had burned it, her eyes shiny with tears of pride and pleasure, her heart filled with devotion. The unexpected warmth and kindness had undone her. Queen Victoria's newest and youngest maid of honour had found her vocation.

George and Alfreda used their time in London well. Firstly, on Alfreda's insistence, they consulted a lawyer about the will; George, who was naturally inclined to laziness, would have given up his grievance by now if she hadn't worked on him. But the lawyer, Antrobus, though reluctant to turn away what might be lucrative business (there being nothing that generated more fees than testamentary disputes), was unable to give them any hope.

'In itself, going to Egypt to work on the Suez Canal cannot be construed as a sign of madness, especially as your late father was an engineer,' he said, putting it politely. 'And as his will was drawn up by his usual man of business, it might be assumed that he, the man of business, would have noticed if the client was not in his usual mental state.'

'But I understand that the solicitor concerned was himself distracted,' Alfreda said quickly, 'having recently suffered a bereavement. His wife of many years, of whom he was very fond—'

'I see,' said Antrobus. He had a fairly clear idea who was the driving force in this matter. 'Well, madam, sir, I cannot say that on the face of what you have told me, there is a case for attempting to overset the will. Of course, the decision must be yours, but you may like to consider before taking matters further that if any clause is the result of madness, all might be. There could be counter-claims by others who have been left out.'

'There are no others!' Alfreda snapped, but George laid his hand on her arm, and she recalled that the younger three children had had no provision made for them at all. Was it possible she and George could end up worse off? She had wanted most of all to humiliate Henry Anstey; but it struck her for the first time that if a fuss were made, it might reflect unpleasantly on them. Did she really want to be the wife of a madman's son?

George was for leaving things be. Outside in the street he said, 'It would cost a fortune in lawyers' fees, you know, with no guarantee that we'd get anywhere. And I don't know but what it mightn't look bad, telling the world my father was queer in the attic.'

Alfreda was ready to save face. 'I'm glad you've come to that conclusion. I felt myself it would be unpleasant to make a fuss.'

'I wish you'd said so,' George said. 'I thought it was what you wanted!'

'You were so determined; as a dutiful wife I had to go along with you.'

'Well, in future, I wish you'd always say what you think. You know better than me about most things. How could you think I'd question your judgement?'

Alfreda left it at that. She must regret the loss of the fortune that went to Edward, but she had more important things to do with George's money than make Antrobus richer.

The London Season was over, but they did a great deal of shopping, looked dutifully round an exhibition, and met Lord Marwood several times for dinner. He gave them titbits of London gossip, and mentioned that he had danced with the daughter of the Duke of Southport. 'A very handsome, spirited girl. Quite ready to accept me as a cousin.'

'We should call,' George said. 'The connection isn't so very distant, and my father was well acquainted with the duchess.'

'She's very approachable, but the duke's a high stickler,' Marwood warned.

Alfreda thought a Turlingham was the equal of any Morland, even one married to a Fleetwood, but said only, 'We will not, if you please, Mr Morland, pay a visit of form at a time when people of fashion have left Town. That would be to show

147

ourselves provincials. We may leave our cards, however. That would be the appropriate attention.'

George had to acknowledge to himself once again that Alfreda was right when a note was brought round to the hotel from the duchess, thanking them for the compliment, congratulating them on the marriage, and much increasing the Morlands' standing with the hotel staff, who were quick to spot the ducal coronet on the envelope.

The other urgent business Alfreda had in London was to engage a lady's maid for herself and a valet for George. He had no objection – he rather liked the idea of dropping into conversation references to 'my man so-and-so' – but he wondered why they need get them in London rather than in York.

'My dear Mr Morland,' she said severely, 'you are a man of position, possessor of a great estate, first in consequence in your neighbourhood: only a London-trained servant, accustomed to the way things are done in the best households, will have the refinement to match your superior requirements.'

'Oh yes, I see,' George said, enjoying this new portrait of himself. 'You are quite right – as always.'

'Yorkshire people may do in the lower positions, but they are too coarse and stupid to make upper servants. Our house must be run efficiently and above all *elegantly*.'

George had nothing more to say, and was quite content to leave it to Alfreda to consult the agency and interview candidates, while he jaunted about the Town enjoying himself. By the time they were ready to leave for Brighton, they were no longer alone. Hayter, a very thin man in his forties, with a chilling manner and a beak-nosed, hood-eyed face to go with it, had taken charge of the large wardrobe of new clothes George had accumulated, and frightened George by disapproving of a purple tweed sack-coat he had bought one day when Alfreda was otherwise engaged and had fancied not a little.

Alfreda was attended by Stéfanie, a short, plump and pretty Frenchwoman with curly fair hair and large pale eyes, who was by no means as young as she looked. She had all the skills needed to turn her mistress out in the best style, but

Alfreda also hoped she would prove a useful ally in bringing the rest of the servants up to scratch. Fanie might look like a little doll, but she had a high opinion of her consequence, as well as a will of iron and a tongue like barbed wire if she was crossed.

The time in Brighton was not an unalloyed pleasure, though each put a good face on it, not wishing to let themselves down in front of the other or the servants. Being alone together for so long was a strain. George had no experience of being with females, and was in constant fear of doing or saying something wrong and incurring Alfreda's contempt. He tiptoed around her, deferred to her opinions in everything, and was so meek and restrained that his erstwhile bosom friends would not have recognised him.

This in turn made him an achingly dull companion to Alfreda, who sometimes felt as though, at a moment when she might have been enjoying herself for the first time in years, she had been saddled with the care of an exceptionally large and stupid child. Each was glad to get away from the other when circumstances permitted. When Alfreda encouraged George to enjoy the company of other men without her, he felt he had married a woman in a thousand, of unique understanding and sympathy. She was careful, however, to do nothing that might burst the bubble of his adoration. He was extremely biddable, and never queried the expense of anything she wanted, and she had not learned to regret having married him.

The physical side of marriage was something she had prepared herself to endure: she knew that some payment had to be made for the security and fortune she was to enjoy as George's wife. She knew nothing about the act itself, but she remembered her mother telling her long ago that after marriage a man did certain things to his wife in the privacy of the marriage bed in order for children to be born, and that while they were unpleasant and disgusting to any lady, it was her duty to bear them with good grace.

On the first night in London, Alfreda felt her mother had not told her the half of it. George came to her in his nightshirt, got into bed with her, and there followed an episode of fumbling and heavy breathing, while he attempted to do

149

something to her that made her eyes stretch so wide in shock she half wondered afterwards that they hadn't fallen out on the pillow. The pain was considerable, but she hardly noticed it, so appalled was she by the discovery of what was involved. She did not wonder something so utterly disgusting was kept such a close secret, for if girls knew beforehand what they were in for, they would surely never marry at all. She supposed George must know what he was doing: he did not seem to have any doubts about it, displaying considerable excitement over the brief transaction, and afterwards kissed her and murmured endearments that seemed to suggest he was perfectly satisfied with the result. Alfreda lay rigid, her fingers locked into the sheets, unable to respond to his grateful caresses, so that after a short while he went away to his own bed, leaving her alone to grapple with this unwelcome new knowledge, and to wonder how she would face her husband in the morning.

Over the weeks of honeymoon she grew more accustomed to it, and began to feel it was a price she could pay. She did not view it as any less foul and degrading, but it hurt less as time went on, and at least it was over quickly. By the second week in Brighton, George was no longer coming to her every night. She couldn't help wondering, however, that God should have arranged things so badly: surely it ought not to have been beyond the Almighty's ingenuity to devise a better way to conceive children, something that did not involve parts of the body no decent person admitted the existence of even to themselves?

George was also wondering what all the fuss was about. Before his marriage he had known in theory what to do – a man who bred horses could hardly be ignorant – and he'd heard excited talk from other young men about the pleasure of it. He'd sometimes had Feelings himself, and wondered what it would be like to Do It, though he'd never been sufficiently tempted to try to find out. When he fell in love with Alfreda he hardly dared think about Doing It to her, and had only allowed his mind to glance at the idea sidelong, for such temerity had seemed too appalling to contemplate. But when it came to it, the reality was a disappointment. The physical rush of sensation was pleasant enough, but it was over so quickly that it hardly seemed worth putting Alfreda through what was obviously detestable to her. She never moved, spoke or responded in any way, and he couldn't rid himself of the feeling that what he was doing was monstrous and that she must despise him for it. He only persevered from the knowledge that it was his duty, and that Alfreda was a whale on duty. But when he missed a night and she did not berate him, he felt somewhat relieved.

He wished he might ask her how often she expected it; but talking about it, of course, was impossible. One day in Brighton, however, she said, 'Mr Morland, when we return to Morland Place, I think we should do something about altering the main bedchamber.'

'Whatever you like, Mrs Morland,' he said, blushing at this approach to the unmentionable subject.

'My visit to Morland Place was short, and I was not able to make detailed observations,' she went on, 'but I remember that the room was vast – quite large enough, I imagine, to divide into two?'

'Oh yes, certainly,' George said.

'It would be convenient if we had bedchambers adjoining each other, with a communicating door, as we had in the hotel in London. In that way, should you ever wish to visit me, you could do so quite privately.'

Should you ever wish – now that didn't sound too bad, George thought. That sounded like an occasional, rather than a regular, onslaught. He had been wondering how he would cope at home if it were expected to be too regular, for his active life left him little energy in the evening. Separate bedrooms! His parents had slept together in the huge bed in the great bedchamber, and he had supposed he would have to do the same. He had not expected to enjoy it much, being on his best behaviour all the time. He couldn't imagine ever feeling comfortable about using the chamber pot in front of her; and, dammit, there were times when a fellow wanted to yawn, or scratch, or break wind in the privacy of his own room!

'I think that would be a very good idea,' he said.

Alfreda looked at him with relief. He was not going to be too demanding a husband, then. For a moment she felt really quite fond of him. 'Mr Morland,' she said tentatively, 'I am so eager to get on with making Morland Place a fit home for us both. What would you think to cutting our time here short?'

'Aren't you enjoying yourself?' he asked anxiously.

'Oh, yes, but one can have too much idleness, and there is so much to be done at home. I'm sure you are anxious about the estate, too.'

He hadn't given it a thought until that moment; but he missed riding, and he supposed at home he wouldn't have to hover about Alfreda all day and worry whether he was doing things wrong. 'If you would like to go home, I should be more than happy to go myself,' he said.

'Good,' said Alfreda. 'Then suppose we leave tomorrow morning? I will tell Hayter and Fanie to pack.'

Henrietta and Manfred had been helping with the shearing all day; Regina hadn't wanted to come, preferring a sedate walk with Katie to pick flowers for pressing in her book. Shearing was another of those times when all hands were wanted. Handling the struggling sheep was men's work, but the women and children helped with catching and penning the lambs, moving the fleeces and gleaning the wisps, fetching and carrying, bringing drinks to the shearers.

It was a warm day with a high cloud cover, and a multitude of little black 'thunder-flies' were making a nuisance of themselves. Henrietta was hot and sticky. Her nose was full of the smell of sheep-yolk where she had mistakenly rubbed it, and her foot was sore where a ewe had stamped on it with her sharp little hoof. But it was good to be here, away from the house, where discord reigned. Bittle was attempting to get things ready for her mistress's return, and the rest of the servants were resisting her with all their skill. They resented her assumption of authority over them, and her unsparing criticism of their unrefined ways.

Though Henrietta felt at peace out here, it was not quiet. The air trembled with the din of sheep, the ewes calling their lambs and the lambs their mothers, and those being taken up to the shearers bellowing with terror.

'Why are sheep so *stupid*?' Henrietta exclaimed crossly, as another ewe was run past her by two sweating men, struggling as hard as she could, ridiculous in her oversized coat of wool. They'd been shorn before: why didn't they remember it did them no harm?

'They're not stupid,' a voice at her elbow said. 'They knaw different things from thee, that's all. God gives 'em a mind for grass and hawks and the smell o' the wind. Tha couldn't tell me when t'snaw's comin', could tha? But a yow can.'

Henrietta turned gladly. Old Caleb looked quite biblical, she thought, a serene figure above the turmoil, his crook in his hand, his dogs beside him. Watch greeted her like an old friend, but Monk stood remote, regarding the sheep with a stern and possessive eye.

'So,' Caleb said, when they'd exchanged greetings, 'tha's got a new sister-in-law?'

'I shall have, when they come back from their honeymoon.'

'A handsome young lady, so I hear tell. Well, 'appen it'll be good for the house; it badly wanted a mistress.'

Henrietta glanced at him curiously, for he had sounded as though he did not think it would be good. 'George is very much in love with her,' she offered.

'I don't doubt it,' Caleb said. 'A man in love is careless, and it has to be said about this marriage, that Master George has upset as many folk as he well could.'

'Upset?'

'Not marrying at Morland Place for one thing. Going in the face of tradition, that was, and there's those that say it'll bring bad luck. The heir allus marries in the chapel. Besides, the estate folk have looked forward for years to the young master's wedding. To see him wed, and share in the feast: that were our right, and we've been denied it.'

'But it had to be a quiet wedding, because of being in mourning,' Henrietta defended. 'A big affair wouldn't have been seemly.'

'What were seemly about goin' to a public 'otel, wi' strangers? And then to go away wi'out even presenting the young lady to her own people? No announcement, no wedding, no feast, no presents – nay, I knaw tha must defend him, miss, and I honour thee for it; but he has set us at naught, an' that's the truth. As if he thought his wedding didn't concern us at all.'

Henrietta turned her head away to hide her chagrin. After a moment Caleb said kindly, 'Nay, Miss Henrietta, don't tha take on. It had to be said, and well tha s'd know it, but it weren't thy fault, and no-one thinks it. Folk have feelin's, that's all. You can't use 'em an' then put 'em aside like machines.' He waved his crook around the scene. 'We skin our hands and break our backs for Morland Place, and it's not just work for wages. We need to know it's appreciated.'

'I appreciate it,' Henrietta said humbly.

He bent a kindly look on her. 'Aye, I know. Tha's'd make a good mistress.' And she felt comforted.

The last of the present batch of ewes was finished with, and released, slim and near-nude, to scamper back to her companions, leaving her great matted outer case behind like a discarded chrysalis. The lambs were in a separate pen, milling about and bawling desperately; now the gates of the two pens were opened and in a white rush like two heads of flood water meeting, thirty ewes and sixty lambs boiled around each other with frantic cries. And yet in a matter of minutes, the bellowing ceased and every dam had been reunited with her offspring.

'Isn't it wonderful how they know each other in all that crowd?' Henrietta marvelled. 'I couldn't tell one from another.'

'Aye, well, the yows can tell, 'at's all that matters,' Caleb said. 'Didn't I tell thee, we've all got different kinds o' wisdom.'

'I don't think I have any at all,' Henrietta said sadly.

'Aye, tha has. Thee and me, an' the yows, an' awd Watch, here, we all 'ave our uses to God, and He values us all the same. Remember that, if they should be harsh with thee sometimes.'

He saluted her and walked off to gather his sheep, before she could ask him *who*.

When hunger told her it must be teatime, she found

Manfred and limped home. The dogs danced up gaily to meet them in the yard.

'Oh yes, bad things, I know I smell lovely! Get down!' Henrietta said, pushing the eager muzzles out of her face. Then she saw there was a heap of luggage on the cobbles by the steps. 'Look, Manny! Georgie must be back! I didn't think they were due for days yet.'

Manny eyed the luggage with interest. 'A lot of it's new. I wonder if they've brought us presents?'

Askins and Baynes came out of the house and applied themselves to either end of a small trunk in a manner that oozed resentment. Askins looked dourly over his shoulder at them. 'Oh, you're back, are you? You've been looked for.'

His glance took in the state of their faces and clothes, and he felt slightly comforted for the sharp words and contemptuous looks the new mistress had directed at him. There'd be some changes made at Morland Place now that one'd got her hands on the reins, and none of them for the better, by his guess. Sour-faced, sour-tongued – and not in her first flush, neither, not by a long chalk! Master George had been properly caught, if anyone wanted Askins's view. A havey-cavey business it was, too: no proper wedding, no feast, no holiday nor bounty to the servants. If the old mistress were here to see it, she'd turn in her grave . . .

Baynes, going backwards up the steps, gave Henrietta a warning look. 'Goin' to 'ave to mind our Ps an' Qs from now on,' he said. 'Best slip up by the backstairs, missy.'

But it was too late. As Henrietta and Manfred followed them into the hall through the great door, Alfreda appeared from the staircase hall with a sheaf of papers in her hand, evidently on some mission. The dogs, flooding past, whirled at her in a cheerful mass, and she flinched back from them.

'I thought I gave orders for these beasts to be chained?' she cried angrily, fending them off her skirts, hitting out at muzzles with the papers. The dogs bounced excitedly, thinking it was a game. 'Askins, why did you not do as I ordered?'

Askins dropped his end of the trunk loudly on the floor and straightened up, jutting his jaw aggressively. 'Told us to bring luggage in, didn't you? I can't do everything at once.'

'Don't be insolent!' Alfreda snapped. 'I *will* not be spoken back to. Obviously you should have chained the dogs first. If you can't use your common sense—' At that moment she saw Henrietta and Manfred and her jaw dropped slightly before she caught it up.

Henrietta thought it best to give a little curtsy as she said politely, 'Good afternoon, Alfreda. Welcome home. Did you have a nice time?'

Alfreda recovered herself. 'Go upstairs at *once* and make yourself decent! How dare you appear in front of me in that state?'

'I didn't know you were here,' she said in a small voice.

'We've been helping with the sheep,' Manny said, his hand creeping into Henrietta's for comfort.

'Helping with the sheep? Have you *no* sense of your position? You are far too old for such pranks, Henrietta. I can see it's past time for me to take you in hand!' She gave an exasperated shake of her head, and slapped angrily with the sheaf of papers at the rump of Philo, who was balancing on three legs while she thoroughly and tactlessly scratched her neck with the fourth. 'Disgusting creature! *Will* you get this dog out of here! *Nothing* in this house is done as it should be. Oh, for heaven's sake,' her irritation revolved back to Henrietta, 'don't just stand there – go! I can't bear to look at you. You're *black*!' And she turned on her heel and strode rapidly away.

Manny stuck his lip out. 'You get black, helping with the sheep,' he pointed out when she had safely gone.

'Well you'd better go an' get yourselves *un*-black,' Askins said without sympathy. 'Leave the box down,' he told Baynes. 'Aye, just where it is. We've got our orders, 'aven't we? Get dogs out, she said. Coom on, dogs! Coom on, then, Fern, Kes! Coom here, Jacko. We know when we're not wanted.' He sniffed. ''Appen we'd better chain ourselves up while we're about it.'

He and Baynes gathered the dogs and went out. Glumly Henrietta took Manny's hand and limped towards the back-stairs.

*   *   *

Bittle hadn't known whether she looked forward to Alfreda's return with more hope or fear. She had not managed to get done what she had been left to get done, and she was afraid that, if Alfreda wanted to dismiss her, she might make that the excuse. But if she was not to be dismissed, the sooner Madam came home and she could go back to being her lady's maid, the better. Apart from that, she longed for order, and she did not doubt for an instant that Alfreda would curb the stubborn, impertinent, contrary Yorkshire servants and make them do as they were told.

The early arrival of the master and mistress filled her with painful hope, bolstered by the cheerful greeting Alfreda gave her as she stood in the hall pulling off her gloves and looking about her. The hope lasted exactly as long as it took Hayter and Fanie to follow them up the steps and through the great door. Bittle had been in service all her life, and she knew the look of a first-class French lady's maid when she saw one. She did not need the introduction which soon followed.

'And this is my old nurse, Bittle,' Alfreda completed it. 'She's been maiding me recently, and she'll be glad to be rid of a very troublesome duty, I make no doubt.'

Hayter gave Bittle a nod of the utmost uninterest, and Fanie turned her pale, bright eyes on her and examined her briefly but with great thoroughness, before giving her a small, tight smile and a little bob of courtesy.

Bittle turned to Alfreda in desperation. 'Madam, if I might have a word—'

'Not now, Bittle.'

'Madam, I beg you—'

'*Not now.*' The cold, sharp rebuke went through Bittle's heart like an icicle. She gave a little gasp, almost of pain, and Alfreda, raising her eyebrows, said, 'I will send for you later. For the moment, you will have enough to do preparing rooms for us.'

'Rooms, madam?' Bittle had been at Morland Place long enough to know that the master and mistress slept in the great bedchamber – a barbaric custom, she thought it. It seemed her mistress thought so too.

'For the moment Mr Morland will have his old room, and

I will have – what was the pleasant room with the blue and white carpet called?' she appealed to George.

'The blue bedroom,' he supplied.

'Just so. See to it, please.'

All day Bittle hovered nearby, holding her tongue and doing as she was bid, running errands and taking messages as Alfreda went through the house like a whirlwind, finding dust, noting marked wallpaper and ragged carpets, ordering furniture moved, making lists, lashing outspoken servants into astonished obedience with her tongue. George escaped with her complete blessing to the stables; the children were out somewhere, thank heaven. There was more to do, Alfreda thought with a mental rolling up of sleeves, than she could have imagined.

In the blue bedroom, housemaids toiled under the basilisk eye of Fanie. Hayter, having inspected the east bedroom with disfavour, had appropriated Battey and Scoggs, the boot-boy, and was gliding about the house picking out the best furniture and hangings which he then made them transport to his own kingdom. The kitchen had been briefly but violently visited, and Mrs Pretty, in a state close to shock, was now frantically working to prepare a dinner that would not bring Mrs Morland's wrath down on her. Atterwith had looked in to express a civil welcome home, and had backed out again hastily when he found himself witness to Alfreda's displeasure that half the luggage was still standing out in the courtyard. Shortly after that, Henrietta and Manfred arrived home and fell into disgrace.

When things were a little calmer, Bittle tracked her mistress down to her bedroom, where she was discussing with Fanie the disposition of one or two small items of comfort. 'If you please, madam,' Bittle said firmly. She was not comforted to see Alfreda and Fanie exchange a swift glance which seemed to speak too much mutual understanding for comfort. Fanie bobbed a curtsy and left the room, and Alfreda turned to Bittle without meeting her eyes.

'Well, now, you will be wondering, I suppose, what your new position will be?' she began pleasantly.

'I was happy enough with my old one,' Bittle said angrily.

She had meant to be conciliating, but her feelings overcame her. 'What do you want with bringing home a foreigner? She's a sly baggage if ever I saw one! And no better than she ought to be, if you ask me.'

'I don't ask you,' Alfreda snapped. 'Fanie is a trained lady's maid. You are not.'

'Not trained? What do you call all those years I've looked after you, if it wasn't training? I doubt she could've managed as well, for all her fancy flouncing about and silly foreign accent. Why, I've worked my fingers to the bone for you, I've made do and mended—'

'Precisely! The circumstances are different now. Your skills were appreciated then, but they are not appropriate to the position I now hold as mistress of a large household. I have a position to keep up.' She allowed her voice to soften. 'Come, don't let us quarrel. I'm not ungrateful, and I know you are owed wages—'

'Wages!' Bittle said in disgust. 'There's no counting what you owe me! And now I suppose you want to pay me off with money and be done with me, and forget where you came from and how you got here!'

That was precisely what Alfreda would have liked, but if Bittle was going to be poisonous, she would prefer to have her here under her eye than spreading the poison round the neighbourhood. She arranged her face into a smile. 'Not at all! How could you think it? You have been a faithful servant and I want you to share in my new prosperity. I have a job for you, if you will accept it – one which you will fulfil to perfection. I want you to take up your old position of head nurse.'

Bittle was too surprised to speak for a moment, and Alfreda went on quickly, 'At the moment there are only Miss Regina and Master Manfred for you to exercise your skills on, but in time there will be new babies in the nursery, and who should I want to take care of them but the good nurse who brought up Kit and me so well? You may arrange everything exactly as you wish, and ask me for anything you need to make you comfortable. And of course your salary will be substantial, to reflect your importance as nurse to *my* children.'

Bittle was silent a moment. Then she said, 'And if I refuse?'

Alfreda's smile glittered. 'I should be sorry to lose you. Have you thought where you would go if you left Morland Place?'

Bittle knew she was defeated. At her age, it would be hard for her to adapt to a new position, even if she could find one. She didn't want to go, to have to get used to new people, to face old age alone or with strangers. 'Very well,' she said, 'I accept.' And she lowered her eyes so that Alfreda should not see the expression in them.

'Good. Excellent. I am glad you will be staying,' Alfreda said, and went on to elaborate on her wishes for the nursery. Bittle didn't listen. She had been humiliated and bested, and she would make someone pay for it. Eyes bent on the floor, she brooded on revenge.

BOOK TWO

Endeavour

Trust thou thy love: if she be proud, is she not sweet?
Trust thou thy love: if she be mute, is she not pure?
Lay thou thy soul full in her hands, low at her feet;
Fail, Sin and Breath! – yet, for thy peace, She shall endure.

John Ruskin: *Trust Thou Thy Love*

CHAPTER TEN

Everyone had talked admiringly of the Prussian army's efficiency, but no-one was really prepared for the speed and ruthlessness with which the war was prosecuted. In a matter of weeks the German armies had pushed the French out of Alsace. Surrounding Metz, they pinned down 173,000 French soldiers with apparent effortlessness, and a huge force sent by Napoleon to relieve Metz was itself surrounded at Sedan, on the river Meuse.

Everything in the war was on an unprecedented scale. The Germans began with half a million men under arms, the biggest force ever seen in Europe. They moved so quickly that within a single month ten battles were fought, with the loss of 300,000 men, killed wounded or captured; and by the 2nd of September they had penetrated a hundred and fifty miles into France, and forced the French Emperor to surrender at Sedan.

In England public support for the Prussians, which had been very strong at the outset, began to waver. Reports were coming back of the brutality of the German soldiers, and their callousness towards the wounded, even their own; and of a growing German hostility towards the English.

Venetia wrote to her parents: 'There's a report from London that the Prince of Wales said publicly he hoped France would win – which the Crown Princess tells me the Queen writes is not true: Bernstorff said it only to make mischief. But Bismarck spreads the lie, to whip up feeling against the poor Princess – *die Engländerin*, as he calls her rudely. I suppose it doesn't surprise me, since it's well known he hates the Princess and her husband. But why should the ordinary people believe it, when England has done nothing but send aid and messages of support?'

In another letter she wrote, 'The French get a large part of their arms from America, and when German soldiers find the French dead holding rifles with names like "Remington" or "Colt", they believe they are English weapons supplied by us to the French. Of course the officers know the truth of it, but they encourage the common soldiers in the belief and their hatred of the English. As a result the field ambulances sent out from England are not being used, though they are desperately needed.'

Venetia found her life one of strange contrasts. There was the cosy domesticity and gentle erudition and culture of the Crown Prince and Princess and their circle; the stiff, formal, military-minded pomp of the Court at large; and the unspeakable horrors to which she was now witness in the hospitals. She was learning with brutal speed the truth of what her mother had told her: that nothing she had read had prepared her for reality.

Charlotte had seen that her daughters were very different from each other, and had tailored their education to suit them. For Olivia, quick of ear and compliant of temper, there had been training in the accomplishments that would fit her for marriage: music, dancing, sketching, languages and conversation. Venetia's strong intellect had craved more sustaining food. While Olivia sang and sewed, she had studied Latin, Greek, mathematics, history and philosophy under a series of tutors.

It was not surprising that she should be interested in medicine, given her background, but the fact was that Charlotte had not anticipated it. Venetia understood the nature of the present compact: she was being allowed to dabble in medicine on condition that she became sickened by it and gave it up. Her stubbornness made her determined *not* to be put off; but the reality of the German hospitals came near to undoing her.

The first thing to hit her was the smell. 'Hospital stink', as it was called, had been known to make visitors vomit when they first encountered it; Venetia fumbled with a handkerchief and made play to blow her nose, while she pressed her lips together hard and swallowed and swallowed, determined not to show weakness. The ward was filthy – it seemed to be no-one's job to clean it. The patients were not washed, nor their bedclothes changed; and since they were soldiers coming from the front, all of them were dirty and most of them had lice. Dysentery was rife, and as there was no proper provision for clean water or sewage disposal, it spread quickly. The bare wooden floorboards soaked up the blood, urine, faeces, vomit and pus that were constantly spilled on them; and in the summer heat, with the windows tightly shut, the odours proliferated unrelieved.

'Oh Mama, you were right,' Venetia thought, struggling with her reluctant body. If the smell made her vomit, the sight of the wounds made her feel faint. At first she could not manage more than a horrified peep without the blood rushing from her head like a panicking crowd fleeing a burning building. A man with his foot mashed shapeless by the wheel of a field gun; the gleam in the glistening red depth of an open wound of the bared bone; men with faces mangled like chewed meat; wounds that heaved with maggots like a restless sleeper under a blanket: one glance, and her senses would try to leave her, to prevent her from seeing more. It took serious effort before she could look steadily for long enough to be able to do anything helpful.

The most common operation – almost the only treatment available – was amputation. In the wards the stumps rested on zinc trays, in which the drips of pus collected into pools. Gangrene announced itself first by the sickly smell; two in three amputees died that way. Those with abdominal or chest wounds almost all died, of loss of blood or the inevitable sepsis; dysentery, typhus, typhoid and pneumonia carried off large numbers who might otherwise have recovered. Only the strongest could survive the hell of pain, suffering, infection and inadequate food which was the hospital, to which the battle wound seemed only an added dimension of horror.

Venetia was sustained by her mulish determination to prove everyone wrong, but once she had overcome her inconvenient physiological reactions, she had no mental aversion to finding herself here. In a way, the very vileness of the conditions was a stimulus, because it was almost impossible, even for someone with so little experience, not to make a change for the better. To see such suffering and to be able to do any small thing to alleviate it was a pleasure greater than anything she had known.

The trained nurses set to work at once to establish some order. Washing the patients and the bedclothes was a priority, together with setting up an invalid-food kitchen – the rations served to the sick and wounded were inedible to any but the strong and vigorous. Cleaning the floors and walls, scouring the utensils, removing slops and finding clean water occupied much of the nurses' time, and they did these tasks in the face of hostility from the military doctors, for they embodied the twin faults of being female and being English. Without the gentle persistence and tact of the Crown Princess they would not have been allowed to remain; only the wounded appreciated their efforts.

Venetia saw that the work of cleaning, organising and nursing was necessary and admirable, but it did not call to her. What interested her was the nature of disease and injury, and their effects on the human body. She saw men alive and cursing who had sustained wounds her reason told her they should not have survived; she saw strong, healthy men dying from disease that left them outwardly almost unmarked. The human frame was mysterious and magnificent in its complexity and endurance, and she came to hate seeing it defeated, in a way which was quite separate from her sadness for the individual concerned. The waste of that miracle made her angry; the dogged and sometimes gallant courage of the men touched her unbearably. She wanted to know more so that she could do something about it, not just feel miserable and frustrated. She saw so many of the medical staff who were ignorant, lazy, arrogant or indifferent, she knew that if only she had the training, she could do better than these butchers in their blood-encrusted coats.

One of them, however, noticed her, and did not seem indifferent to her. Dr Gottlieb was younger than the other military surgeons, and when he saw that Venetia was interested, and did not faint, he encouraged her to follow him on his rounds. Finding her quick and neat with her hands, he let her help him, explained what he was doing, and answered her intelligent questions. From there it was only a step to inviting her to help him in the operating room, where an intelligent nurse could make a real difference. Venetia had to overcome a fresh access of revulsion, but when it was past, she found the work fascinating. Her only difficulty was in remembering not to speak to or ask questions of the other doctors: Gottlieb's preference of her was put down by the older men to a liking for her pretty face, but he warned her that if they had known she was interested in medicine for its own sake, they would have dismissed her from the hospital altogether.

The Princess was concerned that Venetia's nerves and health would suffer from too much exposure to the vapours and horrors of the hospital, and insisted that she worked only in the mornings; and since Venetia could not go there without the Princess's chaperonage, she had to obey. The afternoons, therefore, she gave over to studying – a considerable strain on the intellect since the books available were in German – and to making notes about what she had seen in the wards. And, again on the Princess's insistence, she shared the social life of the circle. She enjoyed walking and riding, but found the evenings tedious, especially when they had to attend court functions and reviews. Venetia missed the freedom and greater variety of home; and she even found that she missed her retinue of amusing young men. German men, she thought, were very dull dogs.

At a court ball one evening she was fanning herself and wondering how soon it would be over, when she was startled from a reverie by someone bowing before her and addressing her in English.

'What an entire pleasure it is to find you here, Lady Venetia! I knew you from across the other side of the room, but thought I must be mistaken – like a man in the desert who sees a mirage of pure, lovely, refreshing water.'

'Lord Marwood!' she exclaimed, smiling warmly. She ought

not to have given him so much encouragement, but it was pleasant to see a familiar face. 'How do you do?'

'Much better since discovering you are present at this Great Exhibition of dullness. *On n'a plus besoin de périr d'ennui.*'

'For heaven's sake, not French – not here!' she said urgently, but his eyes twinkled with mischief.

'What can they do to me that they have not already done?'

'Why, what have they done?' she asked, studying him. He was not really handsome, but he had a most winning smile and a great deal of charm, she decided. His dress uniform fitted his shapely body like a glove, and his hair and whiskers were glossy and magnificent. 'You don't look like a man in durance vile.'

'They have sent me here,' he said. 'A replacement was needed for Campbell at the embassy, and it was our turn to provide one. Unluckily I had just won a very large sum of money from my colonel at cards, and he saw a way of getting his revenge on me. So here I am.'

'Is it a punishment to be sent here, then?'

'Can you doubt it? Not only are the Prussians dull, they also hate the English. But of course, now I discover *you* are here, I see that my colonel has missed his mark. It's not a punishment at all, but a reward I could not have hoped for this side of heaven.'

She laughed. 'You do talk nonsense!'

He brushed his moustache with one finger. 'But charmingly, don't you think? It's my greatest asset, I'm told.'

'You are outrageous!'

'Why, thank you, ma'am. My aim is to please. Would you think me intolerably impertinent if I asked you to dance? I might presume on the privilege of a relative—'

'Oh, please don't,' she shuddered.

'What have I said?'

'Two of my cousins presumed on the privilege of a relative to propose marriage to me just before I left home. Horrible!'

He bowed, offering his arm, and she laid her hand on it, allowing herself to be led into the dance. 'You've made it

168

very difficult for me,' he complained. 'I'm told I make love quite prettily, but if you regard it as a grave offence, it leaves me with nothing to talk of but politics.'

She laughed lightly. 'Oh, you may make love to me if it amuses you, but please don't talk of being a relative. I'm no more likely to marry a cousin than I am any other man.'

'That comment has a depressing ring of finality to it.'

'Do stop flirting for a moment, and tell me how things are at home,' she said, looping her skirt and stepping into his ready arms.

'Well, everyone's out of Town, of course, so I can't give you news of anyone interesting. Oh, except that I hear the fascinating Miss Miles, who had the Town by the ears two Seasons ago, is to marry a very rich, dull man from New Zealand. She met him at Cowes, I believe. Remarkably appropriate, since his fortune comes from sheep.'

'I remember her. I thought she went to Paris?'

'Every English person in Paris left the instant war was declared. You hear them everywhere mourning the death of civilisation – and, looking around, I can see they're right.'

'Ssh! Someone might hear you!'

'What, over this orchestra? How divinely you dance, by the way!'

'I dance vilely, but no flattery is too gross for my craving at present.'

'Then I repeat, you dance divinely. And how little the other couples seem to be enjoying themselves! Look around you, Lady Venetia, at these dull folk, and then imagine the same scene in Paris.'

'Have you been in Paris? Do you like it?'

'It is my spiritual home. Has it occurred to you, ma'am, that this war is a classic conflict between the eternal opposites of human nature – what I like to think of as the Roman principle and the Greek principle.'

'No, it hasn't occurred to me,' she said, 'but I suspect that it's about to.'

He smiled down at her. 'It will give you something to think about when you are mopping brows in the hospital tomorrow

– yes, you see I know what you are doing here! You are the *on dit* of the embassy.'

'Never mind. Tell about the Romans and the Greeks,' she said firmly.

'Well, then, the Romans were efficient, disciplined, orderly, mechanically minded, and a whale on duty. One sees them as rather earnest and dull fellows, but with excellent plumbing! The Greeks were urbane, pleasure-seeking, conversational, and loved music, art and wine. One sees them as charming folk, whose servants would take advantage of them, and who would always be tiresomely late for dinner.'

Venetia was amused. 'And these are the eternal principles?'

'Just so. Everything in life is a struggle between them. We all have seeds of both in us, but some people lean one way and some the other. Now you are seeing the battle on a national scale: the worthy Roman Germans against the frivolous French Greeks.'

'But the Romans were very good at soldiering, weren't they? They conquered most of the world. Surely in any conflict it will always be the Romans who win.'

'But you are forgetting that the Roman Empire did eventually fall. The Romans conquered the Greeks – efficiency, discipline and duty conquered hedonism, laughter and art – but in turn they were conquered from the inside by hedonism and frivolity reasserting themselves. Pleasure will out, Lady Venetia. It can't be denied for ever.'

'What a fascinating theory,' Venetia said. 'And are all nations one thing or the other?'

'Excepting only the English. We combine both principles equally and maintain a perfect balance. That's why we are never conquered, and will never fall.'

'Oh, you mustn't make me laugh so much! People are looking!'

'It's envy, that's all. You must be used to envious glances by now.'

'No, no, it's not envy, it's disapproval! Talk seriously to me.'

'Couldn't possibly,' he said lightly, holding her eyes. 'I should make the most dreadful fool of myself.' She blushed, taking his meaning, and averted her gaze. 'Do you ride out, Lady Venetia? I hope you are not neglecting the fresh air entirely?'

'No, the Princess insists I take some exercise. She is very careful of my health. I generally ride in the afternoon.'

'Would you permit me to escort you tomorrow?'

She felt she ought to refuse him, but he was so refreshing. 'Perhaps your duties won't allow it,' she temporised.

'My duties are more apparent than real, I assure you. I undertake to appear at any hour you name.'

'Very well, then,' she said. 'But you must ask the Princess's approval.'

The Princess was very pleased that Venetia should have an admirer, and one so very handsome and respectable. She fell an instant victim to his charm when he was presented, and since he spoke sensibly to her, she thought him serious and virtuous too. She had no knowledge of his reputation at home, of course, but assumed that as he was a lord and attached to the embassy, he must be someone Venetia's father would approve of.

Venetia did not disabuse her. She enjoyed Marwood's company, and his flirting, and talking nonsense with him. It was a pleasant contrast to the blood, death and horror of her mornings to have him make frivolous love to her in the afternoons. She felt herself in no danger from him: he was not the sort of man she could fall in love with, and he would not overstep the mark in his present delicate situation.

The war continued its vertiginous course. Emperor Napoleon surrendered to the Prussian king, William (the Princess's father-in-law) at Sedan on the 2nd of September and became a German prisoner. Two days later Paris declared the end of the Second Empire and the beginning of the Third Republic, and the Empress Eugénie fled to England. A fortnight later, German armies surrounded Paris and laid siege to it. It seemed that the war was almost over. Venetia was too close to the effects of the fighting to feel any interest in the result of the war, except that she supposed its end would mean her father would recall her to England. It was left to Marwood, of all people, to give her thoughts a philosophical direction.

He was invited to supper one evening with the Prince and Princess and their circle. Afterwards there was music, and then some tables were made up for cards. Venetia did not play whist, and as it was intolerably hot, Marwood invited her to stroll for a few minutes on the terrace. Venetia hesitated, her heart jumping at the idea, but his usual flirtatious manner was absent for once, and he seemed sober and thoughtful, so she accepted.

For a little while they walked in silence, and then, seeming to rouse himself with an effort, he said, 'I have heard some news which will interest you. It seems we are to have the pleasure of receiving your brother into the regiment next month as a cornet.'

'Marcus? Oh, then he has persuaded Papa! I'm so glad for him. He always wanted to be a soldier, like Uncle Cavendish.'

'Your uncle was in the Hussars, wasn't he?'

'Yes, and Grandmother was always against it, so Mama always tried to be understanding about Marcus. Papa wanted him to go to the university, but Marcus always said he hadn't any brains, so the best thing for him was to be a soldier.' She realised suddenly what she had said and blushed, but Marwood only laughed softly.

'He's quite right, of course. Of the two of us, my horse is the greater scholar.'

'I don't believe that,' she said.

'Why, thank you for the compliment, ma'am,' he bowed. 'But remember you haven't met my horse.'

'I wonder why Papa has changed his mind?' she mused.

'A great many minds are changing about a great many things. When this war began, there wasn't a newspaper in the land that didn't applaud the respectable Prussians for attacking the decadent French, and rave about the imperial tyrant Napoleon – for "imperial" read any aspersing epithet you can imagine. But now the papers are full of praise for the gallant French underdogs, while the Germans take the role of the overweening bully.'

'And what has caused this change of mind, d'you think?' She was only half serious, thinking he was talking for her amusement.

But he said, 'The best of all persuaders: fear and self-interest. All those people who admired and praised the German military machine are now looking nervously over their shoulders at our own establishment. You perhaps don't know that our entire army consists of a little over a hundred thousand men, including reservists – and with those we have to man all our scattered foreign garrisons. If we had to send an expeditionary army to Belgium tomorrow, we would be hard put to it to scrape together twenty thousand men. *Twenty thousand*, against Germany's half-million.'

'We are Germany's friend,' Venetia objected.

'But are they ours? And if so, for how long?'

Venetia was thoughtful. 'I remember Uncle Tom – Mr Weston – saying we should be wondering what the Germans will do next with their great efficient army.'

'It's not only that. Every nation is watching this conflict, and when the Germans win, they'll draw certain conclusions from the victory. The whole philosophy of military power is going to change.'

'What can you mean?'

'Simply this: that always before, countries have raised an army in response to a cause. There was a need to fight, and so the men were recruited and armed for the purpose. But now we see a country creating an efficient and professional army and then using it to get what it wants, without any other justification.'

'You mean having the army has created its own cause?' Venetia said.

'Just so. And if other countries copy the example, it will make a very different kind of world altogether.' They reached the end of the terrace and turned to come back, but he stopped, standing in the shadow where no light from the windows fell. His voice sounded cold and old. 'With every nation taking what it wants by force of arms, we shall be living in a state of permanent warfare.'

'I don't believe it could happen,' Venetia said anxiously. 'Ordinary people wouldn't let it.'

'Ordinary people have no choice. It's governments – and generals – who make wars.'

'Yes, but ordinary people have to fight the wars, and in the end they would just refuse to go.'

'You're forgetting, we've just postulated a world in which the armies are made up of permanently employed, trained soldiers. *They* won't refuse to go. It's their whole reason for existence.'

She shivered at his words. 'Don't, please.'

'I didn't mean to frighten you. Forgive me.' He laid his hands on her forearms, and said in a very different voice, 'You're cold.'

'No,' she said. His hands slid to her upper arms, his touch hot on her bare skin. She trembled, her mind dithering with excitement and apprehension. 'I'm not cold,' she said foolishly.

'But you are,' he murmured. 'I can feel you shivering. Let me see if I can't warm you a little.'

He drew her against him, lowered his head, and kissed her.

It was like an electric shock passing through her. She had never been kissed on the lips before – never been kissed at all by any man but a relative. It was a sensation of piercing sweetness. Her insides seemed to melt and she felt warm and helpless, happy and strangely hungry, though for what she wasn't sure.

And then he stopped kissing her. She felt first a surge of disappointment; then social sense returned. She remembered that the first kiss was not supposed to happen until one became engaged: it was a milestone of huge significance. Kisses were for the man one married, and him alone, and Marwood was a loose fish, a gamester, and not at all the sort of man who could be considered for a husband. Besides, he had not proposed: he had kissed her for other reasons entirely. She ought to be very angry. It was insulting of him to have assumed she was the sort of girl he could do it to; and worse still, she had liked it, and, in spite of everything, wanted him to do it again.

All these thoughts took only the fraction of a second to pass through her head while she stared up at him with half-dazed confusion. He was still holding her by the arms, looking down at her with an expression she had never seen before,

174

a hard and predatory look that both frightened and thrilled her.

'Venetia,' he said urgently. 'Kiss me again!'

'No,' she said, as much afraid of her own feelings as his. But here were his lips again, and she was responding, eager head up like a hungry fledgeling. Then she made a violent effort of will and pulled herself away from him. 'I can't!' she said, and, before he could take hold of her again, dodged past him and ran a few steps towards the light.

'Don't run in like that,' he said urgently. 'People will talk.' He had not moved to follow her, and she paused, looking back at him. 'I'm sorry I startled you,' he said in as normal a voice as if they were simply passing in a street. 'I won't do it again. Only you must go back in as though nothing had happened, or there will be scandal.'

His rapid changes of mood confused her, and her anger was aroused. 'You didn't startle me,' she said. 'You insulted me.'

He gave a low laugh. 'Insulted you? No, no, you're quite mistaken. There is no greater compliment than for a man to desire a lovely woman.'

'You had no right to kiss me!'

'Did you dislike it so much?'

'Yes!' she said, but sounded to her own ears not magnificently angry but merely childish.

'Dear ma'am, then I shall not do it again, and beg your pardon most humbly for offending you.'

He bowed, and the smile in his eyes did not placate her but angered her more. He was mocking her! He thought her a silly little miss! 'You shall *not* do it again,' she asserted, trying to regain the initiative. 'I don't want to see you ever again.'

He gave a slightly lopsided smile. 'Your wish is about to be granted – at least, in part. I am recalled to England. The diplomatic situation is growing more delicate, and I am only a simple soldier: my place must be taken by someone with more address. I came this evening to say goodbye to you.'

'That's nothing to me, I assure you,' she said with as much dignity as she could muster, and stalked back towards the saloon, remembering, as she reached the door, to try to look normal, and not as though she had been kissed out there in the darkness. Marwood followed, and the rest of the evening passed without incident. When the card tables broke up, Marwood formally took leave of the Prince and Princess, thanking them for their kindness. He bowed to Venetia, but said nothing more to her than goodbye.

Venetia didn't know whether to be glad or sorry that he was going. Lying in bed that night she thought again and again about his kisses and her own reaction. It *was* an insult, wasn't it? Beauty Winchmore wouldn't have done such a thing – not without encouragement. But perhaps she had encouraged him. Perhaps secretly she had wanted him to kiss her. Horrors – was she *fast*? She had felt – oh, strange and wonderful and different while it was happening. She wanted to feel like that again. She drifted off to sleep, and had disturbing dreams all night, waking unrefreshed. The morning's occupations drove everything but themselves out of her mind; but in the afternoon, when no Captain Lord Marwood appeared to amuse and cheer her, she was certainly more sorry than glad that he'd gone.

The siege of Paris lasted, to everyone's astonishment, a hundred and thirty-one days. The stories that came out of the beleaguered city, of terrible suffering and heroism, of dashed hopes and vain sorties, filled the newspapers in England and aroused the sympathies of their readers. Paris was the world's largest city after London, the best known, and the most magnificent, the very home of luxury; now its poorest inhabitants were brought literally to starvation, and even the wealthiest were reduced to eating the inmates of the Tuileries Zoo to survive. Yet the French would not yield.

Venetia said goodbye to her kind hosts in mid-December, having been summoned home by her father. She arrived in London with very mixed feelings, tired and glad to be home, looking forward to livelier entertainments and a family Christmas down at Ravendene, but regretting leaving her work and doubtful about her future. Olivia was at home and greeted her rapturously.

'You've changed,' Venetia observed. 'You seem quite different.'

Olivia had grown confident, Venetia thought: she was still quiet, but it was a thoughtful, comfortable quietness, as of a grown woman who knew her own mind. Venetia wished she felt like that. 'No, *you've* changed,' Olivia said when she had stopped hugging her. 'You've got so thin! And you look – older.'

'Thank you, love. My youth and beauty quite worn away? But I know what you mean. The things I've seen, Livy! I shan't ever forget them. I suppose this is a bit how Mother must have felt when she came back from the Crimea.' She shook the thoughts away. 'Never mind it now. Tell me all about being a maid of honour!'

'Oh, it's not a bit as frightening as I expected. Just at first when I didn't know what to do, perhaps – but my first waiting was at Osborne, which is much easier than Windsor because it's so small. The gentlemen don't like it there because the accommodation is so cramped, and some of the older ladies say there is nothing to do, but I liked it very much. Such a pretty house, and the pleasure-grounds are lovely.'

'Never mind the house, what about you? What do you do?'

Olivia thought a moment. 'Well, there are lots of rules. For one thing, the Household is in perpetual mourning for the Prince, so the older ladies all wear black, like the Queen, but we maids are allowed white or grey or mauve or purple, because we're young. Well, that's the idea behind it, though my pair, Miss Allerdyce, must be at least forty, from what she tells me. Not that one could tell from looking at her. She's very pretty.'

'What's the Queen really like?'

'She's very nice – as kind as can be – though very particular, of course. She has very sharp hearing and hates doors to be banged, or any rattling noises. Miss Allerdyce sometimes worries her because she wears lots of little bangles and chains and lockets and things, and they clink together when she walks. She said – the Queen was kind enough to say – that she likes me to read aloud in the evening because I turn the pages without rustling.' Olivia blushed a little, recounting the compliment. Venetia wondered that she could be satisfied with praise so small, but there was no doubt she was content.

There were one or two social functions, including a ball at Lady Petersfield's, where Venetia was glad to meet old friends and renew old flirts. She was a little nervous of meeting Lord Marwood again, but he did not seem to be in evidence, and when she mentioned him casually to Lord Freshwater, she was told that he was not in Town, having gone to Morland Place for the Christmas season. Winchmore was also absent, having gone down to his father's estate; on the whole, Venetia was glad.

A few days later they travelled down to Ravendene. Venetia found her brother Henry, the heir, enjoying the hunting, in which his enthusiasm was only matched by her youngest sister Augusta, who at fifteen lived for horses.

'You are going to come out while you're here, aren't you?' Augusta asked anxiously. 'You haven't got so grown up you don't ride any more?'

'Of course not, love,' Venetia said. 'I hope I'll never be *that* grown up!'

'But you've missed the beginning of the season, and we've had some beautiful runs,' Augusta said.

'I was in Prussia.'

'You didn't have to be. You could have come home any time.'

Venetia declined to argue. 'Is there anything for me to ride?' she asked her brother instead.

'Oh yes. You can have Queen Mab, if you like,' Harry said. 'She's as fit as a flea and needs a run – unless you want something quieter? Mab takes some holding when she's corned up.'

Venetia put her chin up. 'I'll ride anything that's fit to go,' she said haughtily.

Harry grinned. 'Good for you! I was afraid you'd grown up and turned mimsy. You can have Tanager, too, then. He's jumping really well at the moment.'

Lord Marcus Fleetwood arrived on the same day by a

later train, eager to show off his uniform and talk about all the splendid fellows and ask Venetia eager questions about Prussian military tactics which she had no hope of answering to his satisfaction.

Fanny had come with the family to Ravendene, and was joyfully reunited with her daughter. Since Emma didn't ride, Fanny was able to have her to herself while Augusta was out hunting. Their long, cosy chats were often joined by Olivia, who didn't care to hunt. She liked the social side of it, and sometimes rode to the first covert for the pleasure of the company and the spectacle – hunting was becoming very fashionable, and it was the done thing to be seen 'out', so there were always plenty of friends – but she didn't see any pleasure in a mad scramble over rough country and being plastered with mud. She always left the field when the first run started, to ride home comfortably with a groom in attendance.

The family party was completed by the arrival of Lord Batchworth, Charlotte's brother, together with his son Lord Blithfield and his daughter Lady Anne Farraline. Blithfield was of an age with the twins and had largely been brought up with them, and the three quickly fell into their old easy intimacy. Lord Batchworth – Uncle Cavendish – was a semi-invalid, having taken a wound at Balaclava which had never really healed properly. He was only thirty-nine, but looked much older, since his hair had turned prematurely white, and his face was much lined with his constant pain. Yet he was always cheerful and interested in everything, could be very droll, and was popular with all his nephews and nieces.

The great love of his life was his little daughter Anne, a dainty, golden-haired seven-year-old whom he called 'Fairy'. She reciprocated his adoration. Her mother had died at her birth, and for her whole life she had sat on her father's knee as on a throne, commanded his devotion and directed his activities and her household. Fairy might well have been the worst sort of spoiled, tyrannical brat, but fortunately her intelligence and her sweetness of nature saved her. Having gone through a stage at the age of three of being impossible and throwing tantrums, she had grown sick of her own bad behaviour and corrected herself. Everyone loved Fairy; and

179

apart from her father, Venetia was her great hero. Venetia was very attached to the little girl, and saw now how much she had grown up in the last year. She saw too that Fairy was worried about her father's health. She had foreseen what it would mean to lose him, and Venetia was desperately sad for the little girl, who had had to leave her childhood so early and face at seven the kind of sorrow that ought to be reserved for a much greater age.

There was no shortage of material for conversation, and Venetia was glad to avoid talking about her own experiences, which would inevitably raise questions about her future, in favour of encouraging Olivia to talk about her life at Court. She had done two waitings so far, the one in Osborne, and one in Balmoral in the autumn.

'We had some excitement while I was there, because Lord Lorne proposed to Princess Louise while we were all out walking near the Glassalt Shiel, and she accepted. Lady Augusta says the last time the child of a monarch married a subject was over three hundred years ago, when Henry VIII's sister married Lord Brandon.'

'Yes, and I hear the Queen isn't best pleased about it,' Batchworth said.

'Oh, but it was partly her idea,' Olivia said. 'She encouraged him to pay court to the Princess. Only the thing is that he has a very disagreeable voice, poor man, because of an accident he had at school, and she likes people with pleasant voices. But she does think he's too forward. It must be difficult for him to keep on being deferential,' she said fairly, 'when he's going to marry into the family.'

'The Crown Princess was very upset about the engagement,' Venetia said. 'She didn't approve of her sister marrying a mere nobleman: she wanted her to marry a Prussian prince.'

'Yes, I know,' Olivia said. 'She sent a letter to the Queen about it, which made the Queen quite angry.'

Batchworth laughed. 'I hear Lorne's father, the Duke of Argyll, said that since his ancestors were kings when no-one had even heard of the Hohenzollerns, he thought he could survive their disapproval.'

'How did you know that?' Venetia enquired.

'Oh, I hear things,' he said lightly. 'It's probably as well there isn't to be another Prussian connection, eh, Southport?'

'The Government is strictly neutral,' he answered. 'You know that.'

'I'm glad to hear that you got out and had some fresh air while you were in Balmoral,' Charlotte said. 'I was afraid being in waiting would mean you'd be shut up indoors all day.'

'Oh no, there were plenty of outings, and walks, and drives, and picnics. It's only that no-one's allowed out of doors before the Queen; and even after that, if you slip out for a breath of fresh air, it's bound to be the very moment she wants you for something.'

'Yes, she has an uncanny knack of knowing when anyone is not where they should be,' Batchworth put in with an amused look. 'You might sit in an ante-room all day and not be called, but venture out for an instant and you become the one person she can't do without.'

Olivia looked reproachful at his levity. 'She likes to know where everyone is, that's all. And we're there to serve her. Miss Phipps says we are the blank pages on which she writes her instructions.'

'Dear Livy, it all sounds very dull,' Venetia said.

'Oh, but it isn't,' Olivia said quickly. 'I thought, with the Queen being broken-hearted, and the mourning and everything, that it would be all solemnity and hushed voices. But she's not like that at all. She loves to have fun, and laugh. When we were at Osborne, she went rowing in the private cove with Princess Christian and Princess Louise, while Prince Leopold and Princess Beatrice were bathing, and the splashing and shouting that went on were like nothing you ever heard! And in Balmoral she dances almost every dance. And the new Private Secretary, Colonel Ponsonby, is very droll, and has everyone in fits of laughter, and the Queen always wants to know what he's been saying, and laughs as much as anyone.'

'It's a pity she can't exhibit more of this propensity for fun to the people,' said Southport. 'Her refusal to be seen in public is causing us problems. She may claim that her widowed state and her poor health prevent her from performing her public duties, but it isn't only the republicans who suspect it's simply because she doesn't want to.'

'The republicans are getting very noisy lately,' Charlotte said. 'I don't know if I mentioned in one of my letters, Venetia, that there was a rally in Trafalgar Square in September, after the French republic was announced?'

'France sneezes, and England catches cold,' Batchworth remarked. 'It's always the way.'

'They were calling for the Queen to be deposed,' Charlotte went on. 'And there've been all sorts of horrid leaflets circulating.'

'Yes, I saw one the other day that said she was putting away a huge sum every year out of her income,' said Batchworth. 'Chiefly memorable for being the first time, I should think, that a Hanoverian monarch has been criticised for thrift!'

'But these things don't really matter, do they?' Harry asked. 'Aren't there always silly pamphlets being circulated?'

'I'm afraid this time it may be more serious,' his father answered. 'We sat it out in '48, but Europe is seething again, and the republican movement is gathering strength. If they should ever get their way, it would be disaster for us.'

'Why, Papa?' Henry asked. 'If no-one ever sees the Queen anyway?'

'Because whatever anyone thinks about the present incumbent, the monarchy gives us stability. Everyone knows and agrees who the monarch is, and who the next one will be, and so the fighting for power goes on at a lower level, where it does less harm. But take away the undoubted head of state, and you will never have agreement again about who it should be. Every minister wants to be president, and every president wants to be king. You've only to read Roman history. It's what the French have learned over the past eighty years, and will have to learn all over again if I'm not mistaken. Take away the monarchy, and we shall have bloodshed and civil war.'

'Can't you explain that to the Queen?' Charlotte asked.

Southport grimaced. '*Somebody* might, I suppose, but I've yet to learn who it is. Gladstone has tried and failed.'

'Gladstone will harangue her like a public meeting,' Charlotte said severely. 'Of course it sets her back up.'

In early January 1871, Bismarck ordered Paris to be shelled. Worn down with hunger, the Parisians now had to endure nightly bombardment which not only destroyed property and prevented rest or sleep, but took a further toll of civilian lives. On the 23rd of January the Foreign Minister of the new French Republic began to treat for peace, and on the 28th, Paris surrendered. The war was over.

Even before that, however, Bismarck had judged the time right for the final act of unification, and persuaded the King of Bavaria to beg King William of Prussia to accept the title of Emperor of Germany – Kaiser, in the German tongue. To emphasise the complete subjugation of France, the coronation of the Kaiser was carried out, on the 18th of January 1871, in the Galérie des Glâces at the Palace of Versailles – a deliberate insult which the French felt very much, and vowed to avenge. William was said to be so little enamoured of his new title, preferring his old one of King of Prussia, that he pointedly ignored Bismarck all through the ceremony. But Germany was united all the same, and Southport remarked to his wife that there would be no end of trouble to come.

It was left to Charlotte to comfort him with the assurance that the Kaiser's heir, Crown Prince Frederick, was a man of education and liberal views – who, moreover, was married to an English princess. 'Which means the next Kaiser after that will be her son, and half English. That must be a good thing, mustn't it?'

CHAPTER ELEVEN

Morland Place gave a ball on Twelfth Night, a culmination of the series of grand entertainments given over the Christmas season to celebrate the end of mourning, and the introduction of the new mistress to the neighbourhood.

The dinner which was to precede the ball was not until eight-thirty, but Henrietta was ready by half-past six. This was not eagerness on her part, but because Fanie had dressed her, and Fanie had to go on to dress her mistress in time to be in the drawing-room at eight, a process which took an hour and a half. So now Henrietta had nothing to do but sit in her room, a prey to unfamiliar feelings.

The room itself was unfamiliar: Alfreda had decreed that it was past time for her to leave the nursery, and had assigned her the red room, a rather dark and dismal chamber which, having been the back part of the east bedroom, had no windows, only a deadlight onto the corridor. Its carpet and drapes (which were yellow, for some reason, not red at all) were old and worn, the wallpaper rubbed, and the furnishings were odd pieces rejected from other rooms. But, least favoured of all the bedrooms though it was, it was hers, a place of her own. She was still not quite used to having it to herself, and sometimes woke in the night listening for the children's breathing and Gurney's snores.

At the moment its deficiencies were illuminated by the unusual number of candles Fanie had demanded in order to be able to dress Mademoiselle properly, and the light seemed to flow and rush about the draughty room like water slopping up and down a tilted vessel. The fire had dimmed to a glow: it wanted making up again, and the old Henrietta would have jumped up and put some coal on, without bothering to ring for anyone. The present Henrietta did not dare, partly for reasons of etiquette (Alfreda would be sure to find out and tell her it was not ladylike) but mostly for fear of her dress. She didn't like to ring, either, knowing how busy everyone would be downstairs.

She had a new gown for the ball, of delicate white figured muslin over white silk. It had been made by a mantuamaker this time, and fitted her rather better than a glove, so there was also a new corset. Waistlines were even smaller this year than last, and Henrietta's figure was changing. Nursery food, which had never been enough for her active life, had kept her too thin. Now she 'ate down', and Mrs Pretty had been replaced by a new cook, Kemp – who called himself *chef de cuisine* – under whose aegis Morland Place dinners were becoming the talk of the county.

The corset was another of the unfamiliar feelings. It gripped her body in a grim embrace, cutting her in half at the waist, and preventing her from expanding her ribs. One of the reasons Alfreda had sent Fanie to dress her was to make sure the laces were pulled tight enough; and Fanie, in a bad temper for some reason, had hauled on them like a dozen sailors on a rope.

'I can't breathe,' Henrietta had gasped in faint protest.

'What for do you want to breeze?' Fanie demanded unanswerably, and gave her an extra tug as punishment for complaining. After the corset there were four petticoats of stiffened white cotton and a top one of the palest pink taffeta with double ruffles at the hem, designed to be seen when the skirt of the gown was lifted. Then the gown went on, and Fanie settled to the long business of putting up Henrietta's hair. She liked doing hair and her temper began to mellow. In a moment she remarked approvingly on the candles. 'I do not like ze gaslight. My last lady 'ad it, and it make 'er look like a *noyée*.'

'Everybody in York has gas now, but we're too far out. We'd have to have a pipe all to ourselves, and it would cost too much,' Henrietta said.

'Candles are better. It is more r-r-romantic,' Fanie said, rolling her r's for effect. 'And better to dress by candlelight, for candlelight – remember zat, Mademoiselle.'

Henrietta agreed humbly that she would, though she couldn't think when she would have a choice in the matter. Fanie brushed and twisted and coiled and plaited and pinned; she wound a string of artificial pearls in and out of the mass, finishing with a spray of silk roses.

'Zere, Mademoiselle,' she said at last, 'now you look varry nice. All zat is needed is a little touch of colour – 'ere.'

She produced from nowhere a tiny pot into which she inserted her little finger and approached it to Henrietta's lips. 'Oh no, Fanie!' Henrietta protested, alarmed.

'Oh yes, Fanie,' said the maid obdurately. 'Why for all ze fuss? Just ze littlest touch in ze world – so! Pinch up your cheeks – so. Now look.'

Henrietta looked. She saw a young lady – elegant, beautifully dressed, with pink cheeks and lips and bright eyes and a crown of thick, soft, chestnut hair. 'Oh!' she said.

Fanie softened a little. She knew everything that went on in the house. She knew her mistress disliked this girl, whose seventeen-year-old freshness reminded her daily of her own wasted youth; she knew that Henrietta in her innocence admired Mrs Morland and wished to be loved by her; and she cared as little for one as for the other. But even this tough and practical opportunist had been young once. She knew how Henrietta must feel on the brink of her first ever ball, seeing herself looking really pretty for the first time in her life, and she sympathised.

'Yes, you look everysing you ought,' Fanie said kindly, and gave Henrietta's shoulder a little pat. 'All ze young men will fall in love wiz you tonight.' She became brisk. 'Now I muss go to my lady. Don't dare to move or you will spoil your 'ead.'

So Henrietta sat still, watching the moving candlelight, trying to work out a way to breathe without using her lungs. The corset was the worst of the new sensations, but her head also felt strange, heavy and full of metal. She experimented with a few gentle movements, but Fanie was a master hand, and it was quite secure. Reassured, Henrietta stood up and tried walking across the room, to see how she would manage the bustle and long train. There was a trick to turning which she was not quite confident she had mastered. And when she danced – *if* she danced – she must loop up her train. She practised that a few times, sure she would make a mull of it when the time came. She dropped her fan and automatically went to pick it up, only to find that because of the corset, she could not bend without turning faint. Of course, she remembered, Alfreda had impressed on her that if she dropped anything she must wait for the nearest gentleman to pick it up for her. She had thought it a silly affectation intended to romance the gentlemen, but she saw now that it had a practical application too. Alfreda, fashionable to an advanced degree, never did anything for herself, but always got someone else – Henrietta or a servant – to do it for her.

Henrietta fetched a chair, sat on it, and then carefully slid forward and reached down until she could retrieve the fan. Then she sat back and thought about her sister-in-law and the difference she had made to the house. Since they could not, Alfreda had decreed (she was very particular about propriety), entertain while they were in mourning, she had spent the first months of her residence at Morland Place cleaning, refurbishing and reorganising it. Henrietta had been made her right hand, doing errands, running messages, writing letters, making inventories. George, having given his wife *carte blanche*, made himself scarce, spending all day out of doors with Alfreda's complete approval, going round with Atterwith trying to learn how the estate was run, and interesting himself in the horses, as he had always done. The only time he was indoors was for dinner every night. Henrietta suspected the new regime of Kemp dinners was equally trying to her and her brother: to George because it was served fashionably late, and he got hungry long before then – she had seen mysterious covered trays being spirited up the backstairs to his bedroom around the old dinner time of six; and to her because, though the food was delicious, she was having to learn company manners, and every meal was an 'obstacle race', full of pitfalls and unfamiliar cutlery.

The other great trial to George was not being allowed to

have the dogs with him indoors. He missed them so much he had taken to having them smuggled up to his bedroom after Alfreda had gone to bed. Fortunately he rose very early out of old habit, and she did not leave her room until the proper, fashionable hour of ten, so he had not yet been caught sneaking Philo out again and handing her over to Baynes at the back door.

So for six days of the week George was pretty happy. On Sundays Alfreda insisted on the whole household going to church twice. This was a terrible trial to George, who had never given a fig for religion, and had always before enjoyed his Sundays on horseback and in comfortable clothes. Now he had to endure hard collars and tight boots and the pain of two hours on a wooden bench, with nothing spared him from Dearly Beloved Brethren to the Prayer of St Chrysostom, and an hour-long sermon to boot. He would wriggle and fidget in an agony of boredom until Mr Hughes glared down from the pulpit and Alfreda fixed him with an awful look.

Alfreda seemed to have no difficulty in keeping still, and sat upright and immobile with her face unmovingly serene. Henrietta, impressed by such patient piety, tried hard to emulate it. She wanted to be good as Alfreda was good, and made every effort to concentrate on Mr Hughes's rambling words and make sense of them. But it was hard; especially in the evening when, after their respective good dinners, Mr Hughes waxed ever more eloquent, while George waned into helpless sleep and received Alfreda's sharp elbow in the ribs whenever he began to snore.

In between the two church visits they had to sit quietly in the drawing-room, with no diversion but to converse or read aloud from divine works. Poor George would cast longing looks at the day outside, but only once had he dared to suggest that horses didn't have Sundays, and that there were things to do up at the stud. Alfreda hadn't said much, but her look was everything, and George had subsided with a red face. Dinner on Sunday was at three, so that the servants could be clear by six for church again, and there was no supper afterwards. George always retired to bed straight after church, saying he was tired; but then rang for a tray of supper to be brought to his room – he had the east bedroom, which was divided from Henrietta's only by a lath-and-plaster wall, and she could hear it all quite clearly. It was as hard for him to live up to Alfreda's high standards, Henrietta thought, as it was for her.

But the house was certainly looking better. Cleaned and polished and cared for as it ought to be, it had emerged slowly from the blurring of long neglect like an archaeological treasure being brushed free of the clinging earth. And the service was already different. Alfreda had purged the staff of members she had said were hopeless of improvement, and engaged an enormous number of extra bodies which she said were needed. There was a butler now, Goole, and the staff were divided and organised into three divisions under him, Kemp and Mrs Holicar, which was how it should be done, Alfreda said.

Things certainly ran smoothly, and there seemed to be servants for everything; but Henrietta regretted the old days when the servants were like friends, and if you wanted something you as often as not went and got it yourself. Now you sat still and rang, and had to wait the ten minutes it took someone to come, find out what you wanted, go and fetch it, and bring it back.

Above all, she had learned, you must not chat with the staff, but must be cool and aloof at all times. 'You are a lady, and must learn to behave like one,' Alfreda told her sternly, and explained how Henrietta's former attitude to the staff had been simply selfish. 'It is quite unkind to encourage them to familiarity, and then have to correct them when they encroach too far. It is more comfortable for them if they know what their place is, and can be confident that you will keep to yours. You should always consider the feelings of inferiors, and not simply please yourself at their expense.'

Henrietta understood now, and tried hard not to respond with the smiles and warmth that came naturally to her, especially towards people she had known all her life. It had been hard to see so many old friends go, and to see others who had stayed keeping their distance, speaking in hushed voices and with lowered eyes. Saddest of all had been the loss of Gurney, who had been a substitute mother to her and the younger children. But with Bittle in charge of the nursery, there was no place for Gurney, she did see that. Alfreda had arranged it that no-one knew Gurney was to go until afterwards, and that she should leave while Henrietta was out riding and the children walking with a maid, so that they should not have to see her leave. It was kinder that way, Alfreda had said, and Henrietta agreed intellectually, though in her heart she still wished she could have said goodbye, and assured herself that her old nurse was going to a comfortable place.

The clock in George's room struck seven. Another hour to go until they would all gather in the drawing-room to receive the guests. An hour and a half until they could eat. She was so hungry! She was sure her stomach would groan and shame her. She'd had nothing since five o'clock tea, and then it had been only two tiny cakes. Alfreda didn't approve of ladies eating very much. She hadn't eaten anything at five o'clock, and never ate much at dinner, either. How did she survive? Henrietta entertained a brief fantasy of secret trays to the blue room too, but then dismissed it. Alfreda would never do anything underhand.

She was too good for them, really; and the trouble she was taking with Henrietta was proof of her goodness, for after all she was only a sister-in-law, not a blood relation. Henrietta could wish sometimes that she was not so good as to try and get a husband for her. Of course Alfreda hadn't said that was what she was doing – she was much too refined – but Henrietta could hardly fail to notice that since they had started entertaining again, there was always an unattached young gentleman who was brought up to Henrietta and left with her. And she could not fail to notice Alfreda's disappointment in her when the young gentlemen lost interest and wandered away. Knowing she was on approval made her self-conscious; she knew she was not pretty, and must therefore sparkle, but she could never think of anything to say, and the thought of marrying any of these young men filled her with embarrassment. So they thought her dull and walked off at the first opportunity, and she felt both humiliated, and ashamed to have disappointed Alfreda.

And tonight – oh, tonight it would be worse than anything, because it was her first ball. She had not been taught to dance until Alfreda, her eyebrows shooting upwards, had discovered the deficiency and given her some hasty lessons in the drawing-room. She played the piano herself and snapped out instructions, while Henrietta stumbled about red-faced in the clutch of Fanie, who was furious at being asked to play the man and pinched her or kicked her shins at every opportunity. Henrietta doubted she'd remember anything if it came to a real dance with a real man; but worse even than that, she was sure no-one would ask her. There in the great hall – cleaned to its former glory, completely free of dogs and clutter, and housing, under the dazzle of the newly polished chandelier, thirty dancing couples and a small orchestra surrounded by potted palms – there she would be exposed before all the finest people in Yorkshire as the dull girl too plain to be danced with; the wicked girl too ungrateful to her sister-in-law to attract a husband.

There was a tap at the door, and Teddy put his head round. 'Are you alone? Oh good!' He came in and shut the door behind him. Henrietta's face lit in a welcoming smile. He was still in his day clothes, and carried about him a faint aroma of brandy and cigars. 'Hullo, sissy! You look splendid!'

'Do you really think so?' Henrietta asked anxiously.

'Top-hole. You're dressed early, aren't you?'

'You're late.'

'Oh, there's plenty of time. It don't take me long to change my togs. I've been on the town with Marwood.' He chuckled. 'You know, I can't help thinking he's not at all the thing! Of course he's splendid company, but inviting him here is like giving a fox the run of the hen-house!'

'What do you mean? He's Alfreda's brother.'

'And she loves him: quite. Still, if I were George I'd worry about him running through my fortune. Stood everyone at the club a bumper of brandy and then wanted to go on to a gaming place! I said I was a good little boy and must go home to change for the ball. He said, what ball?' Henrietta's eyes were wide. 'Oh, don't worry, I hauled him back with me and gave him over to his man.'

'Teddy, he's not *drunk*, is he?'

'No, love, he's too old a hand to show,' Teddy laughed. 'He'll be ready for starter's orders, don't worry.'

Henrietta was still concerned. 'Oh, but poor Alfreda! She ought not to be upset when she's gone to so much trouble for tonight.'

Teddy gave her a grimly humorous look. 'I'll give a guinea old Alfie knows what's what with her brother. It wasn't *his* rhino he was splashing about at the club.'

'Oh, Teddy, you shouldn't talk like that about her!'

'Shouldn't I? I thought it was quite mild really, considering what I might say.'

'But – don't you like her?' Henrietta asked anxiously.

'Do you?'

'She's so very kind to me. And beautiful, and good.'

'Hmph,' said Teddy, hitching one buttock onto the edge of her dressing table and folding his arms. 'Well, she's not very kind to me. In fact, she's made it quite clear that she'd like me out of here as soon as possible, if not sooner.'

'I'm sure you must be wrong,' Henrietta said loyally.

'You didn't hear how she pi-jawed me this morning about the expense of keeping me at Oxford. And whenever we sit down to a meal, I can feel her eyes watching everything I put into my mouth! Besides, Marwood got just merry enough to be indiscreet today: she's told him that since I've inherited half Georgie's fortune, I ought to go and live on it and not sponge on Morland Place.'

'Oh Teddy, no! Not sponge. He must have been making it up.'

Teddy shrugged. 'Well, to tell you the truth, I'd as soon not be here now she's changed it all. It's not like the old Morland Place any more. What do you think of all this fuss and fal-lal?'

'Of course I loved it the way it was,' Henrietta said fairly, 'but you must admit it was shabby and dirty. Alfreda's making it great again. Don't you think it deserves to be properly cared for?'

He shrugged that away too, and said, 'I'm thinking that perhaps I won't go back to Oxford after Christmas.'

'Not take your degree?'

'I shan't need it now I'm not going to have to earn my living. I shall be twenty-one in August, and then I shall be a man of substance, so I might as well start behaving like one. There's Moon's Rush to do up, and the land to get back into good heart – I quite fancy myself the gentleman-farmer.'

'But you can't live at Moon's Rush. It hasn't even got a roof.'

'I've got Makepeace House to live in until I've done it up. There's the business to look over – I ought to understand where the money comes from, as well as where it goes to! And Uncle Henry has said that he'll spoon out the ready within reason, as long as I'm not gaming it away or consorting with bad lots.' He chuckled again. 'I'd better keep shy of old Marwood, or Uncle Henry'll shut the purse again with a snap!'

Henrietta sighed. 'Well, I suppose you know your own mind. It'll be nice to have you nearer home, anyway. Perhaps I'll see you more often.'

Teddy cocked his head. 'Why, you don't think *you'll* be at home much longer, do you? Alfreda means to have you married before spring. Now, don't colour up: you must have realised she was fattening you for the pot.'

'It's so awful,' Henrietta said, putting her hands to her hot face. 'I know she's doing it for my sake, but the men all think me dull, and the thought of marrying at all—'

'I told you, you'll fall in love, and then it'll be all right. It'll happen quite suddenly, I expect. It generally does.'

'Are you in love?' she asked, raising her eyes disconcertingly.

'Every few days, with someone different,' he said lightly. 'But tonight's your first ball, isn't it? That's a great occasion for a girl. Perhaps you'll fall in love tonight.'

'Twelfth Night – Gurney used to say it was the night of prophecy, didn't she?' said Henrietta.

'Yes – poor old Gurney.' His face darkened for a moment, but whatever he was about to say was interrupted by a loud groan from Henrietta's stomach.

She crimsoned with confusion. 'Oh! It's awful! How can I go downstairs? I'll disgrace myself. But I'm so hungry.'

Teddy slapped his leg. 'I'm a mutton-head! I knew there was a reason I came to see you. I've got something for you.' He began to fumble in the pocket of his sack-coat. 'I guessed you'd be starving, so I called in at the kitchen. *Voilà!*'

He drew out a large napkin, which he put down on the dressing-table and unwrapped.

'Game pasties. They got broken coming out of the oven.'

'Oh Ted! Oh, how glorious! But you never got Kemp to give them to you?'

'Lord, no! I waited until he was out of the room and cozened them out of Marlow. Here, let's get a towel to hang round your neck, or you'll drop something down your new gown.'

The golden pastry, shiny on the top, delicately crumbling and buttery where it was broken, and the delicious, moist, savoury filling with its rich gravy, set Henrietta's mouth watering. Mrs Marlow, the pastry-cook who did all the baking – and, incidentally, gave the *chef* someone to be *chef* over – was an artist.

'You are the best brother in the world,' Henrietta said.

He tied her towel round her, pulled up a chair, and they both tucked in, eating with their fingers and talking easily. When the last crumbs had been dabbed up, he fetched a damp cloth from Henrietta's wash-stand and laughingly cleaned her face and fingers.

'There, all innocent,' he said. 'Butter wouldn't melt in your mouth. Oh, no, I forgot, it already has! Well, I'd better go and dress. See you in the drawing-room.'

Alfreda was alone in the drawing-room when Lord Marwood wandered in, dressed but looking distracted, and his eye a little short of lustre. 'Oh, Kit, I'm glad you're early. I wanted to have a word with you,' she said.

'Must you?' he said querulously.

She focused on him. 'You don't look quite yourself. Are you all right?'

'Oh, I'm tol-lol-ish. But what does one have to do to get a drink in this house?'

'No more before dinner,' Alfreda decreed sternly. 'You

drink too much anyway. I suppose you were drinking all afternoon?'

'Dash it, Alfie, it's prophylactic! How am I to face an evening with the good provincials without a little help?'

'Don't be silly. Dinner will be excellent, and the dinner guests are quite up to our standards – well, most of them. You will find it entertaining.'

'Is that a prediction or a command? Oh, very well, but there's the ball afterwards. I draw the line at dancing with the natives, damn it.'

'Don't swear. And of course you will dance. That was what I wanted to talk to you about. I may want you to dance with Henrietta, so you must hold yourself ready and look for my signal.'

He raised his eyebrows. 'A rescue operation?'

She walked up and down the room irritably, her brows drawn into a frown. 'I'm at my wits' end with that girl! I've done everything for her – spent a fortune on clothes – and she just won't *take*. I don't think she even tries. I put people in her way, and she stands there like a stock and won't open her mouth. Well, if she's not asked to dance, *you* must dance with her. I can't have her seen without a partner, or they'll think there's something wrong with her.'

'Not me! She's got two brothers, hasn't she?'

'That would be too obvious. It would look like desperation.'

'But I have to be careful who I dance with. Plain girls always want to marry men who dance with them, and I have other fish to fry.'

'Don't be vulgar.' Her curiosity overcame her. 'What fish?'

'A certain duke's daughter,' he said with a private smile, 'who kisses with unexpected passion.'

She regretted her curiosity. 'And don't be indecent. No, it must be you who dances with Henrietta, to give her cachet. You're so glamorous, other men will follow where you lead.'

'Good Lord, Alfie, she ain't the Dark Continent!'

'She's an albatross, that's what she is!' Alfreda said uncharitably. 'I must get her off while she's young and fresh, or I'll never be rid of her at all without a large dowry. And

I'm determined I shan't be forced to support all Morland's indigent relatives.'

Marwood laughed. 'Oh dear, poor love! And here I am with a Morland pension *and* running up bills for you to settle. Well, I did warn you!'

'I don't begrudge you anything,' she said, her expression softening. 'You're my own flesh and blood. They aren't.'

'Well, Edward Morland has received the message at any rate – he's as anxious to go as you are to be rid of him.'

'Good. The younger ones won't be difficult. Regina is pretty and insipid – just the sort men make fools of themselves over. I shall get her off all right as soon as she's sixteen.'

'And the little boy? Boys are expensive to put to a profession.'

'I shan't. He'll have to be educated, but there are plenty of inexpensive schools in Yorkshire where he can learn arithmetic and a fair hand, and then he can take a clerk's job somewhere.'

'A clerk's job? I say, no, Alfie— !'

'If his father didn't provide for him to have a profession, I don't see why I should.'

Marwood was a little taken aback. 'You sound so grim, love. I don't like to see you growing so hard.'

She looked at him for a moment almost with dislike. '*Growing* hard? You have no idea, have you, of what I've suffered? The years of poverty and humiliation! You think I am the same girl I was at seventeen, before Papa ruined all our lives. Do you think that girl would ever have married a man like George Morland? Well, I did what I had to do, and I don't mean ever to be poor or pitied again. I am going to make Morland Place what Turl Magna was, and I shall hold the place here that Mama held at home.'

'Hmph. Well, you'll do it, if anyone can,' Marwood said. 'And for the sake of peace, I'll dance with the girl if I have to.'

'Thank you,' Alfreda said. She stared forbiddingly into the distance. 'But if she shames me tonight, she'll wish she had never been born.'

'Probably already does,' Marwood said lightly.

Henrietta was not enjoying herself. The scene in the great hall was brilliant, the music was lovely, she was wearing a gown most girls would give anything for: she knew it was dreadfully ungrateful, but she wished she were anywhere but here. The trouble had begun as soon as she had gone down to the drawing-room. The glorious, rich game pasty that had seemed such a good idea when Teddy produced it had not been able to get past the tightness of her corset, and lay seething somewhere under her ribs. She had wondered, when Fanie was lacing her, how she would be able to eat with her stomach fastened flat to her backbone, and now she knew the answer. That was why, she supposed, Alfreda ate so little at dinner. A sip of soup, a fragment of fish, a morsel of soufflé might slip under the fence, but anything bulky was trapped. By the time she sat down at the table the pasty was sending waves of searing acid coursing through her, and threatening to make her belch.

She sat through the endless dinner, picking at the delicious dishes before her, daring to touching nothing; her eyes fixed on space as she tried to control her inner pandemonium. The corset seemed to grow tighter all the time, as though it were a living thing that had got hold of her and was slowly crushing her to death. She was aware of nothing around her, only longing for it to be over.

When Alfreda at last gave the signal to rise, she got up too quickly, forgot to breathe shallowly, panicked when she could not expand her ribs, and swooned. It was horrible: for a moment she thought she was going to be sick. The gentlemen had all risen, of course, and Lord Grey, who was nearest, caught her and supported her, fanning her face with his menu card until she recovered herself. It lasted only a moment, but she was covered with confusion, and dared not meet Alfreda's eyes for fear of what she might see in them.

And now, much later, she was suffering from hunger and indigestion at the same time, which struck her as unfair. She had danced several times, but had not enjoyed it: afraid of going wrong, she had had to concentrate so hard on her feet she had been unable to respond to her partners' conversation.

None of them had asked her a second time, and with each dance it seemed to her more conspicuous that other girls were scrambled for and she was left until last. She had been rescued once from ignominy by kind Lord Grey, and had been obliged to dance once with Lord Marwood, which she disliked very much, for he smelled very brandyish and held her too tightly.

And now, pinned to the spot by Alfreda, she was standing again unpartnered and feeling horribly exposed, while all around her more favoured girls were led onto the floor by smiling young men. At least she would be spared another circuit with Lord Marwood, whom she had seen disappearing with Teddy down the kitchen passage, either in search of food or drink, or bent on escape through the buttery door. But if no-one asked her at all, Alfreda would be angry and think her ungrateful, and, oh! she felt wretched and wished she could go away and hide somewhere.

Suddenly someone was standing in front of her, a male someone, asking her something. She mustered her whirling wits and found that it was Mr Fortescue, the rector of Bishop Winthorpe, who had conducted George's wedding and who, she remembered vaguely, had been at the dinner table this evening. His stern, aesthetic features were softened in a smile; he was bowing. He was the last person she would have expected. She blushed in confusion. Surely he was not asking her to dance?

'I – I beg your pardon, sir? I didn't quite— ?'

'Not at all. I merely apologised, my dear young lady, for my complete inability to dance, were it not for which I would ask you to do me the honour.'

'Oh! Thank you, but I do not like to dance,' Henrietta stammered, and then, remembering Alfreda was beside her, added quickly, 'At least, not very much.'

Fortescue raised his brows. 'Indeed? Then if I am not keeping you from some more desirable partner, perhaps I might persuade you to walk around the floor with me, in lieu of dancing?'

Henrietta glanced doubtfully at Alfreda. Would this count? He was a man, after all. Alfreda gave her a small nod, her expression unreadable. Henrietta looked at Mr Fortescue and smiled. 'I should be honoured, sir,' she said, and reached for his arm almost before he had crooked it, so eager was she to prove to Alfreda that she was trying her best.

Mr Fortescue had been doubtful about accepting the invitation. He had noticed, of course, that the new Mrs Morland had been courting him assiduously, and though he supposed it was flattering to be lionised even by such a woman, an evening spent consorting with inferior minds was not a tempting prospect. He had succumbed, however, to the temptations of the flesh: he was by way of being a gourmet, and Lord Grey had told him that Morland Place dinners were not to be missed.

He had not been disappointed. The dishes were well chosen and deliciously presented, the wines were superb, and the service – *à la Russe* – was excellent. He dined well, and drank deeply. He was pleasantly surprised, too, by the quality of the other guests. He had supposed that they would all be young, frivolous people, and had steeled himself to listen to nonsense; but Alfreda had invited several men of position and education. The conversation at his end of the table had been weighty and engaging, and Mr Fortescue, mellowed by wine and relief, responded eloquently.

It was while he was talking that his attention had been drawn to the young female opposite. By both age and sex she belonged to that division of society that least interested him; but her eyes were fixed on him unwaveringly, and she seemed to be listening with rapt attention. It was the concentration on his words that reminded him who she was – his hostess's sister-in-law, the daughter of the house, who had listened to his sermon at the wedding with such deep interest.

Once aware of her, he found he could not help looking at her from time to time. She was pretty, he thought, in a delicate, spiritual way. He liked her soft hair, her rather pale face, which contrasted delightfully with her very pink lips, and the soulful, almost melancholy look in her eyes. He noted that she barely touched her food: evidently she had a mind above such things, for she looked even at the delectable woodcock in truffle sauce with something like dismay, as though the act of eating were too gross for the transparency of her soul.

Her little swoon when the ladies withdrew was further evidence of her delicacy. He had, of course, not been near enough to help her, but he had been conscious of an unexpected stirring of desire to be the one whose arm went around that utterly tiny waist to support her in her moment of need. Her confusion over the episode had delighted him. He had always thought women rather coarse creatures, much more animal than men. But this young lady, he thought, was different. She seemed to exist on a higher plane.

And now he found her standing apart from the dancing, her pale little face showing how much she was suffering from this exposure to the vulgar entertainments that so pleased other girls. He did not miss her start when he spoke – she had been elsewhere, thinking so deeply she had not noticed him. And he was flattered and unexpectedly thrilled by the eagerness with which she put out her hand to him. As he slipped her hand under his arm, he could not help giving it a little squeeze against his ribs. He quite surprised himself in this – it was out of his character, though he had drunk generously of Morland's excellent vintages – and was almost ashamed when the young female did not even seem to notice, proving herself more other-worldly than him.

The desire to protect her rose up in him again. She was so young, so delicate! All around him coarse and bucolic young men were swinging ordinary girls about the room in the customary manner. Suppose they asked her to dance? He imagined their sweating hands touching her, grasping her fairy-like waist. Suppose one of them married her? The thought of it made him shudder, and yet it was all too likely. He was quite well aware that that was what balls were for, and she was of marriageable age. Perhaps that was what made her so pale and unhappy.

He cleared his throat, and she looked up at him enquiringly – her sad, sweet face and limpid gaze so innocent, so trusting!

'Well, Miss Morland, so you do not like to dance?' he said a little foolishly.

'Not very much,' she said. 'I do it so badly. But of course,' she added hastily, 'it is very kind of Alfreda – Mrs Morland – to go to so much trouble. I did not mean to sound ungrateful.'

He was touched. She was a good girl, and thoughtful. The new Mrs Morland must be insensitive not to notice that her young sister-in-law disliked worldly things. 'You and she perhaps do not share many tastes?'

Henrietta thought of her old life, roaming the country on her pony, helping with the haysel, sitting on the grass and sharing Caleb's onion and cold tea. 'Perhaps we don't, sir. But I'm sure I ought to. She has done so much for Morland Place.'

He noted the wistfulness. Morland Place was becoming famed for its lavish and stylish entertainments, which must be uncomfortable for a spiritual girl. 'You perhaps preferred the way it was before?' he suggested.

'I think I did,' she admitted. 'But I ought not to say so.'

'Your secret is safe with me,' he said indulgently, and she smiled at him in a way that made his heart beat faster. 'I seem to remember that we had a little conversation at your brother's wedding,' he said. 'You told me then that you preferred the life of contemplation and study.'

Henrietta demurred. 'Oh, but I—'

'My dear young lady, I understand perfectly. Not for anything would I wish to compromise your loyalty. Indeed it is admirable. But you must allow me to offer my sympathy. There can be nothing worse than the noise of the world when all one's inner feelings revolt against it. The animus sickens at such coarse food. The soul pants like the hart after the cooling stream.'

Henrietta had little idea what he was talking about, but catching at the odd word – *inner feelings, sicken, pants* – she gathered that he had guessed her secret. How, she could not imagine, unless he had suffered from indigestion himself at some point – it could hardly be that he wore a corset! She blushed and looked down in confusion and said, 'Oh, I hoped no-one would notice.'

'*I* noticed,' he said, delighted with her, with himself, and with the involuntary tightening of her hand on his arm.

'Oh, sir – you won't— ?'

'Have I not already told you, your secret is safe with me?'

Now she looked up shyly. 'Have you – have you suffered in that way yourself, sir?'

'Many times,' he said fervently. 'The world is too much with us, late and soon – squandering the precious gifts of time, of silence – how we lay waste our powers in meaningless frivolity! The serious mind is everywhere despised! I think, Miss Morland, we are alike, you and I, cut of the same cloth.'

'Oh, no!' Henrietta protested, delighted but shocked that one so erudite should think so.

'You are modest, my dear. It is meet in woman, a delicacy of spirit one always hopes to find and yet of which one is so often disappointed,' he said with a sigh. 'To be man's helpmeet, and yet to crave the shelter of his umbra; to support him, and yet to shrink from the brightness of the world which glares upon him—' He talked on, and she gazed up at him, rapt; she drunk with his words, he with eupepsia, claret and port. They had almost completed the circuit, were approaching Alfreda again, the grim landmark towards which he must steer this lovely girl. He noticed how, as she caught sight of her sister-in-law, his delicate companion seemed to shrink in on herself. His protectiveness asserted itself once more, and with fine fervour.

'I return you now to the world,' he said tenderly, 'but do not fear, it shall not always be so.' He unlatched her hand from his arm and lifted it briefly to his lips. 'Andromeda shall not remain chained to the rock. The monster shall not devour her.'

Henrietta rejoined Alfreda in a state of some confusion, pleased that so eminent a man had sought her company, afraid Alfreda would be annoyed that she had not danced. But Alfreda only looked at her with raised eyebrows and said, 'Did I just see Mr Fortescue kiss your hand?'

'Yes,' Henrietta admitted. 'Was – was it wrong?'

'No, not wrong. I was surprised, that was all,' said Alfreda, and relapsed into furious thought. Mr Fortescue? Well, after all, why not? In fact, she wondered she had not thought of it before. A bachelor, extremely well-to-do, and unworldly –

the very man who, if he suddenly fell in love, would not think of asking for a dowry. And why should he not fall in love? He was not likely to notice whether or not Henrietta was pretty, and given that he was a scholar, would probably welcome her being dull. If he could be brought up to scratch, it would not only get Henrietta off her hands, but would reflect credit on Alfreda and the family – the sort of connection that was good both in material and social terms.

She must think how to throw him together with Henrietta again soon. And she must speak to Henrietta about how to behave with him. No, on second thoughts, that might only confuse her, make her more awkwardly self-conscious. Whatever she was doing, it was right for Fortescue. Better let her alone.

CHAPTER TWELVE

The Earl of Batchworth died one frosty morning in February 1871. He was on his way back from the stables, and fell almost on the exact spot where his father had died thirteen years before. His son William became thirteenth Earl of Batchworth still nine months short of his seventeenth birthday; Mr Farraline, an elderly cousin on his father's side, became William's guardian and trustee – and also his heir, until he should marry and beget one.

Charlotte was still at Ravendene with her daughters and Henry when the news arrived, and started out early the next morning on the long train journey to Manchester. Southport and Marcus, who had already gone back to London, would come up in time for the funeral; but Charlotte knew she would be wanted at once by her brother's children.

'He wasn't even forty,' Charlotte said, watching the frozen country pass monotonously by the train windows. 'I wish we had seen more of him in recent years.'

The Southports had their own railway carriage, comfortably carpeted and upholstered like a drawing-room; it was even heated with a small stove, though the cold outside was so intense today they did not take off their outer garments. Henry was in an armchair at the far end, reading the newspaper which he had picked up when their carriage was transferred onto the London train at Rugby. Olivia was sitting at the round table in the middle, doing a dissected puzzle with Augusta to keep her amused, for Emma had stayed at Ravendene with her mother.

Venetia and Charlotte faced each other from opposite

corners of the sofa at the end nearest the stove. Staring blankly out of the window, Charlotte was remembering the first time she had ever seen her brother, as a fresh-faced boy of eleven coming whistling through the shrubbery at Wolvercote, neither of them having any idea who the other was. So fair, so cheerful, so full of the joys of life he had always been. How she had loved him! How proud they had been of each other. He had always wanted to be a soldier, but their mother had set herself against it, fearing it would mean his death. And so it had, of course: his constitution had been undermined by his experiences in the Crimea. Charlotte was glad their mother had not had to witness this tragically early death.

But what would Cav's life have been to him, she pondered, if he had been denied the one thing he wanted to do? It was natural to want to protect your children, and that meant their physical selves first, which you had formed of your own flesh with such travail. You gave them their life to begin with, when you bore them helpless into the world; but it was not yours to hold back from them when at last they put their hands to it, to take their own direction. You had to let them go.

Oh, but not yet forty! She had found him so late; had lost him once before, and suffered this pain of bereavement only to get him back again. But this time, it was final. There would be no reprieve, no laughing, teasing brother to jump up and say *It was all a hoax! Here I am!*

'I didn't know,' she said aloud, 'at Christmas. When I said goodbye to him, I didn't know it was for the last time.'

Venetia examined her mother with newly anxious eyes. Huddled in her sables, with a fur hat pulled down over her ears, Charlotte looked like a chilly bird ruffling its feathers against the deadly frost. Venetia felt the breath of mortality touch her. Uncle Cav was dead, whose warm lips had kissed her cheek in parting only weeks ago. Mama was nine years older, and in this unkind February light looked shrunken inside her furs, vulnerable. One knew intellectually, of course, that everyone must die some time; but there was a deep, blind conviction that one's own mother and father were somehow different. They had always been there, in the world since time began, and always would be, until time's end.

'Would it have made a difference?' she asked, in reply to her mother's last remark.

Charlotte shrugged slightly. 'One always wants to be able to say goodbye. But of course, one would never believe it, even if one was told. I suppose,' she sighed, 'the answer is to say goodbye always as though it were the last time.'

Venetia moved impatiently. 'We can't be always expecting the worst, or we'd be too miserable to live at all.'

Charlotte smiled faintly. 'Of course you're right. God bless the robustness of youth!'

'But you're young too, Mama-duchess. Not even fifty yet.'

Charlotte met her eyes with complete understanding. 'I shan't die for a long time yet, I promise,' she said.

When they stepped down from the carriages at last, chilled to the marrow by the two-hour drive from the station, the house at Grasscroft looked deserted, standing grey and blank-windowed in its February ice-garden. Dusk was coming on, a little misty, the sky dim and pink over the roofs. The horses' breath rose in clouds, and the gravel under their shifting hooves was slippery with frost. The trees were hung so thick with rime, it was like snow, and every blade of grass stood out, sharp, separate and fantastic. The shutters of the upper windows were closed, and no light showed anywhere. A dead house in a dead land, Charlotte thought. Out here on the edge of the moors the bones of the earth lay too close under the surface, barely covered. There seemed nothing between her senses and reality; everything felt too hard, hurt too much.

The great door opened, and a slice of yellow light fell out, making the dusk at once colder. The butler was there, a footman, and two maids, waiting to receive them. They stepped into the hall. Miss Aubrey, the cousin on Cavendish's paternal grandmother's side who had kept house for him, smiled a nervous greeting, and behind her came William, the new earl, slender and young, dwarfed by the echoing vastness of the house. He had arrived only the day before, from Eton. He came forward, trying to be the man and the host, but he had been coping all alone since that terrible moment when the telegraph had arrived to say his father had left him for ever, and at the sight of Charlotte his chin began to wobble. He dragged his lip in under his teeth in an effort not to cry.

Charlotte dropped her reticule and muff and held out her arms, and he abandoned manhood and ran into them, pressing his face into her cold fur and spilling hot tears onto her neck.

'Oh my poor boy,' she murmured, folding a hand about the curve of his fragile skull. He looked so like his father at the same age. Over his shoulder she saw Fairy, her hand in that of a nurse. Her eyes were puffy, and in her face was the starkest tragedy a seven-year-old is capable of realising: the end of childhood, and the knowledge that nothing is safe.

The servants were glad of the duchess's arrival, with her practised authority, her ease of command. They knew what to do, but wanted someone to tell them. The children clung to her; the lawyer, the parish priest, the carpenter, the sexton, the head coachman all wanted instructions. Charlotte felt them leaning against her. She was glad of it, on the whole: it was impossible to be overcome with grief while there was someone else relying on you to maintain normality. And yet, she thought, in all her life she had never been allowed to be overcome, to faint and fail, take to her bed, to step away from duty and be helpless with sorrow. There are those who will always be expected to cope, she thought, with a touch of weary resentment.

When the funeral was over, there remained the question of what to do with Cavendish's children. Old Mr Farraline, son of Cav's grand-uncle, was no help. He had never expected to inherit and had never interested himself in the titled part of the family. He lived a comfortable bachelor life in a small, neat house in Kendal, where he sketched birds in the summer and read books about foreign travel in the winter, and he frankly resented the historical precedent that made him guardian to these unknown children. All he wanted was to get away from this vast, draughty mansion and back to his own house and the ministrations of his housekeeper, who knew exactly how to make him comfortable. He had just had a new patent fireplace put into his book-room where he always sat, and the cavernous chill of Grasscroft was making him appreciate its benefits all over again.

'I have no experience of children,' he protested as often as anyone would listen to him. 'I am a bachelor. I cannot take charge of them. As to the management of the estate, surely that is a task for specialists? I would not know where to begin. I am neither a lawyer nor a land agent.'

Charlotte said privately to her husband, 'It's a pity Cav didn't think to make *you* guardian. As uncle to the children you are surely closer than Mr Farraline – and at least you care about them.'

Southport said, 'I'm only uncle by marriage. And besides, it wouldn't do. It has to be the oldest male member of the family – that's tradition. Your brother knew that.'

Charlotte showed what she thought of that tradition. 'It's odd to think,' she went on, 'that if anything happened to William, Mr Farraline would be the next earl. In fact,' she thought suddenly, 'isn't that a reason for not making him guardian? It would be too easy for him to do William a mischief, and—'

Southport shook his head, amused. 'My dear, you're fair and far out there! There's nothing Farraline would like less than to be the next earl. He's in a terrible quake lest anything should make him stay here half a day longer than he has to. If it were up to him, William would live for ever and have sixteen sons.'

Charlotte began to laugh, and then caught herself up, remembering the occasion. 'But what *are* we to do? The poor children can't stay here, either alone or with Mr Farraline. It's too dismal.'

'I agree with you. In fact, I think Fairy should come home with us.'

'Do you? Oh, bless you! I was hoping she might. She could live down at Ravendene with Augusta and Emma, don't you think?'

'Of course. One more girl in the schoolroom can make no difference.'

'But what about William?'

'I think that must be up to William.'

208

William had been bowed with worry about taking care of his little sister, for he had quickly seen that his cousin wasn't to be relied on. Relieved of that responsibility, he felt able to say that what he would really like was to go back to Eton and finish his last half. 'But would it be all right for me to leave Grasscroft like that?'

'Certainly it would,' Charlotte said. 'I expect Miss Aubrey will stay and look after the house; but if she doesn't care to, a housekeeper can be employed. And the agent can take care of everything else, until you're ready to take over.'

William seemed almost visibly to straighten as the last burden was lifted from his shoulders. 'Then, do you think, Aunt, that I might go on to Oxford, as Papa planned for me?'

'I think it is what he would have wanted,' Charlotte said.

Matters took some settling, and Southport had to return to London before everything was done, though he came back at the weekend to lend his wife his support. Charlotte was three weeks at Grasscroft, and when she finally left Manchester, frozen February had turned to damp March, and there were only a few days at Ravendene before it was time to go up to London again.

Venetia held off from mentioning her own situation until they were settled at Southport House, and the invitations were flowing in for another Season. Then one morning when her mother was sorting through the day's crop of cards, she said, 'Mama, it won't do, you know. I'm sorry if it comes as a shock to you, but your plan to make me sick of medicine didn't work. I can't go through another five months of pointless dancing and flirting. Uncle Cav's death has made me even more sure that I want to be a doctor.'

Charlotte put down her handful of invitations and looked her dismay. 'Oh dear! I hoped you'd forgotten about it.'

'You said you'd help me. I've seen the horrible things now, and they don't disturb me. I must go on.'

'You know how difficult it will be? How men will hate you and ridicule you? You know you will never be accepted?'

'Never is a long time,' Venetia said. 'Things change.'

Charlotte sighed. 'If you are determined on this, I will speak to your father. But it won't be easy. You must leave me to choose the right time.'

It wasn't easy to find the right time. Cardwell's army reforms were meeting increasingly hostile opposition. Each measure had to be fought through, against the rigid traditions and vested interests of the military establishment on one hand, and the civilian's instinctive fear and hatred of the army on the other.

'Wellington was a great hero,' Southport had said to Charlotte once, 'but he lays a dead hand on everything. Whatever we want to change, it's always "The Duke would never have stood for it" – as if we were blaspheming.'

There was so much that was wrong. To begin with, anyone who took the shilling had to sign on for twenty-one years, which, since the lower orders rarely lived to fifty, meant for life. Once in, they were liable to harsh punishments, including flogging. This combination of long service and brutal punishment had made joining the army the equivalent of a harsh prison sentence, with the result that only the worst dregs of society were willing to serve.

'We can't recruit a better sort of soldier unless we treat them better,' Southport said. 'But the officers argue that flogging is the only way to control the sort of rabble they have in the ranks. Someone has to break the circle.'

With enormous difficulty, and against fierce resistence, Cardwell had managed to get a measure of reform through, but the Act of 1868 was a compromise: flogging abolished only in peacetime; and service reduced to fourteen years – still a lifetime to men whose life expectancy was little more than forty.

Popular opinion was so hostile to the idea of a standing army that Wellington had hidden it during peacetime by stationing it in small scattered garrisons abroad. That made effective training well nigh impossible, so in 1869 Cardwell started to bring the troops home, encouraging the self-governing colonies to raise their own local defences; but the opposition was again fierce, this time from the Whig and civilian interests.

And now in 1871 the biggest battle of all was being joined:

the Army Regulation Bill, which, in addition to many other measures, was intended to abolish the system of purchasing commissions.

'The task is sisyphean,' Southport said to Charlotte a day or two after her conversation with Venetia. 'And I'm not even sure it's the right task.'

Charlotte looked her surprise. 'You don't uphold the purchase system?'

'I don't know.' Southport walked about restlessly. 'Tell me, what do you think the army is for?'

'I should have thought that was obvious,' Charlotte said. 'To defend us against attack from our enemies.'

'Then what was it doing in the Crimea?'

She thought. 'I suppose you might say it was defending the British interest.'

'And who is to define what the British interest is? If it can be something as remote as that, it might be anything. That opens the road to the one thing every Englishman dreads: military dictatorship.'

'Surely you exaggerate?' Charlotte said.

'Do I?'

She shook her head, puzzled. 'I don't understand what you're saying. The army's run like a gentleman's club, and purchase is the very heart of the system.'

'Just so.'

'But we saw in the Crimea how inefficient the army is.'

'The question is,' said Southport, 'do we want an efficient army?'

Charlotte was silent, not understanding him.

Later that day, in the drawing-room before dinner, the subject was raised again, this time by Marcus, who was dining with them.

'I must say, sir,' he said to his father crossly, standing before the fireplace with his hands under his tails like someone twice his age, 'that I wish you were doing something else for Mr Gladstone – anything but be Cardwell's right hand. It makes things dashed uncomfortable for me in the mess.'

Southport raised an eyebrow. 'A novel thought, that I should govern my actions by what makes you comfortable.'

'I don't mean to be impertinent, sir,' said Marcus, 'but after all, you did buy me my colours only a few months ago, and now here you are opposing the whole system! Well, naturally the fellows rag me.'

'They would always find something to rag you about,' Southport said lightly. 'You're the new boy. It's traditional.'

Marcus did not see the warning light. 'But this is different. I mean, buying me my colours and then trying to stop others doing the same – well, it looks like hypocrisy.'

Charlotte drew a quick breath, but Southport kept patience. 'What I suffer from, Marcus, is not hypocrisy but ambivalence.'

Marcus frowned, trying to understand. He looked so young, Charlotte thought, young and light and easy, like thistledown, ready to be blown anywhere that pleasured him; while Oliver was weighted with age and responsibility and care. She tried to remember when Oliver had been carefree, and it was difficult. But then, he had always had the dukedom ahead of him.

'But sir,' Marcus said vigorously, 'the army would be nothing without purchase! It's purchase that makes sure the right kind of fellows become officers, fellows like – well, like . . .'

'Like you,' Oliver finished for him. Marcus reddened and was silent. 'You're right of course,' Oliver resumed. 'England has never had the slightest notion of the art of war. Officers are expected to be gentlemen and sportsmen, and to cultivate a languid ignorance of all military skills. Of course, they balance it with a staggering courage in the field, which endears them to the common soldiery, brutes whose whole business is to die brutishly. So, on the whole, the system works. That's the problem.'

'Why is it a problem?' Marcus said. 'We've always beaten everybody. *That's* the proof of the pudding! Look at Marlborough! Look at Wellington! Sir, officering is an occupation for gentlemen. Abolish purchase, and you make it a trade for professionals!'

'A home thrust,' Oliver sighed. 'You come to the heart of my ambivalence. Is an inefficient army preferable to an authoritarian state?'

'Sir?' Marcus was half indignant, half puzzled.

'It seems to me that a standing army is an affront to democracy. If there's one thing this nation stands for, it's the freedom of the ordinary man to go about his business without fear that the government of the day will impose its ideas on him by force of arms.'

Charlotte glanced at him, troubled by the weary anger in his voice. She was following him now, though she saw Marcus was not. 'It sounds as though there's not much ambivalence in the case,' she said. 'You seem to me to be quite decided.'

He turned to her. 'As long as all countries had the same attitude to war, we were safe. But Prussia has broken ranks. The choice now lies between protecting our easygoing civil liberties, and protecting our country from invasion. Marcus's gentleman amateurs couldn't beat a professional army – and soon every European country will have one. Whether we like it or not, we have to remodel along Prussian lines.'

'Copy the Prussians?' Marcus protested. 'Why, one of ours is worth ten of theirs any day!'

Venetia was remembering what she had seen and heard in Berlin; recalling Marwood's words, uncannily chiming with her father's. 'Shut up, Marcus, you don't understand,' she said.

'I understand a lot more about the army than you,' he retorted. 'Professionalism would be the ruin of soldiering! It's a damned disgrace that this Bill was ever presented. In my opinion—'

Southport's temper frayed a little. 'Oh, remind me to ask for your opinion when I want it.'

'It's not just my opinion,' Marcus exclaimed hotly, 'it's everyone's, right back into history! Wellington, Raglan, Panmure, Palmerston. All your own friends, sir, past and present. Everyone supports purchase, apart from a handful of cranks. Cardwell's a damned outsider, and I say—'

Oliver had finally had enough. 'Be silent! I will not be disputed with in my own house.'

Marcus subsided, but with a just-audible grumble that 'Cardwell and Northbrook and the others had better not start on the cavalry, that was all.' The Duke affected not to have heard, and firmly changed the subject, but the atmosphere simmered all evening with Marcus's resentment and Southport's anger.

It therefore proved impossible for Charlotte to find a good moment to broach the subject of Venetia's ambition. There simply were no good moments. When she did take advantage one day of what looked like a patch of sunshine, the thunder clouds rolled in at once.

'No! Absolutely not! I won't have it. You will not, if you please, begin on that nonsense again.'

Charlotte, in loyalty to her own beliefs, as well as to her daughter, persisted a little. 'I don't think it is nonsense, Oliver. She's very sincere in this.'

'This damned woman question!' he exploded. 'It's like a creeping disease. It infects every part of professional life. That damned Garrett female has a lot to answer for – forcing her way into doctoring, worming her way onto the London School Board— !'

'She was elected to the Board,' Charlotte protested. 'She had the largest number of votes of all the candidates.'

'She should never have stood for election,' he snapped. 'Where will it end? Women at the Bar? Women in Parliament? Are we to have shrill harridans haranguing us wherever we turn?'

'We have a woman as Queen,' Charlotte said.

'The Queen was born to her position – and she knows how to behave. Look at that abominable Jex-Blake hoyden and her friends, inciting riots in Edinburgh. Is that the example you want your daughter to follow?'

'No, of course not. I should hope she would behave in a more seemly way. But after all, those women have a cause for complaint. They were refused their rightful admission—'

'Oh, you have it all pat, the revolutionary language! It's clear where Venetia gets her ideas.'

'Oliver, that's not fair!'

'I suppose I should have known, after your own antics, that your daughter would be troublesome, but I did hope some vestige of loyalty to me would have made you keep her in check.'

'She's not a child any more. She has her own ideals—'

'She's no right to have them! While she's in this house she'll do as I say!'

Charlotte tried once more, keeping her voice reasonable. 'Is it so very terrible an ambition, to want to save life? Don't you believe we are all made equal in spirit?'

'We may be equal but we are not the same. There is something grotesque and prurient about this desire to know what is patently not fit to be known by a female. Well, I have more care for her than you seem to. I shall not allow her to debase and unsex herself. And that's my last word on the subject.'

Charlotte was sorry to have provoked him, knowing how overburdened he was with work and worry, and told Venetia that the subject was closed. Venetia, however, would not accept it.

'I'll find a way, in spite of Papa,' she said angrily. 'I'm over twenty-one. He can't stop me doing what I want.'

'Don't be silly, darling, of course he can,' Charlotte said.

And for the time being, Venetia could not see any way of circumventing her father's embargo. She felt lonely and embattled. There was no-one to discuss the problem with. Olivia was in waiting again, at Windsor, where she had been in time to witness Princess Louise's wedding to Lord Lorne. Fanny was still at Ravendene, for she had caught a chill in February, and the country air was thought better for her than Town.

In the end it was to Tommy Weston that she unburdened herself. He called one day, knowing that Olivia was away and thinking she might be lonely. She was 'not at home', but Ungar, the butler, admitted him anyway as a privileged relative.

'You weren't at the opening of the exhibition yesterday – I thought you would be. But I suppose as you're in mourning you aren't going about at the moment?' Tommy said.

'Oh, it isn't that,' Venetia said. 'We're only in half-mourning now. I just don't feel like seeing anyone.'

'Shall I go?'

'I don't count you – you're always welcome.'

'Thank you, ma'am,' he said with an ironic bow. 'Would you like me to stay and chat? Or would you like to go for a walk?'

'Oh, yes, a walk,' Venetia said. 'Anything to get out of this house! Wait while I put on my hat.'

It was a grey and blowy day, but pleasantly mild after the frosts of last month. They crossed the Mall into St James's Park, where daffodils were bending madly under the trees and the surface of the lake was ruffled up like snagged silk. At Buckingham Palace they crossed into Green Park and walked up Constitution Hill. Venetia set a brisk pace as she talked, her black-gloved hand light on his arm, her face under her veil tilted forward as though she could get along faster by willing it. Tommy could tell how agitated she was, because she did not spare so much as a glance at the horses cantering past them on the tan.

'How badly do you want this?' he asked when she came to the end of her fulminations.

'It's *all* I want,' she said. 'Can you doubt it? And don't tell me I don't know how bad it would be. Four months in a war hospital in Berlin is enough to prove anyone.'

'No need to bite my head off,' he said. 'I'm just making sure.'

'Making sure of what?' she said impatiently. 'Tommy, I've read everything I can lay my hands on, my general education is good, I'm intelligent, I learn quickly, and I've had experience of what it's like on a ward. If I were a man, no-one would doubt my sincerity, or my ability. If I were Marcus, Papa would think my ambition praiseworthy. It makes no *sense* to deny me this, simply because I have a female body.'

'A lot of things in life make no sense,' Tommy said mildly. 'You are twenty-one, legally independent. What if you defied him?' Venetia stopped dead and turned to look at him searchingly. 'Go to the hospitals. Apply to the medical schools. Try and find doctors willing to admit you. What's the worst your father could do?'

She tried to imagine it. Her father's wrath – awful! She had always been afraid of him. But what could he actually *do*? His influence was considerable, but not all-pervading. There must

216

be *some* doctors who would not care for his anger. She couldn't apply to the Southport, of course, if her parents were against her; but there were other hospitals.

'He could turn me from the house,' she said at last.

'Yes, you'd have to leave home,' Tommy agreed. 'But there are respectable lodging-houses that take in females.'

'He'd disown me. Refuse to see me. Stop my allowance,' she concluded on a downward note. That was the leveller. The only money she had was from her father; she had no way to support herself without it.

But Tommy said easily, 'Don't worry about money. The thing is—'

'The thing is,' Venetia mocked him, 'that I would have to have something to live on, quite apart from fees, and books, and instruments and I don't know what else.'

'But I've plenty of money,' he said. 'I'd give you whatever you needed.'

Venetia's eyes opened wide. 'I couldn't possibly take money from you!'

'Why not? Don't be silly. I've more than I can ever use, and I'm your cousin after all.'

'But Papa would be furious – your father would be furious.'

'Well, perhaps we wouldn't tell them,' he said indulgently, as though she had said something foolish. 'The thing is, I believe in you, and I think your ambition is splendid. You ought to succeed, and I'll do anything I can to see that you do.'

'Tommy, you're very kind, but I *couldn't*. It just isn't done. Not the thing at all.'

'Then you're not serious about this.'

'I *am*!'

He smiled. 'I never thought I'd hear you saying something was not the thing!'

'I'm not a complete hoyden,' she protested. 'And I couldn't possibly sponge on you.'

He shrugged. 'We'd better turn round. I ought to be getting you back.'

They walked in silence a while, retracing their steps. Then

217

he said, 'I'm glad you aren't serious about it. It would be awful for you, you know – much worse than for Miss Garrett.'

'Why so?'

'Because you are Lady Venetia Fleetwood. And you are very beautiful. Those things would tell against you.'

She made a face. 'Phooey!'

'It's true.' He looked at her in her lavender wool gown and grey paletot trimmed with ermine tails, the neat bonnet under the veil, decorated with a bunch of artificial violets, everything about her elegant, unselfconsciously wealthy. 'How could *you* live in lodgings, and wear ugly clothes, and do ugly things, and drudge and toil?' he said. 'And if you ever were to succeed as a doctor, you would become hard-faced and mannish and be everywhere an outsider, and I would hate that for you. You ought to get married.'

'Oh, of course!'

'No, I don't mean it like that,' he said with a faint smile. 'I mean, I think the married state would suit you, that you would be very unhappy if you never married, whatever else you did.'

'If I were going to be a doctor, I couldn't marry,' she said flatly. 'It would be impossible.'

They were silent a while longer. 'I'm not sure I'd have the courage to go through with it,' she said at last, 'the way you describe it. I'd always pictured having my mother's help. To be all alone, cast out from the family, no Mama, no Olivia—' She shook her head. 'But on the other hand, what do I do with my life? Go to balls and dinners, the theatre, ride in the Row, another Season, and another after that. How could I bear it?'

'That's what you will have to discover,' Tommy said.

March turned to April, Olivia came home again, and Charlotte decreed the girls could come out of mourning. The young people might have been waiting at the street corner, so quickly did they arrive at the door as soon as the Fleetwood girls were known to be receiving. They resumed the social round; but it was not like before.

Venetia did not sparkle; sometimes she seemed positively

irritable towards her former courtiers. At balls she might dance every dance with an almost frenzied abandon, or moodily refuse to stand up at all. She took to walking in the park alone except for her maid, who loathed the exercise and trailed along behind her with her head down and a scowl on her face. She rode in the Row at unfashionable hours, accompanied only by a groom, heavily veiled and hardly acknowledging anyone else who happened to be about.

It was on one of these solitary rides that she encountered Mr Winchmore, who paced his horse alongside hers and addressed her several times before she noticed him.

'You are in an absolute reverie,' he said. 'What is it, Lady Venetia? Can you tell me?'

'Oh, it's nothing,' she said lightly.

'Don't brush me off. You haven't been yourself for weeks now. You danced with Fred Paston *twice* at the Grosvenors'.'

'Did I?'

He smiled, flashing his famously beautiful teeth. 'I *thought* it wasn't intentional. He was quite obnoxious about it all yesterday, until I told him you hadn't an idea he was there at all. Unfortunately, I don't suppose you remember you danced with me, either.'

'I always remember when I dance with you, Beauty. You do it so divinely.'

'Oh my God, she's being kind to me!' he cried, rolling his eyes. 'Anything but that!'

An unwilling smile tugged at her lips. 'Ass!'

'Better,' he said. 'Can't you tell me your trouble?'

'I have something on my mind, that's all.'

'That much is obvious. What is it, goddess?'

She yielded at last. 'My future. What I should do with my life. I can't go on like this for ever.'

'I should hope not,' he said promptly. 'Marry me.'

'I'm being serious,' she chided.

'So am I.'

'Beauty, I can't marry you. I can't marry anyone.'

'Why not?'

'Because I mean to be a doctor.' As she said it, a shaft of watery April sunlight slid through the moving clouds and illuminated the tan before them. She laughed shakily. 'There, you see! The finger of God. Wouldn't you call that a pretty convincing sign?'

'As signs go, it's a good one,' he agreed. 'An eagle dropping a naked child into your arms would be better, but I'm prepared to stretch a point.'

'I'm serious about this,' she said.

'I know you are. I can only beg you not to be. Venetia, don't do this. It will make you very unhappy. It will make everyone who loves you very unhappy.'

'Anyone who loves me ought to be glad I'm going to do what I want.' She drew a deep breath. 'I wasn't absolutely sure until this moment, but now I am. I'm *going* to do it.'

'I'm quite sure your father won't let you.'

'My father can't stop me. I'm over twenty-one. I'm going to leave home, find myself some modest rooms in a respectable house, and badger the medical men until they admit me to their classes and lectures. I shall take a false name and wear very plain clothes so that they'll take me seriously – and they shall, I promise you.'

'What would you live on?'

'Oh, that's all arranged,' she said lightly. 'I shan't need much, anyway. I'm going to do it, Beauty!'

'You can't,' he said desperately, believing her at last. 'You really, really can't!'

'Oh, but I can,' she said, and for the first time she believed it too, right down to her toes.

CHAPTER THIRTEEN

The long day was ending. Sunset had stained the sky and dusk had drained it, and now Henrietta could see nothing beyond the carriage windows but the small moving patch of grass verge and hedgerow lit by the carriage lamps. The train from York had been a slow one, stopping everywhere, and they had not reached Northallerton until five by the station clock. There they had been met by Mr Fortescue's own vehicle, and his elderly coachman had set such a cautious pace over the winding, uneven road to Richmond that darkness had overtaken them. Henrietta had no idea what the time was now, but it felt very late. The coach was stuffy and cold, and she was aching with tiredness and had fidgets in her legs from sitting so long. So much had happened since she woke that morning that a sense of strained unreality had settled over her.

The wedding had been at eleven o'clock (*her wedding* – how strange it seemed to put those two words together!) but she had been awake since before six. The morning had passed in an exhausting slow bustle, with her seeming to be always in someone's way, or not where she was urgently wanted. George had the right idea: he had taken himself out of the way, going up to Twelvetrees very early, coming back only in time to dress. Teddy was not coming until later – he had left Morland Place now and was living in his own house on the corner of Nunnery Lane.

The kitchen had been in a state of siege over the wedding feast to come, and tense with the ongoing clash between Kemp and Mrs Marlow, both of whom had felt it was their right to make the wedding cake. Alfreda had devised a compromise – that Mrs Marlow should bake it and Kemp decorate it – which satisfied neither. In consequence there had been no proper breakfast, just bread and butter on trays taken up to the bedrooms – which annoyed the housemaids, who said they already had too much to do. Mrs Holicar had quarrelled with Goole for using both sculleries for washing glasses when she wanted to be washing china. Fanie had been in a temper because Hayter had commandeered the large smoothing-iron. Regina had hysterics over the curl of her hair not being right, and when Bittle smacked her she threw the pin-pot at her and broke the glass on the mantel clock. And through it all, Alfreda glided with an unnatural, terrifying calm which paradoxically seemed to wind everyone else tighter than watch-springs.

But the ceremony itself, in the chapel, had been beautiful, and a thing of lovely tranquillity by contrast with all the fuss before it. Mr Hughes had presided; the chapel, shining and sweet with beeswax, glowed with candles and flowers. Henrietta had walked up the aisle on George's arm in her gown of white silk taffeta and the veil of Brussels lace lent by Lady Anstey. In a dream she had heard those most familiar of words, *Dearly beloved, we are gathered here in the sight of God*; heard her own voice, faint and childlike, make her vows, and Mr Fortescue's, strong and mellifluous, make his; felt the touch of his hand and watched the ring being pushed onto her finger.

Afterwards in the great hall the tenants, estate workers and villagers had presented their good wishes. Then the cake had been wheeled in – a towering fortress of white sugar-paste on a trolley – and servants, guests and everyone had crowded round, and cheered as Henrietta and Mr Fortescue cut it. Then the guests had retired to the dining-room for the feast, while Goole and Mrs Holicar supervised the distribution of cake and bounties. Henrietta had been glad about that, remembering what Old Caleb had told her. Her wedding, at least, had done right by the house and its people, and perhaps it would make up for the master's.

The feast had been magnificent – though Henrietta's emotions had been too turbulent and her corset too tight for her to eat much of it – and there had been a great many toasts and as many speeches, including one from Mr Fortescue in which he had referred to her, with a smile, as 'my wife', which had made her blush and everyone else, for some reason, laugh.

My wife. She was a married woman; she was Mrs Fortescue. No, it was impossible to believe. It was hardly more than three months since that evening when Mr Fortescue had walked around the floor with her at the ball. Things seemed to have moved so quickly – and in another way to have drifted detached from time altogether. He had dined with them, walked once or twice with her, well muffled up, in the gardens, shown her a courteous attention which both thrilled and terrified her. Alfreda's looks and nods told her that *she* thought he meant something by it; but Henrietta dreaded an embarrassing revelation. She imagined his grave disapproval when he realised anyone could have been so uncouth as to suppose he was making love to her; imagined his disappointment in her that *she* could have supposed it.

Then came the day in February when he proposed to her while they were walking in the parterre. The flowerbeds were bare, the box edging grey with frost, the sky yellowish with the threat of snow. In the still, frozen noon their footsteps had crunched echoingly on the gravel. He stopped and turned to face her, and in a quiet, intent voice told her that he loved her with a great passion, that she was in his thoughts night and day, and that his dearest wish was to make her his wife.

The air had seemed to sing against her ears, though it was a still and windless day; the light had seemed strange and clear, as though she were at the top of a great mountain, seeing things at once vividly close and impossibly far away. His face had been etched against the sky as though it were rimmed in light, the grave, noble features sculpted, surely, by some divine hand. Behind him she had seen a flick of movement as a robin came down onto one of the urns, its breast bright as a rowan berry, and she had wondered at the tiny, sharp perfection of it. She no longer felt the pain of cold in her fingers and toes, or the sting of the bitter air on her cheeks: she might have had no body for all she was aware of it. With a sense of utter unreality she had answered humbly, gratefully, that she wished it too; and he had taken her gloved hand in his, and leaning down had kissed her cheek.

After that, it seemed that the wedding had taken over all of them as though it were a separate entity with a life of its own. Mr Fortescue had suggested they marry in mid-April, for that was a time when he normally visited his other parish, just outside Richmond. The visit there might serve as her honeymoon: the Yorkshire dales were very pretty in spring. She had hardly seen him as the weeks of the betrothal passed in a whirl of visits, congratulations, wedding presents, shopping, fittings and plans. She had been in the grip of an increasing sense of unreality, as though she were reading a story and simultaneously taking part in it; and the moment when he had said he loved her seemed further and further away, receding beyond history into legend or fairy tale.

The carriage slowed from its already slow pace and then lurched violently as it turned a right angle. She heard Mr Fortescue stir in the darkness beside her. He said, 'We're here,' the first breaking of the silence since they had left Northallerton. Now the wheels were grinding over gravel; the carriage swung in a slow arc – round a sweep, presumably – and stopped. A moment later the door was opened and the step let down, and a man in waistcoat and gaiters was holding up a lantern with one hand and extending the other to help Henrietta out.

She stepped down onto the gravel before a square stone house. After the stuffiness of the carriage, the air smelled coldly, freshly green. She shivered a little. There was no moon; beyond the circle of light from the coach lamps was darkness and the night rustle of leaves, and far away the sharp, clear bark of a fox; she looked up at the house, and saw its roof-line black against the starry sky. Someone had opened the house door now, spilling light into the porch, and Mr Fortescue had stepped down beside her, and was offering his arm. 'Come, my dear,' he said. She put her hand (how far away it seemed) on his sleeve and walked forward, through the porch, into a hall.

It was oak panelled, and smelled cold and old, with the faint, sweet odour of dry rot, like a church. There was a long-case clock against the panelling on the right, whose hands stood at just before eight, and which was making throat-clearing noises in preparation to strike. Eight o'clock – imagine! She had been married for almost nine hours.

A woman stood in front of them, in a black dress with apron and cap, hands folded before her; a dark, fleshy face with heavy eyebrows and a forbidding expression.

'Ah, Mrs Allen,' said Mr Fortescue.

'We thought you'd never get here, sir,' she said. 'That Grimshaw drives so slowly.' Her eyes moved significantly to Henrietta, whom she regarded with evident disapproval.

'My dear, this is Mrs Allen, my housekeeper. She and her husband take care of me when I am at Swale House. Mrs Allen – my wife.'

Mr Fortescue seemed to have no difficulty with the words, though they made Henrietta blush again. She moved to shake the housekeeper's hand, but the woman kept hers folded over her stomach as she dropped the slightest possible curtsy, and Henrietta felt snubbed.

'Dinner can be on t' table whenever you like, sir,' Mrs Allen said, turning her attention to her master as though consigning Henrietta to oblivion. For the moment Henrietta didn't care. Someone had mentioned dinner! She scented the air hopefully, but the kitchen must have been very remote or well sealed for there wasn't so much as a hint of soup on it.

'In half an hour, then,' said Mr Fortescue. 'You will show Mrs Fortescue to her room. Oh, and tell Allen to bring up champagne. Mrs Fortescue is not accustomed to wine, but she will take a glass of champagne on this occasion.'

'Very good, sir,' said Mrs Allen, as though it were not very good at all. With a slight bow of the head to Henrietta, Mr Fortescue took himself off to a room across the hall, just as the gaitered man, who Henrietta thought must be a groom, came in with her luggage. He looked old and frail, and the valises dwarfed him. Henrietta felt she ought to offer to help.

'This way, madam,' said Mrs Allen, and led the way upstairs. Henrietta followed, and the man stumped after her with her valises under his arms, their footsteps clonking hollowly on the bare polished boards. Upstairs was a passage with several doors off it, and a further staircase going upwards. Mrs Allen opened a door and stepped back to allow Henrietta to enter. In the lamplight from the passage she saw more bare boards, but with a square of carpet in the middle; no panelling here, but red flock wallpaper, rather rubbed in places; red velvet curtains drawn tight, heavy dark furniture, a high bed with a white counterpane. The man came past her and dumped the cases heavily on the floor, while Mrs Allen lit the candles: two in sconces over the mantel, one on the dressing-table, two in brackets sprouting like antlers from the cheval glass. The room was large, and their light did little to brighten it.

The man had already departed, breathing heavily from his exertions, and now Mrs Allen was withdrawing, saying only, 'Dinner in half an hour, then,' as she reached back to close the door. There were so many things Henrietta didn't know, and would have eagerly asked if the least opening had been granted her. She was confused and afraid, and had no idea what was to happen next or how she was to cope with it; she was tired and hungry and she wanted to go home. The realisation had just come to her that Morland Place was not home any more, and she would not be going back there again.

'Oh please,' she said desperately; and Mrs Allen paused, but without removing her hand from the doorknob or offering to step back inside. Not to that resolutely uninviting face could Henrietta address the babble of questions that tumbled round her brain; but she picked one out of the froth which was, if not the most important, at least the most immediate. 'Must I – should I change my dress?'

Mrs Allen looked as if for two pins she would refuse to answer; but at last she said merely, 'Mr Fortescue always changes for dinner,' then stepped out and closed the door terminally behind her.

Alone in the dimly lit room, Henrietta was close to tears. There was so much she didn't know. She must change, but what into? How fine must she be? To get it wrong either way would be awful. Was this Mr Fortescue's room too? Would he come here in the next half-hour? And how would she know when half an hour was up? Where should she go when she went downstairs? And how should she conduct herself alone at dinner with a strange man whom she must now call husband?

After a few minutes, fear of being late roused her from her useless panic, and she looked round the room. She could not wash, for there was no water: the jug inside the ewer was empty. No fire was lit, though the night was chilly and the air felt damp as well as cold. And no-one had offered to unpack for her, or even to unstrap her bags. Little as she knew about the rules of entertainment, this seemed churlish. Was it because they were so late arriving? If they had come at a better hour, would her reception have been kinder?

She knelt down and unstrapped her bags herself, opened them, took out her brushes, and lifted out the first few gowns, laying them over the end of the bed. It would have to be the dark blue silk, she realised suddenly, because she could not fasten any of the other evening gowns herself, since they fastened up the back. She hoped the blue was fine enough – it had only a moderate bustle and hardly any train, though it was low cut. She had never thought to wonder who would help her dress once she was married. Someone must: she could not pull her own laces to the restriction Fanie and Alfreda thought necessary, and her gowns would not fit without. As she took off her travelling costume she did not even know if the blue silk would fit, for she was laced quite lightly for travelling.

The blue went on, just, though the stitches in the waistband creaked, and the lower buttons strained. She prayed none would go flying off during dinner. With some pushing and pulling she managed to get her bosom in the right position for the *décolletage*. The gown really needed another petticoat to hold the skirt out properly, but she could not now bend down to search for one. With a handkerchief and the water from the drinking-bottle by the bedside, she cleaned the smuts from her face and rubbed her hands, and then did what she could to tidy her hair. The low-cut gown needed a necklace, but she had no idea where the box containing her few trinkets was, so all she could do was to keep on the locket she had been wearing with her travelling-costume. It had been Mr Fortescue's betrothal

227

present to her, and she wore it on a black velvet ribbon, which was not right for the blue silk, but what else could she do?

Was it half an hour yet? There was no clock in the room, and no sound in the house to guide her. She went to the door and opened it cautiously, peeping out. No movement anywhere – no clock in sight, either – but then to her relief she heard one somewhere – the one in the hall perhaps – strike the half. Time to go. She drew herself up, took a few calming breaths, and ventured downstairs.

While she was hesitating at the foot of the stairs, an old man with white side-whiskers that met under his chin came from a passage at the far side with a tray in his hands. They stopped in surprise at seeing each other – though his surprise seemed bordering on disbelief. She blushed, and stammered, 'I – I don't know where to go.'

He roused himself from some mental quagmire and said, 'The master's in the breakfast parlour, madam. If you would follow me.'

He led her down another passage, opened a door for her, and she stepped into a small, cosy, well-lit room, with a young fire burning eagerly in the grate. An oval table in the centre of the room was laid with snowy cloth, china and silver sparkling under a branch of candles. There were armchairs to either side of the fire and a settle under the window, all upholstered in rose pink to match the thick pink and white carpet which covered the floor. The contrast with the gloom of the hall and her bedroom could not have been greater, and she felt suddenly hungry and hopeful.

And there was Mr Fortescue, standing by the fireplace, leaning an elbow on the overmantel and gazing into the flames. He had changed into evening black-and-white, and as he turned to her she thought how well it suited him, and how handsome he looked – if handsome were not too ordinary a word for him.

'Ah, there you are!' he said. 'Well, well. Good. Excellent. We dine quite informally tonight, in view of the occasion and the late hour. The breakfast parlour is not quite – but I thought it might be more pleasant to you than the dining-room, just this once.'

'It is a very pretty room,' she said shyly. Was it possible –
was it *possible* – that he was nervous? He seemed not quite
composed, talking more quickly, moving his hands, glancing
at her and away again.

'Is it? Yes, I suppose it is. The previous occupant had a wife
and daughters, and I believe this was the room the ladies sat
in. Well, now, Allen, is that the champagne? Very good. You
will take a glass, my dear? Good. You must be hungry. We
will sit down at table straight away, if you please.'

He came and drew out her chair for her himself, and then
sat down opposite her. She was rigid with shyness, and kept
her eyes lowered, but felt him looking at her all the same,
as though he were touching her face with every glance. She
hoped he was not looking in disapproval. Was she correctly
dressed? Had she missed a smut?

Allen came to pour champagne into her glass, and then
removed the covers from the dishes disposed about the table.

'Thank you, Allen,' Mr Fortescue said. 'I will ring when I
want you.'

The soft click of the door latch as the servant left them told
her she was alone with her husband. There was nothing to be
done but to look up. He was watching her quizzically. But he
only said, 'We will say grace.'

She folded her hands, and he gave the grace in Latin; she
thought it sounded lovely. After the amen he coughed and
raised his glass. 'To our happiness,' he said; but there seemed
almost a question mark in his tone.

The wine was a beautiful pale gold, and smelled like apples.
She put the glass down, and surveyed the table with dismay.
The whole dinner, it seemed, was there, arranged on the
table in dishes amongst the salts, breads, pickles and fruit.
There was some kind of a fish under a shiny sauce, a roasted
duck decorated with dried cherries, a dish of stewed celery,
another of mushrooms, a small raised pie, something white
and mounded – potato perhaps – and something soft and
pink that looked like a pudding. There was also, just to her
right, a small tureen of soup – carrot, to judge by the colour.
She was desperately hungry and it all looked inviting, but at
Alfreda's dinners everything was handed round by servants.

She hadn't the least idea in the world how to get this food from its containers and into herself. She knew how stern Alfreda was about etiquette, particularly at meals. She was going to be shamed before her husband, and he would despise her for her ignorance and gaucherie.

'Is something wrong?' Mr Fortescue asked after a moment.

Henrietta, locked in a fog of embarrassment, her cheeks burning, said, 'Oh! No – I – no, not at all.'

Another agonising minute passed, and then Fortescue said in a quite different voice, 'Perhaps you would care to help me to some soup, Mrs Fortescue. The bowls are there, to your left.'

She saw the bowls; and a ladle lying beside the tureen. Feeling a complete fool, she served soup into a bowl, looked up, and found Mr Fortescue's hand ready across the table to take it from her. She served herself, replaced the ladle in the tureen, and seeing from under her eyelashes that he was eating, picked up her spoon and began.

The soup was good, and restored her. After a few spoonfuls she had courage to look at him again, and found that he was smiling.

'I see you are wearing the locket I gave you,' he said tenderly. His voice and his expression made her feel warm and weak and fluttery.

'It is my dearest possession,' she heard herself say.

Mr Fortescue was almost as bewildered as Henrietta to find himself in this position. He had woken on the day after the ball feeling bemused and inclined to wonder if he had imagined it all. He'd taken his usual breakfast and retired to his study for his morning's work, but the words on the page would not penetrate his mind, and he saw instead a sweet, suffering face, a shy smile, limpid eyes, thick, soft hair confined with pins and ornaments.

What would she look like with her hair loose? Like a wood nymph, he decided; imagined her bare feet white against the emerald turf of a wood; and had to get up from his desk and walk about the room briskly for some minutes. His mind, usually so ordered, was filled with softly tumbling words, indistinct images – sensations rather than structured thoughts. She had disturbed him in a way he had thought he had gone beyond long ago.

He paused by a bookshelf, hesitated, then drew out an unfamiliar volume, one whose pages he had rarely turned, its fine leather binding almost pristine despite its age, some of its pages still uncut. It was not his usual mental fare; but in his present state of mind, the words, remembered over years, called to him.

She walks in beauty, like the night
Of cloudless climes and starry skies.

He had been in Italy when he was younger, he remembered nights like that. He imagined her there, where the darkness was velvet soft and fragrant with pine and myrtle and the crickets sang endlessly; where the cypresses cut dark shapes out of the starry canopy, and the caressing air, warm as wine, rocked to the distant murmur of the sea.

Too bewitching! Sensuality was something he knew himself vulnerable to, something he had always sought to deny himself. He was about to close the tempting, unfamiliar volume, when the last stanza caught his eye.

And on that cheek, and o'er that brow,
So soft, so calm, yet eloquent,
The smiles that win, the tints that glow,
But tell of days in goodness spent,
A mind at peace with all below,
A heart whose love is innocent!

Yes, yes, that was it! That was what called to him – surely? Not sensuality, but virtue! The heart whose love was innocent; days spent in goodness. That good, sweet, innocent girl was a prisoner of the worldly Morlands – waiting to be delivered by one who could appreciate her qualities! *The smiles that win* – they must be for him alone. When she had looked up at him (*the tints that glow* – her bewitching blush) there had been that in her eyes which he had seen there for no-one else. She must be rescued, and by him: carried away from that place and brought here, installed in his home where her gentle goodness would bloom under his loving care, and in turn inspire him to ever greater work.

He restored Lord Byron to his place, happy with his resolve now it had been given the appropriate form. But he had never courted a woman, and had no idea how to go about it; hardly knew, indeed, how he was to see her, since he was neither an intimate nor a neighbour of the Morlands.

By the following day, the spell was wearing off. It was impossible, he decided, to break the habits of a lifetime, to seek out the Morlands, to endure their company – and for a girl he had seen only twice? A girl – and he a man past the years of folly, who had lived the life of men for too long to change? He would let the cobwebs of illusion dissolve, as they would in time.

And then George Morland had called, on horseback – 'just taking him in on his way', though it was unclear where he was going to or from – to issue an invitation to a day's shooting and dinner afterwards. Fortescue was a fine shot and enjoyed the sport on his own and friends' estates; but then George added rather self-consciously, 'and Henrietta will be there, of course; she will be glad to see you'.

So, he thought grimly, his attention to the young lady had been noted, had it? He acquitted Morland of archness – the young man was plainly ill at ease with that part of his mission. No, it was Mrs Morland who was busy machinating, and the idea revolted him. He was on the brink of refusing the invitation loftily – the vulgar woman should not weave him in her toils! – when he thought of Henrietta, and how she would undoubtedly be made to suffer if he refused. It was only hours before that he had been wondering how to further his acquaintance with her. Fate was evidently taking a hand.

So he drew a deep breath and accepted loftily; gave George some sherry and let him talk for a while about the hunting, the weather and his in-foal mares, and sent him happily on his way; and retired to his fire again to brood over the worldliness of Mrs Morland. How intolerably it must grate on Henrietta's sensibilities.

As the weeks passed he found himself subject to a painful ambivalence. Henrietta was a sweet, sad and innocent creature he longed to rescue, but every time Alfreda helped his courtship along he felt a revulsion. He wanted to back away from her trap – except that it was a trap he had chosen for himself. He ought to be grateful to Alfreda for helping him, and yet wanted to do anything rather than gratify her.

That day when he had walked with Henrietta in the parterre, he had been very far from knowing his own mind. A strange, still, frozen day it was, like a day outside time; every sound magnified in the white silence, so that the gravel crunched like glass, and his voice seemed to bounce off the distant trees and come back to him strangely distorted.

She had listened to him, as she always did, with such intentness she seemed almost to *eat* his words; and he did not doubt that they were a food she craved, trapped as she was in that unintellectual household, where animals and fashion were the sole topics of conversation. He had stopped and turned to look at her intently, and she had stopped too, glanced shyly at him, and then down, her eyelashes making dark crescents on her cheeks. What white eyelids she had, he had thought; like the petals of a camellia, rich, curving and almost translucent. He imagined himself kissing them as she lay sleeping, her loose hair spread about her head like flowing fire; he saw her smooth throat, the tender hollows of her collarbone, brushed with a feather of shadow . . .

The heat of his images burned in the frozen day, his blood rushed, and he had said the words he had never thought to hear himself saying.

Once they were said, there was no going back. Even had it been possible in social terms, he could not have betrayed Henrietta. But as the wedding took over, building a momentum of its own that carried them all along like scraps of straw on a winter stream, he doubted more and more often; wondered whether it had not after all been a trap; wondered even whether he had been mistaken in Henrietta. The indecent triumph of Mrs Morland, the way she pressed him for an early date, the care she took that he should never be alone with Henrietta, reminded him of what he already knew: that he was the kind of match they could never have hoped for. She had no dowry – Morland at least had the grace to blush about that. In the face of Mr Fortescue's grave look he had stammered a little and then blurted out that he would give Henrietta a fine riding horse as a present, and Mr Fortescue's pride had made him respond that he was quite well able to provide his wife with a horse.

And today the wedding – oh the wedding! The chapel itself was interesting, and old Hughes had stumbled through the rite well enough – though Fortescue's astonishment at finding himself on the other end of it had been considerable; but the noise and clamour, the bucolic feasting, the triumphalism, the nothingness of the conversation, had left him with a headache and a feeling of resentment which even encompassed his always-silent bride.

The slow train and the slower drive had aggravated his sciatica, and his silence in the carriage was of repressed irritability, so that when he arrived at the house all he wanted to do was to get away by himself. But when he had changed and taken a glass of sherry, he felt more composed; and when Henrietta came into the breakfast parlour, slender and shy, his resentment against her vanished. He had chosen his fate, after all: he must face it like a man. But still there was trepidation. What did he really know of her? Was she what he had imagined? Had she perhaps been forced to accept him? Or, worse, was she as worldly as Mrs Morland, wanting only a good match? The thought of spending a lifetime with someone like that appalled him.

And then they had sat at the table together, and he saw that she did not know how to manage a dinner à l'anglais. She was ashamed of her ignorance, but he wanted to leap up and shout a paean. She was truly innocent! Not a co-conspirator, but a young girl so little acquainted with the world of fashion she did not know how to eat her dinner! The desire he had felt at first to protect her leapt up again like a stirred fire; he wanted only to know that she cared for him, that she had not been bullied into the match, for the last of his resistance to dissolve.

'I see you are wearing the locket I gave you,' he said

with tender significance, and her cheeks bloomed like rose velvet.

'It is my dearest possession,' she said.

Henrietta enjoyed that meal as no other she had ever eaten. She was hungry and the food, though not a rival to Kemp's, was good; but it was not that, it was the companionship. She had eaten meals at tables with other people present, but she had never before eaten in company as she did with Mr Fortescue that night. He talked – how he talked! – and she listened, ravished by the sound of his voice, the poetry of his words, his mastery of language and thought. Often she did not understand what he was saying, not with her brain, at least, but she felt so at one with him that she somehow knew what he meant, and when to laugh and when to wonder. She drank a little champagne, just enough to detach her from self-consciousness. She smiled, she listened, her eyes now always on his face. He was talking *for her*, and the wonder of it made her confident; and she saw that her appreciation spurred him on into fresh eloquence. His words became more than thought articulated and more than sound; they seemed to have a physical presence, she rode the stream of them as she would have ridden a barebacked horse, feeling its power and its silken heat under her, and the intoxicating wind of speed in her face.

When the eating was over they removed to the chairs by the fire without, miraculously, breaking the mood; and he talked to her of Italy, his travels there as a youth, how it was one of the cradles of civilisation. He told her of white temples and black cypresses, cerulean skies and wine-dark seas, olive groves and oleanders, and the cricket-singing heat that came up from the ground, to meet the sun's warmth that fell like Danaë's shower all around you.

'Danaë, the mother of Perseus,' he said. 'Perseus, who rescued Andromeda from the rock.' He stood up abruptly, and reaching out both hands raised Henrietta to her feet. She trembled at the sudden physical contact, but she was not afraid. She looked up into his face, and he seemed flushed – though perhaps it was the glow of the fire. 'Time to go to bed,' he said. She waited, looking questioningly at him for further instructions. He released her hands. 'Go along,' he said. 'I will follow.'

She went. Stepping out into the hall from the warm, pink-lit parlour was like stepping out of Mr Fortescue's Italy: chill and dark and damp-smelling were the panelled passages and bare wooden stairs. She hurried, hearing her hollow footsteps like someone knocking in nails, hurried shivering to her room. Someone had kindled a fire in her absence, but it was low and almost out, and had done little for the chill of the room; only the bedside candle was alight and its feeble glimmer left all the corners in darkness.

Thinking anxiously of Mr Fortescue's 'I will follow' and feeling she would shrivel with embarrassment if he caught her half done, she dragged her clothes off almost in a panic and put on her nightdress, which someone had laid out on the bed, pulled out her pins and brushed her hair by feel. She was preparing to plait it when she thought she heard a footstep outside, and scampered like a startled mouse into bed, pulling the covers up to her chin. When no-one immediately appeared, she took the time to compose herself, straightening her nightdress and arranging her hair, and then lay with her hands folded over her chest in what she hoped was a proper pose.

But no-one came. Her candle burned lower, and soon she fell asleep; and when it guttered and went out she was far away in a deep dream, and still alone.

She was woken in the morning by the curtains being drawn noisily. Struggling up onto one elbow she saw Mrs Allen fastening them back; across the room a very small, thin maid was on her knees making up the fire.

Mrs Allen turned and looked at Henrietta with disfavour. 'I let you sleep,' she said, in the tone of voice in which she might have said, 'I saw you steal that sheep.'

'What time is it?' Henrietta asked meekly.

'Almost nine.'

'Goodness! I don't think I've ever slept so long,' Henrietta marvelled.

'Mr Fortescue's gone out on parish business,' said Mrs Allen. 'You're to entertain yourself until luncheon.'

The memory of last night flooded back – the rapture and the failure. He didn't come – did that mean he was disappointed in her? Had she upset him? 'What am I to do?' she asked.

Mrs Allen made a small movement of large impatience, the sort which if Henrietta had been a small child might have ended in a slap. 'Goodness, *I* don't know. There's plenty to amuse a person, I should have thought. Now, your water's here, and I'll send up your breakfast on a tray—'

'Oh please, I'd sooner come down,' Henrietta said quickly.

'It'll be much less trouble for everyone on a tray,' Mrs Allen said forbiddingly. 'The dining-room's been cleared and the girl's done the polishing. We don't want another lot of fingermarks.'

'No. I see,' Henrietta said. The maid had finished with the fire, and stood up carefully with her box in her hand and her head bent as though it were hailing. Henrietta sympathised.

Mrs Allen looked to see what she was looking at and said sharply, 'All right, Minney, off you go. You've plenty to get on with downstairs.'

And with that she, too, was going; and though Henrietta had rather do almost anything else, she was forced to call her back. 'Oh, please, Mrs Allen—' She turned. 'Is – is there someone to help me dress?'

'*Help you dress?*' The housekeeper gave her most boiled look.

Henrietta flushed before it. 'I can't do up my own laces, not tightly enough.' Still Mrs Allen stared. 'My gowns won't fit without.'

'Well, I never heard the like,' Mrs Allen said on an expiration of shocked disapproval. Henrietta was close to tears. 'Well, I suppose it can't be helped *now*,' she went on grumblingly. *Now*, Henrietta guessed, meant *now Mr Fortescue's married you*. 'You'd better ring when you're ready and I'll send the girl up.' And with that she went away, her heels clicking angrily on the bare boards.

After washing, breakfast, and the inept ministrations of 'the girl' – who turned out to be another housemaid, Lizbeth, a degree less small and thin than Minney but equally cowed – Henrietta ventured downstairs. The hall was deserted, but the front door stood open on the bright day, and with a sense of relief she ventured out. In her life before George had married Alfreda, she had hardly spent an hour a day indoors; since their marriage, she had hardly spent one outside.

The sky was high and pale, the air clear and with a bite in it, coming off the hills; but where it was sheltered there was real warmth in the sunshine. She stepped out onto the gravel and walked round the house. There was a feeling of spring everywhere. Beside the path a hazel stretched its interlacing branches overhead, bursting with vivid green buds amongst the spent brown lamb's tails that dangled stiffly against the arched sky.

Swale House was square and built of stone with typical Yorkshire symmetry and understatement. The grounds were large, formal gardens leading to shrubberies and a wilderness, and eventually over a meadow to a mossy slope down to a fast-running stream. Smooth and brown and sinuous the water was. On its dark surface drifting swirls of petals, like pale scum, circled, caught on protruding twigs and freed themselves again into spinning fragments. Henrietta went carefully down to the edge, holding the narrow wrist of a young silver birch to steady herself, and saw there were fish in there, lying in the current as effortlessly as if they were in bed, facing upstream and keeping place with little muscular twitches of their tails.

She wandered happily all morning, her spirits rising with every moment out of doors. She was young enough to shrug off disappointment and hope for better things. Probably, she told herself, Mr Fortescue was tired last night, as she was. Mrs Allen might be disagreeable, but, as she had unwittingly pointed out, Henrietta and Mr Fortescue were married now, and nothing could change that. And last evening – yes, last evening had been decidedly wonderful, and surely the evening to come would be too?

When hunger suggested it might be time for luncheon, she made her way back to the house, and came round the side into the sweep again just as Mr Fortescue rode in through the gate on a long-eared bay road horse. Gladness to see him overcame shyness, and she almost danced up to him.

'Well, and have you been waiting here for me all morning?' Mr Fortescue said indulgently. 'Faithful creature.'

She caught the rein, and the bay lowered his head to her, blew into her hands, and decided she was nice enough to rub his itching muzzle against. Bracing herself automatically against him, Henrietta said, 'I've been exploring the gardens. Everything is very beautiful.'

Mr Fortescue dismounted, touched by her enthusiasm, by the unstudied way she greeted him and held his horse, not seeming to mind that it was making marks on her fashionable dress. Bracebridge, the groom, came hurrying out to take the rein from her with a resentful look, and led the horse away.

'I'm glad you found something to amuse you,' Mr Fortescue said, walking with Henrietta into the house. 'After luncheon, if you would care for it, I will take you for a drive and show you the neighbourhood. Richmond is a pretty town, and the surrounding scenery is remarkably fine.'

'I would like that very much,' she said; and probably she would have said the same whatever he had suggested. Just to know that he still wanted to be with her was enough.

So the week passed. In the mornings, Mr Fortescue went about his parish and other business, and Henrietta wandered about the grounds and explored the immediate environs of the house. Swale House stood rather isolated, a little outside the town, and there were no other houses nearby, so she rarely saw anyone other than the servants. The Swale House servants – Mrs and Mrs Allen, the groom Bracebridge, and the housemaid Minney – remained aloof from her. The coachman, Banyard, belonged to the establishment at Bishop Winthorpe, and had come down by train ahead of his master; he seemed to feel himself superior to the Richmond servants, and perhaps to distinguish himself from them he occasionally bestowed a not unkind look on Henrietta, though he did not unbend sufficiently to chat.

But the housemaid Lizbeth was an extra servant taken on

for the occasion, and though she was evidently afraid of Mrs Allen, Henrietta did manage to persuade her to open up a little while she was helping her to dress. From her Henrietta learned that the clerical duties were undertaken for most of the year by a vicar, Mr Herbert, who lived in a small house under the shadow of the church with his wife and six children, but that Mr Fortescue came five or six times a year, and in April and October made a 'long visit' when he generally stayed for a fortnight or more. Mr Fortescue, she said, was very highly regarded, and was asked everywhere to dine, but only gave tithe dinners himself, no doubt because he was unmarried. (She seemed to have forgotten the reason for Henrietta's presence.) When Henrietta's friendliness overcame her discretion, she further vouchsafed that Mr Fortescue was a very nice gentleman and rich as Croesus; that Mrs Allen was an old witch; and that Mr Allen drank, and was not above pinching a girl if she was slow enough to be caught in a doorway when he was passing.

Mr Fortescue sometimes came home for lunch, and sometimes Henrietta was served alone in the small dining-room. But every afternoon Banyard brought the carriage round to the door and they drove out to see the sights: the pretty stone-clad town of Richmond, built around its cobbled square, and the great, grim fortress that loomed over it; the ancient, many-arched bridge; the river which clattered over natural rocky weirs, but upstream ran brown and fast between steep, high banks of hanging woods. They went farther afield, to Bolton Abbey, to Jervaulx, to Middleham where Good King Richard lived in his youth. They drove along the winding roads of the Dales, through little villages, the neat houses tucked down snugly under their stone-pantiled roofs, each with its blowing flag of blue woodsmoke. Mr Fortescue talked of the history and archaeology and architecture of what they saw, and knew many an interesting and recondite fact; but Henrietta ached to be out of the carriage, to be on horseback, to ride up and up to the wild brows where the peat-smelling wind rioted and the curlew-haunted emptiness spread away below you for ever. Did married woman ever do that? Or was it barred from her for all her life?

Occasionally on their drives they would pass someone who would greet them or wave or touch their hat, and Mr Fortescue returned the salutes gravely but never stopped to talk, and never presented Henrietta. In the evenings they dined alone at home, and no-one called. The evenings were less rapturous than the first, for Mr Fortescue talked less, perhaps because he had said so much of what he had to say already. Henrietta could never think of anything to say to him that would be worthy of his intellect; so there were silences, during which Henrietta kept her eyes lowered, and Mr Fortescue looked at her undisturbed. And every night she retired alone, and he did not come to her room.

Mr Fortescue was puzzled with himself. All his dealings with Henrietta had been a struggle between the intellectual and the emotional, in which he hoped the intellectual had prevailed. His first impulse towards her had been an unprompted desire to rescue her, which observation had allowed him to rational-ise: she was in need of being rescued, and he alone could give her the environment she needed and deserved. But having secured her and brought her to his own place, he now could not do what logic and intellect told him he must. He did not know how to approach her. She was so fragile, so innocent; her clear gaze unmanned him. Freed by sleep, his mind was filled with the same sensual images, but in cold consciousness he could not take his passion upstairs to that chilly room and unleash it.

He too remembered that first evening with wistfulness, and at the end of the week, in an attempt to break through his own barriers, he told Mrs Allen that they would take their dinner in the breakfast parlour. 'Light the fire in there this afternoon, to make sure that it is properly warm,' he ordered. 'And be sure there is a good fire in Mrs Fortescue's room, and see that it is kept up. The rooms on that side of the house can be very chilly.'

He had Allen serve champagne to Henrietta again. For himself ordered his best burgundy, and under its influence he rediscovered his eloquence. Henrietta found the confidence to ask him questions, and he endowed them with his own acuity and marvelled at her quickness and wit. When they retired as before to the fireside chairs, he talked for the first time of his own work, and she listened with her usual rapt attention. Suddenly he said, 'There is something I should like to read to you. Will you permit me?'

'I should like it more than anything,' she said at once. 'Is it something you wrote?'

'No, but it is something very pertinent to me,' he said. 'I will fetch the book. Wait just a moment.' She sat looking into the fire. After five minutes he was back with a well-worn volume in his hand. 'The *Metamorphoses* of Ovid,' he announced, resuming his seat. 'I know you have no Latin, but you will forgive me. It is your own story, the story of Andromeda, and poetry is poetry, whatever the tongue.'

He read to her, and she marvelled that someone could be familiar with anything so foreign and meaningless. But he spoke it with great feeling, and she listened, fascinated, to the song of his voice. At last he closed the book and, his eyes filled with a strange, hot light, said in a low voice, 'Go up to bed now. I will follow.'

She went upstairs with a tight feeling of anticipation in her stomach. Surely this time he meant it? She was filled with longing, and afraid at the same time. She hurried out of her clothes and into her nightdress, and while she was still taking out her pins, there was a scratching sound at the door which made her heart jump painfully. Turning, she saw a folded sheet of paper slide under it.

She took it to her bedside candle. His handwriting was small and precise but oddly hard to read.

It said, 'I shall come to you in five minutes' time. Wear nothing but your unbounded hair, put out your candles, lie upon your counterpane, and await my coming.'

She found her hand trembling and her heart crowding up into her throat at these instructions, her imagination giving her an instant, shocking picture of how she would appear to him, naked and uncovered on her bed. But it was exciting too, in a way she had never felt before. She did as he bid her, brushing out her hair, and put out the candles before she removed her nightgown, for she felt too shy to do it in the light. And then she crept up onto the high, white bed, and lay down, drawing as much of her hair about her as she could.

It seemed more than five minutes, waiting in the dark; cold despite the good fire that had been lit for her. But then there was a sound at the door, and it opened slowly, admitting the bending light of a candle. Behind it she could see the shape of someone in a dark dressing-gown, hanging open over a nightshirt, but she could not see past the flame to the face.

Fortescue knew she would not be able to see his face, and it made him feel safe. He slipped out of his clothes at the door, and naked advanced across the room, holding the candle before him. The blurred edge of the radiance reached the bed, revealed her lying in beautiful nakedness, white and soft and curved as a half-opened flower, her masses of hair spread about her, her eyes wide with apprehension, her lips parted with her quick, short breaths. Andromeda chained, in terror of the beast, naked against the whiteness of the rock: his for the taking, for the ravishment which, through consent, attained a delicious ambivalence that was almost unbearably arousing.

He put the candle down on the bedside table, and climbed up onto the rock.

CHAPTER FOURTEEN

Southport looked up in annoyance as someone tapped on his business-room door and opened it without waiting. Now who the deuce was this? If it was Venetia come to make another fuss, he thought dangerously, there would be trouble!

'Have I the right room? Ah yes. I'm sorry to interrupt you, Oliver, but I must speak to you.'

'Fanny?' he said in astonishment. Fanny hardly ever left her own room, and had never come to his before.

'Yes, I knew you would be surprised to see me. I hope the surprise will help my cause along.'

His brows drew down. 'Cause?'

'May I sit down?' she asked mildly.

He stood up impatiently and came round his desk. 'Of course, sit by all means, but I warn you, if you have come to make another row—'

She shuddered. 'God forbid! There's been enough trouble in this house. No, I'm here to suggest a scheme which I hope may save everyone a great deal of pain.' She gestured him to sit down. 'You make me nervous, looming over me like that.'

He sat. 'You, nervous? I don't believe you've ever even been shy. Certainly you've always treated me with a scalding lack of respect,' he said, but with half a smile.

'Were you scalded? I don't believe that. But I'm not afraid of you, if that's what you mean, though I quite understand why everyone else is.'

The smile went in. 'If people were a little more afraid of me, I should not be subjected to defiance and wrangling, day and night,' he said bitterly. 'Do I deserve no peace? Am I not to be master in my own house?'

'That's what I want to explain to you, dear Oliver,' Fanny said. 'The wrangling, you see, does not arise from lack of respect. Venetia is very much afraid of you.'

'Oh is she?' he growled.

'Yes, but because something matters so much to her, it has become stronger than her fear,' Fanny said.

'So you have come to plead for her,' he said with an expression of distaste. 'I might have known it.'

'You're wrong. I disapprove as much as you could wish of the whole thing. No, I've come to warn you. Please—' she lifted a hand – 'please hear me out. It has cost me something to come here like this. And in case you think of mentioning the word "ingratitude", believe me when I say that no-one could be more conscious of what I owe you.'

He looked uncomfortable. 'You have the deuce of an opinion of me, if you think I would throw that in your face.'

She smiled a little. 'Oh, I know that when a man is angry and fretted to death he'll use any weapon that comes to hand. I was trying to disarm you in advance.'

He *was* disarmed, by discovering that there was someone who realised he was fretted to death. 'Well, what did you want to say?'

'That Venetia is determined to try to study medicine, and that if you continue to forbid her, she will defy you. She will leave this house and make the attempt alone.'

'Nonsense. How can she, if I cut off her allowance? Or doesn't she believe I will?'

'She believes it, but it won't stop her. She has been offered financial assistance by someone else.'

His eyebrows shot up in shocked disbelief. 'By whom? Not by her mother?'

'No, no! Charlotte won't help her – not because she doesn't want to, but because she's loyal to you. Does that shake you? You don't know your own wife very well.'

'I do know her,' he said, a little shamefaced. 'I forget sometimes. Not Charlotte, of course. Who then?'

'Tommy Weston.'

'Tommy Weston? The dickens!' he exploded.

Fanny shook her head. 'Oh Oliver! Tommy's been in love with her for years. He knows he has no chance, never has had and never will have, but he'd do anything for her – and without any hope of return, I hasten to add.'

'If he really cared for her, he would not encourage her in this – this – *lunacy!*'

'Well, Tommy is rather given to the women's movement,' she said mildly. 'I understand he has contributed funds to the Society for the Promotion of Employment of Women, and the Cambridge College for Women, and other worthy causes. When you think of his origins, it's hardly surprising. If women had education and the means to employment they would not be victims of the sort of poverty— '

'Stop!' He flung himself to his feet again. 'I won't be lectured on this infernal subject again! Tommy Weston may do as he pleases with his own money, but by God, I'll stop him corrupting my daughter!'

'You can't stop him, for the same reason you can't stop Venetia: because although they're afraid of you, they want this thing more. Oliver, do listen to me, and don't rant. I'm on your side, I promise you.'

Oliver stopped pacing. 'Well?' he snapped.

'I'm not a clever person,' Fanny said, 'and never have been – Uncle Henry always said I had more hair than wit – but I do know about Society, and I know that if Venetia leaves home and lives in lodgings paid for by Tommy Weston, it will cause a dreadful scandal. That's why I have come up with a plan which I beg you most earnestly to agree to.'

'Which is?' he said stiffly.

'That I should rent a small house, and have Venetia to live with me. It will be far more respectable, and safer. I can chaperon her, and I may even be able to influence her. She listens to me. And at the very least she won't be dependent on Tommy Weston's money.'

'Out of the question,' he said starkly.

'Oliver, you must believe me, as one who has been driven to desperation myself, she *will do it*, whatever you threaten. She will leave home, and since I can't bear to think of her living in lodgings, I will be forced to follow my plan anyway. But it would be so much better if it had your consent.'

'If you think I will do anything to lend countenance to this appalling scheme of hers, you must be mad! You seem to forget that I am a man of influence. No hospital will so much as let her through the door once I have made my feelings plain.'

'Oh dear, I beg you won't do that,' Fanny said urgently. 'I wish she didn't want this thing, but she does – and, really, it's not morally bad, is it? There are many people, thoughtful people, who would applaud her. If you agree to her living with me, and pay her an allowance, you will be seen as a liberal thinker bravely prepared to support his daughter in challenging the old order. You will be admired. But if she is seen to be doing it in defiance of you, and you storm about London publicly thwarting her, there will be a far worse scandal. She may never recover, socially – and it will touch the rest of the family too.'

'So I am to condone disobedience and unfilial behaviour because I can't stop it, am I?' he said furiously. 'Fanny, this is blackmail, plain and simple.'

She sighed. 'I wish you wouldn't use such hard words.' She looked at him intently. 'Oliver, tell me truthfully, would you really mind it so much if you weren't in the middle of all this wrangling over the Army Regulation Bill? If you weren't tired and vexed, and if Marcus weren't teasing you in that stupid way?'

The barrier was lowered for a moment, and a weary man looked out at her from his undefended eyes. 'Sometimes,' he said, 'I can hardly rise to face another day. This army reform is killing me; but one cannot step away from duty. Sometimes I think anger is the only thing that stiffens me enough to stay upright.'

Fanny held out a hand in an unconscious gesture of sympathy. 'Then let her go,' she said. 'I will take the best care of her I can, and discourage her, gently, all the while. And if she succeeds in spite of all, you can be proud of her, because it will take great courage, and she gets that from you.'

He stared at her a moment longer, and then turned away

247

bleakly. 'She can go with you. I won't publicly oppose her. But I won't pay her an allowance. If you are fool enough to do this, Fanny, you can pay for it too. As to being proud of her— !'

Seeing she had won all she was going to, Fanny quietly left him.

Many was the time in January and February that Alfreda had thought she would never manage to bring Mr Fortescue up to scratch. He was an eminent man, a scholar, welcomed in the best circles, with refined tastes and the resources to indulge them: what would he want with an untutored girl less than half his age, with neither wit nor beauty? What could she do to bring it about? Not knowing what had attracted him to Henrietta in the first place, anything she did might as easily repulse as encourage him. She decided the only possible stratagem was to impress upon him that he had raised expectations, and hope his gentleman's honour would do the rest. It was to that end she had dispatched George with his invitation and postscript that day.

George had been frankly incredulous when she told him Mr Fortescue was in love with Henrietta. 'What, that rector fellow? But he's an old man – and a regular jawsman too! Damned if I understand one word in three he says.'

'Don't swear, please. The point is not whether you understand him, but whether he is going to offer for Henrietta. Consider this, Mr Morland: he is wealthy enough to take her without a dowry. He may be the only man who would, and since poor Henrietta will have nothing at all, we should encourage him all we can.'

'Well, when you say nothing at all,' George began, a little awkwardly, 'I suppose we may manage to find *something* of a dowry. My father would have expected it.'

'There's no knowing what he may have expected!' she said irritably. 'He seemed very happy to let other people shoulder his responsibilities. And the fact of the matter is that since he robbed you of half your inheritance, you simply can't afford to give her anything. Consider what it has cost you to keep her all this time, to say nothing of the wedding itself, which

I suppose you will have to pay for, since it's plain no-one else will. And if you don't get her off, you will have to keep her for the rest of her life, thanks to your father. She will be a dead weight on the estate, without talking of dowries.'

'I hadn't thought of that,' George said, losing the thread a little.

'So we had better do all we can to get this man for Henrietta, or we shall be bankrupted. The cost of her clothes alone is frightening.'

Her relief when Fortescue finally proposed was tempered only by her fear that, during that interview at which she could not be present to keep George to the line, he might weaken and promise a dowry. But she had worked on him constantly in anticipation, and he acquitted himself well. Fortescue, he told his wife later, had taken it like a gentleman, and merely said that Henrietta was treasure in herself.

But Alfreda could not really relax until the ceremony was over and the bridal couple had driven away. She'd had an irrational dread that when Mr Hughes got to, 'If any man knows any reason,' a dark stranger would leap up from the back of the chapel and reveal the existence of a mad wife locked away in Mr Fortescue's attic. She was half afraid her brother would do it for a lark.

She had been desperate to get rid of Henrietta. What she had suspected in February she was sure of in March, and she was beginning to feel superstitious about having Henrietta in the house at the same time as the new little heir, as though she might have the power to blight his life before it had well begun. She could not admit to herself that there was anything to fear in having a first child at the age of twenty-eight, so she apportioned her uneasiness where her dislike lay. Of course, as a Christian she did not believe in evil eyes and hexes and such pagan nonsense; but it was only common sense to shoo away an owl if it settled on your roof tree. Now, if she could only get rid of the other two . . .

One morning, while she was still in bed, with her morning tray of tea and bread-and-butter on her lap, considering her plan of action, there was a knock at the door, and Bittle came in, in a state of agitation.

'I must speak to you, madam!'

'Good heavens, what is it? Really, Bittle, must you come bursting in at this time of day?'

Bittle's lips were white with fury, and there was a spot of high colour in each cheek. 'Indeed I must, for I suppose you will want to do something about it, though the Lord knows I'd as soon the little wretch fell into the river and drowned! He has run away, the wicked heathen, that's what!'

'Who has? What are you talking about?' Alfreda asked in rising irritation.

'That child, that *Manfred*,' she spat the name, 'has run away. He would not sit down to his lesson this morning, and when I tried to correct him, he *bit* me, the animal, and let loose some wicked language I wouldn't repeat for anything, and ran away.'

Alfreda sighed impatiently. 'Why are you troubling me with this? He will be hiding in the house somewhere. Have him found and punish him how you like. It's a nursery matter. That's what I employ you for.'

'I know very well what you employ me for,' Bittle said sharply, 'and he is not in the house. He has run away from home. He said he was never coming back, and while I don't doubt you'd be happy about that, I thought you might want to make some show of searching for the brat, for your husband's sake. However, it's no affair of mine.' She turned as if to leave.

'How dare you speak to me like that!' Alfreda said furiously, a pang of fear going through her at hearing her thoughts articulated. Bittle stopped and looked at her silently. 'The child must be found,' she said more calmly. 'I don't suppose he's gone far. Some of the men must go and look in the barns and sheds and suchlike places, where children hide.'

Bittle's look was satirical, but she said only, 'Do you want me to give the order?'

'No, Fanie can fetch Mrs Holicar to me. You'd better go back and take care of your other charge.'

'That one wouldn't notice if the house fell down,' Bittle said, and stalked out.

*　　*　　*

Alfreda directed a search of the house first, not trusting Bittle's judgement on the matter; but no sign of Manfred was found. Atterwith, she knew, was out at Thickpenny that morning, so she put the outdoor search in the hands of Grocer, the home yard man who had replaced Askins, and washed her own of it. She had enough to do, with the architect coming that morning to show her the plans he had drawn up for her for the first alterations to Morland Place.

She had forgotten all about it by the time her luncheon was served, but Goole hemmed as he was about to withdraw and said, 'I understand from Grocer that the boy has not been found, madam. Would you wish the search to be extended?'

Alfreda frowned. 'No, no, there's no point. If he's not in the outbuildings he might be anywhere. He'll come back when he's hungry, I expect. The carriage at a quarter before two, Goole: I have morning calls to make.'

Teddy had been out at Moon's Rush that morning, looking at the work there. It was going slowly, because he changed his mind about once a fortnight, whenever he read something in a journal or met a fellow at the club who had improved his own house. The roof was repaired and the immediate jungle of brambles and saplings around the house removed, but the carpenters and bricklayers had got into thoroughly lazy habits. Since they expected daily to have their orders contradicted, they saw no reason to do very much of anything at all.

Teddy didn't mind. He was enjoying himself enormously, finding out about his businesses, playing at being a landowner, and in between, spending money and discovering what a splendid fellow everyone thought he was now that he was an heir. It was lucky, he thought, that he had been brought up under George's shadow, or his head might well have been turned. As it was, he enjoyed all the attention – especially from the young female portion of York's Society – with an amused cynicism. He seemed to be getting through money at an alarming rate, but since Uncle Henry had not yet carpeted him, he assumed that the dibs were still in tune. He hadn't a clear idea of how rich he was going to be, but plainly it was rich enough for the present number of new clothes and fine dinners.

And talking of dinners, he decided he would eat at the club tonight. Makepeace House was convenient, but he didn't like it much – too big and gloomy. In fact, it wanted pulling down, as big old houses were being pulled down all over York. The fine folk mostly lived outside the walls now – even Lord Anstey was building a new house at Clifton, and the ancient, insanitary Anstey House on the Lendal was to be demolished and the site used for new shops and offices. York was a city perpetually in the throes of reshaping itself: the air seemed permanently full of brick dust and the sound of falling masonry, and a walk through any of the teeming streets involved ducking under scaffolding and dodging builders with sharp-edged barrows and loaded hods.

Teddy had eschewed either of his father's clubs as being stuffy, and had chosen instead the new Yorkshire Club, where a very jolly set of fellows was always to be found. The club had opened in 1868, and had its premises just above the steamboat landing on the river, beside the Lendal Bridge. From the dining-room or the smoking-room you could look down at the river, and watch the flat-bottomed steamers ply up and down, freighted with wheat, barley, oil-cake and flour, sugar, cocoa and lemons, sand, gravel and cement. Sitting looking down at the bridge, Teddy often thought how long and hard his father had battled to get it built. The first bridge, which had opened in 1860, had fallen down again in 1861, while Benedict was in America; and when he returned he had other things on his mind. The present bridge, opened in 1863, therefore owed nothing to him, which always struck Teddy as ironic.

He left his horse at the livery stables behind the Jolly Bacchus and walked on down Micklegate. As he turned in to Nunnery Lane, something hurtled out of a doorway and launched itself at him, and had he not put on some weight since leaving Morland Place, he would have been knocked off his feet.

'What the—! Here, steady on!' It was a boy, and Teddy grabbed his arms to fend him off, an instant before he recognised him. 'Good God, Manny!' Manfred was clutching him and panting with some extreme emotion. Teddy tried soothing him, while delicately unhooking the fingers from his clothes. 'All right, old fellow, there there. Quiet down, now. I say, Manny old chap, mind my coat, you know. It's new.' When he had put the boy far enough back to see his face, he found his little brother was weeping steadily, the tears making clean tracks down his dirty face. 'What's wrong? What are you doing here?' he asked.

'I was waiting for you,' Manny said, between sobs. 'I didn't know what to do. Oh, don't send me back, please!'

The hands tightened again, and sighing for his jacket's sake, Teddy said, 'All right, old chap, let's go into my house and talk about it. I expect you're hungry, aren't you? We'll find something to eat, then.'

Teddy's house was kept only by an old woman and her son, who managed between them for his present few wants. She was a good-hearted creature, and tutted kindly over the grubby boy her master brought into the kitchen, but asked no questions, only went about getting together a plate of bread and jam and cold beef and a mug of milk, and then retired discreetly to the servants' hall next door to leave them in privacy. Teddy lit a smoke and sat quietly while Manny attacked the plain fare with a day-long appetite. Only when the plate was clean, did he put his question again.

'I've run away,' Manfred answered, raising apprehensive eyes to his brother's face, expecting an explosion.

But Teddy only nodded, as if it were the most ordinary thing in the world. 'I see. Going anywhere in particular?'

'I don't know. I just – I couldn't – I can't bear it any more!' Manfred cried out at last. 'I hate them! I won't go back. If you make me, I'll run away again, I swear.'

'No need to swear, old chap,' Teddy said. '*I* don't care where you live. I ran away several times myself, when I was your age – when Georgie was horrid or Mr Wheldrake had given me a thrashing. I always went back again, though. Got too hungry to stay out.'

'I was hungry,' Manfred confided, reassured by this confession. 'I haven't had anything all day, not since breakfast, and that was only porage. I hate porage.'

'So tell me, why did you run?'

Manfred looked at him with dark, brooding eyes. 'Do you know what today is?' Teddy looked blank, and Manfred's mouth turned down bitterly. 'You forgot too. Everyone forgot, even Henrietta. Now she's gone and got married, she doesn't care about me.'

Teddy's brain made an heroic effort. 'Good grief, it's your birthday, isn't it? I'm sorry, it slipped my mind, now I'm not living at Morland Place any more. Many happy returns.'

Manfred shook his head; it was too late for that. 'Everyone hates me,' he said, the tears welling up again.

'Oh, here, I say! Just because they forgot your birthday doesn't mean—'

'*She* hates me. She wishes I was dead. That's why she sent Gurney away.' The tears spilled over. 'I can't go back! I can't! I shall die if you make me!'

Teddy threw his cigarette into the fire and came round the table to comfort his brother. Under his coat, the little fellow felt very thin, and he was trembling with either misery or fear, or perhaps both. The tears became more abandoned, and resigning his pleasant dinner at the Yorkshire to oblivion, Teddy took the boy onto his lap and let him sob into his lapel.

Bit by bit the story came out. The cause of the present eruption was Manfred's forgotten birthday: in the nursery some little treat was usually prepared or notice taken on account of the day. When Bittle told him to sit down to his lessons immediately after breakfast he had raised a tentative objection, meaning to remind her of the anniversary, but she had administered a slap to silence him before he could finish, and told him he would forfeit his mid-morning cake and milk for insubordination. The sense of injustice welling up in Manfred had led him to rebel, and Bittle had then decreed the most dread punishment, that he be shut in the staircase cupboard until he came to a realisation of his sins. As she dragged him, pleading and crying, towards the door, he had bitten her in desperation, and in the instant she released her hold, had fled.

At this point Teddy asked, 'Well, I can see why you were

upset, old chap, but being shut in the cupboard doesn't sound too bad to me. Better than a whipping, anyway.'

But Manny's sobs intensified. Incoherent words dropped in tear-soaked clumps, while he clung to his brother as if he would be snatched away. Teddy had been away from home for too many years to know, as Henrietta would have known, that Manfred was afraid of the dark. Bittle had soon found it out, and used it to subdue the boy who was too used to having his own way, in her opinion. The cupboard on the nursery landing, built into the curved wall of the spiral staircase was tiny, cold, and pitch black inside, having no window and a very tight-fitting door. It smelled of dampness and old wood, and since the walls and door were so thick, no sound penetrated it. Shut in here, in utter darkness and silence, Manfred was at the mercy of his overactive nerves and imagination. He lost all sense of direction, space and time, feeling as if he were falling through the darkness of oblivion into hell; in the end, he couldn't even tell whether or not he was screaming.

It was some time before Teddy understood even part of this. He had little imagination himself, and a robust temperament which had always taken things as they came. Thrashings had been frequent when he was a boy, and he had shrugged them off as his lot, and simply learned to avoid them. The horrors that breed in the dark had no substance for him; but he could see how badly his brother was suffering.

Further questioning uncovered a history of cruelty, of repression, beatings and intimidation ever since Bittle had taken over the nursery. Further back still, Manfred had been more affected than anyone knew by the loss of Gurney, who was the only mother he remembered. It was interesting to Teddy that while Manfred was evidently in terror of Bittle, he instinctively assigned the blame for it to Alfreda – a judgement with which Teddy concurred. He knew how he himself had been driven out; and he had seen how assiduously Fortescue had been stalked as a bridegroom for Henrietta. Only the obvious fact that Henrietta wanted to marry Fortescue (something Teddy had shaken his head over wonderingly) had reconciled him to the match.

But what, now, was to be done about Manfred? Naturally Teddy had no hope that he could do anything to change the nursery regime. George had even less imagination than Teddy, and would regard the trials of childhood as something everyone had to go through – as Teddy would have himself, had he not been faced with this miserable scrap of terror on his lap. Furthermore, George would not go against Alfreda in anything.

However, it was his duty to let them know where Manfred was. They would be searching the countryside by now. He stirred; Manfred, who had fallen asleep, woke and clutched him again in an agony of fear. 'No, no, it's all right. You're quite safe. You're at my house. Up you get, old thing – I must be about my business.'

Manfred slid from his lap and looked up at him with swollen, pleading eyes. 'You won't send me back?'

'No, you can stay here tonight,' Teddy said. 'I'm going to hand you over to Mrs Scawton now, for I've things to do.' He called the housekeeper in, and told her to give Manny a bath – for he was extremely dirty after his day-long wandering – put him to bed and take him up some supper. 'And be sure a lamp is left lit in his room at all time. He's afraid of the dark.'

'Very good, sir.' She put a kindly hand on Manfred's shoulder, and he looked from one to the other, still apprehensive.

'I've got to go out,' Teddy told him, 'but I'll come in and see you when I get back. Don't worry, you're quite safe here.'

'So, what's to be done?' Teddy asked when he had finished explaining Manfred's presence in his house.

George, standing by the fireplace, had been moving restively from foot to foot while Teddy spoke, and now said impatiently, 'What should be done? He must come home tomorrow, of course. I wonder you didn't bring him back with you, and save yourself the trouble of an extra journey.'

Teddy sighed. 'I don't think you understand. He's very upset.'

'Oh pish! He ran away from a punishment and now he's afraid to get an extra one, that's all. Good God, we've all been

256

through it! No-one likes a thrashing, but it's part of being a child. It's good for them.'

'Manny's not like us, Georgie. He's sensitive.'

'Sensitive!' George exclaimed contemptuously. 'He hasn't been thrashed *enough*, that's the whole trouble! If he'd had a tutor, like us, all that nonsense would have been beaten out of him by now. Sensitive! It's being brought up by women. A tutor would have made a man of him.'

Alfreda was alarmed. If George took it into his head that Manfred must have a tutor, the expense would be intolerable. Besides, this was a perfect opportunity to get rid of the boy for good. 'I think, Mr Morland,' she said, commanding his instant attention, as she always did, 'that Edward is right. Something must be done about Manfred. It's a problem I have seen in the making for some time.'

'Oh, is it? Well, if you say so,' George said, blinking. 'But what?'

'I think he must be sent to school,' she said.

George took a moment to digest it, and then he looked alarmed. 'School? Eton, you mean? But it would cost a deuced fortune!'

'A tutor would cost as much, I should think, when you take his keep into account,' Teddy said.

'I don't mean to take it into account,' George said crossly. 'You're very free with other people's money! Why don't you stump up yourself, if you're so dashed keen on the idea? You seem to think you understand the boy better than anyone else.'

'I didn't mean Eton,' Alfreda said calmly. 'That would be a nonsense, in the circumstances. There are plenty of schools in Yorkshire, so I understand, where boys are taught to reckon and keep books and so on, and generally fitted to find employment as clerks. The expense, I believe, is quite modest, and I think we should do as much for your little brother.'

'A clerk?' Teddy said indignantly. 'Send Manny to a school with shopkeepers' sons? You can't do that – dash it, he's a Morland! If he goes to school, it has to be a proper one.'

'By which,' Alfreda said coldly, 'you mean a school for gentlemen?'

'Yes!'

'Where he will learn Latin and Greek?'

'And other things.'

'The things a gentleman needs to know – a gentleman with his own independent fortune,' she concluded. 'You have perhaps forgotten that your father did not see fit to provide for Manfred in that way. He has no fortune, and will have to earn his living. An Eton education would be a cruelty to him, giving him tastes above his expectations. Far kinder to send him to a school where he will learn something useful.'

Teddy did not quite give up in the face of this logic. 'As I remember, Papa left it to George to provide for the younger ones.'

'And that is what your brother proposes to do,' Alfreda said relentlessly.

'But not by making him a clerk. Dammit, he could go into one of the professions!'

'If your father had meant Manfred to go to Eton and be put to a profession, no doubt he would have said so. He was quite capable of making it clear what he intended for *you*.'

Teddy flushed angrily. 'So that's what this is about! You've never forgiven me for inheriting the Makepeace fortune, have you?'

Alfreda shrugged coolly in the face of his heat. 'If you feel you have so much closer an understanding of your father's wishes, it is open to you to carry them out.'

'Ha!' said George. 'There it is! *You* don't want to be saddled with all that expense, do you? But you're happy to propose I saddle myself!'

'You were quick enough to saddle yourself with Marwood's expenses,' Teddy retorted. 'Brothers come expensive, don't they, Alfreda? Isn't it lucky for you that Georgie's happy to cast off his own!'

'That's enough of that!' George said, growing angry. 'I won't have any impudence towards my wife! And I won't discuss my affairs with you, either. You send Manfred back here tomorrow, or you can keep him for ever. Make up your mind.'

'You know I can't keep him. Dammit, I don't have a wife or even a household.'

'Very well. Then send him back and mind your business.'

Teddy felt himself on sinking ground. He changed his tone. 'Look here,' he pleaded, 'I'm sure you have Manny's best interests at heart. But if you're sending him to school, don't let that nurse of yours frighten the poor little fellow out of his wits in the mean time. Be a little kind to him.'

George would have replied, but Alfreda silenced him with a look. 'You may be sure that he will be treated as he should be,' she said graciously, and Teddy was forced to be satisfied with that.

The next morning he had the unpleasant duty of telling Manfred that he was going back to Morland Place. 'But you won't be there long. You're going to go away to school – won't that be nice? You'll have a jolly time at school – I know I did – and in the vacations you'll be too old to go back into the nursery, so Bittle won't have anything to do with you.'

Manfred gave him a burning look. 'You promised!'

'I tell you, it will only be until they find a school for you. You can stand it for a few days, can't you?' But he felt very bad about it as he escorted the shrinking child back home. 'Look here, Manny,' he said at last, as they were crossing the drawbridge, 'if you really hate it at school, you can come to me. I can't say fairer than that, can I? Only do give school a fair chance, won't you? Because the Lord knows what I would do with you if you did.'

Manfred was at Morland Place only for two more weeks before departing for school; and during that time Bittle left him alone, on strict instructions from Alfreda not to provoke him. The school was at Oakworth, on the edge of the Keighley Moor, away on the other side of Bradford. Alfreda had chosen it, after enquiry, as being inexpensive, and a good, long distance away, and because it was willing to keep its pupils during the holidays. George did not demur. He had been annoyed and embarrassed by the whole Manfred episode. He was ashamed of having so timid a brother (when George was a boy he had been so manly the nursery-maids had all borne the marks of it) and he wanted to be rid of him as quickly and cheaply as possible. His own son was on the way, and he didn't want him corrupted by Manfred's example.

It had been George's way to get rid of those he disliked. In his boyhood he had got rid of a foundling his father had brought into the nursery out of charity – a weakling milksop like Manfred, called Lennox Mynott – and later he had got rid of his tutor, Wheldrake. In fact, he was half convinced now that he had got rid of his father, too, when he became an embarrassment, by persuading him to go to Egypt. George saw himself as a genial and kindly man, as long as he was not crossed; but anyone who did – by God, they had better look out for themselves!

With Manfred gone, Alfreda now only had Regina to worry about. She had just turned fourteen, and was three years short of the age when she might reasonably be expected to be married off. It was a tiresome age, too – too young to be useful, too old to be ignored – and she was taking up too much of Bittle's time for Alfreda's liking. As her pregnancy advanced her hatred of Bittle was undergoing a reversal. The bad times were fading from her memory, now that she was secure again, and she was more often remembering the good times of her own childhood. Bittle had brought up Alfreda and Kit safely and well, in the days when the Turlinghams were rich, important and powerful. Bittle would understand what was fitting for the child who was half a Turlingham; Alfreda's son would need Bittle's undivided attention.

Alfreda was terrified of the approaching ordeal, and needed someone to turn to. Not to Fanie, not to any servant – certainly not to George – could Alfreda so unbend as to admit her fear, confess there was something that she could not control. It would be humiliating for anyone other than Bittle to know her weakness. She needed Bittle now, and, being Alfreda, hadn't the slightest doubt that Bittle would be glad and grateful to be needed again.

So Regina had to be sent away for a few years. Schools for young ladies were plentiful – she remembered Mrs Holland's in Kensington with a shudder – but they were expensive. Far better if someone could be found to take her in for a few years.

The difficulty was that George was short of suitable relatives: because of his parents' eccentricity, contact had been lost with all the various cousins and second cousins who might have done, and the ducal cousins in London were too grand to be approached in that way.

But then she remembered that Lady Anstey, in her girlhood, had been Benedict Morland's ward; and Lady Anstey had two daughters, Alice and Margaret, who were fourteen and thirteen years old – just Regina's age.

Alfreda thought that it would take some tricky manoeuvring to secure the invitation, but she had not reckoned on Lady Anstey's good nature. She paid her a morning call, and had only got as far as sighing about how much Regina missed her sister and how lonely it was for her in the nursery, especially living on an estate where there were no other girls nearby for her to consort with, when Lady Anstey interrupted.

'Yes, I have been thinking the same myself, and I have wondered – do you suppose she would like to come and stay with us for a while? I know Alice and Meg would be delighted to have a visitor, and our Miss Reagan can just as well teach three girls as two.'

Alfreda felt as though she had thrown her weight on a door and found it open. Lady Anstey added quickly, 'I hope you won't think it impertinent of me to make the offer, Mrs Morland, but you know I have always looked on the Morland family almost as my own children.'

'So I understand from Mr Morland,' Alfreda said.

'And another thing,' Lady Anstey added. 'You will forgive me for mentioning it, but *you* will have a great deal too much on your mind in the next few months to want the trouble of having Regina on your hands.' She smiled. 'There's no need to colour up. I'm old enough to be your mother, my dear, and I've five children of my own! And may I say, I couldn't be more delighted for you and Mr Morland. So do let me take one worry off your hands and have Regina to stay until you are safely delivered.'

So Alfreda had nothing to do but accept gracefully, and to think it would not be her fault if Regina never came back to Morland Place at all.

CHAPTER FIFTEEN

It was more difficult than Venetia had imagined to leave home, even with the help of Aunt Fanny. Her father's coldness was hard enough to bear – she might go, he said, but she could not come back until she had given up this appalling nonsense and was ready to behave like his daughter again – but to see how her mother was torn between them made her feel even more miserable and guilty. Tommy Weston's support of her caused another rift: when it came to it, his parents, though wishing Venetia had not chosen this path, could not but side with their beloved only son, and that brought down Oliver's angry disapproval on them. There was no formal breach, but a coolness now marked the public exchanges between Tom Weston and Oliver, and the Westons no longer called socially at Southport House. In short order Charlotte lost her two closest friends, Fanny and Emily, as well as her favourite daughter.

Venetia's mind and heart were sore with the struggle, the rows, the guilt and the wrench of so many partings, which were like little bereavements. What Fanny suffered in leaving Southport House she was not to know, for Fanny remained uniformly cheerful, and spoke of the 'adventure' with enthusiasm; and Venetia had not the penetration to see behind Aunt Fanny's mask.

But when the goodbyes were over and the move was made, the prospect ahead was tremendously exciting, and Venetia felt more alive than ever before. The place Fanny took was very modest, a tiny terraced house in Bury Street, a narrow street not far from the British Museum. It had kitchen quarters in the semi-basement, a drawing-room and a tiny back parlour on the first floor, two bedrooms on the second floor, and two servants' bedrooms at the top. The bricks of the house were soot-stained and dreary, and there was no garden, only a scrap of a yard at the back. Venetia's heart sank when she first saw it. The stairs were so narrow and dark, the furniture so old and heavy and ugly. She was used to space all around her, and the rooms seemed horribly cramped; she sometimes felt as though the walls and ceilings were closing in on her.

But she was conscious that Fanny was sacrificing a great deal for her, so she only ventured timidly, 'It's – very small, isn't it?' when Fanny asked her what she thought.

'Oh, you'll soon get used to it,' Fanny said cheerfully. 'I've lived in far smaller places, and you'll be surprised how you don't notice it after a day or two. Anyway, what would we want with more room than this? We have a bedroom each, the drawing-room to be smart in, and you can have the back parlour for your studies.'

Venetia wondered how they could be smart in that drawing-room, and imagined – for instance – entertaining Beauty Winchmore there. And then she reminded herself that thoughts of entertaining were to be put out of her head for the next few years, if not for ever.

The house came with staff: a cook-housekeeper, Mrs Lodden, her imbecile son Malcolm, whose muscles were as powerful as his brain was weak, and a maid, Aggie, who was skeletally thin and had a perpetual sniff. Between them they cooked, cleaned, kept the fires and answered the door. A laundress took away the washing once a week, for there was no room in the basement to do it, and nowhere to hang it out.

When Tommy Weston came to see the place, he was as dismayed as Venetia had been; and she now played Fanny's part, and was airily confident that they would do very well. 'We don't need much, you know. We shan't be having *ton* parties.'

'I didn't think you would,' Tommy said with a worried frown, 'but you ought at least to be comfortable, and I don't see how you can be, here. I don't like to see Lady Venetia Fleetwood in these surroundings.'

'Ah, but I'm not Lady Venetia Fleetwood any more, I'm plain Miss Fleetwood. And you don't have to come here, Tom, if it's not grand enough for you.'

His frown cleared. 'Don't be silly. I've been in far worse places than this. It was you I was thinking about.'

Mrs Lodden appeared at the door at that moment. 'There's a big box arrived downstairs for you, miss,' she said. 'Where did you want it put?'

'A box? I wasn't expecting anything.' Venetia turned to Tommy. 'Is this something to do with you?'

'No, word of honour! Shall I go and see what it is?'

Soon a shuffling and puffing on the stairs heralded Malcolm and the carrier bringing the box up, with Tommy directing them from behind. 'Yes, in there. Now turn left – no, the other way – through to the back room. Very good, put it down there – gently, now!'

The two men shuffled out again, the carrier touching his greasy cap in response to Tommy's tip. The nails had been drawn downstairs, and Venetia, on her knees, pushed the lid away and exclaimed, 'Books! Oh, look Tommy, all the medical books from home! Harvey – Hunter – Gray – Snow – all Great-grandmama's bound papers! My mother must have sent them. Oh, glory! I was wondering what I would do without them.'

She was taking out one and then another, caressing their familiar covers as though they were a litter of kittens. Tommy, his hands in his pockets, rocked on his heels and looked about the room. 'You'll need some bookcases in here – or perhaps just some shelves, if the walls are sound enough to hold them. That table will do to work at, I suppose. You might push it under the window where the light's better. Yes, I think you might be quite snug in here after all.'

Fanny appeared in the doorway behind him and said, 'Ah, I wondered what all the noise was about!'

'Look, Aunt Fanny, Mama's sent my books – isn't it wonderful?'

'Very wonderful.'

'Best of all,' Venetia said, turning a glowing face to her, 'is that it must mean they are forgiving me, at least a bit. I wish they had sent a note, though.'

'But what about you, Cousin Fanny?' Tommy asked. He had suddenly wondered what this move must mean to her. The cramped confines and bad air must be material to a semi-invalid. She would not even have a maid here to help her dress and fetch and carry for her, which in her case was not so much a luxury as a necessity. 'Is there anything I can do to make you more comfortable?'

'Oh, nothing at all,' she said cheerfully. 'I need very little to amuse me. I shall miss having a piano, perhaps, but there really isn't room in the drawing-room for one – or there won't be when I have moved in my *chaise-longue*, and I must have that. You know I can't sit for long.'

'You might move that peculiarly hideous cupboard,' Tommy said. 'In fact, I think it has woodworm anyway. Give it to Malcolm to chop up for firewood.'

'Oh, I shall be all right,' Fanny said. 'I have all my music in my head, after all.'

Apart from the smallness and dinginess of their surroundings, Venetia found it difficult to get used to the noise. Southport House was so big it was insulated from street sounds, while inside everyone moved quietly and spoke softly. Here Venetia found at first that she could not get off to sleep at night for the racket coming up from the street – traffic, drunks, dogs, altercations – which seemed to go on all through the dark hours, with only a brief pause before dawn, when it started up again, with the lively addition of street-vendors' cries and draymen's curses. Inside the house every footfall and conversation seemed to be transmitted through the thin fabric of the building with alarming clarity. She wondered how she would ever be able to study.

A few days after Tommy's visit, the carrier called again, this time delivering a small, new cabinet piano, directed to Mrs Fanny Anthony.

'From Tommy?' Venetia exclaimed in delight. 'Oh, he is the kindest of men! I can't wait to hear you try it, Aunt Fanny. How did he find one so neat? I hope the tone is good.'

Fanny folded the note she had been reading, which had come with it. 'Yes, it's from Tommy,' she said. Her cheeks were a little pink as she put the note away in her reticule, without showing it to Venetia. It said, 'I understand what you are doing, and salute your courage, but I fear you will be made too uncomfortable in the process. If ever there is anything I can do to ease the burden on you, I am yours to command.'

The task facing Venetia was a formidable one – in the optimism of youth she had not realised quite how formidable. There were hundreds of medical schools and universities offering courses in medical education, and a score of organising and examining bodies, the main three being the Royal College of Physicians, the Royal College of Surgeons, and the Society of Apothecaries. The Medical Act of 1858 had been intended to rationalise the situation. It provided that all medical graduates should have the same basic qualification (each body set its own examination, but supervision by the General Medical Council ensured that the degrees were roughly equivalent) and that the GMC should keep a register of all practitioners thus deemed qualified to practise.

Of course, it was not necessary to be registered: anyone could practise medicine. But without registration a practitioner could not claim to be qualified. He or she would not be able to serve on a board of health or in any other official capacity; their work would not be taken seriously or their findings accepted. And, of course, they would be unable to attract the fee-paying middle or upper-class patients – and even a doctor had to eat.

In some ways, the existence of the two pioneers, Miss Blackwell and Miss Garrett, had made things more difficult. Elizabeth Blackwell had graduated from an American medical school, where things were easier for women. Coming to London in 1858, the year the Medical Register was first drawn up, she had applied to be put on it, and since the rules said that all holders of a medical degree were eligible, the Council had seen no option but to comply. But to prevent such a thing happening again, they had changed the rules:

in future only graduates of British institutions would be registered.

Elizabeth Garrett had managed to get herself admitted to the examination of the Society of Apothecaries by pointing out that their rules stated that 'all persons' who fulfilled certain qualifications were allowed to take the examination, and that 'all persons' must include women. She passed the examination and was registered as Licenciate of the Society of Apothecaries, but the Society, in fury and chagrin, changed its rules in 1868 specifically to exclude women from then on.

So the authorities Venetia was about to petition were thoroughly on the *qui vive*; but she was too caught up in the excitement of her new life to think about the obstacles. She would have dashed out the first day on her mission, but Fanny exclaimed in alarm that she must first do something about her clothes.

'My clothes?' she exclaimed in astonishment. 'I have more important things to think about than my appearance!'

'That may be so,' Fanny said patiently, 'but if you turn up at a medical school looking like an illustration from the *Journal des Demoiselles*, they won't listen to you for an instant.'

Reluctantly, Venetia had to agree. She had not brought many clothes with her, and had chosen the plainest, but they still had tight waists, modish decorations, draped skirts and bustles, which would inevitably mark her out as a young lady of means and fashion. Fanny sent for a mantuamaker, and in consultation with her had two gowns made for Venetia, which Venetia always referred to afterwards as 'my uniform'. They were of good strong wool barathea, one in dark brown and one in dark blue. The bodice was styled like a jacket with revers and straight sleeves, and with a gored waist over a full but plain skirt, and they were cut roomily so that Venetia needed only the lightest of corsets. She wore them over a white blouse with a high neck, finished at neck and cuff with a neat frill. A simple hair-style, a plain straw hat and low-heeled boots finished the ensemble.

'There, and if I don't look as if I mean business *now* – well, I don't know!' she said, viewing herself with difficulty in the dressing-table glass which was all her bedroom provided.

'You look very determined,' Fanny said. 'Which is just as well, because you will be going to places where the people are not at all what you are used to.'

'The doctors and medical students?'

'They will be bad enough; but I was meaning the patients. Hospitals are always thronged with the poor, the criminal, the mad and the drunk; and the streets around them will be, too.'

Venetia gave herself a firm little nod in the glass. 'I'm ready for that. My hat is secured with my longest, sharpest hat-pin.'

The good thing about Bury Street was that there were several hospitals in the immediate vicinity, and others within reasonable distance. Venetia did not count the Southport: they would be sure to find out who she was, and she wanted as far as possible to remain anonymous. For that reason she decided to call herself Miss Fleet, in case anyone associated the name Fleetwood with that of Southport.

But as it turned out, it made no difference what she called herself, for no-one was willing to accept her under any name. Even to get to see the right person was an obstacle race where every porter, clerk, secretary and assistant set up a new barrier. She walked miles of corridors, knocked on dozens of doors, sat on benches outside offices and on chairs in waiting-rooms, and saw a forbidding 'no' in every face, hatred and contempt in many an eye. It took enormous persistence even to acquire an appointment to see a principal, and then it was only to hear the same 'no', pronounced with as much hostility and considerably more impatience.

Her best hope had been of the Middlesex, where her mother had helped Dr Snow during the cholera epidemic long ago, and of University College Hospital, which had a reputation for liberal thinking. But there was no-one at the Middlesex now who would have remembered her mother, even if she could have invoked her name. She spent many, many days wandering its passages and knocking on doors. Once she passed a group of medical students who looked her over with insolent eyes and made remarks which had her cheeks burning and her palms itching to strike them; on another occasion a drunken porter who offered to show her the way to a certain office led her into an empty room and tried to assault her. Fortunately he was too drunk to do more than offend and embarrass her – she was easily able to push him away and escape – but when she complained to an official about the incident he said to her quite brutally, 'What can you expect? You lay yourself open to such abuse. If you wish to be treated like a lady you must behave like one.'

At the University College Hospital she met generally with cold civility, but with no better luck. Their liberal thinking did not go so far as to allow that women might do the same things as men. As a new approach, she tried interviewing individual practitioners in the hope of getting their support, but most would not even see her. She spent a whole week waiting to see the professor of obstetrics, Sir Robert Kavanagh, whose secretary made appointments for her which the professor did not keep.

One day, waiting in the corridor outside his room, almost an hour beyond the time appointed, she saw him approaching with a group of young men, presumably his students, at a fast walk. He was talking rapidly, and evidently being very amusing, for they were hanging on his words and laughing heartily. Venetia rose to her feet expectantly as the group approached; but they swept past her without a glance, not going into his room but on down the corridor. In desperation she ran after them, crying, 'Sir Robert! Just a moment please! Sir Robert!'

The group stopped; Kavanagh turned and, seeing her, frowned. 'Not now, madam. I cannot see you now,' he said impatiently. 'If you wish to consult me you must make an appointment with my secretary.'

'I *have* an appointment,' she said, aware of the curious looks the students were giving her. 'I have had an appointment every day this week. I have been waiting here for you an hour this morning.'

Sir Robert raised his eyebrows, puzzled. 'Waiting *here*? You are under a misapprehension, I'm afraid. I do not see patients here.' He seemed to be trying to gauge her social position through the conflicting evidence of her appearance and her accent. 'My consulting rooms are in Harley Street,' he continued. 'I shall be very pleased to see you there if you—'

'I am not a patient, Sir Robert,' Venetia interrupted. 'I am Miss Fleet, and I want to become a medical student. I am here to ask your help.'

The students nudged each other at this, and there were broad grins and some whispers. Sir Robert rolled his eyes and said, 'God preserve us! Is nowhere sacred?' He pointed rudely at Venetia. 'Gentlemen, observe: we have here a prime example of the species *mulieris importuna*, a very unpleasant little parasite which attempts to infiltrate the collegiate body and, if not ruthlessly excluded, will multiply and destroy it. You must be on your guard against it. These days it seems to have a wearying capacity for cropping up everywhere.'

His acolytes laughed. Venetia blushed angrily – and was angrier with herself for affording them the amusement of her reaction. Sir Robert was turning away, evidently having finished with her, but she said loudly, 'I wonder that you find it necessary to be so rude to someone who has addressed you civilly. It is not what I would expect of a gentleman.'

The students fell silent, turning their eyes to the specialist to see how he would play this ball. Sir Robert looked her up and down with contempt. 'Madam, I do not find it necessary to be civil to a creature who so far forgets her place. You are a disgrace to your sex. If I had my way, women like you would be stripped and flogged and set to hard labour in a penitentiary. That would teach you to ape your betters. And now I have wasted enough of my time on you. You will leave this building, or I will have you thrown out bodily. Do not have the impudence to address me again.'

Curled up in the corner of the sofa, clutching a cushion to her chest for comfort, Venetia wept. Fanny watched sadly from across the room. It was this sort of humiliation she had hoped would persuade Venetia to give up her plan. However painful it was to see her favourite suffer, it must be for her own good, if it drove her back home at last.

'I know I'm a fool,' Venetia reproached herself through her sobs. 'I ought to have expected it. But I've never been spoken to so. It was so – so cruel!' And she buried her head in a fresh paroxysm.

When the tears were spent she sat up, dabbed hopelessly with her sodden handkerchief, and accepted the fresh one Fanny silently offered. She blew her nose, wiped her eyes, took a few deep breaths, and then said in an almost normal voice, 'There, that's done! I shan't be so weak again. The trouble is,' she added judiciously, 'that I've never been used to argue with older men like Papa. I was brought up to obey, and it's natural to me. I have to get used to conflict – to *harden* myself. My skin is too soft.'

'From what you tell me,' Fanny said, 'you got off lightly today. I'm afraid that won't be the worst abuse you encounter.'

Venetia looked at her shrewdly. 'Oh, I'm on to you, Aunt Fanny! You hope cruel mockery like that will put me off altogether!'

'My dear child, who is it who has left a comfortable home to look after you?'

'You have, and I'm very grateful,' Venetia said promptly, 'but you can't pretend you ever approved of this.'

Fanny thought a moment before answering. 'You're right, I don't approve; but I know what it is to be imprisoned, and the worst sort of gaoler is the sort who only has your best interests at heart. That's why I'm helping you – that and, of course, the hope that I can lessen the damage to you.'

'Shall I be damaged?' Venetia seemed surprised.

'As I have been. If you persist in what you're doing, you may never be accepted in Society again.'

'Why should I care for that?' Venetia said. '*You* don't, do you, Aunt Fanny?'

'Oh yes,' said Fanny. It was all she said, but it was feeling.

'Well, I don't think that I shall,' Venetia said. 'I quite like it down here in the underworld. Things are so much simpler.'

Tommy visited them later, saw the red eyes and heard the day's news. He was obviously upset, though not surprised, at the way Venetia had been spoken to. 'Shall I go round

271

to his consulting rooms and challenge him?' he asked, only half joking.

'Certainly not!' Venetia said promptly. 'You shall not dignify him with such notice.'

'I could break all his windows, then,' Tommy offered. 'Anonymously, if you like.'

'Bless you, Tommy, you dear old bulldog! But I'm over it now. I shan't cry again. I shall gird up my loins and go out tomorrow to fresh hospitals and medical schools new. There are plenty of them. I've lost a battle, but I shall win the war.'

'What a Trojan you are!' Tommy said admiringly.

Aggie came in, a drop trembling on the end of her thin nose. 'Mrs Lodden says, how many is it for dinner, mum?' she intoned, with a copious sniff for punctuation.

'Will you stay, Tommy?' Fanny asked. 'Tell Mrs Lodden three, then, Aggie.'

When the maid had gone, Venetia said, 'You are a brave man. I thought I smelled cabbage soup just now. My delicate palate, reared on larks' tongues, truffles and *foie gras*, is suffering a shock from which it may never recover.'

'Ah, but I'm not such a hothouse flower as you,' Tommy said. 'And besides, I'd sooner a dinner of herbs in the present company than a stalled ox anywhere else.'

Venetia smiled at the compliment, but said, 'If it were only herbs! But Mrs Lodden learned her craft in Scotland, where they thrive on salt cod and boiled sheep's stomachs and the like. You don't know what you're letting yourself in for!'

A few evenings later, when Venetia returned from another dispiriting day of failure, Mrs Lodden opened the door to her, and said, 'I just showed up the gentlemen, miss, which were calling for you. Mr Weston and another.' She eyed Venetia with frank curiosity. 'Will they be biding for dinner?'

'I don't know. Which other?'

'I couldn't undertake to say, miss. He looked a queer sort to me, but if he's a friend of Mr Weston's . . .' She let the suggestion hang, and then added, 'Only, the chicken willn't stretch to four, so if the gentlemen are staying I'd best send Aggie out for a ham or something.'

Venetia couldn't be interested in domestic matters. 'I'm sure Mrs Anthony will let you know,' she said, slipping past Mrs Lodden's solid bulk and running lightly up the stairs. In the drawing-room Fanny was on her *chaise-longue*, as usual, and Tommy was standing by the fireplace, watching the door like a pet dog left behind. In the armchair sat a strange young man with rather shapeless, shabby clothes, and a derby hat which he was turning round and round by the brim in his hands. His hair was light, strawy and rather dull, and seemed to be growing in various wrong directions, as if he had cut it himself without benefit of a looking-glass; his face was pale, his cheeks hollow, and his eyes lacklustre. As Mrs Lodden had said, he was a queer-looking sort; Venetia couldn't place him at all.

'There you are!' Tommy cried, hurrying forward eagerly as she appeared.

She put her hands behind her. 'You're *not* going to try to shake my hand, Tommo?' she teased. 'I'm not so *mauvais ton* as that, I hope.'

He halted and collected himself. 'Of course not. How did you get on today?'

She made a face. 'As badly as usual. Hello, Aunt Fanny.'

Tommy picked up the lead. 'Well, I've brought someone to see you who may be useful to you. This is Mr Mark Darroway. Darroway – my cousin, Miss Fleet.'

Darroway, who had risen, gave her an awkward bow, his hat held to his stomach, but he said nothing.

Venetia nodded to him, and sat down. 'And how is Mr Darroway to help me?' she asked uninvitingly. There was still quite a bit of the duke's daughter in her, and she didn't like having strange young men thrust upon her.

'Darroway is a medical student at the Middlesex,' Tommy said triumphantly.

Venetia felt a pang of jealousy. 'I'm sure I congratulate him,' she said coldly. How was it that this poor-looking specimen was accepted when she was not, simply because he was male and she was female? Where was the justice?

273

'Now don't poker up!' Tommy said quickly. 'You'll be grateful to me when you understand my plan. Darroway has what you have not, and you have what he has not. He's been admitted to the medical school, but the poor fellow hasn't the means to support himself as a gentleman would wish – what with tuition fees, and books and so on.'

Darroway's eyes were fixed on his hat brim during this recital of his shortcomings, and Venetia felt a very slight sympathy for him. Humiliation was a new experience for her, but probably not for him.

'My proposal,' Tommy went on, 'is that he should pass on to you each evening the instruction he has had during the day, in return for an agreed sum of money. He will be kept from starving, poor fellow, you will have the benefit of his training, and the two of you together will be able to worry out anything either of you doesn't understand. A faultless plan, I think.'

It was received without rapture. Fanny reserved judgement, watching the scene silently from the wings. Darroway kept his head down, and Venetia examined him with disfavour, wondering how much this dull creature would be able to impart, even if he understood it in the first place.

She cleared her throat. 'I know you mean well, Tommy, but I don't think it is a substitute for a proper medical degree.'

Tommy smiled patiently. 'I know that! Of course you will still spend your days trying to get yourself accepted somewhere. But at least this way you will be learning something in the mean time. It won't give you the practical experience, naturally, but you'll be moving forward instead of standing still, and that must be to the good.'

She said nothing, and Darroway looked up at last. 'If Miss Fleet doesn't care for the idea, there's no more to be said. I'm grateful to you, Mr Weston, but we mustn't embarrass a lady.'

His voice was low but his accent was quite pure, and his thoughtfulness proved him a gentleman. Suddenly she warmed to him. 'I think we should try it,' she said. 'A trial period, to see how we get on.' She turned to Fanny. 'Mrs Lodden was asking if the gentlemen were staying to dinner.'

Fanny rose nobly to the occasion. 'I hope you told her that they were? We would be grateful to you, Mr Darroway, for your company. We pine for intelligent conversation.'

Tommy had been looking for a student from the beginning, but he needed one who was poor enough to want the money but who could be trusted with Venetia, and both categories were difficult to fill. Medical students paid eighty-five guineas a year for tuition, besides all the incidental expenses, and of course their keep, so they generally came from families which could afford to pay them generous allowances. Tommy had hung around the cookshops, taverns and clubs favoured by students for some time, rejecting out of hand the prosperous and rowdy youths he mainly found there, before he had come across Darroway, hopelessly staring through the window of a chop house he could not afford to patronise.

Mark Darroway came from a large and respectable but impoverished family from Hertfordshire. His father was a country parson, and he had been well educated at a grammar school, but there were insufficient funds to keep him comfortably while he followed his ambition of becoming a doctor. His poor appearance and apathy were largely due to semi-starvation, but he was too proud to accept charity, and Tommy had had to convince him that it was he who would be doing the favour to Venetia.

Venetia accepted him warily, but soon warmed to him. His present poverty was brought home to her forcibly by the fact that he thought their little house comfortable in comparison with his lodgings, and by his obvious enjoyment of Mrs Lodden's cooking. Their first sessions in the small back parlour, with the door to the drawing-room left open for propriety's sake, were stilted and awkward, for he was shy and she was reserved. He was as conscious of the social difference between them as she was, and his manners with her were very formal. But he was used to the easy, teasing give-and-take of a large family in a confined space; and because he had sisters, he was more at ease with the opposite sex than was Venetia, whose brothers had always been brought up separately from her. As better nourishment gave him more energy, he proved a lively companion; and as he lost his fear of her, he talked to her as he would to his own sisters. Fanny, stitching in the next room, often heard their murmured conversations punctuated with bursts of laughter or the slightly raised voices of friendly argument.

Having regard to his poverty, Fanny always made a point of asking him to stay to supper when the study hours were finished. His appetite seemed frightening to her, but however much he ate, he never put on a pick of flesh, and his cheeks remained hollow, though there was colour in them now, and a shine to his straw-pale hair. Supper times were the best part of Fanny's day, full of laughter and fun: Mark was a good mimic, and had a nice sense of the absurd. But though they were all soon on first name terms, it was clear to Fanny that Venetia didn't really see him as a man.

Darroway thought Venetia's ambition, which coincided with his own, admirable, though he admitted frankly that he wouldn't want to see any of his sisters doing what she was trying to do.

'But you're different,' he said, plainly puzzled by his own judgement. 'I don't know why. Perhaps it's being so rich.'

'But I'm not rich,' Venetia pointed out, annoyed.

'Mmm. But you were born it, and that's what matters. You'll always be a rich man's daughter and I'll always be a poor man's son. And in a funny sort of way, it makes us the same, because money doesn't matter to either of us.'

'Oh Mark, you do talk nonsense sometimes!'

'It's not nonsense,' he said easily, 'but it doesn't matter. Let's try and make sense of my chemistry notes again, shall we?'

As spring turned to summer and London grew hotter and grimier, Venetia continued to tramp the streets and knock on doors. The soles of her boots wore thin; the heat and smells of the metropolis and Mrs Lodden's cooking dampened her appetite and she lost weight. Fanny, trapped on a sofa by a window which, if it were open, admitted only smoke and noise and no fresh air, suffered too; but her worries were only for Venetia's health. She hinted to Tommy that he might take Venetia out sometimes to walk or drive in one of the parks, and Tommy needed little encouragement. But he rarely succeeded in detaching Venetia from her books. Even on Sundays she studied, sometimes with Mark and sometimes alone, trying to make up for the lack of the first-hand experience Mark enjoyed.

Mark was frustrated too. Venetia had imagined that once she was accepted by a medical school, everything would unfold before her like a highway to the horizon, but what Mark told her of the course modified her ideas somewhat. The teaching was haphazard, to say the least. Every afternoon at three-thirty there was practical morbid anatomy in the post-mortem room, but that was the only regularity. Lectures in the full range of disciplines were scheduled, but as often as not the lecturer did not appear; demonstration classes would be announced on one of the wards, only to be cancelled at the last minute. And when a class took place, the behaviour of the students was so rowdy it was hard for the studious, like Mark, to benefit from it.

'It doesn't matter so much for some of the men,' he complained to Venetia. 'Those who've got doctors for fathers, or who've served apprentice to one – or even those with natural genius. But men like me suffer a terrible handicap.'

'But what do they do?'

'Oh, they behave like savages! Horseplay and practical jokes – sometimes quite indecent ones. I know some of the professors are eccentric, and most of them are poor teachers, but that's no reason to make butts of them.'

He relayed some of the less repulsive pranks to her as they happened. The botany professor, a mild, absent-minded man, was always a target. One week someone threw a hydrogen sulphide ampule onto the platform, and the smell was so bad the lecture had to be discontinued. The following week two pigeons were let loose, and the students jumped up, hooting with delight, and began chasing them, letting off pea-shooters, jumping on the benches and generally making as much hullabaloo as possible.

'The poor old prof. said, "Gentlemen, if you do not wish

to learn, you are at liberty to leave," and three-fourths of the class walked out,' Mark told her.

'Well, perhaps they won't come next week, and the rest of you can get on,' Venetia said.

'I don't know that botany is such a wonderful thing, anyway,' he said discontentedly. 'I think my time might be better spent elsewhere. They say if you tip the beadle half a crown he'll mark you off for the whole course so that you can get your certificate without going to the lectures.'

'Well and good,' Venetia said grimly, 'but that won't get me *my* certificate.'

'True,' Mark conceded. 'But botany's all rot anyway. I can't see how it's going to help when you're faced with a compound fracture or a breech birth. I say, Venetia, I've just remembered: a fellow I know, Thompson, has got a skeleton to sell. He bought one, and then his pater sent him one. He says he'll sell it for thirty bob, which is jolly cheap, because I've seen one in the shop for two guineas. It would be an awfully good thing for you to have, if you want me to get it for you.'

Venetia smiled. 'Of course, it would be no use to you, would it?'

He grinned back. 'Well, I don't say I won't ever look at it, but *I* haven't got thirty shillings.'

Examinations came in July, and for a week Mark didn't come to Bury Street. Both women missed him a great deal, especially as Tommy happened to be out of town that week too, escorting his mother to the seaside at Eastbourne. The weather was sultry and airless, and never had London seemed so dull and so dirty. Venetia was depressed with her lack of progress, and could not concentrate on her books, feeling that she was getting nowhere and that everything was hateful.

One afternoon Aggie tapped at the door and announced breathlessly, 'A gent'mun to see you, miss.' She looked impressed.

'Which gentleman?' Venetia asked, brightening. Could it be that Tommy had come back early?

278

Aggie frowned with concentration. "'E give 'is name, but I ferget,' she concluded. 'Ever so 'andsome 'e is, miss.'

'Well, show him up then,' Venetia said. She exchanged a glance with Fanny, at a loss to guess who it might be. 'Could it be Harry, or Marcus? I'm sure no-one else knows where we are.'

A firm footstep on the stair resolved itself, to their astonishment, as that of Beauty Winchmore.

'Good God, what are you doing here?' Venetia exclaimed as he stepped in.

Winchmore bowed. 'A greeting of finished politeness. Mrs Anthony, your servant, ma'am. Well, Lady Venetia—'

'Hush!' Venetia stopped him, until Aggie had gone away. 'I'm not Lady Venetia here, I'm Miss Fleet. How did you find me?'

'Oh, through a friend of a friend of a friend,' Winchmore said easily. 'London's a small place, you know. Am I unwelcome?'

'Please, do sit down,' Fanny said. 'We are very pleased to see you. Venetia, where are your manners?'

'Gone a-begging, with my wits,' Venetia said. She stared at Winchmore blankly. 'I can't get over seeing you here.'

'Ditto ditto,' he said. 'Though the setting rather shows you off – by contrast, you know, like a diamond against black cloth.'

'Have you just come to talk nonsense? I hope you aren't here to harangue me. You haven't told anyone else I'm here?'

'Yes, no, and no, to your questions,' he said. 'But did you think you could stay hidden for ever? I didn't even try to find you, knowing your feelings, but here I am.'

'Well, I'm glad to see you, in spite of everything. Tell me what's been happening. Have you seen anything of my family?'

'Your brother Lord Marcus, of course. I'm sure all must be well at home, or he'd have reported otherwise. Oh, and I saw Lady Olivia when I was at Windsor last week. She's in waiting again. She seemed her usual contented self.'

'I'm glad. I miss the dear creature. Has she any new flirts?'

'Not to my knowledge.'

'She seems to have given all that up,' Venetia sighed. 'I know a maid of honour mustn't marry, but given a choice between the two—'

'Well, some of them do seem to dedicate their lives to it,' Winchmore said. 'Like nuns.'

'Olivia shan't be a nun,' Venetia said firmly. 'It would be too much of a waste.'

'And what about you?' he asked.

'I'm going to be a doctor,' she said. 'And that also precludes marriage.'

Fanny thought it was time to intervene. 'Will you stay for dinner, Captain Winchmore? I'm afraid our cook does not produce the sort of meals you're used to, but we will be very glad of your company.'

Winchmore bowed to her. 'Nothing would please me more than to dine with you. But rather than discommode your servants, might I be permitted to play host, and invite you both out to the theatre, and supper afterwards at Shepherd's Hotel?' He anticipated Venetia's refusal and went on quickly, 'I know you are in deep hiding, but I have a very secluded box, and I assure you almost everyone is out of Town, so you won't be seen. And there's a private room at Shepherd's where I dine my aunts when they come to London and the house is shut up, so you can be sure it's both discreet and respectable.'

Venetia hesitated, thinking longingly of the pleasures of the theatre and dainty food again, and Beauty's company. He looked so handsome, so elegant, so much a part of the old easy life, that for a moment she wondered why she had ever set herself on this course. She looked at Fanny for her view, and received a nod and an eager look.

'Then I accept,' she said. 'Aunt Fanny would never forgive me if I denied her a proper meal again, after all this time.' And then, thinking that was a little ungracious, she added, 'Thank you, Beauty. You are a good friend.'

He merely bowed to her, but his smile and his eyes were warm.

CHAPTER SIXTEEN

When Manfred first arrived at Trawden School, he was in a state close to despair, miserable about his past and in terror of his future. He had been robbed of his dear Gurney, tortured by her successor, and finally expelled from his home never, he guessed, to return. And if his wicked sister-in-law had done all this (instinctively he exempted George from blame, having never known unkindness from him) it was certain that she would have chosen a place to send him where they would be cruel to him.

He was escorted on the long journey by Roberts, one of the new footmen, who did not know whether to be pleased at getting out of the house for a spell, or annoyed at being given a job he suspected would reflect no glory on him. He therefore ignored Manfred loftily throughout the journey, sucking on his pipe and staring out of the window, or dozing with his hat tilted forward over his nose. It was a long journey, by railway to Leeds and then to Bradford, then by an old-fashioned coach to Oakworth, where the school's own vehicle met them at the inn. Here the coach was turned round and, after an hour's bait for the driver and a change of horses, set off again for Bradford.

Roberts eyed the school's ancient one-horse phaeton, and decided he would much rather not sample its paces. A quart of ale and something to eat in the inn would be a much better use of his talents.

'I'll leave the boy in your charge, then,' he told the whiskery individual on the phaeton. 'I must take the coach back to Bradford, so I dare say there won't be time to go all the way to the school. Here's his box – can you catch hold of it? Up you get then, Master Manfred. That's right. Be a good boy, now. Off you go, driver!'

The whiskery one looked as though this kind of haste to be gone was not new to him, and he received the boy and his luggage without comment, pulled his hat harder down on his head, and shook the reins. The horse heaved itself into a walk, and the phaeton rumbled off. Manfred looked back to wave goodbye, but Roberts had already disappeared. He felt abandoned, and completely alone.

Leaving Oakworth behind they passed out into open country, a road running across a moor – oh, but such a moor! Dark, grey and drear, running almost flat to the smudged horizon, and seeming empty of all life. Gathering rain clouds added to the brooding air of menace and oppression. It was nothing like Marston Moor, the only other moor he knew. No-one, he thought, could ever love such a moor as this.

The journey was not long, though the slow pace made it seem so, and the driver showed no desire to speak or even look at his charge. He was merely, Manfred thought, a gaoler escorting him to prison – a dungeon most like – where misery and death awaited him. They came in to Trawden just as the clouds were at their darkest and the rain began. The village was a modest affair of huddled cottages and a few scattered smallholdings. The church was large, with a steeple, built of dark stone; slightly elevated, it brooded over a large square graveyard, hedged round with tall trees. Beside the church was the vicarage, a plain, square house of the same grey stone; on the adjacent side of the graveyard was the school.

What the school had been was not clear – perhaps a barn or animal shed, perhaps a large cottage. It was long and lowish; whitewashed, which made it gleam eerily in the rain-dusk; it had a stone roof, and a chimney at one end which emitted welcome smoke. The rain began to drive hard as they drew up in the road before it, flattening the smoke down over the roof, and laying back the horse's ears.

The driver, however, seemed impervious. 'Here y'are, then,' he said, unflinching under his dripping brim. 'Go roun' t'other side. Tek thi bag. Ah'll bring t'box.'

He gestured with a thumb. Manfred climbed down, took his cloak-bag, and hunching his shoulders against the icy rain, trudged down the side of the building towards the churchyard. On this side, overlooking the graves, there were windows, but they were set too high to see into, though Manfred could see a reflected glow as from a fire within. He reached a door, heavy, panelled and shut. He knocked on it, but his small knuckles did not seem to make any impression. At last he tried the great iron ring of a handle, found it turned, and let himself in.

He was in a large room that took up half the space of the building, and went all the way up into the roof. In the end wall, to his right, was a large fireplace housing a bright blaze, with a mesh fireguard all the way round it. The rest of the room was taken up with wooden trestles and benches at which a large number of boys of various ages were working. Over in the corner a man was conducting some kind of lesson with four older boys, who seemed to Manfred on the verge of adulthood. No-one looked up as he came in. Manny felt very small and alone, wet, hungry, tired, far from home. His lip trembled, and he blinked hard to stop himself crying. At any moment now someone would notice him and his new life of torture would begin. However unhappy he was at this precise instant, it was a hiatus, and he wished it might go on for ever.

But one of the great boys looked across and saw him, and in a murmured comment brought the master's attention to him. The master said something in return, put down his book and came across the room. One or two other boys looked up as he passed: the master said sharply, 'No need to stop working,' and the heads went quickly down again.

He was a tall man, clean shaven but for his side whiskers, thin and pale. He was wearing a threadbare and shabby suit of black, a maroon waistcoat, and a large and battered silver watch in his fob. To Manfred, at nine, the ages of adults were an impenetrable mystery, but in fact he was only in his mid-twenties, though there were deep lines in his face, of the sort that are left by childhood illness.

He stopped in front of Manfred and looked him over, while

283

Manfred stared at the watch and felt the rain dripping off the ends of his hair. 'Well, so you're the new boy,' the man said at last. 'What's your name?'

'Manfred Morland,' Manny said in the husk of a voice, and then added judiciously, 'sir.'

'Quite right, we were expecting you. Who brought you?'

'I – I don't know his name. A man with a cart.'

'No-one from home came with you?'

Manfred drooped miserably. 'He left me where the coach stops.'

'Oh. Well, I am Mr Liddel,' the man went on, in a different voice, which made Manny look up at last, because it sounded kind. Liddel was smiling pleasantly. 'Jacob shouldn't have left you down here. I suppose he wanted to get out of the rain. He should have taken you up to the house first, to see the principal.'

'Who, sir?' Manfred was emboldened to ask.

'The Reverend Mr Kettleworth, who owns this school.'

'Don't you own it, sir?'

'No, I only teach here,' said Liddel, seeming to find the question amusing. 'Well, I can't leave the school to take you myself.' He looked round. 'Cousins, come here.'

A boy of about eleven at a nearby table got up at once and came to stand before Liddel, keeping his eyes with remarkable discipline from Manfred. 'Take this boy up to the house – he's the new boy, Morland. Don't dawdle, and come straight back. You can leave your bag here, Morland,' Liddel added. 'Off you go.'

Cousins set off at once, without even looking to see if Manny was with him. Outside it seemed less dark, perhaps because the clouds were lifting a little, or perhaps in contrast, because there had been no lamps inside. The rain was steady, but not as violent as before.

As soon as the door was shut, Cousins turned to give Manfred a comprehensive examination. 'How old are you?' was the result.

'Nine,' said Manny.

'I'm nearly twelve. I've been here a year and two months. I know everything about this place, so if you want to know anything, you can ask me,' Cousins said, lordly-wise. 'What's your name, your first name?'

'Manfred.'

Cousins hooted. 'What sort of a name is that?'

'It's out of a book,' Manny said defensively.

'It's a silly name. Mine's Tom. That's a sensible name. You ought to get a new one, or you'll be ragged.'

'It's not my fault. My mother chose it.'

'You'd better jolly well unchoose it, or you'll be for it!'

'They call me Manny at home, mostly.'

'That's not so bad. I'll call you Manny, and you can call me Tom,' Cousins said generously. He started along the path that skirted the graveyard, towards the house, and Manfred fell in beside him, too interested in this new contact to notice the rain. 'You're lucky, having a mother,' he conceded, 'even if she did give you a silly name.'

'I haven't any more,' Manny said. 'She died years ago.'

'Have you got a father?'

'He died last year.'

'Oh. I never had one at all. Not a father or a mother.'

'You must've had,' Manny objected.

'Well, I didn't. I lived with my aunt until I came here, so there.'

They were almost at the house, and there were more urgent questions to ask. The problem of Cousins's origins could wait. 'What's it like here?' Manny asked.

'Oh, it's not bad. The Kettle's a bit fierce, and no end particular, and the Lid's nearly as bad. That's what we call them,' he explained kindly, 'the Kettle and the Lid. It's a joke.'

'Yes, but what's it *like* here,' Manny urged. They had reached the iron gate of the vicarage and time was running out.

'It's all right,' Cousins said vaguely. 'They make you work desperate hard, and if you get things wrong, they beat you fit to kill. The Kettle thrashed me last week until his arm nearly came off. But the other fellows are jolly. Here we are. Ring this bell. I'd better get back, or the Lid'll be batey as a bull. Cheer-oh!'

285

Cousins abandoned him on the doorstep and dashed away, and Manfred, his resurrected courage destroyed again, found himself trembling as he took hold of the iron bell-handle and pulled. A prolonged jangling sounded deep in the house, and after a moment the door was opened by a severe-looking lady in a plaid gown, with a cap over her hair and spectacles on her nose.

'Boys do not ring the bell!' she pronounced in awful tones. Manfred shrank from her and felt the tears dangerously close to overflowing; and then she stooped to examine him more closely, and said in a completely different voice, 'Why you're the new boy, aren't you? Dear me, I'm sorry, I didn't see you properly. It's so dark out here. There, never mind, don't be frightened. You did quite right to ring. Come in, come in out of the rain.' Manfred stepped into a gloomy panelled hall, and she shut the door behind him, then came to examine him again. 'Why, child, you're trembling! Cold is it? You're not afraid of me, I hope?'

Manfred was too tired and hungry and confused to be able to tell any more what he felt. He gulped like a fish, trying not to cry.

'There, now, don't cry,' the lady said. 'I am Mrs Kettleworth, you know; and you must be little Morland. I am the principal's wife, and I take care of all you boys. You are very wet! Are you hungry, my dear? I expect you are. Come with me into the kitchen, where there's a fire, and we'll get you warm and dry, and Cook shall find you something to eat. The boys' supper isn't until five, and you won't want to wait until then.'

Talking pleasantly, she led Manfred across the hall and down a passage into a large kitchen with a bright fire, where a stout person, hard and red as a rose-hip, in an all-enveloping apron, was chopping vegetables. Manfred, shivering violently, as much from emotion as cold, was placed on a stool as close to the fire as he could bear. Soon a cup of milk and a plate of bread and butter were put in his hands, and then Mrs Kettleworth produced a rough towel and with her own hands dried Manny's hair, talking all the while in a pleasant tone. He didn't know what to make of it. The fire and the food and the soothing voice made him think of the nursery back home, and Gurney. But when was the torture to start? Was it a trick to ambush him?

When his shivering had stopped, Mrs Kettleworth went out of the room for a while, and came back to sit opposite him and say, 'Mr Kettleworth will see you in a little while, when you've finished your lunch. You've no parents, I understand?'

'No, ma'am,' he said.

'Well, then, you must think of Mr Kettleworth and me as your father and mother. We've been such to many boys, I can tell you!' she said with a laugh. 'We are a family here at Trawden, I always say – isn't that right, Cook? And if you are a good boy, obey orders and work hard at your lessons, you'll have nothing to fear. Finish up now, that's a good child.'

She stood up, and Manny heard her murmur to the cook behind him, 'Turned out, poor child, Mr K. says – father's just died and brother doesn't want him. What a world it is, Cookie!'

'Yes, mum,' the cook replied, her low voice only just heard over the rapid staccato of her chopping of a carrot. 'What age is he? Nine? Small for it, isn't he? How long is he to stop?'

'Permanent, so Mr K. says.' The word seemed a foreboding and somehow shameful thing, like a mark of failure, to the listening boy. 'Well, let's hope there's no trouble about the fees. They're supposed to be decent folk, but you never can tell.'

Manfred's interview with Mr Kettleworth was brief. Conducted into a dark, booklined room he stood before a massive desk, on the other side of which was a man with a bald front and long white hair behind, gold pince-nez on a thin, beak-nosed, fine face. Like an eagle, Manfred thought through his weary confusion, not like a kettle at all.

'Manfred Morland,' said the man, consulting a piece of paper before him.

'Yes, sir,' Manny just managed to say.

'You've been sent here to study, to learn what will enable you to make your living in the world. I am here to help you learn. This will be your home now, and I hope you will be happy in it, my boy. What studies have you done at home?' Manfred didn't know how to answer. 'Can you read and write?' Manny nodded. 'Have you studied mathematics? Latin and Greek? History? The globes?' To all of these, Manfred shook his head; but Mr Kettleworth did not seem unduly upset. 'Well, you are young. You will soon catch up.' Suddenly he smiled, and it was like the sun coming out after the darkness of the rain. 'You will be my blank page, and I shall write on you. What did you do at home, when you were not at your lessons?'

'I – I went about, sir,' Manny said shyly. 'About the farms. I rode my pony, and fished, and helped with the sheep. And watched things. Foxes and rabbits and badgers and things.'

Kettleworth nodded. 'You are fond of animals? And birds, too? Do you like birds?'

'Yes, sir.'

'I am very fond of bird-watching myself. I see we have something in common. We shall have some pleasant times in the future.' Manfred dared to smile, and, satisfied, Kettleworth said, 'Well, now, you had better go back across to the school. Report to Mr Liddel, and he will see you settled in. I shall be across myself shortly to take a lesson. Goodbye, Morland, my boy, for the present. I am sure you will be very happy here.'

And Manfred obediently went away, feeling that perhaps, indeed, he might.

Cardwell's Army Regulation Bill contained much else besides the abolition of purchase, but that was the issue that was fiercely fought over. In the Commons a group of colonels devised a new system of opposition: remaining on their feet and talking at enormous length and obscurity, obstructing the Bill and baffling its proponents by the sheer consumption of Parliamentary time.

But at length it was passed, and went up to the Lords, where the battle was renewed. The traditional lines of conflict were much blurred. It was not just a matter of Whig against Tory, or die-hard against liberal; many were the liberals who agreed with Southport's view, and supported purchase because the idea of a well-trained professional army running loose about the country seemed a worse danger than the possibility of invasion.

In the end the Lords voted to shelve the Bill, by a majority which should have meant it was never seen again. But two days later the Government announced that purchase had been abolished by Royal Warrant. There was uproar in both Houses.

Charlotte heard the news from Oliver, who came up to see her in her sitting-room after the end of the morning's Cabinet business and before going into the House. He sat on the edge of her desk and fiddled with her pens as he talked, and she could see that he was frayed with the long battle, in a state of nervous irritation. Still she could not help expressing a worry. 'Doesn't this set a dangerous precedent? Surely using the royal prerogative to overturn the wishes of Parliament is undemocratic?'

'It's not a matter of the prerogative,' Oliver said. 'Purchase was established in the first place by Royal Warrant. All the Queen has done is to cancel that warrant and issue a new one stating that purchase is no longer legal.'

Charlotte frowned at him. 'Oh, my dear, that's sheer sophistry; adhering to the word and not the spirit.'

'The spirit in this case is the nation's desire for an efficient army to protect it,' he said.

'How do you know what the nation desires? That can only be expressed through Parliament.'

Absently he ruined a nib by twisting it between his fingers. 'Don't you turn against me too!' he said, and he sounded close to breaking.

'No, never against you!' she declared quickly. She gently removed the pen from his hands and said, 'You must know better than me, and I respect your judgement, but if any government can overturn Parliament's will by some trick like this, surely it opens the door to dictatorship – the very thing you were so concerned about.'

'Oh Charlotte, if you knew the number of things I have been concerned about! I am so tired of fighting for something I can't entirely justify – against men whose opinions I partly share!'

'I know, love. I do know.'

He rubbed his temples wearily. 'Well, it's over now. And

to soothe your fears that Parliament is being circumvented, I can tell you that the Lords are to resurrect Cardwell's Bill.'

'Because of the *fait accompli*?' Charlotte asked, a little surprised. She wouldn't have expected the Upper House to cave in so easily.

'No, because the Bill provided for generous compensation for the officers affected, and there will be none at all unless it is passed. So the measure will have the democratic approval you seem to crave.'

Charlotte still thought that to force Parliament to approve by use of a trick was not democracy, but she said no more, seeing how tired her husband was. It had been a strain on all of them in the War Office, but especially on him, for he had lost the friendship of many old colleagues – the senior army officers who would never forgive him, and other peers who had taken the opposing side and who felt the Upper House had been outflanked by a blackguard device.

In addition there was conflict at home, for Marcus felt he had been put in an impossible position, and had distanced himself from his father. He had even quarrelled with Harry, who said his first loyalty should be to his father. The twins, who had been inseparable since babyhood, were now suffering under a coolness. Marcus no longer came home, living his whole life in barracks and in the clubs favoured by military men.

To add to this there was Venetia's continued exile, and the estrangement from the Westons, which, though it didn't affect Oliver a great deal directly, made him feel guilty for the hurt he knew it inflicted on Charlotte. Only Olivia gave him no pangs, seeming happily settled in her life of court service, interspersed with quiet months at home when she seemed to do nothing but wait patiently for her next summons. Her only agitation had been when Venetia left home and the Queen had expressed disapproval.

'She says it's not at all the thing for females to ape men like that. She very much disapproves of unwomanly behaviour,' Olivia reported to her mother with breathless anxiety. 'And she advises Papa to force Venetia to come home. A father's authority ought to be absolute, she says; and she says the Prince would never have allowed it.'

'But Olivia,' Charlotte said impatiently, and with some dismay, 'whyever did you tell the Queen about Venetia? Our whole hope was to keep the thing secret.'

Olivia's eyes opened wide. 'But Mama, I can't keep any secrets from the Queen. It would be wrong!'

'I don't mean you should lie to her,' Charlotte said patiently, 'but there's no need to go telling her things she wouldn't otherwise know, and which, frankly, have nothing to do with her.'

'*Everything* has to do with her. She's the Queen,' Olivia said simply. 'And besides, she always finds things out, and then asks why one didn't tell her, and sounds so *wounded*. She always hears everything in the end.'

Charlotte saw that Olivia had a severe case of *crush*, as they said nowadays, and left it at that.

Olivia came back from waiting in mid-August when the Court moved to Balmoral. 'I wish I hadn't had to leave,' she told her mother. She was helping Charlotte with preparations to shut up the house for summer. 'Her Majesty had a sore throat, and one can't help being worried, because she's never ill. She has such a remarkable constitution.'

Charlotte said. 'To bear nine children and still have so much energy is remarkable. My five were enough for me. A card will do for Lady Tonbridge, I think, but I ought to call on the Petersfields. Mary Petersfield has been unwell.'

'I'll start a list, shall I?' Olivia said, and then continued with what occupied her thoughts. 'I hope Balmoral will set her up. She always says the air there is the best in the world.'

'Are the Petersfields going to Balmoral?' Charlotte said in surprise.

'No, Mama, I meant the Queen,' Olivia said patiently. 'Princess Alice is going to visit this summer, too, and she's such a good nurse, she's bound to make a difference. But I wish I could be there. I could cheer her up with music. She likes my Italian songs so much, and none of the other ladies sings in Italian.'

Charlotte looked up from addressing an envelope and

regarded her daughter curiously. 'You are really happy at Court, aren't you?'

'I'm not really happy anywhere else,' Olivia said unexpectedly. 'A card for Lady Hope?'

'I think they've gone down already, but we'll leave one just in case. But isn't it very dull for you at Court, love? The same routine, the same people, the nothing-doing all day long?'

'Oh *no*! It's never dull! There's always something going on, ministers calling, and foreign diplomats – affairs of state, you know.' She nodded impressively. 'And then, the Queen is such wonderful company – so warm and charming.' She sighed. 'I miss it all so when I'm not there.'

Charlotte could not discover that there was any young man at Court or out of it who had touched Olivia's fancy, and concluded that for the moment the crush was all. She hoped her daughter would grow out of it before she was too old to marry, for it seemed a shame that such a pretty girl should become a vestal virgin. 'Put the Morpurgos on the call-in-person list. They're cousins of a sort, and not very well off: one must be extra careful in those cases.'

Charlotte soon had other things on her mind which drove out any concern over Olivia: Oliver came home from Downing Street to announce that he had handed in his resignation to Mr Gladstone. He took Charlotte to walk in the garden for privacy to discuss it.

'I've nothing more to give,' he said. 'The conflict over purchase has worn me out. They used me blatantly as a go-between, and I accepted the rôle; but it's been more tiring than I could ever have imagined. There's still a great deal more to do, of course—'

'Let the younger men do it,' Charlotte said quickly. 'You've earned your rest.'

He stopped and turned to her, taking her hands. 'What would you feel about my giving up public life altogether?' he asked abruptly.

'Could you?'

'Oh, God, yes! I'm so tired, Charley. You don't know how tired.'

'Do you know,' she said with a slow smile, 'I think that's

the first time you've ever called me Charley. You were always so disapproving when Cavendish called me that.'

He smiled too. 'I can't think what came over me. I must be sicker than I thought. But what would you think, dear love, of having me at home all the time? Would it trouble you?'

'I can't think of anything nicer,' she said. 'We've had so little time together. In all our marriage there has always been your public life and mine to keep us busy and apart.'

'Ah yes, that's the other half of the equation: your public work. Could you give it up? Would you be happy to close up the house for good and live down at Ravendene? Walking, riding; I could teach you to fish; local affairs, estate matters. We shouldn't be bored.'

'But we could still entertain sometimes?'

'As often as you liked, down there. One ought to pay some attention to the county.'

'*Noblesse oblige?*' Charlotte mocked. 'That wasn't quite what I meant.'

'Friends too,' he said with a smile. 'We could have house parties in the hunting season. Picnic parties in the summer. It's no distance from London for weekend visits.'

'We'd have to open up Southport House for Augusta's coming out,' Charlotte mentioned.

'Of course. And for Emma's,' he said. She squeezed his hand gratefully for that. He could so easily have punished Emma for Fanny's defection. 'And we'd have Fairy to keep us lively. Could you bear it, do you think? To grow old in the country with me? You wouldn't miss your committees?'

'No,' she said. 'Not if I had your company. But Oliver, what about Venetia?'

He had been smiling in a way that made him look younger than he had for years; but now the old frown came back. 'Not now. I can't talk about her now. If you want to remain in London for her sake— ?'

'No,' she said quickly. 'I want to be with you.'

'I dare say Tommy keeps an eye on her and Fanny,' he said, and it was a concession to her feelings, because he had not even mentioned Tommy's name before. Charlotte wished he could forgive Venetia, for they were so alike, and she believed he had loved her best of all his children. But perhaps that was why he couldn't. She could only hope that time would work its healing, and either bring Venetia home, or reconcile Oliver to her actions.

She said nothing more about Venetia now, as Oliver drew her hand through his arm and they walked on. 'Perhaps,' he said after a while, in a cheerful voice, 'we might start a garden together, down at Ravendene. I've never made a garden – in fact, I've made so little impression on Ravendene, if I died tomorrow it would never know I'd gone.'

'*I'd* know,' she said, 'so please don't.'

'Would you like to make a garden with me?'

She felt a strange, fluttery thrill, almost as though he had asked if she'd like to make a baby with him. 'I'd love to.'

'There ought to be water in it, I think.'

'And a summerhouse, so that we can sit and admire our work,' she said.

Planning happily, they walked on through the sooty London shrubbery, seeing a very different landscape in their minds.

At Trawden the boys lived their whole lives in the schoolhouse. The large room Manfred had first seen was schoolroom, playroom, and refectory. At the trestles they studied and ate, and outside lesson hours pursued their other interests. The other half of the building was on two storeys. On the lower floor was the boys' dormitory, and the upper floor, a strange little chamber with sharply sloping walls, was Liddel's private room.

There were forty boys in the school, in age ranging from eight to fifteen. Some were the children of respectable working folk trying to better themselves, who wanted a good practical start for their sons, or who wanted a son trained up to do the office work of an expanding family business. Others were the unwanted, the residue of various social accidents: orphans, foundlings, the damaged and the illegitimate, for whom there was someone willing at least to pay to have them educated to be self-supporting. The lessons were in English and mathematics, handwriting and book-keeping, together with a modicum of general subjects – current affairs and history and geography – all that was needed for them to find employment as clerks.

The lessons were given by the Kettle and the Lid, and silence and strict discipline were enforced during school hours. Idleness, inattention, or the slightest propensity towards riot were swiftly punished with a beating, and in the first few days Manfred went in fear and trembling, flinching whenever the stick came crashing down on another's flesh. He applied himself with such desperate attention to the work that was put in front of him that he could hardly comprehend it; but no harm came to him, and after a few days he relaxed enough to begin to understand the lessons. As time went on he came to discover that Kettleworth and Liddel knew their pupils pretty well, and a boy who sincerely did his best was not punished.

All the lessons were taken by these two gentlemen, and by a visiting tutor who came in on Wednesday afternoons, when Liddel had his time off – a former military man called Morris, who with very little persuasion from the boys would turn a geography lesson into a spell-binding story of his experiences with the colours.

On Saturday afternoons there were no lessons, and except for those who had extra tuition or domestic duties, the boys could do as they pleased. The school and church were the last buildings in the small village, and the moor rolled like a lapping sea right up to its boundaries, a natural playground for boisterous youngsters who had been mewed up all week, a place where they could stretch their eager muscles without doing any damage. On Sunday the boys attended church twice, and for the rest of the day were required to sit quietly, read the Bible or approved religious texts, and learn by heart a collect, an Old Testament extract, and a piece from the Gospels.

Two boys each week were assigned to kitchen duties, and two to laundry duties. The former helped with the preparation of the meals, which they then helped carry down from the vicarage kitchen. The menu was unvarying: porage for breakfast, bread and butter or bread and cheese for lunch, and for supper something hot, a stew of barley and vegetables, or

295

potatoes, or a large piece of pudding with gravy or sauce. On Wednesdays there was meat, generally bacon, with it, and on Sundays a good dinner of roast or boiled beef or mutton and rice pudding was served at midday, with bread and butter for supper. The food was very plain, but Manfred found there was usually enough of it, and he was not as often hungry as he had been at home.

Kitchen duty was popular with the boys, partly as it took them away from lessons for a short time, and partly because they hoped to filch or be offered something extra to eat while they were in the kitchen. Laundry duty was disliked because it took up the Saturday afternoon free time. The laundry was a lean-to building behind the vicarage kitchen, and the laundress, a sour-tempered woman with vast red arms, laboured there every day on the boys' smalls and shirts. But each Saturday four pairs of sheets were washed, and it was with these that the boys had to help. As there were sixteen beds in the dormitory, each got clean sheets once a month.

Mrs Kettleworth oversaw the domestic care of the boys. It was a nice calculation how to house and feed them out of a fee small enough to be afforded by the sort of families the school was intended to serve. A defaulting guardian could throw the finances into chaos; an unexpected donation from some benefactor could mean extra food or new sheets, or another hundredweight of coal laid in for the winter. It was also her duty to tend their ailments, for the school could not afford to call in a doctor except in the most extreme circumstances. Trawden was not a healthy place, too cold and damp, as the fog that frequently hung over the graveyard attested; and boys in close confinement passed things quickly to one another. There was always a cold going about, and the last boy would not have finished with one before the first boy was starting another. Minor injuries, stomach upsets and chilblains were a constant attrition; infectious disease the thing most to be dreaded.

Manfred found the life spartan and comfortless at first. It was much colder out here on the edge of Keighley Moor than it had been at Morland Place, and though he was not used to sharing a bed, he came to be very grateful for the heat of other bodies under the inadequate blankets. In the schoolroom he began to find the work interesting and stimulating, but when they were not doing lessons, there was no comfortable chair to curl up in, only the same bare trestles and benches, and the places round the fire were always taken by the senior boys. There were no picture books or toys for amusement, only the other boys, conversation, and what playthings they could contrive for themselves. The scene was monotonous and confining to one who had been used to roaming about a large house and estate; his daily life here without any touch of comfort or beauty.

But there were benefits: there was no deliberate cruelty, and his nervous fears gradually faded away, so that his true nature could re-emerge. He had the companionship of the other boys; and as the weather improved, the moors to roam over. And he had the pleasure of acquiring knowledge and training, the delights of an expanding mind. Mr Kettleworth discovered that he was naturally intelligent so gave him extra work to do, and occasionally individual tuition.

Some of the boys with parents who lived not too far away were fetched home on Saturdays, returning on Sunday night; and these were the boys who also went home for the holidays. The boys with no families, who stayed the whole year at Trawden, called them oppidans, and themselves collegers, terms taken from Eton College to distinguish boys who lived in the town from boys who lived in the school. The words were used lightheartedly, and each group claimed to be superior in some way to the other; but as the year broadened and the summer vacation approached, Manfred came to realise that there was a world of hurt underneath the teasing. The collegers laughed, but when the time came and the oppidans were fetched away to homes that wanted them back, they watched the departing vehicles in silence.

CHAPTER SEVENTEEN

August was the month when London traditionally emptied. Parliament went into recess, the great folk closed their houses and went down to the country, and naturally the great medical men, bereft of their patients, went away too. The poor, who had no choice but to stay in London, had to rely on the lesser men at the hospitals and dispensaries.

Venetia was oddly upset when Southport House was closed up. 'I know it's foolish, because I couldn't go there anyway, but I liked the thought of Mama being nearby. Do you think it will ever be opened up again?'

'I suppose Harry will want to use it when he gets older,' Fanny said listlessly. The heat of summer, the confined life she was leading, and Mrs Lodden's cooking were all undermining her health.

Venetia pushed a sticky strand of hair from her forehead. 'Goodness, it's so close! Do you think there'll be a thunderstorm?'

'It might clear the air if there were,' Fanny said.

'The milk was off this morning. That's usually a sign.'

'It's a sign Mrs Lodden didn't get any fresh in.' She watched Venetia cross the room to find a book. 'With all the great men out of London, I suppose there'll be no-one for you to badger,' she said. 'Not much point in your staying in London at all, really.'

'Oh, there's always someone,' Venetia said, missing the wistful tone in Fanny's voice. 'The hospitals don't close, you know, and someone has to run them.'

'Wouldn't a break from it all do you good?' Fanny tried

again. 'Even Mark has gone home to his parents. A few weeks at Ravendene would set you up for the fray.'

Venetia turned. 'It would be lovely to see Livy and Gus, and the boys, and Mama – but Papa hasn't forgiven me yet. I couldn't go unless they asked me.' It struck her at last. 'Poor Aunt Fanny, you must miss Emma so. I should have thought.' She frowned. 'Couldn't you visit, without me?'

'I couldn't leave you unchaperoned,' Fanny said. 'And besides, if you aren't forgiven, neither am I.'

'You must want to see Emma. I wonder if she could come and visit us here?'

'There's no room,' Fanny said.

'Oh, there's always room for the people one loves. She could share my bed,' Venetia said.

Fanny marvelled at this, from the girl who a few months ago had despaired of being able to live in such confined quarters. But she said, 'I don't think I should like to drag Emma from the country to London in August. Perhaps in September or October, when the weather's cooler, I may ask her. We'll see. Don't worry about it.' She hoped very much that in a month or two more, Venetia would have outworn her enthusiasm for this life, and they might both go home permanently.

The rain came down in a torrent the next day. Venetia was out, and Fanny was lying on the *chaise-longue* by the open window, enjoying the smell of warm wet bricks and pavements, the sound of gurgling and rushing in the gutters and down-pipes. She watched, as she watched most days, the theatre of everyday activity below her in the street. The shop-keepers were hurrying to bring in the goods displayed outside; umbrellas were sprouting everywhere like mushrooms. The passers-by without them were sheltering, some huddling in doorways, some hopping from one door to the next in dramatic dashes, others plodding on under the makeshift cover of a folded newspaper. The rain bounced off the road with a hissing noise, dissolving clumps of manure and washing them into the gutters to join the paper, straw and cabbage leaves that always choked them. A window in the building opposite was closed with a bang by an unseen hand; on the next windowsill, a pair of pigeons sat with their drab shoulders hunched in a hopeless manner, like people waiting for an omnibus.

There had been no traffic for a few minutes, and a pi-dog, indifferent to the rain, had wandered out into the middle of the road to investigate a piece of refuse. Now a hansom turned into the street and approached at the usual clip, sending the dog scrabbling for safety. It came to a violent halt just below. Fanny watched the driver receive his money through the hatch; the passenger, invisible to her, flung back the covers and shoved out an umbrella, opened it, and climbed out under its shelter, showing her no more than the ends of his trousers and a very shiny boot – from which she concluded he had not stepped out of doors since the rain began. She was pondering this when to her surprise the umbrella mounted the steps of the house and she heard the sharp rapping of the door-knocker below.

Tommy? she wondered. But he had said he was going down to Eastbourne for a week – anxious and apologetic for abandoning Venetia and Fanny as he had been, he owed the duty to his mother. Beauty Winchmore, perhaps? He might have taken a hansom rather than get a wetting. But why would he call when he knew Venetia must be out?

At last the drawing-room door opened, and there was Mrs Lodden, puffing from the exertion of the stairs, her face all one yawning question as she announced, 'There's a Mr Anthony here to see you, ma'am.'

Fanny's heart jumped so violently it hurt. It couldn't be! It *couldn't* be! Had her husband found her out after all this time? Come to reproach her? To make her go back to him? All the agony of her past crowded into her mind, blotting out thought in a wordless scream of protest. Her mouth was too dry to frame either question or request; but in any case Mrs Lodden had saved herself a double journey by bringing the gentleman up with her – Fanny could see a dark shape moving behind her on the landing. There was no denying him now.

Mrs Lodden stood aside, and a perfect stranger stepped in. Fanny stared at him, her mind whirling uselessly like a wheel out of gear. It was a young man who stood before her, a man in his early twenties; he was formally clad in black frock-coat over grey-and-black striped trousers, a black neck-cloth held with a diamond-headed pin – expensive but discreet – and a black silk top hat in his hand.

'Mrs Anthony?' he enquired.

Fanny still could not speak, but there was no denial in her face. Mrs Lodden, having waited in vain for any enlightenment or command, had no choice now but to leave them; she stepped out and closed the door reluctantly. The young man stood where he was, his pale face set, unsmiling. It was a face of regular features marred by a rather blobbish nose, but would not have been unattractive had there been animation in its expression. He was clean-shaven but for long side-whiskers, a rather old-fashioned affectation for such a young man. His hair was fair, his eyes a pale, bright blue. He was staring at her, gripping his hat brim more tightly than his valet would have liked – and surely he had a valet, for his clothes were expensive and well kept.

At last he said, 'You *are* Mrs Philip Anthony?' His voice was harsh – with emotion, Fanny suddenly realised. A thought was knocking at her mind, which she did not want to admit.

'I am Fanny Anthony,' she managed to say, her voice husky from the dryness of her throat.

The young man's blue gaze did not waver, but his mouth trembled. 'I am Lionel,' he said.

It was a moment of scalding emotion: fear, wonder, regret – embarrassment too. Lionel, Philip's son, the child she had abandoned as a baby and never seen since; the child she had not loved, and had felt guilty about because she had not loved him, because she had left him. Had he come to reproach her now? Perhaps – but there was something else in his eyes. He looked very unsure of himself – very young, and vulnerable.

It was absolutely necessary for her now to speak. She said, 'You will forgive me – I can't rise. Please, won't you come and sit down – here, where I can see you.'

He crossed the room to the chair she indicated, hesitated, and sat, his hat on his knee in the approved manner of the formal morning call. They looked at each other again for another long moment. The embarrassment was wearing off, now they were growing used to the look of each other. She was searching his face for familiarity, and finding a hint of it here and there – and presumably, he was doing the same. He didn't look much like what she remembered of his father. Perhaps he resembled some relative further back. There was a hint of herself about his mouth and chin, she thought; and he had a mole on his cheek just where she had one. It was peculiar and unnerving to see her own ghostly image peep out of this stranger. It was as if someone had stolen parts of her body while she was sleeping.

He cleared his throat and said, 'Are you – do you – are you confined to the sofa?'

She framed the answer for him carefully. 'I am something of an invalid and I go out very little. But I have the use of my legs. The surprise of seeing you took the strength from me. You look – very well.'

He ducked his head from the compliment, like a boy avoiding having his hair ruffled by an aunt. It was a strangely touching gesture, and Fanny did not want to be touched.

'You are not the way I imagined you,' he said, still looking down.

'*Did* you imagine me?' she said. 'I would not have expected you ever to give me a thought.'

He took the question straightforwardly. 'Yes, I imagined you. You were the woman who gave birth to me. I expect all children are curious about those things that appertain to them. But of course, I always imagined you as a young woman, as you were when I was born. It was foolish of me not to have realised that you must have grown old.'

That hurt. 'Yes, it was foolish of you,' she said brittly. 'Time did not stand still for me; but hardship and illness have taken their toll as well.'

He looked up then, a swift flash of blue. 'The hardship was your own choice,' he said. 'You must not expect me to pity you. You left me, without a thought for my welfare, or my father's. Do not ask *me* for sympathy.'

'Have you come here to reproach me?' she asked. 'Is that all? After so long, I wonder you bothered.'

'No, I came to see what you were like. But if my presence

is unwelcome to you, I will leave.' He stood up, and she held out a quick hand.

'No, please don't go. Not yet. I want to know what you are like, too. I'm sorry I spoke sharply to you. But this is very painful to me.'

'Do you think it isn't painful to me?' he asked, a little angrily. 'And to find you here, living in these conditions!'

'How *did* you find me?' she asked.

'I called at Southport House. I thought the duchess would know where you are. The house was shut up and the family gone down to the country, but a servant gave me your direction when I told him who I was. But I never thought Bury Street would be like this, that I would find you living in such squalor. I thought you were well provided for.'

'I am,' Fanny said. 'I have a very comfortable income, but I am living here temporarily for a particular reason, which I won't go into, since it is not my secret to divulge. You need not be ashamed of having a pauper for a mother – I am very well to do.'

He turned his face from her and walked a pace or two up and down the room, and she was sorry to have antagonised him again.

'Lionel,' she said, forcing herself to use the name, 'I'm sorry. Really, I am not managing this very well. Please sit down and tell me about yourself.' He sat, very much on his dignity, and she searched for a neutral question. 'What made you come to look for me? I mean, why now?'

He looked straight at her. 'I came to tell you that my father is dead.'

Fanny kept absolutely still. Philip was dead: her husband still in the eyes of the law, since he had never divorced her; and as long as he lived, a threat to her, for he might at any time have come to force her to return to his house. He was dead, and she was a widow. She was free. His face was suddenly before her in imagination, and she remembered how she had loved him, long, long ago. This pale young man's very existence was owed to that love. She had lain with his father in love, and borne him a son in labour; and if the love had failed, that did not negate it.

'When?' was all she managed to say.

'In May. Just after my birthday.'

'Your twenty-first,' she said, staring at nothing.

'How did you know that?'

'Did you think I never thought of you? I tried not to, but you've been there in my mind like a ghost in the room, always. You and your father. I'm not so good at callousness as I would have liked.'

He did not know how to take that, so he went on with his own story. 'My father told me about you, but though I was curious, I felt it would have been disloyal to him to come and see you while he was alive. Well, he's dead now. I've finished sorting out the estate, and I had a little time in hand, so I thought it was a good time to do it.'

'The estate – in Norfolk?'

'Yes. It's a very large property now – my grandfather's land, plus the additions my father made. He was a good steward, and I intend to follow in his footsteps.'

'You don't have a profession, like him?'

'I've no need. I am a landed gentleman.'

'I don't think your father was a doctor because he had to be,' Fanny said mildly. And then, awkwardly, 'Did he leave – was there no message for me?'

Lioned looked at her steadily. 'No, he left you no message. He never spoke of you. As far as I know, he never thought of you. He told me about you when I was growing up, when I asked him. He never refused to answer a question, but he never mentioned you otherwise. But I thought it was right that you should know he had passed away.'

'Thank you for telling me,' she said. There was a silence. He had asked her no question about herself; she hardly knew what to ask him about his own life. 'I'm sorry,' she said at last, 'if what I did hurt you. I did not do it lightly.'

'I don't think it hurt me. I didn't really know you,' he said calmly. 'I can't say I ever felt the lack of a mother. I was curious about you, I confess, but it was an idle curiosity.'

'Who brought you up?' Fanny asked.

'I had a nurse.' He seemed disinclined to tell her more. Fanny wondered if the nurse had been young and pretty,

304

if she had comforted Philip. He had never divorced her to marry again. Had he really been celibate all that time? And yet she could imagine him remaining celibate, if for no other reason than to distance himself from Fanny's wickedness, so that his disapproval of her could be absolute.

'You have a sister,' she said on a sudden impulse. 'Did you know that?'

His cheeks flamed unexpectedly. 'I have no sister or brother,' he said between rigid lips.

'Her name is Emma. She's almost fifteen.'

He stood up. 'I must go now,' he said without looking at her. Outside the rain had stopped, and the sun had come out again; the roofs were steaming, and a symphony of drips had replaced the sounds of downpour. 'I should not have come.'

'Please don't go,' she said. She felt sore from the scouring of emotion, but if he went she would have a thousand questions unanswered, and a world of self-reproach to bear.

'I must,' he said. 'I have a train to catch.'

'But you'll visit me again?' she said desperately.

'No. There's nothing for me here.' Now he met her eyes. 'I am going to be married. That was another reason for coming here. With Papa dead, I wanted to clear everything up before my wedding.'

Fanny didn't know that she wanted to be cleared up. It sounded too final. 'Married? Is she nice? Tell me about her. What's her name?'

He looked down at her steadily. 'I don't wish to discuss her with you. It is nothing to do with you.'

'Nothing to do with me? You're my son!'

'But you are not my mother,' he said. He must have seen how it hurt her, because he said, 'I'm sorry. I must go now.' He was at the door. 'Don't ring – I'll see myself out.'

'Lionel!'

'Goodbye,' he said, closing the door behind him.

The St Giles Hospital near Moorgate was the next on Venetia's list. She had been told that she must take her application to the Committee of Benefactors: the benefactors were the

305

subscribers to the hospital, and therefore its governors. They met at eleven each Thursday morning, in the committee room, which was to be found off the main front entrance hall.

Venetia arrived at the front of the hospital at a quarter before eleven. It was a noble-looking building from this aspect, with iron railings, a courtyard of neatly raked gravel, a classical façade, a handsome doorway with false columns, and an entrance hall with black-and-white marble on the floor and magnificently framed portraits of benefactors past and present around the panelled walls. It presented a strong contrast to the entrance to the outpatients' department, round the back of the building, which Venetia had briefly glimpsed the day before.

She was surprised, therefore, when she entered the hall to find it full of poor people, some sitting on the hard benches along the walls, others standing quietly in orderly rows, filling the hall but for a wide passage down the middle to allow access to the staircase. Many of them sported bandages, some had missing limbs, digits, eyes. Some had evidently made an effort with their appearance, and sported their tawdry best clothes; others were in their working clothes. Some seemed apathetic with poverty and ill health, others seemed reasonably vigorous.

Venetia asked the porter, a huge beefy man with flourishing whiskers, what they were waiting for.

'It's the grateful cured, miss,' he said, leaning his elbows on the top of his high, massive desk. It was shaped something like a pulpit, and she guessed gave him some protection as well as authority in dealing with the patients, for a great many of the people who frequented hospitals were drunk, as she had discovered by now, and many others were mad. 'Physician-cured that side, surgeon-cured that side.'

Venetia noticed that it was the latter who had the missing limbs. 'But what are they doing here?' she asked.

'Waitin' to see the Benefactors, acourse,' he said, as if she ought to have known; and then seeing she did not understand, he explained, 'See, them as 'as been cured by the 'orspital comes in fust Thursday arter they're discharged, to give thanks to the Benefactors.' He settled to his exposition, evidently enjoying having someone to talk to that he could regard as an equal. 'They goos in one by one – physician-cured fust, see, then t'others – and hexpresses their 'umble gratitude fer the cure. Then the Benefactors hinstructs 'em to visit their parish church and give 'umble thanks to the Halmighty, likewise.'

'Indeed?' said Venetia.

'S'right, miss. Thank the Benefactors fust, and the Halmighty second, seeing has it's the Benefactors as pays down the dust.'

'Well, that's very nice,' Venetia said, still a little puzzled, for there seemed no air of joyous thanksgiving in the entrance hall, even allowing for the diffidence of the poor. 'I'm glad to know that they wish to express their thanks in that way.'

The porter dropped her a ghostly wink. 'Wishes my eye! Obliged to, ain't they? Else they don't get their serstificate.'

'Certificate?'

'To get in again next time they're took queer, see? Them as refuses to be grateful goos on the blacklist, an' then they can die in a welter o'gore outside the wery gate for all hanyone cares, but they wunt get in nor get treated, not if it was ever so.' He grinned and looked around the silent ranks. 'Grateful cured, ey? They better be hemming grateful, if they knows what's good for 'em!'

Venetia leaned a little towards him, confidentially. 'Do you suppose I can get in to see the Benefactors first, before they start going in?' She tried to imply that the power in the matter was his to dispense.

The porter sucked his teeth, flattered and reluctant to disappoint her. 'Oh no, miss, that wunt do. The chief physician an' chief surgeon'll be there already, to present the cases to the Benefactors. They wunt like bein' kep' waitin'; and the Benefactors wunt like their rowtine bein' upset. Desprit formal coves, the Benefactors. Best you wait till afterwards, catch 'em just afore they goos off to the Hangel.'

'The hangel?' Venetia asked, startled, connecting it in her mind with the Halmighty.

'The Hangel 'Otel,' he said, with another wink. 'To conduck the remaining business o' the day – to wit a right-down, four-square, slap-up luncheon, no expense spared. Halways in a good mood when they've nothing in front of 'em but the remaining business, miss. That's the time to hask a favour – assooming it's a favour you're after.'

'Well, yes,' Venetia admitted.

He nodded, taking in her appearance and quality. 'Thought you was,' he said. Another o' them do-goods, he thought; always tell 'em by their plain clothes and earnest hexpressions.

So Venetia waited. Rather than wait in the entrance hall with the grateful cured – who smelled pretty bad in this warm weather – she went outside and walked about, coming back in from time to time to check progress. When the clock of St Giles Without Cripplegate, across the road, chimed the half after one, there were only half a dozen left. The porter was nowhere to be seen, but after a few minutes he came out of the door of the committee room, to say to the patients, 'All right, you lot, Benefactors 'ave gorn. You'll 'ave to come back next Thursday. Eleven o'clock sharp, 'an don't be late. Orf you go!'

Venetia stepped forward. 'Did you say the Benefactors had gone?'

The porter started on seeing her. 'Oh, gorblimey, miss, where'd you spring from? I fergot all abaht yer! They gorn all right – slipped out the side way into White Cross Street. You'll 'ave to come back next week.' He registered her dismay and said, ''Ere, tell you what, though, if you're nippy, you might still catch 'em. They'll just be walking' dahn Fore Street.'

She abandoned dignity and ran out of the hall, down the steps, across the courtyard and out into the street. She was, indeed, so nippy that as she reached the corner of White Cross Street, a group of silk-hatted gentlemen who could only be the Benefactors was just crossing it at the junction with Fore Street. Venetia flung herself across between the noses of a speeding hansom and laden brewer's dray, caught her foot on the kerb and almost went headlong on the far pavement; and as the brewery driver turned the air blue, found herself being steadied by one of the gentlemen, the rearguard of the group, who had turned just in time to see her acrobatic arrival.

'Oh!' she gasped, out of breath, embarrassed, and slightly

shocked by the driver's vocabulary, which contained several phrases that were new to her. 'Thank you!'

The gentleman's left hand was supporting her by her right forearm; now he raised his right hand to his hat, removed it, and said with a glimmering smile, 'Not at all, Lady Venetia. Glad to be of service. It *is* Lady Venetia, is it not? Yes, I thought so, though it's a very long time since I last saw you.'

She stared at him, much discomposed. The rest of the group had walked on, too deep in conversation to notice the drama behind them. Her rescuer was an elderly gentleman, who had evidently once been handsome, and still had the air about him of expecting, not without justification, to be liked. His fine white hair was in strange contrast to his very dark eyes, which embraced her with fatherly and amused understanding.

'I – I'm sorry,' she said, 'you have the advantage of me.'

'Of course I have. You haven't the same incentive to recognise me as I have you. But I am an old friend and colleague of your mother's, and perhaps you will know my name. I am Sir Frederick Friedman.'

Sir Frederick abandoned his lunch with the Benefactors to escort Venetia home – in a cab, since the rain was just starting. When they got to Oxford Street he told the cabman to drive on to Hyde Park, to give him time to get the full story from Venetia. He had no need to tell him to drive slowly: in the mysterious manner of London when the rain starts, traffic had slowed to a crawl.

'I can't take you to my house, or to an hotel, or there'd be scandal,' he said to Venetia. 'One day Society may arrange itself so that innocent conversations between members of the opposite sex can be conducted in places other than carriages, but for the moment this poor, wet horse must be our chaperon.'

To Friedman's willing ear, Venetia poured out her story. She knew who he was, of course: he had been the first chief of surgery in her mother's hospital, and had also operated twice on Uncle Cav's arm. Her mother had spoken often of him as a colleague, friend, and sympathiser with her aims. Charlotte's day-to-day contact with the hospital had long ended, and Sir Frederick had moved on, too, and his name had not cropped up in conversation in Venetia's presence for many years. But even had she known less about him than she did, she would probably still have told him everything. For one thing, he was a senior medical practitioner and willing to hear her out – a unique combination, in her experience; and for another, he was that sort of person.

He listened with flattering attention as she described her experiences and her still unwavering desire to study medicine, and at the end he said, 'You do know, don't you, that apart from the Church you have chosen the hardest nut in the country to crack?'

Venetia was disappointed. Was that all he had to say? 'Yes, I do know,' she said, in a voice so brimming with patient dismissal that he laughed.

'That puts me in my place! I beg your pardon, Lady Venetia. I deserved the snub.'

She blushed. 'I didn't mean to snub you—' she began.

'Oh yes you did, and it was beautifully delivered! You are your mother's own child. I was very, very fond of your mother, did you know that? Well, it was so; and for her sake I would like to help you.'

'I ought to mention,' Venetia said, 'that my ambition is not approved of at home, and for that reason I am going under the name of Miss Fleet.'

'Let me understand: does your mother disapprove of what you are doing? I couldn't undertake to help you against her wishes.'

'It's not that she disapproves: she thinks it will make me unhappy. But Papa is against it, and Mama has to side with him out of loyalty. That's why I left home.'

'You don't live alone?' Sir Frederick asked, alarmed.

'Oh, no! With Aunt Fanny. All very respectable! You see, Aunt Fanny disapproves of the thing itself, but she believes girls ought to be allowed to follow their ambitions, so she's supporting me out of her own fortune; and Papa allows it, while not officially approving, because he doesn't want to upset Mama by disowning Aunt Fanny or me. Is that clear?'

'As Thames water,' Friedman assured her cheerfully. 'Just tell me, if I were to help you get into medical school, would it call down the wrath of your parents on my head? I don't want a furious father beating down my door.'

'Goodness, no! The last thing Papa wants is a fuss. He thinks I'll get discouraged and give it up, but if I succeed I'm sure he'll be proud of me in the end. But *can* you help me?'

He smiled. 'You think I've been wasting your time driving you round the Park in the rain? Yes, I can help you – if you are determined to go on, and can bear the insults and cruel tricks you'll have played on you, and won't faint at the sight of blood, or turn sick at smells and filth, or be frightened by screams and horrible wounds and drunkards and lunatics—'

'I helped in the Prussian military hospitals during the war. Mama said it was as bad as anything she'd ever faced.'

'Very well,' he said. 'I can't help you at any of the big hospitals, I'm afraid, but there is a small hospital in Mercer Street, just off Long Acre, called St Agatha's, where I am professor of surgery, and where my influence is far greater. You will have to satisfy the Board of Guardians at a viva voce examination about your basic education, but from what I've heard from your own mouth, you are well grounded. After that it will be a matter of persuading the heads of the different disciplines to accept you. Most of them will, when they know I support you. If there are any who remain obdurate, you will have to try to arrange private tuition to cover the gaps. This Aunt Fanny of yours – she can afford all this?'

Venetia was in raptures, her eyes like stars, her thin face glowing. The rain had stopped, and now, reflecting her mood, the sun broke through the parting clouds and lit the soaked park into a dazzle of refracting raindrops. 'Oh yes, count on me for that! Oh, how can I ever thank you? It's like a wonderful dream!'

He made an equivocal face. 'Odd dreams you females have nowadays. You ought to marry, like your mother, and be a great lady, not grub about in sick bodies and obscurity.'

'My sister Olivia is the one who has to make the great marriage. She has the face for it. I'm no beauty, as you see.'

'I'm renowned for my remarkable eyesight,' Friedman said,

311

'and I see a very great and rare beauty. But you must follow your spirit.'

'When do you think I can begin?' Venetia asked eagerly.

'The new session begins in mid-October. If I succeed in persuading the Board and the Medical Committee, you will be called for examination some time in September or early October.'

'Not until then?'

'It will take me time to see everyone privately and persuade them. There will be nothing for you to do, so I recommend that you take the opportunity to get out of London for a few weeks. You are looking fagged, my dear, and you will need all your strength for the coming fight.'

Venetia felt as strong as a horse, but she thought of Aunt Fanny, wilting in the heat, and missing Emma. Well, if they couldn't go home, she supposed there were always hotels; or perhaps a rented cottage, where Emma could come and stay. 'I could carry on with my reading,' she concluded aloud. 'It wouldn't be completely wasted time.'

Sir Frederick saw Venetia to the door of the house in Bury Street, but declined to come in, saying that he was late for an appointment. Venetia rather suspected he didn't like the look of the house, and didn't blame him; thanked him again, and went in. The street door had been standing open, so she ran up the stairs without troubling the servants, and burst into the drawing-room crying, 'Aunt Fanny, guess what? I've got the most *wonderful* news!'

She halted abruptly at the sight of Fanny on the *chaise-longue* weeping into a pillow as if she would never stop.

The summer at Trawden, from mid-July to September, proved to be an unexpectedly happy time for Manfred. Once he had got over the initial misery of realising he had no home any more – or none that would welcome him – he settled down to make the most of a wonderful freedom combined with the company of more boys than he could ever have had at Morland Place.

His particular friends were Cousins, the boy he had met the very first day, who had taken a fancy to him and regarded him as a protégé and lieutenant, and Dobbs, one of those with whom he shared a bed. Dobbs was also eleven, thin almost to gauntness and troubled by a persistent cough, but a clever boy with a sardonic humour. He was illegitimate, the son of a young woman of good family who had got into trouble. He had been taken from her at birth and placed in an institution, from which he had been sent to Trawden at the age of eight by the orders of his anonymous grandfather.

The three boys went off together on all sorts of expeditions. Cousins was boisterous, the engine of the trio, egging them on to activities which, if he had his way, were usually dangerous to life and limb. Dobbs was ingenious, thought up unusual new plays, and wrote the script of many wide-ranging adventures. Manfred had country lore, knew the names of plants and the habits of animals, and could find his way over any country and, more importantly, back again. He could make fires, catch fish, snare rabbits, and knew where birds nested. He also had an ease of communication with adults, which neither of the other two did. Under his leadership the boys made friends with the local farmers, helped out with the beasts and the harvests, and were rewarded with wonderful things to eat.

Mr Kettleworth had not forgotten his words to Manfred on their first meeting. He had taken a special interest in him, for his situation was unusual: the school rarely received orphans from good families, and there were ways in which Manny's responses differed from those of the other boys. Kettleworth had given him extra tuition, and watched with gratification how the young mind expanded. Now during the summer, when he had more time to spare, he redeemed his promise to take Manny out bird-watching so that he could get to know him better.

Manfred would have done without the treat, for he would rather have gone roaming with his friends. Cousins laughed at him for his bad luck in 'being under the Kettle's thumb', and Dobbs commiserated that he would undoubtedly do something to annoy the principal and call down punishment on his head. 'It's rotten luck in the holidays, to be in a way to get whopped.'

But, though he never admitted it to his peers, Manfred

actually enjoyed his expeditions with Kettleworth, and as the master's kindness showed through more and more, a warmth developed between them. Brought up by women, with a father too detached to notice him, Manfred had never before enjoyed a man's influence or affection. For Kettleworth, who had four daughters, Manfred began to be the son he had never had. As the summer wore on, he took to inviting Manny back to tea on expedition days. He had never before brought any of the boys into his own home, but when Manfred sat at the table with Mrs Kettleworth and the four girls, it somehow seemed quite natural.

'Next term,' Kettleworth said one day as he was leaving, 'if I can find the time, I will begin you on Latin. You will find it a great help with many other subjects.'

'Thank you, sir,' Manfred said, knowing it to be an honour, but foreseeing the teasing of his friends.

'You will not need Latin as a clerk, of course,' Kettleworth said, 'but it occurs to me . . .' He paused, and then went on, almost to himself, 'Teaching is a young man's business; it needs so much energy. And one day in the not too distant future I shall have to look about me for someone to take my place. Of course, there is no need to think about that now. Not for a long time yet. But it's as well to bear the possibility in mind. Just the possibility.'

Manfred did not understand him, though he realised no reply was wanted. But as he took his departure, to cross the graveyard to the schoolhouse, he had a feeling of belonging which the words had somehow generated, and which he had not expected ever to feel again.

314

CHAPTER EIGHTEEN

Henrietta was in the morning-room writing a letter when a maid came to tell her that Mr Fortescue wanted her in the drawing-room.

In the three days since their return from Swale House Mr Fortescue had been so busy she had hardly seen him. 'Did he say what he wanted me for?' she asked.

'I couldn't say, madam,' said the maid stonily. Sarah was the most disagreeable of the servants, and from the beginning had made her disapproval of Henrietta uncomfortably plain.

Henrietta jumped up and went to obey the summons, hesitating at the door for a moment to get her bearings. The rectory was a large, long house, a Queen Anne hunting box with Georgian wings, and there were ten rooms downstairs, lots of passages and three staircases, so she was still finding her way around. She had been surprised at the size and style of the place, not having realised before what a wealthy man she had married. Her naïve exclamations on first seeing the house had served to reassure her husband that at least she had not married him for his fortune.

When she stepped into the drawing-room – a lovely long, light room with an Adam fireplace at each end and french windows looking onto the gardens – she found Mr Fortescue was not alone. A large, burly gentleman dressed in breeches and boots seemed to fill the room. He had a broad, red face, wispy, curly hair the colour of wheat, and very round, bright blue eyes that he turned on her as soon as she entered, crossing

315

the room with his hand extended and a cheerful smile that she could not help responding to.

'Ah, there you are!' he exclaimed, without waiting for Mr Fortescue to effect any introduction. 'No need to tell me you are the new Mrs Fortescue – your reputation goes before you! Pretty as a picture, they said, and smart as new paint, and I see they weren't wrong!' The big, leathery hand took hers and the other followed to engulf it completely. 'I am Sir Robert Parke, from the Red House, as everyone calls it – the redbrick pile at the other end of the village. Perhaps you noticed it as you passed on your way from the station? I'm sorry I didn't call on you when you first arrived in Bishop Winthorpe, but it happened I was away in York and only got back this morning. But I have hurried the first moment I could to do my duty, you see, and welcome you – which I do with all my heart! I see you stare at my blunt manners, but I'm harmless, as anyone will tell you, though I don't stand on ceremony. You may as well get used to me,' he added with a chuckle, 'for I'm too old to change!'

Henrietta smiled, feeling unexpectedly at ease with this bluff man. 'I am very glad to make your acquaintance.'

'Bless your heart, I think you are,' he said, pleased. 'You have brought us a treasure, Fortescue!'

'Thank you. I'm glad you commend my taste,' Mr Fortescue said drily, looking at Henrietta with a faint but proud smile.

'You will liven us all up, my dear,' Sir Robert went on to Henrietta. 'We shall be very glad to have a mistress up at the rectory again. Fortescue is a great host, you know, a great entertainer – but all in the masculine way. Nothing but bachelor dinners for his scholar friends, which is a great trial to the ladies. The young people find it very dull here. You must let me present my daughters to you,' he said, releasing her hand at last and ushering forward the other two people in the room, who had been hovering in the background: young girls in identical fawn silk gowns with pink trimming, and straw bonnets with pink ribbons, whose fair curly hair and round blue eyes proclaimed their parentage. 'These are my girls, ma'am, Amy and Patsy – twins, as you see, and like as peas. Dashed if I can tell 'em apart half the time!'

The girls curtsyed in unison, staring with innocent, frank interest, and smiling with their father's geniality.

'How do you do?' said Henrietta.

'How do you do? Good morning!' they chorused.

'Mad for dancing, my girls,' Sir Robert said, 'like all young people. Now you are here, Mrs Fortescue, we can hope for livelier times, eh?'

'Do not depend too much on it, Sir Robert,' Mr Fortescue intervened. 'Mrs Fortescue is not addicted to Society. She would always sooner stay quietly at home with a book, like me, than be dancing.'

'Oh? Ah! Well, if you say so,' Sir Robert said solemnly; but with the side of his face away from the rector he dropped Henrietta a wink, which rather shocked her, though in a pleasant way, and made the twins giggle. Mr Fortescue frowned a little, and Sir Robert hastened to cover his tracks. 'Now then,' he said, 'if Mrs Fortescue will forgive me, I've a little business to attend to. I want to talk to you, Fortescue, about those rascally Thomases: something must be done about 'em . . .' He obliged Mr Fortescue to walk off to the other side of the room, leaving Henrietta alone with the twins.

She invited them to sit down, and found them very easy company, for they had no shyness, and talked readily, passing the thread back and forth between them in what was evidently their usual way.

'We're so glad to meet you! We wanted to call on you straight away, but we weren't sure if we should before Papa came home.'

'And we're glad now we didn't, because Papa says we're too young to call on a married woman.'

'Though we're fifteen – nearly sixteen really.'

'And we've been keeping house for Papa for ages. Mama died ten years ago, you see.'

'Oh, I'm so sorry,' Henrietta said.

'It's all right – we don't really remember her,' said Amy.

'We were only five when she died,' Patsy added.

'Papa's heart went to the grave with her. She's buried in the churchyard, just by the north wall. You'll see her grave

– it's splendid, the nicest in the churchyard. It has the most magnificent monument on it.'

'Papa designed it himself. It has weeping angels, and a dear little cherub reading a book.'

'Mama was a great reader.'

'She and Mr Fortescue were great friends, Papa says.'

'She did all sorts of good works,' Amy concluded, 'and she was very beautiful. At least, her portrait is very beautiful, and Perry says she was like an angel.'

'Perry?' Henrietta enquired.

'Our brother. His name is Peregrine, but he doesn't like it.'

'So we call him Perry, because that's what he called himself when he was very little.'

'Of course,' Amy assured her earnestly, 'we don't remember him then, because we weren't born.'

'He's nineteen now. He's at Oxford, but you'll meet him when he comes home in the summer.'

'He was nearly ten when Mama died, so he does remember her, though not very well.'

'I was thirteen when my mother died,' Henrietta said.

'Oh, how sad!' Patsy exclaimed. 'Who brought you up?'

'A nurse, mostly. Though I was left to my own devices a great deal. Who brought you up?'

'We had a nurse when we were small and then a governess; and we have lots of aunts – Papa has six sisters. We had almost too much bringing up for two small females, when you think of it,' Patsy said judiciously.

'That's why we got rid of the governess as soon as we were fifteen,' Amy added. 'Papa said it was a scandal, but we told him we weren't going to learn any more, so it was an awful waste of money keeping her. Are you bookish?'

'No, not at all, I'm afraid,' Henrietta admitted.

The girls stared. 'We thought you must be. Everyone says you are. They say that's why Mr Fortescue married you.'

'Everyone?' Henrietta queried.

'Well, of course everyone's been talking about it ever since they heard Mr Fortescue was going to get married, because no-one thought he ever would. Not that they talk to *us*, precisely,' Amy added fairly, 'but one can't help overhearing sometimes.'

Henrietta found their indiscretion refreshing. Before the advent of Alfreda, she might have chatted just like that, if she had ever had anyone to chat to; now, of course, she was constrained both by what Alfreda had taught her, and by her desire not to offend her husband. Even as the light, cheerful voices prattled on, she cast anxious looks across the room at Mr Fortescue to ensure he was not looking disapproval at her; but he was deep in conversation with Sir Robert.

At last the men returned to them. 'We must take our leave now, Mrs Fortescue,' Sir Robert said, 'and no doubt you'll be glad to be relieved of my two little chattering jackdaws.'

'Oh, no, really, I've enjoyed their company,' Henrietta said quickly.

'I hope you will think of yourself as always welcome up at the Red House,' Sir Robert went on. 'Don't stand on ceremony – nobody does with us. Just walk up any time you feel like it. You will find you'll be seeing a lot of me, in any case, for Fortescue and I own most of the village and the neighbourhood between us, and we are fellow magistrates, as well as being on all the committees, so I shall be in and out, my dear, in and out. By the by—' he added on a sudden thought, turning to the rector, 'speaking of committees, I wonder if Mrs Fortescue would like to stand for the School Board? New blood and so on?'

The rector frowned. 'A very unhappy thought,' he replied. 'You know my feelings about Board schools. It is an abomination to separate religious teaching from education.'

'Aye, but there's no doubt there's a deficiency of schooling in the neighbourhood.'

'I don't agree,' Mr Fortescue retorted. 'The lower orders do not value education, and would not take it up if you offered it.'

'Far be it from me to argue with you, sir,' said Sir Robert, 'but I find all sorts of working folks show an interest when I mention the subject.'

'Then perhaps you should not mention it. In my view it is not only wasteful but wrong to give any man more education than his expectations require. What use raising his sights above what must be his station in life?'

Sir Robert scratched his head a little. 'Well, it's cart and horse, isn't it? Their station depends on their education as much as vice versa.'

Mr Fortescue didn't want to argue. 'If you really feel we need more school places, then let us discuss Church of England places,' he said dismissively.

'But then we get no grant from the Government under this Forster Act, and the rate-payers must pay all; and you know the Nonconformists won't shell out for Church places,' Sir Robert said. 'If the government inspector comes here and makes the judgement that we need places, there'll be no getting out of it, so we might as well get on and be ahead of the game.'

'There are too few inspectors to visit every district,' Mr Fortescue said firmly. 'It may be years before one comes here. I believe we had better wait until it happens.'

'And end up paying for all out of our own pockets – I see it coming,' Sir Robert said with a sigh.

'When the poor parishioners ask for education, we can discuss the matter again. For the moment, I don't see there is any need for change. And in any case,' he added severely, 'Mrs Fortescue could not consider standing for an election. To be involved in competition, exposing herself to public scrutiny and impertinent speculation – *that* is surely not what you could wish for any lady, Sir Robert?'

Sir Robert was not snubbed. 'Oh, I believe we may have very different views of what a lady can bear,' he said cheerfully, 'but I shan't argue with you. You are a good fellow, and if you do canter on the other leg from me, we can still go in harness where we must. Now then, come, girls. Your most obedient, Mrs Fortescue.'

Once it was known that Sir Robert, locally known as the squire, had called, the rest of the Bishop Winthorpe felt licensed to do likewise. In the days that followed, Henrietta spent the hours of the morning call in the drawing-room, besieged by a succession of callers who came to stare at the rector's new lady, to probe her views, examine her clothes and winkle out information about her past. She found the process exhausting, for she was on her mettle the whole time, wanting to do the right thing and make the right impression for her husband's sake, and not knowing precisely what that might be.

It was plain that the marriage was the wonder of the neighbourhood. From what she observed and the questions that were asked, combined with the useful indiscretions of the Parke twins, who called every day at her invitation, she found that opinion about her was divided. The older, more conservative element saw no further than her youth and fashionable dress, and concluded that the rector had taken leave of his senses in the usual, hackneyed way. Those who had heard of Morland Place spread the word that the Morlands were respectable and wealthy, and the worldly set decided Mr Fortescue had merely chosen in the customary manner an heiress of good family for a wife. The younger set noted Henrietta's reserve and shyness, pronounced her bookish, and concluded that they supposed she and the old fellow must see *something* in each other.

Henrietta was not much troubled by any of this; her worries were quite otherwise. She only wanted to be sure that her husband loved and the neighbourhood approved her. On the first count, he had not visited her at night since they came back from Richmond, and when she saw him he seemed polite, kindly, but distant. On the second count, she knew there was an etiquette about returning visits, but didn't know what it was. She wished she had someone she could ask, someone older and wiser than her, but not so much so that they paralysed her with shyness. If only she had a friend like that, she might also ask them what a married women did with herself all day, if she was not, contrary to all reports, of a bookish nature.

The carriage drew up in the paved forecourt of the Red House, and Henrietta looked out of the window at the lamplit steps and the great door open on a glimpse of a hall ablaze with light.

Mr Fortescue said, 'We need not stay very late, if you do not care for it. It is a necessary part of my life, to keep on civil terms with the neighbourhood, but these social gatherings can be very tiresome.'

Henrietta turned back to him, damping down the eagerness in her expression. 'I am not much accustomed to such things, sir,' she said hesitantly, 'but I expect I shall find it very pleasant.'

'You are a good creature,' he said, smiling, and patted her hand. 'We will endure together.'

The door was opened, the steps were let down, and he climbed out, and turned back to assist her. Glowing inwardly from his words and the touch of his hand, she stepped down, concentrating on managing her skirts and train, and hoping her hair would stay put. The youngest housemaid, Maria, had been helping her dress, and had learned to do the simple style Henrietta wore day to day, but for Sir Robert's evening party she had felt she ought to have a more elaborate coiffure. She and Maria had devised one between them, but she wasn't sure it was a success, or that Maria had mastered it.

For his supper party, Sir Robert had enlisted the services of his wife's cousin as hostess, an elegant lady he introduced as Miss Compton and whom the twins addressed as 'Aunt Mary'. Henrietta judged her to be about twenty-five, and thought her very pretty, with smooth dark hair, blue eyes and a lively look. As she made the round of the other guests with her hand on her husband's arm, Henrietta looked across from time to time at Miss Compton and noted that she seemed a general favourite, and that the conversation was always the most animated wherever she was.

When the card tables began to form, Miss Compton came over to the corner where Henrietta was listening uncomprehendingly to the political conversation of the rector and a group of gentlemen, and said, 'Now I must insist on monopolising you for a while. Do come and take a turn or two with me. Mr Fortescue, I am stealing your bride away.'

Fortescue bowed to her without breaking the rhythm of his speech, and allowed Henrietta's hand to be detached from his arm.

'There, that's better,' said Miss Compton, putting Henrietta's arm through hers and steering her away. 'Everyone else seems to know you a great deal better than I do, and that won't do for me, I can tell you! You've been here for two weeks and I haven't called on you, which is shocking of me, but you will have to forgive me. I've been confined to the sofa and unable to leave the house until now.'

'Oh, I'm sorry. Have you been ill?'

'Not ill. It might have been easier if I had been. No, I had a fall out riding and hurt my back, which meant that I was hideously bored for a fortnight until Dr Savage let me up. Don't look alarmed – I'm quite recovered now. It was nothing but a sprain and some bruises, and nobody's fault, unless you count the rabbit.'

'The rabbit?'

'The one who made the hole. My poor beautiful Midnight put his foot down it, and over we went. Thank God he didn't break his leg! But he's been eating his head off in Sir Robert's stables all this while, and he'll be far too full of himself when I do ride him again. I expect he'll have me off in five minutes.' She didn't seem at all alarmed at the prospect, and Henrietta warmed to her.

'Do you live nearby?' she asked hopefully.

'I live in the village, in the house opposite the forge. I hope you will do me the honour of visiting me there.'

'I'd like to very much.'

'Then do! No need to stand on ceremony with me, any more than Sir Robert. He's the dearest creature, don't you think? Treats me like his little sister. Well, though I was Frederica's – Lady Parke's – cousin, we were brought up together after my parents died, so we were always more like sisters. She was ten years older than me, but so full of fun the difference didn't signify. Have you seen her likeness?'

'No, this is the first time I've been to the Red House,' Henrietta said.

'Oh, then you must let me show you. The best one is in the dining-room. Will you come?' Henrietta glanced around doubtfully, and Miss Compton, reading her thoughts, smiled and said, 'No-one will mind, I assure you. Sir Robert's evenings are very informal.'

She led the way out of the saloon and across the hall. The

portrait hung over the dining-room fireplace, and showed a beautiful, dark-eyed woman all in white gauze, against a background of gloomy trees, so that she seemed to float like a lily on dark water.

'Poor Frederica,' Miss Compton said at last. 'She was only twenty-seven when she died – just the same age I am now.'

'It must have been a terrible blow to you,' Henrietta said.

'It was. We were travelling in the carriage together when it overturned. I was hardly bruised, but Frederica broke her neck. I've often thought—' She did not finish the sentence, but Henrietta, glancing at her, guessed it.

'God has His plan for all of us,' she said tentatively, feeling it was almost impertinent to offer comfort to one so much older than her.

Miss Compton gave a little shrug. 'So I came to live in Bishop Winthorpe,' she continued briskly, 'to keep an eye on her children. Sir Robert would have had me live here, in the Red House, but I prefer my independence.'

'Have you no other family?' Henrietta asked. For an unmarried woman to live alone was unusual – not at all the thing, as even she knew.

'Oh yes, an older brother – he ought to be here tonight, the wretch, but I suppose he's been delayed. Officially he lives with me – I am not quite so brazen as to set up house alone, you see! But he travels a great deal. He and I were brought up separately. He was at school when our parents died, and when I went to live with Frederica, he was taken in by another uncle, so we were not very well acquainted. But I love him dearly now. He is quixotic and unaccountable, but he has the warmest heart. Have you any brothers or sisters?'

Henrietta began telling her about her childhood, home and family. Miss Compton listened intently, and as Henrietta was warmed by this obviously genuine interest, she expanded, forgetting to be shy or to worry about doing the wrong thing. She began to feel that here might be the friend she had hoped for, and was sorry when they were interrupted by the twins, who rushed in excitedly, curls and muslin skirts flying.

'Aunt Mary! Quick, quick, Uncle Jerome has arrived! And Papa says we can have dancing!'

In the hall was a tall young man with a dark, vivid face and thick dark hair, and eyes that had the same eager devouring look as Miss Compton's, as if life were something to be consumed avidly and whole. He was being relieved of his cape by a servant, and exchanging greetings with half a dozen people, but he turned at once to receive his sister's embrace with a readiness Henrietta liked.

'You are a wicked wretch to be so late! I thought you weren't coming!' Miss Compton cried.

'I was late setting off, and then Warrior cast a shoe, and I didn't dare come over those horrible flinty roads without one, so I had to knock up the blacksmith in some God-forsaken village,' he said, stripping off his gloves. 'But here I am at last, ready to make amends. Amy, Patsy, if you swing on my arms like that I shall collapse! Don't you know I'm a weary traveller.'

'Oh, nonsense, you're never weary!'

'There's going to be dancing, do come!'

'Girls, do try to behave like young ladies,' Miss Compton said, and turned to draw Henrietta forward. 'My dear, you must let me present to you the person I love best in all the world – my brother Jerome. Jerome, this is Mrs Fortescue.'

Compton gave Henrietta a swift and comprehensive inspection that made her feel strangely exposed, as though he had seen through her clothes and her skin and right into the core of her. His eyebrows shot up, and he said, 'Mrs Fortescue? Not Fortescue the rector's wife? Good Lord! It can't be!' The voice was like Mrs Compton's, musical and full of laughter, but velvety deep. Henrietta, afraid she was being ridiculed, hung back, looking up at him doubtfully from under her brows.

'Your manners, Jerome!' Miss Compton exclaimed, laughing.

'Oh, I mean, of course, that I am honoured to make your acquaintance, ma'am,' Compton corrected himself quickly. He held out his hand, which Henrietta knew from Alfreda was not good form, but the gesture was so open and spontaneous that she took it almost without volition. His grip was firm, and a strange thrill ran through her at the touch of it. 'Your most obedient servant,' he said warmly, looking down into her face. Henrietta felt the contact with him was too close and too personal, and wanted to pull away, as one would from a too-hot fire; but her hand remained in his, and she scorched.

'Mr Compton,' she said faintly.

'It is to you that I must apologise for my disgraceful lateness,' he said, 'for I know that this party is being given in your honour, and I know, moreover, what is due to a new bride.'

'You might also apologise for doubting Mrs Fortescue's credentials when I first introduced you!' Miss Compton said.

'Oh, never that!' Compton replied, not taking his eyes from Henrietta. 'I stand by that, for I was not expecting a bride in the first flush of youth and beauty, like a rose just unfurling its petals for the first time.'

Now Henrietta did draw back her hand, sure she was being mocked, and feeling also that his attention was too prolonged and pointed, given that she was a married woman.

Miss Compton, noting her blush, said, 'Too bad of you, Jerry, to tease so. You are making Mrs Fortescue quite uncomfortable. You mustn't pay him any attention, my dear ma'am. He is a dreadful monkey, but he has a kind heart.'

Compton said, 'I was not teasing, I assure you. But I shall be as proper as a curate from now on, I promise. Did someone say something about dancing?'

The twins almost jumped up and down on the spot with excitement. 'Papa says we may! It wasn't meant to be a ball, of course, because Mr Fortescue doesn't care for them, but Mrs Carstairs says she will play the piano and Papa's sent Dick for his fiddle, and they are rolling up the carpet in the music room. Anyone who wants to can dance there.'

The music room was a large salon leading off the saloon, and already the younger element was drifting towards its doors. As the Comptons, dragged along by the twins, passed through the saloon, Henrietta took the opportunity to return to Mr Fortescue's side. He was listening to the discourse of an elderly gentleman, but he bestowed a look and a smile on her, and took her hand to pass it under his arm. Henrietta felt safe again, and proud to be the object of his attention; she stood as close as she could without disturbing him, and tried to understand what was being said. But out of the corner of her eye she could see the activity round the music-room door, and the strains of music striking up made it harder than ever to concentrate on the abstrusities of government policy.

And then she saw Mr Compton coming towards them. She felt her colour begin to rise, and concentrated her gaze on the old gentleman; but Compton still came, and reaching the group, coughed deprecatingly for attention.

'I beg your pardon, Colonel, for interrupting your most edifying exposition on the Duke of Cambridge, especially as I am an emissary of mere frivolity—'

'You are an emissary of the dickens, Compton my boy,' the colonel said with great good humour, 'and if your impudent tongue don't turn black one of these days— !'

'I hope not,' Compton said smoothly, 'until I have had a chance to beg for Mrs Fortescue's hand. We are having a little hop about in the next room, sir,' he addressed the rector, 'and I hope to make amends for my rudeness in being so late this evening by leading your good lady into the dance.'

The rector frowned, but fortunately for Henrietta her eyes were elsewhere. 'Mrs Fortescue does not care to dance,' he began, but got no further.

'She would be doing me a great service,' Compton said smoothly, 'for nothing else will convince my sister I have been forgiven. Won't you take pity on me, Mrs Fortescue, for just one set? Ten minutes only – it will be a work of charity.'

The music was tugging at Henrietta, and her feet and legs were longing for exercise after so long confined indoors. She looked up at her husband. 'May I, sir?'

His face assumed a blankness. 'Of course, my dear, if you wish it,' he said without inflection. Compton bowed low to him, and crooked his arm towards Henrietta. She took it and tried not to skip with joy as she was led away towards the lights and the music.

The carriage journey home was not far, just to the other end of the village, but they had to wait their turn to get out of the courtyard, which added five minutes. Henrietta did not dare look at her husband. He had not met her eyes nor smiled at her

327

all evening, and had handed her into the coach with a face of stone. They left the lights of the Red House behind and turned into the darkness of the village street, relieved only by a square of light here and there hanging like a yellow painting on a black wall. She felt his presence beside her, near but deliberately not touching; grew more aware all the time of his breathing. In the confines of a carriage they were private and alone, and there might be no other opportunity to speak to him; and she was braver in the dark when he could not see her.

She swallowed the obstruction in her throat and said timidly, 'Are you angry with me, sir?' He didn't answer, and she pressed on in an even smaller voice, 'Have I done something wrong?'

His voice came out of the dark, cold as a tomb. 'No, not at all.'

She despaired. If he was angry with her but would not tell her why, how could she make amends? She would remain forever shut out; she would die in the cold. Her eyes filled with tears and she caught her lip in her teeth to stop it trembling.

He must have felt her sorrow, for he changed position restively, cleared his throat, and after a moment said in a different voice, 'Do you like dancing?'

'I don't know. That's only the second time I've done it. I think so,' she answered. She caught gladly at his words. Was that where she had erred? Oh, to know and be punished and then readmitted to the light of his regard! 'Was it – was I wrong to dance, then?'

'No,' he said at once. 'Not wrong.' He sounded faintly puzzled. 'I did not know you cared for it, that was all.'

Henrietta didn't know what to say. She did not feel forgiven, and yet he had not said she was wrong. They had left the paved part of the street now, and hedges were passing the window in the wavering beam of the carriage lamp. Soon they would be home and the ride over, the chance gone.

As if he had thought the same, he drew a breath and said quickly, 'Henrietta, why did you marry me?'

Even in the darkness Henrietta blushed at so personal a question. She wanted to tell him, but she hardly knew how:

he was so far above her, she dared not use ordinary words to him. She was afraid that one word too many or too few, or just the wrong word, might shatter the extraordinary, unbelievable treasure of being his chosen wife. But the carriage was slowing now, coming to the entrance to the rectory. It was now or never.

'Because I love you,' she said, and her voice was a mere breath, so that with the noise of the wheels on the road he might not have heard.

But he had heard her. His hand came blindly along the seat and she felt the movement and let hers be in the way. He took it. '*Do* you love me?' he asked.

'Oh yes,' she whispered.

He squeezed her hand and let it go. She didn't know what to make of it. The carriage lurched, turned, swayed, pulled up before the house. They climbed out into the cold night air, with a prickle of rain in it, and passed into the dimly lit house. She was walking automatically towards the stairs when he said quietly, 'Are you very tired?'

She stopped and looked at him – a brief glance was all she dared – and said, 'No, not at all.'

'Come to the library, then, just for a little while. Let me read to you.'

Hope leapt up like a small hot flame, and she could not answer for the thoughts and speculations that tumbled through her mind.

In the library sandwiches and wine were waiting, and a freshly tended fire, crackling brightly in the hearth – for it was a cool evening. She let him seat her by it, pour her a glass of wine, and then looked about curiously at this section of his exclusive world while he went to fetch the book he wanted. This was how it had been in Richmond, the second week: every night a reading from Latin or Greek, and the mysterious incantation combined with the wine and candlelight had had a powerful effect on her, so that the mere sound of the incomprehensible words would make her skin run hot and her head feel light. When the book was shut she would go up to her room and wait with mounting tension, and he would come like a creature of myth, a Greek hero borne to her on a wavecrest of words, to ravish her on her white rock with an abandoned passion that thrilled and shocked her.

He had never at any point spoken of or even made reference to their nightly adventure in Swale House; and to Henrietta it was as if there were two Mr Fortescues. One was the grave, formal, deeply intellectual scholar, whom she admired as she would any great prelate or teacher she knew only by reputation; the other was the naked ravisher of her dark hours. Since they had come to Bishop Winthorpe, she had been married only to the former; now it seemed the other Mr Fortescue had emerged again.

He read, and she was transported, first exhilarated and then caressed into a languor by his voice, so that she felt she might have stretched herself out right there on the library carpet in the firelight, without the least fear or shyness. But at last he shut the book and said only, in a voice that trembled slightly, 'Go to your room.'

She went without a word. Maria was sitting up for her, swaying sleepily on a hard chair just inside the bedroom door. She let the maid unlace her and take out her pins, then dismissed her. 'Go to bed. I'll manage myself now.'

Maria curtsyed, shivering with sleepiness, and went away. Henrietta removed the rest of her clothes, and then, standing before the cheval glass brushed out her hair, staring with detached interest at her naked body. Everything about this part of her relationship with Mr Fortescue seemed dreamlike and unreal, could only exist in that other, sorcerer's world of incantation and myth; could not, therefore, make her self-conscious or ashamed of her nakedness. She thought she heard a footstep in the passage outside, blew out the candles and scampered hastily up onto the bed, to arrange herself as she knew he liked it.

In a moment the door opened slowly, and the candle entered, with him a shape behind its halo of dazzle. He came to the foot of the bed, and she stretched herself a little, like a cat, in anticipation. But he did not move. He stood for a long time, looking at her, and then he sighed. That was all – just a small sigh, hardly even a breath in the darkness. But she felt a sadness like a great cold ocean tide rolling in; and without a word, he turned and left her. After the door had clicked quietly closed, she waited for him, unable to believe he would not come back; and waited even after belief left her. At last she grew shivery and climbed in under the bedclothes; and slept with a sense of failure upon her.

On a fine June day, Henrietta walked along the main village street, thinking not for the first time how pretty Bishop Winthorpe was. Though it was only twelve miles from Morland Place, the country was very different, more closed and wooded, the lanes narrower and deeper, and she sometimes missed the big skies she was used to. But the village was a gem of the picturesque. Here were whitewashed cottages with long front gardens full of lupins and beanpoles, roses, delphiniums and cabbages; there neat grey stone houses with lichen-gilded roofs. Here on the left was the Bell Inn, a long house of beams, mullioned windows and a crooked roof tree; a wistaria scrambled along its face, the long pale purple blossoms trembling against the sunlit walls. It was much admired by tourists, and a young gentleman of the loose tie, smock and shady hat fraternity was enthusiastically sketching it, with an enthralled audience of two stout-booted children and a pi-dog.

The central part of the main street, where there was a paved footpath, had several shops: a butcher's, a bakery, a post office, a hardware shop and seed merchant, and a large haberdashery, which was where the ladies of the village congregated to exchange gossip. Opposite this row, on the right, was the church, St Mary's, set up high above the street on a curious knoll. It was a large church with a tall, square tower and a handsome clerestory; behind it, a row of ancient chestnuts spread their gold-green crowns against the creamy blue sky. The churchyard was fenced with iron railings, and half a dozen sheep were grazing the graves, watched over by a barefoot boy, who stood up and saluted Henrietta politely as she passed.

On the left now was the other public house, the Same Yet, a plain stone building whose lack of obvious charm was mitigated for visitors by its curious name. It had originally been called the Seven Stars, but once when it was having a new inn sign painted, the artist had asked the landlord what he wanted on the sign. The landlord had replied, 'The same yet', and the artist had taken him at his word.

Beside the Same Yet was the Copper Kettle tea room, where the visitors who came to admire Bishop Winthorpe on fine days throughout the year might refresh themselves. As well as the tourists enticed by the guidebooks and the amateur artists, Bishop Winthorpe attracted large numbers who came to hear Mr Fortescue's sermons. He was punctilious about taking the morning service himself on most Sundays, not least because large congregations meant large collections. If the acolytes proved to be distinguished, they were sometimes invited to dine at the rectory.

Beyond the church, set back a little, was the village forge and wheelwright's, and here the street widened to accommodate an elongated village green, and the houses of the better-off. At the far end of the green were the railings behind which the redbrick Georgian house of the squire squatted massively, facing across the road the third public house, a little redbrick reflection called the Parke Arms.

Henrietta's destination was Mary Compton's house, and she found, as so often before, that the door was standing open. Miss Compton liked visitors, and stood on no ceremony. Jerome Compton said she must have been an Oxford undergraduate in another life, for she understood the principle of the unsported oak.

Henrietta hadn't known what he meant by another life, and when she did understand, she was a little shocked, though intrigued and stimulated too. Both Comptons had read widely about other religions, and were quite at ease discussing the possibility of reincarnation, just as if the Bible were a mere book and the Christian truth a story you could take apart, choosing and discarding elements as you pleased.

'My dear girl,' Jerome Compton had said once when she – a little hesitantly – protested, 'God gave you intellect for a purpose. How can it be blasphemous to use it? You might just as well say that God gave us legs for ornament and meant us to spend our entire lives lying down.'

And Henrietta had retorted, 'I don't think it's for you to

say what God does and doesn't mean. And don't call me your dear girl. It isn't proper.' This only made him laugh, which made her more upset, until at last Miss Compton brought him to order.

The fact was that Jerome Compton treated Henrietta with a complete lack of ceremony which might have been delightful in any other circumstance, but which made her feel uneasily that she was being disloyal to Mr Fortescue. She did love the excitingly explorative conversations, and the fun the Comptons made, egging each other on to further flights of fancy, but she was put on her guard after she had foolishly repeated something they had said at home.

She had been at dinner with Mr Fortescue and Mr Catchpole, the curate. Catchpole lived at the rectory, and his status seemed to Henrietta uncomfortably ambiguous, not quite a servant and not quite family either. He had a bedroom of his own at the far end of the first floor, whereas the servants' bedrooms were all up in the attics; and he ate his meals with her and Mr Fortescue; but at dinner he always left the table before the dessert was put on. When Henrietta once ventured to ask why, her husband told her rather shortly that such delicacies were too good for him, and that he must cultivate humility.

Henrietta could not see that deprivation made him humble: he seemed only dull and tepidly resentful. He was a thin, elderly man, bald-fronted but with a bolster of thick white hair around the sides, who had the poached eyes, grey skin and coffin breath of a digestive disorder. He performed all the church duties Mr Fortescue did not care for, which tended to be the disagreeable ones, and Mr Fortescue had less consideration for his comfort or convenience than he would have had for any servant. When Mr Catchpole was sent out to the midnight deathbed of a poor parishioner, for instance, Mr Fortescue would not dream of ordering the horses put to for him at that time of night. Mr Catchpole could walk – and did, in all weathers. Henrietta couldn't help feeling rather sorry for him, though she didn't like him and knew he didn't approve of her.

On this occasion the three of them were dining alone, and

conversation had been rather sticky. In a misguided burst of energy she had tried to divert them by bringing up the subject of Mr Darwin's theory of the origin of species. It was something quite new to her when the Comptons explained it to her that morning, and she had found the whole conversation fascinating. She thought her husband and the curate were fascinated, too, as they listened to her in absolute silence. Too late she realised the silence was not rapt but horrified. Her voice trailed off, and Mr Fortescue spoke with forbidding coldness.

'I am shocked to hear such blasphemy from your lips, Mrs Fortescue. Have you no modesty, no decency? Have you no sense of my position?'

Catchpole, looking at Henrietta with loathing, took up for her, knowing argument would only fuel his master's disapproval. 'I am sure Mrs Fortescue would not knowingly blaspheme, sir. Perhaps she does not fully understand the iniquity of Mr Darwin's ideas.'

'Then she should understand!' he snapped. 'The theory expounded in that vile book is in direct contradiction – *direct contradiction*, Mrs Fortescue – of Holy Writ.'

'But sir, it seemed so sensible as it was explained to me,' Henrietta said eagerly. 'And I believe there are fossil remains in the earth that support the—'

'Be silent!' Mr Fortescue thundered. 'Did you not hear what I said? The account in the Book of Genesis was handed down to us direct from God's mouth. All living things were made at the same time, in the seven days of the Creation, in the forms which God saw fit to give them. I will have no more of this wicked nonsense. Who has been putting it into your head? You have not,' a new horror occurred to him, 'brought That Book into this house?'

'No sir,' she said, bowing her head over her plate. 'I'm very sorry to have offended you.'

All in all she had been glad when, at the end of May, Jerome Compton went away on his travels again. He was exciting and rather disturbing, but she had an obscure feeling he was dangerous to her. Her friendship with Miss Compton ripened nicely without him, and she had far more of Miss Compton's attention when he was not there.

She found Miss Compton in her small garden, gloved and straw-hatted and tending her roses. 'Ah, there you are! I was hoping you would come,' she exclaimed with gratifying promptness as Henrietta stepped out from the house. 'Now I have the perfect excuse to stop doing this. A lady is supposed to gain great spiritual comfort from tending a garden, but it bores and annoys me. I wonder why it is that the things that are supposed to give one spiritual comfort are so often tiresome.'

'Are they?' Henrietta asked, startled.

'Why yes,' Miss Compton said with an amused smile. 'Like going to church, for instance. Only fear of censure makes me appear week after week. After two hours on a hard bench in St Mary's on a Sunday morning, aren't you ready to scream?'

'Oh, no!' Henrietta said eagerly. 'It is the best time of the week for me. The architecture, the lovely singing, and most of all listening to such beautiful words spoken in a voice that—' She broke off, embarrassing herself with a sudden memory of candlelight and wine and Latin poetry.

Miss Compton looked at her curiously. 'Ah, yes – well, you are in love, so perhaps it's different for you. Being in love makes the strangest things valuable.' She observed Henrietta's face minutely, and then said abruptly, 'Forgive me, but is something troubling you? I would be glad to help you if I could – even if it is only to lend you a sympathetic ear.'

Henrietta turned to her quickly. 'Oh, if I could tell you,' she said longingly.

Miss Compton drew off her gloves and linked arms with her. 'Come and sit with me in the arbour. We'll be quite private there. You can tell me absolutely anything. You know I am quite incapable of being shocked.'

Miss Compton's small garden was crowded with flowers and shrubs, and a winding path led down to a bench in a sunny corner, sheltered by a framework over which rambled a rose, pink in bud but opening to almost white, whose scent was an elusive dream. To either side lavender bushes overhung the path, and to the background hum of foraging bees, Henrietta at last poured out her troubles to the willing ear, which had expected to hear something else entirely.

335

'I thought when I got married everything would be wonderful, and my life would be orderly and – and complete. But it isn't like that. Mr Fortescue is busy all the time. Well, I know he has a great deal to do, with his estate to manage, and the church and parish business; and being a magistrate as well, and on all those committees, takes up time; and then there's his other parish, and his writing, and he has a great deal of correspondence. But it means I hardly see him at all, except at meal times. Even then, at breakfast he's always reading the newspapers or letters, and he never takes lunch – or anyway, not with me. I have to eat alone with Mr Catchpole, who hates me. And at dinner there's usually a guest or two, Mr Fortescue's friends, and they're all men and scholarly and old, and I never understand a word of what's being said. They just talk about texts and readings and mis-transcriptions and such stuff! And if we do dine alone, there's still Mr Catchpole, and afterwards Mr Fortescue always excuses himself on account of having letters to write or his sermon to compose or something, and I sit in the drawing-room alone and they bring in the tea tray and think – and think—' She stopped herself on the edge of tears.

Miss Compton found nothing in the exposition to surprise her. It was horribly sad and just what could be expected when a girl like Henrietta married a man like the rector. She said gently, 'Well, you know, gentlemen generally are busy. They have their own affairs, which we can't expect them to neglect for us.'

'Oh, I don't mind Mr Fortescue being so busy and clever,' Henrietta disclaimed quickly, 'because he is a wonderful person, so far above me that I'm only grateful he ever looked at me; and I can't think why he did, for I'm not rich or clever or beautiful. But the thing is, I don't know what I'm supposed to *do*.'

'About what?'

'Not about anything. Just *do*. When I was at home I rode about the estate all day and talked to people and helped on the farms and so on, but I was only a child then. I thought once I was married I would know what a married lady does, and I would be good and useful and busy all day long, and people would like and respect me, and Mr Fortescue would love me and approve of me.'

Miss Compton was not tempted to smile. It seemed to her too sad. 'Married ladies generally have a household to run.'

'I can't do that,' Henrietta said glumly. 'Everything runs itself, and the servants hate anything to be changed. Mrs Prosser – the housekeeper, you know – makes believe to consult me every day after breakfast about the menu and so on, but if I ever suggest anything different she says it's not in season, or Mr Fortescue doesn't like it, or the cook's already started preparing something else, so I end up agreeing with whatever she says, which is what she wants in the first place.'

'Elderly servants can be tyrants,' Miss Compton sympathised. 'Your Mr Fortescue inherited them from his father, I believe.'

'Yes, and he likes everything just the way it is because he grew up with it, so there'd be no point in changing anything, even if I was allowed to. The one time I tried to rearrange things in the drawing-room, Sarah came in and let out a shriek so I almost dropped a vase. She spent the next hour putting everything back the way it was, and then made a big fuss of dusting and polishing, saying I'd left fingermarks.'

'Oh dear!'

'So I haven't got a household to run, and I can't spend my time studying, as some people seem to think I should, because I'm not bookish. So what *am* I supposed to do?'

Miss Compton considered. The other thing that kept married women busy – having babies – seemed, from reading between the lines, not to be likely to happen. 'You want to be useful, and not just enjoy yourself?' she asked. Henrietta nodded. 'Then, my dear, the thing is simple. You are the rector's wife. You must do your Christian duty and visit the sick and poor.'

Henrietta's brow cleared miraculously. 'Is that what a rector's wife does?'

'And a vicar's wife, and a squire's wife,' Miss Compton smiled. 'Well, perhaps in the circumstances it's not wonderful that you didn't think of it before. But if it's duty you want, and good works, you should be getting to know your husband's parishioners and tenants, and finding how you can be of service to them.' She wondered Mr Fortescue had not mentioned it himself, but perhaps he was so unused to having a wife it didn't occur to him.

'But – doesn't Mr Catchpole do all that? I shouldn't like to annoy him.'

'I'm sure he visits, but for different purposes. He will point out their shortcomings to them and exhort them to come to church and read the Bible. The lady of the manor brings advice and baby-clothes, medicine and food, listens to their sorrows, tells them how to cure their ills, wash their babies and cook their dinners.'

'Could I really do all that?' Henrietta wondered shyly. 'I used to visit the people at home, but not to give advice, of course.'

'You're very young, I know, but they won't mind that. They'll be the more patient and courteous with you. And it's astonishing how ignorant the poorest of them are – that's why they are poor, of course. However little you think you know, it will be a hundred times what they do.'

Henrietta glowed. She saw herself with a basket on her arm, being welcomed by grateful parishioners. She saw Mr Fortescue looking at her approvingly and loving her for her charitable heart. And it would be something she could talk to him about when they dined together. Perhaps then he might read to her again . . .

'I'll begin tomorrow morning,' she said. 'Tell me how to go on. How do I start?'

'You start,' said Miss Compton solemnly, 'by looking out your plainest gown and stoutest boots.'

338

BOOK THREE

Endurance

I say, Fear not! life still
Leaves human effort scope.
But, since life teems with ill,
Nurse no extravagant hope.
Because thou must not dream, thou need'st not then
   despair.

Matthew Arnold: *From the Hymn of Empedocles*

CHAPTER NINETEEN

The morning-room door opened and Mr Fortescue came in. Henrietta jumped to her feet guiltily.

Her parish-visiting work had made a great difference to her: she was busy all day long, which kept her cheerful, and having a rôle had made her much more self-confident. She blushed and stammered less, noticed more, and was not overawed by people as she had been. Her relationship with Mr Fortescue had improved, too. Her adoration of him need no longer be humbly silent: she had something to offer of herself, something to contribute when they conversed at the dinner table.

Still, it was so unusual for her to see him at this time of day that she assumed she must have done something wrong. His life, when he was at home, was led almost entirely at the other end of the house, in what was called the 'gentleman's wing'. Here were the billiards room, the smoking-room and the gun-room, together with the study and the library, in one or other of which he did his work. Those who visited him on business were encouraged to come and go by the side door, so Henrietta never saw them. He used the smoking-room as his private sitting-room, and from there a back staircase led to the bedroom floor; while a door in the passage next to the gun-room gave onto the path to the stables. Once he had left the breakfast table, he was as absent and unaccountable to her as if he lived in another town, until they were reunited at dinner.

'No need to alarm yourself, my dear,' he said kindly. 'Do you remember what day tomorrow is?'

'Thursday, I think, sir,' she said, puzzled.

He smiled. 'Can selflessness go further? It is your birthday, if I don't mistake.'

'Oh! Yes – I'd forgotten.' She felt foolish and added in her own defence, 'We didn't take much account of birthdays at home, after my mother died. Papa was always too busy to remember.'

'Well, I have not been too busy to remember a certain promise that I made to your brother before we were married,' said Mr Fortescue, evidently much pleased with himself. 'Will you do me the honour of coming with me?'

He held out his hand, and, mystified, Henrietta followed him out of the morning-room, down the passage and across the hall to the open front door. He bowed her through, and there on the gravel of the sweep stood Bond, the head groom, holding the reins of a horse. 'Well?' Mr Fortescue asked. 'What do you think?'

It was a chestnut mare of the most wonderful polished gold colour, very showy, with a long mane and tail and two white socks before, and she was saddled, Henrietta saw at once, with a side-saddle. 'Is she for me?' she asked wonderingly.

'A present for your birthday. I have been remiss, my dear, in not providing you with a mount long ago. You are accustomed to taking riding exercise, and should not have been deprived of it. I can only plead in excuse for my neglect of you the intense and ongoing nature of my occupation with business.'

'Oh, no sir,' Henrietta cried in protest. 'I never thought you neglected me!'

'You have a forgiving heart,' he said, smiling. 'I hope at least that this present will make amends. She is called Ginger, I'm told, and the dealer who sold her to me assured me she is a thoroughbred lady's mount, gentle in temper, and – "fit to go over any country", I think was his expression. She is certainly pretty.'

'She is *very* pretty,' Henrietta agreed. 'I don't know how to thank you! You are very, very kind to me.' She was touched almost to tears by this evidence of his affection; but she could not help her Morland eye noticing the tell-tale ring of white about the mare's eye, or the laid-back ears, or that Bond was

342

standing well back from her, holding her at arm's length and keeping a wary eye on her. 'Ginger' might refer to more than the glorious colour of the mare's coat. And it had to be said that she was too long in the back and her quarters were poor. It hurt Henrietta to think that there was any area in which her husband did not excel, but if he had been anyone else she would have concluded that the dealer had sold him a pup.

She did not, of course, express any of this by so much as a blink. A gift from Mr Fortescue must by definition be perfect. She turned the smiling eyes of love and gratitude on him, and thanked him until he stopped her.

'You have been working very hard lately,' he said, 'and must have some recreation. And I know how much horses mean to you. I hope you will let me see you try her. Won't you go and put on your habit?'

Henrietta was only too glad to rush upstairs to her bedroom. White eye or not, she had not been on a horse since she left Morland Place, and she missed riding very much. Also, not having a horse restricted how far she could go in a day on her parish visiting, and time and energy were wasted tramping over terrible tracks and rough fields which could better have been spent with the objects of her philanthropy.

In no time she was back, in the habit which had been hanging neglected in the wardrobe all these months. Bond had been walking the mare about, and now, while Mr Fortescue stood at the door watching proudly, he handed the reins to Oaks, the second groom, and prepared to throw Henrietta up into the saddle. Ginger flattened her ears and lifted a threatening hind leg as Henrietta gathered the reins, but Oaks had her tight by both bit rings. As soon as she was in the saddle, Henrietta felt the back rise under her resentfully, and the mare fly-kicked.

'She seems spirited,' Mr Fortescue said. 'But the man assured me she's as gentle as a kitten. Walk her round a little, Oaks, let me see how she moves with Mrs Fortescue.'

After a few circuits Henrietta told Oaks to let her go, and she rode by herself around the sweep. Ginger went quietly enough, but Henrietta could feel the ominous silence at the end of the reins of a hard mouth. Still, her paces were good.

Perhaps she had been badly treated, and would respond to kindness.

If only she could ride her across! One had so much less control sidesaddle. She thought of the happy days at Morland Place, riding her pony as if they were one being. But as a married woman, and the rector's wife, it was unthinkable. She might as well have run naked down the village street as ride astride.

Fortescue watched quite content. He was no horse-fancier, and saw nothing wrong with the mare; together she and Henrietta made a delightful picture. His early disappointment in his wife was largely forgotten since she had begun her visiting of the poor and sick: now that she had proved she was serious-minded, he was ready to forgive her for liking the occasional dance, and for rarely picking up a book. In fact, he believed it was really to be preferred that she had no scholarly leanings. The idea of a wife who was an intellectual companion contained a basic contradiction which he now felt it had been foolish to entertain.

Henrietta was young, virtuous, and her shy reserve with him gave her prettiness that air of sadness which had first attracted him to her. He could not regret that he had rescued her from the worldly clutches of Alfreda and George; and the fact that she had not visited them since proved how much she had disliked their sort of life. It did not occur to him, of course, that she needed to be told she had permission to do so.

His life had changed very little since his marriage, for which he was grateful; and he liked being seen with her on his arm on the few occasions they were in public together. As to the other business – the physical or, as he thought of it, dark side of marriage – he could not, of course, tell her that it was her little movement of anticipation that night which had opened his eyes to his own abhorrent sensuality. To have knowledge of one's wife out of duty and for the procreation of children was one thing; but to desire her as he had found himself desiring Henrietta was something else.

That vein of sensuality which he had long fought against had betrayed him. He had given in to it at Swale House; but back at the rectory he had been able to tell himself it had been an aberration, never to be repeated – part of the unreal, dreamlike atmosphere of honeymoon. Then after the ball, when he had been moved by her declaration of love (and was it – oh, surely not! – jealousy?) he was aghast to discover he had been on the point of enjoying the most reprehensible, the most shocking – no, he couldn't think of it! He had caught himself back from the abyss in time; and now kept himself from temptation by having as little to do with his wife as possible, and by treating her, when they were together, with a polite and fatherly distance.

Her taking up parish work had helped to fortify this attitude. While she behaved thus, he could put her out of his mind and forget his uncomfortable, unfulfilled longings for her. He could pretend his marriage had never happened, as long as his life could go on as before. It was in gratitude for this that he had decided she deserved a present, something he knew she would really like. Her thanks and her adoring looks were very pleasant to him, and he was glad he had taken the trouble.

Miss Compton had arranged a riding party: she and Henrietta, the twins, and their brother Perry were to meet at the Red House and ride out to Sheriff Hutton to picnic at the ruined castle. It was a perfect, still September day: a blameless, chicory blue sky above, the woodsmoke smell of dying leaves on the air, and soft sunshine that fell like melted butter over the changing woods. Henrietta was looking forward to the ride very much. It would be the first time she had left the immediate neighbourhood of Bishop Winthorpe since her marriage.

She had met Perry Parke when he first came back from Oxford in July: a bright and cheery young man, with the same curly fair hair and round blue eyes as the twins. He was lighthearted, lazy and good-humoured, fond of his sisters, and ready to do anyone a service if it didn't put him out too much. Henrietta liked him as soon as she met him, recognising the type of her own brother Teddy. Having been brought up to expect to inherit his father's title and fortune, Perry saw no reason to improve himself in any way, and was getting through his years at Oxford in the same way that Teddy had, with dining, playing games, and making friends. He had been a little formal with her at first, because of her married status; but because she was so nearly of an age with him, he soon fell into the way of treating her like another sister.

At their first meeting he had been a little languid after the exertions of the term, complaining that he had been 'fagged to death' with work and worry; his tutor was the 'greatest beast in nature' and seemed to think he had nothing to do but read books and write essays. Since then his nerves had recovered rapidly, and he had been enlivening Bishop Winthorpe with one prank after another. The next time she had seen him, he had been frightening the horses in the village street and putting children and old ladies in jeopardy by riding a machine up and down with great inaccuracy and frequent tumbles.

'It's a *vélocipède*,' he told her, having fallen with it in a heap at her feet. 'It's a kind of bicycle, only better. A fellow at Christ Church had a bicycle, made by his father's blacksmith, but you could only go downhill on it: it was so heavy it took two men to push it back up.'

'That must have been inconvenient,' Henrietta said mildly.

'Well, it was,' he agreed. 'He got me at it once, and I tell you it would break your back to go half a mile on the thing. But this beauty of mine was designed by a Frenchman – I forget his name.' He screwed up his brow. 'Began with an "m". Something French. Anyway, the Coventry Sewing Machine Company made four hundred of them for this French chappie, for sending over to France; but bothered if the war didn't break out over there, so that was no go. So they sold them in England instead – the Sewing Machine fellows did – and, to cut a long story short, I bought this one from a man who was a friend of a chap who knew a fellow who came from Coventry and got in on it at the beginning.'

Henrietta marvelled dutifully. 'I'm sure it's a splendid machine.'

Perry patted it enthusiastically. 'Oh, it is! Much lighter than the old sort of bicycle, and faster, and so easy to ride it's like falling off a log.' Henrietta contemplated the chaos he had left behind him and repressed a smile. 'Well,' he qualified, 'it takes a bit of practice, of course, before one gets the hang of it. But once you hit the knack, you can whizz along like the dickens. It's as fast as a horse – and better than dobbin because you don't need to stable it when you get there, and it never gets tired.'

'But don't *you* get tired?'

'Oh – well – I dare say, eventually. But not for miles. I tell you it's the transport of the future. We'll all be riding them soon – ladies too!'

'I don't think I should dare,' Henrietta said. 'Falling off looks so painful.'

'No worse than falling off a horse.' He rubbed at some mud on the frame. 'Lord, if I ain't scratched the paint! The pater will be furious. It cost rather a lot, you see, and I'd already run through my allowance.'

The assaults on the shins of the village populace ended when Perry cut his head open on a stone, and decided to learn bell-ringing instead. Then there was the scheme for brewing ginger beer for sale to the summer visitors, which was meant to restore his depleted coffers, but ended with an explosion of flying corks and having to pay for several broken windows. Then the purchase of a mongrel dog from a gypsy brought on a craze for ratting, during which Perry went about with bits of court plaster all over his face and hands.

Life had certainly been more interesting since Perry Parke came home. Henrietta only hoped that today he would not have brought with him any of those strange devices for making noise – whistles, rattles and the like – that seemed to fascinate him. Last time she had seen him he had been playing a jew's harp, and she didn't think Ginger would stand for anything like that. Amy had once begged to try Ginger round the paddock, and had apostrophised her as a 'perfect beast to ride', but Henrietta would not allow any criticism of her. There was no denying that she was fidgety and hard-mouthed, and started and jibbed at any strange noise or unexpected movement, but so far there had been no disasters. After two weeks Henrietta was getting used to her, and was beginning to feel confident she could manage her.

They were passing the forge now, where a stoical cart-horse was being shod, and Ginger flattened her ears and began to sidle, disliking the smell of burning horn and the hissing of the bellows. The ploughman holding his horse gestured to the smith, who stopped his work and straightened up to watch impassively as Henrietta struggled to get the mare past. Every horseman in the village knew about Ginger by now, and wondered that Rector should allow his new young wife out on such a bad 'un.

'S'all ah coom an' lead 'er for thi, ma'am?' the ploughman called politely, as Ginger dug her toes in and set her jaw like rock. Henrietta waved a negative. She would master her.

'Gi' 'er a whack wi' thi stick!' the blacksmith suggested helpfully. His assistant, who had been working the bellows, came to the front of the forge to see the fun, taking out a handkerchief to wipe the sweat from his neck. Ginger took exception to the flapping cloth and shot past, giving half a buck and trying to snatch the bit. Henrietta felt she was losing control, but fortunately just at that moment Ginger was distracted by the sight of two horses standing in the road outside Miss Compton's house, being held by a very smart-looking groom. Her ears shot forward and she lowered her head, and Henrietta had her in hand again.

She was as surprised as Ginger, for the arrangement was to meet at the Red House, where Miss Compton's horses were stabled by arrangement with Sir Robert. In any case, she saw that the black was not Miss Compton's Midnight, but a gentleman's horse; the other being presumably the groom's. As she hesitated, wondering whether to stop and ask the groom what was happening, the twins came out of the house, having seen her approach, and greeted her eagerly.

'Hello! It's us – we're here! Do stop! Surprise! You must come in and see.'

Amy caught Ginger's rein, Patsy summoned a loitering boy with the promise of a penny for holding the mare, and in a moment Henrietta had jumped down and was following the twins into the now familiar house. In the front parlour Miss

Compton turned to greet her with a glowing face, transformed with happiness. 'Oh, here you are! Look who has come!'

'Your servant, Mrs Fortescue,' Jerome Compton said, bowing.

'He arrived quite suddenly, without any notice to me, the wretch!'

'When have you ever wanted notice?' Compton laughed, but without taking his eyes from Henrietta. 'Besides, this is my own house.'

'Yes, as if you ever used it! But I might have been out – would have been, if you'd been an hour later.'

'Well, I wasn't, so you needn't shrill,' Compton said.

'I was going to send you word that I wouldn't go today,' Miss Compton said, turning to Henrietta. 'But Jerome wouldn't hear of it. He's going to come with us. Isn't that splendid?'

'Yes,' said Henrietta, but with a private reservation. She wished he wouldn't stare at her, and wondered what he meant by it. His smile looked ironic. Was he making fun of her? 'But if you'd rather stay home – Mr Compton must be tired from his journey—'

'Not at all,' Compton protested. 'I wouldn't miss it for worlds. I'm not the least tired. I've only come from York this morning.'

'Of course Uncle Jerry must come!' Amy cried.

'He will tell us all the history of the place. He knows *everything*,' Patsy asserted.

'I know I will push you two down the nearest quarry if you persist in calling me uncle, when I'm no such thing!' he exclaimed good-naturedly. 'But we should get on. I'll walk up to the Red House with you, Mary—'

'Oh no, you can stay here,' the twins said. 'We'll bring back Midnight with us.'

'I'll go with you,' Henrietta said quickly. 'No, really, it's better if I keep Ginger moving.'

She wanted to get away from Mr Compton: he was making her feel uncomfortable. He and Miss Compton came to the door with her, their arms twined about each other's waists. The boy brought Ginger up, rather glad to be rid of his charge, and Henrietta gathered the reins and her skirt, and was obliged to allow Mr Compton to throw her up into the saddle, there being no-one else to do it, and no mounting-block. Ginger, who had a cold back, laid her ears back as usual and cow-kicked, and Compton had to skip out of the way. He waited to see that Henrietta was settled, and then went back to his sister's side.

Henrietta bent to arrange her skirt, and with her head down heard Compton say *sotto voce* to Mary, 'Good God! What a screw! What is the rector thinking of?' The words seared her with shock, and though an instant later she realised he had not meant her to hear them, still she blushed with anger. What right had such a man to criticise Mr Fortescue, who was as far above him as the stars above the earth? She straightened up, and without another glance at the Comptons, rode Ginger away up the street towards the Red House.

Almost as soon as the party set off, there was a wrangle about their destination.

'I've been talking to some people,' Perry announced, riding his bay Billy one-handed as he turned in the saddle to address them, 'and they say Sheriff Hutton is nothing – just some broken old stones. What say we ride to Castle Howard instead?'

'Oh, yes, Perry!' the twins exclaimed. 'Do let's! It's a famous place!'

'But could we see it?' Miss Compton said doubtfully. 'Surely we'd need an arrangement to go inside.'

'Oh, that's all right,' Perry said airily. 'I know a fellow at the House who knows George Howard. His name is sure to get us in. And besides, the park alone is worth seeing.'

'It's much too far,' Mr Compton said. 'We'd never get there and back, and picnic, *and* have time to look round.'

The twins protested. 'Oh we would! We would!'

'How can you be so horrid!'

'Of course we'd have time,' Perry said. 'We've got all day.'

'Remember,' said Compton, 'it's September, not June. It will be dark by six.'

'We can have a quick look, can't we?' Perry said. 'We needn't spend hours about it.'

'It's still too far,' Compton insisted.

'Pooh! It can't be above ten miles.'

'As the crow flies, perhaps, but twelve or fifteen by the lanes and tracks.'

'We'll go across country, then,' Perry said. 'Pretend it's a point-to-point! Famous!'

'You might spare a thought for the ladies,' Compton warned. 'It would be too much for Mrs Fortescue.'

They all looked at Henrietta. 'Don't be afraid for me,' she said, annoyed. 'I've spent longer days in the saddle than this. I'll go as far as you will.'

'But your mare won't,' Compton said.

'What do you mean?'

'No bone and no quarters,' he said shortly. 'She's a park horse. And, frankly, she's not a lady's ride. The way she pulls, she'll wear you out before you've gone two miles. I can see already you can hardly hold her.'

'Thank you,' Henrietta said brittly, 'but I can manage my own horse.'

'I don't think you can,' he contradicted, shocking her with his bluntness. 'What sort of fool would think of buying such a flat-soled, hard-mouthed— ?'

'Jerome, stop!' Miss Compton warned softly, seeing Henrietta was upset.

'The mare is a present from my husband,' Henrietta said hotly.

'Indeed? Well, I'm sure he is all sorts of an excellent man, but it's plain he doesn't know the first thing about horses!'

'He is, however, a gentleman!' Henrietta snapped in reply.

'Oh, here, I say,' Perry said in dismay, sorry for what he had started, 'don't let's quarrel! Wait a minute, I've just thought,' he added, brightening, 'we can't go to Castle Howard anyway, because John and Sam are meeting us with the picnic at Sheriff Hutton. So that's that.'

After an awkward pause, they rode on, the group stringing out as the lane narrowed, with the twins and Perry in front, chatting and laughing noisily, the Comptons in the rear talking quietly to each other, and Henrietta on her own in the middle. Ginger jogged and pulled, and Henrietta brooded angrily on Jerome Compton's rudeness. Why did he have to come along and ruin everything, she thought resentfully. They would have had such a nice ride without him.

A while later he left his sister and rode Warrior up alongside her, to say quietly, 'Mrs Fortescue, I beg your pardon for being so infernally rude.' She did not answer, staring angrily ahead, and he added in a rueful tone, 'I really am desperately contrite. Please forgive me, for the sake of the party if nothing else. I will perform any penance you care to name, rather than have the day spoiled.'

'I have no intention of spoiling the day,' she said stonily.

He looked at her profile for a moment and then said, 'Look here, I was wrong to express myself as I did, but I was prompted only by concern for you. That mare's as hot as Hades, and hard-mouthed into the bargain. She's not safe, you know.'

She scowled. 'I know nothing of the sort! And if you intend to continue abusing her in that ill-mannered way—'

'No, no, I promise you, I won't say another word!' he said hastily, holding up his hands in surrender. 'She shall be an equine paragon if you please, if you will only forgive me. Name my penance! Shall I crawl through thistles? Eat worms? Anything to have you smile again!'

The faces he pulled were ridiculous, and she wanted to laugh, but she would not give him the satisfaction. She bent her head a cool fraction and said, 'I forgive you. There! Now please stop annoying me.'

He let out a whoop that made even Warrior throw up his head, and had Ginger jogging sideways. 'She forgives me! The day is saved! And Englishmen now abed shall curse themselves they were not here—!'

'Jerome, do stop!' Miss Compton called. He continued to clown enormous relief, and Henrietta kept her lips tight closed against a smile, feeling sore inside and confused, and half wishing she had not come.

As the ride progressed she wished it more, for Ginger did not settle. She jogged sideways and tossed her head, fly-bucking and pulling. Henrietta's arms ached with holding her, and the jolting made her head ache. She was enormously relieved when they reached the village of Sheriff Hutton.

The grey stone ruins peeped over the cottage roofs in a way that reminded her a little of Richmond of sacred memory. The servants were waiting at the castle in the Red House brake, loaded with the picnic things, and halters for tying up the horses. Henrietta was glad to dismount and hand Ginger over. Her muscles were trembling and her back ached from the continuous effort, and there was still the ride home to come; but she shut her mind to that, determined to enjoy this part of the day at least.

The rugs were spread, the picnic was laid out: a wonderful array of pies and pasties, rolls, *pâté de foie*, potted crab, tomatoes stuffed with forcemeat, cheeses, fruit, cakes and jellies. 'And what's this?' Miss Compton enquired, lifting the lid of a basket. 'Oh, heaven! Oysters! The first of the season for me – though I suppose you've been revelling in them, wherever it was you were,' she added sternly to her brother. 'We must have them first. Crack them for me, darling, and keep them coming. What is there to drink with them? Don't tell me!'

'Sir Robert is the best of men,' Jerome agreed, discovering the champagne. 'Mrs Fortescue, let me fill a glass for you. I'm sure you need it after your heroic struggle.'

He looked so demure and yet so knowing, she could not resist any longer, and laughed. After that, the slight constraint in the atmosphere relaxed. Both men exerted themselves to be entertaining: Compton told what he knew of the history of the place, and then had a good-natured argument with Perry about whether King Richard III was a good or a bad man, with Perry outdoing himself in absurdity, since he knew almost nothing about history and invented the most ridiculous 'facts' to support his case.

When the remains of the picnic were cleared away, a pleasant digestive somnolence came over them; the afternoon was warm and soft, the air a little hazy. The twins went to look for blackberries – there were plenty of brambles growing over the ruins – while Perry lay on the warm turf and propped himself against the footings of a vanished wall to smoke. The Comptons strolled away arm in arm, talking in low voices, and Henrietta wandered off to explore the ruins without any great urgency.

Some time later she scrambled down from a wall into a square of green sward like a carpeted room, with a broken doorway leading to half a flight of stone steps. Standing in the middle, wondering what sort of people had lived here and what they wore, she realised that she could hear the Comptons talking on the other side of one of the walls. She was about to reveal herself when her own name caught her ear and she held her breath.

'Your Mrs Fortescue is quite a stunner in her way,' Compton was saying.

'Do you think so?' Miss Compton replied idly.

'She's improved immeasurably since I went away. So much more poise, more confidence. What has she been up to?'

'Finding her feet. I persuaded her to take up her parish duties. I suppose that's made the difference. Of course you would notice it more than me, since I see her almost every day. But she's a sweet girl.'

'Oh, your universal "sweet" won't do in this case! She's neither pretty nor conventionally "nice" – as you women will say in your loose, ignorant way – and all the better for it. I'm sick of self-conscious flirts.'

'Yes, I'll bet you are,' said Miss Compton, laughter in her voice. 'Like a greedy child sick of sugar cakes, having consumed too many of them!'

'Hush, you brazen girl! I've done no such thing.'

Henrietta was beginning to move away quietly, not too upset by what she had heard; it was nice to hear oneself praised, though she felt they had discussed her too freely. But then Compton went on, and she waited, guiltily, for more, unable to tear herself away.

'I tell you she has a certain something,' he said, sounding almost puzzled; and then added more heatedly, 'But what the *devil* does that mouldy old rector mean by marrying her?'

'Hush!' Miss Compton said urgently. 'Someone might hear.'

'Oh, they're all blackberrying. We're private here. I tell you, Mary, it makes me mad! Old satyrs like that have no business snatching up young heiresses and locking them up in their horrid castles! It's a sin against nature!'

'Nonsense! When did you ever care about nature? You're sophistication incarnate!' She sounded as though she were trying to tease him away from the subject.

But he said, 'I'm serious. Don't you hate the very thought of it?'

'It was a love match,' Miss Compton said. 'She as good as told me so herself.'

'She couldn't love him, a dried-up old man like that,' he said moodily. 'Besides, it's killing her. Don't you see that look of hers – like a caged animal. You can't shut up a wild thing like that.'

Miss Compton said lightly, 'Dost thou affect her, brother mine?'

'Oh bosh!' he said crossly. 'I just hate waste, that's all. And I tell you what else – that mare will give her trouble before the day's out.'

A stone slipped under Henrietta's shoe. The rattling sound was small, but startled her from her stupid reverie. She removed herself hurriedly and quietly, back the way she had come. When they all met up again, it was plain they had not realised she had been there.

But Henrietta was quiet on the way home; tired, sore of heart, confused and worried. Ginger, refreshed by her rest, jogged and pulled, went sideways, flung her head up and down. Eventually Henrietta said in desperation, 'Shall we canter a little? Ginger is so eager to get home she's shaking me about, and a run might settle her.'

It annoyed her when everyone looked to Mr Compton for his approval; and annoyed her even more when he said, 'Are you sure you'll be able to hold her?'

She remembered his slighting words about Mr Fortescue. 'Remind me to come to you when I want lessons,' she snapped. 'However, as I've been riding since I was two years old, I think I might manage.'

Compton glanced around. They were crossing open grazing, and he thought they couldn't get into much trouble. Perhaps a good run would quiet the mare down. 'Very well,' he shrugged. 'But let me go first, and try to keep her behind Warrior. He'll go steadily. The rest of you keep well back from her, and don't turn it into a race. Are you ready?'

He put his black into a canter. Henrietta tried to hold back for a moment or two to give herself some space, but Ginger was so eager to go she whirled on the spot and then reared. One of the twins gave a little shriek of dismay and Miss Compton called, 'Be careful!' Henrietta hit the mare on the shoulder and she dropped, and then broke into a jarring trot, her head up and her jaw braced against the bit. Henrietta was being shaken almost out of the saddle, and in self-defence put her into a canter, which at least was easier to sit.

Hearing the hooves coming up behind him, Compton glanced back, and assessing the situation decided the only thing to do was to wear the mare out: she was not as fast as Warrior, so she would not pass him, and there was plenty of room to gallop her to a standstill. He eased his hands and Warrior's pace increased.

Ginger wanted to race, but she hadn't the legs of the big black. Unable to catch up, she settled down to a hard canter. It was faster than Henrietta had ever ridden, and she felt a thrill of fear; but it was easier to sit this pace than the usual jogging, and after a moment she began to enjoy it. It was exhilarating to feel the wind whipping past her cheeks and the urgent drumming of hard hooves on the dry ground.

Warrior was slowing now, and Henrietta tried to take up a little on Ginger's mouth, but her neck only went flatter, and the drumming faster. She realised she couldn't stop her. The open field was running out: there was a tall, thick hedge ahead. Surely she wouldn't try to jump? She saw Compton look back. He must have understood, for he began to turn Warrior in a slow arc away from the hedge, hoping that Ginger would follow. Henrietta leaned on one rein, her breath coming short and hard with fear and exertion; and the mare began to turn too, following the black's lead. She was slowing, too, beginning to tire. Relief strengthened Henrietta, and she pulled more confidently at the hard, set mouth.

All might have been well, had not a bird got up right under Ginger's nose. Henrietta never saw what it was –

a skylark, perhaps, nesting in the field – but there was a rattle of wings and a small, swift movement, and Ginger gave a great panicking breenge and leapt sideways. Henrietta managed to stay on, but lost a rein; Ginger accelerated, head up, and banged into Warrior's rear; Warrior kicked, Ginger bucked, and Henrietta parted company with her.

She had a brief, interesting sensation of flying, and then the ground came up and hit her with sickening force. She did not lose consciousness, but all the breath was forced out of her, and for a moment she couldn't see or think, flattened into a horrible black fluttering of shock. Then slowly the darkness receded and sounds returned.

'Aunt Mary, Aunt Mary, is she dead?'

'Don't move her. She mustn't move.'

'Oh my God, suppose she's broken her neck!'

'Don't get too close – give her air.'

'How will we get her home?'

'Can't one of you catch the horse?'

'She's not dead. She's breathing.'

She was. The black fluttering in her chest turned into breaths: in and out; oh blessed air! She was looking at the sky, and the grass was cold under her head. Then the awareness of pain seeped in, slowly at first, but rapidly swelling to a level of jangling that made her nauseous. It was Jerome who was on his knees beside her, and somehow that didn't seem surprising.

'Don't move,' he said to her, seeing sense return to her eyes. 'You may have broken bones. I'm going to check. Don't be afraid.'

The two sentences didn't seem to make sense together, but then she realised he meant don't be afraid of his hands. In normal circumstances she would object violently to his touching her like this, but she thought him silly for supposing she would play propriety at such a moment. It was all she could do not to be sick; but as the nausea passed she knew that the pain was only that of landing so hard, and that there was nothing seriously damaged. He tested her legs and neck, and was working down her arms when she said, 'I'm all right.'

His hand closed round hers, and she held onto it, finding it comforting. She tried to sit up.

'Don't,' he said.

'I'm all right,' she said again, and pulled herself up by him to sitting position. He passed his arm round her back to support her. 'Dizzy,' she said shortly, as a last black swirl passed her eyes. She saw the others standing near, the twins clutching each other, Miss Compton kneeling nearby, her face white, Perry keeping back, holding Billy and Midnight. Warrior was loose, peacefully cropping the grass nearby. There was no sign of Ginger.

She took a deep, quivering breath, and tried to smile at Miss Compton, who seemed the most distressed. She remembered that she had seen her cousin Frederica die with a broken neck, and said, 'Nothing broken.'

'Are you sure? Are you really all right?' Miss Compton asked, unable to believe it.

'Just bruised. I had the breath knocked out of me.'

'You came the most awful purler,' said Miss Compton with a shaky laugh. 'They must have heard that bang in the next county.'

'Landed on her back – more luck than sense,' Jerome said, and he sounded angry.

Henrietta looked at him. 'Where's Ginger?'

'Taken off. Where she is now, I neither know nor care. With luck she'll break her neck and that will be that.'

Henrietta pulled away from him. 'Don't say that! She might be hurt.'

His anger exploded. 'Hurt? It's a miracle you aren't dead! What could possess you to come out on a screw like that, you little idiot!'

'It wasn't her fault!' Henrietta flared. 'A bird startled her.'

'A bird!' he cried in disgust. 'You should never have ridden her. You knew you couldn't hold her.'

'I had her in hand. I was stopping her when the bird—'

'You were not stopping her! She got away from you, and one way or another you were coming off! It was only a matter of time! You risked your silly neck because you wouldn't admit you couldn't hold her. Some ridiculous pride, or misplaced loyalty, or—'

Belatedly the tears came, and Henrietta's storm of weeping

silenced him. The others were staring at him, shocked. He tried to comfort her, but she pushed him away violently, and Miss Compton gave him a meaningful look and took his place. She soothed Henrietta, stroking her hair, and supplied a handkerchief. The storm was as brief as violent, and was soon over. Miss Compton helped her up, straightened her clothes and found her hat while Henrietta blew her nose and dried her face.

'I'm sorry,' said Compton when she was composed again. 'I shouldn't have shouted at you. I was so worried about you I forgot myself.'

Henrietta shrugged his apology away. Her bruises were beginning to stiffen, settling into a steady ache. But how was she to get home without Ginger?

'Do you think you could ride Amy's horse, if we helped you up?' Miss Compton asked. 'I'd give you Midnight, but he's still fresh and he's not an easy ride.'

'And what will Amy do?' Henrietta asked.

'I'll take her up in front of my saddle,' Compton said. 'Warrior can carry two.'

'Or you can ride Billy, and I'll walk and lead you,' Perry offered.

Henrietta gave a tired smile. 'Two miles in those boots? I can ride, it's all right. I'm only a little bruised.'

But getting up onto Amy's bay Treasure was more painful than she expected, and riding woke the ache to a jangle again, so that it took all her character to keep going without complaint. Never had two miles seemed longer, and never had the rectory looked more welcoming than when at last it came into sight.

The vigour of youth soon worked on Henrietta's shaken nerves, and after a few days she felt perfectly all right again, though she had some interestingly coloured bruises. Ginger had been found wandering half a mile from the place of the accident by a farmer. She was slightly lame, and he had stabled her and, once enquiry had established where she came from, had sent word to the rectory. Bond went over there to have a look at her, and finding she had a slight sprain which needed rest, asked the farmer to keep her for a few days.

He went back on the Saturday to bring her home, and it was the sight of Ginger being led down the village street that provoked Jerome Compton to seek an interview with the rector. He was shown into the study, where Fortescue was working on his sermon for the following day, and was not best pleased to be disturbed.

'Mr Compton. An unexpected pleasure. I hope no-one is ill?' he said drily, to convey that nothing less than illness ought to have interrupted him at such a time.

Compton stood square on, balancing lightly on the balls of his feet, his hat held in both his hands, looking as if he might spring at any moment. Had he been a cat, his tail would have been lashing.

'My business with you will not take long, sir. I have just seen the chestnut mare, Ginger, being led home. I wondered what you meant to do with her.'

The rector's eyebrow climbed. 'Did you, indeed? Now why should you wonder that? Have you a desire to purchase her?'

'You will be selling her, then?' Compton asked tautly.

'Mr Compton, I fail to understand what your interest in the matter can be,' Fortescue said, his voice hardening.

'My interest, sir, is in seeing that Mrs Fortescue does not ride that mare again. It is not safe.'

'*You* have the audacity to address this subject to *me*?'

'Because I have seen the mare in action, which perhaps you have not. Which, I would say, *certainly* you have not, or you would never have suffered Mrs Fortescue to ride out on a hard-mouthed, hot-headed, long-backed screw like that!'

Fortescue rose to his feet behind his desk. 'What possible concern is it of yours, Mr Compton?'

'The concern of having witnessed an accident which should never have happened. It's a miracle she was not killed!'

Fortescue snapped, 'I will thank you to mind your own business, and leave me to mind mine. Mrs Fortescue is my wife, and I do not care to hear her name on the lips of a man of your stamp.'

If Fortescue's anger was cold, Compton's was a flame. He seemed to spit and sparkle with it like a newly lit fire.

'Her name could just as easily be on a headstone, since you see fit to send her out on a horse not fit to pull a cart! Good God, man, how could you even come to buy an animal like that? If you take so little care of *your wife*, someone else must do it for you!'

Fortescue came round the desk in a sudden movement, his usual scholarly calm shattered by an uncontrollable upsurge of emotion. 'And that someone else is to be you, is it? By God, sir, I will see you dead first! I have never liked you, Compton, or what you stand for. Nothing is sacred to you. Everything is to be questioned and sullied by your impertinent, undisciplined mind: every tradition, every teaching, every decent precept! You think you know better on every subject than a thousand years of dedicated scholarship! Better than God Himself! But I tell you when you have cut down the rules that shelter man on this earth, you will have loosed a mighty roaring wind that will sweep you away along with all the other works of the devil!'

'You are mad,' Compton said, recoiling from the ferocity of the attack. 'I thought you were only bigoted and blind, but I see now you are quite mad!'

'Leave this house, sir, and do not dare to enter it again!'

'I'll go! It gives me no pleasure to talk to you. I came here only because my sense of duty—'

'*Duty*, you call it!'

'Yes, my duty to try to protect a helpless young girl from the ignorant folly of an old man who would sacrifice her to—'

'*Get out!*' Fortescue almost shrieked. 'I know what's in your mind! Get out, and never dare to come near us again!'

Andrews, the butler, tapped at the door and opened it at that moment; behind him Jenks, the footman, looked anxiously over his shoulder. 'Beg pardon, sir, but is everything all right?'

Fortescue did not speak; he and Compton held each other's gaze for one more moment, and then Compton turned and left without a word, brushing angrily past the servants in the doorway. He felt he had not handled matters well. He had

probably done Henrietta more harm than good by his inter-
ference; and he wondered at himself, who was usually so well
in control, so languidly amused at the follies of the world.

Fortescue waved the servants away, and sat down abruptly
behind his desk again. He was trembling all over, and when he
thought over what he had said, and what Compton had said,
a groan escaped him, and he put his head in his hands. What
madness was this? Was it his, or Compton's? What terrible
force was breaking through the order of his thoughts, like
something rupturing the earth's crust? Did that appalling
young man really covet his wife? And was that reason enough
for Fortescue to want to kill him?

Mr Fortescue did not appear at the dining table. Andrews, his
face a mask of discretion, delivered the message to Henrietta
that the master was much preoccupied with business and sent
his apologies but would not dine. Henrietta and Mr Catchpole
had to make do with each other's company, and the meal
passed silently, for neither by this time had much to say to
the other. News of the violent quarrel in the master's study
was slow to seep through the house: Andrews swore Jenks
to silence in such terrifying terms that it was supper time
before he even divulged it to Oaks, his particular friend;
while Mrs Prosser, who had got it from Andrews within the
hour, sat on any speculation amongst the maids so firmly that
Mr Catchpole only gathered that something had happened,
without knowing what.

Henrietta went early to bed, knowing nothing about
Compton's visit; but the house felt restless, and she was
anxious about her husband's unusual absence from dinner,
and could not settle to sleep at once. She sat up in bed
reading half-heartedly; heard the creak overhead which was
Mrs Prosser going into her room, the last of the servants to
bed. Silence descended; and then the door to her room slowly
opened.

Her heart hammered. 'Who is it?' she whispered. Candlelight, then the candle itself; her palms grew damp; and Mr
Fortescue came in and closed the door behind him. Her heart
was running like a hare: why was he here? He never came to

her like this, without the poetry first. Had he come to berate her? Was he ill? He stood just inside the door, looking at her, the candle held to one side so that for once she could see him, though she could not read his expression. He was in his bedgown, which was hanging loosely open over his nightshirt, his head bare.

'Sir?' she managed to say.

He shook his head, and made a gesture for her to be still. He crossed to the bed and put down the candle, stared at her a moment longer, and then pulled back the bedclothes in one quick movement. Her instinct was to catch at them, and he took her hands and unfolded the fingers, not roughly, but firmly. She glanced up nervously at his face: it was closed to her and grim – but with concentration, she thought, not with anger or disapproval.

He was her husband, and therefore her master; and more than that, he was infinitely her superior – her lord. She did not resist him. Working in this strange silence he pulled off her bedgown, dragging it over her head and dropping it on the floor, and pushed her down onto the mattress. He took out of the pocket of his bedgown two silk stockings which he tied round her wrists, and then to the bedposts. She lay helpless with her arms stretched out and up, trembling at the strangeness of it, but she was not afraid of him, only of his disapprobation. She began to speak, to ask him – she hardly knew what; but he stopped her, putting a finger against her lips, and the gesture reassured her. Whatever strange ritual he was working out for himself, it was not a punishment; he meant no harm to her.

He took time to arrange her hair over the pillows, and then stood for a long moment looking down at her, his eyes opaque, swaying a little, as though with the rhythm of the sea. She imagined in the room's silence the sound of that tide of words on which he had come to her before. Perhaps, she thought, he was listening to it too, rolling inside his head to crash on this beach where she lay bound like a sacrifice.

And then in two swift movements he took off his garments, and climbed up onto the bed.

CHAPTER TWENTY

It was not strictly necessary for George to attend the hiring fair. Atterwith did all that was necessary; but in the sixteen months since he had inherited Morland Place he had become more and more interested in how things were run. Besides, it was an opportunity to meet old friends and other farmers and landowners; and besides again, Alfreda was near her time. The atmosphere at home, with its emphasis on female suffering, made him feel irrationally guilty.

He strolled about examining the men and women seeking new positions, all dressed in their best, many in the decorative smocks or carrying the symbols that marked out their calling. The horsemen were kings, stood proudly, talking amongst themselves, not seeking the eye: it was for the employers to court them, not vice versa. Ploughmen, shepherds, beastmen of all sorts were the next in rank. Among the labourers he took mental note of those who had been at the fair last year, and would be again next: the bad hats who'd been dismissed, and the restless ones, who would not stay more than a twelvemonth in one place. At the bottom end of the scale came those who not only tried to catch the eye, but sometimes called out or touched one's sleeve – the old, the infirm, the simple, the unfortunate, all who were desperate for a position. George hurried past them with averted eyes.

He also hurried past the section for domestic servants, where there was always a fresh crop of girls, going into service for the first time, and loitering nearby a gaggle of noisy youths trying to flirt with them. George had no time for that sort of thing. The last great upset in the house had been caused by the discovery that one of the numerous new maids was pregnant. Alfreda had thrown grand hysterics – something for which she had developed a talent in the last couple of months – and insisted George undertake the inquisition and sacking of the girl. He had protested that it was not his business, which had provoked fresh paroxysms from Alfreda; and then when he did her bidding, the wretched maid burst into tears and made him feel most awkward. He hated women's tears: he never knew what to do about them.

He supposed Alfreda had a right to be fidgety – even mares were known to have uncertain tempers when they were near foaling. When she was in one of her takings, only Bittle could comfort her. It was all Bittle these days in the struggle for power in the house: Fanie was nothing now that she could not dress Alfreda like a fashion plate. Bittle rejoiced in her restoration. She had had nothing to do since Manfred and Regina went away but prepare the nursery; but once the little heir lay in his cradle under her care, she was fixed for ever. George suspected she encouraged Alfreda in her vapours to make herself important, but in fact she was as far from wanting Alfreda to be agitated as it was possible to be: a live healthy baby was to be her salvation.

He was so deep in thought he cannoned into someone coming round the corner, and had taken off his hat with a vague apology before he realised that it was his brother.

'Hello, old man,' Teddy said cordially. They eyed each other with interest. They hadn't met for some months, and each saw a change in the other. Teddy's clothes had undergone a sobering – he looked more like a gentleman and less like a bright lad; George was in riding coat and breeches, of course, but they had far more of fashion and less of comfort about the cut, and his boots would not have disgraced Rotten Row. Teddy had filled out more solidly since he came of age and into his fortune; while constant activity and less of the comforts of home in recent weeks had fined George down somewhat.

'Well, well, well,' George said, at a loss for anything better to say.

'Come to see the fun?' Teddy asked. 'Or are you here on business?'

'Oh, just amusing myself,' George said. 'Seeing who's about. I might be in the market for a new head man up at Twelvetrees. Old Sibthorpe's getting past it – his rheumatism gets worse. But we'll see, we'll see. What about you? Taking on new men?'

'Not this sort. My workers seek me out, you know. And my domestic set-out is nothing like yours.'

'Yes, I hear you manage wonderfully on one and a half in help,' George said, with a little of a sneer.

Teddy rode it out unconcerned. 'It's not quite so dusty as that. But I only keep a bachelor household – whereas I hear you've got an indoor staff to rival Belvoir Castle these days.'

'Nonsense!' George said, pleased. 'But there's no sense in being uncomfortable. Alfreda likes things done properly.'

'Ah yes, how is she?'

'Not in best fig, but that's to be expected. The youngster's due any time.'

'Ah! Well, my best respects to her, and I hope all goes well.'

'Thank you. So where are you off to, if you're not hiring?'

'I was going up to the club for a bite to eat. Why don't you join me?' he added in a surge of cordiality.

George frowned a little. 'At this time of day? I never take lunch, you know.'

'Lunch?' Teddy grinned. 'This is breakfast. I was up late with a bunch of very ripe lads. But come on anyway – do! Take a tankard of ale with me, if nothing else – or a glass of wine, or whatever you fancy.'

'Oh, very well.' George fell in beside him, curious to know more about his brother's life. Teddy had come of age in August, and now had full control of his fortune – that property which should have been George's own. He'd like to know what he was doing with it.

At the club he meant only to take a glass of ale – the Yorkshire did a very good October – but the sight of the cold table overcame his resolve, and he sat down at length opposite Teddy with half a cold roast pheasant, several slices of pink, fragrant ham, and a wedge of the best game pie in the city. Teddy took the game pie, and kedgeree, and in deference to the fact that this was his breakfast called for half a dozen sausages.

They chatted at first on neutral subjects, feeling each other out: the weather, the price of wheat, the various improvements that were going on in York.

'And what about your building scheme?' George asked. 'Pass the mustard, old fellow. The last I heard, Moon's Rush was still a ruin.'

'Not quite – the roof's on and the walls are sound. But I can't make up my mind to go and live there – too far out of the city. I like to have people around me. I'm not ready to settle down on an estate yet. To tell the truth, I'm not sure I'm cut out to be a landowner.'

'No, I never thought you were,' George said complacently. 'It takes a certain kind of gentleman to understand the land. Of course, I was brought up to it, being the heir from the beginning. And Alfreda comes from the landed aristocracy.'

'You're right,' Teddy said meekly, spooning pickles onto his plate.

'I know I am. You're more the modern-minded sort of fellow who likes machinery. I suppose Father realised that when he left you those grubby workshops of Makepeace's.'

'Right you are! Soot and grub, that's my mark! Some more ale? Oh, waiter! Leave the jug, that's a good fellow. You know, George, I begin to think Moon's Rush is wasted on me – the house and the land.'

'I should about say it is!' George said eagerly. 'You've never done anything about bringing the land back, have you? It's a crime to let acres lie idle – and you'll have thistles and brambles and seedlings growing up all over it if you don't mind out, and then it'll be the devil to clear.'

'I know,' Teddy sighed. 'It worries me sometimes. I just don't know what to do about it.'

George put down his knife and tried not to look too eager. 'Let me have it.'

'Eh?'

'It's simple. You don't like the land, and I do. You've no use for it, so let me have it.'

Teddy let the idea sink in slowly. 'I know you always wanted it,' he said.

'Oh, land is land, you know,' George said casually. 'I thought it would be a good addition to Morland Place at one time, but I'm not so sure now. There are other parcels I've got my eye on – but I hate to see good land wasted like that. Just as a favour to you, I'd be willing to take it off your hands.'

'Take it?'

'Buy it, I mean. Buy it, of course. Not,' George added quickly, 'that it's worth much. It will cost money to get it right – that has to be reflected in the price.'

'Ah yes, the price,' Teddy said thoughtfully. 'You see, the thing is, I'd be glad to let you have it, but I don't really need money.'

'Don't need money?' George said, amazed at the blasphemy.

'I only have a bachelor establishment, and I've no plans to marry. I have plenty for my needs.'

'Well, if you're that flush, you can give me the damn' land,' George said, half annoyed, half joking. It was unnatural for a man not to want money.

'I don't think I could do that,' Teddy said. 'That would be like snubbing our father – saying his gift to me was worthless. I'll tell you what, though – I'll swap it with you.'

'Swap it? Are you potty? Swap it? We're talking about land, not a game of marbles.'

'Look here, Georgie, you love the land and I don't. On the other hand, you've got those dirty old factories in Manchester that you hate, and I quite like factories. So why don't we swap?'

George was a slow thinker, and not a noticing man, but he couldn't help feeling he had been manoeuvred up to this point. Yet Teddy's face was a study of disinterest, and he couldn't for the life of him see what the trick might be. The land was valuable – good farmland was going for anything up

368

to forty years' purchase these days – and placed as it was, could only become more so. And he had no value for the factories. They brought in an income, but he only had a half-share, and the manager was always telling him they needed capital spent on them. Besides, they were far away and he had no time to visit them, and he couldn't be bothered with it at all, he really couldn't.

'Let me be clear,' he said slowly. 'You want to give me the land and the house at Moon's Rush, in exchange for my share in Hobsbawn Mills?'

'And the railway shares,' Teddy added calmly.

'Oh, and anything else?' George said ironically. 'What else are you going to add at the last minute?'

'Nothing else. Just the mills, and the railway shares. It makes it nice and neat – you don't want to be bothered with that industrial stuff. You're a landowner, Georgie, the squire, the lord of the manor.'

'All right,' George said. 'You're on.' He held out his hand across the table. 'But no welshing, mind! Once we've struck palms, that's it.'

'Of course, no welshing,' Teddy said. 'We're brothers, aren't we? Anyone would think I was trying to do you down, instead of doing you a favour.'

They shook hands across the table, and then George grinned and took up his knife and fork again. 'You were right about this game pie – I shouldn't mind another bit,' he said, so as not to let Teddy think the deal meant anything to him; but inside he was rejoicing. He had got back the land his father's will had cheated him of – and got it back for nothing, without parting with a penny piece!

Teddy called for the waiter to bring more game pie, and thought that it was almost too easy, like taking a toy from a baby. The factories and the railway shares for that rubbishing piece of land! And old Georgie was gloating away as if he'd done a deal on the Crown Jewels.

'We'd better get Arthur Anstey to draw up the exchange, just to make it all fair and legal,' he said casually. 'I'll speak to him this afternoon on my way home, shall I? Try some of this pickle with the game pie, old man – it's first rate.'

George was half-way home, idling along with the reins slack and his mind elsewhere, when he met one of the young grooms on horseback coming to find him.

'Sir! Sir! Mr Goole sent me – it's Mrs Morland, sir.'

Crusader jerked his head and snorted as George's hand shortened rein convulsively. 'Is it the baby?'

'Yessir. Mr Goole says to find you and tell you the mistress 'as gone to her room, an' the doctor's been sent for,' the boy vouchsafed breathlessly.

'Very well,' George said, and put Crusader into a canter. When they reached the yard George slithered off and flung the rein to the groom without a word. The boy watched him run for the house, impressed with this evidence of concern: normally the master was full of orders about Crusader's welfare – and he never ran.

George found the household in a turmoil. Those who had something to do were in the minority: mostly the servants were milling about the hall or peeping from the kitchen passage, talking in low voices and patently waiting for some spectacle. George emitted a few angry barks and cleared the area, leaving himself with Goole to deliver the bulletin.

'Madam – ah – went into travail two hours ago,' the butler said, evidently uncomfortable with the subject matter. 'She has retired to her bedchamber with her maid and Mrs Bittle. The midwife arrived a short time ago and ordered the doctor to be sent for. I regret I have no further information.'

'Very well, I'll go up,' George said, trying to sound unconcerned. He thought a moment. 'I'd better change,' he added. Alfreda would object to the smell of horses in her bedroom. 'Where's Hayter?'

'He is upstairs, sir.'

George took the stairs at a run and on the upper landing met his man with an armful of brushes and nightclothes. 'Hayter! Where the deuce are you going?'

Hayter turned martyred eyes on him. 'To the east bedroom, sir – your old room. I took the liberty of ordering the bed made up for you there. You will not, sir,' he anticipated George's next outburst, 'wish to remain in your own chamber during the proceedings. I regret to inform you that the new walls are not sufficient to render the matter impenetrable to the ear.'

'Good God,' George said. 'Well, as you please. If you think it necessary.'

Hayter's expression was martyred. 'Most necessary. I am informed by Mrs Prosser that these matters commonly go on for many hours.' He bowed and continued on his way.

George stood hesitating on the landing outside the bedroom door. The great bedchamber was no more. He remembered a week in the early summer when the house had reverberated to hideous, heavy blows, and the air had shimmered with suspended dust, as the estate masons had smashed the massive stone surround of the fireplace with mallets, and tore down the lath-and-plaster internal walls of the dressing-room.

Before that, of course, all the furniture had had to be removed, and Gowthorpe, the estate carpenter, had come up with his lads to dismantle the massive Butts Bed, in which generations of Morlands had been born and died. They had drawn out the long tapering pegs of wood which held it together, gently knocked it into its component parts, and taken it away.

George had come home to find them reassembling it in the north bedroom. '*She* wanted it got rid of,' Gowthorpe had complained as he shuffled backwards with one end of a massively carved tester-beam. 'Burned for firewood, like enough.'

George, torn between shock and loyalty to his wife, started to speak and changed it to a cough.

'Huh!' Gowthorpe grunted. 'I told her. History, that is. A hairloom. You'll bring bad luck on this 'ouse if you go brekkin' it up like that.' He eyed George cannily. 'I told her *you'd* never stand for it.'

So the bed had been saved; but everything else had gone. Once there had been a vast chamber with dark beams lifting into a shadowy, vaulted ceiling, dark-panelled walls, a huge fireplace that could consume half a tree, and broad, polished oak floorboards shining like dark water. Now there were two modern, low-ceilinged rooms, each with a small, neat patent fireplace, bright wallpaper, and new carpet underfoot covering most of the floor. There was a communicating door between the bedrooms, and each had a dressing-room and closet leading off it with a return door to the passage so that Fanie and Hayter could come and go.

'Everything neat, convenient and proper,' Alfreda had said with satisfaction, and had ordered a wonderful new commode for each closet and a large bath for each dressing-room.

She could not, of course, have anticipated the one inconvenience to the new arrangement. George ventured into his own room, and the noises from next door drove him hastily out again. Fanie was just coming from Alfreda's room.

'What's happening?' he asked her.

She looked pleased with herself. For weeks Bittle had been queening it over her and she had been sulking, but with the new turn of events Bittle needed help and Alfreda had refused to have anyone near her but Fanie. And Fanie had a large family of nephews and nieces back in France and the absorbed interest in childbirth of her peasant origins. In fact, as was being proved, she knew far more about the process than Bittle, who had only ever dealt with the results.

'Oh, it will be a ver' long time yet, monsieur. Not per'aps until tomorrow morning. You need not wait. One will tell you when it is done.'

'Can I see her? Does she ask for me?'

Fanie gave him a pretty smile. 'But no!' she said, as though he had asked something childishly silly. 'Madame does not wish anyone to see 'er like zis. I will tell 'er zat you 'ave askéd after 'er. Zat is enough.'

'But is everything all right? Will it be all right?' he pleaded.

'Oh yes, why not?' Fanie said with reassuring promptness; and then, bold in her female supremacy, she patted his forearm. 'Better you go 'way now – it is no place for a man.'

Remembering the noises, George agreed with her and, glad to have been excused, he hurried away to the other end of the house.

Fanie was right. The hours passed. The doctor came and went

away, saying he was not needed yet, came again and went away again. Goole enquired about dinner and was sent away with a snap and a black look. Later he brought a large supper on a tray and was not rebuffed. George wandered from room to room downstairs, trying to avoid seeing the procession of women going upstairs with their smug air of busy-ness which he was beginning to hate. There was something gruesome about it: temple virgins preparing one of their number to be a blood sacrifice. Mrs Holicar had joined the inner circle now, and the laundrymaid who was a mother of ten.

The doctor came again and stayed. All the clocks in the house struck midnight and the small hours began. There were difficulties, it transpired. All was not going as it should. For the first time George wished they had a chaplain so that some more powerful help could be invoked. He went into the chapel and knelt and tried to pray, but he could not think of anything to say. He was not in the habit of talking to God. But he went to church every Sunday: his membership was paid up. Surely God would know what he wanted? He left the chapel and wandered again, and wished Alfreda had not banned all dogs from the house. It would have been comforting to have a heap of warm, unconcerned, loving bodies against his knees, rough heads and smooth ears to caress. He thought of going out to the kennel and fetching Philo or Bran, but it seemed too much effort; and probably unfair to Alfreda, going behind her back when she was helpless.

The dark outside grew grey at last, and he leaned against the drawing-room windows with his breath feathering the cold glass, and stared at the autumn mist over the moat, roiling like steam on the water, blanking out the world except for the shadow of a hedge, a ghost tree. Unseen, the sun came up, and the mist was suffused with slowly spreading gold; and then it began to thin, and the world assembled itself gradually into lines and shapes, startlingly near after the distanceless white.

The door opened and the lamp man came in to collect the lamps for filling, followed by a housemaid to tend the fire. They both started when they saw him, but he waved to them to continue. And then, in the open doorway behind him, Mrs Holicar appeared.

'The baby's born, sir,' she said without preamble. Her eyes were red with lack of sleep. George stared at her, numb from the long waiting, unable to speak. 'It's a boy.'

A boy! A son! It had never occurred to him at any point that the baby might be a girl, but now she announced it he realised belatedly that there had always been one chance in two. He felt a huge gratitude. A son! The heir to Morland Place.

He found his voice, dry with long unuse. 'Healthy?'

'Yes, sir. It seems so.'

'And – and Mrs Morland.'

'It was hard for her. You'd better talk to the doctor about that.' Belatedly she saw the two servants with their mouths open and their ears on stalks. 'Get on with your work! If you'd like to come upstairs, sir,' she added with a significant nod towards them, 'I'll get Doctor Winchester to come out.'

There were servants everywhere – going about the normal morning routines, of course, but lingering in case they might overhear something – and Mrs Holicar had to install him in the long saloon for privacy. There was a delay before Winchester came, and then he had his sleeves rolled up and blood on his shirt, which George tried very hard not to look at.

'The child is well formed,' he said. 'He is sleepy, as is to be expected after a long labour, and a little small, but he seems healthy. We will know better in a day or two. However, it has not gone well with the mother. There were complications, and her age was somewhat against her.' He met George's eyes gravely, and George shivered involuntarily. 'There were times when it was touch and go. She is resting now, and out of immediate danger, but I would not be doing my duty if I were not to tell you that we aren't out of the woods yet. We may still lose her. I will do everything in my power, it goes without saying, but I must make you aware of the possibility.'

George found his voice at last. 'May I see her?'

'In a little while. I will send for you. In the mean time, perhaps you would like to see the baby? I'll have the girl bring him out.' At the door he turned back. 'You will need a wet-nurse for him. Have you anything arranged?'

'I – I don't know.' George felt foolish – but these were women's matters.

'I'll ask the nurse. If not, I know a very good girl. I can send her up straight away.'

He went. In a little while, Katie came with the shawl-wrapped bundle, gave him a shy smile, and laid it in his arms. 'It's so tiny!' he breathed in alarm. The eyes were sealed, the pinched little face closed and silent, as if he had already gone away, after so little time in the world.

'You must be glad it's a boy, sir,' Katie said to help him along, seeing he hardly knew what to do or think. And then, to her horror, she saw tears filling the master's eyes and spilling over his lower lashes. 'Let me take him,' she said quickly, but he shook his head, holding the tiny thing closer that had cost so much to bring to being.

For two weeks Alfreda hovered between life and death, and the baby lay unmoving and uncrying, as though he could not decide whether or not to stay until the other issue was settled. Dr Winchester called several times a day, and on his recommendation a specialist nurse was brought in, much to Bittle's annoyance. George saw Alfreda only once in that time, a brief visit on the first day. He was shocked at the evidence of her suffering, plain in her haggard face and shadowed eyes. After that she would not let him near her again. She had seen too clearly in his expression the reflection of how she looked.

At the end of the fortnight Winchester pronounced her out of danger, provided no infection developed, but she was still bedridden and in a great deal of pain. It was a month before she got out of bed for the first time.

By then the baby had improved, was feeding well and was more alert, though still very small. When he was placed in Alfreda's arms, she was torn between resentment that so insignificant a creature could have caused her such torment, and a fierce tenderness for him. Her child – the last of the Turlinghams! He should not die! He must live, and inherit Morland Place, and be a great man!

He had been baptised without a name by Mr Hughes on

his first day of life. It was not until he was two months old that Alfreda was able to leave her room for long enough to attend his christening in the chapel. He was given the names James Edward Benedict – Morland names, but James was also the name of Alfreda's father, so it united both families.

Knowledge of the quarrel between Jerome Compton and Mr Fortescue gradually spread through the village, and since nobody but the two protagonists knew what it was about, everyone was free to supply his own matter. Andrews knew only that voices had been raised and his master had told Compton to get out. The doors were thick and he had heard no more than that; but he had more than once heard Mr Fortescue at dinner deploring Compton's views, particularly his espousal of the Darwinian theory, and he had once hinted that he suspected Compton did not believe in God. It was not difficult therefore to attribute the quarrel to religious differences, and this became the favoured explanation.

It was the end of the week before it got back to Henrietta, through the agency of Amy Parke, who heard it from her brother Perry; and by that time Jerome had embraced the better part of valour and departed for a friend's house in Scotland for some shooting. Henrietta visited Miss Compton, who asked after her physical well-being, mentioned briefly that Jerome had gone on his usual visit to his friend Maitland, and turned the conversation gracefully to village matters. Henrietta took her tone from Miss Compton's, and seeing these two were friends, the neighbourhood had to keep its speculation to itself thereafter.

Mr Fortescue never mentioned the subject to Henrietta, and she put the quarrel down to Darwin too, and dismissed it from her mind. A week after Compton's visit to the rectory, Henrietta was in the morning-room working on her diary – she had lately begun to keep a note of her parish visiting, partly to keep track of who was due a visit, who was suffering from what, and who had had the baby-clothes last – when Mr Fortescue came in.

'Do I disturb you, Mrs Fortescue?'

Henrietta stood up. Since the evening of Jerome's visit,

Mr Fortescue had visited her twice more at night in the same manner, but in the daytime his demeanour was so normal and unchanged that she was beginning to be able to detach herself as he did, and not confound herself with the sudden memories his appearance provoked. 'No, sir, not at all,' she said.

He came over to the desk to see what she was writing. 'Ah, I see that I do, but I hope the interruption will not be unpleasant to you. I have been talking to Bond, my dear, about the mare. Perhaps I should have done so at the beginning,' he added, as though to himself. 'He thinks that perhaps she is not suitable for you. What is your opinion?'

'I can manage her,' Henrietta said quickly.

'Your horsemanship is not in doubt,' he said, unexpectedly kindly, 'but after the accident—'

'It wasn't her fault, not really. A bird got up under her feet and frightened her.'

'But Bond thinks she is unsafe, and not a comfortable ride for you.'

'She is difficult to handle,' Henrietta admitted, 'but – well – she was your gift to me. I don't want to part with her.'

He paused for a long moment, and she wondered if she had offended him; but at last he said, 'You are very kind. But if I replace her, the new horse will also be my gift. And I should feel happier to know that you had a safe mount.'

'Thank you, sir,' said Henrietta, deeply touched. 'But what would happen to Ginger?'

'I could not sell her, knowing her to be dangerous.'

'You wouldn't – not shoot her?'

'That is what Bond recommends. Her temper is not good enough to breed from her.'

Henrietta's hands came out in appeal. 'Oh, *please* not! I'm sure it isn't her fault. If I promise not to ride her, won't you please keep her? She can be turned out to grass. I'll willingly go without a horse, if only you won't kill her.'

'What tender concern for a dumb beast!' Mr Fortescue said, half amused, half touched. Was it for his sake she valued the animal so much, or was it just her nature? In either case he would not deny her. In the daylight hours, at least, he could show his love for her in an appropriate way. He locked away the knowledge of his dark visits to her in a part of his mind he never examined. 'If it means so much to you, we will keep the mare. But I will buy you another horse – you must have the means of exercise you are used to. This time, however, I shall take advice. Do you think Sir Robert Parke knowledgeable about horses?'

'Oh, yes sir. Very much so.'

'Then I shall consult him about the best way to proceed.'

Sir Robert undertook to make enquiries for a suitable horse, but warned that it might take time. Meanwhile Henrietta walked to her sick and poor, and Ginger, reprieved, was unshod and turned out, much to Bond's disgust. He saw no point in wasting good grazing on her; but Henrietta went every day to visit her, taking an apple or a carrot or some other treat. With nothing else to do and no other company, Ginger gradually came to enjoy these visits, and would whinny and come to the gate when Henrietta appeared; and Henrietta harboured secret plans one day to break her in again and reschool her from the beginning.

Still no new horse was forthcoming when a letter arrived from Regina – still with the Ansteys and looking like to stay there – telling of the birth of the new heir to Morland Place. Henrietta wrote to George and Alfreda with her congratulations but her letter was not acknowledged. She was a little hurt; but indeed there had been no communication between her and Morland Place since her marriage. Of course, she had never expected either of her brothers to write – that was women's business – but it seemed Alfreda had given it up too. Perhaps it was always that way with married women; certainly she wrote to Regina less often now that she had parish work to do.

Bishop Winthorpe was a prosperous neighbourhood. The squire and the rector owned the majority of the land, but there were also several yeoman farmers, a breed dying out in most parts of England, but still common enough in Yorkshire. The prosperity and comfort of these farms varied enormously. On one, for instance, the labourers, men and women, were housed in two buildings like cattle sheds, presided over by elderly female caretakers, and fed on bread and dripping, pease pottage, cabbage and beans. On another, no larger, the farm servants lived in the farmhouse and ate princely pork and potatoes at the farmer's table.

Amongst the cottages there was even wider discrepancy. Most had only one room downstairs, and in the worst cases the room was virtually bare, with only a table and a few plain chairs or stools for furniture, an old potato sack on the earth floor for a hearthrug. At the other end of the scale she visited bright and cosy cottages with upholstered chairs, dressers of crockery, pictures on the walls and colourful rag rugs on the floor.

It seemed to depend on the skill of the housewife at managing, and how many mouths there were to fill. Marriage meant continuous childbirth: she visited cottages where the wife had borne eight or ten children, sometimes more, and was worn out with it, dragging herself, toothless and apathetic, about her work with a baby on her arm, another in her belly, and three or four little ones underfoot. And when the woman died, either from exhaustion or complications, the man was often left with no choice but to marry again, for someone had to mind the children left behind while he was out at work; then more babies would come along. Henrietta knew one family where the fourteen children came from three different mothers. It was no wonder, she thought, that abstention from the pleasures of the flesh – even within marriage – was regarded as a virtue.

In some households the woman also went out to work, leaving the smallest children to the care of the next smallest, or to the old who couldn't work. Once Henrietta found two babies, one a few weeks old and one over a year, in bed with a sick and bedridden old man. When she gently remonstrated with the mother, the woman only gave her a hopeless look and asked what else could she do? Someone had to take care of them while she worked. She earned eighteenpence a day following horses around the pastures and breaking up their droppings with a long fork.

But it was not always so cheerless. In households where the progeny were more spread out in age, the older ones were out at work or even married before the youngest were born. Girls went into service as soon as they were eleven or twelve, easing the burden on the house and even sending a little money home; boys could begin farm work at ten. Even the young ones were set to whatever they could do – bird-scaring, gleaning, stone-picking, horse-holding – to earn a penny here and there, or perhaps payment in kind – milk, potatoes, beer, coal.

The worst misfortune was for the man of the house to fall sick or injure himself, and then a family could go from moderate prosperity to desperate poverty in a matter of weeks, for the way they lived left no reserve to draw on. Old age was also much to be feared: when a man or woman could no longer work, if they had no family willing to support them, they would simply starve to death. Now that factory conditions had improved so much and the work was steady and the wages good, the worst of poverty was to be found in the countryside.

Henrietta pondered these matters as she went about her duties. She saw one brisk woman managing a houseful of children, keeping them clean and civil and feeding everyone adequately, while another in almost identical circumstances was sunk in apathy and muddle, her children wild as animals, half naked and half starved. What caused these differences she did not know. Could it be that some people were just born with the ability to manage and others were not? It was sometimes canvassed at the rectory dinner table. Mr Catchpole asserted that poverty was caused by vice, and when he visited the least favoured his message was simple: read the Good Book, go to church, sin no more, and comfort will follow. It was a reasoning accepted and understood by most of the lower orders, and few of them thought the worse of Catchpole for voicing it. As they saw it, it was a clergyman's duty to tell them such things.

What Mr Fortescue believed was harder to fathom. Henrietta sometimes thought that his mind was fixed on such high things, he did not really see his parishioners at all. When they came to him for spiritual advice, he gave it carefully and freely, and they went away comforted even if they had not understood what he said. They never went to him with earthly problems: it didn't seem appropriate.

It was November before Sir Robert found the right horse for Henrietta. It was a grey gelding, pretty enough to satisfy Mr Fortescue's wishes, with darkish dapples and a near-white mane and tail. He had excellent paces and a soft mouth and was as gentle as a kitten. Mr Fortescue queried whether a lady could ride a male horse, and Sir Robert told him that in his opinion, the notion that females could only ride mares was nonsensical, and that geldings were generally more reliable in temper. Mr Fortescue remembered his resolve to take advice this time, and paid the reassuringly large sum for Starlight without demur.

Henrietta was delighted with him. He was a full hand bigger than Ginger, but she felt perfectly safe on him. Her only difficulty was in mounting if she ever had to jump down for any reason; but he stood so quietly that she only had to find something high enough to stand on. She became adept at gauging gates, walls and tree stumps and, this mastered, found a new degree of freedom.

Christmas – her first as the rector's wife – was a happy time. She was kept very busy as the day itself approached, trying to make sure that all her poor families had something extra by way of food and fuel, and at the same time helping Mrs Prosser and Andrews – the wonder of it! – with the arrangements for Christmas Eve, when the rectory opened its door to all the neighbourhood children, the rector addressed a homily to them, and then gave each of them a present, with cakes and lemonade. The same evening the Red House held a supper party, the centrepiece of which was the lighting of the candles on the Christmas tree (a modern innovation of which the rector would have none at his own house), with a cold buffet and hot punch afterwards.

Christmas Day was busy, with three services of which the rector took two himself, and in the afternoon the Quarter Day visit of his tenants; and there were always neighbours 'dropping in' and carol singers stopping by, all of whom expected refreshments to be served. On St Stephen's Day – which they called Boxing Day up at the Red House – a party was got up to go to the nearest meet. Henrietta hunted Starlight for the first time, and found him everything she could wish for. They would be hunting from Morland Place, she thought, and remembered suddenly the Christmases of her childhood, with the fetching of the yule log and the service in the chapel, brilliant with candles, and the tenants and servants crowding into the great hall, and later the mummery and fun of Twelfth Night. Then she turned her mind resolutely from it. It would not be like that now; and it was not her home any more.

On Boxing Day evening the Red House gave a grand ball. Mr Fortescue suggested Henrietta would be too tired after hunting to attend it, but when the time came she found herself wonderfully revived. Perry Parke had come home for the Christmas season; Jerome Compton had too, and Henrietta thought there might be some little awkwardness in meeting him again, but when she first encountered him, at Miss Compton's house a few days before Christmas, he seemed in high spirits, quite unaffected. He did not see Mr Fortescue until Christmas Day at morning service, but the two met at the church door with formal civility, which was all that was required, and if the rector did not shake Compton's hand, only Miss Compton noticed the omission.

At the ball Henrietta kept close by her husband's side at first, though the lights and music and chatter of other groups beckoned to her strongly. She tried hard to follow the conversation he was having with the older and more staid gentlemen in this quiet corner. Looking at his grave profile as he listened and spoke, she could not equate him with the man who came, very frequently in the past few weeks, to her bedchamber at night. The things he did there seemed odd to her, though she had nothing to compare them with; but she did not doubt he did them in love. She was always moved to wonder that he should love someone as ordinary as her.

But the music tugged at her mind like a child tugging at a sleeve, and her head kept turning of its own volition towards the door of the room where the dancing had begun. When Perry Parke at last came to ask if she would like to dance, she was half grateful, half embarrassed as she refused.

Perry made a civil protest, but he was eager to get back to the fray and went off to find someone more accommodating. Fortescue turned from his conversation and said, 'What did that young man want, my dear? To dance with you? Do not disappoint our friends on my account. You know I do not dance, but if you wish to, pray do.'

Henrietta was just about to answer when Jerome Compton arrived at her side, bowed to her, and said to the rector, 'Sir, may I solicit the honour of Mrs Fortescue's hand in a dance?'

Henrietta did not miss her husband's involuntary frown. 'Oh, but I don't mean to dance,' she said quickly. 'Not tonight.'

Compton gave her an amused glance, then looked again enquiringly at her husband. She realised that her hasty denial had made it seem as though Mr Fortescue had ungenerously forbidden her, which was not at all the impression she wanted to give. Fortescue said evenly. 'Pray dance with Mr Compton, my dear, if you wish. I have no objection.'

So there was nothing for it but to place her hand on Compton's arm and allow him to lead her away. But as she approached the music her spirits rose and her feet longed to be off. Compton looked down at her with a smile. 'What energy! No-one would think you were out for four hours today!'

'It was an excellent hunt, wasn't it?' she said, turning to him eagerly. A waltz was playing, and they closed and whirled away with the unconscious ease of otters slipping into a river.

'Yes, and your new horse went well.'

'He was perfect. But how did you know that?'

'I was watching you, of course.'

'I didn't see you.'

'No, because I was behind you all the way. I was taking my young horse quietly. But your grey didn't put a foot wrong.'

'And we had such a splendid run!'

'Yes, the weather was just right. The only drawback of such a mild Christmas is that without a freeze there's no skating.'

'Oh, yes, I love to skate! And I love the snow, too. I remember one year it started snowing just when we were coming home with the log, and when we got to the top of the slope down to the house, there it was all edged with snow, like white fur. It looked so pretty!'

'It must be a fine place, this Morland Place of yours,' he said, thinking what a crime it was for all this young rapture to be wasted on a dead stick like Fortescue.

'It is,' she agreed, and then the joy faded a little. 'But it's not my Morland Place any more.'

He changed the subject quickly. 'You dance remarkably well.'

'Do I? I haven't had much practice – but I do with you, I think,' she added innocently.

He resisted the urge to pull her close to his heart. 'Then we should make sure that we dance together often. One should always promote the best. Look at poor Parke with Miss Corby! He looks as though he's steering a cart with only three wheels.' Henrietta tried not to laugh, because it wasn't charitable. 'Miss Corby is a very nice young lady, but she had no sense of rhythm. Now, don't you think it's better for the world to increase its stock of excellence? It's like doing good, you know: the more you do, the more there is in the world.'

'I suppose you're right,' she said doubtfully, 'but I can't help thinking—'

'Yes?'

'That you're bamboozling me,' she finished.

He laughed. 'Without a doubt! But in the best possible cause.' And he whirled her fast round a corner so that she hadn't the breath to ask him what the cause was.

It was soon after Christmas that she began to feel unwell. It began with occasional bouts of indigestion, which surprised her, because she had always been able to eat anything. But she put it down to over-indulgence at Christmas, and tried to ignore it. She was in any case very busy. The weather had broken at last, and the cold exposed the weakest points in the parish, and brought on illness.

The first time she was sick, she thought she had caught something from one of the poor she visited, and was rather frightened; but no other symptoms developed, and she didn't like to consult Mr Fortescue's doctor, Mansur, who was a grey and grim old fellow with a forbidding manner. But the sickness continued: first thing in the morning it struck her, though it wore off after a couple of hours and she was able to go about her work. Her breasts were very tender, too, so that confining them in a corset was painful. That, however, was something she could not tell anyone, not even the maid who laced her up.

And then one day when she was visiting Mrs Harris, the ploughman's wife who had recently laid-in of her fifth, she came over faint while leaning over the crib admiring the child, and swooned dead away on the bedroom floor. When she came to herself Mrs Harris was holding a burnt feather to her nose while her eldest daughter, Fanny, rubbed her hands.

'I'm so sorry,' Henrietta muttered, confused. 'I don't know what came over me.'

'If I was you, mam,' Mrs Harris said, 'I wouldn't wear such tight lacing. It's not good for you, in your condition.'

'Condition?' Henrietta queried vaguely; but she was not as innocent as she had been before she began parish visiting, and she blushed deeply as a thought occurred to her. She met Mrs Harris's eyes appealingly, and Mrs Harris, unexpectedly quick on the uptake, sent Fanny out of the room. A few questions and answers were exchanged, and then Henrietta burst into tears.

'Why, mam, don't upset yourself! It's the most natural thing in the world, and nothing to be afraid of,' Mrs Harris cried, distressed.

'I'm not afraid, I'm h-happy,' Henrietta sobbed. 'Are you s-sure that's what it is?'

'From what you tell me, mam, I'd say it was certain sure.' She patted Henrietta's arm. 'You go straight home now and tell Rector. He'll be as pleased as punch, I warrant you. Eh, what a happy day! And there's you bringing baby-clothes to the likes of me! You'll be stitching your own from now on.'

CHAPTER TWENTY-ONE

In September 1871 Venetia passed her viva at St Agatha's with ease; but it was not in even Sir Frederick's power to have her entered there as a medical student. After long debate between the dean, Mr Bentley, and the treasurer, Mr Linscourt, Miss Fleet was admitted as a 'lady amateur'.

'Which means,' Sir Frederick explained, 'you have no status at all, and may be asked to leave whenever it suits them; but it is a foothold, my dear, a foothold. Bentley and Linscourt have no personal objection, but they feel the rules don't permit them to go further.'

'And what about the fees?' Venetia asked.

'They can't let you pay student fees, of course, but I know you don't want to be taking advantage of the situation, so I have suggested they accept a voluntary donation of the same amount – that is, eighty-five guineas.'

'Thank you. I am determined to pay – or at least, Aunt Fanny will be paying for me, but I'll reimburse her as soon as I can.'

'Very well. By the by, Bentley and Linscourt know who you are, but urge you not to let anyone else know your real name. It would cause resentment.'

'You needn't worry,' Venetia said. 'I have to keep the secret for my father's sake.'

As soon as matters were arranged, Fanny wrote to Charlotte. She was longing to see Emma again, and to breathe some country air before settling down for the new term. Surely now that Venetia had proved her seriousness, she might be readmitted to the family circle?

Charlotte took Fanny's letter to Oliver and argued the case as fervently as Fanny could have wished.

'You see she's over the first hurdle, and you can't deny she did it through persistence and strength of character. Won't you accept what she's doing now, and forgive her?'

It took a little work, but the duke was already feeling much better for having given up his War Office work, and relaxation and fresh air down at Ravendene were mellowing his temper. 'I don't want to deprive you of your daughter's company,' was all he would say at first; later he admitted, 'What she has done has taken courage, I'll say that for her.' Finally he reached, 'I wonder how the experience has changed her? I should like to see her again.'

So in the last week of September Fanny and Venetia took the train down to Northamptonshire, and there was reconciliation. Charlotte hugged them almost impartially, and then the rest of the family crowded in. Marcus was with his regiment, but William and Harry were there, wanting to know all about Venetia's adventures, and called her 'a trump', while Fairy was wild with excitement about the whole thing. With her father there was still a little reserve on his part, and awkwardness on hers; but she had never been on intimate terms with him, and was not disappointed with the advance she had made. He welcomed her gravely, kissed her forehead in blessing, and said, 'You have done what you set out to do: I congratulate you for that.'

'Thank you, Papa. But I've only just started. I hope to make you proud of me when I am a qualified doctor.'

'You mean to go on, then?'

'More than ever,' she said. He sighed and left it at that. She could see he still didn't like it, and was careful not to talk about it when he was in the room.

Olivia greeted her with hugs and kisses, but her mind was evidently on other things. The family had barely arrived at Ravendene when the news had broken that the Queen was seriously ill at Balmoral. The sore throat Olivia had been worried about had worsened rapidly. She was running a violent temperature and suffering from pains in the joints, and an affliction something like gout. Olivia had been so worried that it even moved the duke, who had never much interested himself in his second daughter, to set up a telegraph relay via various friends in official circles so that news from Balmoral would reach them as early as possible.

It was not good news. The Queen's condition worsened in the cold and damp of her Scottish home: chills, aches and shiverings added to her sufferings. It was said that Jenner, the Queen's physician, believed she was dying. When word came that an abscess seemed to be rising on her arm, everyone at Ravendene was inevitably reminded of Cavendish, and a sombre mood settled over the house. Olivia was distracted, and wanted to rush to Balmoral at once, even going so far as to look up the trains.

'But darling, you can't go unless you're summoned,' Charlotte pointed out. 'And there'd be nothing you could do if you did go.'

'Yes, I know,' Olivia said, and continued to suffer in silence.

Jenner summoned the surgeon Joseph Lister to lance the abscess in the hope that it would give the Queen relief, and with the unspoken acknowledgement that it could not now make her worse. Charlotte was interested to hear that it was Lister who had been chosen, knowing something of his experimental work in combating infections. The professor had developed an antiseptic spray which filled the operating room with a fine mist of carbolic acid, soaking the patient, the instruments and the wound, and his results had been remarkable.

'My dear old friend Dr Snow was sure that infections are caused by organisms in the air, but of course most medical men still disagree fiercely,' Charlotte said to Venetia during one of their long conversations. 'It could make a great deal of difference for it to be known that the Queen endorses his theories.'

'Do you really think so?' Venetia said doubtfully.

'Why, yes! It was the Queen who made anaesthesia acceptable by having it herself. She could do the same for antisepsis.'

The operation had gone well, and though there was no

miraculous recovery after it and the Queen remained ill and weak, she did improve a little. By the time Venetia and Fanny came to Ravendene, Jenner seemed to think she was out of immediate danger, and Olivia's worry was more chronic than acute.

Venetia was not inclined to waste her precious time at Ravendene being gloomy with her sister. She was glad to be in the country again, to enjoy the freedom of walking and riding over the familiar fields; to hear the sounds of nature outside her bedroom window at night, and to be in rooms where the walls were a significant distance apart. Sometimes, remembering the cramp and stink of Bury Street and the humiliations she had endured, she was close to thinking herself a fool for ever having started this business.

Beauty Winchmore was staying with friends nearby – how coincidentally, she couldn't tell – and came over every day. Venetia was happy to see him, and they rode out alone together in the park like old friends. It was clear her mother entirely approved of his presence, for she invariably invited him stay to dinner.

'Perhaps, since there are quite a few families down, we should give a ball before you go back to London,' she said casually one day. 'Nothing very great, just a dozen couples or so, all friends – what do you say? You haven't had any dancing for a long time, and young Winchmore does dance beautifully.'

'I know that look, Mama-duchess,' Venetia said. 'You're plotting – and it's no good, you know. I like Winchmore very much, but I can't get married. Marriage means babies, and how can a woman doctor have babies when her every moment must be taken up with trying to hold her position?'

'I only suggested a dance or two, that's all,' Charlotte protested, looking wounded.

'No, you didn't! But I'll dance with pleasure. You must make up your mind to the rest.'

So the ball was a settled thing; and the Westons came down for it, now that Tommy was forgiven. Venetia was relieved that her mother had her two closest friends restored to her again.

Fanny, accepting now that nothing was going to put Venetia off her chosen course, thought there was no need to go on punishing herself. She decided to give up the house in Bury Street and rent a larger and more comfortable one which she had heard of in Bedford Square.

'I'm glad,' Winchmore said to Venetia as they rode side by side across the park. 'I hated to think of you living in that place. It was hardly decent – not at all fitting for Lady Venetia Fleetwood.'

'How often must I remind you that I'm not Lady Venetia any more?' she said in exasperation.

'You can say it as often as you like, but that don't make it so. You're a duke's daughter, and however hard you run, you can't get away from that.'

'We'll see,' Venetia said, not wanting to argue with him. 'I'm glad we're not going back to Bury Street, so let's agree on that and leave the rest. Oh, how quickly this time has gone past! Now there's only the ball tonight, and tomorrow left.'

She glanced across at her frowning companion, and felt a pang at the familiar beauty of his profile against the pink sunset sky. What would it be like, she wondered, to be an ordinary girl, and fall in love and be married? It would be easy to fall in love with Winchmore – and sometimes, compared with her chosen path, the conventional fate beckoned like a soft bed. But could one lie in bed all one's life? Wasn't that why she had rebelled in the first place? She sighed.

'You will come and see us sometimes, when we're back in London, won't you?'

He turned to her, his face lighting. 'I was hoping you'd want me to. I should like nothing better. I'll be in Town again a week or so after you, and I'll call on you straight away, if I may.'

'We might receive you properly this time, and give you dinner,' she laughed.

He smiled at her tenderly. 'Will you dance with me tonight, lovely Venetia?'

'Of course – but don't get sentimental. You won't sway me from my course.'

'I won't try,' he promised. 'Not yet, anyway. I'll wait until

390

you're sick of it all, and then appear to you in the guise of St George.'

'You still don't understand, do you?'

'No – and I don't think you do either. A woman has a different nature from a man. You will find the work repugnant, distressing. Your delicacy will be outraged every minute.'

'And if I don't find it repugnant, you will find me so?' Venetia said. Her manner was joking, but she was serious underneath. Winchmore didn't answer, the thoughtful frown back between his brows, and she was sorry. She would be sad to lose him as a friend, and she was afraid that it might be inevitable.

One of the benefits of the new house was that there was room for Emma. She went back to Town with her mother and Venetia, looking forward to the new experience, though sorry to be parting from Augusta. 'But you can come back for Christmas,' Charlotte said, 'and London is a very exciting place.' Augusta was equally sorry to be parted from her friend and somewhat peeved at staying behind, but Charlotte did not think Fanny could cope with two girls; and besides, Oliver would never have consented to the ruination by association of another daughter.

He had, however, decided to pay Fanny for Venetia's keep, though he begged Fanny not to tell Venetia about it. 'I *don't* approve,' he said, 'and I don't want her to get the idea that I do. But it's not right for you to continue to foot the bill.'

Fanny was glad of the money, not so much for herself, for her needs were not great, but because she did not want to diminish Emma's eventual fortune. The mills were not bringing in as much as they used to, and Venetia had been a drain. Emma had no name and no family, and Fanny wanted to be sure that she would have a sufficient income to keep her decently, so that she should not be forced into marriage by the lack of alternatives.

Bedford Square was only a short walk from Mercer Street, and on the first day Venetia scorned Fanny's idea of taking a cab, though she would have to pass through some poor streets.

'I must begin as I mean to go on, and that's to be as like the other students as possible. Besides, how can I isolate myself from the poor when I'll be treating them every day?'

St Agatha's Hospital was an old building, formerly a merchant's house, of red brick with white copings, much stained with London soot. It had three storeys and a basement, and sat directly on the street with no forecourt, only a flight of shallow steps up to the main door. Behind, a jumble of additions and short wings had been tacked on over the years as its uses changed, and beyond its scrap of sooty garden loomed the back wall of Delafield's brewery.

Taking her courage by the scruff of the neck, Venetia marched up the steps the first day in a well-cut, plain gown of black silk, with her hair neatly but becomingly pinned. She did not want to attract the wrong sort of attention, but neither did she want to appear an ugly bluestocking, which she guessed would set up just as many backs. Her first problem was simply finding her way around the warren of passages, staircases and rooms off rooms off rooms. On the ground floor, as well as administrative quarters, there were lecture rooms, the outpatients' rooms and the dispensary. The wards were on the first floor and the operating rooms and laboratory on the second. In the basement were the dissecting room, various stores, the laundry and the kitchen.

She was received at first with a certain stiffness by the nursing staff, which melted gradually when they found she spoke sensibly, valued their help, and did not 'carry on' with any of the medical men. There was as yet no regular training scheme for nurses at St Agatha's, but many of the older nurses, coarsely spoken and uneducated as they were, had experience and knowledge enormously valuable to her.

Her fellow students received her with a mixture of shyness and intense interest. Some were stand-offish and disapproving, some were friendly and polite, and some, no doubt through awkwardness, swung too far the other way and were over-familiar. It was here that she found her upbringing helpful: the daughter of a duke was exposed from an early age to all sorts of social situations, and learned how to deal gracefully with people. She was accustomed to being flirted with by young men, but that was something that must not happen here; yet she wanted to have a cordial relationship with them, not to keep them at a distance with haughtiness. She learned quickly how to check boisterousness with a raised eyebrow before it went too far; but also to accept without reaction things which in normal circumstances would never have been said in her presence.

That she was successful was proved when, after a couple of weeks, one of the students, Tucker, said, 'I must say, you ain't a bit like what we expected. When Old Bill told us you were coming, we were all agog.' Old Bill was what they called the dean.

'Yes, and we thought you must be a gorgon,' his friend Anderby agreed.

'Henderson said you'd be as ugly as a horse's arse, with shapeless clothes and a hat like a coal bucket.'

'I must remember to thank Henderson,' Venetia said.

'Henderson's an ass,' said Quinton shortly. 'Can't forget his guv'nor's one of the Benefactors. Filthy rich, the Hendersons – brewing and animal feed, you know.'

'Never mind Henderson,' Tucker said. 'We all think you're very jolly. And 'strordin'ry brave to throw in with rough chaps like us.'

'Rough? You must think I'm made of paper,' Venetia said. 'I have two brothers: I'm quite used to slang and knockabout.'

It was not all sweetness. Venetia heard some ill-humoured comments behind her back, and several along the lines that 'a man wouldn't want his sister doing such things'. A group that centred on Henderson complained in advance of any evidence that the teaching would be toned down to accommodate a female and that they would receive inferior training because of her. But on the whole the students thought it was all rather a lark, and went along with it, at least partly in the hope of seeing the great men of the medical staff discomfited. They were a high-spirited crowd, and lived for those pleasing little diversions that lifted the tedium of the working day, like letting loose a monkey in the laboratory, or concealing a rotten fish in the lecture room. They spent their evenings in

393

pubs and music halls, augmented their incomes by poaching in the country around London and selling the result to their landladies, and amused themselves with gambling on horse races, and the all-night poker game set up by the night porter on the midwifery ward.

But Venetia's interest in her fellow students was perfunctory. She had more important things to think about, and every day was crammed with stimulation, interest and sheer hard work. She was glad now that she had had those months of study with Mark Darroway, for it had at least broken her gently to the effort of continuous application. But after a few weeks of falling exhausted into bed the moment she had finished supper, she got her second wind. 'I've never felt so alive,' she said to Fanny and Emma.

It was a long day for her. Aware that she was under a disadvantage compared with even the least favoured of the male students, she knew she must do more than them just to stay abreast. So she rose at six every morning and put in an hour's preparatory study before setting off for the hospital. She arrived at eight so that she could attend the dressing round in the surgical ward. The ward sister was a friendly woman, and very knowledgeable, and was willing to help Venetia by explaining much that was too basic for the medical staff to tell her. Treatments and terminology they took for granted she had to learn; and there was always something new to observe.

From nine until ten there was a lecture, which many of the students missed, either because they had woken with a thick head after too much indulgence in porter and pigs' trotters at the Canterbury the night before, or because they had bets to place or racing papers to read. After that there were the Resident Officers' rounds, the medical from ten to eleven, and the surgical from eleven to twelve. Both Mr Vandyke, the surgeon, and Dr Welby, the physician, were courteous and helpful to her. Venetia liked Dr Welby better, because he spoke without reserve and used the proper medical terms for everything just as if she were a man. Mr Vandyke, who was older and more formal in his manners, sometimes made her uncomfortable simply because, feeling there were things a gentleman could not decently say to a lady, he sought for euphemisms and oblique ways of referring to conditions and bodily parts. But he was impressed with how much she knew, and praised her quickness of mind and her 'lady's hand', which he said was ideal for surgery – small, strong and dextrous.

Between twelve and one, when the other students were eating, reading or generally amusing themselves, Venetia arranged privately with Mr Frapham, the apothecary, for her to attend the dispensary, where he instructed her on materia medica as he went about his duties.

Between one and three the consultants visited the wards, and from three until five there were more lectures. First year lectures were in physiology, botany, chemistry and materia medica. The chemistry lecturer, Professor McBane, was a dry and elderly Scot who liked Venetia, appreciating her ready grasp of the purely intellectual side of his subject, which bored most students. Her early studies in mathematics and philosophy paid off now, and McBane made rather a pet of her, often addressing himself to her when he went further into a piece of business than the syllabus demanded, and keeping her back afterwards to show her extra experiments, or new work he was doing.

She already had the good will of Mr Frapham, who lectured on materia medica; Mr Howden, who lectured on botany, hardly noticed whether he had any students or not. He was an eccentric man who spoke in a monotonous mumble, never looking up from his notes, and paying no attention to anything that might be going on in the room. Venetia didn't feel she got much from his lectures, especially as the only students who didn't cut them seemed to attend purely for the purpose of seeing how far they could go with the old fellow. He was remarkably impervious: the only time he abandoned his place was when they threw 'stink-bombs' at him.

It was fortunate for her that the physiology lectures were given by the dean, Mr Bentley, who was very much on her side, for it was in this area that prudery was most expected. An article in a journal discussing why it would be impossible for any woman to become a medical student had emphasised that 'knowledge of this class' would cause 'extreme repugnance, amounting to disgust' to a girl, and that no decent man could ever bring himself to speak openly about such things in mixed company.

Before the first lecture, Venetia sought out the dean and begged him not to make any omission or alteration in his usual lecture on her account. 'I must and will learn everything, and I don't want to be the cause of any lowering of standards.'

Bentley said, 'I am at one with you on that score, Miss Fleet. Besides, I've always thought it a piece of amazing hypocrisy to balk at teaching women physiology when we make nothing of instructing female nurses on the wards in the same language.'

Venetia smiled. 'And after all, how can anything God made be indecent? The human body is a miraculous thing.'

'We agree then,' Bentley said pleasantly. 'But you will oblige me by sitting in the middle of the front row, so that the other students won't be continually looking back to see if you are blushing.'

In the evenings Venetia studied, with the help of Mark Darroway.

'I thought you wouldn't need me any more, when Weston told me you'd got into St Agatha's,' he said gladly the first time he called at Bedford Square.

'On the contrary, I need you more than ever,' Venetia said. 'I'm on my mettle now. I have to be better than everyone else, just to be as good.'

Mark said, 'But if you'll take a bit of advice from a humble fellow student – don't be too good. If you show the men up too much, they'll turn against you.'

'I get on very well with the other students,' Venetia said.

'I dare say. But there's naturally talk about you, and the St Agatha's men are already being taunted by the meds from other schools. They take it in good part because most of them think you won't stick it and it's all a bit of fun, but they won't relish having their noses put out of joint.'

'Do you think I'm going to pretend to be stupid, or deliberately fail just to salve their pride?' Venetia said impatiently.

Mark only shrugged in his mild way. 'You must decide for

yourself. But they won't like being made to look nohow by a girl. I only say don't make too much of a show.'

By the end of November Venetia had settled in and was finding her feet, and was no longer so exhausted at the end of the day. But she was at the hospital six days a week and studied every evening, and had no time for the new season of plays and concerts. Tommy was a frequent visitor at Bedford Square, and with Venetia always preoccupied, found Emma a willing substitute. He took her to the theatre, and to exhibitions and other respectable events. Emma was pleased and grateful, and the two struck up quite a friendship. Both had come from the humblest origins, and it made a bond between them. Fanny watched with amusement and pleasure, and also with something of a pang, for Tommy was just the sort of man she would like for a husband for Emma, and she could see that Emma had a slight crush on him; but Tommy treated Emma like a little sister. His heart was still hopelessly Venetia's.

Beauty Winchmore did not come back to Town as promised, for his father, Lord Hazelmere, had died at the age of sixty-two. He had left the Blues, and was now much involved in estate business. 'I suppose we'll have to stop calling him Beauty,' Venetia said. She was disappointed that he had not come to redeem his promise of amusing her; busy as she was, she would have found time for him.

Now that she was readmitted to the family, there were letters to enjoy. Olivia's next waiting began in the second half of November, and she wrote from Windsor, where the Queen had just returned from Balmoral.

'I'm so terribly shocked at the sight of Her Majesty. Seeing her for the first time it's plain how ill she has been. She must have lost two stones in weight! I wish those hateful people who criticise her could see, and then they'd be sorry. I'm thinking of that wicked Sir Charles Dilke and his speeches, and Mr Chamberlain. I can't understand how anyone can listen to them.'

For the past eighteen months, republicanism had been smouldering like a heath fire, breaking out here and there in little spurts of flame, in speeches, rallies, newspaper articles and questions in the House. During the Queen's illness, the republicans had kept quiet, for the nation's sympathy was obviously engaged by the royal suffering; but now she had recovered, Sir Charles Dilke, the radical MP for Chelsea, had made a ferocious speech in Newcastle, attacking the cost of the Civil List and asking what return the taxpayer got for his money.

'The Queen is particularly hurt by his attacks,' Olivia wrote, 'because she has known him since his childhood – his father helped the Prince set up the Great Exhibition. She remembers once stroking his hair – Sir C.D.'s, I mean – and says she supposes she must have stroked it the wrong way. It is so *like* her to jest about what hurts her most!'

When Venetia wrote back, she had a political encounter of her own to report. 'A card was left while I was at the hospital by a Mrs Fauncett, with a message that she would call back the next evening. I had no idea who she was, but Aunt Fanny recalled that Papa's Uncle Alfred married a Miss Fauncett, so we presumed her a relative. She arrived looking not a bit like her name, but young, not much more than twenty-five, and *very* smart in pale lavender, her hat a profusion of ribbons, the apogee of à-la-modality. Revealed that the Miss Fauncett Aunt Fanny mentioned was her husband's grandfather's sister. Claims therefore cousinhood of a sort – quite enough for her purposes, which were to inveigle me into going with her to a political meeting.

'I must have been a disappointment to her – politics make me yawn – but Tommy was there and gave her quite enough encouragement. Her particular hobby-horse is the Women's Suffrage Committee, which I thought must have quietly died when it failed to get women householders the vote in '67 (a modest enough ambition one would have thought, there being only ten such in the country!) But no, they exist, and hearing of the bold Miss Fleet who has joined the medical students at St Agatha's she came to get me to add my weight to the rope.

'I told her I hadn't the least interest in the vote, having quite enough on my plate as it was, and she harangued me (though in a very musical voice) about my duty to my less fortunate sisters. And then Tommy joined in the general censure and not only told *me* I ought to join the movement, but told *her* she ought to be pressing for the vote for *all* women, not just householders – the biter bit! She left at last with his promise to come to a meeting, and mine to think about it – which I shall when all other matter for thought is used up!

'A shocking waste of an evening, and I am now behind with my studies as the next day the new Lord Hazelmere returned to Town (in *great* beauty, I may add) and insisted on taking me to the Royal Opera House. Lady Petersfield chaperoned, and Patti and Mario sang "Romeo and Juliet", but Baby Sutton and Sammy Cleveley were in the box too and fell on me like drowning men, full of questions I dared not answer. They chattered so incessantly about my absence from Society and Freshwater's engagement to Cordelia Stratford that I hardly heard a note of the opera. There was just as much noise from the boxes on either side, too – like starlings in a roost. A true music lover like you would have died of rage!

'I must mention that Lord Marwood was in the pit and kept staring up at me as though he'd never seen a woman before. Hazelmere was most diverting, muttering about "impertinence" and damning his eyes. As soon as the interval came he snatched me away to walk in the loggia, I'm sure as much to avoid Marwood as to make love to me. But Marwood came and found us and flirted quite appallingly with me, which made poor Beauty mad. All in all I enjoyed this little taste of the high life, but the next day I was back at the hospital and suddenly it all seemed a distant and not very interesting dream.'

It had been raining all day, and the short December afternoon was closing in, dark and dirty; the streets were full of wet horses and clashing umbrellas, the hiss of wheels and the gurgle of gutters. Venetia had forgotten her umbrella, and rain was dripping off her hat brim onto her nose and down her neck. As the lamps were lit in succession along the street, it seemed instantly colder and darker outside their circle.

She found Emma on her knees in front of the drawing-room fire. Emma turned a rosy face to her. 'Hello! You're early! I'm just making toast, and you shall have some.'

'Thanks, I'm starved. I haven't eaten all day.'

Fanny said in concern, 'Venetia, your skirt! Wet to the knees! And your collar's damp.'

'I left my umbrella at the hospital.'

'Why didn't you take a cab?' Emma said, easing a piece of toast off the fork with flinching fingers.

Venetia gave a short smile. 'It's plain you've never tried hailing one in the rain.' She went to the fire and spread her skirt to the blaze.

'Hadn't you better go and change into some dry clothes?' Fanny asked. 'You don't want to catch a chill.'

'Toast first – bless you, Emma! Is there any tea?'

'It's coming up,' Fanny said. 'Are you all right? You seem rather down-hearted.'

'Oh, I've made the most awful fool of myself, and probably given myself a black that will never be expunged,' Venetia said lightly, flopping into a chair; but despite her joking tone, Fanny could see that her face was tired and anxious.

'What happened? Can you tell us?'

Emma held out a plate. 'You shall have the first two slices,' she said. 'I've buttered it, but you can have jam too.'

A single tear escaped Venetia's eye, before she took in a shaky breath. 'Don't be kind to me, Em, or I shall howl.' She took a bite of toast, chewed and swallowed. 'But I was right, I know I was – and Mama would have agreed with me. I bet she would have said what I said.'

'Oh dear,' Fanny said. 'Have you upset someone?'

'Not someone, Aunt Fanny – just the greatest of the great, Sir Davies Grenfell himself! He was operating this afternoon, and we were all sent in to watch.'

Emma knelt up straight and stared. 'Oh Venetia, you didn't watch an operation! Was it awfully grue?'

'Grue?' she asked vaguely. 'Oh – no, not really. It was too interesting to be horrible. I must admit I was nervous at first when we all filed into the theatre, wondering how it would affect me, but when some of the fellows edged me down to the front so that I'd be able to see, I knew I wouldn't dare faint or they'd all see me. The first few moments were bad – my heart was beating very fast and I felt a bit light-headed

400

– but after that there was too much to take in even to think about fainting.'

She stopped, remembering. The theatre was on the top floor, of course, under a glass roof to give the best possible light; the operating floor was sunk like a bear pit within a semicircle of raised stands, stepped upwards, each with a rail along it for the students to lean on. The operating table was in the middle of the floor under the roof-light, its surface scarred and stained rust-coloured, with sawdust scattered thickly round it like a butcher's block. Venetia recalled the smell of the sawdust, sharp and pleasant, and the hint of charcoal from the brazier, over to one side, in which the searing-irons were kept hot. But neither smell quite obliterated the flat metallic smell of blood. There were dried splashes of it up the panelling of the pit, and old dark stains in the wooden floorboards.

She had thought for a moment with scalding pity what it must be to be a patient waiting for the knife, and to see this place; and then the fascination of the business had driven the patient as a person from her head. Grenfell, a tall, heavy man with bushy hair and piercing eyes, was reputed to be enormously skilled. He certainly had great presence, and exuded confidence, working with swift, sure movements. The operation, for the excision of a tumour, was carried out under anaesthesia, and Grenfell had time to point out various features of his work and the pathology. 'You see, here, gentlemen . . .' he said; and, 'What you must remember, gentlemen . . .' He made no mention of Venetia nor looked in her direction, for which, on the whole, she was grateful.

He had entered the arena wearing a coat so soaked with blood and matter that it was impossible to tell what colour it had originally been: as Tucker whispered to her, it was stiff enough to have stood up on its own. As Venetia knew, all the medical staff had an old frock that they wore in the dissecting rooms, and the surgeons wore the same one for operating. All through the operation, Grenfell wiped his hands down the front of the filthy coat before returning them to the abdominal cavity, and used the tails to wipe his instruments.

His dresser, standing by, had a coat which was well on its

way to emulating that of his master, and he was wearing the first two suture needles, already threaded, stuck into his lapel, the long ends of silk trailing to the floor. When more were required, he sucked the end of the silk to make it easier to thread. And when Sir Davies complained that a knife was not sharp enough, the obliging dresser took it from him and stropped it briskly against the sole of his shoe.

It was only now, seeing these things for herself, that Venetia realised fully what before she had only read about. Post-operative infections carried off the majority of surgical patients, and the general opinion was that infection was generated from within the patient in some way, or was simply an inscrutable act of God. But was not this, as Professor Lister postulated, the likely source of infection? Had Grenfell not read of Lister's experiments? Ought not someone to point out to him what he was doing?

When the operation was finished, Grenfell, evidently pleased with himself, genially invited questions. Plenty were forthcoming, and the great man played up to the students like an actor on a stage, eliciting laughter and admiring gasps. Everyone thought Grenfell a wonderful fellow, and Tucker whispered to Venetia that they were 'deuced lucky to get him'. Friedman, he said, was a regular stick, dry as dust, and never joked with the students. Venetia listened in silence; but the thing on her mind wouldn't go away, and at last, when the flow of questions slackened, she found she had put up her hand almost without volition.

Grenfell turned to her at last, raised his eyebrows as if in surprise, though he must have known who she was. 'I see we have an interloper in our midst, gentlemen!' he said. There was laughter – good-natured, but alert. Eyes turned to her, bright with anticipation of some entertainment. 'I must congratulate you, madam, on witnessing the operation without swooning – or at least, I *suppose* I must congratulate you. There is a school of thought which says it would have been preferable for you to have swooned, but we will have none of it here – eh, gentlemen?' More laughter. 'Well, well, our hard-headed visitor has a question, I believe? Something, let us hope, about flowers or poetry?'

Venetia lifted her voice above the sniggering. 'What proportion of your patients survive this operation?'

'A home question!' Grenfell said, smiling round at the other students. 'More than one in three. Almost forty per cent, in fact, Miss – er—' The dresser whispered. 'Miss Fleet. Ten years ago the survival rate was negligible.'

Venetia was trembling all over with her own daring, but forced herself to go on. She was glad to find her voice was quite steady. 'Sir, are you aware of the work of Professor Lister in Glasgow? He has cut his mortality rates fifty per cent by use of antiseptic routines.'

A deathly hush fell. The students had been quiet before, but now their silence was breathless. Grenfell's eyes narrowed and his nostrils flared, but when he spoke again, his tone was bantering.

'Gentlemen, if my ears don't deceive me, our interloper has just asked me why I don't *wash my hands*.' The students laughed at the absurdity of it, and there was an edge to the laughter, the excitement of the crowd at a public execution.

'Cleanliness, and the use of carbolic acid—' Venetia began, but her voice shook now, and slid into a squeak.

Grenfell was on her like a soft, deadly cat on a very small mouse. 'You seem to be widely read, Miss Fleet: it is a pity you have not read to better advantage. It is a pity, indeed, that you have not confined yourself to the sphere God designed you for, rather than intrude yourself into a world for which you are not fitted by nature or intellect – if one can apply such a word to the female of the species.' His sharp look round the theatre hooked appreciative laughter. 'Since, however, you have so far abandoned modesty as to thrust yourself into our midst, let me remind you that I have been a practising surgeon for twenty years. When you can say the same, it may be appropriate for you to voice your opinions, and perhaps then they may be taken seriously – though I would recommend you not to advise your eminent colleagues to soak themselves in a substance more usually employed to drown the smell in sewage works!'

The last words produced a gale of laughter. Venetia had to hold the rail to stop her knees giving way, and though she longed to show she was not cowed, she could not find even a thread of voice to answer him with.

Grenfell eyed her with relish and continued. 'This, you see, is the real difficulty of admitting ladies to our world, gentlemen. We shall all have to mind our p's and q's from now on. Hand-washing is only the beginning. Soon there will be books on medical etiquette. The correct form of address to a patient one is about to cut. Whether one should keep one's hat on during amputations. How many cards to leave during a Caesarean section!'

Each sally was greeted with roars of appreciation, while Venetia stood as though bound to the stake, concentrating on not crying. When at last he had had enough, Grenfell said, 'That is all for today, gentlemen,' bowed and left, rubbing his hands and talking in a low voice to the dresser who bobbed along at his side like a sycophantic tug.

'Oh poor Venetia!' Emma cried when the tale was told. 'No wonder you look so glum. What a hateful monster!'

Fanny chose her words carefully. 'You knew that it would be difficult before you began, Venetia dear. But I'm sorry he should have amused himself at your expense.'

She looked up with her eyes full of hot tears. 'I was right, I know I was! Why won't they even look at Lister's results?'

Fanny said, 'Gentlemen don't like to be told things by ladies – and I'm sure surgeons don't like being told things by students.'

'That's what the dean said afterwards. I was sent for out of class – everyone looked at me as I walked out. They all knew I was being carpeted. It was so humiliating. Old Bill was pretty nice about it, really—'

'Old Bill?'

'The dean, I mean. Mr Bentley. But he told me there isn't a surgeon in London who would have taken such impertinence from me – *impertinence*! – and that Lister is a crank and no-one takes him seriously – he has the whole operating room filled with his spray and the surgeons have to work soaking wet. He says our great men would be laughing-stocks if they accepted that sort of nonsense. He said I was pretty lucky Grenfell had reacted as he did.'

'He'd complained to the dean?' Fanny put in.

'First thing,' Venetia admitted glumly.

She stopped, thinking of those hot, embarrassed minutes of her interview with the dean. 'You are here on sufferance, Miss Fleet, and if you alienate too many of the staff – or indeed the pupils – you will be asked to leave. I don't ask you to be mute: it's important that you speak up when questions are asked in class or on teaching rounds. You can learn more by answering a question wrongly than by listening to someone else give the right answer. But you are not here to promote your theories in competition with those of the medical staff. For heaven's sake, use your common sense! And have a little discretion.'

'So what did the dean say?' Fanny asked.

'He told me to guard my tongue in future.'

'Is that all? He didn't dismiss you?'

'Well, that's not so bad, is it?' Emma said.

'It was the way it was said,' Venetia explained. 'And if I'd been a male student, Grenfell wouldn't have dreamed of complaining to the dean. He'd have forgotten about it the moment he left the theatre.'

'But you're not a male student,' Fanny said bracingly, 'and there's no sense in wailing about what can't be changed. You must cope with things the way they are.'

'Yes, I know. You're right,' Venetia said, straightening her shoulders.

'Have some more toast,' Emma said sympathetically. 'As you're home so early, what do you say to going to the Women's Suffrage meeting? Tommy was here earlier to say he's going.'

'Do you want to?' Venetia asked in surprise. 'The last thing I want is to have my nose rubbed in the "woman question" all over again.'

'Mama, can't we go?'

'If you really want to, love. You don't mind, Venetia?'

'No, I'm going to curl up on the sofa with a book, and in all probability fall asleep before I've turned two pages.'

'How dull!' Emma cried. 'I hope I'm never that old!'

At the end of November the Prince of Wales had fallen ill

with typhoid, and the Queen hurried to Sandringham to be with him. In December Olivia, still in waiting, wrote that his life was despaired of.

'The Queen sits with him all the time. She will hardly let anyone help. Miss Allerdyce says that it must remind her of the Prince Consort's last illness, which was typhoid too. The most awful thing is that the Prince Consort died on the 14th of December, and now the Queen has a terrible dread that since the PoW has the same sickness, he will die on the same day. She has quite convinced herself, and it's dreadful to see how she suffers.'

On the 13th of December, the Prince of Wales was so ill that the doctors thought the Queen's premonition would prove true. The papers were full of it, and a mood of sombreness was over the country. But on the morning of the 14th, it was reported that the crisis had passed, the fever had broken, and the Prince of Wales was sleeping quietly.

By the time Olivia came home for Christmas, it was clear that he was recovering, and the nation had broken out into a frenzy of monarchist loyalty. The newspapers proclaimed thanksgiving for the double delivery of the Queen and the Prince of Wales in a few short months. Sir Charles Dilke was shouted down in the Commons when he stood up to pursue his republican agenda, and at meetings up and down the country, republican speakers were drowned out by bands playing 'Rule Britannia' and crowds singing 'God Save the Queen', and many were forced to flee for their safety.

'Well,' said Oliver to Charlotte, 'that's done for the republicans this time round. We won't hear any more from them.'

Olivia said, 'I wish I could live at Court all the time. I hate being away.'

And Charlotte said, 'Venetia and Fanny and Emma will be down next week, and everything will be perfect for Christmas. I can't wait to hear how she's been getting on. Henry, what is there for her to ride? She'll want to hunt while she's here.'

Despite what Mrs Harris urged, Henrietta did not immediately tell Mr Fortescue. For one thing, she still wasn't sure that was what ailed her; and for another, she was too shy to bring the subject up. The only times she saw him were at dinner, when they were never alone, or when he came to her at night, when speech was forbidden. As to seeking him out to broach a subject of such delicacy – if it was impossible in imagination, how much more so in reality?

Two weeks passed, the flux was due and did not come. She wished there were some authority she could consult, but Dr Mansur was a close friend of the rector's, and that would be as bad as asking the rector. To consult another doctor would be to insult Mansur; the only close friend she had was Miss Compton, and it was impossible to ask her about something only a married woman should know.

One day after breakfast Mrs Prosser was 'consulting' her on the day's menu as usual. Henrietta was feeling more than usually green, and held up her hand half-way through. 'Please, settle it how you like. You know better than me, anyway, what the master likes.'

Mrs Prosser was arrested by the unexpectedly tetchy tone. She looked at Henrietta's averted profile for a moment, and then said, 'Beg pardon, madam, but are you quite well?' Henrietta looked at her sharply. 'You haven't eaten enough to make a hen fat these last few mornings, when you're usually so fond of your breakfast.'

'Oh, don't talk about food!' Henrietta begged, and then met the housekeeper's eyes and blushed vividly. 'I think I'm

407

– that is, I don't know for sure, but – there may be a little one on the way.'

Mrs Prosser began to smile. 'So that's it, is it? Well, I never did!' She clasped her hands over her stomach, beaming. 'To think of it! There hasn't been a baby in the rectory nursery since the master himself. It was just what we were hoping for, Andrews and me, ever since the master brought you home. Eh, a baby in the house! I wish you great joy, madam, with all my heart.'

Blinking in this sudden unbending and warmth, Henrietta said, 'Thank you. I'm very pleased, of course but – well, it doesn't feel very joyful at the moment.'

'The sickness? Oh, that will pass, don't you worry, and then you'll feel as well as Bell Hill!'

'Did you feel like this?' Henrietta asked shyly.

'Bless you, I was never married! Housekeepers are always called "Mrs", didn't you know that? Same as cooks. No, I was never wed, nor yet was Andrews, and I must say we'd quite given up all thought of it for the master when, all of a sudden, there you were.' She looked awkward suddenly, and her eyes shifted away from Henrietta. 'We may have been a bit stiff with you at first, Mrs Fortescue, and if we were, I take leave to beg your pardon, from both of us. We were afraid—'

'Yes, I know,' Henrietta said quickly, to save the housekeeper's pride. 'You thought everything would change. I expect I'd have felt the same.'

'Oh no, madam! But we're glad to call you mistress now, indeed we are,' Prosser said warmly. 'And is the master pleased? I wonder he hasn't said anything to Andrews.'

'He doesn't know.' Henrietta met Prosser's amazed look. 'I didn't know quite how to tell him.'

'No, of course not,' Mrs Prosser said. As shy and innocent as a new lamb, she heard herself telling Andrews. If you'll believe me, John, the poor little thing didn't know how to give her own husband the news.

'Do you really think he'll be pleased?'

Mrs Prosser made an unfinished gesture, as though she would take Henrietta's hands. 'Indeed he will! You mid tell him this evening, madam, after dinner. When he takes his tea with you in the drawing-room: you'll be nice and private, and have all the time in the world.'

'But perhaps he won't take his tea with me,' Henrietta said. He hardly ever did.

Mrs Prosser almost winked. 'Leave me alone for that. Andrews and me'll make sure of it.' She turned to go, and then turned back. 'Oh, and madam, you ought not to go riding any more, not a-horseback. Let me send word to Bond not to bring up the horse.'

How they managed it, Henrietta couldn't guess, but true enough, Mr Fortescue arrived in the drawing-room a few paces in front of the tea tray, and took his seat at the opposite side of the fire. While Andrews poured and handed, Henrietta stared at the flames and tried to assemble her thoughts, and Fortescue picked up the paper from the table and leafed through it without interest. When Andrews had gone, he put it down again, cleared his throat, sipped his tea, and said, 'Well, my dear, I hope you don't object to my company.'

'Oh, no sir! I'm glad of it.'

He studied her a moment. 'You were very quiet during dinner. Not that you aren't always so, but more quiet than usual. Is something the matter? Are you worried about anything?'

Henrietta sought for the right words to tell him, but there seemed none that could be addressed to such a man. If only he would understand without her having to say the words.

'I sent word to Bond not to bring Starlight up this morning,' she said. 'I think I ought not to ride any more. Not for a while.'

There was a long silence. The tips of Henrietta's ears burned, her heart pattered along like a pony trying to keep up with a horse. At last she could bear it no longer, and looked up at her husband. His face was expressionless, and he seemed to be having as much difficulty in finding words as she. But when he spoke, it was with a scholar's precision.

'Are you with child?'

'I think so,' she whispered.

'You *think* so?' he said sharply, as though rebuking a student for imprecise thought.

Henrietta's eyes filled with tears. 'I've never done it before,' she said apologetically.

'No. Of course not.' He stood up abruptly and walked up and down the room. 'You must see a physician, of course.'

'Dr Mansur?' she asked in a small, appalled voice. 'Must I?'

He turned back to look at her. She was so young, so small, dwarfed by the high back of the fireside chair. All his original passion for her flooded him on the instant, burning through the layers and layers of thought and reason and self-analysis that had crusted over every unfettered impulse year after year. She was with child! His seed was now cradled within her white body. His seed – his child! He wanted to snatch her up and crush her to him; he wanted to take hold of her and carry her away, far from the world, to some place of pure feeling where nothing would ever come between them. He felt, for that one burning instant, all-powerful, young as flame.

He crossed the room in two swift paces and flung himself at her feet, catching her hands from her lap and pressing them to his lips, his cheek, his lips again.

'You're pleased?' she said hesitantly.

'Pleased?' He released her hand and drew her against him, resting his head against her breast, and she dared, trembling, to touch his hair, and then stroke it. She felt hollow and shaken with the wonder of it, that he should love her so, that he should be brought thus supplicant to her feet, and she the giver, the possessor of riches. She almost wished they could both die then and there, so that the moment need never end.

The clock struck, and its silver sound burst the delicate bubble that held them. Self-consciousness woke abruptly and reminded Mr Fortescue with its customary sneer that he was kneeling on the floor in an absurd embrace with his own wife. He released himself awkwardly and stood up, walking away from her to brush down his clothes and straighten his hair.

'Ha-hm!' He cleared his throat sternly and turned again, avoiding her eyes. 'Mansur must be consulted,' he decreed. 'There's no need to colour up. He is a physician, after all. You may have your maid with you while he examines you – or perhaps you would prefer Mrs Prosser.' She looked so downcast that he felt a pang. 'Come, my dear, Mansur is not an ogre. There's no need to fear him.'

'No sir,' she said, but without conviction.

'And you are quite right, you must give up riding entirely.'

'But how shall I do my parish work?'

'There is no need for you to continue with that in the circumstances,' he said. 'In fact, you must avoid places of likely infection. No risk must be taken with the child, or with your health.'

'Then – what shall I do all day?'

He frowned. 'How can you want occupation or amusement? If bringing a child into the world is not enough for you, there is a library full of books in the house.'

She bowed her head. He was right, of course – he must be right, since he was who he was.

In April 1872 Alfreda celebrated her full recovery from childbirth by visiting the attics of her house for the first time. Mrs Holicar accompanied her, resigned to some further upheaval. Changes were a nuisance and always involved extra work and amazing amounts of dirt, but to Holicar's mind the changes so far had all been in the right direction, enhancing the importance of the house and thus her own status as housekeeper. The number of servants under her had increased enormously, as labour was divided into ever more discrete tasks. In the old master's day, for instance, the footmen had filled the lamps and trimmed the candles; now there was a lamp man whose sole business it was. The housemaids did not carry up water any more: there was a water man, a tall and burly youth whose slow wits were no impediment – in fact, were even an advantage, since trudging upstairs with cans of water suspended from a yoke, and trudging downstairs with chamber pots to empty and wash was hardly exciting work. The nursery had its own footman and laundress, as well as Bittle, and under-nurse and a maid, despite there being only one occupant.

Of course, all these servants had to sleep somewhere, and that somewhere was in the attics. That alone wouldn't have been enough to engage Alfreda's interest, but a housemaid having got herself pregnant, the mistress wanted to know how it could have happened.

Stepping off the bare wooden backstairs, Alfreda found herself in a strange and shadowy place, a warren of passages and little rooms which had been created by erecting partitions in the roof space between the upright supports and the beams. In the centre of the space, where the roof was fifteen feet above, these partitions did not go all the way up, providing privacy only if no-one made the effort to look over them. These rooms were of varying sizes, from singles and doubles up to dormitories of six or more beds; some led off each other without access to a passage; none had fireplaces or windows. All light under the roof was provided by candle, and the fire risks were so great and obvious that there were buckets of water standing about at strategic places, against which the unwary Alfreda stubbed her toes more than once.

Round the edges of the roof space, under the slopes, partition walls reached full height, but the extra privacy was counterbalanced by a loss of head-room. The senior servants preferred these rooms, and some of them had their own small fireplaces, with flues made of iron sections tacking erratically round the rafters until they could tap into one of the main chimneys.

Alfreda inspected Mrs Holicar's room – a bare little space of iron bed, wooden chair, wash-stand and chest of drawers – with indifferent eyes, but the sleeping arrangements of the generality of the servants horrified her as she walked from room to room. Bare and inhospitable, they were chilly with the brisk April wind that was finding its way in through every crack and fissure: roof spaces were deliberately kept draughty, to prevent damp and rot.

'This is far from satisfactory,' she said at last. 'In fact, I will say without hesitation it will not do at all! Changes must be made at once.'

'Yes, madam?' Mrs Holicar said. She had not expected such tender concern from this mistress.

Alfreda turned to her, skull-like in the light from the candle she held. 'Male and female servants all in the same place, with free access to each other! Rooms leading off rooms! Single bedrooms for junior servants! No wonder the unpleasant incident occurred. It's a wonder to me it does not happen more often. Arrangements like these are a clear incitement to immorality!'

'Yes, madam,' Holicar sighed.

'There must be complete separation of male from female servants. We must have a partition – the full height of the roof – right across the whole building, with the men one side and the girls the other. And there must be a separate entrance to each, to avoid any possibility of contact.' She looked around. 'I suggest the girls have this side, and use the backstairs. The men can have the other side, and we will have the nursery stair extended up into the attic to make an access for them. You and Goole will be in charge of behaviour up here, and you must see that strict discipline is maintained at all times.'

'Yes, madam.'

'Lights out at a regular time, and no talking or laughing after that. And there must be no single rooms for junior servants,' she added, outraged at the thought. 'The youngest girls must be four to a room at the minimum, and you must make sure that there is a steady girl in each room, and that the flighty ones are kept separate.'

'Very good, madam,' said Holicar. She approved whole-heartedly of the morality of the arrangements, but she had hoped there might be some improvement to comfort at the same time. It was bitterly cold up here in winter, and lying in bed staring up at the rafters and the bare underside of the roof tiles was depressing.

'I shall speak to the master about it straight away,' Alfreda concluded. 'I look to you, Mrs Holicar, to ensure there is no improper behaviour during the transition period. Such an upheaval can present opportunities to the light-minded.'

She went downstairs, glad to get back to the light and comfort of the rest of the house, and hurried to the drawing-room to warm her chilled fingers. As the blood returned to her extremities, her thoughts began to flow, and taking up her writing-case, she sat by the fire and began to sketch out her ideas. She was deeply occupied when Goole came in and announced, with the hint of disapproval of a man who didn't like surprises, 'Lord Marwood is here, madam.'

She put her writing aside and stood up as Marwood brushed past the butler and came to catch her hands and kiss her. She freed her hands and turned her face away from his lips, but waited until Goole had closed the door to say coldly, 'What are you doing here? I was not expecting you.'

'That's not very welcoming to your only brother,' he said in hurt tones.

'My only brother! So you do remember that? I only wondered, since you haven't been near me for nearly a year – despite the fact that I almost died in childbirth.'

'Now, Alfie—'

'*Don't* call me Alfie! And don't think you can wheedle me, either! You haven't even *seen* your nephew, and he's six months old!'

'Is he indeed? Doesn't time fly? But I don't see much point in visiting babies. They don't appreciate it.'

'*I* would have appreciated it,' Alfreda said bitterly.

He gave her his most winning smile, head slightly on one side. 'I know. I've been a rogue and a "will'n", as our old groom used to call me, but it ain't because I don't care for you, Kitten. I've been busy and you've been increasing and – frankly – I couldn't have borne to see you all pale and suffering. That's why I waited until you were well again.'

'You lie,' she said, but without heat. He was so handsome; she had to forgive him. 'What have you been busy about?'

'Oh, regimental duties, you know; and trying to recoup my fortune,' he said vaguely. 'You are pleased to see me, aren't you? I found I had time on hand and decided just on impulse to dash up and see you. I couldn't wait any longer to find out how you were – and I see at a glance you are in fine fettle! I have to go back again tomorrow, so don't waste time being cross with me, dearest, but tell me all your news, and all about the latest feats of my "nevvy". I know he must be a remarkable child. Is he walking and talking yet? Has he painted his first masterpiece or made his first speech to the House?'

It was a fine performance, but Alfreda knew him very well.

With little trouble she picked out the one significant phrase in his babbling brook of speech. 'What do you mean, trying to recoup your fortune? Have you been gaming?'

His bubble burst, he said in his ordinary tones, 'Straight to the point, eh, Alfie? Yes, I've been gambling, but not on the cards and dice, so you needn't give me that look.'

'Horses, then,' she said flatly.

'Only a little. Mostly it was the Stock Exchange. Well, that's respectable enough, ain't it? I thought it must prove better than the Regiment of Fifty-Two, but—'

'Oh Kit!'

'I had damned bad advice,' he said peevishly, 'and from the most plausible fellow, too. Swore I'd make a fortune.'

'Doesn't it occur to you,' Alfreda said patiently, 'that if anyone knew how to make a fortune, he'd make it for himself, not give the secret away to anyone else.'

'You don't know men,' he said loftily. 'We're a brother-hood. We like to help each other.'

'You're a brotherhood of boobies,' she said. 'How much did you lose?' He didn't immediately answer, and she looked at him with rising suspicion. 'Tell me that you aren't in trouble. Tell me that you haven't come here to ask me for money.'

He gave her a weak smile. 'M'tutor told me never to tell a lie.'

'But Kit, you had all that compensation money from the War Office for your commission! It was thousands.'

'What do you think I speculated on the Exchange with?'

'All of it?' she said, aghast.

''Fraid so.' She sat down, thinking of the thousands and what she could have done with them. She had thought her brother was set up for good. With his pay, his annuity and the interest from that, he ought to have been comfortable. Marwood sat down opposite her. 'But look here,' he said at last, losing patience with her silence, 'you've got plenty – or Morland has, which is the same thing. You won't begrudge a little bailing-out to your only brother, who loves you?'

She shook her head, but he saw it was not a negative, only exasperated wonder. At last she said, 'Kit, you must marry and have children.'

'What? This is a new start!'

'I'm serious. For the sake of our family. Little James is of our blood, but he's not a Turlingham in name. Besides, it's the only way to solve your problems. You must marry an heiress.'

He smiled and patted her hand. 'You dear old thing! What inducement do you think would make an heiress marry me?'

'You're handsome, you have a name and a title. It happens all the time.'

'*You* find me one, then.'

'You don't want to marry a provincial. It's bad enough that I had to.'

'Poor Kitten, is he very horrid?'

'Oh, he's no trouble at all, really. In fact, I'm rather fond of him. But living up here – well, it wouldn't do for you. You are the Viscount Marwood. Surely there is some girl of fortune you could marry?'

Marwood looked thoughtful. 'It's funny you should say that, because I saw the eldest Southport girl a few months ago, at the opera, and it was obvious from the way she looked at me that she remembered our pleasant little encounters in Berlin with fondness. There was a definite something between us over there, but of course I knew in England that Southport would never entertain me for a son-in-law.'

'Well, then, what's the use?' Alfreda said impatiently.

'Wait, I haven't told you all. There's something odd about the situation, because Southport House is closed up, and the duke and duchess are living permanently in the country now. Southport's retired from government altogether. So what is Lady Venetia doing in Town all alone?'

'Of course she's not all alone,' Alfreda said. 'She must be staying with some relative.'

'Ah, but which? And where? I can't find out what should be a very simple piece of information. And there are the oddest rumours going about Town that I can't make head or tail of.'

'Who was she with at the opera?'

'Hazelmere, the booby, but he won't tell. I've pumped him

416

like a municipal fireman but I can't get a drop out of him. There's something odd going on.'

'Well, if there is, what use is that to you?' she asked impatiently.

'The girl is Southport's daughter. He's fabulously rich. So's her mother. There must be some way I can use the situation. If she's turning out difficult, they might be grateful to a titled man willing to give her his name. If she's in trouble, I might be able to help her. One way or the other, the cards must fall to my advantage.'

She shook her head again. 'I don't like it. I can see you getting yourself into trouble. Better you come and stay with me and let me find you a Yorkshire heiress.'

'No, love, I'm keeping you as a last resort. But forget about it now. Tell me about your plans for this old place.'

She let herself be turned. 'Well, George has been complaining about having no billiards room.'

'Quite right! No gentleman's house should be without one.'

'There was some talk of putting a table in the long saloon upstairs, but I have a better idea . . .'

Teddy hadn't anticipated any particular consequences from his ownership of the railway shares: he just had a fancy to have them, in memory of his father. He was surprised therefore to be visited by a delegation from the directors of the North Eastern Railway, consisting of Lord Anstey, Mr Bayliss and William Pobgee of the firm of solicitors Pobgee, Pobgee and Micklethwaite.

'We've come to talk to you about the new railway station,' Anstey said, settling himself in the offered chair and looking round curiously at the drawing-room, stiffly furnished with the taste of fifty years ago, and exuding the dim comfortlessness of a room seldom used.

'Oh, there is going to be one, then?' Teddy said, perching himself on a slippery horsehair-covered sofa. On this very sofa, his benefactress, the Mrs Makepeace who had left everything to his father, had breathed her last, as the obliging Mrs Scawton had told him, but he didn't think about that. He had grown up in a house with many ghosts, and a crypt full of coffins underfoot, and the dead didn't bother him a bit.

'That is the question. It's a great nuisance having a station that's a terminus, with no through line; on the other hand, building a new station looks likely to be difficult because of the terrain, and therefore expensive.'

'Why difficult?' Teddy asked.

'Because trains can't go around corners. The through line will have to join up with the existing lines to the north in gentle curves, and fit into the bend of the river. Because of the limited space, the station will have to be built on a curve. It presents quite a problem of engineering.'

Teddy grinned. 'It's a pity my father isn't alive. He'd have rubbed his hands at the thought of it!'

'That's rather why we've come to you,' Bayliss said.

'I'm not an engineer,' Teddy objected.

'But you're a shareholder and your father's son,' said Pobgee. 'And in addition you own the rackety slums along the south end of Thief Lane, which is the only place the station can be built.'

'Ah,' said Teddy, enlightened. 'So you want to buy the land from me?'

Lord Anstey smiled. 'We thought you might like to involve yourself a little more closely than that. You see, we need a committee to look into the matter, to canvass opinion, investigate options, assemble estimates – eventually, if it's decided to go ahead, to commission an architect and get in tenders.'

'The committee will have to have a chairman,' said Bayliss.

Teddy looked from one to the other. 'You mean me?' he said in amazement.

'Why not you?'

'I don't know anything about railways – not above what I've heard my father say in passing, anyway.'

'That doesn't matter,' said Bayliss. 'A chairman doesn't have to be an expert – he employs others for expert advice. What he has to do is to supervise and collate. For that he needs a general intelligence—'

'Which you have in abundance,' Lord Anstey said.

'A knowledge of the people involved – which you also have – and an ability to get on with them.'

'And he has to have leisure,' Pobgee finished. 'All of us have professional calls on our time, but it seemed to us that you have yours at your disposal.'

Teddy grinned. 'You mean I am an idle devil, with nothing to do but amuse myself and get into trouble!'

'Not quite that,' Pobgee protested politely. 'I know you like to interest yourself in your business, but perhaps it doesn't take up quite *all* your time?'

'So all in all,' Bayliss finished, 'we thought it was something that might appeal to you.'

Teddy thought, but not for long. He had felt life was rather flat recently, and it would be nice to be involved with something that had a forward momentum and a tangible result. The alternative would be to marry and have children. 'Very well, I'll do it,' he said.

Pobgee was worried by such haste. 'No need to decide at once. There's no hurry. Take time to consider.'

'What is there to consider?' Teddy said easily. 'I should like to do this. Papa was in at the very beginning of the railway here: I'd like to do it for him, for his memory.'

Shown into the small sitting-room at the rectory, Teddy could not immediately see his sister. After the brilliance of the June sunshine outside, the room seemed dark, except for the oblong of pure light which was the window. And then a movement drew his eye to the sofa, and a glad voice cried, 'Oh Teddy!'

'There you are!' He crossed the room. 'I hardly expected to find you indoors on such a fine day. I half thought it would be a wasted journey, but I had to see a man in Bugthorpe, and I couldn't be so near without turning out of my way just to say hello.'

'I'm so glad you did! It's so good to see you, after all this time.'

'Hey, now, don't smother me,' Teddy said, laughing. He looked about for a chair and drew it up. His sister was lying on the sofa covered in a silk shawl, patterned in exotic colours with dragons, fish and Chinese ladies on bridges. 'This is a very splendid affair,' he said, fingering the fringe. It embarrassed him to look directly at her, for the shawl was covering but not concealing a large bulge.

'Miss Compton gave it to me. She's a neighbour – and a friend, too.'

'I'm glad you have agreeable people nearby. But what are you doing on the sofa? You're not ill?'

'I'm having a baby,' she said colourlessly.

'Well, I know that, foolish! Regina told me.'

'Oh. You didn't write, so I didn't know you knew.'

'I'm no hand at letter-writing,' Teddy said easily. 'That's a female's business. I half think,' he added, 'that it's the main reason men get married.'

'I wrote to George, and he didn't write back either.'

'I shouldn't mind it. He's more or less thrown us all off, since he married Alfreda. I only live a mile away and I never see him, unless I bump into him in town. Anyway, they're a great deal too busy changing Morland Place to have time for anything else.'

'How do you know if you never see them?'

'The whole of York's talking about it. It'll be a miracle, from what people say, if there's one stone left standing on another when they've finished.'

'You don't mean it? They're not really pulling it down?' Henrietta said, hauling herself up a little.

'You'd think so, from the outrage of the Historical Society!' Teddy chuckled. 'It's the kennels that are being pulled down at the moment, to build what George grandly called a gentleman's wing.'

'Oh, yes – Mr Fortescue has one here.'

'Has he? Well, George is mad for a billiards room, it seems, and there's to be a smoking-room and something else, I forget now what it was – Jack Bryan told me about it, because his guv'nor's drawn up the plans – but the important thing is there's to be a door from the new wing into the yard so that Georgie can have his dogs in with him. Did you ever hear the like?'

'He was always very fond of his dogs.'

420

'Yes, but to let his wife ban them from the house, and to have to go to such lengths to get them back! It beats all.'

Henrietta frowned. 'But what's to become of the kennels? Are they giving up hunting?'

'No, quite the opposite. Alfreda's mad for it – it's all the go now for ladies to hunt, isn't it? There's to be a new kennel block built out past the easter barn – I think Jack said a stable too. Something very great, at any rate.'

'It doesn't sound too bad,' Henrietta said, comforting herself. The thought of Morland Place being changed had shaken her. Though she might never see it again, it was something to know it was still there, and still the same. 'Why should the historians object?'

'Oh, it isn't that, so much, but the changes inside that Alfreda's ordered. She finds the drawing-room too big and gloomy, apparently—'

'Yes, she always said so.'

'So it's to be divided to make a smaller drawing-room and a small sitting-room for her. And all the panelling is to be torn out. That's what incenses Mrs Havergill, because apparently it's priceless mediaeval linenfold or something, rare as rocs' eggs – though for my money I agree with Alfreda. Not that I'd dare remove it if it were me, but those who think panelling's so wonderful should try living with it! Oh, and there are to be modern windows and a modern fireplace, and something's to happen to the ceiling, which upsets the historical folk because of the plasterwork.'

'I always thought the ceiling was beautiful,' Henrietta said wistfully.

Teddy shrugged. 'It's their house to do what they like with.'

'With Alfreda in her sitting-room and George in the gentleman's wing, they'll never see each other.'

Teddy didn't comment. Though George had told him at the time of the wedding that he was in love with Alfreda, Teddy didn't see how he could have been, and put the declaration down to mere correctness. He wondered if all this frenzy of building might be Alfreda's way of keeping him

421

interested in his home. After all, George was only twenty-three, and young men had been known to rove.

He changed the subject. 'But you didn't tell me why you're lying on the sofa, instead of being out in this lovely weather.'

'Dr Mansur says I must lie down every afternoon,' Henrietta said, in a voice devoid of light. Teddy looked at her properly at last, and saw that her face was puffy and her eyes red, as though she had been crying, not just now, but often. 'And anyway, if I go out I'm only allowed to walk about the grounds. I've walked about them so much I know every blade of grass.'

'But – then – what do you do all day?'

She shrugged. 'Lie on the sofa.'

'You must be moped to death,' he said. 'You have friends to visit, don't you? Or to visit you?'

'I can't see people in this condition,' Henrietta said, waving a hand at herself. 'It wouldn't be decent.'

'Decent be damned! Who says so?'

'Everyone.' She gulped. 'Mr Fortescue.'

'Fortescue said it wasn't decent for people to see you like this?' Teddy asked in amazement.

'He – he sent a message by Mr Catchpole. Something about being a vessel filled with the Holy Spirit and not spilling any.' She began to redden with suppressed tears. 'Mr Catchpole wouldn't look at me while he said it. And he doesn't eat at the same table with me any more. Not that I like him anyway, but—' The tears spilled over. 'Oh Teddy, I'm so miserable! I'm on my own all day long and I never see anyone! I have to eat alone and – and Mr Fortescue never visits me. I think he doesn't love me any more!'

She broke down in sobs, and Teddy, feeling wretched and awkward, leaned over and patted bits of her, and then, taking his courage by the scruff, manoeuvred himself onto the sofa and with difficulty took her into his arms. She sobbed with huge abandon, like a dam breaking, and at one time he was afraid she would hurt herself. He had no experience of sobbing women, or indeed pregnant women, and didn't know what to do. But at last it eased off, and he thought it must be like a violent rainstorm, noisy at the time, but clearing the air.

The two handkerchiefs he had about him were entirely inadequate to the task of mopping her up, and using his wits he fetched the white cotton runner from a nearby table and, rather shamefaced, Henrietta used that too. She was sitting up now, shoulders hitching with dying sobs. 'I'm sorry,' she said at last.

'No, no,' he said. 'But look here, Hen, this is all wrong! A woman having a baby is supposed to be happy, isn't she?'

'How can I be happy when he doesn't love me any more?' she said simply.

'Of course he loves you. Why shouldn't he?'

'I don't know,' she said sadly, staring down at her hands. 'I only know he doesn't. He keeps away from me entirely, and if I happen to cross the hall when he comes into it, he turns away to avoid me. He won't look at me. He thinks I'm ugly.'

'Oh, nonsense! Of course he doesn't.'

Henrietta didn't argue. She knew what she knew, though it was hard to explain it to anyone else. That wonderful moment when she had told her husband about the baby had been followed by several weeks of great happiness; there were no more night visits, of course, but during the daytime he spent more time with her, and was gentle and tender towards her, talking of his plans for the child, which she enjoyed, and the philosophical meaning of fatherhood, making reference to classical and biblical examples, which she didn't understand.

But then it had begun to change. As soon as her pregnancy started to show, he began to withdraw from her; and though he had never said so to her, she knew that she repelled him. The spiritual idea of having a son to follow him, the miracle of new life, were intellectual concepts to thrill him, but the physical manifestation he could not bear. As her belly started to swell he loathed the sight of her, even as he loathed himself for his part in having made her so. Henrietta did not understand this intellectually, but she knew it at a deep and wordless level.

And as his twin loathing grew, he felt compelled to shut her away. First she was not to come to church, then she was not to leave the house or see any outsiders, and finally he imposed this isolation on her. Only thus could he confine his feelings, which threatened to rampage out of control. She ate alone, and sat alone. The servants were not to disturb her, attending her only if she rang, and remaining with her only long enough to provide what she had rung for. They were not to talk to her. When she walked in the grounds, the outdoor staff were instructed to keep out of sight.

The rules were explained as Dr Mansur's: her condition was delicate and if disaster was to be averted she must not be upset or excited in any way. Complete rest and quiet were necessary at all times; and as being stared at upset her, she was not to be seen. To the servants it seemed reasonable, and the fact that Mrs Fortescue spent so much of her time weeping seemed only to prove that her nerves were fragile. They joined him in shunning her, out of the kindness of their hearts.

Teddy had got in to see her only because Prosser and Andrews both happened to be out, and Jenks, the senior footman who answered the door, supposed a member of the family would not come under the visiting ban. He had gone to ask Mrs Fortescue tentatively if she would see Mr Edward Morland, and her eager affirmative had seemed enough. He had shown Teddy in, and hurried back to Mr Andrews' pantry where he had been reading the racing paper and enjoying a drop of port which he had salvaged from last night's decanter before it went to be washed.

Henrietta said at last, sighing, 'I am ugly. He's right. No-one wants to look at a pregnant woman.' She lifted her eyes. 'You didn't want to yourself when you came in.'

Teddy, embarrassed, couldn't deny it. 'But everything will be all right after the baby's born, won't it? In the mean time, what about this friend of yours, Miss Whatsername, who gave you the shawl? It might be embarrassing for a man to see you increasing, but she'd visit you, surely?'

She shook her head. 'Mr Fortescue says it isn't decent.' She made an effort and conjured up a watery smile that hurt Teddy more than anything else he had seen or heard here. 'Never mind about me, Ted. I'm just so glad to see you. Tell me more news. Tell me what you've been doing. Have you see Regina lately? Have you heard from Manny?'

*　　*　　*

Teddy left her at last apparently much happier – or at least more cheerful – and rode off down the village street with a thoughtful frown. This marriage business was stickier than it appeared from the outside, and the more he saw of it, the less he wanted any of it for himself. He liked flirting with girls, and enjoyed being made to feel handsome and clever by them, but he was well aware of the trap they represented and was careful never to give any of them – or their mothers – the idea that he was serious. He had no desire for children; and for the other business, there was the accommodating girl – the one he had bought Henrietta's silver necklace for – in York, and another, now, in Leeds that he visited when he wanted a change. And that seemed to cover it.

A man on horseback approaching from the other direction drew rein, and Teddy looked at him automatically, then halted. 'I say, don't I know you?' he said.

The other fellow considered him. 'You do look familiar, but I can't place you.'

Teddy screwed up his brow in thought. 'Oxford, wasn't it? Weren't you at the House?'

'Balliol,' he said, 'and not in your time, evidently.' He was plainly older than Teddy. 'But used to visit a Christ Church man – Perry Parke.'

Teddy laughed. 'But I know Perry! We must have met in his rooms. I'm Edward Morland.'

'Good God, no wonder you look familiar! You must be Mrs Fortescue's brother. Now I know, you do have a look of her. I'm Jerome Compton. Parke's father married a cousin of mine.'

'Yes, I'm sure I remember you, now,' Teddy said. 'Didn't you have a nice little liver-spotted pointer bitch?'

Jerome laughed. 'Dolly? Yes, everyone remembers her. She died of hard-pad two years ago, poor bitch.'

Teddy was looking round. 'And now I come to think of it, doesn't Parke live somewhere hereabouts?'

'Yes, in the Red House, at the end of the street. There are quite a few House men in the neighbourhood. You didn't come to Bishop Winthorpe to visit him, then?'

'No, I've been to see my sister.'

'Ah! Look here, Morland, I live just here. Won't you come in for a bit, take a glass of something, have a jaw?' Teddy hesitated, and he added, 'I've a particular reason. If you're not too pressed for time.'

'My time's my own,' Teddy said. 'I'd be pleased to.'

'Good fellow.' The groom took the reins of both horses, and Jerome led the way in. 'I live with my sister Mary, and she'll be very glad to make your acquaintance.'

Teddy stopped and struck his forehead. 'Curse me for an idiot! Compton, of course! Henrietta only just now mentioned a Miss Compton, who gave her a nice silk shawl.'

'Mentioned her favourably, I hope?'

'Said she was a friend.'

'Good. That makes things easier. Mary!' He looked in at the sitting-room, and then the back parlour. 'Ah, there you are. I've brought you a visitor. Here is Henrietta's brother, Edward Morland.'

Mary Compton, rising to her feet from the table where she was potting cuttings over carefully spread sheets of newspaper, looked eagerly towards them. 'Mr Morland! You can't think how glad I am to see you. Have you seen Henrietta? Ah! Then you can tell us what's wrong with her.'

Teddy was not one for betraying confidences, and he would not normally have discussed anything so delicate as Henrietta's condition with anyone, leave alone two comparative strangers; but the interest of both Comptons was palpable and earnest.

'There's evidently something odd going on,' Mary Compton said at last, thoughtfully. 'I've tried many times to get to see her, and been denied. I was told that her nerves are affected and Mansur decrees complete quiet.'

'Her nerves seemed all right to me,' Teddy said, 'and she never had them before. She was the strongest, healthiest girl you ever saw back home. And she was so glad to see me, it quite shook me. I think she's moped to death, shut up in that house on her own all day.'

'Anyone would be,' Mary said. 'It can't be wise. If Mansur decreed it, he's an old fool. I don't go to him – Savage is my physician.'

426

Jerome got up and paced about restlessly. 'I don't believe Mansur decreed it. This is some freak of Fortescue's!'

'Now, Jerome, be careful what you say,' Mary warned.

He turned. 'He's taken some mad notion into his head about her, and this is the result. I tell you, the man's unhinged! I've watched him for a long time, and there's something not right about the way he behaves towards her. Well, what the devil did he mean by marrying her in the first place? It's monstrous!'

He's in love with her, Teddy thought in surprise. Now what the deuce!

'She doesn't come to church on Sundays now,' Jerome went on. 'What sort of man prevents his wife from attending service? I think he's mentally unbalanced.'

'He doesn't behave like a madman,' Mary said, 'but he has seemed a little odd lately. His sermons – have you noticed, Jerome? – they're getting extremely strange. Longer and longer, rambling, and full of peculiar references to the most obscure texts. But he always was something of a recluse – well, not that exactly, but he never saw anyone but his fellow scholars. Everyone was surprised when he married. Probably he's just going back to his old ways.'

'Without a thought for her needs!' said Jerome angrily. 'Why was she ever made to marry him!'

'She wasn't,' Teddy said. 'She wanted to. I never understood it myself, but she was definitely in love with him. I think she still is – at least, she's very unhappy because she's afraid he doesn't love her any more.'

'Why, what does he do to her?' Jerome asked sharply.

'Oh, nothing. I mean, she never sees him, and if they bump into each other, he hurries away and won't look at her.' Teddy glanced from one to the other uneasily. 'I say, I shouldn't really be telling you these things. You won't— ?'

'You're quite right to tell us,' Mary soothed him. 'We have nothing but the warmest regard for your sister, and we're worried about her. And of course we will never reveal to anyone what you've said.'

'That's all very well,' Jerome said impatiently, 'but what are we to *do*?'

Teddy shrugged unhappily. 'I don't see there's anything you can do. You can't interfere between man and wife.'

'There's certainly nothing *you* can do,' Mary said to her brother. 'In the circumstances, it would be very wrong.'

He looked at her quickly, and a message passed between them. Jerome subsided a little and stopped grinding his teeth.

'It's not as if he's harming her,' Mary went on. 'If he ignores her, it may be unpleasant, but it won't kill her.' Jerome said something under his breath. 'I suppose I might go and see Mansur.'

'He wouldn't talk to you,' Jerome said. 'A physician can't talk about his patient to anyone else.'

'That's right,' said Teddy.

'And Mansur's an old friend of the rector's. He'd always side with him.'

'Then I must just make renewed efforts to see her,' said Mary helplessly.

'They won't let you in.'

'Mr Morland got in.'

'He's her brother.' Jerome's face lit suddenly. 'Wait, I have it! Hasn't she – haven't you – a sister?'

'Regina, yes. She lives with some friends of ours in York.'

'How old is she?'

'Just fifteen. Why?'

'Wouldn't she like to go and stay with Henrietta? A nice, long visit?'

Mary clapped her hands. 'Jerome, that's the answer! How can the rector object? A married woman often has an unmarried sister to stay with her – even to live with her. Mr Morland, would this sister come, do you think?'

'I expect so,' Teddy said. 'I could ask her. But are you sure the rector would allow it?'

'There must be a way to ensure it. We must work out how it's to be done,' Mary said.

CHAPTER TWENTY-THREE

At the end of June 1872 Venetia sat her first papers, and in July was called to the dean's office to receive the results.

'I am pleased,' said Bentley, though he didn't look it, 'to be able to inform you that you have passed all your class examinations with honour. Here are your certificates.'

'Thank you, sir.' Venetia took them with a smile that trembled slightly. The dean, after some hesitation, shook her hand.

'Congratulations, Miss Fleet. Only two other students reached the same standard. You can be justly proud of your efforts,' he said gravely. 'However, though I dislike to inject a sour note into the proceedings, I must warn you against allowing it to be known that you have achieved honours in all subjects.'

'Sir?'

'I shall tell no-one, but if it should get out, it will make you very unpopular.' He met Venetia's eye for a moment, and then to avoid the clear gaze he walked across to the window and looked out at the sooty brick wall which was all his view. 'No-one supposed that you would persevere – not even I. We admitted you as a favour to Sir Frederick, and out of respect for your mother's work – by the by,' he added, looking back at her, 'why didn't you go to the Southport?'

'My father disapproved, and though my mother supported me in principle, she wouldn't embarrass my father,' Venetia said dully. The shine was being taken off the moment.

'Ah! Well, to resume, I, like everyone else, thought you would find the work too disagreeable and too difficult, and give up. Even Sir Frederick, though he didn't say as much, gave a hint that if we were to indulge you a little, you would soon leave of your own accord. Most of the seniors accepted the situation on that understanding.' He shrugged. 'As for the students, they will not like being outshone by a female. They are already made fun of by the students of other schools. They take it in good part, but if it appears that you may be a serious rival rather than just a larky girl—'

'Yes,' Venetia said, 'I understand. A woman is for decoration, for the amusement of men in their leisure hours. We aren't human beings, with capacities and desires and ambitions, we're toys without minds of our own.'

Bentley raised his eyebrows. 'Don't rant at me, Miss Fleet,' he said, quite mildly. 'I had thought you pleasantly free of that propensity.'

'I'm sorry sir, but it's hard not to be angry. How would you feel if the cases were reversed, and you found that whatever you did, and however well you did it, you could never be judged on your own merits?'

'Perfectly infuriated,' Bentley said. 'I do enter into your feelings, which is why I am supporting you.' He stared out of the window again. 'But I think you are a rare case, a lady with a masculine cast of mind – and I certainly hope that you *are*. God made us different for a purpose, and the thought of every business and profession being overrun and degraded by chattering, flapping females, while homes stand neglected and children go untended, fills me with horror.'

Venetia was silent, too offended to speak.

'However, as I said, I will support you, and so again I advise you to keep your success in the class papers a close secret.' He came back to his desk and sat down. 'Term ends in another week, and the winter term begins in October. Will you be going out of Town?'

'I think I must, at least for a while. My Aunt Fanny, whom I live with, isn't quite well. She needs country air. We'll probably go down to Ravendene – my father's place in Northamptonshire.'

Bentley nodded, tapping a finger thoughtfully on the desk top. 'Next year will be a hard one for you. It would benefit you a great deal to have some more clinical experience before it begins.'

'Sir?'

He looked up and met her eyes, and she was surprised at the cordiality in his expression. 'If you would care to come back to Town early – say, at the beginning of September – I can put you to work in the receiving room. You will see more there in a day than you could read about in a week. But it is not pleasant work, I warn you.'

Venetia smiled. 'If I'd wanted pleasant work, I should never have begun this,' she said. 'You are *very* kind, sir.'

He waved her thanks away. 'And while the students are absent, I may find time to give you a little private teaching in anatomy. I anticipate that difficulties may arise in that area when term begins – but we will cross that bridge when we come to it. Well, Miss Fleet, shall I see you in September?'

'Oh, yes! And thank you – more than I can say!'

'Well, well, off you go,' Bentley said with a private smile.

She was walking down to the lecture room on the day before the end of term, in company with Tucker and Quinton, when Sir Frederick Friedman appeared, walking towards them. He nodded pleasantly to the men, and smiled at her. 'Ah, Miss Fleet! A word, if you please.' She stopped, and the other two walked on, casting back glances of open curiosity. 'I understand congratulations are in order,' he said when they were out of earshot.

'Thank you, sir,' she said. 'I believe you didn't think I would stay to the end of term?'

He laughed. 'Bentley's a blabbermouth! But no, I didn't think a gently born girl like you would be able to stand it. You have, and with honour, and that's to your credit. And you are to come back early and work in the receiving room?'

'Was that your doing?' Venetia asked, eyeing him narrowly.

He spread his hands. 'Guilty as charged. I put the idea to Bentley, but he made no difficulty about it. He is a good fellow, and very interested in our little experiment.'

'The experiment being me? Well, whatever the motive, I am grateful to you both.'

431

'You've changed, you know,' Friedman said thoughtfully. 'You're much more self-confident. A woman, now, not a girl. And you still like the work?'

'It is more fascinating even than I expected,' Venetia said.

'It is,' he agreed, 'the most exciting profession in the world.'

Venetia grinned. 'Which is why you want to keep it to yourselves, of course. Don't let the girls play!'

'You are growing saucy,' Friedman said, laughing. 'Be off to your lecture. You're going down to Ravendene this summer? Give my regards to your dear mother, if you please.' And he was off down the corridor, chuckling to himself.

Tucker and Quinton had waited for her at the head of the stairs. 'What did the old boy want with you?' Quinton asked, with more openness than good manners.

'Nothing in particular,' Venetia said; and then realising that that would not do to avert curiosity, she added, 'He was asking after my mother. He's an old friend of the family.'

'Oho!' said Tucker. 'So that's how the milk got into the coconut!'

Venetia brazened it out. 'You don't think I got myself admitted here without *some* string-pulling? Really, gentlemen, use your wits!'

'Funny sort of old family friend,' Quinton said. 'Can't see any of ours helping to get my sister into such a scrape.'

Venetia, with Fanny and Emma, went down to Ravendene on the day after term ended. Emma was most unwilling to go, complaining that there was nothing to do in the country and that London was the only place to be, summer heat notwithstanding. But her real reason was so close under the surface that even Venetia, preoccupied with her own affairs, knew that Emma had got a crush on Tommy Weston, and didn't want to leave Town while he was there.

At Ravendene, however, Emma was seized upon instantly by Augusta, and borne away to the old nursery, with Fairy pattering in their wake. Augusta was just about to be seventeen, and plans were in hand for her come-out the following spring. Emma's birthday was two days before Augusta's. 'I *wish* you weren't a year younger,' Augusta said over and over, as if repeating it might bring it about. 'It would be such fun to come out together. I'd really almost rather not come out at all, as do it without you.'

Olivia was home from waiting at Osborne, full of royal family chatter. Mr Gladstone had presented the Queen with what he rather grandly called 'a Plan of Life' for the Prince of Wales, who was getting a reputation for being addicted to idle pleasure. Gladstone's idea was that the Prince should be made Viceroy of Ireland, which would help attach the troublesome province to the parent country, and also give him a taste of his future regal duties. Gladstone proposed that the Prince should spend four or five months in Dublin, three months representing the Queen at Court in London, and the rest of the year on military duties.

'The Queen didn't like it at all,' Olivia said.

Charlotte was amused. 'I shouldn't think the Prince would, either! It sounds rather a grim routine for a man who loves horse-racing, dining and the theatre.'

'The Queen was terribly offended,' Olivia said. 'She said the Prince's future was a matter for her to settle.'

'Gladstone is very tactless,' Oliver commented. 'He has no notion of handling people.'

'And the Queen said that Ireland was in no state for experiments, but Mr Gladstone still wrote again and urged the plan on her. But you know, though she's very fond of the Prince, I think she worries about him being king one day,' Olivia confided. 'I think she thinks he's too frivolous. I overheard her say something about it to Princess Alice.'

Prince Leopold, the Queen's youngest son, had also been the subject of much royal debate. He had finally won permission to go up to Oxford, against stiff opposition from the Queen.

'She's afraid he won't take care of himself properly if he's out of her sight,' Olivia said. 'She worries about him so much, and he's always been dreadfully reckless.' Leopold was a haemophiliac, a fact which was meant to be a closely guarded secret, though it was quite widely known at Court. 'But Princess Louise said to me the other day that she thinks he'll probably behave better at Christ Church because of not feeling he's being watched all the time. She thinks it's that that makes him rebel. Oh, by the way, Venetia,' she went on, 'Princess Louise knows about you studying medicine, and she thinks it's perfectly splendid. She's all for women doing things. She said to wish you the very best of luck – only I'm not to let the Queen know she said so.'

Venetia took the opportunity to reveal to her interested family that she had been offered outpatient work in September. 'It's a tremendous compliment that Old Bill is willing to take time and trouble over me,' she said. 'He told me he didn't think I'd stick it out. I suppose this is my reward for surprising him.'

'It will be useful experience for you,' Charlotte said. 'But don't you feel you ought to have more of a rest? You've been working very hard.'

'Oh, I'm not tired at all,' Venetia said. 'Everything is so *very* interesting, and it seems the more I do, the more I can do. I never get those awful fits of lassitude that used to come over me after a morning of idling about and reading on the sofa. I'm sure all the vapours and nerves and ailments women suffer from are caused by boredom, pure and simple.'

Charlotte caught Fanny's expression, and said, 'I wouldn't be too quick to say *all*, love. Your Aunt Fanny is looking far from well.'

'Oh, I didn't mean you, Aunt!' Venetia said quickly. 'I know you aren't fanciful.'

Fanny made an equivocal face. 'Thank you for that! But, Venetia dear, I have to tell you that, much as I love you, I can't go back to London with you again. I'm really sorry to disappoint you, but my health won't stand another winter of it.'

Venetia was aghast. She held herself back from protesting, because now she really looked at her, she could see how poorly Fanny was. 'I – I see,' she managed to say at last. 'But – then – what will become of me? I suppose I could live alone.'

'Not on any account in the world,' Charlotte said quickly, catching her husband's expression. 'Now, don't look so tragic. I wonder if Tom and Emily might not have you to stay?'

'That will do a great deal for her anonymity,' Oliver remarked.

'Oh, I think she might pass there, if she's careful. It's not as if they entertain much any more.'

'But haven't you heard?' Venetia said tragically. 'They're giving up the London house and going to live in Eastbourne, for Aunt Emily's health.'

'Tommy's taking over the house,' Emma put in with some satisfaction.

'I can hardly stay there with just Tommy in residence,' Venetia finished, giving her a distracted look.

'I'm glad you realise that, at least,' Charlotte said. 'But it's not so bad. We'll be opening up Southport House next year for Augusta, and I'm sure we can contrive somehow to hide you away – can't we, dearest?' She threw an appealing look at her husband.

Venetia didn't wait to hear his answer. 'But you don't understand – I must go back in September!' she cried desperately. 'I can't wait until March or whenever you go up. I can't miss half a term, *and* the extra work Mr Bentley's arranging for me. I must go up in September, or everything will be ruined!'

'What a lot of passion to spend on something so little worth the expense,' Oliver said. 'You might as well put an end to this nonsense, because I tell you once for all I will not have you at Southport House while you are masquerading as a medical student. It seems I can't stop you making a scandal of yourself, but I will not be seen to condone it.' And with that he left the room.

Venetia watched him go with bitterness. After all she had achieved, she was no further forward with him than before. But there were other things to think about. 'I can't give up now,' she said urgently to her mother. 'I passed with merit, among the best three in the class. There must be a way to go on.'

Charlotte was thoughtful. 'If you are really determined, then we shall have to try to find someone else to chaperon you. Do you remember, Fanny, when you and I were young, we set up in our own little house, with a distant cousin for decency?'

Fanny smiled. 'Yes, and how shocking some people thought it! Have you got any more suitable cousins?'

'It must be someone old enough to give propriety, but young enough not to disapprove,' Charlotte said.

'And needy enough to take on the job,' Fanny added.

Charlotte pondered, and then said, 'Do you know, I think I have it. What do you think to cousin Marianne? She's unmarried, but she must be nearly forty now, which is quite old enough to play chaperon.'

'You mean Marianne Morpurgo?' Fanny said. 'Yes, she's very lively and forward thinking. And she's quite used to going out and about alone, poor thing, so she'd be up to all the rigs.'

'Do you think she might agree to do it?' Venetia asked.

'The Morpurgos aren't very well off,' Charlotte said. Peter Morpurgo had inherited his parents' business, a riding school in the Bayswater Road, and though it had the most fashionable customers, he and his wife had a numerous family to support. 'And I know Marianne feels badly about continuing to live with her brother and being a drain on his household.'

'Why didn't she marry?' Fanny asked. 'She's pretty enough.'

'She was disappointed in love,' Charlotte said. 'The man jilted her. It was a shocking thing.' She turned to her daughter. 'Well, what do you think? Shall I write and ask her?'

'Oh, this instant, if you please! Thank you, Mama-duchess! I knew you would turn up trumps.'

'She hasn't said yes yet,' Charlotte cautioned. 'Don't get too excited.'

But Miss Morpurgo was very taken with the idea and expressed herself willing almost by return of post. Before the next question – where Venetia and her chaperon should live – could even be raised, Emma had entered an impassioned plea to be allowed to join the household.

'You're much too young,' Fanny objected, ambushed by the question which she ought to have foreseen.

'But Mama, I'm not a child. I'm sixteen, or I will be by September. Lots of girls are married at sixteen.'

'That has nothing to do with it.'

Emma shifted ground. 'If Cousin Marianne is old enough

to chaperon Venetia, she must be old enough to chaperon me.'

'You ought to have a governess,' Fanny said. 'What do you suppose you're going to do in London without me to give you lessons?'

'I'm too old for lessons,' Emma said quickly. 'You know I'm not bookish like Venetia, and there's no use in pretending I've learned anything in the last year. What I need to know is how to go about in the world, and I should think Cousin Marianne would be just the person to show me.'

'Whether she is or not—' Fanny began.

'And anyway,' Emma added irrepressibly, 'with Venetia at the hospital all day and studying all night, what is poor Cousin Marianne to do with herself? I think Aunt Charlotte has recruited her under false pretences: I'm sure she doesn't know she'll be condemned to lonely solitude for six days out of seven.'

Fanny laughed in spite of herself. 'Lonely solitude indeed!'

'*Dearest* Mama, look at all the advantages if I go to London: I'll keep Cousin Marianne company, be an extra chaperon for Venetia, *and* I'll learn how to conduct myself so that when I have my come-out I'll make a tremendous splash and have dozens of offers right away. If I stay mewed up in the country I'll be just another awkward schoolgirl. Now *do* say yes!'

'I'd have thought you'd want to stay here with me,' Fanny said. 'To say nothing of Augusta.'

'Well, I love you, of course,' Emma said judiciously, 'but I know you depend on getting me off respectably, so naturally that's on my mind. And as for Gussie, she'll be going to London anyway in February or March for her launch.'

Fanny sighed. 'I suppose I shall have to give in. If Marianne says she will take on the extra responsibility, you may go.'

Miss Morpurgo expressed herself willing to have Emma's company, and it was decided then to keep the Bedford Square house, with Fanny sharing the expense with Charlotte. Fanny was sorry to see her daughter go, but the past year had tired her more than she knew until the house was quiet again and there were no more calls on her attention. Then she became aware of the desperate aching of every fibre, and the longing

437

just to lie still and gaze out of a window at the spreading green of the park. She was fifty-one, and had gone through a great deal in her life. Now she rested, and let her mind drift back over the years. Sometimes she dozed, and it was hard to tell which were her waking and which her sleeping dreams. She thought of her home in Manchester, and the dirty streets and smoky mills; the wide open spaces of Grasscroft, where Charlotte's mother and stepfather had treated her like their own child, and Cavendish had been her honorary brother.

She did not think of Philip Anthony, her husband: it was too painful. But she thought of Lionel, and wondered if he was happy with his bride, and if he had made her a grandmother yet. She thought a great deal about Peter Welland, with whom she had shared the worst hardships: kind Peter, who had loved her, and given her Emma. What contrasts her life had encompassed! But she had been useful, at last, to Venetia: she could claim that. Now it was time to rest.

She must have been sleeping, for she suddenly became aware of Charlotte leaning over her, a hand on her shoulder, saying, 'Fanny, are you awake? There's a visitor for you.'

She struggled to full wakefulness. A visitor? Could it be Lionel? But the young man who placed himself in her line of vision, though the same age, was of a very different cut.

'Mrs Anthony – or may I call you Cousin Fanny? Am I disturbing you?'

Fanny stared, her mind still clogged. Who was this dapper young man, dressed rather townishly for Northamptonshire, but with evident expense – a well-built fellow with a long, sharp-chinned face, brown eyes, and a hint of fox to his dark hair? And then the cobwebs of dream dissolved and she remembered the telegraph that had arrived to say that Edward Morland had come to London seeking an interview with her, and learning she was at Ravendene, begged leave to come down and speak to her.

Fanny smiled at last and held out her hand. 'So you're Benedict's son. I'm very glad to meet you. You have a look of your mother about you, I think.'

'Thank you, ma'am. I count that an honour.'

438

'Well, so you should. Sit down, and tell me how things are at Morland Place.'

Teddy waited for Charlotte to sit, and then drew up a seat for himself. 'I don't live there any more, so I can't tell you much – except that George and his wife are making something very splendid of it. Expense is no object. I fancy they have Castle Howard or Blenheim Palace as a model.'

Fanny didn't know how to take this, and said instead, 'They had a child, didn't they, a son? Are there any more yet?'

'No, just the one boy so far. James, they called him—'

'Oh, after his great-grandfather?' said Fanny. 'That's nice. And where do you live?'

'In York. I have a house there. I inherited it from my father, along with some small factories and a drapery business and one or two other things.'

'Business must be good,' Charlotte said. 'You look very prosperous.'

'It is,' Teddy said. 'York is a very coming place, with plenty of wealthy residents. Besides, with drapery and leather goods one can hardly go wrong. Every lady wants new gowns, and every gentleman needs gloves, boots and whips. It's business I've come to talk to you about,' he concluded.

'Shall I leave you alone?' Charlotte asked, preparing to rise.

Fanny stayed her. 'No, please. I may need your advice.'

'I hope you will take advice, Cousin Fanny,' Teddy said. 'I have a proposition to make which I think will benefit us both, but you ought to consult your man of business about it.'

Fanny looked puzzled. 'I can't think what it can be about except Hobsbawn Mills. But doesn't your brother own the other half of them?'

'He used to,' Teddy said simply. 'We swapped.'

'Swapped?'

'Didn't your agent tell you, then?'

'I don't know. Perhaps he did. I don't read the letters with great attention, I must confess. I've so much else on my mind.'

'Why did you swap?' Charlotte asked. 'And for what?'

Teddy gave her a limpid look. 'I had a piece of land Georgie

439

wanted. I thought at first I'd like to be a squire, but when it came to it, it wasn't to my taste. Georgie didn't care about the mills, and I enjoy messing about with my own little factories, so it seemed the obvious thing to do.'

'Obvious,' Charlotte agreed drily.

'So we are partners, then,' Fanny said. 'And you've come to make yourself known to me?'

'Not just that; I've an offer I'd like you to consider. You know, of course, that the return from the mills has been falling for some time?'

'That much I did gather,' Fanny agreed. 'Fortunately I have other investments, and my expenses aren't great, but I have a daughter to settle. Have you some scheme for making them pay?'

He nodded. 'The machinery is old and inefficient, and some of the working practices ought to be improved. And the mills need a closer eye kept on them. The manager's a good man, but when the owner don't show up from year to year, everyone gets lackadaisical.'

Fanny looked dismayed. 'You don't propose I go up there?'

'No, I propose you sell your share of the mills to me,' Teddy said. 'They need capital investment, and I'd like to sink some money into them and get them up to scratch; but, frankly, I don't fancy stowing my blunt in them while I've only got a half-share. And divided ownership is inefficient. I want full control if I'm to take the risk.'

Charlotte said, 'I expect I'd feel the same if it were my blunt.'

'I don't doubt it, ma'am,' Teddy grinned. The duchess wasn't a bit stiff or difficult to talk to. He'd felt rather intimidated when he arrived and the butler walked him through acres of rooms stuffed with family portraits, but he almost felt he could have called this nice lady with the tired face 'Cousin Charlotte'.

Fanny said, 'I think I could part with the mills now without any pain. I shall never go back to Manchester, and it seems a waste to have them run badly for want of the right owner. But how will I know what's a fair price? It's Emma's fortune I have to think of.'

'I've no wish to cheat you or your daughter,' Teddy said. 'I would suggest that each of us appoints an independent valuer, and let them come to an agreement. But you oughtn't to make a decision about selling right this minute. Take your time to think about it, and consult your man of business first.'

Fanny smiled. 'You are a nice boy. But I think I'd sooner have the money to put safely in the Funds for Emma. What would she do with some old mills up in Manchester?'

'Would you want to sell Hobsbawn House, Fanny?' Charlotte asked. 'It's your childhood home.'

'I shall never go there again,' Fanny said, 'and what I love of it is all up here.' She tapped her brow. 'Do you think anyone would buy it?'

'Oh, certainly,' Teddy said. 'It's in a prime position. Some-one would pull it down and put up shops or offices in its place. That sort of thing is going on in the heart of most old cities. It's how I'm going to finance my scheme – by selling Makepeace House.'

'And where will you live then?' Charlotte asked, seeing that Fanny, for all her words, was rather shocked at the idea of Hobsbawn House being demolished.

'At the club,' he said promptly. 'A man can be very comfort-able there.'

'You may get married,' Charlotte said. 'You would want a house then.'

'Not me! I can't see the point of it, unless you have to marry money, or you want an heir. Well, I've money enough, my businesses to keep me amused, good fellows at the club for company, and I've no desire at all for children.'

'You might fall in love,' Fanny said, amused.

'Oh, I pray not!' Teddy said, with a pantomime of horror that made both women laugh.

As inevitably as the summer brings the swallows, Venetia's arrival in Bedford Square brought Tommy Weston and Lord Hazelmere to her doorstep like two rather wistful ghosts on a haunting. Emma seized Tommy's attention with an address that made Miss Morpurgo look at her thoughtfully.

Hazelmere was in plaintive mood. 'Have you heard, Edith

Wood is to marry Holford, after all the times she's turned him down? And Baby Sutton has offered for Cleveley's sister.'

'Dear me, what a lot to happen in August,' Venetia murmured. 'It's supposed to be the month without news. Which sister?'

'Frances.'

'The giantess? Poor Baby, he'll be completely overlaid – like a piglet, which I've always thought he rather resembles.'

Hazelmere didn't laugh. 'Everyone seems to be getting married,' he said discontentedly.

'Now, Beauty, don't start that! Besides, it isn't true. Look at Cocky Landsdowne: he's been run after ever since he could walk, without getting caught. By the by, did you know he's gone to the War Office, now Northbrook's got India? I wonder how he'll get on with Cardwell?'

'Hang Landsdowne! Hang Cardwell!'

'By all means! Then there's my sister Olivia – she's still single, and very pretty. Why don't you pay court to her?'

Hazelmere looked at her seriously. 'Would you mind it if I did?'

Venetia paused. Her life was full and fulfilling, her energies were all taken up with the furthering of her studies and potential career; she treated Hazelmere as an annoying thing that buzzed in her ear. And yet, the thought of the rest of her days with no Beauty arriving to tell her the gossip, take her to the theatre, admire her – the thought of Beauty making love to some other girl – no, it was not to be borne.

'Of course I'd mind,' she said lightly. 'You're very amusing when you aren't steeped in melancholy.'

Emma called across at that moment. 'Venetia, Tommy suggests we all go to Maidenhead on Sunday. Shall we? Oh do say yes!'

Venetia roused herself. 'Maidenhead? How *demi-monde*! Tommy, I'm ashamed of you!'

Marianne laughed. 'Come, do you think I'd agree to it if I thought there was to be any dalliance of that sort?'

'Oh, be assured there will be plenty of it,' Hazelmere said, cheering up at the prospect of a whole day with his adored. 'It doesn't follow, however, that we have to fall in with the customs of the natives. Lady Venetia, I'm accounted a fair hand with oars or pole. Could you fancy the decorative part of the, business? Sporting a parasol and trailing your fingers in the water?'

'Take your turn, Hazelmere,' Tommy said sternly. 'I mean to be showing off my prowess to the ladies.'

'A picnic!' Emma cried. 'Oh, and could we have tea at a hotel, on a lawn? I saw a picture of it in a magazine. I'm sure it was Maidenhead.'

The next day Venetia started work in the receiving room of St Agatha's. It was a large, bare hall on the ground floor, with its own door to the street. The plaster walls were painted grey, and it was furnished with nothing but rows of deal benches, and a strange leather-covered bed, like a *chaise-longue* with no back, on which the worst accident cases were laid down for examination. The room was never cleaned, and the benches and walls were grimy from contact with unwashed clothing, while the bare wooden floor had soaked up all manner of bodily fluids. The smell was terrible, and reminded Venetia of the wards in the military hospital in Berlin; but it was only on first entering each day that she noticed it. The nose can only bear so much before losing the power of distinction – which was why, she supposed, the poor never smelled themselves or each other.

The receiving room was in the charge of the 'residents'. Each week two senior students were appointed, who had to deal, under supervision of the dean, with all the surgical and accident cases coming into the hospital. During that time they had to remain on the hospital premises, sleeping in a room set aside for the purpose, and provided with their meals – porage for breakfast, bread and cheese and beer for lunch, and a good solid dinner in the evening.

The work was hard and the flow of patients never ended, only slackening in the early hours of the morning, between the last of the night revellers and the first of the workmen. St Agatha's being set in a poor quarter, there were always cases of infectious disease – typhoid, typhus, tuberculosis and dysentery – together with the other results of poor food and bad sanitation, and the constant stream of chronic infections about which nothing could be done. There were drunks who had fallen and hurt themselves, or had fought each other with fists, bottles and knives, prostitutes who had been beaten by their customers or pimps, or were dying in the last stages of venereal disease.

Long hours and unsafe conditions led to many accidents at work: ruptures, crushed fingers and toes, head wounds, eye injuries. Since the hospital backed onto the brewery, many came from there. Not a day passed without someone being carried in on a plank with the red bone ends of his broken legs sticking through his trousers, or hopelessly coughing blood from a stove-in chest. There were street accidents – people run down by traffic, or struck by objects falling from windows, roofs or scaffolding. There were domestic accidents – scaldings and burnings were the most frequent, followed by accidental poisoning, usually of children.

The standard of care given was low: there were so many cases, the time spent on each was usually no more than two minutes. Venetia found that the residents varied enormously in skill and intelligence, and in their attitude to her, but from the best of them she learned a great deal. The nurses were a tough and sometimes foul-mouthed body, but only the hardiest could survive in that environment, and their experience was so vast they often put the students right. One or two of the residents were hostile to her, but on the whole she was welcomed, if for no other reason than because she was another pair of hands to help stem the tide of work.

Strangely enough it was not the outpatients but the dissection work the dean arranged for her that caused the breach with Beauty Hazelmere. He came to visit one evening and found Venetia alone in the drawing-room; Miss Morpurgo and Emma were upstairs changing, having just come in. Venetia was curled up in the corner of the sofa with a book on her knee. For a moment she didn't see him in the doorway – the maid knew him well enough to accept his assurance that he could show himself up – and he was able to observe her as she sat in a cradle of firelight, which turned her cheeks to gold and her hair to flame. Usually so sleekly groomed, she looked just then softly ruffled, and very young.

'You'll ruin your eyes, reading by firelight,' he said to break the spell – she moved him too much for safety.

'Hello!' she said cheerfully, looking up. 'You're right. I rang for reading candles, but I suppose Lotty's forgotten. If only one were rich enough for gas lighting!'

She could be rich enough, if she married him; but nobly he refrained from saying so. 'Dare I hope it's a novel you're reading? Something improving, like *The Dairyman's Daughter*?'

'Do you realise if this were thirty years ago you'd be exhorting me not to waste my time with novels?' she said, inviting him by a gesture to take the other end of the sofa. 'Mama says they were considered works of the devil in her young day.'

Hazelmere was used to her language and didn't flinch. 'A book of sermons, then?'

'Foolish! It's Quain's *Elements*.'

'Elements?'

'*Elements of Anatomy*. I began dissection today. The dean arranged it so that we had the room to ourselves for an hour—'

Hazelmere was staring. 'Dissection? You don't mean – cutting up dead bodies?'

'Not a whole one, of course. That doesn't come until much later. Bodies aren't as easily come by as you might think.'

'Please don't joke,' he said painfully. 'Are you telling me Bentley actually allowed you to cut up human flesh?'

'Oh Beauty, don't be tiresome!' she exclaimed. 'Must we have the same argument time after time? You know what I'm doing.'

'I know about your treating the sick and I've come to bear it,' he said gravely, 'but this is something different – something much worse.'

'How is it worse to cut up dead bodies than live ones?' she said impatiently.

'I don't know, but it is. It's – indecent! Besides,' he went on hastily, seeing her anger start, 'you don't cut up living bodies.'

'I will do, when I do the surgery course, so you may as well get used to it.'

'No, surely not!' he was horrified. 'Surely they wouldn't make you do that? They can't be so – so completely without scruples as to ask a lady to perform a task so indelicate and revolting?'

'Oh, don't talk such rubbish!' she interrupted. 'What do you think I'm trying to do at the hospital? Learn to hold patients' hands while the men get on with the real work? My whole struggle every day is to do what the male students do, and not to be patted and put aside and protected. If you haven't understood that, you haven't understood anything!'

'Perhaps I'm very stupid—' he began, and she snapped at him.

'It seems you are.'

'Thank you,' he said, with dangerous gravity.

It was possible to lose him, she saw, and it made her angrier. 'You disapprove of what I'm doing, don't you?'

'You know I do,' he said quietly.

'Well, if you disapprove of that, you disapprove of me, and I don't care to be surrounded by people who are always judging me and finding me wanting. And I don't care to have the same boring argument every time we meet. So you can take your pious face—'

'Pious?' His nostrils flared.

'And boring!' she cried. 'Oh, go away and leave me alone!'

He stood up. 'You don't mean that?'

She cared for him, and she'd mind very much if he went away; but she was hurt and disappointed that he would not give her his unconditional support. 'I always mean what I say,' she said.

'Then – goodnight, Lady Venetia.' He bowed, and left her.

A moment later Marianne Morpurgo came hurrying in, still adjusting her cuffs. 'I thought Lord Hazelmere was here,' she said, surprised. 'Lotty said—'

'He was here, but he went,' Venetia said without looking up from her book.

'Oh.' Miss Morpurgo studied the bent head for a moment, thoughtfully. 'Will he be coming back?'

'No,' said Venetia, turning a page.

Marianne Morpurgo proved an undemanding chaperon. She saw her business, as far as Venetia was concerned, as simply living in the same house to appease convention. Venetia could come and go as she pleased, without Miss Morpurgo's ever asking a question – an arrangement Venetia thoroughly approved of. Emma, being so much younger, was another case, and Marianne never let her stir out of doors alone, though she was flexible about who the companion must be. But Emma's new-found interest in the women's movement turned out to coincide with Marianne's long-founded one, which gave them lots to talk about and plenty of things to do together. Marianne knew Mrs Fauncett, as well as other leading lights of the women's movement.

Venetia got used to coming home after a hard day at the hospital to find the drawing-room full of ladies in uncompromising hats talking hard about the inequalities of life, and drinking endless cups of tea. She wondered sometimes if Marianne were quite the right companion for Emma, for having been jilted by the man she loved, she had become something of a man-hater, and Emma was beginning to pick up a certain hardness of speech and boldness of manner that Venetia didn't think Aunt Fanny would like.

Tommy Weston was around as much as ever – perhaps more so, now that his parents were not in Town and he had given up his secretarial job. That he noticed the change in Emma was made clear one evening in the drawing-room when a group of the friends was arguing about higher education for women. Venetia was at the table in the window, trying to shut out the noise and concentrate on her dissection notes: Mr Bentley had given her a whole arm that afternoon. Tommy, sitting at the other side of the table, watching the group discontentedly, leaned across at last and spoke in a low voice to Venetia.

'I don't like to see Emma so suddenly up to everything,' he said. 'She's so young, it's not becoming.'

Venetia dragged herself away from the *supinator longus* and the *flexor carpi radialis* and looked over at her young cousin, who was laughing and talking nineteen to the dozen. 'One gets these enthusiasms at her age.'

'Yes, but why must she be enthusiastic about this?'

'I thought you were very keen on the woman question,' Venetia remarked.

'So I am, but I don't want to see Emma becoming one of those hard-faced females who stride about with their hands in their pockets and talk contemptuously about men,' said Tommy. '*You* aren't like that, in spite of the things you do. You manage to stay feminine and ladylike.'

'Much obliged to you,' said Venetia with a grimace. 'But I'm older.'

'That's my point,' said Tommy. 'I don't think Marianne is quite the thing, you know. Or, at least, she's not the right person to take care of Emma.'

Venetia put down her notes. 'Oh dear, don't you really think so? I wish you hadn't said that. If Emma is taken away, the whole scheme will fold and I shan't have a chaperon. And I don't think Emma would settle in the country again. Tommy, you don't really think there's any harm in it?'

He sighed, and said, 'I shall just have to provide a counter-influence myself. Perhaps if I take Emma out to exhibitions and driving in the Park and so on, it might give her something else to think about.'

'Of course it would,' Venetia said. 'What a good person you are, Tommo!' She wondered if Emma's attachment to him was somehow rubbing off, and making him fonder of her. It would be to everyone's benefit if he transferred his affections from Venetia to Emma; and stranger things had happened. After all, few men had the heart to go on loving with no encouragement; and he and Emma would deal excellently together.

'I don't know what we should do without you,' she said on an impulse of affection, laying a hand on his arm. 'You won't get disgusted with us unnatural females and abandon us, will you?'

'Of course not,' he said a little gruffly. He tried to pluck up courage to lay his hand over hers, and achieved it just as she removed hers and went back to her studying. He changed

448

his hand's direction in mid-stream and converted the gesture into a scratching of his nose, embarrassed even though no-one could have noticed. Why was he always so dashed awkward, he chided himself. If only he could be as easy with Venetia as he was with Emma!

One evening Lord Marwood came out of the carriage-maker's on Long Acre where he had been looking at a sporting vehicle he was toying with buying. He couldn't afford it, but if he could touch Alfreda for a little more juice, it occurred to him he could do pretty well out of making wagers on his own prowess, for he was a better driver than most of his acquaintances gave him credit for.

For the moment, however, his penury was such that his evening's entertainment would have to be as cheap as he hoped it would be cheerful. He thought he'd just trot up to the Oxford Music Hall and see what was what. The new female singer, Little Nelly Kelly, was quite an eyeful; and for half a crown he could get the best seat and a five-course dinner.

He crossed the road and cut down Mercer Street, his hat on the back of his head, swinging his cane and whistling 'I Don't Know What's To Do', Miss Kelly's latest song; but half-way along he stopped abruptly, whistle suspended, and then shrank back against the railings to make himself invisible. He could hardly believe his eyes, but the woman who had just come out of the main entrance to St Agatha's in a smart, close-fitting jacket trimmed with velvet and a black straw hat was Lady Venetia Fleetwood! What could she have been doing in there? She turned away from him up the street, heading for the Seven Dials, and he fell in behind at a discreet distance, his mind working.

Could it be? Could it possibly be? He had heard rumours that she was doing something unusual, and he remembered how in Berlin she had gone to the hospital every day to help nurse the wounded soldiers. Since it was impossible that she could have gone to St Agatha's as a patient, she must have gone there for some other purpose. As a benefactor she would not need to conceal herself or her purpose: she must have gone there as a nurse or – he remembered the fuss there had been over Miss Garrett – perhaps even a medical student.

The figure ahead of him was moving briskly through the increasing crowds with an ease that spoke of long experience. It was not the first time she had walked this route. He kept behind her, his height making it easy for him to keep in sight over the crowds the smart hat with its artificial flowers and purple grapes nodding with the movement of her agile walk. He tracked her all the way to Bedford Squre, watched her go in, and concluded from her manner that it was her home.

He stood sucking the head of his cane for a few moments, then turned and set off for the Oxford. It was well known that medical students were fond of music halls, and it shouldn't be difficult to find one who was willing to be befriended and would talk about the strange female at St Agatha's. Once he knew all about her, he would have the power he needed. He remembered her passionate response on the balcony of the palace in Berlin. If she was cut off from her family, she would be little use to him as an heiress; but *déclassée* she could still provide him with a great deal of pleasure.

CHAPTER TWENTY-FOUR

Henrietta's baby was born on the 9th of September, without any great difficulty: a girl, rather small, but seemingly healthy. Henrietta was disappointed when the midwife first told her that she had not had a boy, for she knew every man must want a son, and that to have a girl first was a kind of failure. But as soon as the tiny thing was placed in her arms, and she looked for the first time into her daughter's face, she fell in love. How could anything so small be so perfect? And how could anything so perfect deserve less than absolute love and devotion?

The first person outside the birth chamber to see the baby was Regina, who hurried in as soon as she was permitted, to congratulate Henrietta on a safe delivery. Rather gingerly she held her diminutive niece. 'I'm glad you had a girl,' she decided. 'Girls are nicer than boys.' She eyed her sister curiously. 'Was it really terrible – having her, I mean? It does seem awfully odd, when you think of it.'

'Don't think of it,' Henrietta advised. 'Not for a long time yet.'

'Well,' Regina equivocated, 'I am fifteen, so it might not be so very long, you know. What *was* it like?'

Henrietta shook her head. 'I can't tell you. There aren't words that could make you understand. No-one could have told me, beforehand. But no, it wasn't terrible. And it's worth it. Look, isn't she complete? Her tiny nails! And her ears!'

'I think she's sweet,' Regina said loyally. 'And I'm sure she'll get prettier soon. She looks like a little old man.'

'Nonsense!' said the midwife sternly. 'She's a bit crumpled, that's all.'

'Yes, like a butterfly when it comes out of the chrysalis,' Henrietta said. 'What a nice idea.'

'Well, ma'am, it's to be hoped that her father thinks so, whenever he comes to see her,' the midwife put in, taking the chance to voice her disapproval. Mr Fortescue was from home, visiting some friends in Oxford. A telegraph had been sent when Henrietta went into labour, but he had not returned nor replied to it, and the midwife thought this callousness of no mean order. Henrietta defended him, saying that probably the message had gone astray; but secretly she suspected that he had gone away to Oxford precisely because he knew the baby was due, and didn't want to be in the house when it happened.

It was true that there was nothing a gentleman could do to help; and probably it was very unpleasant to them, even if they didn't actually witness it. Mr Fortescue was dedicated to the life of the mind, and she was beginning to understand that he did not like things of the flesh to drag him down from that rarefied sphere he inhabited. Still, there was a hurt place in her heart, however much she reasoned with herself. It was his child as well as hers, and he ought to have been at hand for its birth.

Her life had been improved immeasurably by the advent of Regina. She wasn't sure who she owed that to: it seemed to be Dr Mansur who told Mr Fortescue that she needed company and suggested asking Regina to come and live with them; but who it was that put Dr Mansur up to it, she didn't know. She put aside any notion that Mansur had thought of it for himself.

Regina had been doubtful at first about changing the excitements of York for the quiet of a country village. But Lady Anstey had told her it was her duty, and Alice and Margaret had seemed envious that she was to be companion to a grown woman and no longer under the disadvantage of the schoolroom.

Henrietta had found her sister much improved by her stay with the Ansteys, more sensible, better informed, and less absorbed with herself and her appearance. They had been glad to see each other again, and had plenty of old times to talk over to keep them occupied while the last weeks of pregnancy passed quietly. Regina was flattered to find herself of such importance to her sister; and Henrietta promised her plenty of society once she was out of confinement. 'It's a very nice neighbourhood, and there's lots going on – parties and outings and so on. And some very nice young people. The Parke twins are about your age – I know you'll like them.'

Though Henrietta instructed Mrs Prosser to send a second telegraph to Mr Fortescue, announcing the birth of his child, he did not return. Instead a telegraph arrived to say that he was going directly from Oxford to his other parish at Richmond. Henrietta received this news in tense silence. It was hard to see this as anything but a deliberate avoiding of her, for it was not yet his time for Swale House – October was when he usually went. Besides, his journey would take him through York, only an hour from home. Surely any normal, eager husband would break off to visit his wife and child at such a time?

It was the thing that finally swung Mrs Prosser over to Henrietta's side. To the cook, who was very much Mr Fortescue's creature, she said only that it 'seemed queer the master should not come home first' when there had been no request from Swale House to bring forward the visit; but to the month-nurse she expressed herself more forcibly.

'I don't know when I've been more uncomfortable, seeing Mrs Fortescue so brave about it – putting on a good face, though her poor heart must be breaking, for she's devoted to him, you know, always has been. I never thought I would see the day when I would shake my head over anything the master did, but it has to be said, nurse, it's not right.'

She showed her feelings by addressing Henrietta with a greater warmth than ever before, and continually urging meals on her, bullying the cook – who had thought to have a lazy time of it until the master came home – into devising ever more elaborate dainties to tempt her. Henrietta found it hard after a week in bed to feel any appetite: she was bored, and wanted to get up, and go out. A beautiful Indian summer was laying its benign hand over the park beyond her window, and she knew from other years exactly how the soft air would smell, and how the fields and hedgerows would be full of rustling activity, of birds and animals surprised again by the sudden plenty of fat berries and hips, ripe seeds and nuts.

The month-nurse told her she must stay in bed for three weeks, in her chamber for another week after that, and within the house for a further two, before she could with decency venture abroad. But Henrietta felt perfectly well after ten days, and Regina's docile company was not enough to keep her occupied, especially when Regina could go out of doors for her walk every day, and came back frustratingly deficient in the sort of detailed description Henrietta craved. The nurse relented and let Henrietta out of bed after the ten days, but was so shocked at the idea of her leaving her chamber before three weeks *at the very least*, that Mrs Prosser took a hand, and said to Mrs Fortescue that if she would stay put, she would persuade Nurse to let her have a visitor.

So Mary Compton came, bringing with her such a breeze of wider spaces that Henrietta had never loved her more. She brought Henrietta flowers, Michaelmas daisies and some heads of blue hydrangea, and one perfect rose, separately, to put in a glass by her bedside. 'You look so well, I can't believe it,' she said. 'I've never seen a newly delivered mother before: I wasn't allowed a glimpse of Frederica until she was a month from the ordeal, so I assumed you would look like the survivor of a battle.'

'I feel perfectly well,' Henrietta said, 'only longing so to go out, you can't imagine.'

'That much I *can* imagine,' Miss Compton laughed. 'I am charged with all sorts of messages, from all the Parkes, and the whole of the village at large, but as they all amount to the same thing I shan't bother to remember them. But Jerome wishes me to convey to you his most particular congratulations and warm feelings, and to couch it in such terms as are appropriate, so consider it done, if you please, because I haven't an idea of what they might be.'

'Thank you,' Henrietta said, lowering her eyes.

'And he says,' Mary went on, noting it, 'that as soon as you are allowed out of your prison – no, those words are

454

mine, not his – but as soon as you want some fresh air, he is at your service to drive you and your sister anywhere you please. And me too, if you will have me along.'

Henrietta looked up, and saw in Miss Compton's face the knowledge of Mr Fortescue's neglect, and a feeling of bitterness against him came over her, that he should have exposed her to the speculation of outsiders. It was the first time she had ever had a critical thought about him, and it unnerved her. Was it possible for her to be right and him wrong about anything?

Fortunately there was no need for her to say anything in response, for the nurse came in with the baby, and demanded admiration for it. Miss Compton looked dutifully, and Henrietta, piqued, took her daughter into her arms and demanded more specific praise.

'I'm sure she's everything you say, but the truth is I don't much care for small babies,' Miss Compton said. 'When she's older, when she can learn to ride, I shall be her devoted slave, I promise.'

Henrietta only smiled, looking down into the small face. The child had uncrumpled, as the nurse promised, and she seemed to Henrietta the most beautiful thing that had ever lived. She was awake more, too, and looked back at Henrietta now with those strange dark-blue eyes, that she thought were like the eyes of a god, human in appearance but not in thought, seeing things mortals did not see. Miss Compton has never had a child, Henrietta thought, and therefore cannot understand this beauty and wonder. Twice in a very short time she had found herself making a judgement of people she had previously reverenced. Was she changing? Motherhood proverbially did change girls to women, but somehow she had never thought of proverbs or universal truths applying to her. She had always been Henrietta, the same from birth and to the end of time, as though she had stood outside life looking in. Now she had slipped into the stream, and was swimming along with everyone else. She was going to be a real person from now on; and the thought did not displease her.

Mr Fortescue cut short his visit to Swale House. Their surprise at seeing him could have been due to nothing more than his being before his usual tine, but he chose to see it as a criticism of his not going home to see his wife and new child. He told himself firmly that it was his imagination: Mrs Allen had no particular liking for Henrietta, or for his matrimonial state. He told himself they did not stare at him, or talk about him in the kitchen in low, disapproving tones.

Women had babies every day of the week, and gentlemen of affairs did not customarily notice their offspring until they reached the age of reason. That's what he told himself: but the fact was that his experience in the business was very small and third or fourth hand at best. Most of his friends were bachelors, and they were not, in any case, the sort of friends who would discuss such personal matters.

He knew that Henrietta would have expected him to come home, and that she would be hurt that he had not. A child. A baby – a daughter! He didn't know how he felt about that. The possibility of breeding had been something purely academic to him when he married Henrietta: a logical possibility, but not realised in any imaginative way. He saw now that he had not realised anything about his marriage. He had been as much a victim of unregulated fancy as any woman. He had been 'in love' in precisely the way he had always despised in other people, having no regard to reality.

He had devoted his life to reading about classical heroes and heroines – Paris and Helen, Antony and Cleopatra, Troilus and Cressida – and knew all about undying passion, the love that endured to the grave, when it was framed in deathless prose. He had loved Henrietta in that way, and seen her as the tremulous Andromeda, gauze-draped, upon the sea-lashed rock; white arms, fragile as coral, reaching out in appeal, a delicate hand starfished against the wine-dark sea.

But in fact, like any ordinary fool in love, he had invested the object of his passion with qualities she did not have. He had seen young men in drawing-rooms (and not-so-young men, for that matter) hang simpering and glazed of eye on the words of tawdry young women plying arts too transparent to cover the base animal underneath. He acquitted Henrietta of having applied such arts – she had, at least, been artless; but he had imagined a great soul and a noble mind, because that was what he wanted.

And what had he now? A human, earthly, earthbound woman. Women had no soaring, no intellect, no urge to rise, to attain: they were concerned only with their incestuous, myopic view of themselves, suffocatingly obsessed with their vile bodies. Oh, their bodies! Pregnancy, childbirth, were the gross extreme at the other end of the universe from the beauty of literature, of art, of devotion, the place where he wanted always to be. It was, he thought, the most sardonic of God's jests against mankind: childbirth was the punishment inflicted after Eden, for Eve's sin; but God had not removed from Man the desire to be winged. The casual, cruel power of God, who could create things of staggering beauty with such ease, and yet enjoyed a humour as black and glittering as obsidian, was something Fortescue had been acquainted with all his life. It was this God of barbed beauty that demanded his absolute, and yet bitter, love and devotion.

For two weeks at Swale House Mr Fortescue shut himself away in dark musing; and at the end of that time emerged, like a man recovering from fever, to the acknowledgement that he lived in the real world, and in that world he had a wife and now a child from whom he could not escape or be severed. He wished with a brief and instantly suppressed passion that Henrietta had died in childbirth; and then he knew that he must go home, pay the formal visit to her that convention, the world, his neighbours and household would expect, and find a way to live with the situation.

And even as he thought it, he realised that she had been very little trouble to him in the time they had been married, and that, with some careful adjustment, a comfortable *modus vivendi* could be achieved. All that he had lost, now he was able to think about it rationally, was his dream. Ah, but that was such a loss!

Andrews and Mrs Prosser were waiting for him in the hall as he stepped through the door of the rectory, Andrews with his usual schooled indifference of expression, Prosser with a look of faint, cool resentment.

He handed his gloves to Andrews. 'Where is Mrs Fortescue?' he asked.

Prosser answered, 'She's in her room, sir,' and managed to imply that if he had done as he ought, he would have known where she was.

Fortescue returned her a look as cold as her own. 'Go and inform her that I shall do myself the honour of stepping up and speaking to her in a quarter of an hour's time.'

Mrs Prosser may have thought he might have asked if his wife wanted to see him at all, but she did not dare say so, or disobey a direct order. He had meant to give Henrietta time to prepare herself – adjust her dress and so on – but as she was already dressed, the quarter-hour was just enough to discompose her. She arranged herself on the *chaise-longue*, in a chair, her hands in her lap, on the chair arms; touched her hair, rearranged the folds of her gown, licked her lips, folded her hands in her lap again. The clock ticked impassively, indifferent as Andrews to her anxiety.

And then there was a tap at the door, and he came in. She had recreated him extensively in her imagination over the past few weeks, but now here he was looking exactly as he had always looked, and her ungoverned heart jumped at the sight of him. For a fleeting second she thought how it would be if he crossed the room in three strides and snatched her to his breast, kissed her and told her he loved her. She would have died for him gladly if he had done so.

But he closed the door precisely and stood before her, his eyes not quite meeting hers, and said, 'I trust I find you well?'

An enormous calm came over her. 'Thank you, I am very well,' she said. 'Too well to be still in my room, but the nurse insists.'

'I believe there are conventions about such matters,' he said. He cleared his throat, disturbed by even so tangential a reference to the business he had run from.

'Won't you sit down?' Henrietta said. There was a chair matching hers on the other side of the small round table, and he took it, so that they faced each other across the table top. Behind them the window was partly open and the soft air blew the muslin curtain fitfully. He did not say anything for a long time, sitting studying his hands, which were clasped together on the table. She looked at them too, and saw the loose skin over the knuckles and the slight chalkiness of the nails – not a young man's hands. She remembered briefly and involuntarily, as a lightning flash illuminates the unseen country at night, those hands on her body as she lay sprawled naked on her bed in the sea of her hair. The memory drove a sharp pang deep into her vitals. She drew a breath, and dared to look at his face.

She had loved it so long, and perhaps never really seen it, for looking at him had been like looking at the sun. Now she saw the real, human man of flesh and blood: his colourless skin, the slackness under the eyes, the slight reddening over the cheekbones. With the magnification of this new scrutiny, she observed the creases of his upper lip, the faint silver of the nascent bristle coming through on his cheeks and chin since his morning's shave. She saw the loose skin under his chin, the deep frown lines on his brow, the intricate convolutions of his ear: her husband, the man she was bound to live with and serve for the rest of her life. She had loved a dream, a god who walked the earth in mortal disguise. She saw an ordinary man, no longer young, much troubled; and she loved him too. It was a very different love – not a helpless and fearful adoration, but a love that saw clearly and accepted, a love that gave rather than hoping to receive. She felt – yes, it was true – almost *motherly* towards him. Towards Mr Fortescue!

He looked up at last, and she did not flinch from eye contact. He seemed, she thought, rather puzzled as to what he should say or do.

'Well,' he said. 'So – so I am to congratulate you on a safe delivery? I trust you have given thanks to Him, in whose hands you were, for the happy outcome?'

'Yes,' she said simply. 'And I hope you did, too.'

Her directness disconcerted him. 'Indeed, indeed. God is very good.' He cleared his throat again. 'So you have a daughter.'

'*We* have a daughter,' she said. 'Nurse will bring her in a moment. She is very beautiful.'

'I'm sure she is,' he said awkwardly.

'You must decide on a name for her,' Henrietta said, 'and then we must have a christening, with a party here afterwards. I hope you will perform the ceremony. Mr Catchpole does not like me, and thoroughly disapproves of having a baby in the house.'

He looked at her quizzically. 'You have changed.'

'Have I?'

'You speak your mind so boldly,' he concluded.

'I'm a mother now,' she said.

'So you are.' It seemed both amusing and piercingly sad. The pure and innocent child he had married was now this amiable woman, whom he did not know, and could not love.

She must have sensed something of his thoughts, because she said abruptly, 'What is to happen now?'

'Now?' He pretended not to understand her. He could not talk as women talked of emotions and feelings and such things. 'I must go back to Richmond tomorrow. When I return, you may have the christening. Arrange it with Mrs Prosser as you please.'

'You're going back to Richmond? When you've only just come from there – and before that, Oxford?'

'I have business to perform,' he said, frowning. 'It is not for you to question what I do and where I go.'

'No,' she agreed, but she still looked at him steadily, without a blush for his rebuke. 'But it seems to me your business is all that you care for. Why did you marry me? You are never with me.'

'A man's life and a woman's are separate things,' he said.

'Even when they are married?'

'Of course,' he said, and his confidence returned, for this was something he must know more about than her. 'A man has matters of great import to occupy him: he must go out into the world and do battle. A woman's life takes place wholly in the home.'

'The home,' she repeated. 'My all in all is to be these four walls?'

'A home is more than the fabric of the house,' he said sharply; and lest she ask him for clarification on that point, which it would have puzzled him to give, he added, 'You have a child. A woman's greatest contribution to the human condition is the rearing of her children.' She said nothing, as if she thought he had not finished. 'So you see, my dear Mrs Fortescue, we each have our separate sphere in which to exercise our different abilities, and that is the way it has always been. If you had other expectations, I am sorry, but it was the fault of your upbringing. Husbands and wives in our stratum of society do not huddle together like pigs in a sty, constantly tumbling over each other's concerns. That idea, I'm afraid, is the product of vulgar and sentimental novels.'

'I don't read novels,' Henrietta said calmly, which he knew was true. 'I don't know what I expected. But I understand now. I shall not trouble you again, sir. But will you answer me one last question?'

He eyed her unwillingly, afraid of what it might be. 'Very well,' he said.

He was right to be wary. 'Do you love me?' she asked.

For a scalding moment he remembered her in the garden when he had proposed to her, her frozen velvet cheek turned up for his kiss; and in the parlour at Swale House the night he had first read to her, exalted with love; and the silk of her naked flesh under his hand, the hot, troubled look in her eyes when he ravished her. But it was too much to bear: the reel of images burned through and disintegrated, like paper in a furnace, leaving no trace.

'I have towards you every proper feeling of a man for his wife,' he said. Did she sigh, just a little? He was relieved from hearing what her response might be by the entrance of the nurse with the baby in her arms.

'Here's your daughter, sir,' Nurse said, perhaps a little pointedly. 'Would you like to hold her?'

Fortescue would have refused indignantly, but he was given no choice, for the bundle was thrust upon him, and he took it in pure reflex. He had held babies before, of course, many times – he had christened a hundred of them – and his arms knew what to do. He reverenced them theoretically as the vessels of new souls, but in reality regarded them as unpleasant, moist, snuffling, malodorous animals. But the first touch of this one was different. He looked down into the small, calm face, and felt a shiver deep inside him, of something in him that before had only thrilled to the sound of great literature or great music. The nacreous skin, soft and clear as a river-washed pearl, the tender rose-coloured lips, the ultramarine eyes, were an expression of absolute beauty, of a soul not yet tainted by the flesh it inhabited. And *he* had made her – with God's help. He had only ever made words before, never anything tangible. He had loved the beauty of the prose he created, and was proud of his skill; but this was something so infinitely more complex and beautiful he felt a great tremor of love and fear. She was perfect, and given to him to keep from danger. How could he save her from the world? He touched the miniature hand, and the fingers curled round like soft, clinging tentacles, blindly trusting, demanding protection.

Henrietta spoke, intruding on his moment of perfect communion, dragging him back to reality. 'She ought to have a name, sir. Will you choose one?'

With one last covert look at the little face, he gave her back to the nurse with a fair appearance of indifference. 'Elizabeth,' he said, 'is as good a name as any.'

The christening was held on the 25th of October, when the baby was just over six weeks old. The day was unseasonably warm, and the party afterwards spilled out of the french windows of the rose drawing-room onto the terrace and lawn. Henrietta had invited everyone, neighbours, family, and Mr Fortescue's academic friends, wanting Elizabeth to have the best possible launching into the world. Mrs Prosser had put her best foot forward and persuaded the cook to do the same; and he had hardly needed encouragement to show off his prowess in a great decorated cake. The children from the village school, of which Fortescue was a governor, came in white dresses to dance a country dance on the terrace, to the accompaniment of two fiddles and a fife, and there were speeches, and gifts, and a great deal of champagne.

George and Alfreda sent their excuses, and Henrietta had not really expected them, but Teddy was there, and so was almost everyone else she had invited – including all the dry scholars who had come out of wonder that the aesthetic and celibate Fortescue had burst forth like a dead stick into blossom. There was such a crowd, Jerome Compton's presence went unnoticed by the host.

'I hope this marks the end of your imprisonment,' he said pleasantly to Henrietta. 'It seems unfortunate that you should have missed such a fine autumn. Perfect riding weather.'

'Oh don't tease me! Don't you think I've seen every day out of the window what I've been missing? And even now the nurse has left dire warnings that I should not venture on horseback for at least six months, if ever again, indeed.'

'I can't get over the change in you,' Jerome wondered. 'You were such a little mouse before, and now here you are challenging the good conventions of motherhood!'

'Motherhood is what's changed me,' Henrietta said. 'She is lovely, isn't she?'

'Isn't who?'

'The baby, of course!'

'Oh! Yes, a very fine specimen, as far as I can tell – but I warn you I'm no expert.'

'Then you must take my word for it,' Henrietta said promptly. 'And now she is properly launched, tomorrow I shall begin my new life.'

'That sounds very alarming. What do you mean to do?'

'I don't know yet. But it will be different.' She thought of the long months of her pregnancy, walled up without company, like an ancress, but not of her own choosing; and before that all the months, with Mr Fortescue and before that with Alfreda, when she had waited passively on someone else's will, afraid to move or speak for fear of doing or saying the wrong thing. How silly she had been! She felt the strength of herself, like a flower unfurling, like a wind rising. There was so much she could do, now that she had decided to decide for herself. She didn't yet know what those things might be, but she was going to find out. The mother of a miracle like Elizabeth must have power to perform any mere mortal act she chose.

Jerome watched the thoughts fleeting through her face

like cloud shadows running across the fields. 'If it were not impertinent to suggest it, I would recommend that any new life ought to begin with a plan of serious reading.'

'Reading!'

'Don't look so appalled,' he said, amused. 'It isn't as dull as you might think. In fact, it may be the most exciting activity of all. Consider what ground it covers, both in space and time – dimensions immeasurable.'

'The only proper book I've read is *Pilgrim's Progress*,' Henrietta confessed. 'But you see . . .' she hesitated, and with a flash of insight he understood that her difficulty was not disinclination but the fact that the library was Mr Fortescue's territory.

'We have a collection of books at home – Mary and I,' he said diffidently. 'Nothing like the rector's, of course, but all well-loved favourites. We would be pleased to lend you anything you fancied – and to guide your choice, if you did not think that a presumption.'

She thanked him, pleased with the idea. 'It would be like visiting your favourite places and being shown the nice things about them. I wish I could show you mine, but they're real places, and they're all at Morland Place.' She thought suddenly of Old Caleb, sitting on his knoll and gazing out over the open moor where the sheep were spread, like mackerel clouds across a green sky. A stab of homesickness came and went.

He said, 'But of course there must be outdoor things, as well as reading. The day will come when you are able to ride again—'

'Oh, I don't listen to Nurse's old wives' tales,' she said firmly. 'I am perfectly well enough now to begin, and I mean to, first thing tomorrow.'

'Then perhaps you'll allow Mary and me to call for you?' he said quickly. 'It would be an honour to attend your first horseback venture. Does your sister ride too? I'm sure Mary would lend her other horse.'

'That would be kind. I must speak to Mr Fortescue about getting a horse for Regina.' She amazed even herself with those words. 'And another thing: Ginger has been idling about in a field for long enough. I mean to break her in again, and make a decent horse of her. I know I can do it. I'm sure she's only difficult because she's been badly treated in the past. Poor thing, she ought to be given another chance.'

'It would be an interesting project,' Jerome said cautiously, thinking of the danger to her.

'Yes, and I need a project,' she said.

'Would you consider accepting some help? There is a fine schooling paddock at the Red House, and Sir Richard's head man, Tobin, is very good with nervous horses.'

Henrietta smiled. 'If Sir Richard doesn't mind, I'd be happy to work on her there, under Tobin's eye – and under yours, I've no doubt.'

He raised his hands in a little gesture of wounded innocence. 'I wouldn't dream of trying to impose my will on you, ma'am.'

'Yes you would, in an instant, if you thought you knew better than me!' she laughed. 'But I shall give as good as I get. I was brought up with horses and I've ridden all my life. You may give your opinion, however. I'm strong enough to withstand that!'

'I think you are strong enough to withstand anything,' Jerome said.

And she thought, yes, I am, I really am. I shall ask for what I want, and I shall have it; I'm not afraid of Mr Fortescue, or anyone. It was the end of childhood, and the beginning of being grown up, she thought, and there was a sadness in that, because it also meant the end of illusion. But the world before her was much bigger than the one behind her, and she would know more of it, and possess what she knew.

In February 1873 Southport House was opened up again, and the duke and duchess came up from Ravendene for Augusta's first Season. Emma covered her disappointment that she was not sharing it by telling Venetia in offhand tones that she really didn't want to be brought out in the old-fashioned way because it was an insult to women to parade them like cattle in a market for men to pick over.

But Miss Morpurgo said privately to Venetia, 'It's just as

well Emma is younger than your sister, because the duke would never have consented.'

Miss Morpurgo was right. The duke was grateful to Fanny for keeping Venetia out of trouble, but there was no getting away from the fact that she was an adulteress and Emma was illegitimate. Fine people to associate with his daughter at her come-out! It would have been disastrous for Augusta to have the top people stay away from her ball, and not invite her to their parties; it would harm Olivia too. There was trouble enough as it was, with some of the leading military families still not having forgiven him for the abolition of purchase; and he had to reason long and hard with Charlotte to make her understand why Venetia must not come to Southport House at any time.

Charlotte protested. 'You let her come to Ravendene.'

'You must see that it's different in the country.'

'Then I'll visit her at Bedford Square.'

'You mustn't do that, either. It would be known about instantly.' He read her expression and said impatiently, 'This is Augusta's time. Don't sacrifice her advantage for the sake of defying me.'

Charlotte coloured. 'I don't object to things to annoy you, but because I think they're wrong.'

Oliver passed that. 'At all events, Society has its rules and Augusta will have to live by them, so let's give her the best chance we can. I know you want to see Venetia,' he added more kindly, 'but wait until the summer. A few months won't make any difference, will they?'

Harry and young Lord Batchworth, who were at Christ Church together, were to get permission to come down to London to attend Augusta's ball. Marcus, settling in to a life in the Blues and finding his own easygoing personality was making him friends in spite of his father's crimes against the army, was resuming normal relations with his family, and would be at the ball too. It was only Venetia who would be absent, and Charlotte minded it very much, though she did her best to hide her feelings for Augusta's sake.

Augusta had grown up almost as pretty as Olivia, and with

a more winning personality. She would have no shortage of partners, it was plain, and would be able to take her pick from the beaux of the Season. As soon as the knocker went up on the door, it was never still. With Olivia and Augusta both at home – both pretty young women with good dowries – there was every reason for unattached gentlemen to call, and where they were, other young ladies would naturally congregate. Had Venetia been been able to observe the 'morning callers' she would have been amused to see Fred Paston's contortions as he tried to pay court to both sisters at once. In fact, many of her former beaux went to try their luck with the younger Fleetwood sisters, as Weston, who had come up to Town on business and called at Southport House, reported.

'But Olivia seems to assume that any courting that goes on is directed towards Gussie. The most accomplished flirts in Society leave her cold. Your mother says that since she went into waiting she lives for nothing but her court life. Everything outside the Household is a mere shadow to her.'

'But she's only in waiting three months of the year,' Venetia protested.

'Yes, and your mother was distressed at the thought of such a pretty girl becoming a vestal virgin; but it seemed to me that Olivia's conversation was notable for the number of times a certain Mr Du Cane came up in it. I wonder if her dreamlike air of not being quite with us is entirely due to her love affair with the Queen.'

'Who,' Venetia asked, frowning, 'is Mr Du Cane?'

'Charlie Du Cane,' Weston enlightened her. 'He's one of the equerries. A very decent fellow – quiet, but with a nice sense of humour. One of Ponsonby's acolytes, and all the better for it. He's a little older than her – early thirties – but he'd make her a splendid husband.'

'Husband? Has it gone so far, then?' Venetia asked in surprise.

'My dear child, I don't know,' Weston said. 'All I'm doing is some surmising based on your sister's never-very-expansive conversation. Whether he is in love with her or not I can't tell you, but I can say he's the last man to lead a girl on to

467

false expectations. *She* certainly seems more than passingly interested in *him*. Pining to get back to him. I only hope,' he added with a frown, 'that she isn't after him solely because being married to a permanent household officer would allow her to stay at Court all the time. I should hate such a decent fellow to be taken in.'

After a moment of astonishment, Venetia realised she was being roasted, and laughed. 'Well, I hope it does come to something, and he does marry her,' she said. 'Poor Livy's life seems horribly dull to me as it is.'

Weston almost asked about her and Hazelmere, but forbore. Instead he said, 'What about that cub of mine. Is he still proving more useful than annoying to you?'

'Tommy's a good friend,' Venetia said firmly. 'And, much as I hate to admit it, it *is* a comfort to have a man's protection. Not that we've needed protection, but it's nice to know that it's there in the background, should one need to call on it.'

'And what about little Miss Emma?' Weston asked shrewdly. 'Is her crush reciprocated, or does it run in one direction only?'

'Oh, Emma's just a little girl,' Venetia said.

'Not so little any more,' Weston said. 'Sixteen is old enough to be in love – and one can only admire her taste in turning her affections on my son. But I can't tell what Tommy thinks about it.'

'Should you mind?' Venetia asked curiously.

Weston hesitated a telling moment. 'It would be nice to have him married and settled. His mother would like to be a grandmother before it's too late.'

'But?'

Weston sighed just perceptibly. 'She's not what I would have chosen for him,' he admitted. 'With his background he can't be too careful about his connections.'

'Tommy doesn't think like that.'

'Of course not – that's what parents are for, to think the sensible, unattractive things that need thinking. But on the other hand, I can't afford to wait much longer. I shall be seventy if I live to my birthday, and if I'm to see him married, I shall have to take what I can get by way of a daughter-in-law.'

'I never know how seriously to take you,' Venetia complained.

'That's my great charm,' said Weston.

CHAPTER TWENTY-FIVE

Venetia had no leisure to mind about being denied Southport House, or being exiled from Augusta's come-out. Her second year was proving harder than her first. The work was more exacting, both physically and mentally. Her time in the receiving room had been enormously valuable both in giving her clinical experience, and in hardening her to the unsavoury aspects of the work. She could now face everything that was put before her unflinchingly; and she found the lectures in the principles and practice of medicine easy to absorb.

The lectures in descriptive anatomy and physiology were harder, because they related to nothing she knew in practice, and the Latin terms were difficult to remember. It sometimes seemed that every new muscle and bone she committed to memory pushed another one out. To add to her difficulties, since Christmas Mark Darroway was no longer helping her, his own studies now taking up too much of his time; though she suspected there was pressure on him from his fellows at the Middlesex not to be siding with the enemy.

Practical anatomy and dissection classes had begun, and though the dean had managed to give her one or two private lessons before the term began, the demonstrator, Dr Clarke, supported by some of the students, declined to have her in the class.

'It is undesirable in every respect that ladies should come into contact with such foul scenes,' he said, 'and especially in the presence of members of the opposite sex. Indeed, it is immodest and unbecoming in any lady to request such a thing. It would unfit her for the sphere of usefulness for which God has designed her.'

And the students signed a memorandum which they presented to the dean, saying that it was unfair that they should be handicapped by the presence of a female, which would inevitably cause the lectures and demonstrations to be diluted and curtailed out of deference to her modesty.

'But I don't want anything to be altered for my sake,' Venetia protested when the dean showed her the memorandum. 'Quite the contrary. I want to learn *exactly* what the students learn.'

Bentley shrugged. 'Unfortunately, my hands are tied. I cannot oblige the demonstrator to take you; and if the students are against it, it would be unwise of me to continue your private lessons. I'm sorry.'

This was a great blow to Venetia. Practical anatomy was essential, and a large part of the course.

'You must understand that it is the students' fees that pay for the medical school,' he went on, 'and if they withdraw, we close. It's only a minority of them who signed the notice,' he added, to comfort her. 'Many of the students support your efforts. But the minority have influential parents and friends. You will have to find some other way to get in your anatomy practice.'

It was not the only problem: the midwifery lecturer, Mr Sennett, had refused point blank to have her in his class or on his ward rounds. 'It's madness,' she complained to Marianne at home. 'He wants to prevent a woman from studying the one thing that only a woman can do. I had thought it would be the one part of the course no-one could object to my studying.'

Sir Frederick, who met her in the corridor soon after the ban became common knowledge, tried to explain. 'Midwifery was the one area of medicine where, historically, women were accepted. Having so recently got them out of it and slammed the door, the luminaries of the College of Physicians are anxious to keep them out. They fear you might be the thin end of the wedge.'

Her beginning her second year had polarised the staff and the students in their attitude to her. No-one expected her to persevere: that she had, won her the admiration of some, and they were now firm in their support of her. But those who disapproved of her activities were angry that their tolerance had not been rewarded, as it should have been, by her giving up. From now on, their opposition would be more open.

So in addition to the work and study, Venetia now had to spend time canvassing other hospitals and schools to see if anyone would take her on for the missing classes.

There was little time for social activities. Tommy Weston continued to call to try to divert Emma's mind, and make Venetia love him. As the weather improved he sometimes persuaded Venetia to go out for a drive with him on a Sunday, or took all three ladies for an outing, to the river or the countryside, or to some notable spot. In the evenings she would hardly ever go out, having too much studying to do, and preferring, if she was not working, quiet conversation by the fireside to anything livelier.

But Marianne warned her that the life of a recluse would make her dull, and said there was nothing more likely to jeopardise her success in her field than being perceived as a grim bluestocking with only one topic of conversation. 'You need to broaden your horizons,' she said. 'Why don't you come to meetings with me and Emma sometimes? I'm sure you'd find them interesting.'

Eventually Venetia allowed herself to be persuaded; and both Emma and Tommy were delighted to have her along. She was doubtful herself as to what use it would be to her, and suspected the people she met would be the very sort of dull women with hobby-horses Marianne didn't want her to resemble. But though there were some women like that, there were others who were well-educated, cultured and amusing, and who carried their obsessions lightly. And, to her surprise, there were a lot of men at the meetings, too: eminent men who came to give lectures, but also some who came to listen and mingle.

'Did you think I was the only man in England who cares about women's rights?' Tommy asked her when she commented on it.

'Well, I did, rather,' she confessed. 'And I half wonder

472

whether some of them don't just view it as a way to meet females without too much competition!'

Marianne Morpurgo had a wide acquaintance within the field, and through her Venetia met Barbara Bodichon, a cousin of Miss Nightingale, who knew her mother: she had worked with her and Cavendish's father over the Divorce Act of 1857. Mrs Bodichon was secretary to the Women's Suffrage Committee and tried to get Venetia interested in the idea of the vote for women, without much success.

She also met Emily Davies, whose particular interest was higher education for women. She and some associates, including Mrs Bodichon, had started a college for women in a house at Hitchin in 1869, with six girl students. It had thrived to such an extent that in 1871 a public subscription had been got up for a proper building to house it, on a piece of land at Girton, two miles from Cambridge, to which it was about to move.

Venetia found the meetings generally interesting and the lectures sometimes stimulating. It did, she acknowledged, broaden her mind to see her struggle to become a doctor in the wider context of other women's struggles. But the world of the 'woman question' was the one in which her personae, of Lady Venetia Fleetwood and Miss Fleet, met and overlapped, and she was disconcerted to discover how many people knew that they were one and the same. It began with Mrs Bodichon, who knew her as Lady Venetia Fleetwood, asking her to contribute an article on her experiences as a medical student to the *Englishwoman's Journal*, a radical paper she partly financed. Venetia refused the request quickly and firmly, imagining how popular that would make her at St Agatha's; but asked Mrs Bodichon how she had known that it was she.

Mrs Bodichon looked surprised. 'I didn't know it was meant to be a secret. "Miss Fleet" is not much of a disguise, is it?'

'The very fact that I use a false name, I should have thought—' Venetia began.

Mrs Bodichon gave a quick, tight smile. 'Oh, to the world in general, perhaps, but not to us, surely? There are few secrets in our small world. You are quite a heroine to our circle, especially to the younger ones. They bask in your reflected glory, you know.'

Venetia was not pleased about this. It annoyed her to have her efforts, which took so much personal energy and will, subsumed into some larger and more general movement, and particularly to have them laid claim to by women who had never done anything for themselves. And further, from what she had seen, she had little trust in the discretion of the movement's disciples. If her secret were as widely known as this, how long could it be kept from the medical world, and how soon would it be before the sort of scandal broke that her father had been afraid of?

But before any of those fears could materialise, something disturbing happened from an unexpected direction. One evening she went to a meeting of the Society for Promoting the Employment of Women, dragged out against her will by Marianne and Emma. It was cold, wet and blustery, March going out like a lion, and the proper sort of night to stay at home by the fire.

'But that's what everyone will think, and there'll be a poor turn-out,' Marianne said, 'and it will be dreadful to let down Dr Harrison, when it's taken almost a year to persuade him to come and talk.'

'And it's at Mrs Beck's house, which is only in Rathbone Place, hardly any distance,' Emma put in.

'What will he talk about?' Venetia asked reluctantly. 'Is he a medical doctor?'

'Oh, no, he's a doctor of divinity,' said Marianne. 'He's talking about Women in the Scriptures. Mrs Beck is hoping that afterwards we can get a debate going about the Church's rôle in determining women's status. It's a very important subject.'

'Yes, I quite see that,' Venetia said. Several of the refusals she'd had from anatomists to her request for tuition had mentioned God, Eve, Adam's rib and such related topics. 'All the same—'

'Oh do come,' Emma urged. 'It will be so dull without you, because Tommy isn't coming. Mrs Beck sent a note

474

this afternoon asking us especially, because of not letting Dr Harrison down, so we have to go. *Please*, Venetia.'

So Venetia went; and, as she was being divested of her wraps in the hallway, the first person she saw through the door of the drawing-room, talking to Mrs Fauncett, was Lord Marwood. He saw her, too, and as soon as she entered the room he approached her with a deep bow and a friendly smile.

'Lady Venetia, what a pleasure! This evening seems brighter already.'

Venetia looked at him with blank surprise. 'Lord Marwood! What are you doing here?'

'My dear ma'am, it's a public meeting, though held in a private house,' he said, seeming amused at her bluntness. 'I was given to understand all were welcome.'

'All who are interested in the subject,' she said. 'I hope you haven't come to sneer.'

'What *do* you think of me? I shall be on my best behaviour, as always. Besides, I'm told Dr Harrison is a notable speaker.'

'I wonder who told you that?'

'You wonder, rather, who introduced me to the Society,' he corrected. 'It was Mrs Fauncett who brought me. I understand she is a relation of yours.'

'A distant cousin. Is she a relation of yours as well?'

'An acquaintance, merely – a good one, though recently made. We share a keen interest in the advancement of women's rights. Why do you look so sceptical? It's not polite to doubt my bona fides so openly – though I admit it does make you more interesting than conventional politeness would.'

She drew back a little. 'Why should you suppose I wish to be interesting?' she said coolly.

'Ah, no, don't frost me! I thought we were old friends, since we saved each other from boredom in Berlin. I expressed myself clumsily. Everything about you interests me; but of course I don't imagine for an instant that you do anything with the intention of affecting the world one way or the other. There was never a more unselfconscious creature in existence. There! Is that handsome enough for you?'

She could not help smiling, though there was a suspicion at the back of her mind that being amused by him was dangerous. Whatever he said, she didn't believe he was here because he was interested in women's rights. She had no doubt he was pursuing some ulterior motive. Probably he was interested in one of the women here tonight; and as she thought it, she remembered with an inward shiver the time he had kissed her on the terrace at the palace. The feelings he had aroused had shocked and unsettled her, and she had taken good care never to be in a position where they could be unleashed again. She amused herself by trying to determine, as he chatted to her, which female he was after. Marianne and Emma joined her, and he was charming to them, altering his tone subtly to suit each of them as he addressed her – the complete chameleon. Emma was obviously impressed with his looks and address, and was flutteringly attracted – though being in love with Tommy, it was a superficial attraction. To Marianne he spoke only of the Cause, and in such serious, sincere tones that she took him for a true believer and accepted him on such instantly intimate terms that he might have been her or Emma's brother.

When the lecture began, Marwood helped all three of them to seats, and then took up his position at Venetia's side. The talk was *very* dull, and Venetia listened with a mixture of pain and indignation that she had been dragged away from the fire on a horrible March evening for this. There was, however, a kind of unconscious humour in Dr Harrison's delivery, for his deep feelings about the place of women in the world was obviously at odds with his intellectual decision that they were men's equals. The contortions into which he twisted his ideas and his grammar to avoid the conflict were the only amusement she got from his talk. It was soon evident that Lord Marwood felt the same. His sidelong looks and suppressed smiles were for her, his co-conspirator; and when the applause at the end began, he leaned over to whisper, 'I once saw a man at a fairground, an Indian fakir, who could knot up his body in the same miraculous way that our good Dr Harrison knots up his mind. He was called the Human Turkshead.'

476

'Ssh!' said Venetia, and bit her lip to stop herself laughing while she applauded harder than ever.

After the talk, Mrs Beck served refreshments, and the members and audience mingled and chatted. Marianne and Mrs Fauncett were soon head to head in deep conversation, and Emma rushed away to talk to a girl of her own age who came to many of the same meetings with her mama. It left Venetia easy prey to Lord Marwood.

After a few opening comments about the talk, he said, 'Your sister is taking the Town by storm, I understand. I've heard her described as the prettiest débutante of the Season.'

Venetia smiled coolly. 'The daughter of a duke is always the prettiest girl of the Season. It's the politeness of self-interest.'

'How harsh you are with human folly! But in your sister's case, the politeness is no fiction.'

'Oh? You've met her?'

'I've seen her,' he amended. 'She was pointed out to me at the Grafton House ball. I have not, sad to say, been invited to any of the private parties she has graced.' He eyed her curiously. 'Oddly, I'm told that you have been conspicuous by your absence from the same parties. Can it be that your family doesn't approve of what you are doing?'

She looked at him sharply. 'What do you know about it?'

He bowed slightly. 'A little more than the rest of London. The wildest rumours are flying about, but I have the satisfaction of knowing about St Agatha's.'

'How do you know?' she asked angrily.

'You needn't be alarmed – I shan't tell anyone. Though I wonder how long the secret can be kept. London – or the part of it that matters – is a very small place, and the more interesting the secret, the more it struggles to escape.'

'Interesting!' she said with some bitterness. 'I wonder you are willing to be seen talking to me, knowing what you know.'

He raised his eyebrows. 'But I'm entirely on your side. It takes great courage to be different, and defy public opinion.'

'You admire me for it?' she said with plain disbelief.

He smiled his most charming smile. 'You can't think how much! I know what it is to be an outsider. But let me assure you, from my longer experience, that the view from the rim of the world is wider and more exciting than from its still centre.'

She said nothing. She was grateful for his support, but wished it didn't come from such a source. It was not like being approved by Lord Hazelmere.

As if he had read her thought, he said, 'By the by, I saw Hazelmere at Grafton House – the first time since he sold out. He looked extremely miserable. I can't suppose he's still grief stricken over his father's death, so I conclude he has some other misery. Can you enlighten me?'

'I'm afraid not,' Venetia said, a little tersely. 'Lord Hazelmere does not call.'

'Ah,' said Marwood, and changed the subject. So Hazelmere disapproved, did he? All the better. Marwood wanted to be her sole supporter: there was power in exclusivity.

Tommy Weston came into the drawing-room one evening to find Venetia alone, standing by the fireside, her elbow on the mantelpiece, looking a little flushed.

'Was that Marwood I saw going away down the street?' he asked.

'Yes. He's just left.'

Tommy frowned. 'I wish you wouldn't encourage him, Venetia.'

'He doesn't need encouraging,' she said lightly. 'He manages quite well on his own.'

'Don't joke. I don't like tripping over him every time I come here.' He saw her brows draw down, and realised he had chosen the wrong words. 'What I mean is – well, he's not received in a lot of places.'

'Nor am I – probably in all the same places,' Venetia said in a hard voice, 'so I dare say we match pretty well.'

'Don't be silly. You and he have nothing in common. He's not a good influence, you know.'

'Oh Tommy, I'm old enough to take care of myself!'

Tommy doubted it, but shifted ground a little. 'You may

be, but Emma isn't. I don't think Fanny would like to know that he was hanging around her daughter.'

'Marwood doesn't hang around Emma. Besides, Emma doesn't know he exists.' She left the mantelpiece and walked a restless step or two. 'Don't fuss, Tommy. I know what I'm about, and I'm not in any danger from Lord Marwood, I assure you. He amuses me, that's all. He tells me the gossip, and flirts with me, and – well, it's pleasant. Now that Beauty doesn't call—'

She stopped abruptly. It was probably not tactful to mention Beauty to Tommy – Tommy who had never defected, never allowed his disapproval to show; who was unfailingly present, and helpful, and without whom she could not have managed to do what she did.

'Hazelmere would call if you sent him word, I'm sure of it,' Tommy said quietly. When you loved someone, you wanted the best for them, and Tommy didn't want Venetia to associate with a rogue like Marwood, even if it meant encouraging his real rival for her affections.

'And I'm very sure I shan't send him word,' Venetia said sharply. 'I won't be looked down on from a virtuous height. When Lord Hazelmere is ready to accept me as I am, he can come and apologise.'

'All the same—' Tommy persisted, and she interrupted him impatiently.

'Oh, don't preach, Tom! I've enough to put up with, without that.'

Tommy let it go, and changed the subject, not wanting to annoy her. 'Are you going to the lecture tonight?'

She made a face. 'I think I've had enough lectures today. Besides, I don't like the speaker – pompous and patronising. No, I shall stay home with my books and have a quiet night by the fire. You're going, aren't you?'

'I was only going to escort you all there, and then go on to the club. Hampton wanted me to make up a four at whist.'

Her expression softened. 'Good for you! You ought to have a little pleasure sometimes, Tommo. The bent bow, you know!'

'But I don't like to think of you all alone.'

'I like to be alone,' she assured him. 'I'm surrounded by people all day long. It makes a restful change.'

When they had gone, and she settled down again by the fire, she found that the solitude gave her thoughts too much freedom: they went off in unwelcome directions. She felt restless and unhappy. She loved her work, but was frustrated by the resistance to her, which seemed to be growing rather than diminishing. She still hadn't found anyone to teach her practical anatomy, and she was beginning to dread the arrival of the post with its cold or outraged refusals. And the handful of students who were against her seemed to be growing: there were looks and whispers, and it was noticeable in the lecture rooms who would sit near her and who wouldn't. It would only take someone to discover who she really was, and the fat would be in the fire good and proper.

She missed her family, and the hurt of being excluded from Augusta's Season was greater than she had expected. She missed Lord Hazelmere too – she hadn't anticipated how much. Life without him had lost a significant part of its savour, and she realised that, though she had dedicated herself to doing a man's job, she was still woman enough to want a man's company. Tommy was wonderful, and she was grateful for all he did for her, but she didn't love him – not in that way. Now that Beauty was gone, and it was too late, she appreciated what he had meant to her. Perhaps she had always loved him; but she'd squandered him, believing that he would always be there, at her beck and call.

Marwood was a poor substitute, of course, but at least he amused and excited her – and perhaps, she thought ruefully, with a little belated self-knowledge, part of what she liked was knowing that everyone else would disapprove of her friendship with him. Tommy certainly did; Beauty would if he knew. To be truthful, she disapproved herself, and her intimacy with Marwood had grown more quickly over the weeks since that first meeting than she had meant it to. He was certainly encroaching, and she felt sometimes that he treated her too familiarly.

Ah, there was a revelation about herself! She was still, underneath it all, Lady Venetia Fleetwood, the daughter of a duke, and she expected people like Marwood to know their place. She was too good for him, and he ought to have known it; but there was something faintly thrilling about knowing that he might overstep the mark again, as he had done before. He knew something about her that no-one else did, and the awareness ran like an underground current through all their meetings. She told herself that if he did go beyond the line she would stop him with an icy look, and throw him out on his ear; but she didn't really think it would ever come to that. His skill was in flirting along the very edge of the boundary, which gave her all the thrill of safe danger, or a dangerous safety, if there could be such a thing.

She did feel, on nights like this when there was time for reflection, that it was wrong of her to enjoy it; but then she told herself that it served Beauty right – as if that were an answer. She never asked herself what Marwood wanted out of the situation. She simply assumed he found it amusing in the same way she did.

The club was crowded, and the whist players made a quiet pocket in a blanket of noise, attracting a group of onlookers who formed a silent wall round the table and blocked out any view of the rest of the room. It was only between rubbers when some people drifted away that Tommy looked up and saw Lord Hazelmere across the room.

'Would you excuse me?' he asked his companions on an impulse. 'I should like to stretch my legs for five minutes.'

'Good idea,' said Hampton. 'It will give me a chance to send for some more drinks. Can't see a club servant in this crush.'

'What about some sandwiches, too, Bertie?' said Lord Bollo. 'If this is goin' to be a long session, I'll need some nourishment for the old brain.'

'Food ain't going to help you,' Cuthbertson said cheerfully. 'Can't feed what don't exist!'

Tommy left them to it and edged his way through the crowds to where he had seen Hazelmere. He had moved on, and it took Tommy a few minutes to find him, standing watching a cheerful game of poker in a corner by the door.

'Hello, Weston,' he said when Tommy accosted him. 'How are things?' He looked, Tommy thought, as though a light had gone out inside him, and his heart sank. It was the same look Venetia had these days, when she thought no-one was watching her. It was a case between them, then. He had always known loving her was hopeless, but since she and Hazelmere had quarrelled, he had allowed himself, foolishly, to think there might be a chance for him after all.

'How are things with you?' he said. 'Haven't seen you for an age.'

Hazelmere shrugged. 'Well, you know I was told I wasn't welcome around Bedford Square.'

'That's nonsense,' Tommy said.

'It didn't sound like nonsense at the time.'

'My dear chap, you give up too easily! You don't have to take for fact everything a lady says when she's in a temper.'

'Is this you giving me lessons on the fair sex?' Hazelmere asked with a faint smile.

'Only if you need them,' Tommy replied genially. 'You ought to know by now that what females say has to be translated like a foreign language. You can't just take it literally.'

'We're not talking about ordinary females. We're talking about Venetia.'

Tommy grew serious. 'She misses you,' he said. 'I wish you'd go and make peace with her. I don't like to see her so unhappy.'

'Unhappy?'

'It's easy to forget, given all the extraordinary things she achieves, that she's a woman like any other, when it comes to things of the heart.'

Hazelmere laid a hand on Tommy's arm. 'You're a good fellow, Weston. I understand what you're trying to do; and I'd run to her so fast my boots would burst into flame, if only she'd give me the slightest sign. But I can't impose myself on her.'

'Then you're a fool,' Tommy said firmly. 'I wouldn't let her go out of idiotic pride, if it were me she favoured.'

'I am proud,' Hazelmere acknowledged, removing his hand. 'Shouldn't I be?'

482

Tommy shrugged. 'That's your affair. But she is too, and the two of you will have nothing but your pride to keep you warm, if one of you doesn't swallow it. But I've no right to lecture you – forgive me, won't you? It was only my fondness for my cousin that made me speak.'

'Of course – I understand,' Hazelmere muttered, a little blankly.

'My game is about to resume – I must go,' Tommy said, and took his leave. As he went back to the table, he smiled to himself, satisfied for the time being. He had planted the seed. Time would tell if anything came of it.

When Lord Marwood left Venetia, it was with the impression that she was going to the lecture that evening with Miss Morpurgo, Emma, and Tommy Weston. Weston, her faithful watchdog! There was no point in his putting himself through the torture of another of those tedious meetings if Weston was going to be hanging on her sleeve, growling at strangers. He went instead to his club, and with the intention of drowning his sorrows – which were many, and mainly financial – had a number of brandies in quick succession.

His life was in a rut. He was bored with the army, which seemed to him no fun any more, now that Cardwell's reforms had replaced all the spirit with common sense. But he had spent his compensation money, and without his army pay would have nothing to live on but his poor little annuity and whatever Alfreda gave him. It was no way for a gentleman to live. He needed to marry an heiress; but the idea of some coarse factory owner's daughter offended his Turlingham pride. He had thought Lady Venetia might serve, but he had spent a great deal of time with her without discovering how to make use of her. He enjoyed her company, and found her amusing and stimulating, but that was not enough for a man with his debts. There was no doubt that her involvement with the hospital made her accessible as she had not been before; but did she still have a dowry? Had she been cast off by her family? It rather looked that way – he couldn't find that she had been near Southport House all year – and yet on the other hand she was not living in poverty, and her cousin

Weston hung about her as if she were a piece of Sèvres he'd been told off to guard.

He had hoped that Southport would be grateful to him for taking her off his hands and giving her a name, and in that event he had intended to behave extremely well by her and give her no cause to regret marrying him. He liked her spirit, and was attracted by that vein of passion he had uncovered in her. But it was difficult to gain the gratitude of a man he could not get to see, and who seemed, for all he could gather, to be indifferent to the danger his child was in.

Things were getting desperate. Little as he wanted to force the pace, he was beginning to think he would have to. Thus he was thinking when, tossing back another glass, he caught sight of Tommy Weston standing in the doorway of the next room in conversation with someone he couldn't see. He put down the glass, his mind running. If Weston was here, he wasn't at the lecture with Venetia, and in that case, Marwood might as well be. He got up went out, collected his hat, and out in the street hailed a growler to take him to Manchester Square, where the meeting was.

The lecture had started by the time he got there, but he told the maid who admitted him he would slip in quietly at the back of the room. However, a comprehensive scan of the heads, hats and profiles told him that Venetia wasn't there – though he spotted Miss Morpurgo and Emma, and drew quickly back out of their line of sight. If she was not here, then presumably she was at home: she wouldn't go out without a chaperon, and he had never learned that she had one except the Morpurgo woman. And Weston was at the club! What an opportunity! He hurried out again past the surprised maid, snatching up his hat, and hailed another cab.

At Bedford Square, the maid seemed doubtful about admitting him. 'I'm sure *my cousin* will want to see me,' he said, trying to exude familial confidence. 'Just step up and ask her, will you?' She could not well refuse, and let him into the hall to wait; he let her get up the first flight and then followed her quickly and quietly, so that she was still explaining matters just inside the open drawing-room door when Marwood came up behind her. It was as easy as that.

'Oh, very well, Lotty,' Venetia said, amused at his daring, and bored with her book, of which she had been reading the same page for an hour without taking in a word. 'Come in, Lord Marwood. Is something wrong?'

When the girl had gone, he crossed the room to stand before her. 'I went to the lecture, but you weren't there.'

'Evidently,' she said. 'Was it a good one?'

'I didn't wait to find out. It could have no possible interest for me after that.'

'For shame,' she said. 'Is your interest in the women's cause so shallow?'

'If you call that shallowness, then yes, it's so shallow it wouldn't drown a fly.' He sat, uninvited, on the edge of the sofa beside her. 'But the most exciting cause in the world would not stand comparison with making love to you, lovely Venetia!'

Her heart began beating fast, but she drew back and looked at him loftily. 'It is *Lady* Venetia to you, Lord Marwood.'

He grinned. 'But it is Miss Fleet I am addressing – the lovely and unconventional Miss Fleet, who defies Society and dares anything. Miss Fleet will not deny me.' He caught her hand and lifted it to his lips. The heat of his breath and the brush of his whiskers made her skin thrill.

'You presume altogether too much,' she said, finding it strangely hard to breathe. She was acutely aware of his strong male body close to hers. 'I should not have admitted you.'

'Oh, you should! Don't recant your courage,' he said, looking up from under his eyelashes, his lips still poised over her hand.

Courage? she thought. No, it was foolhardiness. All the trouble Aunt Fanny and her mother and Tommy had taken to guard her, and here she was allowing Marwood to kiss her hand! She stood up, so that he was obliged to stand with her. 'I think I must ask you to leave,' she said. She said it firmly, but she used the words 'I think', which made it sound less determined than she meant it to.

Marwood grinned. Standing up she was much more

vulnerable than sitting down. He let go of her hand and put his arms round her. 'That's better,' he said, pulling her close, and kissed her.

For a second Venetia did not resist. His lips, warm and smooth, brushed hers and sent a shock like lightning through her; his hands were hot on her back, his lean, hard body against hers. The sleeping animal in her stirred and lifted its head. He felt her response, and gleefully drew her tighter to him, his mouth becoming urgent. She smelled the brandy on his breath, and pushed him away, ashamed of herself. She had allowed him in, had encouraged him, and it was disgraceful and wrong. But after all, no harm had been done. No-one but her would ever know.

'How dare you?' she said. 'Leave at once!' She stepped back from him and walked to the door.

'Leave? Oh no, I don't think so,' he said. Before she could take hold of the doorknob, he reached past her to hold it shut; and she turned, effectively into the circle of his arm.

'What are you doing?' she said.

'What do you think I'm doing, foolish creature,' he said, sliding his arm round her waist.

'But I've asked you to leave. Let me go!'

For answer he put his other arm round her as well, and she leaned back away from him, pushing at his shoulders. He was hard and strong, and she felt a pang which was not yet real fear.

'Don't fight it, Venetia,' he said, smiling down at her. 'We've been playing a pleasant game all these weeks, but now we've the perfect opportunity, and there may not be another for a long time.'

'What do you mean? Opportunity?'

He bent his head and kissed the bare skin of her neck. 'Opportunity,' he repeated. 'Don't pretend you don't know what I mean. You want it as much as I do. I can feel it.'

Now she understood at last. She gasped the cold oxygen of fear. 'No!' she said. 'Let me go! How can you? Don't you know who I am?'

'I know who you were, and that only makes it more exciting. But you're not Lady Venetia now, are you? So don't pretend a virtue you don't have. What Miss Fleet does won't surprise anyone. Let's go up to your room and be comfortable. I can show you a world you've barely dreamed of.'

She felt almost faint with shock. He was not just proposing to kiss her, but to – to – *mate* with her. She didn't have any social vocabulary for it, because it was something so utterly unthinkable. He proposed they should do *that*, and thought that she would be willing, because she was no longer a decent female with a reputation to sustain. She was a ruined woman in his eyes, and therefore fair game. Frantically her mind sought about for escape.

'The servants!' she gasped, still pushing ineffectually at him. 'Lotty saw you. She let you in!'

'I'm sure you know how to keep her mouth shut,' he said. He sounded amused. He still thought she was willing; that she was only worried about being found out.

Outrage gave her strength; and perhaps he had slackened his grip somewhat. She pushed him determinedly away and fumbled with the doorknob; dragged it open, her heart battering against her chest like a bird caught in an attic. She was out into the passage and reached the stairs before he caught her again, his arms going round her from behind.

'Upstairs, is it?' he murmured against her ear. 'Oh, my lovely one, we're going to have such a time! Save all this energy for upstairs.' He pulled her round and against him again, fastening his lips on hers so that she could not cry out. Crushed against him, her mouth covered, she could hardly breathe, and she felt herself growing faint.

When she was helpless, Marwood meant to pick her up and carry her upstairs; then, he believed, her real desires would overcome her childhood prudery, and she would yield to him. She would make a wild and exciting mistress, he suspected; and the duke would surely then want to persuade him to marry her. If he didn't – well, Marwood would at least have had the pleasure of her. He pressed his lips harder against hers, and felt her fluttering resistance grow weaker.

Tommy Weston didn't know what made him break off the whist game when he did. It should have gone on all night, for Hampton and Cuthbertson were keen players, and Bollo had money to burn and would play anything with anyone for as long as required. But a growing feeling of unrest spoiled Tommy's concentration, and when the next rubber, a short one, ended, he made his excuses. 'I'm not feeling quite well,' he said. 'I'm sorry to break up the game, but perhaps someone else will make the four.'

'I thought something was up,' Hampton said. 'You haven't been playing your usual game. I hope you aren't ill?'

'It's nothing, just a headache,' Tommy said. 'If you'll forgive me, I'll go home.'

'Get straight to bed with a hot whisky,' Cuthbertson advised. 'There's a lot of influenza about.'

Out on the street Tommy called for a cab, and climbed in.

'I ain't a mind-reader, guv'nor,' the jarvey said after a moment, looking in through the hatch.

'Oh, sorry!' Tommy hesitated, and then told him to drive to Bedford Square. Venetia was alone at home, and any chance to be with her was hard to resist. Perhaps if he told Venetia how unhappy Hazelmere looked, she might relent towards him, he offered himself as excuse.

Lotty opened the door to him. 'Is your mistress still up?'

'Oh yes, sir,' she said. 'There's another gentleman with her.'

'What gentleman?' Tommy said, puzzled; but even as she spoke Marwood's name there was a slight sound from above. His imagination told him more than he had any right to know by natural means. He dropped his hat and ran for the stairs. At the top of the second flight was a scene that made his blood run cold: Venetia clasped against Marwood's body, their mouths clamped together – but her arms were not round him, and her hands were up against his shoulders in a defensive position.

'Let her go, you swine!' he shouted, leaping up the last of the stairs. Marwood, startled, lifted his head, and then as Tommy launched himself at him, thrust Venetia ungently away, so that she staggered backwards and banged into the wall with a cry. Tommy tried to strike the taller man, who parried the blow and grabbed Tommy's wrist. Then the two

488

of them were locked in a fierce grasp, grappling with each other in breathless silence. Tommy was smaller and slighter, but by far the angrier, and Marwood could not subdue him. They reeled forward and then back; and then Marwood's foot slipped over the edge of the top stair.

Venetia screamed. The two bodies broke apart as soon as they fell. Tommy slithered a few steps, and then caught at a banister, and, flailing, came to a halt. Marwood went down backwards, flying half a dozen steps before his head and neck made the first contact. Striking the stair flipped him head over heels, and he bowled like a hoop down the rest of the flight, before being stopped by the wall of the half-landing.

Lotty came running up the other flight, and let out a shriek. Tommy sat up, rubbing his jangling bruises. Venetia moved to the top of the stairs, her face white, and her knuckles went to her mouth. Marwood, crumpled up against the wall at a peculiar angle, limp as a puppet whose strings had been cut, had not moved.

CHAPTER TWENTY-SIX

When Lord Hazelmere reached the house, he found the servants gathered in a white and whispering group in the hall.

'In the drawing-room, my lord,' said Sam, the footman. 'I'll show you up.'

'No need, I know the way,' he said. He did not waste time on questions. The message brought to him at the club had said only that there had been an accident and begged him to come at once, and was signed Weston. It must be Venetia, his heart said; but he could not speculate on what had happened. He seemed to be gripped in an iron frost; he could feel nothing.

In the drawing-room there was Weston, looking dishevelled, limping slightly as he walked up and down the room; and Venetia, ashen-faced, sitting in the chair by the fire and shivering. Hazelmere was across the room in a second, and on his knees, holding her hands and rubbing them. They were as cold as two stones from the sea-bed.

'What happened?'

Tommy told him in a few sentences. It had seemed natural to send for Hazelmere, though he was not family, and he was glad now that he had, for Hazelmere did not exclaim or fuss, but asked a few quiet questions, and took over everything.

'Where is he?'

'In the dining-room. Sam and I carried him in there.'

'You're sure he's dead?'

'Quite sure.'

At the words, Hazelmere felt Venetia shudder; but she

490

spoke up with amazing calm. 'I think his neck's broken. It feels very loose.'

'You examined him?'

Venetia looked weary to death. 'I'm the one who has the most experience.'

Hazelmere didn't argue with that. 'Has a doctor been sent for? No? Then that must be done.' He got up and rang. 'Are you hurt, Weston?'

'Just bruises.'

'And you, Lady Venetia?' He was reluctant to ask this question. 'Did he hurt you?' She shook her head listlessly. Sam opened the door. 'Send at once for Doctor . . .' He looked enquiringly at Venetia, and she shrugged. They had never had to call one since they had been here. 'Whichever doctor is nearest. Tell him as little as possible, but bring him here at once. You'd better go yourself. And make sure the other servants stay in the house and don't talk to anyone. This must be kept as quiet as possible.'

'Yes, sir.'

Hazelmere gestured him to stay put. 'Where is Miss Morpurgo?' he asked Weston.

'They've gone to a meeting. Manchester Square.'

'I'll write a note,' said Hazelmere. 'Send someone else up, Sam, to take it. Someone reliable.'

When he had gone, Hazelmere went to the side table and poured two glasses of sherry, all there was on the tray. He took one to Weston, and then gently pressed the other into Venetia's icy hand. 'Drink it,' he said. 'You've had a shock. It will make you feel better.'

Venetia met his eyes. 'I shall never feel better. It was my fault, Beauty. All my fault.'

'It was an accident,' he said.

'But he wouldn't have been here if I hadn't encouraged him. I've been so stupid.'

'You did what you felt you had to. Thank God you're all right.'

Her eyes filled suddenly with tears. 'I'm glad you're here,' she said; and distantly, beyond all the distress and horror of the moment, a faint trumpet sang in his mind.

Hazelmere, alone at first, and later with Weston's help, saw to everything; and it was not only Venetia who said, more than once over the next few days, 'Thank God for Beauty'. It was her only comfort, that he had come so readily to her aid. Everything else was horror.

'I've ruined everything,' she said as Hazelmere, coaxing her like an invalid, took her for a walk round the garden. She was pale and drawn, her eyes red-rimmed with tears and lack of sleep. 'Not only my own life, which would have been justice of a sort, but everyone else's too.'

'It was an accident,' he said. 'Don't be so hard on yourself.'

'Who else should I blame?' she said bitterly. 'No, let me feel it as I ought. If I hadn't let him in – if I hadn't allowed him to develop the acquaintance in the first place—'

'He was a bad lot, Venetia,' Hazelmere said firmly. 'You weren't to know how far he would go. How could you? And the fall was the merest bad luck, or he would have left chastened under his own steam when Weston got there. An accident, that's all – and the inquest will confirm it.'

Venetia shuddered. 'The inquest! I hate that word! Don't you see, Beauty, I've brought ruin on us all? No chance of keeping it secret after that. No chance of being privately sorry and getting over it. Accident or not, it will be the subject of a public hearing, the story will be told, and the newspapers will be full of it. The scandal will be terrible. You can't doubt that.'

He was silent, not knowing what to say.

'Everyone will say, "That's what comes of girls stepping outside their own sphere. That's what comes of women trying to be men."'

It was what Southport had said to him, his first reaction. 'No-one will say that,' he said. 'Why should they?'

'I'll be thrown out of the hospital,' she went on relentlessly, 'and that's my personal punishment. But Tommy's killed a man, and will have to live with the knowledge – and maybe with people whispering that perhaps it wasn't such an accident after all. And my family will be dragged into the scandal. Augusta's come-out will be ruined. She won't get invited to parties – no-one will come to hers – no proposals of marriage. Olivia will lose her court position – the Queen won't keep her with a scandal in the family – and the nice equerry she's in love with will never marry her. Papa ashamed. Mama heart-broken. Emma taken away from London and Tommy. And it's all my fault.'

They reached the end of the walk, and he turned her to face him. 'Have you finished? Then listen to me. Your nerves are shaken by what's happened, and no wonder; but you are not in the best frame of mind to judge the situation. Believe me, things are not as black as you think. Try not to give in to despair. I always thought you had great courage. Show it now by holding fast.'

She stared for a long moment, and then tried to smile. It was a shaky effort, but he recognised it for what it was. 'You are very good to me,' she said.

'Nonsense,' he said, pleased.

'Did you really think I was brave?'

'Always – even when I thought you were wrong. *Especially* when I thought you were wrong.'

It was Hazelmere who went to Southport House to interview the duke and duchess and assure them that there was nothing to be gained at this point by taking Venetia away from Bedford Square (Charlotte's idea) or visiting her there to harangue her (Oliver's) about her conduct.

'It is a bad business, but I hope it might be got over without too much damage. Everything can be explained away, and there is no need that I can see for a scandal, if we all behave naturally. I would advise, therefore, if you'll forgive me, that you do nothing and say nothing just at present, until I've had time to speak to the authorities.'

'But is Venetia all right?' Charlotte asked him urgently.

'Lady Venetia has great reserves of courage. She is holding on very well.'

'And Emma?'

'Emma has Tommy Weston, which comes to the same thing.' Hazelmere permitted himself a smile. 'Lady Venetia has told me that it has long been Emma's mother's wish to see her and Weston united. I believe this event, horrible as it is, may have done the trick.'

It was Hazelmere who interviewed the coroner and the Commissioner of Police, and who almost single handed, like Horatius on the bridge, held at bay the hordes of press reporters who swarmed around the front door like ants smelling sugar. Fortunately, of the only two people who had actually witnessed the accident, neither had been under any temptation to talk about it, even to the servants. All the servants knew was that Lord Marwood had fallen downstairs. Hazelmere told the press the tale in the most simple terms and with such a limpid expression of innocence that it was hard for them to find the slightest shadow to take hold of and exploit. Lord Marwood was a cousin by marriage of all three ladies, and moreover shared an interest with them in the women's movement. There was nothing at all out of the way in his calling at Bedford Square. Ditto Mr Weston. Mr Weston had arrived just as Lord Marwood was leaving. Lord Marwood's foot slipped and he fell, breaking his neck on the stairs. Mr Weston, in trying to catch him, had fallen too, but fortunately sustained only bruises. Everyone was deeply sorry about the accident, and the most heartfelt condolences had been sent to Marwood's only close relative, Mrs Morland at Morland Place.

The press hounds, baffled, were flung back and lost the scent, given no opportunity to ask the one question that might have proved hard to answer: why was Lady Venetia living in Bedford Square in the first place, and not at Southport House? They went away with the vague impression that it was something to do with her interest in the women's movement, which made sense, since it was enough to annoy any father, but respectable enough not to make much of a story.

'They don't seem to have got hold of your double life as Miss Fleet,' Hazelmere reported back to Venetia, 'and with a little luck, I see no reason why they should.'

Venetia was hard to comfort. 'It will all come out at the inquest,' she said dully.

'No it won't. You won't have to attend the inquest. I've

494

arranged for it to be conducted as quietly as possible. Weston and I will handle everything, and all you'll have to do is write a statement that Marwood slipped and fell, taking Weston with him.'

'You want me to swear to a lie?'

'How is it a lie? He slipped, didn't he? You told me so yourself. What happened before that is no-one's business but yours.'

'But Tommy was struggling with him.'

'When Marwood slipped, Weston says he held onto him to try to stop him falling. What happened the moment before—'

'Is no-one's business,' Venetia finished for him. 'Beauty, is this right?'

'Was it an accident?' he asked her levelly.

'Yes!'

'Then let it be,' he said. The calm assurance of his voice was balm to her bruised heart and soul. It was like her old nurse's hand on her shoulder when she was a child and had got into one of her frenzies. *Let it be.* Oh, to relinquish responsibility to someone else!

'Are you sure it will be all right?' she asked after a moment.

'Quite sure,' he said. 'I've got everyone on my side. They'll move heaven and earth for me, to protect my fiancée from scandal.' She looked up sharply. 'Naturally,' he said carefully, 'you don't have to marry me. I'm not trying to blackmail you. It's just that I had to have a good reason for being busy in the matter. And everyone loves a lover, as they say. When it all dies down, we can "part" by mutual agreement, if you want, and no-one will think anything of it.'

'If I want,' she repeated. She studied his face gravely.

'But you might want to consider the benefits of not parting,' he went on, with a quirk of his lips.

'You don't want to marry a ruined woman,' she said blankly.

'You won't be a ruined woman if you marry me,' he said. 'The Winchmores are a very old and respectable family. The whole world knows we wouldn't marry anyone in the least suspect.'

Her defences wavered, and she almost smiled. 'Oh Beauty!'

'Are you going to call me by that old nickname for ever? My given name is John, you know.'

'I didn't know. I always thought John was a rather dull name.'

'I'm a dull fellow. Respectable and dull.'

'Never that – not you. But I can't marry you.'

'Why not?' he asked. Her words had shaken him; he'd thought he was winning.

'Because I want to be a doctor. What I said before is still true. If you disapprove of what I want to do, you disapprove of me.'

He swallowed so hard she could almost see all her iniquities go bobbing down his throat like so many badly tied bundles. 'If it really matters so much to you, I won't stand in your way. I'll even help you.'

'You can't mean it,' she said in flat disbelief. 'No man is that noble.'

'Of course I mean it.' He grinned suddenly. 'It might even be fun, setting the respectable world spinning counter-clockwise! More fun than the pranks we used to get up to in the mess – God, it seems a thousand years ago!' She was thoughtful, and he said, 'It's customary to give an answer, you know, when someone proposes to you. But before you do,' he forestalled her, suddenly nervous, 'I should mention one more thing for you to consider.'

'What's that?'

'You were worried about the effect on your sisters. But if you and I announce our engagement and Southport House is convulsed with joy about it, everyone will forget the other business, there'll be no scandal, and your sisters can be bridesmaids at our wedding. And everyone knows there's nothing like one wedding for bringing on another – or even two others. Olivia and Augusta will be next.'

'That's your argument?' she said incredulously. 'Marry you to save my sisters?'

'That's it,' he agreed. 'Do you think it's a trifle thin? It sounded better inside my head.'

'You don't say anything about loving me,' she said diffidently.

496

'Didn't I?' A slow smile spread from his lips to his eyes. 'Say yes, and I'll tell you in great detail all about loving you.'

'Yes,' said Venetia at last.

At Morland Place, the building work on the new wing was halted. Half built, it had the look of something half demolished, a melancholy ruin. In the house, pictures were turned to the wall, looking-glasses covered in black gauze; the servants were issued with weepers, and Battey, the first footman, with brand new black livery in which to answer the door. Bittle, red-eyed with weeping for her first and beloved nursling, needed no encouragement to put baby James into mourning. He was eighteen months old, walking and talking now, and if it seemed odd to the nursery-maid to see the chubby child toddling about in a black dress, it seemed only right to his mother.

Alfreda sat hour after hour in the drawing-room, her hands in her lap, staring at nothing, while in her mind she revisited endlessly the scenes from her childhood when there was just Kit and her, and they were happy. In that place the sun always shone; in that place she and her brother were Turlinghams, and the world was a place of beauty and order.

George had been shocked, of course, at the news of the accident (and a little puzzled and intrigued about the circumstances: how had Marwood got to know Lady Venetia so well? And what was she doing unmarried and living away from home?) He was deeply upset at his wife's unhappiness; but in his private heart he couldn't help thinking it was for the best, all in all. Marwood had already proved himself expensive, and seemed likely to be more so, and who was going to have to stand the dust? Why, George, of course. He couldn't refuse Alfreda anything, and she couldn't refuse Kit anything, and George had already been wondering how big a call on the estate his gaming and raking brother-in-law was going to be. And if Marwood was going to break Alfreda's heart, he reasoned, it might as well be this way, and get it over with, as go on draining away at her drop by drop over a lifetime.

Marwood's body was to be brought to Morland Place to be

buried. George had offered that straight away, and had won a look of gratitude from Alfreda – in which there was a hint of puzzlement he didn't discern. Turl Magna had been sold, and there was nowhere else Kit might have called home that his body could have been sent, but Alfreda was surprised at how glad she felt that he was to be buried here. For the first time she really appreciated the antiquity of the house, the presence of the ancestors in the crypt beneath the chapel. Kit would lie there with the Morlands; and when the time came, Alfreda would lie beside him; and one day his little nephew, James, too. Kit wouldn't be alone, and lonely. It came to Alfreda, in thinking about it, that Morland Place had worked its way into her heart. It was her home now, and if she didn't quite think of herself as a Morland, as least she thought of Morland Place as belonging to the Turlinghams.

Perhaps it was time, she thought, to see about giving little James a brother. It was a good thing not to be an only child: not for anything would she have missed having Kit, and James ought to have the chance of the same comfort. George hadn't troubled her, of course, since the baby was born. He was a perfect gentleman in that respect. When the funeral was over and a decent period had elapsed, she would invite him to visit her again. No doubt he'd appreciate the compliment – the honour, even – she was paying him. Another boy, she thought; and then, perhaps, a girl. It might be pleasant to have a little girl to dress up.

Around her the house revolved on its axis of daily routine, the numerous, well-trained servants going about their appointed tasks, keeping the immaculate interior spotless. She had made such a difference to it, and remembered the chaotic and shabby place she had come to as a bride. It was *hers* now, by virtue of making her mark on it; but there were still more things to do. For instance, they would have to call in Mr Hughes to conduct the funeral, and she didn't like Hughes. He had too independent a spirit, did not treat her with enough deference, did not always come instantly running when she sent for him.

'Mr Morland,' she said as they sat at dinner (though she had no appetite at the moment, the ritual was observed to a nicety), 'I have been thinking that we ought to have a chaplain.'

He looked up, surprised. 'My dear?'

'Morland Place always had a chaplain, and we ought not to let that grand old tradition lapse. And besides, baby will be wanting a tutor soon, if he is to grow up as we want him to. You would not consign him to petticoat government?'

'Oh, no, not at all!' George said quickly. 'I had a tutor, and it did me the world of good. But shan't he go to school, Mrs Morland? To Eton, like your brother?'

'Yes, in time. He will make his friends there – it's important that he should mix with the right people. But he must have a tutor first. We must think how to go about finding a suitable man.'

'Perhaps we should ask Fortescue,' George said thoughtlessly.

Alfreda's lips tightened. Fortescue had served his purpose in ridding her of Henrietta, and she was glad sometimes to drop his name into conversation when it suited her, but she did not want any closer relationship with that branch of the family. 'I think not,' she said sharply. 'You will consult the Archbishop. That is a much better plan.'

'Yes, of course, the Archbishop. I should have thought of that.'

'And – Mr Morland?'

'My love?'

'When all this is over, I have other plans for the house.'

'Whatever you want, shall be done,' George said happily. 'I have plans for the land, too. There are two parcels I'd dearly like to buy, to round off the estate. They will be expensive, I'm afraid, but—' But now Marwood is dead, we can afford them, was the end of his sentence, though he didn't say it aloud, of course.

But it will be worth it if it adds to our consequence, was how Alfreda finished it in her head. A silence fell, in which the only sounds were the tiny clink of soup spoon on china from either end of the dinner table. Even with all the removable sections out, the table was too big for two, and separated them too far for comfortable conversation! The room was too big for the table, too, so that Goole stood several feet behind Alfreda's chair, watching for her signal that she had finished. Battey stood at the other end of the universe behind George's chair, watching for Goole's signal. When the time came they would glide forward to remove the soup plates. Their skill and pride was in doing it as far as possible simultaneously, like two parts of an oiled machine. It was a ritual which might have seemed very far removed either from the ingestion of nourishment, or the enjoyment of a social occasion, had any of the four people in the great, chilly room thought of that.

DYNASTY 1: THE FOUNDING

Cynthia Harrod-Eagles

Set in the years 1434 to 1486, the first glorious volume of the Dynasty series is an enthralling historical novel with the Wars of the Roses as its background. Power and prestige are the burning ambitions of domineering, dour Edward Morland, rich sheep-farmer and landowner, as he sets out to arrange a marriage that will secure his empire's future. And Robert, his son, more poet than soldier, idolises his proud young bride, Eleanor, ward of the influential Beaufort family.

Used to gentility and grace, Eleanor is outraged at having to marry the son of a Yorkshire sheep-farmer, but she must obey despite her consuming secret passion for Richard, Duke of York. Time creates a bond, both passionate and tender, between the apparently ill-matched husband and wife; for Eleanor's warmth and her love for life are as great as her rigid sense of justice. This remarkable woman is at the centre of a pageant which blazes with colour and life.

Robert and Eleanor's marriage is the founding of the Morland Dynasty. Life holds for them prosperity and success – all too often mingled with tragedy as they are embroiled in the civil strife which has divided families and sets neighbour against neighbour.

978-0-7515-0382-1

DYNASTY 21: THE OUTCAST

Cynthia Harrod-Eagles

England in 1857 is stable and prosperous. Benedict Morland seems settled into a comfortable routine of estate matters and civic interests. But his orderly life is shaken when a mysterious orphaned boy arrives on his doorstep. No one – least of all his wife Sibella – can understand why Bendy should take Lennox Mynott into his household.

In London, Charlotte's step-father persuades her to support the new Divorce Bill, which serves only to deepen the rift with her husband, Oliver. Should she accept the comfort she is offered from an unexpected source, and give up all hope of reconciliation with the man she still loves?

Forced to remove Lennox from Morland Place, Benedict takes him to America to join his daughter Mary at Twelvetrees Plantation. As Lennox, an outcast no longer, finds a new life, a family, and a cause to fight for, Benedict becomes enamoured of the Southern way of life, just as bitter civil war is about to destroy it for ever . . .

978-0-7515-2317-1

To buy any of our books and to find out
more about Sphere and Little, Brown Book Group,
our authors and titles, as well as events and
book clubs, visit our website

www.littlebrown.co.uk

and follow us on Twitter

@LittleBrownUK
@LittleBookCafe
@TheCrimeVault

To order any Sphere titles p & p free in the UK,
please contact our mail order supplier on:

+ 44 (0)1832 737525

Customers not based in the UK should contact
the same number for appropriate postage
and packing costs.